Oyoshi, exquisitely lovely, supremely sensual, she had risked disgrace to give herself to Jinsuke body and soul, and to hazard the most sordid scandal to bear his child.

Susan, a foreigner, a barbarian, yet when this beautiful woman and Jinsuke came together, no barriers of race and background could restrain the desire that consumed them both, and no taboos could stop their fulfillment.

Jinsuke had been chosen by the noble samurai warrior Sadayori to serve his country—and now he would be forced to decide how to love, how to live, and, perhaps, how to die. . . .

HARPOON

"A robust tale . . . memorable characters . . . superb!"   —*Chattanooga Times*

HARPOON

C.W. NICOL

A SIGNET BOOK

NEW AMERICAN LIBRARY

Acknowledgments

To the Fisheries Research Board of Canada, for giving me the privilege of working on whales; to Kyokuyo Whaling Company, for permission to sail on their catchers; to the Canada Council, for a grant; to the Whaling Museum of Taiji and all of its staff, for a base and for invaluable assistance; to the Japan Whaling Association, the Taiyo Fisheries Company and the Nippon Whaling Company; to Kyodo Whaling Company, for the privilege of sailing with whalers in the Antarctic; to many Japanese friends; to my wife; and last but not least, to the Japanese Department of Immigration for letting me be in Japan: Profound and respectful thanks!

SIGNET TRADEMARK REG. U.S. PAT. OFF. AND FOREIGN COUNTRIES
REGISTERED TRADEMARK—MARCA REGISTRADA
HECHO EN CHICAGO, U.S.A.

SIGNET, SIGNET CLASSIC, MENTOR, ONYX, PLUME, MERIDIAN and NAL BOOKS are published by NAL PENGUIN INC., 1633 Broadway, New York, New York 10019

First Signet Printing, May, 1988

1 2 3 4 5 6 7 8 9

PRINTED IN THE UNITED STATES OF AMERICA

*To Captain and Gunner
Shoji Mineo*

Note to the Reader

A glossary of Japanese terms
can be found on page 506.

Chapter One

He was on the cliffs of Taiji, looking out toward the Pacific. It was the time of pampas grass, bowing silver heads to the wind, time of late swallows, darting for insects, time of the passing of the cold rains that chilled the hills and the dense forests that crowded right to the shores of this most southerly part of the fiefdom of Kii.

The sun was warm, and waves of a storm that had raged for two days were smashing out the last of their energies on the rocks, the cliffs, the jagged islets that seemed to claw at the Pacific like the talons of a dragon.

Saburo, eleven years old, looked away from the fleet of whaling boats, dark shapes like many-legged waterbugs on the glare of the sea, and let his eyes scan the horizon. Out there and beyond, the ocean colors changed with that mighty current which was the highway for the behemoths they called *isana*—"brave fish."

Dawn was the best time for spotting them, when low and gentle rays of the rising sun would catch the plumes of vented breath, illuminating the drops of oily moisture, so that the watchers at the lookout points could see the great beasts at considerable distances.

Saburo scanned from west to east, from dark to light. He could see nothing yet, and wriggled his buttocks with impatience on the thin straw matting, glancing at the old man beside him. Old Toumi seemed cheerful enough this day. The signal flags and pennants were all ready, the wind was dying to a lusty buffeting, and out of the predawn dark the morning was unfolding with the promise of warmth. The old man kept fussing, checking things, talking sometimes to himself, sometimes to Saburo.

In the village, people tended to be wary of the old man, saying that his temper shortened as his teeth grew long, but what they did not know was that his precious sight was failing, and that Saburo, third son of the harpooner Tatsudaiyu, had become the old man's eyes.

There were other watchers, of course, but still nobody could identify a whale and predict its movements as well as old man Toumi. In fact, his very name was in truth not a name, but a title, meaning "far-seer," and for generations his family had waited on these cliffs, eyes ranging the ocean for migrating whales.

"Oy, Saburo," said the old man, "you still scan too quickly! You must look slowly, give them time to come up and blow. Don't try to hurry them from up here, they'll hurry right enough once your father pricks them. Ah, but we're going to spot a fat one today, I can feel it! We'd better keep a clear eye out, I wouldn't want those fellows at Kandori Point to spot them before we do!"

He squinted fondly at the shaven top of the skinny little boy's head.

"Take slow breaths, Saburo, slow and easy, and keep a little strength in your stomach. Try to breathe like a whale does, think like a whale does."

"*Hai,*" said Saburo, never taking his eyes from the sea.

Behind them was a little shrine at which they prayed each morning, yanking first on the rope to make the round bell clatter and arouse the god. It was said in the village of Taiji that one whale on the beach meant wealth for seven villages, although Saburo had his doubts about that, for although he was only eleven years old, ever since he could remember there had been whales pulled up onto the beach, and still his father and uncles were not at all wealthy. They were not poor, of course not, and their house was stoutly built and clean, even if it was rather small. However, apart from the extra gifts and treats they received from the Taiji and Wada families—the net masters—the whalers still got a ration of only a single *sho* of unpolished rice each day, and that was hardly enough to make anyone rich.

Saburo dared not say such a thing, but he always felt that his father should get more than the rest of them, more than anybody, more than even the lord of Shingu castle, to whom the village owed allegiance. But no one could ever voice such a thought, and besides, his father didn't seem to mind.

As the sun edged up over the rim of the world, the fleet waited, twenty-five boats strung out in a curving line upon the sea, with the lead boat, marked with its phoenix emblem and its stripes of blue, white and red, holding the center. Saburo's sharp eyes could just make out the tiny figure of his father, standing just aft of the long, black, curving prow. The great orb lifted and turned to gold, and the boy could begin to discern the various colors and patterns that distinguished one boat from another.

On a bush beside Saburo, a spider waited in the center of its wind-touched web. The spider was black, yellow and red, patterned as intricately as any piece of enameled jewelry, indeed, as beautifully as any of those painted and lacquered whaleboats, which, like the spider, were waiting and waiting.

"Grandfather," said the boy, using the polite honorific, "what was the name of the first Wada, the one who thought of using nets to catch a whale?"

"Yoriharu-sama," replied the old man. "It was Wada Yoriharu. One day he saw a cicada struggling in a spider's web, and he thought that if such a thin little web could catch such a fat cicada, then men could catch even a whale with a net of strong ropes. You shouldn't forget that, for that idea made Taiji what it is today, and changed the whole fortune and history of whaling. They have copied us and learned from us all over Japan."

"I didn't forget about the web and the rest," said Saburo, "but I can't remember names." He voiced another thought. "Was it the spider who gave us the idea of decorating the boats with colors and patterns?"

Saburo half glanced at the spider and pointed to it, yet still kept his attention as best he could out to sea. The old man followed the boy's pointing finger. The spider was the most common of its kind in these parts, so common that one stopped noticing them, and yet their beauty was remarkable, although sinister. It had long legs, banded with black and yellow, tinted with ruby red, and the pattern on its back was painted with a brush too fine for any human hand or eye. They called it a "whore spider" but why he didn't know, and he certainly wasn't going to tell the boy that either, otherwise he'd get badgered with questions again. He sucked in his breath and thought.

"Who knows? Maybe you should ask Uncle Takigawa?" The Takigawa family were the hereditary boat painters of the village.

"But we shouldn't be thinking of spiders now, should we?" All wrinkles, the old man smiled at the boy, remembering that it was he who had admonished the boy to treasure and train his eyes, to look far, to count stars, to look from dark to light, slowly, always to give the mind time to digest what the eyes saw. To an untrained watcher, even the fattest of whales was but a mite out there on the expanse of ever-moving ocean. Saburo chanced a grin at Toumi, then looked out to sea again.

"Ah! I see dolphins! Heading south, out past the boats!"

"Good," said the old man. He cupped his hands and pretended to shout. "You little fellows, bring the big fat ones to play, won't you?"

They both sat, the old man and the young boy, watching and enjoying each other.

The traveler approached them so silently that neither Saburo nor old man Toumi was aware of his presence until a deep voice spoke out from behind them.

"If all of us Japanese were so vigilant, then we would have little fear of the enemies from the sea."

Saburo and the old man turned in fright and shock, at the unexpected intrusion, at the cultured accent, at the word "enemies." They saw a man, a stranger, his face hidden under a wide conical basket hat. Upon his *haori* jacket they saw an unmistakable crest of three asarum leaves in a circle, and at his hip two swords were stuck in the sash, and even though the hilts of those swords were covered and laced with protective cloth, so that they could not be drawn, the two felt terror, and threw themselves on their knees, the old man babbling an almost incoherent apology for not having noticed the stranger's approach, having his, no, their backs to him, although this one was but a boy, and the whales . . .

The stranger removed the wide hat and, with a smile, made a slight bow. Switching into a more familiar speech, though still not Taiji or fishermen's speech, he told them not to apologize.

"Please, keep your eyes on the sea," he said, "that is your duty."

The old man exhaled loudly at the word "duty" and touched his head to the ground again.

The stranger ignored him, gathered up the pleats of his skirtlike *hakama* and sat upon a rock, removing the big sword from the sash and laying it beside him. Although the stranger's clothes were dusty and worn, their quality was excellent. This was no impoverished *ronin* come to swagger about the village and make a nuisance of himself. The old man was still terrified, well aware that this was a man of status. Why would such a man suddenly appear? With no

12

servants or attendants, and walking, not riding? Yet the samurai seemed perfectly content to sit still, looking out to sea.

Out at sea, too far for the hull of the ship to be visible from shore, Captain Bartholomew Riggs of the U.S. barque *Midas* looked down from his own clean bridge to the filthy, oily decks, where a spiral blanket of sperm-whale blubber was being lowered on a creaking boom to the men who jabbed and heaved at it with their prickers, blubber spades and knives. The captain bellowed at them.

"Keep those damned fires hot, or you'll all be going where it'll be hot enough to melt the blubber off your own lazy backsides!"

A change of wind flapped sails and wafted rich black whale smoke toward him.

A boy ladled the browning, shriveled "biscuits" of rendered blubber from the try pots and pitched them into the fire below. Captain Riggs glanced sideways and cursed again. Like as not, another storm was chasing the tail of the one they had just ridden out, to the cost of all but the last of his extra spars. The boats too had seen a lot of wear, and one was half wrecked, staved in by a wild gray whale. Every day the lubber of a carpenter was whining for lumber as if they could just go waltzing in to the nearest timber dealer and buy his best. Damnation! He couldn't break off the hunt now, head for Hawaii, with whales blowing every day and empty barrels still in the hold!

Far to the west, a line of steep mountains straddled the horizon, with towering pillars of clouds rising from the peaks. The captain snapped open his telescope and perused the peninsula, or big island, or whatever it was. There were no charts of this place, none at all. All he could see were hills upon hills, losing themselves in haze. There would be inlets and bays and quiet harbors there, and damn it, if he could only sail in, find shelter, drop anchor, get spars, take on clean, fresh mountain water, some vegetables, chickens, goats, maybe even buy some trinkets for his daughters back home in San Francisco . . . but there was no point in thinking about that. The stories told about the natives who inhabited that coast would make the boldest captain wary.

The ship was drifting with the current, moving slightly away from land. With luck, the wind would stay calm for long enough to get the three killed sperm whales alongside flensed and cooked. Then he'd beat further offshore. With one last look around the decks, he nodded to his second officer and stomped below to his own tidy little cabin.

At sea the captain was known for being a foulmouthed old tyrant, as well as a damn fine whaler. Yet Captain Riggs prided himself above all in his education. There were no spelling mistakes or grammatical errors in his log.

He took off his jacket and sat down at the table to enter the day's catch, carefully inking in three immaculate little drawings of sperm whales in the margin. It was the twenty-third of October, in the Year of Our Lord eighteen hundred and forty-six. The captain carefully blotted the log book and put it away before taking out a fresh sheet of vellum. He would pen yet another letter to his friend and former school chum, Congressman Pratt, of New York.

"My dear Pratt," he began, in his strong, copperplate lettering, "I beg to draw your attention once again to the reprehensible and intolerable situation which presently troubles this most distant fleet of the United States, fishing as we do for the whale oil that lights the lamps of those centers of civilization and Christianity, centers which seem so far and dear to us voyagers as we stand, here at sea, off these most dangerous shores of the archipelago of the Japans . . ."

Up on deck, his men toiled like demons, feeding the maws of the ship's own deity, the Baal in duplicate, the fiery twins, the red-brick try pots and their belching smoke and fire.

Saburo stood, pointing. "Look! Smoke! Out on the horizon!"

What could it be? There was no island out there. The old man took up the precious telescope and made a show of looking, although his eyes were too dim to discern anything but a faint black smudge.

"May I?" The samurai stood and came beside him, slipping the sword back in the sash. Old man Toumi bowed and held the telescope out to him in both hands. After a long look the samurai spoke with sudden vehemence.

"It is a barbarian ship, and on fire."

The old man's mind raced. "Respectfully, sir, but I do not believe it is on fire." The old man was confident of his knowledge, if not of his eyes. "It is surely a whaling ship. They say that the barbarians render oil from the whales they kill at sea, cooking the blubber in fire pots which they set in the middle of their great black ships, and huge ships they must be, big as towns, for they live aboard them, and come from distant lands for whales."

"How can you know that?" demanded the samurai, his

14

tone harsh. There was a strict Tokugawa edict that forbad any Japanese to go out of sight of land or to have any contact with foreigners. Here not even a single whaleboat or net boat could be built without a license issued by the administrators of the feudal lords of Kii.

"Forgive me, sir, merely stories we hear . . ." The old man bowed.

"Stories?"

"It is said that the Tosa men saved a few of the hairy devils when their ship was driven onto rocks by a typhoon. Rumors reach us, and as we also are whalers, we remember such things. Strange fellows, barbarians! Are there no whales on their own shores?"

The samurai grunted as if in thought. He had known about shipwrecked barbarians, but he had not known of the cooking of whale oil on their ships. He had been more concerned with reports of the size and design of the cannon and swivel guns that even these civilian vessels carried, weapons powerful enough to rake or sink any Tokugawa ship, if not to bombard a small town.

"Have such ships come closer into shore here?"

"No, sir, not here." The old man swept one arm in the direction of the rugged coast, where tattered rags of surf streamed from half-submerged rocks and reefs. "It is too dangerous, for anyone except we who were born to navigate these waters."

True enough, thought the samurai, and that truth was one great strength. The barbarians must never, never learn these waters!

A fleeting fantasy came to him again, of a seashore confrontation with a few, no, a dozen of those hairy half men. His hand stole to the hilt of the long sword, finger feeling the silken cords, the ridges of hilt bindings under the cloth, the sharkskin of the long handle. Then angry at himself for indulging in fantasies, he pushed the thoughts of blood away and looked back to where the bay curved to a small harbor, sheltered behind an island. All around the harbor was a jumble of tiled and thatched roofs, shoving against the lower slopes of the densely forested hills. We can defend those hills forever, he thought, but not the town.

Like most villages and towns along the coast, Taiji was cramped for space. Houses stood shoulder to shoulder, facing each other across narrow streets, pushing right to the edges of the high-tide marks.

Another cry from the boy broke his thoughts.

"A blow!"

"Angle?" asked the old man.

"Straight. It looks like a right whale."

"Why?" asked the old man.

"The blow goes straight up," said Saburo, "then it sort of divides, and it's a fatter blow than that of a humpback, and not as high as the blow of a fin or a blue whale . . . Oh, there it blows again!" His boyish voice piped even higher in excitement.

"Quick, Saburo, get those flags up . . . two black with white centers. Hurry, before those fellows at Kandori see it!" He raised a conch to his lips, took in a deep breath, and sounded a long, mournfully triumphant note, whose echoes had barely died before Saburo raised the black-and-white pennants that licked at the wind like striped tongues. Answering notes came from Kandori, to the southwest, another lookout point, then more notes from the lead chase boat.

Saburo ignored the waving of signal sticks on the boats and kept his eyes out to sea.

"Moving southward, less than one *ri,* and definitely a right whale!"

"Has it got a calf?" asked the old man.

"No, I don't think so. It's just a lone right whale, and a big one," said the boy. The old man took up a signal stick, a thing that resembled a long-stalked chrysanthemum whose flowers were made of a big white cluster of paper petals. He waved it with large, straight-armed movements.

"Saburo, look for me, tell me if there is an answer from Mukaijima!"

Saburo took the telescope and looked landward. He focused it on the watch house that stood on the high point of the island that sheltered the harbor. Then he swung across the short stretch of shallows, deepening to a channel, searching the beach in front of the Asuka shrine.

"Ah! Kakuemon-sama is coming down the beach, and he has seen our signal." He kept the telescope on the figure, waiting impatiently for a reaction from it. "Yes! The signal has gone up! Hunt!"

Old man Toumi blew the conch again, but by now the net boats were racing into position, reaching out like horns. Now the chase boats darted forward, beautiful boats, each with its own design of phoenix, paulownia, chrysanthemum, pine, plum blossom, bamboo, intricate patterns set upon bands of the brightest colors, enabling any boat to be distinguished at a distance. The fleet was a coordinated body,

16

with each boat having its own status and position, and each man knowing his place, for where a man stood and what he did in the fleet were almost totally determined by birth and tradition.

The samurai watched them with admiration as they moved out, like a body of disciplined cavalry, red pennants streaming from the tall bamboo poles at their sterns, just as horse-riding warriors would lash pennant poles to their bodies as they charged into battle.

He heard a sound, a scuffle, and spun around.

Breathless with the exertion of scrambling up the cliffs from the rocks below, Toumi's youngest son, Kakichi, ran toward them along the narrow pathway. In one hand he held a fishing pole, in the other three rock bream and a black-striped parrot fish. When Kakichi saw the stranger, his dress, demeanor, swords, he skidded to a stop and threw himself on his knees, bowing. Beads of sweat trickled down the shaven top of his head.

"Sir, this is merely my idle son," said the old man, although it was he who had told Kakichi to go and catch lunch, and even which rock to fish from and what bait to use. The samurai laughed goodnaturedly.

"So, we catch both big and small here, do we?" He glanced over to the ever-ready embers of the signal fire. "And I thought that this was for making smoke, but it would seem it is for cooking fish. Good idea! Good idea!"

Kakichi flushed with embarrassment, but the samurai held up one hand.

"No apologies are needed." He laughed again. "Your little brother has eyes good enough for the two of you."

"They are not brothers, sir," said Toumi. "This boy is the third son of the harpooner of the lead boat. He and my worthless son are second cousins. This lad is too young to go out with the fleet, but he likes to come here, with me."

"A blow! A blow!" Saburo, who had been keeping his eyes out to sea, called out again. The whale had surfaced after a long dive. "It's moving away from the coast!"

The old man forgot all about manners and turned his back on the samurai again to wave the signal sticks, one in each hand this time. His signals were answered from the line of chase boats, and a group of them began to speed even faster, as fast as their mirror-smooth, black lacquered hulls would let them, the men straining at the eight long sculling oars, racing to cut across the path of the escaping whale. Boat wakes scrawled white on the surface of the sea.

Wheeling around and reaching ahead of the whale, the boats now began to drive it. Even up on the cliffs one could hear the thump of mallets on oar stems, punctuating the chants of the men. Thump! Thump! Thump! Tens of mallets beating, with the impact of wood on wood resounding through the hulls of the boats even stronger in the sea than in the air above it. By now the half-moon set of great rope nets was closed, and the chase boats began to head the whale toward it.

"It's going toward the nets! Toward the nets!" shrieked Saburo. "Ah, it's turning, running on the surface like a dolphin!"

The old man signaled frantically, and two chase boats, chrysanthemum and plum, sped out to head it off, their beat even faster and stronger now than the rest of the fleet's.

Crescendoing over the sea and hurled back by the cliffs, the chanting, lusty voices of well over three hundred men, marked by the beat of mallet and drum, by the creak of oars and stamp of bare feet, rose up and filled the ears of the watchers, pulling them to the race and drama spread out below them.

"Brave music!" exclaimed the samurai. The sound recalled to him the reverberation of great battle drums, drums that made bones tremble, drums that had stayed silent for far, far too long now. He was a *bushi,* a warrior, samurai, and thus in status far above these men he now watched, but still he couldn't help admiring them, even feeling a little envious, facing as they did danger, their prey, their opponent. He had trained all his life to face danger and perhaps death, but his enemies were out of reach, and he wielded sword, halberd and spear only in practice, not in gripping reality, as did these whalers.

In the prow of the leading chase boat, Saburo's father, Tatsudaiyu, stood calmly, one harpoon under his left arm and another on the rest in front of him. The first semicircular set of nets was ready, and beyond it the net boats were speedily running out a second set. This was a big whale, and it could run through the first nets, tangling and slowing itself in the meshes, movements hampered by floating beams and tubs that would clatter and thump along its broad back and sides.

The whale was bolting, terrified by the din of mallets and stamping feet. Its huge tail thrashed, swirling round patches on the surface of the water, and behind it the men strained and chanted at their oars, sweat streaming down chests and backs and darkening the red folds of their loincloths. The phoenix boat drew ahead, black hull knifing whitely.

Now Tatsudaiyu raised his right arm in salute to the whale, calling to it. His men roared and pushed their boat forward in a burst of speed. Tatsudaiyu transferred the first harpoon to his right hand. It was a light weapon with a thin rope attached to it, into which shavings of white wood were woven. The smoothed base of the harpoon shaft rested in the palm of his right hand. His left hand gripped the shaft lightly, while the right arm was held straight down and back, left hand at right breast. His eyes were on the whale, always on the whale.

The black back broke surface, breath whooshed and the blow wafted back at them, and just then Tatsudaiyu with a swift and powerful flexing of muscles flung the harpoon skyward. Up and up it arced, rope streaking like a kite tail, then it reached its zenith and plummeted downward, burying itself deep in the whale's back.

Feeling the prick, the whale dived, but the buoyant line traced its underwater flight, snaking along the surface. Tatsudaiyu made a sharp cutting motion to the right, then lifted the second harpoon off its rest. This one was heavier, and attached to a thick rope and a grappling anchor. His second stood ready, keeping the lines clear so they wouldn't tangle when the anchor went overboard. He and Tatsudaiyu needed no speech between them. They had been together on this boat for ten years now, and within another two or three years the second might get a chase boat of his own.

The foot stamping and mallet pounding had stopped aboard the leading chase boats now, and their chants grew even stronger, coming up from deep in the bellies of the men at the sculling oars.

Tatsudaiyu glanced left and right, seeing that first and second chase boats were in position. Their harpooners, or *hazashi,* would wait for him to make this next throw before they took turns to dart forward like dogs on a boar.

The broad-muscled and deeply tanned chests of the men glistened, bare legs flexing against the movement of boat, oar partners shoulder to shoulder, eyes ahead, long hair blowing beneath headbands, chants syncopated, and seconds with voices rising in what sounded almost like a lament. Even after a hundred, two hundred, no matter how many whales, this creak of oars, the roar of their song, the rush of white water along the hull, the cut of the high, sharp prows, the wind in his face, all of it filled Tatsudaiyu's deep chest with an excitement that was almost too hard to bear.

"Hahhhhhhh! It comes!" he cried, taking his own breath as the breath of his quarry jetted to the sky where soon his second harpoon would arc. Scents of the whale blow drifted back at him as he saw his harpoon come down deep and hard into the base of the whale's tail, just before the frenzied animal tried to make another dive. His second tossed the anchor overboard and the phoenix boat dropped back.

With wild yells, the second boat darted forward, harpooner poised and ready.

On the phoenix boat a young man was scrambling to get another harpoon and coil of line from beneath the deck boards, but Tatsudaiyu's second waved him back to his oar. Tatsudaiyu would use no more harpoons on this whale. Instead, Yosuke, his second, pulled out the long, double-edged, broad-bladed killing spear and slipped off its wooden sheath, before making a small bow and passing it to his chief. Tatsudaiyu laid it ready on the rest.

Other chase boats moved forward and one after another their harpooners hurled irons. The great fan of the tail raised and smacked the sea with a crash, showering the nearest boats with water. Harpoon lines were streaming and tangling, attached variously to long floats of bamboo, or tubs, or anchors.

Now the whale drove into the first nets, breaking attaching ropes and bringing a clutter of beams and meshes and tubs all around itself. Even as it did so, another harpoon arced down and bit deep. The whale tried to dive, but it could not, and its head, bonneted with barnacles and long-stemmed parasites, came high up out of the water.

Iwadaiyu, harpooner of the second boat, urged his men forward again, then looked back over his shoulder and nodded to a young man, his second, a tall, heavily muscled young man with deep eyes and a hawklike nose. Rowers called out encouragements to him as he steadied his nerves and got ready to face the danger and difficulty of the task he must now perform. For Taiji whalers this was the most crucial task of all in securing a whale. He readjusted the wooden sheath of the long knife tucked into his loincloth, determined to do his job well, or die in trying.

The thrashing, agonized whale was struggling against the ropes and meshes, one flipper so tangled that the animal had trouble maintaining equilibrium. Iwadaiyu's chrysanthemum boat came close, being careful to stay clear of the whale's frenzied tail.

"Now!,' cried the harpooner, and the youth dived into the water, swimming with a few strong strokes and grasping for a hold in the tangle on the whale's back. With herculean effort the whale managed to dive, but the young man clung fast, despite the painful pressure in his ears. His lungs almost burst, but the young man clung like a louse, vowing to himself that even if it took him to the very bottom of the ocean he would never let go.

Up the whale came, breaking the surface and exhaling violently, blood streaming from its wounds in scarlet ribbons. Hand over hand the youth edged closer to the blowhole, and as he neared it the whale whooshed breath again, the sound almost deafening him. The young man, straining his utmost, held on with one hand, and with the other freed the knife. The whale rolled over and struggled down again, down beneath the cold green waters, trailing those ribbons of scarlet. The flukes thrashed and made clouds of bubbles, white as the irregular patches on the whale's belly. All along and around the huge body, the lines and tubs and beams bumped and tangled, threatening to enmesh the human clinging to the whale's back. Men died doing this, and that was why it was such an honor.

Surface! The young man sucked air gratefully. By now he was right up to the blowhole, which jetted right by his face in a hot, moist rush. Down again went the whale, but not as deep, for it was exhausted. A net tub banged against his leg, but the young man ignored the pain, and while clinging to a net mesh with his left hand, he cut with the right, making a hole through the whale's septum, through the tough divisions of tissue in the blowhole.

The whale thrashed and made another attempt to dive, but the cut was made. The young man kicked away, careful to avoid the flukes. Then, with knife raised triumphantly above his head, he surfaced. The other whalers cheered, and eager hands pulled him into the boat.

Jinsuke, eldest son of Tatsudaiyu, had cut his first whale, and bravely too.

A second young man dove into the water with a rope around his waist. He swam to the whale, scrambled up its back, and threaded the rope through the triangular cut.

Jinsuke was aware that his leg was grazed and bleeding, and he felt stiff and battered, muscles burning, but a hearty slap on the shoulder from his captain and the laughing praise of his comrades made that all seem nothing, nothing at all.

"Jinsuke, you are indeed your father's son, and we'll make a whaler of you yet!"

Watchful but silent, Tatsudaiyu looked across to the boat of his best friend and saw his son. His chest swelled, and he grasped the killing spear that one day his son would grasp. Without looking back at his own crew he chopped at the air with his free hand. The boat dashed forward, just as the whale hit the second line of nets, coming almost to a stop. With a cry, "Eiiiy!" Tatsudaiyu hurled the heavy, broad spear between the whale's ribs.

Iwadaiyu's boat came in from the other side, and steel flashed. Now flanking the whale, the harpooners Tatsudaiyu and Iwadaiyu thrust again and again, drawing their spears back on their braided pulling lines.

Green sea turned deep red, and the red to frothing pink as the whale fought against the binding of ropes and impediments.

Now the whale began to lash from side to side and the chase boats drew back. The end was close now. Broader, heavier *moso-bune,* or carry boats, banded black and red, two of them, moved cautiously into position. Each of these broad boats carried fifteen men and eight oars, but as they closed in on either side of the whale, the four oars on the inside of each boat were shipped. Offside oarsmen kept the two vessels in position, the floundering, weakened whale between them. The men who no longer had oars to handle took ropes and dived under the whale and the tangle, carrying ropes from boat to boat.

Two great beams were lashed across the whale's back, so that the boats became pontoons with the whale between them.

Now the terrible final lancing began, the men on the carry boats readying themselves to leap overboard should the dying beast thrash with enough violence to tip them over. Again and again the lances darted and soon a rain of heavy, thick blood jetted from the blowhole and fell on the men. Quivering in death throes, the whale stretched out its body. They could hear the crack of tissues in the spine, and then came an awful, low-pitched sound as the whale vented its death cry.

The gape drooped open. The small eyes filmed. The blowhole relaxed. A silence fell upon the whole fleet. But for the lift and fall of the ocean swell, the boats and the men were motionless. *Isana*, the brave fish, was dead. Speed and peace to its soul! From the throats of three hundred Taiji men, a chant of blessing and gratitude swelled, deep and soft as the wind.

At the clifftop lookout at Tomyosaki, old man Toumi sighed and bowed out to sea. He turned to signal a kill to Mukaijima, which set off a scurry of activity on the sloping sandy beach in front of the shrine.

Kakichi began to fold and store the pennants carefully, flags, signal sticks, telescope and conch, and to carry them up to the little watch house.

"We did it, sir, we got a whale today!" said Saburo to the samurai, who had said nothing, but just stood there, one hand gripping the covered hilt of his sword.

A clanking rattle came from the shrine, as the old man yanked on the rope of the bell. Then he clapped his hands, bowed, and gave thanks. The deity within kept silent, but no doubt watched over the sea, the men, the boats, and the soul of the whale too, and the old man felt a great thankful reverence in his heart. He stood there, a little old man with a sparse gray topknot and failing, rheumy eyes, until the first smells of roasting fish tickled his nostrils.

Saburo had brought twigs and built up the fire, and Kakichi spitted the fish and stuck the pointed sticks around the fire, angling toward the heat. It would take a long time before the whale was landed, and they were hungry, and thirsty too.

The old man bowed again to the open doors of the shrine then scuttled around to the back of the wooden building and reached underneath, his hand closing on a large brownish earthenware jug. He went around to the front again and filled a cup to lay before the deity, then carried the jug by its string to the fireside.

"Kakichi! Cups! Hurry!" The old man bowed to the samurai.

"Sir, we are poor wretches, with little to offer a guest, but if it does not offend you, will you taste this worthless stuff? Not fine sake, unexcusable, but . . ."

The samurai suppressed a grin. Peasants and fishermen were not supposed to brew rice wine, but he was not at all surprised that whalers did. Kakichi brought him a teacup.

"We have taken a fine whale this day, sir," said the old man, "and although what we have is not fit for an important person like you, it might refresh you. This evening I'm sure you'll have a fine feast."

The samurai glanced at him, noting that although these Taiji folk were bolder and more familiar with him than fishermen from another village might be, there was no disrespect intended. He took the proffered cup and held it while the old man poured a thickly white brew. In his turn, the wily old man had sensed a tolerance quite unusual in this stranger, otherwise he would never have dared take another cup and share the contents of this flask. The edicts of the Tokugawa *bakufu* government in Edo were strict, and divisions between classes, what they could wear or do, were clear.

"I keep this for the god," said the old man, waiting for the nod that told him he could fill his own cup. "When we get a big whale, a right whale, I think the god would prefer not to drink alone. Ah yes, sir, a fine whale, a fine whale!"

The samurai raised his cup. "Then I toast the whale, and the whalers, and the men of Taiji!"

He sipped the rich fermentation, milky, dew-cooled and potent, as nutritious as it was strong. "Ah, old man, it is a long time since I have tasted such good *doburoku.*" He sipped again and breathed a sigh of pleasure. This was not the clear wine of the towns, nor the exquisitely refined wine of his lord's castle, but the whitish homemade brew made from fermented rice in earthen pots, probably hidden underground somewhere. The drink of ordinary folk. But how much better it tasted in this place, with the open sky and the cries of birds, with surf crashing on the cliffs below. and the fragrance of fish broiling over a simple fire, and on the wind, the distant chant of brave men.

He had walked long and far, setting out when the moon was high. His path led him through a forest of cedar, pine and white oak. Each gust of night wind brought a shower of golden needles, and memories, memories . . . Then on up through a steep grove of bamboo he went, hearing the feathery tops sway and dance. On and on he walked.

Long and tiring though the hike may have been, like all such walks it imparted peace, and when at dawn of this morning the path had led him to the edge of this cliff, with a vista of red-gold sky and gleaming ocean, he, the *bushi,* master of sword and spear, man of steel and ice, had almost wept. Not with loss and pain, nor in secret as he had done so many times, but with sheer open joy at the beauty of his homeland.

Now, with wine in his belly and with its sweet aftertaste lingering on his palate, a pleasant languor came over him.

He leaned back against a cherry tree that grew by the rock he sat on, and watched the flight of a black swallow-tailed butterfly. As it fluttered and dipped, another image came to him, a dancing figure, of even more grace and beauty, with long silken sleeves moving like wings, body slender as a wand, hair black and shining, more lustrous than the wings of this . . .

"Sir, will you have some more?" asked the old man, kneeling before him with the flask. The samurai held out his cup.

"What happens with the whale now?" he asked gruffly, taking his eyes away from the butterfly and looking out to sea.

"Those smaller boats are net boats and barrel boats, see how they are scattered? That's because they are picking up equipment. It's all wet and tangled, a long hard job, especially after a whale that fought like that one. The whale is hugged by the carry boats, with a towing line through the blowhole to keep the head up and make it easier to tow. Three chase boats, in line, help to haul. Sometimes, when wind and tide are against us, we have to use more boats, but it's good today, and three chase boats and the carry boats will get the whale in by late afternoon."

The samurai calculated quickly how many men were pulling at the oars to bring the whale in. Four oars on each outer side of the carry boats, twenty-four more oars on the chase boats, and two men to each oar, except the paired stern oars of the chase boats.

"Fifty-eight men," he muttered.

"Grandfather, the fish is ready," said Saburo. The smells of broiled fish made the warrior's belly growl, and annoyed at himself, he stood and stretched.

"That barbarian ship has gone," he said.

"They drift with the Black Current," said the old man, "following the whales as they move north and south . . . er . . . or so we foolish whalers believe here."

Ranging the whole length of our land, thought the samurai grimly.

The chants coming over the sea now were of a new tempo. They could hear more drums now, and even flutes, as well as the deep sound of conches, while all of it blended and wove patterns around the lilting voices of the chant leaders. The harpooners were standing in the prows of their boats, feet braced, bodies and arms weaving in dance, the whalers' dance. They made movements in the air with white-tufted signal sticks, in time with the song, movements that symbolized waves, storms, wind, whales, and the flight of a well-hurled harpoon. The men at the oars roared the chants, each boat competing yet complementing the chorus. None of the words made sense to the samurai, but the triumph in them was clear enough.

"The whale was expertly killed," he said, and still standing, sipped at the brew again.

"Ah, thank you, indeed it was, sir," said the old man, "and not too many irons in it. Sometimes a whale takes fifty or sixty harpoons."

"In that case it is well named. Brave fish! It would require a heroic man to endure so many thrusts from arrows, spears or swords. But tell me, why so many harpoons? Can they not aim for the vitals?"

"Ah, they do, sir, but when you chase a whale you see only the back. The vital points are small and fewer than in men . . . er . . . or so I have heard. The chief harpooner will try to hit a spot we call 'zebi.' That's near the tail, above where the whale hides it genitals. A good strike there will make the whale flutter about, and more lines can be sunk into it. However, if somebody hits the *zebi* a second time, the whale will wake up and shoot off like an arrow. Tatsudaiyu-san often hits the *zebi* so hard the first time that they can secure and kill without using nets."

The samurai drew parallels in his mind with the art of Yawara, at which he was adept. A trained man could strike at an enemy with fist, the sword edge of a hand, or the spear of stiffened fingers, and cause him to go into shock, a shock from which he could be revived by another, carefully placed blow. Then again, when a foe had both arms raised for a down cut with a sword, even a shallow thrust with a sword point, just below the sternum, would momentarily halt the cut, paralyze him.

"Are there other points?"

"There is one spot in the whale's cheek which paralyzes it, and a cut to the great artery in the tail base will make it bleed to death. But mostly the whale must be thrust between the ribs, into the lungs. The blubber is thick, and the ribs stout, with much meat between them, so it is not an easy kill."

"Grandfather, if we don't eat the fish soon, it will burn."

The old man turned to the samurai again. "It is vulgar food, sir, but freshly caught, and the morning grows late. You must be hungry, sir. Won't you take some fish?"

The samurai almost refused, at which by custom he would be asked again, and again he would refuse until they finally tried to insist, but suddenly something in him rebelled. Because of the open sky? The long distance from the conventions and rules of the castle? Or the bracing wind from the sea? Or was it the brown, honest, open faces of the old man and the two boys. He smiled and inclined his head.

Saburo laid the biggest fish on a broad leaf of bamboo grass and brought it over to him. Kakichi had cut and peeled twigs to make chopsticks, and shyly he handed a pair to the samurai, apologizing, head low. The samurai smiled at them both, and the boys stepped away several paces to let him eat.

So good it was! Far better than any food he'd taken in the past ten months, and better than all the delicacies they had plied him with in the castle at Wakayama. Succulent white flesh of broiled fish matched the sweetness of wine. It awoke an appetite he had thought gone forever.

The smaller boy approached him again, timidly, in his hand another folded leaf.

"Excuse me, sir, would you like this?"

"What is it?"

The boy held it out, too shy to speak. The samurai took it and opened the leaf to see pieces of sweet yam, cooked with a little rice and salt. Simple, good food. He looked up at the boy's face, seeing eyes that shone back at him like pebbles wetted by surf, and he felt a wish: if only he had a son.

"*Itadakimasu,*" he said, gruffly, and popped a piece in his mouth. "Mmmm, delicious." He handed the bundle back. "You eat, lad, it'll make you grow strong. Your mother is a good cook." He felt a sudden warmth in his heart for this polite little boy in simple peasant clothes of threadbare cotton, with feet bare and dirty, and legs scabbed with scratches.

"Give me one more piece, please," he said, and Saburo's face flushed with pleasure.

"We can't eat such good stuff in town." The boy bobbed his head and started to go away.

"Boy, why does your father throw the harpoon up into the air? Why not throw it straight at the whale? Do you know?"

"The point goes in deeper when it falls down like that, and if it goes in straight the chin piece on the side of the harpoon won't pull out. But if you ask my father, maybe he'll show you."

The old man looked up from his fish and spoke sharply.

27

"Saburo! Don't be rude! What can we country bumpkins show an educated gentleman?"

The samurai laughed. "Many things! About whales, about the cooking of fish and brewing of *doburoku*!"

But even as he laughed, the samurai's military mind was digesting what the boy had said, and what he had seen. He had an old scroll at the castle, done before the Tokugawa regime cut Japan off from the rest of the world. The scroll showed in detail the tactics of ancient archers from the barbarian kingdom, across on the other side of the world. A rare scroll it was indeed, one he showed to none other. It showed men arranged in lines, facing charging, mounted, armored warriors. The archers fired all at once, first one line, then another, firing the arrows into the air. If the scroll was true, then those arrows, falling like rain, were piercing armor and flesh at a hundred paces.

He had other scrolls too, brought from Nagasaki, describing the use of mortars of Hollander type, and of similar weapons cast by the converted barbarian called Anjin, back in the time of the first Tokugawa shogun, Ieyasu. These weapons, fired by black powder, hurled heavy missiles into the air to come down on enemy fortifications and structures behind high walls.

He mused . . . There is nothing, he thought, that we Japanese have not already learned about or discovered, but do we use them or modify them? He reflected too that if only the whalers were of *bushi*, or warrior, status, even of low rank, they could be trained to make a fast, effective inshore fleet of fighting men who knew how to face great danger on the sea, who knew how to operate in trained, disciplined coordination. His mind moved with the beginnings of a battle plan.

If the boats were all black, and the men in dark clothes, instead of gaudy designs and red loincloths, surely they could move over the water just before dawn, getting quickly up close to an enemy ship, under the muzzles of the cannon. Also, the boats were very, very swift, and would be difficult to hit. And each boat carried fifteen men easily . . .

"Thank you for the feast." He stood and bowed. The old man and the two boys bowed back, more deeply.

"Sir, we came across to this point by boat," said the old man. "The boat is small and disgracefully dirty, but it is a quicker means of getting to Taiji than by walking all around the bay. If it suits you, will you permit us to row you over?"

"If I won't inconvenience you," replied the samurai.

The two boys tidied up the remains of the meal and doused the fire. A shrike called noisily from the bushes, a sign even in balmy Taiji that autumn was here. On his walk, the samurai had stopped and watched one of these birds, its eye bold with a streak of black, impale a small green frog on a thorn. The frog writhed on the thorn the way the samurai had seen tortured criminals writhe, and he had reflected at that time that life, whether it be for frogs, whales or men, could be as full of cruelty as it was of kindness. He slipped the sword and sheath back into his sash.

"This way, sir," called the old man, beginning to lead the way down the steep cliff path, sending red land crabs scuttling out of the way.

While Yosuke was wiping and drying the long blade of the killing spear, Tatsudaiyu stood at the prow, half smiling at the jokes his men yelled across to the other boats. The phoenix boat by right would be the first back at their base on Mukaijima, back to the warehouse and shops. Tatsudaiyu's lance and harpoons would be the first to receive attention there. In fact, his were the only weapons that got the personal attention of the toolmaker himself. All others were dealt with by the blacksmith.

Tatsudaiyu's hand rested on the smooth paintwork of the gunwale. He felt its warmth, and in that warmth remembered the firmness, the warmth of his wife's thighs when first he married her, and even now, nineteen years later, it stirred him. The exertion and excitement of the hunt were subsiding, giving way to other feelings, to a quiet spring of joy that grew and widened, until his voice, stronger than the voices of all the others, lifted out in song, and his men chanted and roared out the chorus, verse after verse. Other boats took it up and threw it back. With a signal stick in his right hand, Tatsudaiyu began the whalers' dance. The black prow of the phoenix boat knifed shoreward, the red kill pennant fluttering out like the tail of a rooster.

On the beach beside the shrine of Asuka, Taiji Kakuemon was joking with the *naiya danna,* the warehouse boss. Already a crowd of women, children and old folk were crowding the bamboo fence that separated the flensing and processing area from the rest of the beach. On the matted floor of the watch house, three uniformed men were chatting and sipping tea with noisy slurps, while two others, long staff in hand, checked people coming into the flensing area.

"I wonder how much meat those rogues will try to hide away today?" Kakuemon spoke, looking over the jostling scene. His was the responsibility of the entire operation, of an industry in Taiji which employed over seven hundred men at the peak of operations, and which sent whale meat, oil, meal, sinew and baleen all over the country.

"The last time we brought a right whale in, they caught old Hikohei's woman trying to sneak out with a cut of the best tail meat stuck down her crotch."

The *naiya danna* laughed wheezily. "I heard about that. She told the watchman she was having her monthlies when he spotted it, and her at sixty or more . . ."

They both guffawed.

Kakuemon had quietly instructed the watchmen to turn a blind eye to the men stealing a little piece here and there, but to be severe on anybody trying to get away with the best cuts, reserved for the lords of Kii and both the shogun's and the emperor's palaces . . . and, of course, to influential people . . . He shook his head and thought that if the authorities knew where some of the meat had to be rescued from, his head would be displayed somewhere on a board.

Wada Kinemon, Kakuemon's cousin, came hurrying toward them. He had taken the path around the bay from his house and was out of breath. Wada Kinemon was in his fifties, slight of build, face haggard. It was he who had persuaded the *han*, or fiefdom, to let him and his cousin run the Taiji whaling business without any direct supervision from the castle at Shingu. However, whales and weather had not favored them, and he was constantly afraid that the blame might be placed on him.

Like Kakuemon, Wada Kinemon held the *bushi* status, and was entitled to wear two swords, the *hakama* and the *haori* decorated with the family crest. Their status was also indicated by the special way their topknots were tied and looped over half-shaved heads.

"A visitor is coming," he said. "Hurry, clean this place up and get some cushions. What do you think you are, you men, sitting around drinking tea, get out and watch that fence! Is everything in order at the warehouse? Any boats damaged?"

The *naiya danna* bowed.

"Everything is fine, Wada-sama."

Wada looked around nervously, wishing he'd had warning.

"It's an official, all the way from Wakayama castle. Ota village passed word to me of his coming. He was there yesterday, looking around the harbor, asking questions. He should be here now. I pray that no accident has befallen him, it's quite a rough walk. I've sent four men back to look for him, with a palanquin."

"An official? From Wakayama? But we deal with Shingu."

The castle of the lord of Shingu controlled the estuary of the Kumano River, down which came rafts of valuable lumber. Fishing was excellent in that area too. The lord of Shingu was ultimately responsible for the Taiji whaling. Lord Mizuno was a vassal of the Tokugawa shogun, standing under the banner of the powerful castle and lord of Wakayama. It was most odd and worrying that a visitor should not come through Shingu, even though Shingu was farther along the coast. The two managers walked out of earshot of the others.

"Do you know who he is?" asked Kakuemon. "How many in his party? Why did he not come by ship?"

"It's incredible, but he's alone, and he walked, nearly all the way, from Wakayama!"

"Alone? A Wakayama *bushi*? He walked, you say?" Kakuemon couldn't believe it. No official would travel alone. This man must be some wandering *ronin* who had slipped past the border guards. Well, he'd quickly be taken care of if he tried to make trouble in Taiji!

"This is a very special man, it seems, an unusual fellow, with quite a reputation as a swordsman. He is supposedly one of the favorites of the daimyo, and related somehow to the daimyo of Hikone. He served in the Wakayama Department of Internal Administration, but what he's doing now, nobody knows. He's young, twenty-five or twenty-six, and very well thought of. They say he walks everywhere, visiting all the villages along the coast, taking notes, and they say too that he doesn't appear to be short of money."

"Hmmm, no *ronin*, then. But what, a spy? For what reason?"

"I have no idea, but we have nothing to worry about, do we." Kinemon's face betrayed what he really felt. "Our taxes and contributions are all paid, the records in order, the boats licensed."

The chanting, drumbeating fleet was in sight now, easily heard from the beach. Men stripped to loincloths stood ready beside three great capstans, their ropes and toggles run out to the water's edge.

Another, smaller boat was coming in ahead of the rest,

though, and one figure in that little craft had already attracted attention.

Standing in the stern, Kakichi sculled. His last strokes sent the prow scraping up the sand. Old man Toumi and Saburo jumped out to pull the bow a little farther up. Matsudaira Sadayori, warrior administrator of the daimyo of Wakayama castle, stood and jumped out lightly. He stood waiting by the waterline, while Taiji Kakuemon and Wada Kinemon approached to greet him. He saw anxiety in their faces, and suppressed a smile. These men had nothing to worry about, not from him, for Matsudaira Sadayori was no longer concerned with taxes and tributes and the punishment of offenders. His concern was for the integrity of the entire sacred nation of Japan.

Chapter Two

Sadayori sat on a hastily brought cushion placed on the rather grubby mats of the watch house overlooking the beach. A cup of green tea and a small plate of sweet bean-paste cakes was set beside him.

He had expressed a wish to observe the whole process of cutting up a whale, and now the three capstans, powered by brawny men who strained and pushed, bodies at an angle, feet driving deep into sand, were heaving their thick ropes against the tail of the whale. Hoarse shouts and a drumbeat kept their efforts in time with each other. Looking at the men, Sadayori thought that any one of them might make a wrestler.

Tail first, slowly, slowly, the whale moved up the beach until its bulk was halfway out of the water and the immense weight of its rotund body proved too much to move any farther.

Sadayori was so curious and enthralled that he almost left his place and went down among the workers. Such a huge animal it was, and extraordinarily vast cavern of a mouth it had, so curved in the jaw, with a strange kind of fence of fringed plates hanging from the roof its mouth. So that was what they called the "beard" was it? Strange! Kakuemon came and sat beside him.

"It is unusual for us to take a right whale so early in the season. In fact, this is the first one. Your arrival brought good fortune. At this time of the year we usually only get the perfume whales."

"Perfume whales? Ah yes, I've heard about them, they have a strange but precious substance in their guts, don't they?"

"Ah yes, indeed, 'dragon dribble' we call it, used as the base of the best perfumes. They also give us fine ivory, very hard and durable, and their oil is excellent, the best there is for lamps. The meat is very dark, though, and most people prefer the meat of bearded whales. We Taiji people eat it, though, usually sun-dried. The meat of this whale will be of the very best, and I do hope that you will be able to grace my poor house with your presence this evening. We shall serve some sashimi and other treats from this one, and you can judge for yourself."

Sadayori inclined his head. "It is too much of an intrusion. I gave you no warning. I had thought to find a room at a local inn."

Kakuemon looked shocked. "Oh, not at all, please, not at all. My house is meager and our fare poor, but we welcome visitors, a chance for conversation and news. Please, do stay. At least I can guarantee that you'll never taste better whale meat."

Sadayori smiled. "Then, I accept, and look forward to it with pleasure, but please forgive me, for I come empty-handed."

Kakuemon shook a hand in negation. "No, no, no! That is no worry at all. Your conversation is a precious gift to us, so isolated are we!"

He got up. "Excuse me, I must oversee the measuring of the whale."

From a small boat one official took a marked line of silk. They measured from blowhole to anus. This was a really big whale, the head alone standing much higher than a man, while its flukes were four arm spans wide.

Now the flensers, with rough straw sandals to give their feet a grip on the slippery, rounded flanks and back, climbed up onto the whale and knelt there, awaiting orders. They too were stripped to scarlet loincloths, with headbands of cotton around their foreheads. The blades of long-handled knives pointed to the sky.

"Rather like *naginata*," murmured Sadayori, who was proficient in the use of the deadly long-handled halberd. The whalers' knives were broader in the blade, and cruder, but looked as if they could quickly be used as a weapon if needed. He watched with extreme interest.

At a signal from Kakuemon, the chief flenser bowed deeply, his men following suit. Then he stood, gripped the long handle with both hands, and made the first, swift cut. With surgical precision they lay bare the red flesh, slicing through ten inches of tough blubber as if it were nothing but bean curd. From the blowhole, they cut along the back and sides. Capstan men ran out with ropes and toggles which were fitted through quickly cut buttonholes; then, with yells and shouts, the capstans turned, blubber ripping off in sheets, peeled back as a man would peel an orange.

"A skillful dissection," said Sadayori to the man beside him, "but there is a certain pathos in seeing such a vast creature stripped of its protection, of its strength, of its very shape. It fought bravely, I saw."

"Then you saw how our men prayed for its soul," said Kakuemon. "Yes, we feel the sadness of death too, but against that sadness is the joy of having such a fine gift from the sea, and we waste nothing. We use the meat, the oil, the sinews, the bones, the plates of the baleen too."

"Even the entrails?"

"Oh yes, those inner parts are a delicacy. They are washed and cut into small pieces, then broiled, or cooked in miso. The men love it, and say it makes them strong inside too. I don't mind it, although I must confess a preference for the meat, especially the fatty meat near the tail."

Sadayori said nothing. He didn't think he'd like to eat entrails, although he had once heard that communities of castaway criminals on some of the offshore islands actually got to prefer the taste of fish entrails and claimed that the eating of such stuff kept away sickness. Perhaps this was true of whale guts also. Certainly the local men were the biggest, strongest-looking fellows he had yet seen on his travels. His eyes ranged over the scene.

To one side was a line of try pots, with conduits leading to cooling and storage vessels. He wondered briefly why there was no black smoke, as they had seen from that barbarian ship, but Taiji folk, far from burning the "biscuits" of cooked and rendered blubber, saved and drained them for cooking in *oden* soup. They were delicious.

A line of seated men was cutting the big blocks of blubber into strips. Another line of men was using hammers to break up bones into easily cooked fragments from which the oil would be rendered, after which the bone fragments would be cooked again, then smashed to make bone meal.

Scuttling between the whale and various work positions, pairs of men with poles and dangling hooks brought large portions of meat and blubber to be worked, always under the careful eyes of the staff-bearing overseers.

Kakuemon smiled. "These people love whale meat, you know, and they try to deceive us, hiding meat wherever and whenever they can. The men will try to slice a piece, then drop it in the sea or kick it into the sand. Their wives or daughters will use any pretext to get inside the enclosure, pick up the meat, hide it in their clothing. Of course, we know, and we let them get away with a little, but if we were not vigilant, they would steal everything but the blowhole."

He pointed to the crowd waiting by the bamboo fence, calling to their menfolk inside. Sadayori laughed, but his eyes kept going back to the careful, dexterous movements of the long-handled knives.

"I notice that your men never cut a tendon," he said.

"Oh no, tendons are much too valuable. They are dried and sold to the armor makers, or to those who make musical instruments."

"Where does the meat go?"

"The best meat is shipped in tribute to the imperial court in Kyoto, to the palace of the shogun in Edo, and also to Lord Mizuno in Shingu. And of course, to the daimyo of Wakayama."

"Ah yes," said Sadayori, "I have tasted your meat there. It was preserved in salt."

"That is what we call 'Matsuura-zuke' or 'Kamakura-zuke'. Perhaps the method of keeping meat was handed down from the times of Kamakura rule?"

"All good things we have been given by our ancestors," said Sadayori, a trifle pompously.

"The rest of the meat goes to Zakota, to the market at Osaka, and to the markets in Ise and Nagoya. The oil goes all over the country. Buyers sail into Taiji from as far as Kyushu to bid for it. Bone meal is sold as a fertilizer. In fact, next month a ship will arrive from Hiroshima to take back a cargo. And do you know, sir, that oil of an inferior kind is used to kill insect pests in paddy fields? Such oil is boiled with vinegar . . ."

Sadayori's host rattled on about the hundred and one uses to which whale products were put, but his own attention had now shifted to the stretch of water between the beach and the island base, where the crews of the boats were now carefully taking their craft out of the water, laying them on timbers above the high-water marks, and placing heavy rice straw mats over them. The upended boats shone like beetle wings, not a wisp of weed on those polished black hulls. Sadayori had never seen such wonderful boats, nor such fast ones, and he reflected that those boats could be easily carried overland.

Meanwhile, at Mukaijima, the warehouses and workshops were a bedlam of banging and shouting. Clash of anvil and hammer mingled with the hiss of bellows, the roar of flames on hot coals and above it all the yelling of harpooners trying to persuade a blacksmith for some special favor, while the blacksmiths shouted back, complaining about the number of badly bent irons.

Outside, rope and net makers grunted and chanted as they hauled sodden masses of tangled cordage out of boats and spread them out to effect repairs.

"Eiyy! Yoh! Eiyyy! Yoh!"

Coopers thumped away with mallets, shaking their heads at smashed tubs, and everybody seemed to be busy, noisy and excited, for it was a fine whale, and there was much to be done. All was bustle and rush, but Tatsudaiyu stood aloof, patiently watching the toolmaker put the final touches of a smooth whetstone to his killing lance. The edge was sharp enough to split a hair.

Tatsudaiyu had put his short quilted jacket back on, tied low down on his hips with a sash into which he had thrust the long case of his tobacco pipe. On his feet were straw sandals.

He looked up to see Saburo come running, dodging the busy men and their piles of equipment. The boy had crossed over from the beach in their little boat, together with old man Toumi. He just remembered to make a perfunctory bow and greeting to his father before bursting into speech.

"Father, there was a great person, a samurai-san from the castle of Wakayama, and he came up to where we were at the lookout and watched with us. He said many admiring things about Taiji people and about mother's food I had with me, for lunch, and he saw you kill the whale and asked me how you throw your harpoon . . ."

Tatsudaiyu gently pulled the boy's ear. "So much talk, like a tide coming in through the narrows!" Saburo was always so full of affection, energy and enthusiasm that a man couldn't get angry with him for long.

"And did he admire your dirty face too?" There was a smudge of charcoal on Saburo's cheek.

"Go and find your older brother," said Tatsudaiyu, "and we shall all go to the bath house early."

Saburo ran off, and with a word to dismiss his second, telling him to stow the killing lance carefully, Tatsudaiyu sauntered down to the water's edge, where old man Toumi was waiting with a boat to ferry them back.

By now the flensing and disposal of bones and parts was almost finished and the try pots were at full cook, filling the village with the heavy, rich smell of whale. Word came out from the office by the shrine that the whalers could go and collect their small ration of whale meat, but Tatsudaiyu's ration would always come first.

The hills around the crowded street and small houses and shops enveloped the village in shadows that spread across the bay, and in the sky above, the crows were gathering to head inland.

The main room of the Wada house was wide and airy, its wooden ceiling, screen frames and beams all of the best-quality timber, of various kinds. There was a fresh spring smell of new mats that reminded Sadayori that the tip of this peninsula was the most southerly point of Honshu. An arrangement of late lilies in the alcove below the deer-antler and whale-ivory sword rack gave him a small pang of loss. He sat in the position of honor, with his back to the alcove, and beside him knelt a young servant girl, a pretty thing in her early teens, with big, dark, deep-set eyes and a fine straight nose, with hair very thick, black and glossy. Taiji women were famous for their looks, but this was the first really attractive girl he had seen here. His attention was drawn to her hands, which were very slim, holding a sake flask of delicate and colorful design matching the small cup he held. He recognized both as coming from a kiln in Kanazawa, on the coast of the Japan Sea. Wada was no country bumpkin then, but a man of taste, and means. The girl smiled and filled the cup. Sadayori gazed down through the clear liquid at a design of two cranes, white bodies and yellow wings, upon a squared background of rich green. On the inner sides of the cup were patterns of unusually vivid colors, whorls and circles, set on a pattern of rice sheaths. Looking even more closely into the cup he saw that the breasts of the cranes, the undersides of their necks and the tips of their primaries were all etched in russet. Feet and tiny eyes were jet black, and perfect. All of this was inside the cup, below the sweet, clear, relief-bringing liquid, but the outside of the cup was just a dullish brown. He closed his eyes and drained the sake. The girl went to fill it right away, but with a delaying gesture Sadayori raised the cup to look more closely, seeing that there was a fish-scale pattern, very faint, and around the base, where only somebody who was really interested might look, was a circle of deep maroon, with a whirling design of what . . . pine leaves? Clouds? And when he looked more closely at the outer sides, the color hinted at bands of different hues, as he had seen upon the sea that morning, so perhaps the design was not of fish scales, but of waves. He grunted softly with appreciation and held the cup out for the girl to fill it again.

The girl spoke. Sadayori came out of his reveries and looked at the cup, into its bottom again, before lifting it to his lips. Cranes, symbols of long life, of happiness, of fidelity. Sadayori sighed softly.

"Sir, won't you try the sashimi? It is very good."

Despite the country accent, her voice was soft and polite. She dipped a thinly sliced square of fat-marbled tail meat for him. He took it, relishing the taste of meat, nutty and tender, and the salty piquancy of soya sauce and grated ginger.

On the low table before him other delicacies were carefully set out, on fine but not overly ostentatious dishes, the foods nestling on fresh broad leaves. Slices of sea fish sashimi, abalone and squid, with one plate holding a large red sea bream, its flesh carefully sliced, yet retaining the original shape of the fish. Once in a while its gill covers moved, so fresh was it. The table also held a dish of small cubes of broiled whale meat, and there were sweetfish, dusted with salt and broiled over charcoal. There were vegetables, and a fragrant soup of parasol mushrooms, always so good in autumn.

Wada Kinemon came in and bowed.

"Fetch the crayfish from the kitchen, hurry," he said. The girl put down the sake flask, bowed, and left. Wada picked it up and held it to refill Sadayori's cup again.

"This is a feast," said Sadayori. He raised his cup again, then reached out with the flask to fill his host's.

"How is the health of our lord at Wakayama?" asked Wada.

"Our lord is well," Sadayori answered briefly. It was not exactly the truth.

"We heard rumors that this summer the castle was struck by lightning and that the towers of the upper pagoda were burned and must be rebuilt."

"Unfortunate, but true," said Sadayori again, pouring for his host once more, "but lightning tends to strike high places."

They both sipped at the warmed sake. Sadayori did not

want to discuss affairs at Wakayama and his last comment made that quite clear. Wada was still curious, though, and tried again.

"We heard the glad news that a son has been born to our lord . . ."

"Yes." A weak, sickly baby that did not seem likely to survive. Who was to know that this child was destined to become the fourteenth shogun of the Empire of Japan?

Sadayori brought the conversation abruptly around to his real reason for coming here.

"Wada-san, you are aware, I'm sure, of the sighting of barbarian ships off this coast? The peninsula of our fiefdom is a large one, reaching well out into the Pacific, and this village maintains alert lookouts, from dawn to dusk, right at the tip of the peninsula. Do you not sight these black ships more than most?"

"Yes, our men mention such things," said Wada.

"It would be helpful if you could arrange that such reports be written in careful detail and forwarded to the Department of Internal Administration in Wakayama, to me," said Sadayori. A wave of relief, quite masked, swept over Wada. So this was not a visit about revenues, taxes, boat licenses, more demands!

"Certainly we can do that," he replied, "although the foreign ships are always so distant that the matter has not seemed to be of importance."

Sadayori's voice had an edge to it. "It is important."

Wada inclined his head. "The reports will be sent."

"Good. Then question the men at the lookouts about one that even I saw, today, and include it in your first report, please."

Wada tensed a little. "Should copies be sent to Shingu?"

"Only if you think it needed, but these matters are vital, and I must get them."

"I understand."

Sadayori looked through hooded lids at the top of the older man's shaven head. He lifted the sake flask and held it in a gesture of reconciliation.

Wada was now aware that despite his lack of escort and fanciful entourage, Sadayori was a man of power, a man to be obeyed. He edged forward a little and held his tiny cup with both hands for Sadayori to fill it.

"Last summer a barbarian ship actually had the temerity to enter Edo Bay," said Sadayori.

"Yes, even in Taiji we heard that. But they were sent away in shame, weren't they?"

News of the abortive American attempt to open up official conversations with the government of the shogun had reached every corner of the realm. They said that a common soldier had struck a senior American officer, Commodore Biddle, when he was transferring from one boat to another. Incredibly, the Americans had not dared to fight, to retaliate, and neither had that officer been shamed into suicide. To the Japanese, that could only mean that the Americans were too soft, or cowardly, or totally without honor, or all three. They would not have understood that the Americans were under strict orders not to cause trouble.

Despite the strict security about these matters, there were other rumors that a certain Captain M. Cooper, of a whaling ship called *Manhattan,* while returning from the northern hunt out of the Banks Island base of Sachs Harbour, had rescued four drifting Japanese fishermen and landed them safely on the Boso Peninsula. The whaler had then sailed to Uraga, at the mouth of Edo Bay, and there obtained provisions and water. They had been unmolested, and to Sadayori and many like him this was an unforgivable lapse. The barbarian should have been attacked and punished, and damn his cannon, and the four wretches with him.

Sadayori took another thin slice of tail meat and dipped it in the sauce. Again his thoughts strayed to his last meeting with the daimyo of Kii, Tokugawa Nariyuki.

The meeting had started off well, with Sadayori laying out sheets upon which he had drawn up details of the increased sightings of foreign ships, as well as military information, most of it secret, obtained from other fiefdoms. Of particular interest were the activities of another Tokugawa daimyo, Nariaki, lord of Mito, who was busily drilling troops, stocking up a huge arsenal of matchlocks, flintlocks and bladed weapons, as well as casting cannon and mortars in readiness for war with the barbarians. Yes, the meeting had started well, but then his lord had changed the subject and begun to talk of Sadayori remarrying.

"All this interest in war, this concern for the protection of our domains is most commendable, but I think it is hiding something else in you. Recently you have been moping and pacing like a sick tiger. You have also become a terror, a devil in the exercise yards and in the dojo, cracking heads and breaking bones. It all comes back to me, you must realize that. They say you snarl, you shout, you are ferocious and dangerous. Also . . . ." He paused, looking directly into Sadayori's eyes. "Reports about your drinking disturb me."

Sadayori had been shamed. It was true. He offered to commit seppuku that very evening.

"No," said the daimyo.

"Then let me take the tonsure, lord, become a monk."

Nariyuki laughed. "This domain has seen enough trouble in the past with warrior priests! No! I need you!" His voice became unusually gentle. "I feel a great loss too, for she was, after all, a dear cousin of mine, and a delightful girl. But she is gone. Gone. And I have decided that you will remarry next spring. A suitable woman will be found for you."

Sadayori choked off the protest before it came to his lips, although the dismay in his face showed for an instant. How could he bear the thought of another woman taking her place? Since his wife had died, trying to give birth to what would have been their first son, the ghost of her memory had never ceased to walk beside him. His lord glimpsed the tormented dullness in Sadayori's eyes. He fanned himself and looked up at the pattern of curving growth lines in the high wood of the ceiling.

"What a stubborn, thickheaded, impossible fellow you are! You say you want to become a Buddhist monk? A bald head with a stick? Very well, I won't permit that, but I'll give you a task that is just as good, if only to get you out of the way for a time. You are ordered to go and inspect each and every coastal town and village in Kii. You will go alone, with no attendants, and you will tie that sword of yours with a cover. You will not ride, but walk. When you return you will prepare a detailed thesis on how our domain can be defended from invasion. I will give you two years to do this, during which you must report in person to me once every six months, hiding nothing. You may visit whomever you wish, talk to whomever you wish, and practice martial arts until your arms fall off. However, I will forgive no fighting. And the next time I suggest marriage to you, you will obey me."

Sadayori bowed, very deep and very low. He understood, and tears of gratitude came to his eyes.

"Go now," said the daimyo.

After Sadayori had backed out of the chamber, the senior councillor who had been kneeling silently beside the daimyo began to remonstrate with him.

"My lord, it will appear as if he goes from you in disgrace, and people will despise him for not taking the way of seppuku. He has been troublesome, but he is loyal and intelligent, and nobody has a better grasp of military matters than he, not even yourself. He does not deserve this! How can a man of his rank go without attendants, like a wretched *ronin*? Sire, I beg you, reconsider!"

"Matsudaira Sadayori is one of my most trusted and dear retainers, and if you don't see it, you disappoint me. There is much pain in him, and it begins to fester. He must be alone, he must at the same time touch the pulse of life again, for now he only wants to die. Let him be tied to life, with a task I know he believes to be vital, let him walk in the midst of life. You know, I envy him, it is a task I've often dreamed about for myself, just to walk the land and get to know it, with no interruptions. No, this is no disgrace for him. Enough, I have decided. Prepare any documents, passes and money he might need, and tell nobody."

The councillor bowed.

Sadayori jerked his mind back to the present, to this elegant room in the house of a net master of a whaling village.

"Did you know," he said, his tone affably changing, "that over a hundred years ago, the eighth shogun, Tokugawa Yoshimune of Wakayama, patterned some of his warships after the whaler's design, and kept these warships in Edo Bay?"

"Yes, my grandfather often told us that. After all, our chase boats are the swiftest boats ever built, and they carry fifteen men and their equipment."

"Could such boats be built in large numbers today?" asked Sadayori.

"It would cost a fortune, but there are still skilled boat makers who can do it, both here and in Koza. The boats are very finely built, the wood is stronger, thinner and lighter than in ordinary fishing boats and must be well aged. Also, the lacquering of the hulls takes a lot of time, and it is vital that this be done with much care, for it is the smooth finish of the hull that gives the boat that extra speed."

Sadayori nodded.

"We run a fleet of twenty-five boats," said Wada, "although in times past we had as many as fifty boats and crews. Whaling is a very expensive business, and for some reason the big whales do not travel past our coasts in the numbers they did in former years. Now, with the cost of everything rising, we cannot think of adding more boats."

"So whaling is expensive," said Sadayori, raising his cup, "like war."

At that moment Taiji Kakuemon joined them, kneeling and bowing deeply beside the sliding screen door.

"Do excuse me, I had to take all the written offers from the oil merchants and go through them, and it had to be done in time to load the ships so that they could catch the tide."

"Oh, come in, Taiji-san," said Wada, glad that his cousin had at last arrived and would take some of the pressure of conversation with this hard-faced young man. Sadayori made a slight bow in Kakuemon's direction.

"You were right, this whale meat is the most delicious I've tasted," he said.

Taiji Kakuemon came in and took his place while servants bustled in with dishes of broiled crayfish and more flasks of warmed sake.

"I was asking about the time it took to make a whaling boat," said Sadayori, "and I am also interested in what it takes to train a crew of men to move such a craft with the speed and skill that your men do."

Kakuemon, bowing again and accepting his first cup of sake, looked into the samurai's face. He cannot be thinking of using our men to fight, he thought, composing himself before he made his answer.

Meanwhile, in the house of the harpooner Tatsudaiyu, the evening meal of yams, long onions and whale meat was simmering in an iron pot. Saburo's belly was rumbling from the smells that wafted from the tiny earthen-floored kitchen. Twigs crackled in the hard-clay cooking hearth. Saburo went out and poked at the fire.

"Be patient, supper will be ready soon," his mother said. She was kneeling behind her husband, combing out his long hair, ready to tie it up with a hand-rolled twist of paper into a topknot. Jinsuke sat across from his father, waiting his turn, and the middle brother, Shusuke, was out in the back, splitting wood.

"Saburo, you spotted the whale first again, didn't you? That was a good whale." Jinsuke wanted very much to talk about the whale, his whale.

"Yes," said Saburo, turning to grin at his older brother, "and we saw a foreign ship too, making black smoke while they cooked oil. Father, what do they do with the meat?"

I suppose they salt it and put it in barrels. They say

44

foreigners eat more meat than we Japanese do, even the meat of cattle and pigs."

Saburo made a face of disgust at the thought. "I wish I could have a good look at the ship, it must be wonderfully big for them to live on it like they do," he said.

Jinsuke laughed. "Those hairy fellows would gut you and salt you and put you in a barrel too."

"The samurai-san said that we Japanese must always watch out for them," said Saburo. "He said that they are our enemies, and one day we will have to kill them."

Tatsudaiyu spoke in his deep, gruff voice. "Whalers' business is not to kill other human beings, but to hunt whales to feed people. We take life to give life, and perhaps Shaka-sama can forgive us for that. When we take a whale we do so with respect. Those foreigners are hunting whales too, far offshore. They have not tried to attack us, or kill us, so what they do is of no concern to us." He glared at his youngest son. "I will not tolerate talk of taking human life under this roof. Understand?"

"Yes, Father," said Saburo, with a bob of his head.

Jinsuke was about to say something, but his mother gave his hair a warning tug. Jinsuke had no liking for samurai, swaggering oafs who thought themselves so superior. He picked up the bamboo flute he had made for the festival and squinted through it. "Spot another whale for us tomorrow, Saburo," he said.

Saburo's mother finished tying her menfolk's hair and hurried out to the kitchen. Tatsudaiyu called out to her.

"Onui! Bring warm sake and two cups, for me and your eldest son. He cut his first whale today." It was the first mention of the fact, and Jinsuke nearly burst with pride.

"Now," said his father, "what about a wife? You'll be nineteen next year. Do you have somebody you would like to have approached?" It was typical of his father, firm and strong though he might be, that he always asked people their feelings before he came to a decision.

"There is nobody, Father," said Jinsuke, but that was not true, for Jinsuke had cast longing eyes on Oyoshi, daughter of Takigawa, the boat painter. But he could not admit to that, for Oyoshi was still only twelve, with tiny breasts barely beginning to bud. How could he, a man nearing nineteen, a whaler, tell his father that?

At the time of the festival last year, when he had been among the gang of young men pushing, shoving, shouting, carrying the deity's carriage, the *omikoshi,* through the crowded streets, Jinsuke had caught a glimpse of Yoshi's slender calves as she fled from the noisy gang, running with other girls, squealing and shrieking. Her limbs were more than a child's, less than a woman's, they were long and straight, smooth and lovely, and Jinsuke could not stop his thoughts from wandering to where they led, to where the first soft black down must surely be growing.

"I don't think that anybody can cook as well as Mother," said Jinsuke, "no matter how hard Mother tries to teach her. I'm in no hurry to wed."

It wasn't true. He wanted to marry Oyoshi as soon as she was old enough. He was grateful as well as hungry when their mother brought in the iron pot, a wooden ladle and bowls for the food.

Three days later, on this southerly tip of the Kii Peninsula, there was another storm. It brought in the bloated carcass of a whale and left it stranded on the rocks of the arm of a small bay, a line of cliffs jutting out into the sea, just a short walk away from the village. The whale had been stripped of blubber, the head case had been bailed out, and the long, narrow lower jaw was gone. However, none of the meat, its surface now gray and green with decay, had been taken. Gas in the rotting guts had floated the whale from the sea bottom where it had been dumped.

There was some talk between Wada and his cousin of salvaging it, despite the foul smell, to cut out the bones and render them for oil and meal, but luckily for the workers who would have been assigned to the task, high seas on the next tide carried the stinking thing away before the overseers made their decision.

Chapter Three

All morning they rode the swell. There was fog, not enough to call off the vigil, but too much to hope for a whale sighting at any distance. The fog made it chillier than usual, and the whalers wrapped their thigh-length quilted coats around them and squatted down below the gunwales, out of the wind. Just one man stood by the sculling oar in the stern, keeping the boat in position, while another stood watch at the prow.

Jinsuke always found inactivity irksome, and for the past half hour he had been diving off the stern, going down to one of the many underwater peaks. He had brought up enough spiny crayfish and ark shells to give his boats mates a tasty treat to supplement the boiled yams and rice they had brought with them from home.

Amidships, a sandbox had been set, and the boat boy had an iron kettle on the boil, ready for tea, on top of the little clay oven. He knelt beside it, fanning coals, humming tunelessly to himself. If they sighted a whale, the fire would immediately be doused and the sandbox stowed under the deck boards.

Jinsuke hauled himself out of the water and wiped his body with his head band, wringing it out over the side. He retied his dripping red loincloth, pulled it tight, flapped out the wrinkles, then slipped on his quilted jacket. The boat boy passed him a cup of hot tea, which he gratefully accepted.

"*O-kini yo!*" he said, thanks in the Taiji dialect, which most outsiders would hardly understand. Sipping noisily, Jinsuke looked around at the gray-white veil of fog.

"No whales yet," he said, "so maybe you can broil these things." The boat boy glanced at Iwadaiyu, the harpooner, who nodded. At his captain's agreement, for he took orders only from him, the boy laid out more pieces of charcoal and fanned vigorously, getting them hot enough to broil the crayfish and shells. Meanwhile, the men took their lunch boxes and helped themselves to tea.

Only one other boat was visible in the fog, and on it Jinsuke could see Saburo, his youngest brother, sitting by the side, dangling a fishing line in the water. Jinsuke grinned. Saburo would be content to do that for hours, not caring whether he caught a fish or not. As for diving, few of the whalers cared to spend much time in the water once the trees had changed color, and there was no other man who could go as deep or stay down as long as Jinsuke. In Taiji, the women did not dive, as did the *ama* of other fishing villages.

The other men voiced their thanks to the boat boy as they took the coal-hot seafood, blowing on their fingers, cracking open the crayfish, or prying out the meat from the coiled ark shells with the ends of their chopsticks.

Two years had passed since Jinsuke had cut his first whale nostril. His shoulders had broadened and he had gained height, standing six *shaku* tall, big even among Taiji men, who were usually taller and certainly stronger than the men from most other coastal villages. The only other community whose men could equal them was Koza, another whaling village down the coast. Koza was younger in tradition than Taiji. There was a friendly rivalry between the two, and there had been many marriages between the sons and daughters of Taiji and Koza.

Jinsuke had passed his twentieth birthday and was officially recognized as a man. He was exceptionally handsome, nose big and straight, eyes set wide, and very black, teeth that were white, large and well set in a jaw he inherited from his father, a jaw betraying a stubborn nature with its squareness and with the powerful cheek muscles that rippled and twitched if ever he got impatient or annoyed. On the hunt, his long hair, shaved on the top, was let down to his shoulders, and it tended to curl at the ends, bleached slightly red by sun and salt. He was very popular among the whalers, many of whom said he would turn out to be an even better harpooner than his father, in whose footsteps he was meant to follow, as first-born son. If Jinsuke had any faults, they came from his quick temper and his stubbornness.

Jinsuke sucked the last of the meat from the crayfish and tossed the remains over the side. There were goose pimples on his bare legs, and the salty wetness of his loincloth made him feel uncomfortable. Oh, for a whale! To Jinsuke it was the chase, the kill, the dancing and songs that followed that were the most important things in his life. Those, and the troubling fantasies about Oyoshi. His mind had slipped into thoughts of her, her virginal body and full-lipped mouth, her long neck and gracefully sloping shoulders, when the watcher bellowed, making him come back to reality with a start.

"Flag! Flag!" He pointed toward the Tomyo lookout, and there, just visible above the fog that hung low on the sea, there was a big black pennant fluttering in the winds at the high cliff.

"Makko!" yelled Iwadaiyu, and the men jumped for their oars. Steam hissed as the boy doused the coals. From the fog came the answering notes of Tatsudaiyu's conch. Iwadaiyu lifted his conch and blew back. The men waited.

"Can you see it?" said the man close to Jinsuke.

"Not through this soup. We'll have to rely on signals from the lookouts. Stop talking and listen!"

Another signal urged them farther out to sea. From three hundred throats, the battle cry of the whalers echoed through the fog from boat to boat.

"Yooooii! Eheeeeeeeii! Eheeeeeeii! Yo . . . *YOH*!" The boats leaped forward. Cold quickly vanished from Jinsuke's body as he sculled, shoulder to shoulder with his oar mate. They could not see the other boats, but the conches boomed regularly.

After ten minutes of rowing, the chrysanthemum boat burst out of a bank of fog. Even had the men looked back they would not have seen new pennants going up on the cliff. The pennants signaled "no hunt," for the beach master, seeing the signal sticks indicating thick fog, had decided that it was too risky and that a boat might get lost in the fog and go too far out into the great Black Current. Fog dulled echoes, confusing the conch signals, and banks of it rolled thickly, as if clouds had dropped from the sky to roll around and play on the sea. Their boat was all alone in a hemmed-in patch of clear light and Iwadaiyu was pointing ahead, and as they strained to see, two vague shapes grew clearer. From the venting whoosh of a blow, there was little doubt that one of the shapes was a whale.

"Makko . . ." One of the shapes was that of what the Taiji men called "perfume whale," and they could see even at a distance that it was a big bull. The phoenix boat slipped into the lead, and the other boat followed, noting harpoon-

ers' hand signals that told the men to scull quietly and slowly. They got within fifty boat lengths when they saw that it was indeed a big bull whale, fast to a line, and in the final stages of lancing.

Leaning hard on the lance, body straining from toes to fingers, his thigh tight against the bracing board, Tovey Jacks thrust the iron shaft between the whale's ribs. He felt it go through a lung again and pushed on until he felt the resistance of the tough-sided aorta. He grunted, took a quick breath, and shoved the point through the elastic walls of the great vessel. The whale shuddered, jerking the lance out of his hands.

"Back off!" he yelled.

The man at the tiller, a huge red-haired giant, roared with excitement. "There she blows, my beauties! The chimney's afire!"

Blood jetted from a curiously angled blowhole and spattered over the sea. Three blows, one after another, the last blow ending in a clotted scarlet dribble.

"Whadya say, Tovey, forty barrels?" yelled the red-haired man.

"Aye, bungholes and all!" Tovey kept his eye on the whale, weakened and exhausted from the harpoon and the long pull against the whale boat, from two deep dives, and from a previous lance thrust that had pierced a lung but had not gone deep enough to kill. The whale lay dying now, rolling from side to side, snapping the long narrow jaw with its twin rows of peglike teeth.

"Gonna stick him again, Tovey?" shouted the man at the tiller. Tovey waved one hand, still keeping his eye on the whale but turning his head so that the others could hear.

"No, mate, he's a goner. Just back off a couple more strokes, he's about to get the jitters up."

Even as the men pushed on the oars, the bull started to thrash his flukes in a welter of spray, twisting his body so that the head loomed right out of the water. He died in a last convulsive flurry.

"Right you are, lads," yelled Tovey, turning back now to grin at his crew. "Get a line on him and we'll pull for home."

He took a large, grubby, red-and-white-spotted kerchief from his neck and wiped the sweat from his brow. But the other men did not move.

"Get a move on, put your backs into it, you lazy bags of

horse—" He was turning again to curse at them, but he caught sight of what they had already spotted, for the other men were facing the stern of the whale boat, and from behind two strange boats were approaching, silent, swift, high-prowed and brilliantly colored.

The man at the tiller, O'Hara, turned to look back. "Mother of God," he whispered, "the heathen is upon us!" He lifted one hand to cross himself.

Tovey Jacks reached slowly for the hatchet that was kept up near the bow and hid it behind his back.

"Hold steady, lads, not a move lest I give the word." The only weapons they carried were a spare lance, a few harpoons, a boat spade, a hatchet and the knives they kept at their belts or down their shirt collars. They numbered a mere six men, tough and willing, but not much of a chance, thought Tovey, against what a quick count made thirty men who looked like they knew their stuff, in boats that seemed to be a kind of war canoe.

At Tatsudaiyu's command the Taiji men stopped sculling and let their boats slide toward the strangers and the whale they had killed. None of the Taiji men felt hostility at this point, and certainly no fear, only an overwhelming curiosity. Whalers! These barbarians were whalers, from across the other side of the ocean, and what strange whalers they were! A salt-grayed boat with no colors or decorations, only six men in it, and no nets, no other boats. Curious indeed!

Tatsudaiyu called out a polite greeting in his own tongue, but the six foreigners just stared back, silent and tense. Tatsudaiyu saw danger in the eyes of the huge man at the tiller, and he understood. Slowly and carefully, he lifted the harpoon off the rack beside him and pointed to the line attached to it, then to the dead whale. He smiled at them, touching his own nose with his forefinger, then pointing to the dead whale and to the strangers. Then he laid the harpoon back down. Tovey Jacks let the breath whistle out of the side of his mouth.

"Well, I'll be a diddled duck! Rest easy, lads, they be whale men, come over for a friendly gam!"

The Yankees burst into a sudden gabble of laughter and shouts. Two of the oarsmen, one white, one black, stood up and waved their hats. At this animated outburst the Taiji men laughed and waved too, loud and happy, and all tension was gone. The phoenix boat glided alongside the Yankee whaleboat, shipping oars. Men grasped the gunwales of the foreign boat, looking at the six men's faces to see if they would resent this intrusion.

"Oh, how strange!" exclaimed one of Tatsudaiyu's crew. "These fellows are all different colors!"

Several of the Taiji men commented on the huge size of the Irishman, and on the red of his hair. Others remarked on the black skin and crinkly hair of the second oarsman, while others noted the long, lank, grubby blond locks that straggled from under Tovey Jacks's blue knit cap.

"They sit down and pull on their oars," said another man. "That must be heavy work!"

"And uncomfortable!"

"The men at the oars face backward and can't see where they're going!"

Jinsuke, though, had noted something far more vital. He called out to Iwadaiyu. "Captain, please look. In the whale they have killed there is only one harpoon, and two other wounds."

Both harpooners had noted this, and were greatly impressed. Tatsudaiyu pointed to the harpoon shaft, which was now bent over the dead whale's back like a pin. He held up one finger and said "one" in Japanese. Tovey grinned back and held up one finger himself. Yes, just one harpoon. Tatsudaiyu pointed again to Tovey, and then to the harpoon, and made a throwing gesture. Tovey shook his head and pointed to O'Hara, which greatly confused Tatsudaiyu, who could not have imagined that the man now at the tiller of the boat would be the man whose task it was to sink the harpoon, after which he would change places with Tovey, who in the meantime had been at the tiller. Then it was Tovey who lanced. Tovey looked at the excited Japanese arguing this point among themselves, not realizing what confused them.

"Show His Nibs that iron, O'Hara, the one old Jimmy Temple made."

Like the harpoon now in the whale, the one O'Hara hefted was fitted with a toggle head. This was the first year they had used the toggle-head harpoon, made and invented by James Temple, the blacksmith uncle of Nat Temple, their second oarsman. O'Hara passed the harpoon along to Tatsudaiyu, who took it in both hands, raising it slightly and making a slight bow as he did so. His men crowded and craned to see it. Tatsudaiyu felt the sharpened tip, moved the head on its hinge, and marveled at the simple, logical ingenuity of it. A harpoon such as this, once well placed, would never pull out! Somehow, he determined, he would talk to the Taiji blacksmith about it, although such a harpoon would be quite a break with tradition.

Iwadaiyu asked permission to step onto the phoenix boat, then went aboard at Tatsudaiyu's word. He glanced at O'Hara, who smiled and then he too handled the American harpoon.

"These barbarians are not fools. This is a clever thing, and just one of them has held the whale."

"It is a large bull too," said Tatsudaiyu, "and they let it pull the boat, with a lot of line let out. See those tubs?"

Sometimes, when they were sure of a relatively easy kill, the Taiji men let the whale pull the boat, although they did not have the simple but ingenious way of laying lines that the Yankees did.

Tovey Jacks couldn't understand anything of what was being said, but he was sure of the drift of the talk. He started to point out things in his boat, the line tubs, the harpoon rest, the wooden board against which the harpooner and the lance men braced thighs, the hatchet for cutting lines in an emergency, the small wooden bailer.

Iwadaiyu made a drinking motion, pointing to the bailer, and Tovey laughed. No, he said, shaking his head, making a diving motion with one hand, and pointing to scorch marks over the bollard where the rope ran out.

Jinsuke exclaimed, "They pour water over the rope, it goes so fast it burns!"

Tatsudaiyu nodded yes, such a big perfume whale would dive deep and fast, and if not wetted, the rope would burn. He lifted his own harpoon off the rack and handed it to O'Hara, who turned it over, hefting it. He grinned at Tatsudaiyu and raised his eyebrows, yes, it was a good iron, but a bit light. He passed it back.

Meanwhile, Tovey had taken out his pipe, filled it from a leather-and-oilskin pouch, and lit it. He took a couple of puffs, then held up the pouch, offering it to the Taiji boat captains. Both of them took pinches of tobacco, although only Tatsudaiyu had his tiny brass bowled pipe aboard, wrapped in the sash of his quilted jacket, which was now folded and put away.

"Beautiful boats they be, Tovey, all painted with pretty pictures, birds and flowers and such, and shiny and bright, like a church window. There's money in that boat, you know." O'Hara was much impressed.

"Aye, and a brawny bunch of monkeys for a crew," said Tovey, who had never seen men so uniformly fit, brown and strong, although even the biggest of them would come up to only just about the Irishman's chin. He shook his head.

"You can see they gets home cooking, mate," he said.

"Not a sore, nor a mark of scroff or scurvy anywhere. A fine bunch. Damn good job they be friendly!"

In turn, the Japanese could not stop staring at the strangers, all dressed differently, in clothes that were patched and scruffy, reeking of whale oil, sweat and tobacco, and of long months in damp quarters.

"They smell," said one oarsman, "like badgers."

"The poor fellows are a long way from their wives, they have no women to look after them, that's why."

Iwadaiyu pointed at the whale. *"Kujira,"* he said, *"Makko kujiira."*

Tovey caught on. He answered in English. "Sperm whale," he said.

Iwadaiyu got stuck on the first word, and O'Hara thought the Japanese sounded like "mackerel."

"A bejazus big mackerel, boys," said O'Hara, shaking his head.

"Sperm," repeated Tovey, slowly.

"Soo . . . pah . . . moo," said Iwadaiyu.

"That's it, mate, sperm, you know, like the old Portuguese hand-pump drill." Tovey laughed and made obscene gestures, pointing at the whale's head. The Taiji men stared blankly, but Jinsuke burst into laughter.

"I understand! I understand! They name the perfume whale after a man's sex juices, because of the head oil—you know how it turns white when we bail it out, just like that stuff. Don't you understand? They make jokes! Whalers' jokes!"

Now the rest of the Japanese began to laugh, as if it were the funniest thing they'd ever heard. Tovey glanced at O'Hara, who grinned and shrugged. "Well, I suppose it is a queer name, right enough, when you think about it."

The thump of a signal cannon cut short the gesturing and laughter. Tovey shielded his eyes and looked out to sea. It was their ship. The fog had almost cleared and they could see her now, about a mile or so away. Tatsudaiyu heard the gun and saw the ship.

"To oars! Their mother ship approaches! We must leave immediately, unless the men on the ship misunderstand and think we are attacking these men! To oars, to oars!"

He and Iwadaiyu bowed courteously, as if to equals, and Tovey took off his cap. Then with shouts and waves the three boats separated. Tovey had a sudden impulse. He reached into the pocket of his pea jacket, his hand closing on something white and hard. He yelled back.

"Ahoy! Catch!" With a powerful throw he hurled the object in the direction of the nearest boat, but the lift of the swell put his arm off and the thing clunked against an oar and plopped into the water. Japanese never throw things at another person except in anger or insult, and the action startled the two men whose oar the object had hit. But Jinsuke was quick. He dived over the side, with strong breaststrokes and frog kicks, going down fast to the whitish sinking object. It almost got too deep for him, but he reached out his right arm and just managed to close his fingers on it. Then he shot to the surface, holding it above. Tovey gave a cheer and waved his cap.

Jinsuke's friends pulled him aboard. He opened his hand.

"What is it?" asked Iwadaiyu.

Jinsuke handed it to him, and they saw that it was the tooth of a sperm whale, a big one, and on the ivory was a bold design, etched in black lines. A closer look saw that it showed ships, boats, whales being struck, and on another side a strange fruit and a scroll of lettering none of them could read.

"It is a gift to us," said Jinsuke in awe.

"How embarrassing, and we had nothing to give to them," said Iwadaiyu with a worried frown. He handed it back to Jinsuke. "You keep it."

Jinsuke protested, but his captain was adamant.

"If you had not dived for it, this present would now rest on the bottom of the sea, and that would be an insult to those men and would bring us bad luck. It would be bad luck for you to lose it now, so keep it, and this boat will find fortune and take many of those supamu whales."

Jinsuke was filled with pleasure and thanked his captain profusely. He wrapped the scrimshaw in his quilted jacket and put it away in one of the lockers. They began to head back to shore.

On that day the Taiji men spotted no more whales. The sighting of the foreign ship was reported to the office, and thence eventually to the authorities in both Wakayama and Shingu. However, as to their meeting on the open sea with the strangers, the whalers in the two boats promised to keep strictly silent. It would mean less trouble that way.

Chapter Four

The urge to cough gripped his chest in bands of iron. He held it back, though, determined to finish the last two strokes of his brush to an exquisite paulownia on the side of the new chase boat. Then and only then did he cough, shoulders racked, face reddening, a large blue vein swelling at one temple. His daughter, fourteen, took the brush from his hand and gently thumped him on the back.

"Please, Father, rest today. You work too hard."

"Do not worry yourself," he said, gasping for breath. "It is only a slight cold."

How could there be rest for him? He had no son. His only male child had died at birth, followed soon by his wife, who died a year later in giving birth to Oyoshi.

Oyoshi now took her father's quilted jacket and laid it over his shoulders.

"Please, Father, come home. I'll make you miso soup, and some hot sake with an egg beaten into it. You'll feel better tomorrow."

Saburo was standing very still in this dust-proofed, immaculately clean section of the boat shed. He had been watching the artist, his eyes following every movement. He spoke now.

"Please, Takigawa-san, do what your daughter says. If you permit me, I'll clean the brushes for you. I'll move very carefully, and I won't raise any dust. I've watched you do it, so I know how."

The boy's voice was so earnest that Takigawa turned to him and smiled.

"Thank you, Saburo, I'll accept your kindness. But come

along to the house afterward, and we'll share some soup or something. Let Oyoshi put something into that bottomless belly of yours before you go running home and eat everthing your mother has prepared."

Takigawa and his daughter left, and Saburo set to work. He loved to handle the brushes, and he loved even more the brightness and aroma of the paints, the glisten of color and design upon well-lacquered wood. He admired Takigawa more than any other man in the village for his skills. The others often made jokes about him, for he was frail, stoop-shouldered and not as brown or big as they were; but Takigawa could create such beauty, and they could do nothing like that.

The whaling fleet had not gone out that day. There had been four days of wind and fog. During this time Jinsuke had done little but lounge around, sip tea, and chatter about the barbarians, although his father had sternly forbidden him to mention the subject to anybody outside the house. Careless talk could bring a lot of questions, perhaps even punishment for the whole family. The Tokugawa edicts strictly forbade any contact with foreigners, and *bakufu* or *han* laws commanded that if a son or a daughter committed a crime, then punishment would be meted out to mother and father as well.

"Damn the Tokugawa!" said Jinsuke hotly. His father was silent for a while, then came over and suddenly slapped him, hard.

"Do you want to see all of our heads on a board?"

Jinsuke bowed low. "Forgive me, Father, forgive me, but can you imagine how many whales we could take if only we had a big ship and could follow the whales wherever they went? How rich the whole village could become!"

"And how could we get the whales to a suitable factory? Do you think they can do on a ship all that we do here? No, Jinsuke, our way has evolved to be the best and only way for us. Let the foreigners do what they do, their way, but for us it is not only stupid, but dangerous to dream about copying them. Now I order you, hush this chatter. I was interested too in what we saw, but I will store that experience away, keep the knowledge to myself. I order you to do the same."

Rain lashed in from the ocean, four days of rain, obscuring the hills, but when it ceased, a double rainbow hung over the mountains toward the shrine of Nachi.

Takigawa put on an old kimono and stepped out of the house to watch it.

"Ah, see those colors," he said aloud, to nobody in particular. "Would that I could imitate the heavens with my brushes, but I never shall. Hmmm . . . with a rainbow over the mountains, the boats are sure to go out tomorrow."

Oyoshi called from inside. "Did you say something, Father?"

"No, nothing. Oyoshi, come on out, the rain has stopped, let's take a stroll."

Takigawa's old, worn wooden *geta* clopped on the cobbles. After the rain, he thought, everything is so clear. Rocks on the jetty walls glistened wetly, small crabs scurrying together with the curious-looking sea lice, big as large beetles. The smells of charcoal and cooking fish hung about the narrow streets, and near one house he could see a neighbor's wife puffing down a bamboo tube to get the fire going, then fanning it, slapping the fan against one hand as she looked up and called out a greeting. Oyoshi walked just a little behind her father, and they passed a group of young men, with Jinsuke standing in the center of them. He looked so handsome, his long hair all shining and black, tied in a rakish topknot that bulged over to one side, the sash of his cotton kimono tied low on his hips, a folding fan thrust into it. Oyoshi hung her head shyly. Jinsuke bowed to her father and gave Oyoshi a smile.

"Takigawa-san, a fine evening it is, isn't it? Will you and Oyoshi be at the festival tomorrow?"

"Of course, although I hope there will not be too much rowdiness, not like last year."

Jinsuke grinned. "Why, you have nothing to worry about, Takigawa-san, your contributions have been generous."

The other young men all laughed.

The autumn festival in Taiji had a boisterous vigor beneath which flowed a deep, dark current of release from restrictions, and potential violence. The *omikoshi* was carried through the streets at night, its way illuminated by hand lanterns and flaming torches. It was a rowdy affair, and the young men who carried the shrine all had their faces painted white and black, a disguise they sometimes used in the darkness to settle any old score that had been simmering for a year. Moreover, they might also make things unpleasant for anybody who had not made what they, the young men of Taiji, thought to be a suitable contribution to the festival funds. And festival funds, of course, went mostly to buy sake for the young men who carried the *omikoshi* and the older men who lit the way.

Yet despite this undercurrent of threat, the festival was also a wildly happy time. On the day before, men went from house to house, dressed in kimonos of black and blue, performing the lion dance to the tunes of drum and flute. An expectant air hung around the village, and even the kites seemed to dance on the winds, their fluting cries joining in. People laughed and called out when they passed each other.

Jinsuke had been looking forward to it for months. The night of the festival would be the only time that he could talk to Oyoshi without starting a landslide of gossip. He had made Oyoshi a comb, and only on the festival night could he give it to her. It was a beautiful thing, made of baleen. He had softened the baleen in hot water before cutting and shaping it. Then, when it hardened, he polished it first with sharkskin, then with his own hands, and finally with a soft cloth. The comb was strong, but half-transparent, line-fine turtle shell, with the colors of roasted tea and fine ink, streaked with pine-needle brown. When nobody was around he would take it from its hiding place and gaze at it, imagining how the comb would look in Oyoshi's hair.

The day drew near. Jinsuke could hardly sleep. Over the past two years he had resisted all efforts to interest him in other girls, but his father was patient with him and was sure that his son was keen on somebody. Besides, Jinsuke's mother was still young, and had no need of another woman in her kitchen. It could wait.

Oyoshi would be of marriageable age in another year or two. Jinsuke's mind was filled with a thousand pictures of her, growing more beautiful each day. He had seen the way she looked at him, and he guessed that she liked him too. He would find out soon, and meanwhile, the moon grew fuller, day by day, and Jinsuke sat outside the house in the late evenings, practicing the flute.

On the night of the festival the family had a meal of marinated pilot-whale meat, miso soup and rice cooked with red beans, an extravagance that even Tatsudaiyu, chief harpooner, could rarely indulge in. Jinsuke was bubbling, joking with his two younger brothers.

"It might get wild tonight, boys, so you'd better stay out of the way," he said.

"Not me," said Shusuke, "I'm going to be right beside you. I don't want to miss the fun."

Shusuke had grown robust. Four years of rowing a net boat and hauling whale nets had broadened his back and shoulders and thickened his arms. The two grinned at each other. Tatsudaiyu, eating quietly, looked up, bowl in one hand, chopsticks in the other. He finished chewing, swallowed, and his sons stopped talking.

"Do not jabber at meals. And another thing, although I'm not so old that I forget how young men need to get wild once in a while, I warn you that it will be me who gets wild if anybody gets hurt. You must not forget the meaning of this day. The god was brought up from the sea, at night, and it is this god who honors our village. Make sure that you honor the god. Bang on a few doors and shutters if you must, but if there is any real damage to old Sahei's house, then I will know who is responsible, and there will be a couple of damaged heads in this house afterward. Understand?"

"*Hai!*" came the answer. The boys ate in silence.

Before the open doors of the Asuka shrine, a great bonfire threw sparks high against the dark backdrop of the hill from which ancient trees loomed over steep slopes. The *kan-nushi*, the Shinto priest, resplendent in white robes and with the small black ceremonial cap perched on his head, stood in the light from the fire, waiting. He bowed as the Wada and Taiji families came to pay their respects. Several of the older men now brought torches, bundles of split pine, which they laid with the ends into the fire. These brands would light the way for the god-seat shrine, the *omikoshi*.

Saburo was strangely ill at ease this evening. He sat alone on the deserted beach in front of the long outer walls of the Wada house. Behind him a big natural rock archway yawned blackly. A shrike called. With a twig, Saburo scrawled designs in a patch of sand, not noticing how time passed until he heard the shouts—"*Washoi! Washoi!*"—coming from the opposite beach. Slowly he stood up.

The *omikoshi* was being carried through the streets by pushing, pulling, shoving, bobbing opposites, the reds and the blues. The streets resounded with their shouts and reeked with the smoke of the torches.

Here in Taiji, the *omikoshi* was not the elaborate mobile shrine, gilded and carved with a pagoda roof, the kind commonly seen in other towns. It was a simple, sealed barrel, watertight and lashed to a pole. The deity was inside the barrel, the very same and secretive god that had come up from the sea, long ages ago. Few knew now what form the god had taken, but they knew the deity was there, and that was enough.

Saburo had made his way around the beach and was in the shadows, watching. Somebody clutched at his sleeve.

"Saburo, are you deaf? I said good evening to you!"

He turned to see Oyoshi, looking very pretty in her kimono, with her hair done up and pinned with a small silvery-gold ornament from which something dangled and glittered each time she moved her head. Her looks astonished him, and Saburo's first impulse was to blurt out how lovely she looked, but then he found himself resenting that Oyoshi had leaped out and away from girlhood and, it seemed, from him. He was gruff with his answer. Oyoshi made a little pout at his surliness and flounced off to join two friends.

Saburo pushed himself against a wall as the scrum of reds and blues weaved and bumped on past. They seemed to be fighting against each other, and the ride of the god in the sealed casket was rough and erratic, yet full of wild vigor and joy, and it made progress, scattering watchers as it went. It was as if the god had come to life and was goading the reds and blues.

Voices harsh and hoarse with shouting, they made it to the beach where the whales were always winched up, but they did not stop, they went on into the sea whence the god had appeared. Pushing and shouting, they went on out until those brave fellows who stayed with the crazy chariot were way out of their depth and had to swim, still clinging to the pole of the *omikoshi,* which floated. Saburo saw that his two brothers were there in the water, face paint smeared with sweat and seawater. He wondered about himself, for unlike other boys of his age, Saburo had no urge to take part in this one day, although that was something he could never dare confess.

Oyoshi stood right in the sand by the water's edge, clapping her hands delightedly, and looking at her, Saburo felt again very disturbed, very young and inadequate.

Out of the sea the young men came, cotton kimonos dripping, many having lost their straw sandals by now. They staged one more noisy demonstration on the beach before the god, now wilder than ever, made them struggle back and forth, back and forth, up the stone steps and into the shrine of Asuka, now to slumber in solemn, undisturbed quiet for the rest of the year.

The crowd clapped and cheered. Now the hot sake would flow and the young men would all get drunk and be watched, chided, praised and finally cared for by the older torchbearers. The rest of the people would meander among the festival stalls, buying roasted tidbits, listening to stories, and there were all kinds of games to play. For the young people of Taiji, for a few hours, this was the most joyous occasion of the year, for they could be unchaperoned and free, and even if boys talked with girls, there would be no gossip, no enraged fathers or complaining mothers. And despite the lights, the bonfire and the torches, there were still plenty of shadows where a pair might hide for a while.

Oyoshi moved away from the bonfire and lanterns, and suddenly, from a shadow, somebody took her arm, making her gasp with fright.

"Oyoshi, it's me, Jinsuke. I want to talk to you."

"Oh, Jinsuke-san," she exclaimed with relief, "I'm so glad it's you. I thought it might be one of those ruffians who always tease me."

"Oyoshi, I have a present for you," he said, holding out a little package. Her eyes widened, and she hesitated to take it, not knowing what to say, but he kept his hand out and Oyoshi bowed, only just able to stammer the words to thank him. Jinsuke was struggling to find words too, but when they came they were direct and blunt.

"I like you, and it's you that I want to marry. I'm waiting for you and for nobody else. Do you understand, do you?"

Eyes wide, Oyoshi nodded, but he gave her no time to answer or say anything and went striding off into the night. Later, as she walked home, chest aching with excitement, she bumped into Saburo again.

"Saburo," she said, "tell me why your brother doesn't get married. He's very handsome, and a lot of girls say they like him."

"Maybe he thinks the same as me . . . that girls are foolish!"

Then Saburo spun away from her, away from the crowds, the laughing and singing. Somebody threw more wood on the fire and sparks writhed and whirled into the darkness like the tail of a dragon. As for Jinsuke, drunk with more than mere sake, he had his arms around the brawny shoulders of two oar mates, and was singing as loud as he could.

Two days later, while Oyoshi was washing rice bowls, she wondered why her father was so quiet. He sat by the hibachi, poking at the charcoal with iron chopsticks, a quilt over his legs.

"Yoshi," he said suddenly, "you grow fast. You look so

62

much the way your mother did when I first married her. Soon I suppose we will have to find a suitable young man for you." He looked across the rim of his teacup at her. "You know that I have nobody to carry on with my work, with my name, no son to support me when I get too old to work, which won't be long now. I could have married again, but somehow you were all I needed then, and you were such a good girl, right from the time you first started to walk. I can't bear the thought of you leaving this house, and I'm thinking of asking a go-between to look around for a suitable young man for us to adopt. I don't want you to go off as a bride to another house where the mother would treat you like a slave. No, I wouldn't want that at all."

He sipped his hot tea noisily. "Don't you think that my idea is the most sensible? You and I get along so well together, don't we?"

Oyoshi knelt across from him, hands in her lap, eyes down. "I don't want to leave you, Father," she said in a small voice, and her heart was torn, for she knew it was out of the question to adopt the first son of the chief harpooner. Even a family of less importance and standing would not let a first son go, never. It would have to be a second, third or fourth son, and even then it would be a touchy business for a *nakodo* to negotiate. Yet, as Oyoshi looked at how thin and drawn her father was, the way he hunched over, she wanted to weep, for she knew he would die very quickly if she left him.

"Go and fetch my bag," he said.

She did so, and from it he took a small piece of broken boat planking, upon which somebody had painted a spider in a web, and a black swallow-tailed butterfly struggling against the meshes.

"Do you know who did this?" The question was sharp, and her father was looking at her strangely. Oyoshi put one hand to her mouth.

"Oh, Father, Saburo didn't mean any harm . . . it's just that he admires your work so much, and wants to be like you. Don't be angry with him, please! He only uses the paint that sticks to the lids of the pots."

Takigawa turned the piece of wood around in his lap and looked at it for a long time.

"His use of color is childish and the strokes are on the clumsy side here and there, but on the whole this little piece is not bad at all. I like the idea of the black butterfly and the spider, he must have got that from Taiji legends and thought out his own theme. Not many could do that."

He looked up. "No, Yoshi, I'm not angry, not angry at all. I'm pleased." He gave a little snort. "Who would have thought it of a whaler's son! Yes indeed, the lad has natural talent. It surprises me that he learned to do this just by watching me at work, although when I come to think of it he's always asking questions. Promising, promising."

He held out his cup for more tea, then sat for a while, not saying a word, the piece of painted wood still in his lap. Eventually he sighed and nodded to himself. "That Saburo is a good boy, and he grows fast."

Oyoshi stifled a gasp. Oh no, Father could never think of that, oh please, not that! Her father said no more, and carefully put away the little piece of painted board.

In quantities and quality of meat and oil, a humpback whale was almost as valuable to Taiji as a right whale. The baleen was much shorter and coarser, and most people preferred meat from the right whale, but a humpback was nevertheless a good whale, and when they got one that day the whalers were served sake as they came in. They did a dance right on the beach, with everybody laughing and pointing, enjoying it immensely.

After the flensing and packing of the meat was done, Jinsuke left the sound of hammers breaking bone behind him, and with a large piece of red back meat, and another, smaller portion of the marbled fatty tissue from the ventral folds, he headed toward the Takigawa house, hoping to find Oyoshi at home. Why had she not come to the beach?

Calling out, Jinsuke slid open the front door, and to his shock he found Saburo sitting in the little central room, just to one side of the entrance and little porch. He was talking with Oyoshi's father, relaxed, sipping tea as if he were a member of the family. Jinsuke stood rigidly in the doorway, staring at Saburo, but talking to Takigawa.

"Forgive the intrusion. I thought you might like some meat. They are poor pieces, but caught fresh today." They were, of course, excellent pieces.

Takigawa turned on his cushion, making a slight bow and smiling genially. He moved a thin, threadbare cushion to his side and beckoned Jinsuke to come in.

"Saburo," he said, "take this meat from your brother and put it in the kitchen. Oyoshi will see it when she comes in.

Jinsuke, you are so kind, all the time, we are indebted to you, indeed, indeed. Come in, come in and have tea."

Jinsuke inclined his head. His hair was still long and stiff with salt, for he had not been home or to the bath house yet. Bristles grew on the shaven part of his pate, for it had been several days since he had attended to it. His eyes glittered in the mahogany hue of his face and in one cheek a muscle spasmed. He had taken off his headband and it now dangled loosely in his sash. With a sword and a breastplate he would look just like a pirate, fierce and unforgiving. Saburo felt ill at ease. Jinsuke spoke sharply to him.

"Hey, you, did you get wood yet?"

Only the day before, in clear view of everybody, Saburo had placed three bundles of wood right in the kitchen. The question, and the harsh way it was asked, surprised him.

"Yes, I did it yesterday," he said, nettled. Of the three brothers, Saburo was the least likely to neglect chores.

"Well, there are plenty of other things to do. You should not bother Takigawa-san." He stared meaningfully at the teacup and at the treat of fried rice from the bottom of the pot set on a wooden platter between them. Annoyance flickered over Takigawa's face, and Saburo spotted it. Quickly he bowed and gave thanks, saying he must leave. Jinsuke stalked out ahead, leaving the meat on a board on the floor, beside the door.

Takigawa sighed. "Ah ah, these young whalers are as arrogant as samurai. They think they do everything and run everything around here."

He picked up the meat, wrapped in rice paper and dripping with blood, and took it into the kitchen. It really was annoying, such an interruption, just as he was starting to describe to young Saburo the preparation of colors that would last for years against sun and salt water.

Strangely uncomfortable, Saburo followed the broad brown back of his older brother, his straw sandals scuffing. When they got up to the turning of the lane Jinsuke stopped and glanced around, as if to check that nobody was there. His face was a thundercloud.

"Why do you waste so much time at that house? Don't you know the old fellow is ill and gets tired easily? Oyoshi has enough to do without you hanging around uninvited!"

Saburo was normally frightened at answering back to his brother, but this was unjust. "Uninvited? I'm not uninvited! Takigawa-san himself asks me to come around. He even teaches me to draw things!"

Jinsuke's heart froze. He took a slow breath and stepped closer to Saburo, pushing down the rage in his belly.

"Fool! We are whalers, not paint daubers! Your place is in a whale boat!"

He seized Saburo by the right wrist, so hard the bone seemed about to break. He pulled the arm out straight and shook it as he spoke.

"This was meant to hold an oar or pull a rope, not to play with a brush! Have you no respect for our father, for our ancestors? We are whalers, do you understand? Whalers!"

He let go. Saburo was frightened and said nothing, though resentment surged within him. Saburo was not the first son, and could never be a harpooner. To him, no task seemed meaner than having to wait for hours in a crowded boat, then having to stand and sweat behind an oar, just so a bully like this could throw his damned harpoon and have the whole village admire him. *"Hai,"* he said.

As for Jinsuke, he was already experiencing a young man's hell. He was well aware that Takigawa would wish to adopt a young man, rather than let his daughter go and his name die out. He was also aware that he could never be a candidate for that. Oyoshi filled his fantasies so completely. He could not, would not relinquish her! There was nobody he could confide in with ease, and Oyoshi, in his thoughts, was wanton; Jinsuke feared that should he give away just a part of his thoughts, then all the rest would tumble out too. Yet speak he must, before it was too late, speak before this business with Saburo took root too firmly in Takigawa's mind.

Jinsuke had to wait several days before he could catch his father alone, but at last, one evening, Jinsuke found his father by the boat house. Nearly everybody was gone, and Tatsudaiyu was inspecting the hull of the phoenix boat. There was a long scratch on the black finish, from a bent harpoon that had been pulled out of the back of a whale and gotten tangled in the net. In the rush and fury of the chase nobody had noticed the sharp bent metal, and when the phoenix boat darted in for the first lancing, the tangled net and the harpoon had scraped along the side.

"No good, no good," muttered Tatsudaiyu, running his big callused hand along the scar. It would have to be smoothed with sharkskin and fine sand, then carefully relacquered, and that took time. It would have to wait until the migration of the whales was over.

He looked up at his son with a rueful smile. "If boats were human they could heal themselves, but they aren't and we harpooners must take more care to look after them. You know, it's not the harpoon that gets the whale really, but the boat. Too bad, too bad . . ."

"Father, may I speak?"

Tatsudaiyu nodded.

"Father, I wish to marry the Takigawa daughter, Oyoshi. Will you please arrange for a *nakodo* to approach her father? Please, Father!"

He fell on his knees in the sand, bowing low at his father's feet. Tatsudaiyu bent and grabbed Jinsuke's arm, pulling him gently, and when his son looked up, Tatsudaiyu saw the plea in his eyes, naked, almost pathetic. He realized then how hard it must have been for Jinsuke to tell him, and he did not laugh. He gazed into his son's eyes and nodded slowly, sucking in a breath.

"So, that is it? The secret you've kept locked away? I understand, and I will ask old man Toumi to act as *nakodo*. But you know, it will be difficult. Takigawa has no son and only one daughter. He must be thinking of taking in a son-in-law to carry his name, and his work . . ."

"But Father, would he not be proud to be linked to our family? I will be a harpooner soon, and you are the chief harpooner in the whole of Taiji! We could look after him . . . What I mean is . . . I could look after him, when he gets old."

Tatsudaiyu held up one hand, silencing him. "Takigawa may be not as well off as some, but he is a proud man. It is not fears for old age that would bother him, but the loss of his craft, his family name, the whole tradition of his ancestors. He won't want that to die with him. It would be easy if he had another daughter, but he doesn't. But say no more, I will speak to old man Toumi. Be patient, but I warn you, don't get your hopes too high."

Slapping his son on one shoulder, Tatsudaiyu changed his tone. "Come on, let's go home together."

On the rocky shore of the seaward side of Mukaijima there were tasty little oysters, various kinds of winkles and plenty of young sea lettuce and laver. Oyoshi had gone round at low tide and was gathering them for supper when Jinsuke came hopping from rock to rock to find her. Nobody was around. It was the day after he had spoken to his father.

"Oyoshi, I was looking for you."

She was startled. Was something wrong . . . her father
. . . She put one hand to her mouth.

"I need to talk, to tell you something."

Oyoshi looked around, worried, for if anybody saw them
alone like this, there would be a scandal. Taiji thrived on
gossip.

"I have asked my father to arrange for a *nakodo* to go and
talk to your father. I want to marry you, as soon as possible.
Do you understand?"

Tears formed in Oyoshi's eyes and she turned away from
him.

"Oyoshi, what's wrong, don't you like me?"

"No, it's not that. I like you more than my own life, more
than anybody, and that you think well of me gives me more
joy than I can say. But my father . . . my father will never
agree, and I can't . . ." She hid her face in her hands and
wept. Jinsuke held her gently by the shoulders, and unresist-
ing, she let him enfold her in his strong, brown, smooth
arms.

Almost a month had passed and no word or reaction had
come from Oyoshi's father. Had his answer been favorable,
they would by now be exchanging betrothal gifts, and invitations would be sent to Tatsudaiyu and Onui to visit the
Takigawa home.

One day, however, Oyoshi's father arrived at Tatsudaiyu's
house, bringing a sea bream baked in salt and wrapped in
fine woven grasses. Sea bream was a gift of celebration, so
could that mean he would agree? Yet when Tatsudaiyu
looked into his eyes, he knew that was not so. Behind
Takigawa stood old man Toumi, looking very grim. Takigawa
was invited in and he at first declined, but with much bowing
and cajoling at the entrance he came in and settled himself
on the tatami by the door, refusing to come deeper into the
room, refusing to use a cushion. Onui poured tea.

For a long time they chatted aimlessly about the weather,
the whales, the state of the yam fields and vegetable plots,
the awful rise in rice prices and so on, but everybody knew
that Takigawa had come to say something that was not easy
for him. Tatsudaiyu glanced at old man Toumi, feeling a
touch impatient. Why did the old fool relish such moments?
Tatsudaiyu was a man who preferred to drive the lance
home as soon as possible. Old man Toumi cleared his throat.

"With regards to this affair . . . er . . . of young Jinsuke

68

. . . er . . . this family has always had the greatest esteem for the house of Takigawa . . ."

Tatsudaiyu waited while the old man launched into a complete family history of both houses, a long-winded recitation that sounded as if he had been practicing his polite forms.

". . . and presses most sincerely for the marriage with Oyoshi." He sucked in breath and bowed. "So please consider this and give us a favorable answer, we beg of you."

Then the old man sat back on his heels, looking rather pleased with himself. Takigawa had gone white and tense. He bowed, not letting his head come up from the mats for a long time.

"Yoshi is still young, not yet turned sixteen, and it seems early for a decision yet."

Tatsudaiyu's voice was deep and strong. "Takigawa-san, let us forget this formality. You and I are old friends. Our children have played with each other since they were little. You were there when Onui and I were wed, and we attended your wedding. Tell us frankly. Do you think that anything will change our friendship? Oyoshi is not too young to be betrothed, and my son can wait for the marriage if that worries you. I think, however, that I know your dilemma. Tell us your answer. The answer we hope for will give us much joy and will bond two fine families together, but the other answer will not shock us too deeply. We can understand. Speak now. Do you forget whose house you are in? This is the house of Tatsudaiyu."

Takigawa bowed again, forehead touching the mats, voice cracking with emotion. "I respect this family more than any other. I can never forget that it was your wife who gave her breast to my daughter after my wife died, and helped me so much with the things I couldn't do for her. Over these years you have shared so much with me, and I and my daughter are indebted until we die. Yoshi has found sympathy and kindness in the heart of your eldest son, and that is too much of an honor for us. From my heart, I try to pull up words, but I can't. Despite this, despite all of this, I must beg forgiveness. I can only refuse permission for the marriage. I have no son, and Yoshi is my only daughter. I must adopt a son . . ."

Takigawa kept his head down, not looking into their faces, until Tatsudaiyu let out a big sigh. He glanced at Onui.

"We guessed, of course," Tatsudaiyu said, "and it was inconsiderate for us to press the matter, but my son Jinsuke begged me to do so. He likes her very much, and it is going to be hard for him. I, however, have three sons, so how can I think ill of you for wanting a son to take your name and continue the Takigawa line? If I had a daughter like Oyoshi it would tear my heart to let her go. No, no, we understand. We will pray for your happiness, for you and Oyoshi. Come now, let this not affect how our friendship has been. Onui, fetch sake!"

His wife went out into the kitchen.

"As for young Jinsuke . . ." said the old man.

"I will tell him," said Tatsudaiyu with a tone of flat finality.

Chapter Five

From the convoluted caves and twisted rock formations of the cliffs of Onigajo—"Devil's Castle"—Matsudaira Sadayori had walked four of the seven *ri* along the longest beach in the fiefdom of Kii. He had been thinking, his thoughts jumbled with the threats of the future and with ancient stories and myths of the place he had just left. Onigajo was once the lair of the pirates of Kumano, and in ancient times, it was said, devils lived there, red and blue. Were those ancient ogres in fact barbarians? Eventually driven out and destroyed by early emperors? It was known that the first Son of Heaven, the Emperor Jimmu, had come to Kii and defeated many adversaries. Perhaps he had driven out devils too?

Sadayori's straw sandals, crunching in the shingle, were beginning to wear through, and his *hakama* and *haori* were sticky with salt. Surf roared. Regiments of waves marched shoreward, striding out of the Pacific. So vast, so awesome it was! Why should such an ocean carry enemies to this ancient and sacred land? Why could the ocean not swallow them up and turn their bones to sand?

Sadayori had walked almost every beach in the fiefdom of his lord, and what he had learned troubled him deeply. He had come to know each bay, inlet, landing place, jetty, wharf, fishing village, harbor and town. He knew, and had mapped and sketched, all the places suitable for the emplacement of cannon. He knew the numbers and availability of all ships and boats. All of this he had reported to his lord and to the regent, as well as to senior Tokugawa officials in Edo. One of these great men, Ii Naosuke, had been more sympathetic, or more willing to listen, than the rest, who were so deeply entrenched in hardheaded conservatism that they seemed more like fossils than true defenders of Japan and her ancestors.

The bitter, inescapable truth was that Japan was just not strong enough, or organized enough, to defeat a full-scale foreign invasion. The *bushi* could fight in the hills and forests forever, living like beasts, and no doubt preying on peasants for food. Or they might choose to die on the beaches, killed at a distance by grapeshot, exploding shells and rifle bullets. Neither course of action would save the nation.

Tokugawa edicts limited the size and design of ships, and the route and width of roads so that only foot travelers and mounted men could move on them, and such things would prove both a blessing and a curse in the event of invasion. It was true that those laws were wise and had protected the nation up until now. Like a fine strong fruit tree it was, but now thieves were at the garden walls and the gardeners should be open to new ways to stop the thieves before they climbed over. Why should the foreigners have more powerful ships, more powerfu weapons than Japan? For instance, Sadayori had seen a smuggled rifle that could actually fire bullets one after another, with a lever mechanism, a weapon that could hit and kill a man at hundreds of paces. What did Japan produce? On the island of Tanegashima they were still making matchlocks, muzzle loading, fired with a rope fuse that was easily extinguished, weapons that were marvelous in finish and decoration, but which could kill at perhaps a hundred paces, at the most. It enraged Sadayori to accept it, but Japan was hundreds of years behind, and despite what conservatives said, Japanese chivalry and the warrior's code were not enough to defend these shores.

This surely must be obvious to those in power, but how many of them were really doing anything about it? The barbarians continued to nibble away like rats at the edges of a rice bale. Only a year before, an American naval commander had secured the release of shipwrecked Americans who had been imprisoned in Naha. That year too, beacons had flared along the Kumano coast when two American whaling ships had landed at Oshima, and their crews had fired rifles, robbed, and thoroughly made a nuisance of themselves. And such an insult had gone unpunished!

Had Sadayori been responsible he would have returned the barbarian prisoners to their navy ship in two batches—heads in the first batch, bodies in the second.

Sadayori had heard that the Satsuma clan, the powerful warriors who controlled southern Kyushu and the Ryukyu Islands, had been consulted in Edo about overtures from the

French, and it was also known that they were actually carryng on limited trade with the French, despite the laws against it.

He stood, gazing at the sea, as if daring it to produce enemies right then and there. Ah, but it was a simple solution in a sad life, to imagine dying gloriously in defense of this sacred soil! Yet he knew that what was more important than personal release was surely an adequate defense—cannon, rifles, a navy of big and well-armed ships. The so-called warrior class must again learn humility and truly learn to fight!

Sadayori stopped walking, raised both arms and breathed deeply. Cold air blew in from the sea. White upon blue-gray shingle, the surf was in continual turmoil. Behind, the land was a hundred tones of green. All these months spent in reaffirming his country's vulnerability tormented him, and in his imagination he saw great ships, heard the roll of guns and the crashing of shells, saw boatloads of men in ugly tight uniforms. Unconsciously, one hand fiddled with the cords that still tied down and covered the hilt of his sword. Then suddenly, like a pheasant leaping skyward from a silent bush, the long sword was in his hands, slicing the air in a pattern, silvery blade dipping and swooping, then coming to a deathly stop. Another swift movement and a gentle snick and the sword returned to its scabbard. Tension drained from him.

He looked around, but nobody was there, and briefly he worried that the blade, a priceless heirloom that had been in his family for two hundred years, might be damaged by the salt air.

He shook his head. The sword was his soul, the symbol of his caste, his vows, his pride. And in a way too, it was a symbol of a terrible weakness. He retied the cords and hurried on his way. That night he would take special care in cleaning the blade.

His destination was the town of Shingu. Tales of those sea pirates who once used the caves of Onigajo had started the germ of an idea in his mind, and in Shingu there was an old friend of his father's, a man who would listen, and of whom, perhaps, he could beg a favor.

Three days later, with a letter concealed under his sash, Sadayori headed from Shingu toward Taiji, intending to break his journey at Katsuura, a larger, more well-known resort town with hot springs and a harbor safely hidden among islands and winding, high-walled rocky inlets. Katsuura was a favorite stopping place for those travelers and pilgrims who came to visit the shrine at Nachi.

It had been a long walk, and he ached all over, so Sadayori decided to avail himself of a hot bath and well-prepared seafood at a small inn close to the harbor and the teahouses. The following morning he could take a boat across the Bay of Moriura to Taiji.

Like most coastal spas, Katsuura was known for pleasures not normally associated with pilgrims, but since the death of his young wife Sadayori had never used a woman's body. Despite this, he still enjoyed being fussed over and liked to bask in small flatteries or laugh at women's banter. Thus, after a long soak in the bath and a good meal he called for a geisha to serve him.

She was a country girl, but pretty, and she tried very hard to be sophisticated. She fed him small pieces of seafood snacks to go with the sake she served, accompanying herself on the samisen as she sang to him. Sadayori sat by an open window on the second floor of the inn, the girl beside him. He was wearing only a light summer kimono, but after nearly two hours in the bath he felt no chill, and his body was glowing with the mineral heat of it.

There was a drinking place up the street, rowdy with young men calling for sake and jesting with each other. It was obvious from their accents that they were local men.

"Oh, those Taiji men, they are always like that when they come to Katsuura!" said the girl, as if apologizing. "If they annoy you, sir, I'll send somebody to go and complain."

"Taiji men, are they? No, let them be, I don't mind."

In these past months Sadayori had so often enjoyed the simple hospitality of fishermen and farmers that he had become more tolerant. He cocked his head, smiling at some of the outrageous things they yelled at each other. The girl clicked her tongue with annoyance and strummed the samisen loudly.

"Play me folk songs," said Sadayori. She had a sweet voice, and three young whalers, stepping outside to urinate, paused and listened. Sadayori clapped and she put the instrument down to fill his sake cup again. He hummed a melody he had heard, ages ago it seemed, on the cliffs of Taiji.

"Can you play that one?"

"Oh, I know it, sir. Those noisy whalers are always singing it when they come over here."

"Do they come often?"

"Only when it is out of the season for whales, sir."

"For women?"

She put one small hand to her mouth as if out of shyness. "Yes, sir, and for drinking too, and they are always so boisterous. Things are very quiet in Taiji, they don't have any entertainment there really."

Sadayori nodded. He had discovered how disciplined the whaling communities were. Even the outlawed *yakuza* thugs were scared to go near them. He glanced out of the window and saw that the three young whalers were still outside, as if they had enjoyed the girl's last song.

"Please play that whalers' song now, with lots of vigor."

The twang of the chords rang down the street, and in a loud voice, imitating the accents of Taiji, she began to sing.

> *"Seni ga harande,*
> *Umeba kosso . . ."*
> When the belly of the right whale swells,
> and in due course she gives birth . . .

The three whalers joined in delightedly from outside, and soon the men inside the shop added their lusty voices to the chorus. "Ey! Yoi! Yoi!"

> *"Oki ni ya, o-semi ga*
> *Yaiyaran!"*
> And out at sea, those great right whales
> Will never become extinct!

Then came the shouts, as if they were all at their oars. "Ah! Hoi! Hoi!"

Verse after verse, on and on went the song, and the girl, after a while, red in the face from trying not to laugh, for some of the verses were impromptu, made up on the spot by the men below, and very rude and very funny, gave up singing and just strummed.

Jinsuke had come out of the shop into the street. He was fairly drunk and was going through a dance, a pantomime of waves, rising and falling, of taking up the harpoon, of hurling it.

When the song was finally finished, Sadayori brought out some coins from the wallet in his sash.

"Here, go and buy two large flagons of sake. Take them to those outrageous fellows down there and thank them for the song."

The girl took the money, bowed demurely, and left the room. Sadayori sensed disappointment in her, for she had probably expected him to ask her to stay and sleep with him. He sighed. Life was so simple for the ordinary folk, as long as they didn't break the laws, and Sadayori often envied them, especially those whalers. If he were not a samurai, then he too could be down there, singing, getting rowdily drunk, ending up in the arms of a woman he could forget the next day. But he was a samurai, and a very proud one, and he would not take a woman who was not of his class.

The next morning, after another long bath, it was not a design of clouds or mountains that he drew on the blade of his sword with the fine talcum he used to clean it. The whalers' song still rang in his mind, and he drew waves on the blade. Then he wiped away the waves and drew instead a whole fleet of high-prowed boats, line in line, toward the point of the blade.

As he was performing this daily task, an older maid brought him tea, keeping a respectful distance from him. He took out the wad of tissues that he held in his mouth to prevent the moistness of his breath from touching the cold steel.

"I usually do this at night," he said, voice gentle. Sadayori knew of the fear the common folk had at the sight of a drawn sword, and he did not enjoy that fear. He wiped the blade clean and slipped it back into the sheath, where the wavy, tempered, razor-sharp threat of it would no longer disturb the woman. He reached for the tea.

"Ask the master to arrange for a boat. I wish to cross over to Taiji." The maid bowed, looking surprised.

"Taiji, sir? There's nothing there . . ."

"Oh yes there is!"

She looked at him.

"Yes, yes, there is something in Taiji, don't you know? Fast boats and brave men!"

The maid, taking the tray with her, left the airy little room, with the early-morning sun sweeping the pale yellow mats. Out in the bay, steam from the hot *onsen* waters flowed out in a fan on the surface of the cooler sea, making curtains of gold and silver mist. Sadayori got to his feet and slipped into the *hakama*, getting ready to go, his mind full of plans, plans that would bring wealth and pride to the whaling communities, and Taiji would be the first step.

He carried a letter from the castle at Shingu with orders that one whaleboat and crew be selected from Taiji and another from the sister village of Koza. The boats and men were to go to Wakayama city and hold a race for the entertainment of the daimyo. No doubt both villages would be

76

puzzled, and perhaps even fearful, but they would obey. Of course it was not just the entertainment of high officials that Sadayori had in mind.

He had timed this race and demonstration with a visit from the lord of Hikone, Ii Naosuke, a man who had taken great interest in the Wakayama house and its affairs, a man of growing influence in Edo. Dare Sadayori hope to talk with this great man? To try to convince him of the need to raise fast-hitting coastal defense forces, using at first whale-boats, with black lacquered hulls, manned by brave men who knew the sea and who knew rough weapons. Yes, such men could be trained to fight if those blinkered Edo *bakufu* officials could only see it. There would be samurai officers, one or two to each boat at first, men who were stationed at the whaling villages and in charge of the fleet when they went to war, and in charge of an arsenal, not only of weapons to be issued in emergencies, but with fire pots and black-powder grenades that could be hurled at the barbarian ships. They could strike out, like sea wolves, just as those long-ago Kumano pirates did. Were not the whalers descended from such men? They should be used now to defend their own coasts! Eventually, surely, they could be the nucleus of a strong navy!

Wada Kinemon, who had entertained Sadayori on his first visit to Taiji, had died, leaving his title and duties to a sixteen-year-old son, Iori. When Sadayori appeared in the village and arrived at the whaling office, the boy was obsequious and polite, but on reading the letter from Shingu, he passed it with visible anger to his father's cousin, Taiji Kakuemon, and began to bluster.

"This is most unorthodox! We cannot spare the men and boat, and it is such a long and dangerous journey. All the way to Wakayama? Who will pay the expenses? Really! Uncle Taiji, tell him . . ."

Sadayori looked at him coldly, and the boy shut up. "That is an order. Do you wish to disobey?"

Taiji Kakuemon spoke. "Certainly not. Which boat would you prefer, sir? And shall I dispatch a runner to Koza?"

"Any of the chase boats you think worthy of appearing before the lord of this fief. And no, I will take the letter to Koza. You will ready a boat and crew for me by tomorrow morning. I will sail in it and we will stop along the way at Koza. We will stay two days there, then go on to Wakayama. Make sure the men have some provisions to take with them."

The two Taiji net masters stared at him as if he had lost his senses.

"In a boat, with the whalers? You, a gentleman? But those boats are all open, not suitable at all, and there are no facilities for a guest. Oh no, that's dangerous, out of the question!"

Sadayori smiled. "Danger? Comfort? Are those the words of *bushi*? What does a samurai have to do with such notions? It is I who must take responsibility in this matter, and I will take the boat. Understand?"

The two men bowed. Actually, there was no mention in the letter of an officer riding in a boat, that had been Sadayori's idea.

Kakuemon turned to young Wada. "Iwadaiyu's boat is the best one, I think." He spoke then to Sadayori. "That is the chrysanthemum boat, the second boat in the fleet. Forgive us, but it would not be good to send the lead harpooner, just in case a stray whale is sighted."

Sadayori nodded, and Kakuemon called for one of the watchmen to run up to the harpooner's house to tell him to report to the office.

"Matsudaira-sama, will you honor me by staying at my meager house?"

"No, thank you, I won't intrude. There is an inn, is there not?"

"Yes, but it's rather small, and . . ."

"I will stay there. When you have finished with the boat captain tell him to bring his second and come to see me tonight, after the evening meal. I wish to give them instructions."

Neither Kakuemon nor Iori pressed invitations, and Sadayori knew that this time he was not really welcome. With a small bow, he walked away.

Stern though he seemed, inside he was bubbling with excitement. He had dreamed of going out to sea in one of those swift chase boats, and although he would not admit it to a soul, he would even have loved to be able to go out with them when they killed a whale.

Chapter Six

"What? Make warriors out of fishermen? It
would be easier to breed flying fish from
turtles! Preposterous!" In the long room in the castle at
Wakayama, the voices of several other councillors were raised
in outrage and argument. Not all were as opposed to
Sadayori's ideas as they seemed to be, but they were all too
afraid or too disunited to say so. The daimyo of Wakayama
was but a child, and it was the regent and the daimyo of
Hikone who were the actual rulers of the fiefdom. On a dais
at the end of the room, these two men sat, little tailed hats
of office perched on the tops of their shaved heads, dressed
in magnificent brocades, with wide shoulders that stuck out
like wings, and wearing court *hakama* so long that the only
possible gait was a slow, careful shuffle.

Sadayori felt the eyes of the lord of Hikone, Ii Naosuke,
bore into him, but he kept his head down, in a deep bow.

As the councillors shouted their remarks across the free
space between where they knelt, in two ranks, Ii Naosuke's
mouth was set in a tight-lipped, cynical line. What was
wrong with a young, sincere warrior who had so thoroughly
researched the coast, and who was trying to find a solution,
albeit an overly simple one, to this most urgent need for
national defense? In Ii Naosuke's opinion, all such young
men should be listened to, no matter how outrageous their
ideas might seem. He glanced sideways to the regent.

"On whose orders did this man research the coasts?" He
knew, of course.

"Our late lord, sir. He gave direct and personal orders to
the senior councillor."

"And this man has spent how many years in research of the coasts?"

"Three years, I believe. It was my . . ."

"Then don't you think that he deserves a few minutes of our time to listen to him? How many of the councillors have visited the coasts in the past two years?"

There was a murmur of protest. This time the regent raised his voice.

"Quiet!" The room fell silent. "Matsudaira, continue!"

Sadayori bowed again, then raised his head from the tatami and looked directly at Ii Naosuke. He was tanned in the face as dark as a peasant, but when he spoke, it was with the most refined and polite forms of speech possible.

That day, several of the senior councillors, the young daimyo and these two eminent men before him, so eminent that they received the title of *kami,* or deity, had watched the Taiji and Koza boats race and maneuver in the bay. The whalers had stood to their oars dressed only in headbands and red loincloths, and many who watched clapped their hands at the speed of the boats and the skill of the men, and marveled at their powerful bodies. "Like wrestlers!"

The thirty men on the boats, on the way up from Taiji to Koza, and from Koza to Wakayama, had been encouraged by Sadayori to practice a few of the less vulgar and boisterous verses of their song, and they performed these, to the delight of the crowds and guests.

"May I remind my lords, most humbly, that chase boats of this design were built and taken to Edo during the time of our most illustrious eighth shogun, Yoshimune of Kii, a century ago. That most esteemed personage, renowned for his wisdom, saw the potential of such boats in war. They are not mere fishing craft, sirs! They are faster by far!

"The whalers have faced great perils at sea and are highly trained. They do not operate as other fishermen, but in disciplined, coordinated fleets, responding to complicated signals with prompt efficiency.

"Moreover, my lords, the whalers of this coast are descendants of the sea raiders of Kumano, who were feared in battle since the times of Genji, when, my lords, it was the Kumano warriors who changed the outcome of battles. That is all history we all know well. Thus, what I propose I do with great thought and reverence to the history and needs of this land."

Sadayori paused and looked around the room. He was a natural orator, and his travels and exercises had given his voice and manner a vigor and resonance that most city-bound samurai did not have.

"My lords, may I have permission to exhibit a certain unusual weapon?"

One of the councillors closest to the dais turned, face whitening with anger, the stiff shoulder silks trembling as rage shook his body.

"Matsudaira! How dare you disgrace us! A weapon? In this room, in front of these august personages? Have you lost your mind?"

Another councillor shuffled forward on his knees.

"He should be ordered to cut his belly!"

"Does he think this is a dojo?"

"Disgraceful!"

But Sadayori did not bow his head down this time. He knew that Ii Naosuke was a master of several fighting arts and would be intrigued. He was right. Ii Naosuke gestured with his fan.

"Gentlemen! Gentlemen! Are we or are we not *bushi*? Are the swords we carry for decoration? I for one am certainly not terrified or dismayed at the sight of a weapon. No, I am interested. Let those of you who are nervous leave us, and let this young samurai show us this unusual weapon." He laughed. "Matsudaira, do you intend to attack anyone?"

Sadayori bowed low again. "If I have committed an insult, my lord, allow me to take any punishment you choose, but I really believe that you would be interested. If, after seeing it, you are offended, then I will take my life, this very evening."

The room fell silent at his boldness and the conservatives fumed inwardly, guessing that this young upstart was gaining favor.

"Bring the weapon!" ordered the regent, and Sadayori bowed and stood, retreating to the entranceway, outside which armed guards stood. In seconds, one of them brought him a long object wrapped in purple silk and tied with a tasseled cord. Sadayori brought it forward at arm's length and laid it before the dais. He moved back, as if to let one of the councillors unwrap it.

"Show us," commanded Ii Naosuke.

Sadayori removed the covering to reveal a massive, double-edged, pointed blade, razor sharp, fixed to a stout handle of white oak. It looked like an oversized spear. Ii Naosuke stood, shuffled a few steps forward, and hefted the weapon.

"Rather cumbersome, but fearsome indeed. No doubt

very effective in the hands of a powerful man. I have never seen such a heavy double-edged weapon before. Is it from China? It is certainly not European. Have you mastered its use?"

"No, my lord, I have never used it. I doubt if any samurai has mastered the use of this *ken* in the last two hundred years, even though it is Japanese, and a traditional weapon. It is a whaler's weapon, my lord, a lance used to dispatch a harpooned whale. Those burly fellows you saw racing chase boats today, they, my lord, kill far bigger prey than barbarians, and they know how to use such things. Under proper supervision, I know they could be trained to be as good as the Kumano raiders were in time past."

Ii Naosuke put his head back and laughed, his deep voice ringing from the wooden ceiling. "Ah, young fellow, what can we say? Yes, indeed, I'm sure that those burly fellows in the red loincloths are lethal with this thing. And they also use long-handled cutting knives like the *naginata,* don't they? Yes, yes, I've seen pictures. And you'd have them butchering barbarians, would you?" He brandished the killing lance and laughed again. An attendant came forward to take it from him and remove it from the room.

Now another councillor spoke out, but no longer in the condemning tones they had hurled at the young samurai before.

"My lords, it is true that in times past, when the country had internal wars, we levied soldiers from the peasantry. But that was only in times of war. The times now are difficult perhaps, and yet, does not the long peace of the Tokugawa regime continue to ensure His Imperial Majesty's tranquility? Are the peasants not content and settled with their correct station in life?"

At this, Sadayori, who had talked and shared the simple food and dwellings of the peasants and fishermen and who knew that they would suffer greatly under foreign invasion, spoke out: "Sir! There is a severe threat of barbarian attack! And do we forget the rice riots? The rebellion in Osaka? The peasants are not—"

"Silence!" The regent roared at him and Sadayori's stomach knotted. The councillor continued, the lines of his mouth and cheeks drawn in supercilious disapproval.

"To suggest that we train whalers to become a fighting force is a preposterous notion, preposterous and dangerous. It would give them an idea, would it not, that they were on a par with the *bushi.* They are simple men, with simple thoughts, carrying out the duties that heaven has allotted to them. Strength and vigor they have, yes, and they are brave, no doubt, but this is because they are assured of their station in life and protected by us. How can we dare to alter that? That they are descendants of pirates is another matter. Surely, to re-create the moods and habits of pirates would be disturbing."

A ripple of laughter ran down the ranks of councillors and Sadayori gritted his teeth.

"Surely," said the councillor, "it would be evil to give them the idea that the tools of their trade might be used to kill men. Under the wise edicts of this land the peasants are forbidden to carry arms. A wise law indeed! So this thing we have seen must remain rooted in their minds as a tool, not a weapon, otherwise they will think we have relaxed the laws, and that will only lead to more troubles. I agree with young Matsudaira that we should improve our fighting ability at sea, but with warriors, not fishermen!"

The long hall resounded with murmured agreement, and Sadayori could only fume inwardly. He bowed again, feeling the steady, cool gaze of Ii Naosuke upon him.

Later that night he was discreetly summoned to Ii Naosuke's apartments. In an adjoining room the night quilts were already laid out, but the lord was still fully clothed, at a low table, reading scrolls by the light of two shoulder-high paper-screened oil lamps. Silently, attendants ushered Sadayori in, then knelt outside on the polished wood of the corridor. The lord came directly to the point.

"I am intrigued by this idea of sea squadrons. Tell me more." Ii Naosuke used a speech form as adopted by a teacher to a beloved student and Sadayori felt a jolt in his chest.

"I do not envisage just a single squadron, as you realize, sir, but many, located at each whaling town. We should start at Kii, where we have the oldest whaling tradition and two villages with over five hundred seagoing men. After we train them we should encourage fiefdoms all over the nation to follow our example. We would have thousands of sea fighters and hundreds of swift boats, all on the paths of the whales, which is on the route the foreign ships take too. Each unit would have a small garrison of samurai, not too many at first, so as not to overextend the budget. They would have a stout arsenal of weapons, just as country homes have warehouses to safeguard possessions from fire. The samurai would maintain discipline and give the men the extra training they would need for combat. They would drill the whalers in the use of suitable weapons."

"Suitable weapons? Tell me, what are suitable weapons for whalers?" The tone was gentle, but dangerous. However, Sadayori was compelled to speak boldly.

"Their natural dexterity and strength is in the use of harpoons, lances, long-handled flensing knives, short knives, hatchets and such. Give them even rudimentary training in combat and they could be useful at the kind of close-quarter fighting that would be expected on the decks of an enemy ship."

"Indeed. And what of the officers who would lead these pirates of yours?"

"Young, vigorous samurai, my lord, skilled with the sword and armed also with pistols, for the barbarians use such things. I would recommend that one man in each boat should also be trained in the use of a large-bored short-barreled gun that would fire a massive charge of spreading shot. Each boat should carry, in combat, grenades and fire pots, as well as grappling hooks. None of the men should wear armor, for it would impede swimming and fast, agile boarding of an enemy vessel."

"Ninja training . . ." Ii Naosuke was thoughtful. "And what would these men be doing when not training or fighting? Are you suggesting that they be paid a stipend? The country cannot afford it."

"No, my lord, they should carry on whaling and maintain their correct social status, although being with one of these units would bring even more pride to them. There is financial distress in the whaling communities, and equipment is getting run down. Should the government finance the building of new, all-black boats, suitable for both whaling and war, then the industry would greatly benefit. With more good boats they would take more whales, and the government would reap extra taxes from the whaling while at the same time developing a sea force standing at the ready all along the coast." Sadayori's eyes glittered as he spoke. "I envisage a force of swift, silent black boats, the men and officers in black uniforms, a force that could strike under cover of darkness, when enemy cannon would be ineffective."

"Seagoing ninja?"

"Similar, my lord, yes, but trained in disciplined war, not spying and assassination."

"And otherwise, how would they engage a foreign warship? Those boats would be blown to smithereens."

"Either under cover of darkness," replied Sadayori, "or with speed, courage, and the spirit of the Japanese, which is superior to the barbarians in all ways. Some boats would draw fire, but they are small and fast and not easy to hit. Others would dart in as they do with a whale. I believe that lines could be fastened to the ship with harpoons so the chase boats could haul close enough to throw fire pots, grenades and grappling lines. Other boats could be loaded with black powder and flaming oil and sent to ram the enemy. Perhaps an intruding ship could be impeded by the great nets the whalers use, especially in vulnerable harbors. There are surely many possibilities, especially with men who are so expert with boats and harpoons."

"You say that they could fix lines to a ship with harpoons?"

"Yes, my lord. Those men throw harpoons very hard and high, with force enough to penetrate deep into a whale's back. If enough harpoons were thrown, then a chase boat could be hauled right up to a ship. I even believe that some of the better harpooners can throw with enough accuracy to hit an enemy sailor or officer and yank him out of his ship."

"The enemy would cut the lines," said Ii Naosuke.

"Yes, but boats would harry them from all sides, get in under the cannon."

Ii Naosuke lapsed into thought. Perhaps this scheme actually did have merit. Often a simple solution was very effective in war.

"Sir, if you had seen these men close in and kill a great whale you would understand my enthusiasm."

"Hmmm. I would like to see one of these men throw a harpoon. Arrange it for me."

Sadayori bowed, deeply grateful.

"I begin my journey to Edo tomorrow. Wait for me beyond the city limits, in a place that has few people around and suitable range for the throwing of a harpoon. I will order my retinue and escorts to pause there. You and your harpooner wait along the route. You may bring unarmed servants, but no more than six. The servants will keep nosy peasants away. Is that understood?"

Ii Naosuke clapped his hands and an attendant brought a simple roasted tea. Ii Naosuke looked across the rim of his steaming cup and asked another question. "You have read the works of Watanabe Kwazan, of Miyake, have you not?"

Sadayori caught his breath. Watanabe had been arrested and sentenced to death for the anti-*bakufu* opinions in his writings. He had been a student of European sciences and had strongly advocated the opening of the country to foreign commerce. Perhaps out of mercy, the *bakufu* had later commuted the death sentence to life imprisonment. But Watanabe was stubborn, and dedicated to his ideas, and while in prison he passed writings out to his friends. When this was discovered the infuriated Edo government vented its anger on the daimyo of Miyake. Wishing now to atone for the distress caused to his lord, Watanabe killed himself.

"Watanabe Kwazan also strongly advocated the need for coastal defense," said Ii Naosuke.

"Yes. I have read his books, sir." It was a dangerous admission. Ii Naosuke nodded.

"Do you also hold the opinion that we should open the country to foreign trade?"

Sadayori looked briefly into the broad, strong, stern features of this ambitious and powerful man, one who had seen much hardship in his early years, a man who was proud, but not vain, bold, but at the same time cautious. He knew he must answer truthfully.

"The thought does not please me, my lord, but I believe that we need to import armaments, and we eventually need to have strong warships. If so, we must pay for those things. However, we can never permit barbarians to come and go freely. We must have it all under our control. My true desire is to have nothing to do with them, but if we stubbornly take that stand, the barbarians will surely invade. They have done so in the case of every other country and land."

Ii Naosuke nodded. "So you know what happened in China, don't you? You know of the war the English fought to open Chinese ports for their trade in opium? The Chinese were defeated and shamed. Of course, they do not have a true warrior class, nor do they have modern guns."

There was silence between them. From outside came the cries of a patrolling night watchman, and the click of his signal clappers as he banged them together and called out a warning to take care of fires.

"So, you have read the works of Watanabe. What of Takano Choei?"

Sadayori's face was a mask, for this was dangerous. This man had the power of life and death over him. Were these merely casual questions?

Takano was a friend of Watanabe and like him had strongly criticized the *bakufu* and its policies. He studied under many famous people, including the "Hollander" Siebold, who had been given permission to stay in Japan and teach medicine and surgery, and who had even been allowed to travel to Edo. He had been imprisoned for getting his hands on a map of Japan. Like so many of the outspoken critics of the *bakufu*, Takano had become famous, as a doctor and a scholar, but he got himself into trouble for his opinions and officials outlawed him. He fled to Edo, living there in disguise, but still translating foreign writings. He was a formidable expert on foreign military science. They arrested him once, but he escaped in a fire.

Not only had Sadayori read his books, but he admired Takano, and through secret connections from other fiefdoms he had even arranged a meeting. He and Takano had discussed the nation's problems until the early hours of the morning.

A week later, Sadayori was horrified to hear that *bakufu* soldiers had been sent to arrest Takano, who killed two of them and then killed himself. If Sadayori's link with this radical should come out, Sadayori would no doubt be required to take the short sword to his own belly. Ii Naosuke kept on looking at him, waiting for his answer.

"I confess that I have read the works of Takano Choei, my lord."

"So have I. But you understand, don't you, that zealots can do as much harm as they do good—to the government, to themselves, and to their friends. Take care."

Ii Naosuke smiled. "You know, I greatly admired your grandfather. He did much for the country. Go now, and let me see this harpoon thrower tomorrow."

Sadayori bowed and backed out of the room, closing the sliding screen doors behind him. He had been warned, and he was aware now that *bakufu* spies were watching him.

Not wishing to arouse people, he did not take a horse, but walked down to the beach where the whalers were sleeping under their upturned boats, awaiting final orders from him, and no doubt anxious to return to their villages and boast of all they had done and seen. The night air was cool, but his thoughts boiled like a pot on a brazier. What was the true significance of Ii Naosuke's last remark? Sadayori's grandfather, Matsudaira Sadanobu, had died twenty-one years before. Sadayori could barely remember him. He had been one of the senior advisors to the shogun and also minister of war for the Tokugawa regime. Under his orders, the Tokugawa army had been reorganized along European lines, with infantry, cavalry and even artillery. The times were troubled then too. The Russians were pressing for trade, and

they always took more than they asked for. Matsudaira
Sadanobu had ordered a very careful inspection of the coasts
and built forts to discourage landing. Many of his notes and
scrolls and a few copies of his written orders to the Tokugawa
military authorities had come into Sadayori's hands, so in a
way he was carrying on with his grandfather's work. Was Ii
Naosuke's remark intended to encourage him?

He reached the beach. The two upside-down chase boats,
supported by deck boards to make a lean-to shelter, looked
like crouching monsters in the flickering glow of driftwood
fires. Some of the men sat around the fires, some slept on
mats, set under the boats on the sand. As the samurai
approached, three men leaped to their feet to face him,
harpoons at the ready.

"It's Matsudaira," he announced, and they lowered their
weapons and bowed to him.

"Good evening, sir!" the men chorused. Iwadaiyu stepped
forward and bowed again.

"Thank you for the treats, sir, we rarely enjoy such things."
After the races the men had been sent polished rice, dried
laver and even pickles all the way from Kyoto, as well as one
basket of live eels, broiled and marinated yellowfin, best
quality soya sauce, fresh oranges and sake. Indeed it was a
feast for them.

"You did well. The lords were pleased."

The tall, broad, jowly harpooner-captain from Koza joined
Iwadaiyu and echoed their thanks. Jinsuke stood in the
background.

"Choose one harpooner and bring your best harpoon, the
one you can throw farthest and hardest, and meet me one
hour's walk along the road to Osaka, soon after dawn tomorrow. Only one of you may come."

"A harpoon, sir?" asked Iwadaiyu.

"Yes. You will demonstrate in secret to the Lord Ii
Naosuke. In secret, you understand? And come with the
harpoon covered. If you are stopped by any castle guards or
strange samurai, say you were ordered to come to look for
me. Say no more. Understand?"

"We understand," said Iwadaiyu, but he felt worried, and
even afraid to be ordered to do such a thing.

"And if anybody ever talks about this I will cut out his
tongue. Understand?"

They did. Sadayori bowed and bid them good night, and
walked off into the darkness. When he was out of earshot
the whalers erupted into excited discussion.

*   *   *

Sadayori and his servants, and the young harpooner Jinsuke waited. Great pines with branches that shaded the road framed a clear patch of ground from which Sadayori's servants had cleared the tall pampas grass and other weeds. Four servants with long staffs kept curious peasants and early-morning travelers away, and a screen of bamboo and white cloth surrounded the place.

The procession wound its way toward them. Loud cries ordered all to stand off the road, fall to their knees, and keep low. The procession numbered several hundred men, led by mounted cavalry and men with tall whirling pennants who walked in stiff-legged ceremonial gait. There were pack horses and servants on foot, special boxes carried on poles, and several lesser palanquins with their armed guards, but the center of the procession was the heavily guarded palanquin of Ii Naosuke himself.

Sadayori and the others were to the side of the road, kneeling on the grass. Orders were shouted up and the captain of the guards, on horseback, raised his hand and brought the cumbersome procession to a stop. Flanked by swordsmen on foot, the main palanquin had halted right beside the small kneeling group.

"Is everything ready?" demanded the captain, a bannerman. He was curt and cold, looking down at them disdainfully.

"Yes," said Sadayori.

The captain nodded to one of the samurai by the palanquin, and this man went down on one knee beside the small sliding door, speaking in low tones. The lord did not leave his conveyance, but slid open the door so that he could see.

"Proceed," said the captain.

A square of thick red-painted boards was placed on the ground at the far end of the enclosure, put in such a way that it could be easily seen from where Ii Naosuke was. Sadayori bowed again, in the formal way of the warrior, first his left hand, fingers held stiff, then his right hand touching the ground before he lowered his head between them. He raised his head slowly, leaving his hands on the ground as he spoke.

"Does this man beside me have permission to stand and to demonstrate the throwing of a harpoon to His Most Honorable Lord of Hikone? I vouch for him and will take all responsibility for his breach of etiquette. I am Matsudaira Sadayori, samurai, retainer of the lord of Kii." He lowered his head again.

The captain saw Ii Naosuke's nod and answered that permission was given. Had it not been, Jinsuke would have been cut down the moment he got to his feet. Jinsuke stood, trying to control the trembling in his legs. His hair was carefully done up in a topknot, and he wore a new quilted jacket tied with a sash. Around his head was a neatly fastened headband of white cotton. He bowed toward the palanquin, turned, and slipped off the loose sleeve of his right arm and shoulder, baring them as an archer might. An attendant shuffled forward on his knees, handing him a harpoon. The guards tensed, watching like hawks, some horrified at what was being permitted here, a naked point bared, a mere whaler standing.

Jinsuke now held the harpoon under his left arm, as if he were in a chase boat, nearing the whale for the first throw. With slow deliberation, partly to calm himself and concentrate, partly so that each movement could be observed and understood, Jinsuke shifted the butt of the harpoon so that it rested in the palm of his right hand, while his left hand, held across his chest and over his right shoulder, guided the shaft. He braced his legs wider. The point aimed skyward, and the line was carefully coiled behind him, not held by a second as it would have been in a boat. Breathing deeply, he tensed the muscles of his stomach, keeping his eye on the target. With a sudden yell, he hurled the harpoon. It arced upward, turned perfectly, trailing line, then dived down, smacking loudly right into the center of the boards.

Now Jinsuke yanked on the line and pulled the harpoon and the target with it, across the ground toward him. Then he turned again, went down on his knees before the palanquin, and bowed in the way Sadayori had shown him.

Ii Naosuke ordered the guards to bring both target and harpoon to him. They did so, laying it where he could see how the steel head had pierced a board and bit the underside with the barb.

"Matsudaira Sadayori, come here."

Sadayori glanced at the captain, who made a small nod. He approached and knelt.

"A mighty throw indeed!" Ii Naosuke then lowered his voice so that only Sadayori and the closest, most trusted retainers could hear. "I will be in Edo in a month's time Come to my residence. There are things I would like to discuss with you."

Sadayori's heart quickened. The nearest guard handed him a small brocade bag. Inside was half of an official wooden seal which would permit him to pass the checkpoints along the route to the capital. It also contained a few gold coins. Quietly, the door of the palanquin slid shut.

Sadayori and Jinsuke stayed where they were until the tail of the procession had moved out of sight. Then Sadayori stood, called Jinsuke to him, and handed him three small paper-wrapped oblong packages. They were gold *ryo*.

"Two of these are for your boat masters, one is for you. The expenses of your journey have already been paid in silver and rice. This money is a reward for doing so well, and will also ensure your silence. But I am curious why Iwadaiyu did not throw."

Jinsuke couldn't say that Iwadaiyu had selected him because he had become as good a harpooner as his father, perhaps even stronger.

"Iwadaiyu, my captain, has a slight strain in his shoulder, sir, and he insisted that a Taiji man should throw. He said it had to be me."

Sadayori nodded. "Well done. When will you captain your own boat?"

"Next year, I think, sir."

"Next year? Very good, and what will be the design?"

Jinsuke looked up at the tall trees that threw their shade on them. "I shall ask for it to be the pine-tree pattern, sir."

Sadayori smiled at him. He paused before leaving. "You will say nothing about this morning's events. If I hear a lot of gossip, I will know whom to look for in Taiji, and I shall be asking questions about a certain illegal meeting, at sea, between two Taiji chase boats and a boat from a barbarian ship. Understand?"

Jinsuke whitened. Which drunken idiot had talked? Probably to some Katsuura teahouse girl, trying to impress her! Curse whoever it was!

"I will not talk, sir."

"Good. I shall trust you, then." He turned to his attendant, a gray-haired man with quick eyes. "Take this man back to his crew and see that they have enough to eat and drink before they set off for home." His face broke into a smile, which he turned on Jinsuke.

"Give my regards to everybody. I enjoyed sailing with you."

Jinsuke smiled and bowed back, suddenly liking this usually quiet, stern man. He bowed and started to follow the attendant, when Sadayori called out to him.

"Again, tell me your name, whaler!"

"Jinsuke, first son of the *hazashi* Tatsudaiyu," came the reply.

"I'll remember that name. One day I might have use for that strong arm of yours."

And with that he walked back to a grove of trees, hidden from the road, where his horse and groom waited for him. Jinsuke was too delighted about the gold to think seriously about what had been said to him, and already he was wondering what fine presents he could buy before going home, perhaps in the city, presents to take back for his mother and Oyoshi.

Back in Taiji, however, a decision had been made that everybody except the fifteen men on the chrysanthemum boat knew, a decision by Takigawa, the boat painter, father of Oyoshi. Had Jinsuke known, that oblong gold coin would not have felt so warm and heavy in his hand.

Chapter Seven

The gulls of winter had given way to the swallows of spring, who brought joy to the skies with their aerial courtship and made the narrow lanes of Taiji busy with their darting quest for nesting sites, new and old, under the eaves. Soon the Taiji folk would be putting out little boxes to keep the white droppings off the streets and the fronts of their houses.

Pink blossoms flamed then scattered on the cherry trees beside the Wada house and along the pathway to the Tomyo lookout. In wayside grasses the violets grew, blue and tiny. Here in Taiji the spring came quickly, much sooner than in Osaka or Edo. Spring came, enhanced into summer with a profusion of flowers, lilies along the shore, with the delicate splashes of mountain cherry giving way to the richer purple of azaleas, and with fragrant honeysuckle along the paths.

In winter the sea was crystal clear, but in these warm months plankton bloomed, and different, more colorful fish began to move in.

The weather was good, and the Taiji men hunted every day. Whalers reported that the warm current had swung in closer to the coast this year, and there was a mixing of waters within easy reach, where whales were feeding. Fishermen also had good catches, but they brought news of sharks; they had landed three hammerheads, bigger than men and ugly as a devil. On hearing about the sharks some of the men didn't want to go whaling, but the net masters were firm, and they had no choice.

It was an unusually warm, sultry day, overcast yet bright, with the sea a blend of harsh, strong gray and deeper green. A "look-alike" whale, so called because it resembled the sardine whale, and also a gray whale had been spotted, and the chase order went out, the pennants signaling that the men should go after the look-alike. However, the gray whale panicked at the booming underwater din, and it made a sudden turn, driving in a frenzy through the net, tearing out a section and going on, trailing ropes, tubs and beams in a tangle.

Sweating with effort, the shouting crews of the two lead chase boats managed to get close to the fleeing whale and hit it with two harpoons. The gray whale breached, twisting its body against the tangle and hitting the sea with an awesome clatter and splash, tearing one of the irons out.

Now the whale made another run, avoiding a third chase boat and dolphining along the surface at great speed, dragging remnants of gear along with it. The men strained harder, muscles of arms and shoulders bulging, sweat running in rivulets, each oar blade moving like the tail of a swordfish. At Tatsudaiyu's signals the chase boats split into two groups, eight boats each, with one group going after the wild gray whale, and the other going for the more docile but highly valuable look-alike whale.

Iwadaiyu's group pursued the gray whale for two hours, until it seemed that their aching arms would turn as wooden as the oars they worked. But at last the whale began to tire. Iwadaiyu got up close enough to hurl another harpoon, which hit beside the blowhole, biting deep. This harpoon trailed a line and a float tub. The whale made a shallow dive.

Now Iwadaiyu's boat came close. The tub bobbed up and they could see the "color" of the whale underwater and knew where it would surface. Another harpoon soared into the sky and struck.

"Captain!" cried Jinsuke, letting the second line with another tub go overboard. "There's a line fast by the blowhole, let me dive and cut!"

Iwadaiyu signaled a negative, it was too dangerous to jump onto the whale yet. The whale came up again, head straight out of the water as far as the fins, "spy hopping," watching for its tormentors' next move. The mottled gray skin and the little eyes just above the down curve at the edges of the gape were so clear, and all around the whale was a welter of blood and tangled ropes like a grotesque collar. The chrysanthemum boat darted in and another of Iwadaiyu's harpoons struck. Ignoring his captain's refusal, this time Jinsuke dived overboard and in a few strokes reached and grabbed at the tangle of lines and rope meshes on the whale.

The whale slid back down in the water until it gained enough depth to make several immensely powerful strokes with its flukes that sent it into a backward breach, smashing one oar and showering the men with a wave of water. They feared for Jinsuke, but he hung on, despite abrasions and bruises all along his left arm and side, from being slammed and scraped against the barnacle-encrusted head.

The whale made another bolt for it, with Jinsuke still hanging on, trying to crawl closer to the blowhole for a cut. He should have remembered how wild a gray whale could be, but now he felt he could not let go and thrust free and face the unspoken derision of his boat mates. The whale thrashed and twisted, and after being dragged through the water almost out of sight of the chase boats following, Jinsuke was swept off.

Gasping for breath, Jinsuke broke surface, his knife still in his hand. He was much chagrined. With slow, painful strokes, he began to swim toward his boat, wondering why his comrades were shouting at him as they rowed, and why Iwadaiyu was waving a lance. Was he that angry?

At the surface of the water, Jinsuke looked around, and for the first time since he was a small boy he felt real fear. A big dorsal fin was chasing him, the fin of a shark.

Small sharks were common in these waters, but this was a big blue shark, attracted by the scent of blood in the water, blood from both the whale and Jinsuke's scrapes. Jinsuke remembered what he had been taught and treaded water, quickly unlooping his red loincloth, letting it trail out behind him. Whalers believed and told each other that this would distract a shark.

The monster made one pass, and Jinsuke ducked his head under to see it better. It was huge, the water making it seem even more so, and he could see the cold eye, the line of gill slits, the huge sweep of its tail, its head making a strange, stiff, side-to-side swing. It came at a rush, and he felt the roughness of its skin as it swept by him and tore at the red tail of cloth. Jinsuke surfaced in panic and yelled, seeing his boat speeding toward him. The shark turned. Jinsuke took a deep breath and ducked under, trying to punch at the shark's snout with his left hand while he struck with the knife in his right hand. The knife was ripped from his grasp. Numbness.

Somebody grabbed at his hair and yanked him into the boat. The shark had torpedoed at him again, its gills bleeding from a knife slash, but it missed his legs and struck an oar. Jinsuke stood, cursing. Iwadaiyu's face was a mask of horror. The shark rammed the boat and Jinsuke tried to steady himself by grabbing at a comrade's shoulder with his left hand. But he couldn't. He stumbled. He couldn't grab anything with his left hand. It was gone, from the elbow down, and his own blood was spraying over the oarsman's shoulder and back, spurting from the stump, vivid scarlet, spraying now on the legs of another man, while they all just stared at him.

Jinsuke screamed a curse at the shark. Sky and sea began to be sucked into a vortex of blackness. He roared again, screaming at the beast, then snatched the harpoon off Iwadaiyu's rest, taking it with one hand and hurling it with the last of his strength at the ugly snout-faced monster in the water. Then the sky tipped up, there was a rushing sound, and blackness swept him away.

Tatsudaiyu's look-alike whale escaped, and his group turned and went to help secure and kill the gray whale. He and his men were exhausted, and they wondered why Iwadaiyu's boat wasn't there. As they began the long tow back, he called over to the paulownia boat.

"Where are the chrysanthemums?"

The harpooner in the bow just stared at him, his face expressing nothing. "Gone back," came the curt reply.

When Tatsudaiyu and his men reached Mukaijima he was at first angered to see Iwadaiyu's boat there ahead of his. The *naiya danna* ran down to them, obviously distraught.

Tatsudaiyu leaped ashore, heart gone chill. "It's my son, isn't it! It's Jinsuke!"

He saw tears in the man's eyes, and he almost struck him, wanting to know. The *naiya danna* tried to speak but the words wouldn't come. His face muscles worked, twitching around the mouth.

Tatsudaiyu took him by the shoulders and shook him. "Dead? Dead? Speak!"

The man gasped it out. "No, not dead, but hurt, badly hurt. Shark. Come, they wait for you."

They ferried Tatsudaiyu across to the beach in front of the Asuka shrine, where a small crowd of workers and a few villagers were watching silently. Kakuemon came down to the boat. Tatsudaiyu looked beyond him to the sand, where, with a rope around its tail and a harpoon deep in its back, a long familiar shape lay, a thing with a huge maw of triangular white teeth. Beside it stood a couple of flensers, grim-faced, their long-handled flensing knives at the ready, as if standing guard.

Kakuemon bowed. "An accident, a terrible accident. It is your eldest son. He's at home now. We've sent a boat for a doctor from Katsuura. The men did what they could for him, but it's serious."

Tatsudaiyu pointed with a trembling finger at the shark, hatred and rage in his voice. "It was this thing? His leg? Both legs?"

Kakuemon shook his head. "An arm. The shark took his left arm. He went into the water to cut the blowhole and the whale dragged him off, so the boat couldn't get to him in time. It wasn't Iwadaiyu's fault, Jinsuke disobeyed him. Jinsuke fought the shark, knifed it in the gills, then it bit his arm off."

Kakuemon was breathing with difficulty. In the back of his mind was his own awesome responsibility, for he had insisted the men go whaling, despite shark warnings. Tatsudaiyu stared at him, then looked around for Iwadaiyu. Had he found his friend then, he would have killed him. Placing an eldest son on another man's boat was the tradition in Taiji, and it was also a sacred trust, the ultimate expression of friendship between harpooners. As such no son sailed on his own father's boat.

"Did those fools stop to harpoon a shark?" he shouted, and people around winced in embarrassment at how Tatsudaiyu betrayed emotion. Kakuemon looked into the stern, brown, deeply lined face.

"No. Jinsuke did it. He was dragged into the boat, then he stood, and drove a harpoon into the shark and killed it. The head of the harpoon must have cut the spinal column. Incredible strength, the strength of a god. Tatsudaiyu, you must understand, they had to bring that thing back."

Tatsudaiyu covered his face with both hands and Kakuemon reached out and touched the broad shoulder of the man.

"Go home, go home, he needs you. They tied the wound with a line and bound it with salted cloths. He's a strong, brave young man, but now he needs his father. Go home, old friend. The doctor will come in a few hours. Go home." Then the aging net master did an unheard-of thing. In front of many people, right on the beach, he dropped to his knees and bowed, his head touching the sand.

Tatsudaiyu stared at him, his mind blank. Jinsuke had lost an arm. Then he turned, pushed through the onlookers, and ran home, his second running after him.

Slowly Kakuemon rose to his feet and brushed the sand from his *hakama* and then spoke curtly to the *naiya danna*.

"Get the *bozu* down here. Tell him why."

The other man looked blank.

"Go get him, don't you see . . . the arm . . ."

The man blanched, then went. Kakuemon roared at the people to get away and ordered the watchmen to drive them back with their staves. From the point came the drums and chants of the rest of the fleet. Soon the whale would be here, and this matter had to be taken care of quickly, and the beach purified. He called to an attendant.

"White cloth. White cloth! You heard me, now!"

The man ran off. Kakuemon shouted again.

"Keep those people away!" The watchmen began to swing their staffs and the onlookers backed off. A figure came down the beach. It was the *bozu*, the priest of Junshinji, the Buddhist temple. A white cloth was brought and laid on the sand close to the shark. Kakuemon turned to the chief flenser.

"Please, cut."

The man made a slight bow and changed his grip on the long handled knife. He stepped forward and made a long, deep slit in the belly. The priest came forward. Kakuemon turned and walked up to the office, calling an attendant after him.

"See that the flensers and the *bozu* are paid for this, and see that they have sake. They won't want to eat, but give them sake. Understand?"

The man understood.

"Kakuemon-sama . . . should the shark be cut up and dried? The liver . . ." Seeing the thunder in the net master's face, he fell silent.

"Hire a fisherman and tow the cursed thing out to sea!"

Above the shrine of Asuka, which faced the sea and protected whalers, kites mewed. Darkness licked the sky to the north.

Chapter Eight

Taiji Kakuemon was selling off the remaining barrels of whale oil. Most of it was second grade, or even third grade, and would eventually be emulsified with vinegar and spread on rice paddies. This mixture weakened the delicate skins of caterpillars and damaged their eye spots, while the oil film that spread out thinly on the water killed off mosquitoes and other air-breathing insect larvae. At the same time the oil-vinegar mixture was easily broken down by bacteria, fertilizing the paddy as well as protecting it from pests. Kakuemon stood outside the office, accepting the envelopes which contained the bids of the merchants. Some of these men had come a long way, from even as far away as Hiroshima. He took the last envelope and asked the men to wait while he went in and opened the envelopes before a witness. The tubs of oil were already stacked on the jetty, ready for loading. Another figure appeared from behind the group of merchants and Kakuemon gave a start. This man carried two swords.

"Taiji-san, excuse me, but when your business is finished there is something I would like to discuss. I will wait at the shrine."

Kakuemon's eyes widened in recognition, and he bowed deeply.

"Matsudaira-san, welcome back to Taiji. Yes, please excuse me for a short time. I must take all bids at the same time and place."

"Of course, you must finish." Sadayori made a slight bow and walked away.

The business was transacted swiftly, with no quarrels. The oil went to the merchant from Hiroshima, who had placed his bid deliberately high, perhaps because he had invested so much time and effort to get here, or perhaps he had researched the rising prices of this commodity at the Goto Islands, at Iki and Ikitsuki and at other whaling stations close to the Nagasaki market, with which he was also dealing. Kakuemon reviewed the documents and put his seal on them, leaving the details of loading and payment to the clerk.

He hurried over to the shrine, sending a messenger home first, to warn of a possible guest. He found the samurai gazing reflectively at the stone lions that stood guard at the entrance of the shrine. They were fierce, those lions, though small. Hearing footsteps, Sadayori turned. He made the usual comments about the weather and the state of the seasons, then came quickly to the point.

"I have come about the young whaler, Jinsuke, son of Tatsudaiyu."

"Ah yes, thank you. His wound seems to have healed completely. Doctor Itoh, whom you sent from Shingu, was extremely skilled. Far more so than the Katsuura doctor we first used. Is it true that he learned techniques from the Hollanders at Nagasaki? Truly, without his skill, and the infusions of herbs and poultices, the young man would have died. We are all deeply grateful for your kindness."

"I'm glad he was of help," said Sadayori, "and it was fortunate that both he and I were visiting Lord Mizuno at Shingu when we heard of the accident. I would recommend, though, that you send a letter of appreciation, some small gift perhaps, from the whaling group to the regent at the castle in Wakayama. It would make it, shall we say, easier for the doctor. Doctor Itoh Kansai happens to be the lord's personal physician."

Kakuemon sucked in breath and bowed again. "We are indeed indebted!"

"Ah, but not to me, to the regent, who gave his permission for the doctor to come, and to the doctor's great skill. You know that the Tokugawa place the whalers in high esteem. Especially such a courageous young man. But permit me to come to the point. I have come to beg a favor."

Kakuemon looked at Sadayori's face. "Of course, anything."

"I would like to see that the young man gets a pension. It will be confirmed, I'm sure, through Shingu, or maybe even through Wakayama, but that might take time, and I would like to hasten the procedure myself."

Sadayori did not say that the pension he mentioned was

entirely his own idea and would come from his own estate. He continued. "It would be convenient if the sum, either in silver or in rice, be paid through the offices of the whaling operation in Taiji, discreetly. Can that be arranged? Your offices, naturally, could receive a fee for handling the matter."

Again Kakuemon sucked in breath. This was most generous. "Of course we will arrange it. I will see to it personally. There will be no requirement for a handling fee. That is a most humane and generous gesture. Would you like to see the young man yourself? I can have him brought here, or to my house if you prefer. You will of course stay and have supper with us. Our house is very mean, and small, but . . ."

"Thank you, but no. It is better if he is left alone for a while, but please give him and his father my respects. If the story is true, it was an extraordinarily courageous action."

"Killing the shark that bit his arm off? Oh yes, it is true. Fourteen men saw him do it. But you will stay, won't you?"

Kakuemon wanted to talk, to hear news, and he pressed, but Sadayori declined, saying that he had already arranged passage in the ship which was loading, and would sail with the tide. He did not say that he was en route to Kyoto. He smiled and bowed, and walked off toward the jetty

As for Jinsuke, they had to tie him down with sashes for a week to prevent him from tearing the dressings from the stump. His fever had raged, and indeed, had it not been for the skilled doctor Sadayori had arranged to be sent, fatal infection would have spread through his body.

The doctor had recommended that they take Jinsuke either to a small island or to the heights above the town, where cool breezes prevailed. His parents followed the doctor's advice, preparing a small but clean hut that the family had beside the vegetable plots on the heights, which they used to store tools and to take the noon rest when working up there. It was on the way to the lookout point at the Tomyo cliffs, and somebody, usually his mother or Saburo, was with him all the time, and old man Toumi dropped in every day too.

The fever went down and the wound healed, but now Jinsuke had to face the true loss. It took two arms to operate the heavy sculling oar, and two hands to throw the Taiji harpoon. As for Tatsudaiyu, who had been so proud of the son who would succeed him as harpooner, he grieved inwardly, almost as if that son had died.

Jinsuke went into depression and thought of throwing himself off the cliffs, or even of impaling himself on his father's killing lance. Tatsudaiyu understood the awful black maw that threatened Jinsuke, and talked to him.

"You are my son," he said, "and you have the heart and spirit of a whaler. Yes, you have lost your left arm, and your place in a boat, but you have not lost your heart, or your spirit. That right arm of yours is better than two arms of any other man. All the troubles that you must face I know you can face, and you have your family with you. Why don't you let me arrange it for you to become a watcher, or a beach overseer? I'm sure Wada-san and Taiji-san will permit it."

Jinsuke shook his head. "As you said, Father, I am, or was, a whaler, and a whaler who cannot whale would not enjoy the sight of others doing the hunt. No, I'll find something else to do."

"Good," said Tatsudaiyu. He had been sitting cross-legged on the mats of their little living room, sipping tea. He stood straight up.

"Come, Jinsuke, come outside now."

Puzzled, Jinsuke followed him. With his right hand Tatsudaiyu picked up a piece of wood and put it on a chopping block. Then he took a heavy, thick-bladed curved machete and split it.

"There," he said, "your mother needs wood, and that right arm of yours needs exercise. Start now."

For the first time in weeks, Jinsuke grinned. That same day they got word of Jinsuke's pension, and it was just a little more than he would have made as a harpooner.

Within his own family, Jinsuke became gradually less introverted. However, with Oyoshi he was very distant, almost to the point of being surly. While he was sick she too had visited him every day, often coming early with old man Toumi, bringing little treats and things she had cooked. As he got better, and was moved back down to the town, Onui gently reminded her that her father had refused the marriage, and that it was not proper that she should come so often. The ties and links of childhood were replaced by the walls of maturity, and inside, Oyoshi hurt, for herself, for Jinsuke, for her father. She hurt too because of the dislike she found growing inside for Saburo—poor, kind, gentle, enthusiastic Saburo, who spent all the free time he could with her father, cleaning brushes, mixing colors, sometimes even helping fill in colors on the paintings. And all the time Saburo was not aware of what her father had in mind for him. She would look at Saburo as he bent over a piece of work, seeing in him traces of his older brother, yet not so

102

strong, not so powerful, not so . . . Just thinking of Jinsuke made her squeeze her thighs together, made her feel embarrassed with her own body.

Meanwhile, more and more she found favor with the young men of Taiji. She had become a true Taiji beauty, a beauty among women who were renowned for their exotic looks, deeply sculptured features, voluptuous bodies and willowy limbs. It was said that the ancestors of Taiji had been pirates, who raided ships coming out of the Seto Inland Sea, killing the men and carrying off the more attractive female passengers to be their wives. That is why Taiji women were the most beautiful, albeit the most strong-willed, of any in Japan.

No matter how the other young men paid her compliments or looked at her, Oyoshi had thoughts only for Jinsuke. She couldn't understand herself, but she found him even more attractive now, with that empty sleeve on the left side. It was wrong, but she couldn't help feeling a little glad, for it was as if the loss of that arm had brought the arrogant young harpooner down—or was it up—to the status of herself and her father. Could this accident make their union possible? She reflected on all these things, and took to walking by herself, trying to find escape from the narrow streets and watchful eyes of the little town.

Then, one day, Jinsuke spotted Oyoshi talking to another young whaler. It meant nothing, but she was laughing, and she touched the young man's arm, and he joked and touched her shoulder. Jinsuke knew that as children they had been in the same little temple school together, and that this particular young whaler was the favorite clown of the fleet, and that the encounter was natural and brief, but he found himself smoldering with jealousy.

The next day, when the fleet was out, and old Takigawa had gone over to the boat sheds at Mukaijima, Jinsuke went around to her house. Oyoshi was at home, mixing pickles in a tub of miso paste. As Jinsuke came in she gasped with surprise and pleasure and rushed to wash her hands.

"Jinsuke-san! You look so well! Oh, do come in, oh, the place is so untidy!"

Jinsuke said nothing, but kicked off his straw sandals, stepped up, and pulled her to him in an embrace. She tried to push away, but even with only one arm he was too strong.

"What's the matter? Don't you like me now that I'm a cripple?"

"You don't behave like a cripple!" she retorted, face flushed. "You behave like a ruffian!"

He let her go, stepped back, and sat down cross-legged on the mats.

"Forgive me, Oyoshi, it's just that I still keep you in my heart, although I know that I'm no longer good enough for you and that you must look for better chances. That's the way it is, isn't it?"

She flared up with anger at him. "You don't understand anything, do you? It's our situation! Why can't you work toward making that situation better for us? You give me gifts, you make promises, you say you want to marry me, you embrace me, but do you try to make anything work? Oh yes, I've had plenty of offers, plenty of young men would be glad to live under this roof, but you are too proud to see how difficult it is for me and my father. You are proud, stubborn and stupid, but you certainly are no cripple. That shark bit off only an arm, didn't it? Or did it bite off something else that I can't see?"

Jinsuke colored, jumped to his feet, and slapped her. Crying with the mark of his fingers white on her cheek, she ran from him to the corner of the little room. He followed and seized her, pulling her to him.

"Oyoshi! I'm sorry, forgive me, forgive me. I love you. I was jealous, even though I have no right to be."

She slowly enfolded him in her arms. "I want a child with you, only you, and I don't care what my father or anybody else says." She didn't think then about the words, but let them release in both herself and Jinsuke a passion held in restraint for as long as either of them could bear.

Saburo had not gone out with the fleet that day, having found some excuse to stay in the workshops at Mukaijima. Early in the afternoon, Takigawa asked him to return to the house for some small thing. As he slid open the door of the Takigawa house, he stopped, hearing sounds, a whimpering, the harsh gasp of a man, movement, wetness. Not understanding, and a little afraid, he went to the inner door and slid it partly open. There, in the room, his brother was lying between Oyoshi's wide-spread thighs, his buttocks naked, while Oyoshi had her kimono up around her belly. Her head was back, eyes closed, mouth in a round, open circle, face flushed. His brother humped, like an animal, thought Saburo, and Oyoshi moved to him.

Blood rushed to Saburo's head and he almost fainted, seeing things, hearing things. Colors! Flesh brown and paler

104

olive, near white, purple, shocking, blended black! Yet more than the colors and the movement it was the sounds, the grunting, whimpering, animal sounds. Saburo wanted to scream at them, but instead he backed away slowly and left. Once into the street, he ran.

When their lovemaking was over Oyoshi went out to wash herself, to stop the bleeding with tissues, to wipe the stains off the mats. The room smells of chestnut tree flowers, she thought, and tingled. Within herself she felt defiantly proud of what she had done, although behind the defiance there was also shame. She hadn't wanted it to be like that. But no matter, Jinsuke was hers, hers! She tightened the muscles of her body, reluctant to let anything of him go from her. Jinsuke sat up now, cross-legged, his loincloth retied and his kimono readjusted.

"Won't you give me some tea?" he said as she came into the room. He didn't really know what to say, except that he loved her, loved her as he would love no other.

Saburo did not even go back to the workshop. He could not face Takigawa-san after what he had just heard and seen. Instead he took a small boat and sculled it out of the harbor, then let it drift, feeling the sun reflect warmth on his face. For the first time in his life, gentle Saburo had wanted to rage and kill, not only his eldest brother, but her too, she who had been like a sister to him throughout his childhood. He understood many things now—about her recent coldness to him, about Takigawa's friendliness—and in knowing he loathed his own naiveté.

For the next two months, Jinsuke and Oyoshi made love whenever and wherever they could, until it was obvious to even the blindest of gossips that there was something between them. They didn't care.

Chapter Nine

For the two months he had been in Edo, Sadayori had reported every morning to the Tokugawa Kobusho, the elitist *bakufu* school of martial arts. The huge school was a long walk from where he had a house, a good brisk half hour along the outer moat to the Kudan area, but he enjoyed the early-morning bustle of the huge city. A letter with Ii Naosuke's seal upon it permitted him to train in both of the sword styles officially adopted by the Tokugawa, even though one of them was supposedly reserved for the high-ranking *hatamoto*, or bannermen.

The Yagyu Shinkage Ryu, or Yagyu New Shadow Style, encouraged large, full movements. Samurai trained here with sword-length *shinai* made of finely split bamboo, over which a red-lacquered leather covering was stitched. This training device was very pliant, so that short, sharp movements only made the thing wobble and bend, at first infuriating and frustrating for anybody who was used to training with the white-oak *bokuto*. In this style, only flowing, wide, committed movements were suitable, and it taught a bold and dignified beauty that Sadayori especially liked. And naturally, the *bakufu* hired the very best of teachers.

The second style, which Sadayori had first learned from his father, was the Ono Hai Ryu, a powerful, practical style intended for battle. The unarmed combat, or jujitsu, was most satisfying. He spent two hours in each class.

Then, apart from the training at the Kobusho, which only a *bakufu* samurai could attend, he was also encouraged to train in one of the town dojos. He had heard a saying among swordsmen about the town dojos, five of which were very famous. "For status it's the Momoi dojo, for technique it's

Chiba, but for power it's Saito." Sadayori already had status and technique, so he chose power.

Although he was extremely busy, with new students flocking to him, not only from the warrior class, but artisans and merchants too, the sensei Saito Yakuro took to him and even gave Sadayori private lessons. The style, rather fancifully called the Shinto Mumen Ryu, or Way-of-the-Gods, Non-Invocating Style, was vigorous and powerful, and the dojo seemed to attract many passionately patriotic young men from all over.

He found more companionship in this town dojo than he ever found in the status-conscious Tokugawa schools, but it took him a while to get used to the freethinking, outspoken ways of the students. They discussed everything, not only martial arts, but even a topic as dangerous as politics.

Like all *bushi*, Sadayori had been raised to believe in Bushido, in martial ways and correct manners. He was educated and well-read, and he understood administration. Loyalty, obedience, the willingness to die—these were all things that he did not question. However, his isolation from the silken rooms of the courts and his solitary travels and studies had opened his eyes to the beauties, strengths and weaknesses of his country, and indeed he felt it to be his country, felt and thought beyond the confined, secretive, self-centered views of the fief.

One day, after he had been going to the dojo for a month, and they had finished a particularly exhausting session, the students and their teachers were sitting and drinking a cool, refreshing tea of roasted adlay seeds, talking, as usual. Sadayori found it uncomfortable when the topics veered to current politics, but when one young samurai from Izu spoke out strongly against the *bakufu* he felt angered and shocked.

"The shogun and his councillors are nothing but traitors, either traitors or cowards! What are they supposed to do? What is the duty of the shogun? It is to repel barbarians, right? Does he do that? No! We must all prepare to fight, or the foreign ships will come, as they came to China, and make slaves of us all. We can't rely on the shogun, I tell you!"

Seeing the expression on Sadayori's face, the young man turned on him. "Matsudaira-san, you're from Kii, so that means that you are a Tokugawa man, yet you come to train here. Does that mean you're a patriot—or a spy?"

There was a silence. Sadayori put the cup down and got to his feet.

"Are you challenging me?"

"Matsudaira! I'll permit no dueling between members of my dojo! Ozaki! Apologize!"

The Izu man was several ranks lower than Sadayori, and no match at all for him, but he had the kind of wild courage common among the dojo members. He flushed and bowed.

"Forgive me if I offend. I only wish to speak frankly, and I believe that all Japanese must unite and fight the foreigners, but the *bakufu* seems to be like an elephant, stuck in the mud."

"I understand your feelings, and no, I did not come to spy, but to train. Let us forget it."

He bowed to the teacher, to the rest of the students, then turned at the entrance to bow again. The teacher called out to him.

"Come tomorrow!"

"Hai," said Sadayori. As he strode down the dusty street, one of the merchants' sons hurried after him.

"Matsudaira-*sempai,* let's walk together."

Sadayori stiffened a little, for he was still not quite used to being addressed by other classes in such a familiar way. On the other hand, although the son of a merchant, this fellow was a likable sort, and he worked and trained with extreme diligence at the dojo. For some reason, probably his father's wealth and some service he had done for the government, the man had won the right to wear a single sword.

"Don't get angry with Ozaki-san, he means no harm, but he's such a zealot, and the whole of Edo is boiling with politics nowadays, isn't it? Things aren't what they used to be."

Sadayori grunted and stepped aside to avoid being hit by a two-wheeled pushcart, piled high with fresh vegetables.

"It is dangerous to criticize the authorities," he said stiffly.

"Indeed, but then everybody does it, you know. Me, I just ignore it. Politics is not my business."

"Yet you, a merchant, learn to fight," said Sadayori.

"Everybody should be able to defend himself," said the broad-shouldered young man with a grin and a shrug. He spotted a friend and waved. Sadayori almost winced at the raucous yell of greeting.

"Say, won't you come and eat with me? I know a place just close by that gets the very freshest fish from the market, every morning, the best Edo-mae sushi you've tasted. Come on, it's cheap, let me treat you."

Sadayori stiffened at the familiar tones but the fellow didn't seem to notice. Did he presume that training in the same dojo made them equal? He shook his head.

"No, thank you, not today."

"That's a pity. Another day, perhaps." He made a little bow and grinned again. "Tomorrow, at the dojo." Then, shouldering his way through a knot of people who had gathered to watch a street juggler, he was gone.

Although the familiarity of the young man annoyed Sadayori, there was truth in what he had said. People, especially young and usually poor samurai, had become loud and daring in their criticisms of the government. Cracks were appearing in the structure of the *bakufu*. The current shogun, Ieyoshi, was not a strong man, neither in body nor in spirit, and a very different kind of man from his forefathers, who had unified the nation by force of arms and superior cunning and intellect. Ieyoshi had succeeded his father at the age of forty-five, and the pressures of office seemed to be too much for him. There was much intrigue in Edo and elsewhere.

Sadayori's present lord had ascended to nominal control of the huge fiefdom of Kii at the age of three. He was the first son of Tokugawa Naritomo, but he had been raised by the former daimyo of Kii, to whom Sadayori had once felt the strongest allegiance. The present lord of Kii was not even six, and the affairs of the fiefdom were managed by a regent and councillors, and for none of these did Sadayori feel the respect he had felt for his old daimyo.

"He died before he made me marry again, even," thought Sadayori, still saddened by the loss of a lord who took such close interest in his men.

The daimyo to whom he now owed allegiance was a spoiled child, always crying about something or other, although that was perhaps not surprising. *Bakufu* laws demanded that a daimyo spend alternate years in Edo and his domains, and thus the child was always having his surroundings changed. Whatever, Kii needed a powerful lord, said Sadayori's inner voice, not a child, not in times like this!

As a child, the boy's name had been Kikuchiyo, but since ascending to the lordship of Kii, that name had been changed to Tokugawa Yoshitomi. Who could have guessed it at the time that this child daimyo was destined to become the fourteenth shogun, his name again changed to Iemochi?

As for Sadayori, in these past few years he had made

contact with men of vision, often from different clans and fiefs, and this had begun to erode his own conservatism. Perhaps, as many of these men had argued, the future of Japan lay in the hands of bold, brave, intelligent men, able men who were not shackled by outdated laws.

Sadayori felt that war with the foreigners was inevitable. So what would be the symbol to rally the whole nation? If they were to defeat well-armed invading barbarians, the nation must fight as a whole, but which of their leaders were fit to unify the scattered armies of so many fiefdoms?

Wherever young samurai gathered, in closed rooms or in the town dojos, they argued that the central light of the nation was, and always had been, the sacred person of the emperor.

Up until now, Sadayori had believed that the Tokugawa rule protected the imperial house and served it faithfully. But many were saying that Tokugawa control merely isolated the emperor, hid him away so that his light could not shine on his troubled subjects. Uneasy at heart, Sadayori was inclined to agree.

He had to return to Wakayama soon, and there he planned a meeting with a certain courageous young man. A samurai was trained for action, and Sadayori began to consider what action he personally could take.

The walk from the neighboring village of Ota took about forty minutes. Sadayori approached Taiji by way of a narrow back road that led through the forest. Summer was dragging its tail into autumn, and in other parts of Japan it would be winter soon, although here there were harebells along the roads, and insects making songs.

He came up above the town, and sat and rested until a small boy came past, carrying a load of kindling. With a copper coin he sent the boy to fetch Jinsuke, son of Tatsudaiyu. Then, leaning against the trunk of an ilex tree, he waited. It was not long before he heard somebody coming up the steps that led through the graveyard.

As Jinsuke approached, he had to look up at the samurai, standing there in a kimono of dark blue and a *hakama,* striped, of a darker hue. He looked imposing, and although Jinsuke felt a touch annoyed at being summoned up here, he realized that whatever it was the samurai had to say to him, it was important.

They greeted each other in the proper way, and Sadayori asked him if he had any pain in the lost arm. Jinsuke shook his head.

"Much has happened since you threw a harpoon for me. They are hunting whales today, are they not? I smell it in the air."

"Perfume whale," said Jinsuke, then, lamely, "they make good oil, and there are a lot of them out there now." He didn't know what to say.

"You no longer hunt the whale, or ride the waves, and the many names of the winds lose meaning for you. I can surmise that life itself seems without meaning at times?"

Jinsuke looked with surprise into the samurai's face, then touched the stump of his arm, hidden in the pinned sleeve of his short kimono. Sadayori smiled.

"Watch," he ordered, then stepped backward a few paces. He crouched slightly, put one hand behind his back, and crossed his right arm over to snick open the catch in the sheath of his long sword. Then with blinding speed he drew the sword with one hand, slashing through a piece of bamboo that grew beside the path, cutting it cleanly. Then, still not using his left hand, he slipped the long sword back into the sheath just before the cut bamboo toppled against its neighbors. Jinsuke looked at the fallen bamboo, then at Sadayori.

"You have never seen a samurai draw a sword, let alone cut anything with it, have you, whaler?" Sadayori glared at Jinsuke, who shook his head.

"It is usually done with two hands. It took me many hundreds of hours to be able to do that with one hand. Can you think why I should bother?"

"No, sir. However, you are kind, and I am greatly honored, but a whaler's harpoon is thrown with two hands, the left to guide, the right to give power to the flight."

Sadayori took the end of the cut bamboo and pulled it free. "Trim this," he said curtly. Jinsuke looked at him.

"I have nothing to cut it with."

"Go and fetch something. I will wait."

Sadayori sat by the tree and stared into space. Jinsuke turned, and trotted down the steps. While he was gone, Sadayori questioned himself. Was it right, what he was doing? Attacking the barriers of class like this? He questioned himself, but he was sure he was right. Jinsuke came back, bringing the machete. He glanced at the samurai, then began to trim the bamboo.

"How long should I cut it, sir?"

"As long as a harpoon."

The bamboo was at one end as thick as a man's wrist, and not easy to cut. Sadayori watched from the corner of his eyes. When the work was done Sadayori slowly stood up and took the cut length of bamboo, hefting it in his right hand. Then, saying nothing, he hurled it like a javelin into a bank, six paces away.

"You see? There is not only one way to throw a harpoon. Primitive men have used spears and harpoons for thousands of years, throwing it like that."

"But, sir, in Taiji it is not thrown that way."

"No, it isn't, is it? You are not supposed to know this, but a certain young man from a good family in Tosa . . . you know where that is, don't you?"

"Yes, sir, of course, it is in the northern part of Shikoku. They have whalers there too."

Sadayori continued. "That's right. Anyway, as a boy of fourteen or so he was out in a fishing boat and got swept out to sea, where a barbarian ship picked up him and his companions. He went to a foreign school and eventually sailed on a foreign ship, an American ship, a whaling ship. He learned much of their ways. I have had the chance to question him about this, as he took the risk and returned to Japan, where the government forgave him. He tells us that aboard those ships they use men of many nations, and that their strong men hurl a harpoon, heavier than the Taiji harpoon, with one hand. He tells me that they take many whales, these foreigners. I want you to come to Edo. Sail with a ship carrying timber from Shingu. I will arrange a secret meeting for you with this man who knows foreign whaling ways. I believe that it is possible for you to hunt whales again, perhaps on a foreign ship. If you agree, I will try to arrange this. I need a man of strength and courage who can gather information for me about those ships, who will serve me faithfully, and in secret." He stared at Jinsuke.

"Jinsuke, son of Tatsudaiyu, will you do it?"

Jinsuke threw himself to the ground and bowed.

"Very well. Go to Shingu in three days. Here is a pass for you, and money for the voyage." He handed a purse to Jinsuke. "But I warn you. If you betray what I have told you it will cost you your life, and mine. Understand?"

"I won't talk," said Jinsuke. Sadayori nodded. For the first time Jinsuke noticed the lines of hardship and stress around the samurai's eyes and mouth.

"You will be met in Edo. We know when the timber ships

112

come in. Obey me, and I will see that you are taken care of."

Saying no more, Sadayori turned and headed back along the path to Ota.

Jinsuke went back to the house. Only his mother was there. Excitement welling up inside him, he fidgeted, then took the piece of scrimshaw from out of its hiding place, turning over the heavy lump of ivory in his hand, staring at the design, black on white, of boats in a sea full of whales, and he saw that one of the tiny figures in the bow of a boat was raising a harpoon aloft, about to sink it into a bull whale—with one hand! He turned the tooth over, staring at the letters he could not read, wondering what they meant. Would he really be able to hunt whales again?

That night, when his father and brothers returned, he made his announcement.

"Father, Mother, I am leaving to go to Edo. I have been offered a job overseeing the unloading of our fief's timbers. I have accepted it."

Tatsudaiyu just stared at him.

"Edo? Timbers? What do you mean? This is a whaling family, have you forgotten that? Think of your mother! You can't go to Edo!"

"Father, I am going. I gave my word."

"To whom?"

"I can't say."

His father roared at him, raged at him, but Jinsuke was adamant, and when both parents kept on at him he got up and stormed out of the house.

"I can't have a place on a whaling boat in Taiji, can I? Then I'm going to find something else to do, something I want to do! Leave me be!"

He waited for the following day to see Oyoshi, and went boldly to the Takigawa house, not caring what anybody said.

"Oyoshi, I've got to leave for a while, to go to Edo."

She gasped and he took her to his chest, stroking her hair.

"Don't ask why, I can't tell you, but it is very important to me. You wait, and I'll come back and marry you, no matter what anybody says."

Oyoshi cried, and Jinsuke even regretted saying yes to the samurai, but he had given a promise, and he could never go back on that.

"Oyoshi, wait for me, you'll see, everything will be fine."

She pulled him into the room and unfastened the obi of

her kimono. "Come, come into me, I want you inside me," she said, the tears running down her cheeks.

A month after he left, Oyoshi started to get sick in the mornings, and to crave the salty-sour pickled plums. She also developed a great aversion to the mere scent of the cooked pilot-whale entrails that her father loved so much, and she could not go near the beach when the men were processing a whale.

Finally, as the realization of it came to her, she went to the only woman she could trust. She went to Onui, Jinsuke's mother. They wept together.

Chapter Ten

Jinsuke was on deck, gazing at the coastline. The ship had passed the checkpoint at Uraga, where the bay of Edo narrowed like the mouth of a bag, through which hundreds of ships passed every day, all built exactly to *bakufu* specifications, keelless, square-sailed. An almost unbroken line of townships rimmed the western side of the bay, with houses and sheds and other buildings crowding right to the shore. Upon cliffs and promontories there were no houses, for upon these crouched batteries of cannon. The shallows of the bay, close to shore, were forested with the upright bundles of sticks on which the people cultured various edible seaweeds, and fishermen were everywhere, sculling their boats and ignoring the ships that came to and fro, carrying rice from the north, early season oranges and lumber from Kii, sake, dried fish and abalone, and a thousand other products without which this great city of the shogun would starve to death.

Jinsuke became aware of a crewman standing beside him. "So many houses!"

The man laughed. "Wait 'til we get up past Yokohama into the end of the bay, where the Sumida River enters, then you'll see. Thick as ants, they are. We can't bring enough lumber for them. You know what 'the flowers of Edo' are, don't you?"

Jinsuke shook his head.

"Fires! No sooner do they build somewhere, they go and have a great fire somewhere else and burn half the place down! Good business for Shingu, though! We can't bring the lumber in fast enough!"

Jinsuke shook his head with a mixture of wonder and horror. "How many people live in the city?"

"Who knows?" said the sailor. "A million, maybe?"

Edo, for the last hundred years of the Tokugawa rule, was one of the largest cities in the world, if not the largest. It was certainly larger than Paris or London. By the end of the eighteenth century the commercial quarters alone boasted a population of more than five hundred thousand, and this figure did not include the hordes of warrior administrators and guards who safeguarded the business of the *bakufu,* and who accompanied the feudal daimyos who were obliged to spend every other six months, or every other year, in residence in Edo. These lords, when not in Edo themselves, were also obliged to leave their wives and children behind as hostages in the city. At this period there were two hundred seventy-six daimyos, each of whom, depending on status and means, had a host of guards, attendants and servants.

Five major highways radiated out of the city, linking the main cities in the land. These roads were always busy with travelers, with pack horses, with the processions of the daimyos as they came back and forth.

There were canals too, supplementing the traffic that had moved for centuries on the Sumida and Tama rivers, and from the Tama, water was carried underground in hollowed-out wooden pipes to supply each part of the city.

In the center of Edo reigned the castle of the shogun, the mightiest and most impregnable fortress in Japan, whose massive, carefully calculated sloping rock battlements acted against the enormous weight of water in the moat to make it balanced and safe even from earthquakes, while within were spacious parklands and mansions.

It was a city that only a handful of Westerners knew anything about, a magnificent, sprawling city that was at the same time very vulnerable—to blockade, to fire, to earthquakes.

A young man was waiting at the dock to meet Jinsuke. They had a four-hour walk through the city to Sadayori's house, which formerly belonged to his father, now dead. The house was in the suburb of Kojimachi, close by the Hanzo Gate of the shogun's palace. The confusion of sights and sounds, the unbelievable crowds, the curtain-fronted shops, the great palace and proudly strutting samurai, the shouting of merchants and the passing of the chanting palanquin-bearers had Jinsuke in a daze. As they had to walk right around the moat, elegant with swans, Jinsuke asked if the young man who was his guide had ever been inside the palace.

"Not me, but the master goes in on business quite often.

He's well connected with some very important people, you know. Say, are you tired? Shall we rest?"

"No, I'm not tired," answered Jinsuke.

When they reached the house, a meal of broiled fish, miso soup, pickles and rice was ready for them, and after the meal Jinsuke's guide took him to the nearest public bath house. When Jinsuke returned he found that new clean clothes had been laid out for him. There was a dark blue tunic that came down to his thighs, a wide sash to tie it, cotton trousers that reached to his ankles, and even a pair of new wooden *geta*. He was admiring these things when one of the maids, a plumpish woman in her thirties, came to tell him that the master would see him in the morning.

Jinsuke awoke to the chatter of sparrows in the eaves, and lay for a while, staring at the wooden ceiling, puzzled at the rhythmic knock he had heard all night, a sort of pleasant, hollow but soft sound, knock, knock, knocking in the darkness. Now, from outside, came an occasional piercing yell. He dressed and crept out. From the kitchen came the clatter and chatter of women preparing breakfast and the crackle of burning wood under the rice pots. The air was chill.

Jinsuke followed the sounds of the knocking and the yells, and rounding a corner he found a narrow pathway, with stepping stones set in deep green moss, leading to an inner garden. There, at one end, Matsudaira Sadayori was exercising with a heavy wooden practice sword. His face was wet with sweat, despite the early morning chill, and the muscles of his forearms, exposed beneath the sleeves of his kimono, were swollen and corded with prolonged effort. In a corner of the garden stood a paulownia tree and a tiny grove of bamboo, in the shade of which nestled a small rock pool, into which flowed a trickle of water, falling first into a length of bamboo on a pivot, which filled and dipped, filled and dipped, its butt striking each time on a rock. The knocking sound. The rest of the garden was composed of rocks, moss and shrubs, the whole of it sheltered from the view of outsiders by the rooms and annexes of the house, which all faced inward.

Sadayori sensed a presence and stopped. He put the wooden sword down and took several deep, stretching breaths. Without looking toward Jinsuke, he called out.

"Jinsuke! Fetch me a bucket of water from the well!"

Jinsuke looked around and went to pick up a small dipper that lay beside the rock pool.

"No, from the well, around beside the kitchen. Bring me a bucket of water, quickly!"

Jinsuke found the well and came back with the water. Sadayori had stripped to his loincloth. He took the bucket of ice-cold water and poured it over his head, then began to rub himself with a small hand towel.

"A hot bath at night and a cold splash in the morning—I never catch a cold, you know, never have." He put his kimono back on. "Now, go and get breakfast. When you've finished, come to my room." He pointed to a large, airy room whose sliding doors and screens opened right onto the garden, facing southeast.

"Jinsuke . . ."

"Yes, sir?"

"Don't ever creep up on me again. Understand?"

Jinsuke flushed with embarrassment and made a short bow before leaving, not forgetting to take the bucket back to the well.

Breakfast was delicious. There was hot miso soup, rather saltier than he was used to, with small cubes of tofu and soft green *wakame* seaweed, a grilled pilchard with grated radish and soya sauce, pickles, green tea and white rice. Jinsuke ate four bowls of rice and nobody scolded him. In his whole life Jinsuke had eaten white rice only five or six times. They couldn't grow rice in Taiji, and it was very expensive. From the way nobody said anything about this luxury, it would seem that such delicious rice was common here. He looked at the faces of the servants. There was the young skinny fellow who had come to the docks to find him. There was an old fellow with just one front tooth, the gardener. Four women, one quite old, forty or more, then the plump one, and two dumpy maids, twenty or so. They had open, pleasant faces, and had it not been for their lack of color, Jinsuke would have guessed them to be country people, although they did not speak with any strong accent, and the skinny young fellow seemed to be trying to affect the harsh slur of Edo.

He gazed at the young maids, wondering if he could bed one or both of them sometime, but then memories of Oyoshi came flooding back to him and he felt suddenly lonely.

One of the young maids jumped up at a call and came back carrying a tray. Jinsuke glanced at the remnants of the meal and saw that apart from a raw egg, the master ate no differently in the morning from his servants.

"The master asks for you to go and see him now," she said.

* * *

118

Sadayori knelt, his back very straight, before a small desk that faced the sliding screen that opened onto the inner garden. The room was airy and bright, though a bit chilly for Jinsuke, used to the warmer climate of Taiji. From under the eaves came the slight tinkle of a wind chime. The room was large, ten mats, with a *tokonoma* alcove, in which lay Sadayori's swords, long and short, resting on deer antlers. Beside the swords were a strange-looking rock and a tiny flower arrangement. Behind lay a scroll of poetry written in very strong black lines.

> Dew rusts the fallen blade
> Nightjar calls
> Passing thunder.

In another part of the room was a little doorway, leading to an alcove in which things for the tea ceremony were kept, its doorway blocked now by a triple-section folding screen, a very old one by the looks of it, its reds and greens dulled by time, and the gold leaf just faintly catching the morning light. Sadayori was reading a book on the desk before him, turning the pages with great care.

"Jinsuke, come in. You read, don't you?"

Jinsuke stepped in and knelt on the mats beside the door.

"I can read characters, sir, but I haven't read many books, I am not an educated man."

Sadayori turned to face him. "But you can read. That's good. I find little patience with men who cannot read or who scorn the written word. Words can be as powerful or as dangerous as blades, you know." He glanced toward the resting place of his swords.

Jinsuke said nothing. In truth he had hardly ever read a book. He had been taught to read and write at the little temple school in Taiji, but unlike his brother Saburo, he never found much time for books, or for inkstone and brush. Sadayori closed the book and looked up. He reached into his sleeve and brought out a small purse, from which he counted one silver coin and several copper ones.

"Today I want you to walk around the city and enjoy yourself. You've come a long way. Take lunch at an eel shop or somewhere. Edo food is good, and there's much variety. Be back by nightfall. You are going to meet some gentlemen, and I want you to describe to them how you maneuver the boats in the whaling fleet and how you go about taking a whale."

Jinsuke flushed and stammered a little.

"Sir . . . I am not good at speaking, and with gentlemen . . . I . . . er . . ."

Sadayori answered gently. "I want you to do your best. These are special gentlemen, very interested in the sea and ships."

"But sir, I might disgrace you, I might use the wrong speech and offend them."

"You won't. Just tell us about whaling as if you were describing it to another whaler from a different part of the country. You won't be alone. A Tosa man will be here too, and he's from a fishing family. By the way, he's a whaler. I mentioned him before."

Jinsuke's eyes widened at this.

"Yes," said Sadayori, "he was a whaler on a barbarian ship. What he has to say should be interesting to you, I'm sure. Go now. I have letters to write and I must be off to the dojo."

Jinsuke thanked him and left.

The suburb where Sadayori had his residence was one of the most exclusive in the city. The high-walled gardens and homes of *hatamoto* lined quiet, graceful avenues, interspaced with groves of waist-high tea bushes and tall mullberry trees. On the first hour of his stroll Jinsuke passed so many well-dressed samurai and their attendants, either on foot, on horseback or in palanquins, that he stopped doing the polite, deep bows that would have been demanded in Kii. Yet nobody seemed offended at all. Sometimes a lady, her high-coiffed hair covered, would pass by with a servant, and Jinsuke marveled at the richness of the silken kimono and obi. Fish merchants with large round wooden trays on a yoke went from mansion to mansion, carrying big fat sea bream, nestled in fresh greenery, and all kinds of other delicacies that made Jinsuke's mouth water.

On he walked, feeling as if he had entered a brand-new world, on to a little valley beyond the outer moat. Here the contrast was striking. In narrow, muddy streets between ramshackle houses built wall-to-wall in slovenly lines, women yelled out gossip to one another, and dirty, scruffy children with runny noses played and cried in raucous bedlam. People stared and children pointed at the broad, tanned, burly young whaler, who stood over a head taller than any of the men and weighed at least four *kan* more than most.

120

Half lost, he turned down an alley. Two men stepped out and blocked his path.

"Looking for somebody?" they demanded in ugly, harsh tones.

Jinsuke noted that one of them had a hand slipped out of the sleeve of his gray kimono, and hidden in a cotton belly-band, probably at the hilt of a concealed knife.

"Indeed," said Jinsuke, "I am a stranger to Edo and would like to find somewhere to eat."

"Eh?"

The shorter of the two nudged his friend. "Man says he's hungry."

"Hungry?"

A crowd of people gathered around them.

"Where are you from, anyway?" asked the man with the hand at his belly.

"I am from Taiji, in the fiefdom of Kii."

"What?"

Jinsuke angered a little. Did these oafs not know Kii?

An old man in the crowd yelled out.

"Kii, you idiot, on the Seto Inland Sea, where the oranges come from, right?"

"Shut up, grandpa," said the first questioner, and then to Jinsuke, "How do you write this Daishee place?"

With the edge of his *geta* Jinsuke wrote the two characters for *thick* and *earth* on the ground, and everybody peered.

"Taiji," he said, "the oldest and best of all the whaling towns."

"Whaling?" The two men looked at each other. One grubby little boy tugged at Jinsuke's clothing, begging for a coin. An adult cuffed him and the child yelled and was cuffed again. Jinsuke looked more closely at the shorter of the two men, who had a scar across the back of his wrist and a slight squint.

"Why do you question me? Are you city officers?"

The two nudged each other and laughed, and others in the crowd snickered. Then one of the men slipped arm and shoulder entirely out of his kimono, exposing the lurid tattoo of a serpent and hydrangea blossoms, purple, red, blue and black, the mark of either a gangster or a construction worker, perhaps both. Jinsuke was not impressed.

"Oh, you poor fellow, you seem to have a skin blemish," he said, and the crowd roared with delight. From behind, a middle-aged man built like a barrel pushed through the crowd.

"I am Mankichi, chief carpenter. Are you lost, stranger?"

"I am Jinsuke, son of Tatsudaiyu, harpooner."

The barrel-shaped man's jowly face broke into a huge grin. "A whaler! Indeed! Otosuke! Sahei! Why do you bother this gentleman!" Otosuke and Sahei bowed and cleared a way through the crowd.

"We don't have too many strangers in Yotsuya," said Mankichi, "and we keep a watch out for snoopers around here. There are some people who don't want to be found, you see. You're a big fellow, and, forgive me for saying, with one arm, so perhaps they thought you were one too.

"One what?"

"A member of a society, you know."

"Me? A *yakuza*? Oh no, I'm a whaler!" He touched his empty sleeve. "This was indeed taken in a fight, but not by a sword, by a shark."

Mankichi was profoundly impressed. He turned around to the two men, who were now following. "Hey, you two, this Jinsuke-san here is my friend, you hear?" Then he turned back to Jinsuke. "Looking for somebody?"

"Not really, but I don't know Edo and I hoped to find somewhere to eat."

"What would you like?"

"Eels, perhaps?"

"Eels! Good, good, I know just the place!" He grabbed Jinsuke's arm and turned down an alley that led to a small side canal. Dilapidated buildings crowded the banks, and from one low-roofed tiled building with an open front came the fragrant smoke of broiled eel. The four men ducked under the curtain to see platforms of raised mats and low tables. The shop owner stood by the front, fanning charcoal and turning the split, sauce-dipped eels.

Mankichi insisted on treating Jinsuke, and he had several portions of the delicate, juicy eels, as well as several more sticks of broiled eel heart and liver, and again, white rice. The harsh and abrupt speech of the three men no longer bothered Jinsuke and soon the Edo men had him laughing with their easy humor.

"So you see, this fellow spreads around the rumor that there's a giant lurking on the road out of town, grabbing people and eating them. Then he gets a really big piece of bamboo, thick as a woman's thigh, and he rams it full of shit. Then he carefully pushes the shit out, get it? So it looks like an enormous turd, lying there beside the bridge. What a panic! They all thought a giant had shit there and the next

122

day there were Tokugawa samurai swarming all over the place, looking for the giant. Really had them fooled, he did!"

Jinsuke roared with laughter. And when they were leaving, Mankichi absolutely refused to let the whaler pay; he insisted that they walk back with Jinsuke to the end of the wide, mulberry and cherry-treed avenue on which Sadayori's house stood.

"Come again one evening and we'll show you the Yoshiwara," said Sahei with a leer and an obscene gesture with his little finger.

"Nice young ones you can get your whaler's eel into," said Otosuke.

Jinsuke grinned and said good-bye, then hurried off down the street, feeling that he liked Edo after all.

That evening, after training at the Saito town dojo, Sadayori brought some guests home, and after supper Jinsuke was called in to meet them. They didn't give him their names, but they treated him with courtesy. One of the gentlemen, a samurai, leaned forward and tapped his pipe out on the edge of the ceramic charcoal brazier that warmed the room.

"Tell me, Jinsuke, how many men are in the boats?"

"The minimum equipment we need for a whaling operation is fourteen chase boats, each with fifteen men; eight net boats, each with thirteen men; four carry boats, each with fifteen men; one barrel boat, with eight men. That's a total of three hundred eighty-two men in the fleet." He paused. "Then there are the flensers too, on shore."

Sadayori spoke, as if prompting them. "And your father, Tatsudaiyu, is the head of that fleet, is he not?"

"Yes, sir."

The oldest of the four visitors spoke, glancing at Sadayori. "Indeed, that is a large force!"

"Taiji is probably the largest of them all," said Sadayori, "and, as Jinsuke says, the oldest. Other areas are operating with somewhat smaller crews. In Taiji, though, that is a minimum. They have in the past operated with an even larger fleet. Not far away is Koza, another whaling town, and the Taiji and Koza men often combine operations. Together they can put over five hundred strong, brave seamen out."

Sadayori reached for a scroll and passed it to the older man, a vigorous-looking person in his early forties, with a high, intelligent forehead and intense eyes, hair slightly touched with gray at the sides. He was Sakuma Zosan, noted authority on Western gunnery and naval subjects, scholar of the science and language of the Hollanders.

"I have prepared this list and map of all the whaling stations," said Sadayori, "together with the numbers of boats and men currently in use, with diagrams of ideas for their deployment in emergencies, training methods, tactics and so forth. Would you please peruse it at your leisure and give me your advice and comments?"

"I will return the scroll to you in a few days."

A younger man spoke up, also a samurai. He directed his question to Jinsuke.

"Can all the men in a whaling crew use a harpoon and a killing lance?"

"Only the first son of a harpooner can become a harpooner, sir. That is the rule. However, all the men have seen it done many times, and many of them take part in killing the little black pilot whales when they are driven in numbers. They are all very strong. However, harpooners have secrets, taught to us by our fathers and by our captains."

"Fathers and captains?"

"Yes, sir. You do not sail in your father's boat. You must become a second in another captain's boat, and he is responsible for training."

The young samurai nodded and turned to Sakuma. "Sensei, if I may be frank, I am impressed by what Matsudaira-san and this man have to say. It would seem that the whalers are a very well disciplined group, and, as Matsudaira-san has stressed, with proper leadership and training . . ."

His teacher held up his hand. "Yes, but let's discuss that later, Yoshida." He turned to Sadayori. "Afterward, there are several points I would like to go over with you, if I may."

Sadayori exchanged glances with the three samurai guests and nodded.

"Later, then. Gentlemen, we have another man to talk to us this evening. He has some very interesting and disturbing things to tell us. It took courage on his part to come here, as he is being closely watched."

Yoshida Shoin spoke abruptly. "Was he followed tonight?"

Sadayori smiled. "I have taken precautions," he said, then continuing. "This man has had an experience that, as far as I know, no other Japanese has had. He has lived among the Americans for ten years and has sailed with their ships and traveled all across their land. He is a young man, twenty-five, but he has risked his life to return to our country, and to tell us what he knows."

He turned and bowed slightly to the stocky young man who had been sitting quietly throughout, watching and listening to Jinsuke with great interest. He was dressed well, but not ostentatiously, and appeared to be a *bushi* of low rank. His name was Manjiro, and the *bakufu* had recently elevated him to the warrior rank and given him the right to take a surname—Nakahama. They did this because what he had to say was of very great interest. Thus Manjiro was not executed for illegally leaving the country. Moreover, it would not be dignified for officials of the Tokugawa to spend so much time talking to a person of peasant stock. Manjiro bowed very deeply and began to retell his story.

"I am a Tosa man, from a little village on the outer coast of Shikoku Island. One day I went for what was supposed to be a short fishing trip with four fishermen, without telling my poor parents. A storm blew up, and the boat was taken far out to sea. We thought we would be surely drowned, but we were eventually marooned on a small uninhabited island. This was in the month of January, and we were in dire straits.

"When first we spied the foreign ship we were both glad and afraid, but they sent a boat to us and took us out to the ship, where we were given food and drink and treated with much kindness. That ship was the *John Howland*—a whaler.

"They knew they dare not come to Japan, and they took us to tropical islands, far, far away in the Pacific, to a place called Hawaii. Hawaii is a kingdom of powerful dark-skinned people, but the Americans have much control there, and their whaling ships and trading vessels frequent Hawaii in large numbers. Here the other Japanese were put ashore, but the captain took me to his home on the eastern coast of America, to a town called Fairhaven, in the state of Massachusetts. He treated me like a son, and gave me an education, sent me to a school, and had me specially tutored in the language and customs of America.

"When I became older I sailed with the whaling ships and rose to be an officer. Later, I traveled to a place called California, where there is much gold. I worked hard and found gold enough to pay for my passage back to Japan, aboard another American ship traveling from Mexico to China. I yearned for my homeland and wanted to tell everybody of what I had seen and learned.

"I went ashore with two other Japanese at Mabuni, in Okinawa. The people turned me over to the local authorities. I was taken to Naha, held and questioned there for seven months by the Satsuma authorities. I feared I would be executed, but they were greatly interested in my story and treated me well. From Naha I was sent to Kagoshima, and questioned there too, even by Lord Shimazu himself. He then sent me to Nagasaki, where again I was questioned. From Nagasaki, under the protection of the Satsuma clan, I was sent to Edo, where I have been questioned on various matters."

Sadayori spoke, his voice very soft. "Nakahama-san, why have you not written a book about this adventure?"

"I am forbidden to, sir. As I am forbidden to speak publicly about any of my experiences."

Sadayori turned to his guests. "Gentlemen, I would first like to discuss the reasons why so many foreign ships have appeared off our coast. Afterward, perhaps, if there is time, we can ask our visitor more questions, but I should warn you that he must return to his quarters before it gets too late."

They nodded. Manjiro continued.

"As I heard it, a merchantman, passing in Japanese waters on his way from China, spotted many whales, and told his friends. It was about thirty years ago. At first two ships came to hunt in our waters, one English, one American. The whaling ships, especially of America, will eagerly follow whales no matter where they be, leaving their home ports for one to four years. Anyway, the two ships that came first were very successful and soon filled all their barrels with the oil from the sperm, I mean, the perfume whales, an oil which is greatly prized in America for lighting lamps and lubricating fine machines.

"News of the success of these two ships spread quickly, and two years later thirty ships hunted what they called the 'Japan Grounds.' Now I would guess there are around seven hundred ships visiting the waters near Japan each year. More than half, two-thirds I should say, are American."

Yoshida Shoin could not contain himself. "Seven hundred ships, you say? Seven hundred?"

"Yes, sir," said Manjiro, "you see, whaling is very important to some nations, and most important to America. When I was an officer on an American whaling ship, America alone had seven hundred thirty-five whaling ships, or to be exact, six hundred seventy-eight ships and barques, thirty-five brigs and twenty-two schooners. Each of them would carry four to six whale boats."

"How many men?" asked Sadayori, leaning forward, eyes glittering.

"It differs from ship to ship, sir, but a four-boat ship would have at least thirty-five men."

"Cannon? I hear they carry cannon." It was Sakuma who spoke.

"Yes, sir, but not as big as the navy ships, and only a few. They carry them and use them for signaling boats in fog, or for defense. Some places, like the savage islands in the South Seas, can be dangerous, and the natives will attack in war canoes. The whalers carry muskets, rifles, pistols and cutlasses, locked carefully away, except when the ship is attacked."

"So, these American whaling men will fight?" asked Sadayori.

"Oh yes," said Manjiro, "they will fight, although they prefer to be peaceful with everybody, except maybe when they get drunk. They are good fighters. In America, every man has the right to carry arms and defend himself."

The samurai looked shocked at this, and Manjiro said it with almost personal pride. Jinsuke sensed that Manjiro must be a pretty tough man himself, to have lived with those men and to have made them take his commands. Sadayori looked round at his guests to see if the words had sunk in. Manjiro continued.

"Whaling is a very important industry to American. About seventy thousand people are connected to it, working for it in some way. The industry is worth seventy million dollars."

"How much is that in Japanese coin?"

Manjiro thought for a while. "I can't say, sir, because Japanese money, both gold and silver, is so much debased nowadays. America has much gold and silver, and their coins are not debased. However, I suppose one dollar is worth about one silver *bu,* so it would mean at least fourteen million gold *ryo.*" While the others exchanged glances, Manjiro thought again. "But in reality, I would say that the American silver dollar is worth two or three times the *bu.*"

The third guest, Katsu Rintaro, shook his head and sighed. The shortsighted policies of the *bakufu* in debasing currency contributed only to a growing strain on the economy. Manjiro spoke again.

"The whaling people in America are putting a lot of pressure on their government, they and the traders and missionaries, to get ports in Japan open, so they can get shelter, water and supplies."

Sadayori interrupted. "Nakahama-san, you have told us only about whaling ships. What of other ships?"

127

"America has hundreds of other ships, merchant vessels that travel to Europe, around the tip of South America, to lands all over the world. America is a new land, a very vigorous land, and it has a powerful navy which has fought two successful wars. Those navy ships are far bigger and stronger than any whaler. They have great cannon which can send exploding shells for long distances, with accuracy too. America is not alone either; England and France and several other countries have strong navies."

"What of our Japanese ships, the forts along the coast— what chance do you think they would stand against the kind of warship you have talked about? Against an American warship?" Sadayori looked straight at Manjiro's face as he put the question to him, but Nakahama Manjiro stared down at the tatami.

"I am forbidden to talk about such matters," he said.

Sakuma chided him. "You have told us much already. We are not fools. We can make guesses. But please, trust us, we will not repeat your opinions to others."

Manjiro looked up. "I'm sorry, sir, but they wouldn't stand a chance. Our ships are pathetic, they would be blown out of the water, raked with shells, ball, chain shot, grapeshot. The forts would never stand up to the bombardment of a warship, and the cannon we have would not reach them. Even a small American or British fleet would destroy any of our coastal towns. They could be driven off perhaps, but at terrible cost, and as for Americans, if they are driven off in war, they always come back. They are very stubborn and proud people. If I may say something, sir . . ."

"Go ahead," said Sakuma.

"Perhaps it would be wise to be friends with America. They don't want war, nor do they want to take Japan. They just want safe ports. I'm not so sure about the British or the French, though. They are very greedy nations, and they take colonies all over the world. If Japan were friends with America, the British and French would not dare attack."

"We need no barbarian friends!" retorted Sadayori.

Sakuma made a slight bow to Manjiro. "Thank you for your frankness. I have another question. Do you think the American navy will come?"

Manjiro nodded. "I am sure they will come, one day."

"Where will they come first?"

Manjiro inclined his head to one side. "Of course, I don't know, but they already have a lot of trade with China, and as Okinawa would be a convenient place on the way, I

128

wouldn't be surprised if they came to Okinawa first. Maybe the British will try too, though, for they have fought and defeated China, and they control India too. The British navy might come and take the Ryukyus by force. They are very strong. Only America, which used to be one of their colonies, has fought and defeated them." He shrugged, with a faint smile. This brought a flood of questions which he tried to answer.

Eventually Sadayori called a stop to the session. He excused Manjiro, saying to the other samurai that he had to leave. Manjiro bowed, then stood. Jinsuke, at a glance from Sadayori, stood too. Sadayori excused himself and went out into the corridor with the two ex-whalers.

"Nakahama-san, thank you," he said courteously. "It will take a little time to call a *kago* for you. My servants have prepared a simple meal. I would appreciate it if you would excuse me, and if you would consent to share the meal with Jinsuke here. He too is a bold whaler, like you, and maybe you have things you could talk about."

Sadayori had guessed shrewdly. Although Nakahama had easily slipped back into the social mores and class barriers of his native land, ten years of living with the Americans had made him a different man, interested in other men, especially whalers, and Jinsuke was a likable fellow, and both of them were in their early twenties. Manjiro smiled.

"In an hour, then, a *kago* will come," said Sadayori. "My men will make sure you are not watched or followed." He made a short bow. "And now, if you will excuse me . . ."

Manjiro returned the bow and followed Jinsuke and a maid to a room that had been set aside for them. In the middle of the room were two small tables set with food and drink. Jinsuke could sense the maid's puzzlement over the fact that he, who was not a samurai, should be treated so specially. But she also knew that in Sadayori's household such thoughts were kept silent. The two men were left in privacy, as the master had instructed.

Manjiro looked around the room. It was a simple room, not used often, with pine-tree designs on the sliding doors and shoji screen. It had a small *tokonoma* alcove, with a flower arrangement and a hanging scroll of a snowy mountain.

"Despite everything, it's good to be back in Japan," he said, smiling at Jinsuke, who took the warmed flagon of sake and poured it for him.

"Matsudaira-sama told me about you," Manjiro said, raising his cup and waiting while Jinsuke raised his while he in turn took the flagon and poured it for Jinsuke. They drank to each other, not knowing where to begin.

Saying nothing, Jinsuke put his hand into his tunic and pulled out the scrimshawed whale tooth and related the story of meeting the foreigners at sea, off Taiji. Manjiro whistled and picked it up with a delighted grin, turning it over in his hand. He looked at the lettering on one side, and read it out in accents so foreign that Jinsuke just couldn't follow.

"Midas—that's the name of the ship," said Manjiro, "a barque, by the look of the etching on this side, so it has six whale boats. It's American, see the flag? Then here, in English, it says 'May all she touch turn to gold.' It's like a good-luck charm. Midas was a king of ancient Greece, a country in Europe. Anything he touched turned to gold."

"But you said 'she.' "

Manjiro chuckled. "Yes, it's a funny thing to us, but they call their ships 'she' even when the ship has a man's name."

He turned the tooth around and around, squinting at the whale hunt, with a bull sperm whale making an enormous wave with his tail and a boat halfway out of the water. In the bottom right-hand corner of the picture were some tiny letters. He squinted at them.

" 'Tovey Jacks.' " He looked up at Jinsuke and repeated the name. "I would say that this is the name of the man who carved this, the man who tossed it to you. You say he was in the bow of the boat and they had a dead whale? That would mean he's an officer, one of the mates. I don't know him, though. Pity, isn't it—that would have been interesting. This is quite a present, they spend hours and hours doing these. Ah, see this on this side? It's a plant called a pineapple, it has a sweet fruit, and the whalers take them home with them from the tropics. It's a good-luck charm too. But . . . you haven't shown this to the authorities, have you?"

Jinsuke shook his head.

"Don't," said Manjiro, "they'll take it off you and ask you stupid questions until your ears are worn down to stubs."

He laughed and poured more sake for both of them. "Here's to the whalers, and your secret friend, Mr. Tovey Jacks, wherever he might be!"

Jinsuke raised his cup and downed it. He found Nakahama Manjiro a rather odd but certainly amiable fellow. He ate in silence for a while, wanting to ask a question, but too shy to do so outright. He made small talk, feeling increasingly annoyed at himself for letting these precious minutes go by.

Finally, he took a breath, picked up the tooth, and pointed to a tiny figure in the bow of a whale boat.

"This man is throwing a harpoon with one hand. Is that the way the foreigners do it?"

Manjiro looked up at him. "Not usually. Most of the time they get up very close and pitch the iron with two hands, or thrust it into the whale, like this." He made motions, indicating a downward thrust, with the butt of an imaginary harpoon in his right hand, holding also with the left. "Some men grip around the pole like this too. They don't throw it up into the air like you fellows do, though. I suppose there are some men who throw one-handed, like those Eskimo fellows up in the icy north. Wait, though—ah yes, Matsudaira-sama asked me that same question a month ago, when I met him, and I remembered a big Hawaiian harpooner, a huge man he was, and he always threw with one hand."

He looked at Jinsuke and smiled, as if reading his thoughts. "It's a difficult life on a whaler, hard work, danger, poor food, dirty, smelly . . . but those men really know how to catch whales."

"I'm sure we Japanese are better," said Jinsuke.

"We should be better, and we could be better, but we aren't," said Manjiro. "We don't have the ships. I listened to what you said. You said it took three hundred eighty-two men to take just one whale. The Yankee whalers do it with one boat and six men. One whaling ship will take as many whales in a year as your village does, and if the captain knows his stuff, and they have good luck, they'll take more. The ships follow where the whales are, you see, and after they kill the whale they flense it alongside the ship, then boil out the oil aboard and store it in barrels."

"How do they pack the meat? The ship must be filled with meat. Do they take a load of salt with them? And who saves the sinews and bones?"

Manjiro laughed. "They don't keep the meat, or the bones. They just take the blubber, the head oil and the teeth, and when they get right whales they take the baleen, that's valuable."

Jinsuke was incredulous. "They don't take the meat?"

"No, people don't eat whale meat in America, they have so many cattle, sheep, pigs and so forth. They don't need whale meat. Anyway, when I was with the Americans we couldn't carry enough salt for it, and besides, if we tried to sell salted whale meat, they would think us crazy." He laughed at the idea. Jinsuke shook his head, quite shocked.

"That's a waste, a bad, bad waste. The gods will punish them for abusing the gifts of the sea like that." Jinsuke had heard those stories about the barbarians eating cattle and other four-legged animals, which was a sin and would send them straight to one of the hells, but to think they would prefer such meat to whale meat was too awful to think of. Manjiro could see what he was thinking, and changed the subject.

"It would be good if the whaling ships could call into ports in our country," he said, a little wistfully. "They could get good men, like men from Taiji or Tosa, and those men would be able to sail all around the world and see how things really are."

"I would like to go on a whaling voyage, I really would," said Jinsuke, "but with this . . ." He glanced down at his empty sleeve.

Manjiro spoke again. "A good man like you, who knows the waters, the winds, the whales, they'd take you, in spite of that. You'd have to be able to climb the rigging, and do a lot of difficult things, but I reckon you could do it. You'd have to have a very strong arm, of course, to row a boat and do all those things, but you could do it. When we want to, and are earnest, we Japanese can do anything." He smiled at Jinsuke, who filled his sake cup again.

"If I was a whaling captain, I'd take you."

From outside came the clack! clack! of a passing night watchman, slapping his blocks of wood together and calling out to take care of fires. The maid called softly and slid the door open.

"Sir, the men have come with the *kago*."

Manjiro thanked her and stood up. When Jinsuke stood he realized how much bigger and broader he was than the guest, and this man had been a whaling officer, and had seen the world! He followed him down to the front entrance. Sadayori was waiting. He bowed and thanked Manjiro for coming, then slipped his feet into wooden *geta* and went outside. Manjiro bowed.

"Thank you, Matsudaira-sama. I only hope that more people of intelligence will have an interest in modern ships and in what is going on in the seas of the world."

Sadayori nodded but said nothing. He and Jinsuke watched as the *kago* bearers jogged off into the night. Jinsuke turned and bowed to Sadayori.

"Sir, I can't tell you how grateful I am that you permitted me to speak with Nakahama Manjiro-san."

Sadayori grunted, looked at him for a few seconds, then turned and went back into the house. As Jinsuke walked around to his own room he could hear voices raised in argument from the second floor of the main house. Sadayori and his friends talked until dawn crept into the Edo sky.

After a couple of weeks in Edo, Jinsuke was beginning to feel bored and out of place. Then, one morning, he was called to Sadayori's study. Sadayori looked up from his low desk.

"Jinsuke, I'm going to Nagasaki. You'll come with me."

The young whaler's face brightened at the news. Then, very quietly, Sadayori asked a question.

"Would you like a chance to try to become a whaler again? On a foreign ship?" The question hit Jinsuke like a bolt.

"But it's against the law!"

"I know, but I think the laws will change, as the country will change. Hard, dangerous times are ahead of us, and we need to know what the foreigners are doing, so we need men to go on their ships, like Nakahama Manjiro. I can't go, neither can he, but because of your accident, you are surprisingly free." He stared into Jinsuke's eyes. "You wanted to die, didn't you? I read it in your eyes one time. Well, death is nothing, but this mission is more than death. Here in Japan you cannot be a whaler, the laws prevent you from doing most other things, but if you will take the risk, and go abroad for us, when you come back I vow you will not be punished. It may take years, but one day you will return, and I think you will tell us all of lands you have seen and whales you have killed."

Jinsuke sat silently, heart beating hard in his chest.

"If you agree, we will smuggle you out to the Goto Islands, and from there to Okinawa, the Ryukyus. I have somebody I know down there, somebody my father knew before he died. His name is Kinjo, and he will give you some training that you might need until we can smuggle you out to China. From China you can go by foreign ship to America."

Sadayori picked up a sheet of paper and handed it to Jinsuke. Jinsuke opened it, and found it quite unintelligible. Sadayori laughed.

"It's in English, written by Nakahama Manjiro. It says you are a whaling man, honest and good with a harpoon. If we get you out to China, this letter might be of help. Take it and hide it carefully if you want to risk this adventure. If the officials found it then we'd all be in serious trouble. I don't

133

want to be asked to commit seppuku, not just yet!" He laughed again.

Jinsuke looked down at the paper. Images tumbled in his mind, of the glorious days with the whaling fleet, of Iwadaiyu, of his father, of the songs and dances the whalers did, of festivals, of his dreams of captaining his own chase boat with the pine-tree design, and of sweet, lovely Oyoshi.

"Although I am not wealthy, neither am I poor," said Sadayori, "and if I can, if the laws will ever permit it, I will provide the money to build a whaling ship such as Nakahama talked about, if you would captain it and lead a crew of Taiji whalemen to sail to distant seas in quest of whales. It would make a difference to Taiji too, wouldn't it?"

Jinsuke looked into the samurai's face. "I would go anywhere you want me to, with or without the dream of a great ship."

"Good," said the samurai, then, softly, "I'm sorry, but you cannot tell anybody about this, not even your family."

"I know that, sir," said Jinsuke, feeling a great heaviness in his chest.

Sadayori stood with a fluid movement and went to the little alcove adjoining his study. He moved away some boxes, and there, from among the tea bowls, the iron kettle, the whisks and other paraphernalia, he produced two cups and a small sealed flagon. He placed a cup before Jinsuke, opened the flagon, and poured. Then he poured for himself, with great ceremony. Jinsuke's heart filled, and tears came to his eyes. This man of the *bushi* class chose to drink with him, a crippled whaler. Sadayori raised his cup.

"Come back safely, Jinsuke, son of Tatsudaiyu. *Kampai!*"

"*Kampai,*" echoed Jinsuke.

Chapter Eleven

On the azure and limpid waters off the outer edge of the reef, Jinsuke paddled, slowly and easily. The polished and padded stock rested on the thick muscles above his collarbone, braced lightly with head and neck, while his right arm dipped, pulled, twisted, keeping the slender *sabani* on course. He had carved the paddle himself, and used it now as if he'd been born with it.

He scanned the horizon, taking in a slight change of wind, the ring of high white surf like a brilliant collar around the neck of Ie Island, and in the air the indescribable, subtle scents left from last week's typhoon.

The bottom of the *sabani* was vivid and glistening with the colors of a dozen fat fish, colors now beginning to fade in the sadness of life ending. He pulled a square of matting over them. The sun, high in the sky, was fierce.

Jinsuke preferred to use a spear, not the hook and line. He would peer over the side until he saw a good spot, anchor with line and rock, then dive down deep into that wondrous world of table coral, of huge anemones like flowers, of long-spined urchins and a host of fish that danced in costumes of unbelievable colors. He took care to avoid the fire coral, the black and orange posturing of lionfish with their painful spines, the holes that might hide needle-toothed moray eels and any other poisonous creatures, some of which he had known from the seas of Taiji, and many others which his teacher, Kinjo, had warned him about.

As he dipped his paddle, a turtle saucered its way below, and then he saw a sea snake, undulating along an underwater ravine. In all the movement and color of this sea, Jinsuke found peace and strength. He had been muscular and strong before, but now his muscles were even thicker, and of a different tone. Whereas before he had been brown, now he was of a deep mahogany, skin glistening as if polished, and his hair hung long and loose about his shoulders, or, on shore, tied up and pinned in the Okinawan way.

Training under the master Kinjo, gruff-voiced, surly and ugly though he was, had given Jinsuke greater depth, greater understanding of things that moved and lived. And far, far greater strength.

It had been hard to win the master's attention, for despite the gold that came by circuitous route to the master's hands, Jinsuke had not been trusted, and the Okinawans spoke almost all the time in their own tongue, totally different from the Japanese of the main islands to the northeast. However, Jinsuke waited patiently and quietly, spending his days by the small hut that had been rented for him or in the sea, swimming. A few suspicious Okinawan men, fishermen mainly, had come and talked with him; he convinced them he was not a Satsuma spy, and as he talked in sparse sentences about his former life, the quiet, kindly islanders had taken to him.

The Satsuma clan of southern Kyushu, very warlike and powerful, with more samurai per capita than any other clan in Japan, had conquered the Ryukyu Islands, including Okinawa, as well as other southern islands, like Tanegashima, where the Portuguese had landed and taught the Japanese how to use and make firearms. Because of this, Satsuma had a monopoly on sugar, which was produced in the Ryukyus with what was virtually slave labor. This cruel domination gave the islanders little reason to love outsiders, especially those they called "mainlanders" from Japan. Still, they were a basically welcoming, happy people, and finally, after Jinsuke had met Kinjo and delivered Sadayori's letter, in which Sadayori described how Jinsuke had lost his arm while fighting a big shark, the master and the others were impressed. Long ago Kinjo had incurred a debt of gratitude to Matsudaira Sadayori's father, now dead. He agreed to conduct Jinsuke's training. The old man, in his sixties, was a master of a secret style of fighting, totally different from, and perhaps even more dangerous than, the jujitsu and Yawara styles of the samurai.

One evening Kinjo came to Jinsuke's hut. "Stand," he said, in his strongly accented Japanese.

Jinksuke stood there while Kinjo walked around him, looking. Kinjo finally grunted.

"You're a boat man. Deep, rooted stances. You've got a bit of strength, but you're not too flexible, probably slow as

136

a turtle too. No high kicks, no jumps. Waste of time. Follow me."

Jinsuke followed him along a narrow pathway to a clearing in the thick jungle, to one side of which was a row of domed graves, peculiar to the islands and quite unlike the simple carved headstones of the mainland. A post was embedded in the ground, the top bound with a pad of woven straw. Kinjo adopted a low stance in front of it and slowly executed a punch. He repeated the movement, many times, speeding up until his fist moved so fast it was hard to see, and with such power that the post bent and thrummed with each blow to the pad.

He called Jinsuke over, made him do the same thing, correcting the way his feet were planted, the way his knees and toes pointed, the level of his shoulders, the way the fist twisted as it struck, the way to exhale and tighten the muscles of the abdomen.

"Every day you do five hundred of these, both sides, left and right."

"Both sides? But sensei, can you not see . . ."

The master slapped him, making Jinsuke stagger to his knees, ears ringing.

"Both sides! I see as well as you do, if not better, mainlander. We will balance that body of yours, or in a short time your spine will begin to twist, and you will know pain and lose what puny strength you think you have. You have movement in that stump, don't you? It still lives. Do the movement with your body, legs, hips, chest, shoulder. Then imagine the forearm and fist you once had, and put even more effort into that memory. And never, never question me again unless you think you can stand up to me, or I might just decide to break the other arm. Understand?"

Jinsuke fell to his knees, thanking him.

Weeks went by, and Jinsuke did as he was told, and each day Kinjo came to watch, saying little, but making small corrections. Calluses formed on Jinsuke's fist, and he gained movement in the stump, and he could now hold things by squeezing it against his chest. Kinjo taught him to execute a simple front kick to solar plexus height. He added more exercises to Jinsuke's training schedule, which included running along the beach and up steep slopes and through the shallows. The number of daily punches was increased to a thousand, and he was taught a method of striking with both edges as well as the back of the hand.

"When you properly gain balance," said Kinjo, "I can

teach you to block with that shoulder. Work hard. Next month you will begin to learn *kata*."

After months of training Kinjo brought five of his other pupils. They were all advanced. Jinsuke had begun to learn the formal sequences of movements, the *kata,* and as he sweated and tried to emulate the others, he found he could lose himself in this art and began to wish that he could spend many years as a pupil of Kinjo. He watched the others, with their powerful, graceful, blindingly fast movements, and he watched them train with special Okinawan weapons, most of which were adapted from ordinary tools. They trained with sticks and sickles, with the *sai, nunchaku* and *tonfa.*

"I will begin to teach you the *sai*," said Kinjo. "It's like the weapon your mainland authorities use, the *jutte,* although the *sai* is much better. It is an ancient weapon, and properly used, it can combat a sword, if you're good, although that would take ten years or so. Mind you, most of those sword-carrying, swaggering mainland fools don't really know how to use the things they carry anyway." He smiled an inward smile of dark, deep satisfaction.

Thus Jinsuke began to train in the use of the *sai,* the killing iron, a steel truncheon the length of a man's hand and forearm, slightly tapering to a wicked but heavy tip, with curving double tines. With this weapon, usually held one in each hand, you could strike, punch, thrust, chop, hook and block, with the weapon magnifying the moves of the unarmed art. The master found it grimly amusing that he should be teaching a mainlander to use a weapon, when it was mainlanders who had so long forbidden the Okinawans to carry them.

Jinsuke was receiving other secret lessons too, from a young man who had been a clerk at an English firm in China, his father being Chinese. Jinsuke was beginning to learn English, first with the names of whales and sea terms, words useful around docks and ships. The lessons were tedious for him, but he did his best, knowing that if he was to ever sail on a foreign whaling ship this knowledge would be vital. He didn't have too much trouble picking up the lettering, for he had learned the three writing systems of Japan, which were far more complicated, but the sounds of the language seemed even more outlandish than the Okinawan tongue, which he was struggling to pick up too.

The lessons had to be conducted after dark, when Jinsuke would make his way along a narrow, unlighted path to the frail young teacher's house, carrying a lantern when the moon was out, fearful of encountering the deadly *habu* snake.

One night, when they settled in the room and the teacher had taken out the forbidden books and dictionaries he kept hidden in a wicker basket, beneath the mats and floorboards of the house, Jinsuke sensed that his teacher was excited. He took paper and drew various whaling weapons and tools, made in the American style, then pointed to them one by one, making Jinsuke say the names out loud in English.

"Harpoon."

It had taken him an hour to learn to pronounce that well at first.

"What's this?"

"Brubbah say!"

"No, it's a blubber spade. Repeat . . . *blubber spade.*"

With furious concentration Jinsuke repeated it until he got it right. Then came "lance," "boat spade," "hook," then the names of the English tools too—prickers, blubber knives, strand knives, tail knives, bone wedge, pick-hack, cosh, grapnel. After an hour of it, Jinsuke's jaw ached, but the teacher's eyes twinkled with amusement.

"Now, Jinsuke, once more through it all. If you get it right I'll give you a prize."

Jinsuke groaned inwardly, but imagining himself on a foreign whale boat, on some exotic sea, he went slowly through the whole list as the teacher's bony finger pointed from one drawing to another.

"Excellent! Now come with me."

Wondering what the prize might be, Jinsuke followed the teacher out of the house and down to a shed where gardening tools were kept. The teacher stopped by the shed and gestured for silence. He went in and came out with a long and heavy bundle wrapped in cloth. He handed it to Jinsuke, who took it, then followed the teacher to the gate.

"Keep this prize hidden. Such things are not forbidden, but they are foreign, and the Satsuma authorities will question you about them. They came to me secretly, with this letter, from Nagasaki."

He handed Jinsuke the letter and bid him to be careful. With the bundle over his shoulder and the letter inside his tunic, Jinsuke went home.

Once back in his hut, to the flickering yellow light of an oil lamp, he cut open the bundle to find an American harpoon, a long, petal-bladed killing lance and a razor-sharp blubber spade. The letter was short and unsigned, but in Sadayori's hand.

139

"Practice," it said.

Jinsuke went outside and gazed at a sky bright with stars. He raised the harpoon as if to prick one from above.

"*O . . . kini . . . yo!*" he cried in his Taiji dialect, his heart bursting with gratitude for the samurai who had befriended him.

Now, every day, apart from the fighting art and the English studies, he spent three hours or more hurling the harpoon at a bale filled with sand. His range and power increased, and eventually he could hit the target with enough force to bury the harpoon deep at twenty feet and more, and he was confident that he would better that range.

The master Kinjo took a great interest in this, but offered no advice or comment, until one day he announced that they would go together and harpoon sharks. Jinsuke killed one shark a little bigger than a man, with a throw so powerful it severed its spine. It gave him savage delight and Kinjo clapped with approval before helping to haul the shark, their third, into the *sabani* and smash a powerful clenched hammerfist to its brain.

"Jinsuke, I don't know how long you can avoid the attention of the authorities, but I am glad that I agreed to train you, and I am sure that one day you will again hunt whales."

When they got to shore and butchered the sharks, with Jinsuke helping, wrinkling his nose at the slightly acrid smell, Kinjo went on. "It's not going to be easy to get out of Okinawa. They've brought some new inspectors in from Kagoshima, and things are tighter than usual."

"When the time comes, I'll know," said Jinsuke, "but in the meantime I have no words to thank you, sensei, for helping me to be whole again. I wish I could stay here longer, these are such lovely islands, and the sea is a heaven, and you Okinawan people are like my people at home, so proud, so kind, so friendly."

"Yes," said Kinjo softly, "we were free once, with our own kings, our own laws, but we were defeated by the Satsuma, and made slaves, forbidden the true rights of men to determine what they must do and carry arms as warriors should. However, we have a hidden steel, and one day we will show you mainlanders that we have more spirit than any of those conceited fops who prattle on to each other about Bushido, yet who, here in these islands, make pregnant women in their last month leap a ravine to see if they are strong enough to bear children, and who cull the old and infirm of other islands as if they were chickens." He spat in the sand. "You have no idea of the inhuman cruelty of Satsuma samurai, and mark my words, one day Okinawa will become a battleground. I hope I don't live to see it, but even if I don't I will have passed on teaching, not how to fight, but how to face loss with courage. You, Jinsuke, are the only outsider I have ever taught. Don't ever betray the core of what I taught you, don't ever fight for vain reasons, be humble and gentle, but if you fight, fight to destroy the enemy. Those who make a virtue of fighting are less than animals, but sadly, there are many of them, and that is why men such as us have to prepare. I can see violence in your future, so never forget what I say. Be whole, be strong, be gentle, and don't ever fear losing. Now come, let us drink!"

Together they drank the fiery *awamori* until Jinsuke got so drunk that Kinjo had to hoist him over his shoulder and carry him home.

The next day Jinsuke woke up late, his mouth dry as a hot Okinawa beach, his head pounding, eyes red-rimmed and sore. There was a great commotion outside, excitement, people shouting. He staggered to his feet and quickly tied his loincloth. When he gazed out into the bay, alarm, astonishment and a strange elation jolted him into wakefulness. There were ships in the bay, huge ships, black, masts as tall as the tallest trees, ships more threatening, more magnificent than anything Jinsuke had ever seen.

Now at last he had something to report to Matsudaira-sama! The barbarians had come! He ran into the house and put on his tunic and pants then rushed to his teacher's house.

"Where is the sensei?" he asked a few of the Okinawan pupils to whom the teacher taught Chinese characters and poetry. They pointed out to the great black ships.

"They have taken him out there to the ships, to interpret."

"Have they come to fight us?" asked Jinsuke.

"The sensei said before he went that we were not to panic. They are American ships, and they come in peace."

Jinsuke bowed his thanks, then went down to the beach where he kept his *sabani*. He wanted a closer look.

Out on the biggest ship, a vain, pompous, but extremely competent naval commander called Perry had come with orders from his government to lead an expedition to Japan.

In November of 1852, final orders were issued to him. His mission would be to effect an arrangement with Japan to ensure the protection of American seamen and property wrecked on the Japanese islands or driven into Japanese harbors by inclement weather. He was also to secure permission for American ships to enter one or more selected ports in order to obtain provisions, water, fuel and so forth, and to refit if they were damaged. A lesser objective was to secure a base that could be used as a coal depot, for the navy and the merchant marine were switching to steam. Perry himself was in the forefront of leading the navy's gradual transition from sail to steam, and this objective of gaining a coal depot was dear to his own visions of America's future in the Pacific. Finally, there was consideration of a base for commerce.

Up until now, all Western approaches and requests to Japan had been gentle, but this expedition was expected to produce results, and for this a powerful show of naval force was planned, with big steam auxiliary gunboats and large numbers of well-armed marines.

The USS *Mississippi* sailed from Norfolk, Virginia, heading first for the China coast to meet up with the rest of the fleet. Its journey portended the end of Japan's long isolation. Thirty-two years had passed since the *Maro*, a Nantucket whaler, and the *Enderby*, a whaler from Britain, had first hunted the Japan Grounds.

Jinsuke, paddling quite close to the nearest ship before a boat full of armed Satsuma officials came and shouted angrily for him to keep away, knew that change had come, and could not help being excited by it. He turned for shore, remembering now the small, foreign folding brass telescope that Sadayori had given him at Nagasaki. He thought of a quiet place where he could spy on the ships without being caught, but more than anything now, he envied men who could sail on such mighty vessels.

Chapter Twelve

Oyoshi's swelling belly became obvious. Had she been a weaker person, or had she not believed in the right of Jinsuke's baby to life, and in her own love for Jinsuke, she would have thrown herself off the cliffs. Instead Oyoshi became stubborn and defiant. She was positive that Jinsuke would return to marry her. The Taiji gossips, not with intentional malice perhaps, caused great distress, especially to her father. He refused to talk to anybody, and in his heart he had conceived an utter hatred for Jinsuke. In the end, Tatsudaiyu went to speak to him.

"Takigawa-san," he began, kneeling awkwardly on the tatami, "what I have come to say I must say clearly, without lies, without ceremony. Your daughter bears the child of my son, it is no secret between us. We have not seen or heard of my son for six months, and in another two or three months your daughter will give birth. I know my son, and I know it was never his intention to run off and leave her in this plight. He has always loved and wanted to marry Oyoshi, and when he returns, he will marry her. So let us be happy, you and I, that we will both have our first grandchild."

Takigawa was silent for a while, but then with sudden emotion he shouted, his voice cracking.

"Never! Jinsuke will never marry my daughter! I would kill her, and the child first! Then I'd kill myself!" Tatsudaiyu's voice turned cold and hard.

"No. You will not harm either the child or Oyoshi. You may be her father, but I, Tatsudaiyu, have an interest in the life she carries in her. Know that!"

Takigawa stood, making as if to shake a fist, but a terrible bout of coughing racked him, and he crumpled to the floor.

Oyoshi, who had been waiting and listening outside, came running in with a cup of water. She tried to help her father sit up, but he pushed her away, took the cup, and dashed the contents in her face. He turned to Tatsudaiyu, unafraid, despite the great difference in size and strength between them.

"I have but one thing to suggest, only one thing, and that will be done properly, through a go-between. Now leave me alone!"

Tatsudaiyu nodded and got to his feet. He could not really blame the man. He stood by the door and turned to look back. Tatsudaiyu was tall, broad-shouldered, deeply tanned, quiet, his hair just beginning to turn gray. He looked down sadly at the two of them, and through her tears Oyoshi looked up at Tatsudaiyu and felt confidence in him. She was angry with her father, and hurt, but motherhood lent a sense of rightness in herself.

"Please forgive my father, he is ill, and distressed."

Takigawa flew into a rage again and tried to slap her, but she ducked back away from him, and he was not strong enough to follow her.

"Please, it's all right," she said to the harpooner, and he nodded again, and left. After he had gone, Oyoshi sat, gazing at the weave of the matting, wondering where her lover could be and why he did not return or send for her.

Two days later a suggestion came to the house of Tatsudaiyu through old man Toumi. It stunned them all. Saburo sat there, shaking his head from side to side. The old man finished talking, sucked his teeth, stared at his pickled plum, and slurped noisily on his tea, and getting nothing but a hard request for time to think, he left.

For a week Saburo said nothing, and nobody in his family felt any reason to push him, despite the obligations that Tatsudaiyu's family now had for the Takigawas.

"Why me?" asked Saburo to his father. "Father, wouldn't it be better for us to send a message to Jinsuke, and make him come back?"

"You know we've tried," his father answered, "but there is neither shape nor shadow of him. Listen, son, you know the village gossip, it hurts all of us. But also, to have you for his adopted son was Takigawa-san's dream. I saw that years ago. You are a good boy, gentle, and skilled with a brush. But . . ." He paused, and sighed, and ran his hand over his shaven pate. "If only Jinsuke and Oyoshi . . ."

For Saburo it was sheer torment. When he looked on

144

Oyoshi, even more beautiful now in the flush of pregnancy, he found that image, the sight of her on her back, thighs wide, and his brother, buttocks naked, thrusting between them. He felt strange and tight inside, even a little sick to think about it. He gazed at his father, then lowered his head.

"Father . . . please . . . I can't."

"Whatever your decision is, you are my son, and I will stand by you."

Tatsudaiyu reached out in a rare gesture of affection, touching the youth on his shoulder. "Think about it, though. Jinsuke is gone nearly eight months now, and when he left he must have been stupid not to guess that Oyoshi might carry his child. On the other hand, you like Oyoshi, you two were like brother and sister. Think well, make your decision, and your father will stick by you. You know that."

It was an impossible situation, something had to be done, and the focus was on Saburo. Saburo had grown to love old Takigawa almost as much as his father, and Saburo wanted to go to the ailing painter and tell him of his feelings for Oyoshi, of his inner rage at his brother, and of how he loved Takigawa's world of shape, color and beauty, how he would rather paint than do anything else. Then he wanted to tell Takigawa that he could not marry Oyoshi.

However, when Saburo made up his mind and confronted Takigawa in the boat shed, then began haltingly to try to explain how he felt, Takigawa broke down, leaned against the gunwale of a half-decorated boat, and wept as Saburo had seen no man weep before. Saburo was greatly moved. He could not bear his distress. He left the boat shed abruptly and climbed to the top of Mukaijima, and there he prayed at the little shrine, begging for guidance, for something.

That evening, straight after supper, he went to the Takigawa home, even though he should have gone through old man Toumi. Oyoshi served him tea. Silence. She avoided his eyes, and there was no warmth in her movements at all. Saburo spoke.

"I have not consulted the go-between about this because I wanted to see how you both feel. Takigawa-san, you have been both teacher and second father to me, and your work, your world, is more important and interesting to me than any other. Oyoshi is pregnant by my brother, and she should marry him. For me to marry Oyoshi, in the normal sense, would not be proper. On the other hand, my brother has gone. Nobody knows where he is, or when or even if he will return. It is not fair that the child should suffer because of my brother. Jinsuke has not been in Taiji for eight months. I fear he may never return."

Oyoshi was about to give an angry retort to this, but Saburo looked so serious, and so sad. Her father glared at her. Saburo continued.

"Oyoshi has always been like a sister to me, and I still think of her as a sister. Therefore, if she agrees, willingly, I will go through a marriage ceremony with her. Perhaps the marriage will not be a normal one, for we do not want to be married to each other, and I would think of her as my brother's wife, not mine. Can you understand that?"

Takigawa had gone very tense, and he trembled and looked at Saburo's face, taking deep breaths.

"I would come into this house through the marriage, be Oyoshi's husband in the eyes of society, but between Oyoshi and me will be the relationship of brother and sister." He stopped, then stressed something important. *"Elder* brother, elder brother and younger sister."

Now Oyoshi looked up at him.

"If Oyoshi marries me she must treat me with respect," said Saburo. "If Jinsuke returns, I would be willing to divorce her, then she can leave with him. Whatever, the child must not be born in this village out of wedlock. I know that Oyoshi has nowhere else to go. That's all I have to say."

Tears trickled down Takigawa's sallow cheeks, and Oyoshi, eyes wide, stared at Saburo for a while and then bowed, both hands on the mat before her.

"Saburo-san, you have a big heart. Thank you, for my father, for me, for the baby."

"Well? What is your answer?" asked her father tightly.

"We will go to Toumi-san and ask him to arrange everything." She looked steadily at Saburo again. "You would keep your promise? About being an elder brother to me? About not trying to . . ."

"I keep promises," said Saburo.

Saburo and Oyoshi were married just ten days before she gave birth to a healthy, squalling boy. They called him Yoichi. It was the second month of the lunar new year. Saburo moved into the Takigawa house and officially became an apprentice boat painter.

Village gossip did not completely die down. Everybody knew that Oyoshi and Jinsuke had been seeing each other. The marriage, however, now confused the whisperers at corners, and the men, especially the whaling men, would not permit such talk at home. Such things could not be waved about like washing on a bamboo pole. Oyoshi's late pregnancy at the time of marriage, and what went before must now be pushed into the past, for the sake of the whole village. Oyoshi had been married. The third son of the leading harpooner had been adopted into the Takigawa house. Everybody should be happy for that.

Tatsudaiyu, however, knew that although the surface was calmed and face saved, there was a murky silt of hidden scorn, even pity, behind the now friendly greetings and smiles in the village. He felt a deep responsibility for this. He himself had been the one to go to the Wada family to ask them to help trace Jinsuke.

Outside the two families concerned, only old Toumi knew the truth for certain, and although he was a garrulous old man, in something like this, where he was the go-between, he could be trusted.

One evening old man Toumi had come over to Tatsudaiyu's house and was enjoying a dish of squid, the flesh so fresh that it was almost transparent.

"Do you know," said the old man, "that if you wash a body and help put it in the coffin, then go fishing, you'll catch a lot of fish, especially squid."

He dipped a tasty morsel into sauce, popped it into his mouth, and chewed vigorously. Tatsudaiyu filled the old man's cup again with milky, home-brewed sake. He ignored the statement, for his mind was filled with other things.

"Young Saburo is being treated coldly by the people in this town," Tatsudaiyu said.

The old man stopped chewing. Tatsudaiyu's bluntness never ceased to amaze him. Tatsudaiyu went on.

"They have no cause to treat him this way. It is wrong. I would rather die myself than have him be unhappy, when it was his good heart that saved us from disgrace. Jinsuke had better not come back here. I won't forgive it."

The old man sighed. "There are people who go around with plantains, looking for dead toads," he said, referring to a Taiji superstition that said that if you covered a dead toad with a plantain leaf, it would come to life again.

"This dead toad must never come to life," said Tatsudaiyu.

The old man popped another piece of squid into his mouth and waved one hand in front of his face in denial.

"No worry, no worry! This old man has been lazy, enjoy-

147

ing your kindness all the time. Now, though, I will act. This squid is delicious, isn't it?"

They finished the plate in silence.

The next day old Toumi made a point of visiting Iwadaiyu. Although Jinsuke's disappearance was a matter that Iwadaiyu himself would never broach, the old man artfully steered the conversation toward the subject.

"Ah, that young fellow, a very proud one," Toumi said, "and if you ask me, he couldn't stand being around and not going out with the whaleboats. I told him he could find a place with the watchers, but he wouldn't listen." The old man gave a snort. "And where would you fellows be without us watchers?"

Iwadaiyu inclined his head. "We all work together, that is why we can catch whales."

"Maybe he'll come back, maybe not," said the old man.

Iwadaiyu, with the straight ways of a harpooner, knew what the old man was trying to get at.

"He had good reason to come back," said Iwadaiyu.

The old man pursed his lips and folded his arms, his back straightening.

"Things are never the way they seem, you know. It takes skill to watch things and then know what is really happening. Yes, that Jinsuke, I've known him since he was a baby. A very proud fellow, that one, proud like his father, and just as stubborn." Iwadaiyu nodded. "Tatsudaiyu never liked the idea of a son of his, even a third son, taking so much interest in painting, you know." The old man noisily sipped his tea. "Oh, I always knew the boy was different, Saburo, I mean. Saburo used to spend a lot of time with me, up at the lookout, always pointing out colors and patterns on birds, leaves, even spiders. Yes, yes, the boy had a fine eye, even when he was young, but it wasn't really the sort of eye that we watchers have. He could watch well enough, but he fidgeted, always wanting to do something with his hands. Fidget, fidget." Old Toumi gave a little laugh. "Takigawa's grandmother on his mother's side and Onui's grandmother were sisters, you know, so the boy probably had quite a bit of the painter's blood in him. He wasn't like his brothers. He never had that, if you forgive me for saying, that whaler's toughness and bluntness about him, even though he was deep. With Saburo you didn't always see what he was feeling or thinking"—he paused—"or doing." Toumi shifted his position on the cushion and gave a sigh.

"Jinsuke hit him once, you know. Jinsuke was so proud of

being a whaler. Me, I felt sorry for Takigawa, even though I managed to work it all out for him in the end. But if you put two young people together all the time, what can you expect? Myself, I couldn't blame them, they were young. Now Jinsuke kept trying to see young Oyoshi, thinking he could talk to her, but you know young people, talking doesn't help, does it? Mind you, I did get angry with the first harpooner for opposing the marriage for so long, even if the shock of Jinsuke getting injured like that, and losing his status in the boat, and then going off without a word was a hard blow to him. But I told him he had another fine son, a strong, steady, willing lad too, so what did it matter if the third one got adopted? But he's a stubborn fellow! He knew he'd have to give in in the end, the way things were. They make a fine pair, though. Saburo is such a nice young man, a good boy, very kind at heart." The old man took another noisy sip of hot green tea.

"How's Shusuke coming along? Will he make a harpooner?"

Iwadaiyu had not missed any of the intention of the old man's rambling speech. He smiled.

"Well," he said, "given a few more years, he'll be good. He's not as wild, and he doesn't have that feel for the whales that his brother had, but he's strong and, as you say, steady."

"I always have maintained that Taiji was too small to ignore people's good qualities," said old man Toumi. "Those who speak ill of others always end up with bad breath."

"That's true," said Iwadaiyu.

The next day, Iwadaiyu's wife took Oyoshi some dried persimmons, and made various excuses and apologies for not having come before to congratulate her on her new son.

The rumor of Tatsudaiyu's initial opposition to the marriage spread quickly, and it was Tatsudaiyu himself who confirmed it, recognizing the hand of the cunning old man. He was standing and watching his second untangling a harpoon line and laying it ready in a tub.

"Never get impatient with a tangle," he said. "If you get stubborn and pull too hard, the tighter things get. Things must be untangled gently, otherwise you'll end up having to use a knife, and that does no good, does it? Treat a tangle with patience, otherwise you'll have to go back and start at the beginning."

For Tatsudaiyu, a man of few words around a boat, to have uttered such a monologue about a harpoon line had to have more than surface meaning. His second looked up at him, but Tatsudaiyu had turned away.

"So that's the way it was," the man thought, and went back to coiling the kinked-up line.

In a month or so, whatever it was that had been rankling folks had cleared. Saburo and Oyoshi were once again greeted with genuine warmth on the streets.

The Takigawa house was small, and Saburo and Oyoshi slept in the same room, with the child between them. Saburo never expressed his feelings, but few things gave him such pleasure as watching the baby suckle at Oyoshi's full, darkly nippled breast, and as time went on, in his heart the child, if not the mother, became his.

Chapter Thirteen

Jinsuke was writing a letter, leaning heavily on a low, rough table he had made from driftwood boards.

"The big black butterflies are playing among the scarlet blossoms. We have had heavy cloud and wind, and rain, and as usual it is very hot. I trust that you, sensei, are in good health although Edo is hot, and pray that everybody at your fine house in Edo is well . . ."

He put down the brush and rubbed his eyes, which smarted from trying to make letters in the weak yellow light of a single oil flame. He had always hated writing, right from the time when his parents had made him go to the little temple school in Taiji. He was also more than aware that his letters and words were far too crude to be read by an educated and sophisticated gentleman like Matsudaira Sadayori. However, his duty was to inform, and tomorrow he could smuggle a letter, through his teacher, out on a big junk that was leaving for Nagasaki in the morning. He dipped his brush in the ink again and dove straight into giving details. Size and number of the American ships, where the guns were, how many men he had counted on them. He described how boats had taken out gifts of food, from a feast prepared especially for the foreign admiral by the high official of Naha. The ill-mannered foreigner had refused to attend the feast, so the food was being sent out on boats to the tall black ships.

"The people here say that the foreigners intended to force their way into the palace at Shuri, even though the Ryukyu dowager and the young prince were ill. Some armed foreigners forced their way into a public meeting hall, and although the people were frightened, they did not actually harm anybody.

"Other men have long, sharp cleavers in scabbards at their sides, with a round guard over the handles. They have long guns that do not load from the muzzle, but from the back of the gun, which has no fuse . . ."

He dipped the brush again and wrote an angry sentence, but after he wrote it, he almost tore the letter up. But it was the truth, the Matsudaira sensei had told him to write only the truth, as he saw it.

"Those Satsuma soldiers have done nothing, and have stayed away, sending only the usual spies who inform if we go near the foreigners, while the officers just order us to stay away and hide. We men ignore them, because we want to see. The foreigners are totally unafraid and bold, and they laugh and smile a lot while the Satsuma samurai hide."

Apart from watching the ships, Jinsuke had been observing the goings-on in Naha, trying to watch and listen for what was happening ever since the ships had been sighted. Through a relative of Kinjo, Jinsuke had managed to get himself hired as a porter when a party of the foreigners made a trek across the island. The foreigners were such curious creatures, with their tight clothes, tubes for arms and legs, with nowhere for air to cool their bodies. Almost everything they did was amusing, their habits, loud voices, constant laughing and smiling, large, exaggerated gestures and bright red faces. However, as he carefully noted in his letter, their weapons were far more sophisticated than the matchlocks he had seen before. They put up pieces of wood or fallen fruit and shot at them with remarkable accuracy, and when Jinsuke later went to inspect, he found that the holes of the bullets went deep into the tree trunks where they placed their targets. One of the foreigners even shot a raven, quite far off and high in a tree, although why they did that was beyond Jinsuke's comprehension. The gentlemen who seemed to be in charge and most likely officers treated their men like boat mates, and one had even helped Jinsuke hoist up his load, and had smiled at him and slapped his shoulder in a gesture that had to be comradely. They certainly were difficult to understand, those foreigners. He wrote and wrote, and in the end he had a quite bulky package to hand over.

At the end of the letter he puzzled again for polite phrases, but he could not find them.

"And so have I seen and heard these things. To my respected master, from Jinsuke."

He folded the letter and slipped it into a package of oiled paper, tying it neatly. Then he blew out the oil lamp and went to his mats for a few hours of sleep. Tired as he was, his mind could not help wandering back to the sights, sounds, smells and people of Taiji.

Jinsuke rose before dawn to deliver the letter to another man who would see that it got aboard the junk. Then, as was his habit, he took a stroll along the beach, from where he could see the great black ships.

Had any of the Taiji people seen him here, they would not have recognized him. Apart from the even deeper mahogany of his tan, he now wore a single garment of brown cotton, tied with a sash. He no longer shaved the top of his head, and he wore his thick long hair secured at the top of his head by a pair of star-headed brass pins, thick and pointed, which, as Kinjo had taught him, could be very evil weapons. To any casual observer, he was Okinawan.

What might have seemed to be his most distinguishing feature, the lack of a left arm, had paradoxically given him more anonymity, because strangers did not want to stare at his affliction and did not look closely. Knowing eyes might have sensed a strength and freedom in his manner and gait that were out of place.

Three Satsuma officers were making their way along the beach. Jinsuke was not the object of their attention, for one of them was pointing to the boats returning from the biggest of the black ships. They were all talking excitedly, but although they were Japanese, their dialect was as unintelligible to the Taiji man as were the several languages of Okinawa. Not wanting to attract attention, Jinsuke sauntered back up the hot sands and made his way along a winding street, soon out of sight. The street was bordered with coral walls and was shaded by the broad leaves of palm and banana trees. A Naha citizen of rank, resplendent in salmon-colored robe and blue sash, and with silver pins in his hair, passed by Jinsuke without giving him a glance. Jinsuke began to hum a local tune. He was thirsty, but filled with vigor, and was looking forward to meeting Kinjo, who had come in on a rare visit to the city.

Sketching from the deck of the flagship *Susquehanna*, midshipman Charles Olderby inked in the figures of the three swordsmen who strolled along the shore. With their baggy

153

pantaloons and the awkward angles at which their swords stuck out from their hips, and the broad hats which protected their shaven pates from the hot sun, they were most exotic, and he tried to capture that in his drawing.

He did not consider himself an artist, but he did find that drawing helped to fix in his memory the many wonderful scenes and creations he had seen on this voyage. He worked carefully in the large leather-bound notebook of fine vellum that his father had given him. All officers kept logs and diaries, and these were all likely to be seen by the commodore, and the young midshipman fancied that careful drawing such as his might please him. At the end of this expedition, when all logs had to be handed over, Olderby would hope that someday he might retrieve his own record.

Olderby was a lanky boy, just eighteen, with sandy hair and skin much freckled by the tropic sun. His uniform and trousers felt hot, and he half wished that he could wear the looser-fitting white duck trousers and blouses that the sailors wore, or their broad-brimmed hats with the ribbons trailing down the back of the neck.

"Hey, that's not bad, Charles."

He turned to see Mr. Draper, one of the two daguerreotypists.

"Oh, it's just a scribble, a foolish hobby to keep me occupied."

Draper chuckled and slapped him on the back. "What's this, young fellow? You mean to tell me that you are not kept busy enough with daily drills?"

Olderby grinned. "Those I can do without thinking now. I am become an automaton in the service of Congress and the commodore. The drills do much for my body, but little for my mind now that I have learned right, left, port and starboard."

Discipline in the squadron had been tight. Boat drills, fire drills, battle drills—all keeping the Americans ready to face any emergency. There was some grumbling about it, partly because the islands were so peaceful, and the inhabitants, even if inhibited, seemed clean, courteous and quite unwarlike. The women were hidden away, apart from old crones, but there seemed to be no lack of alcoholic beverages ashore. And yet, despite the grumbling, the Americans knew that this was not yet Japan proper, even though there were some Japanese warriors around, and they had all heard of the fierceness of the Japanese, of what they had done in the past to missionaries and the odd sailor. Beheading, impaling,

154

crucifixion, burning, all kinds of horrors. Olderby glanced toward those three Japanese warriors on the shore and could imagine them coming for him, long swords raised, eyes coldly slanted, faces contorted with fanatic Oriental hate. He was glad of the drills.

"If you get a chance to go ashore," said Draper, "I'd be mighty pleased to show you our little operation. We have a small house near a village called Tumai. If constant surveillance by the curious won't bother you too much, we could take a little walk around. It's a delightful place, the neatest, cleanest community I've seen anywhere, and a far cry from China, mark you."

"Why, thank you, Mr. Draper," said Olderby. "I'll bear it in mind. Actually, I'm going ashore on June sixth, although I expect to be occupied then. The commodore is going to visit the palace."

"Even though the old queen is supposed to be sick?"

So everybody had heard that story too. Rumors spread quickly on ships.

"Perhaps he thinks the marine bands will brighten things up for her."

They both laughed.

Boat crews drew alongside. The men came aboard and stacked arms. The boats were raised on their davits and made secure. After being dismissed, Olderby heard one of the men speaking excitedly to a mate.

". . . Ever see such fish? The brightest blue you could imagine, and thousands of them! Tell me now, have you ever seen anything like that?"

The beauty of the islands seemed to affect them all, and Olderby longed for shore leave.

In the early morning of June 6, wind and rain lashed the surface of Naha harbor. Midshipman Olderby looked dismally at the rapidly hurrying clouds, anticipating the discomfort of a heavy, soaked uniform. However, by nine that morning, patches of blue sky appeared and the rain stopped. A signal was hoisted aboard the *Susquehanna* and from all the other ships the boats pushed off. After they had gone, the commodore's barge pushed off. By the time Commodore Perry had stepped ashore, two hundred marines, as well as artillery men, were standing at attention in the shade of a grove of trees beside the road that led to the palace.

Olderby's crew rested on their oars, watching the parade and the hundreds of natives who had come to stare.

"Makes a guy think Old Bruin is off to the palace to marry the old gal, not just to have tea."

Another oarsman made a far more ribald comment and there was a welter of sniggers.

"Silence in the boat!" called the young midshipman. "Any more nonsense from you men and you'll be on report!"

He turned his face away so as not to betray the suspicion of a grin, and found himself under the steady, unwavering gaze of a native, a muscular man, taller than the rest, and with no left arm. Olderby met the stare and for an instant felt he had been here before, in another life. Despite the sun, which now shone warmly through the racing clouds, Olderby shuddered.

Jinsuke turned away to look at the armed men under the trees, standing like wooden dolls, in straight rows. He thought of the first time he had seen foreigners in a boat, off Taiji. Those fellows were not so neat, but none of them looked like mere boys. But then, he thought, whalers grew to be men fast.

An important person wearing a long coat with a lot of gold on it and a large hat shaped like a cut watermelon walked slowly down the lines of men, none of whom even bowed to him, just staring straight ahead, holding their long guns with the knives at the end. Behind this man was an officer who actually had his sword drawn, holding it upright in his right hand, the blade facing forward in a ready position, as if he might cut at his superior.

It's the barbarian admiral, thought Jinsuke, seeing how the important one and his two officers would stop from time to time and stare closely at the soldiers in line.

All of a sudden, they started to shout out, almost like dogs barking. This at first startled everybody, but at the shouting the lines of foreigners began a kind of stiff-legged dance, forming lines and starting a procession. The procession had two cannon and big flags, followed by a group of several men carrying drums and huge instruments of glittering brass. The cacophony was astonishing!

Now the admiral, for surely that was who he was, mounted a big chair carried by eight Chinese. It was a garish thing, painted, and hung with trimmings of blue and red. On either side of it marched huge, heavily armed fellows. Behind the chair came more men in long coats with silver buttons and with swords hanging at their sides. Behind them came coolies, carrying gifts.

As if the loudness of the first group of musicians wasn't

enough, another gang followed, music blaring, drums banging, with one enormous thing making sounds that seemed ten times louder and many times deeper than a conch-shell signal.

The lines of soldiers now moved, all together, in exactly the same timing, left, right, left, right, while their right arms swung with big, funny movements. With guns and long knives held at their shoulders, they looked like farmers going off to their fields with mattocks.

The noise, the shouting, the tramp of feet, the way the soldiers looked straight ahead and moved so stiffly—everything was almost overwhelming in its newness, but Jinsuke felt no fear. This procession was fun, new, exciting. It was nothing like the procession he had seen of the daimyo, back in Wakayama, where he and the other people were required to prostrate themselves under fear of death. So, all these soldiers and officers and guns had come, but they hadn't hurt anybody, had they? Was Matsudaira sensei wrong about invasion?

Jinsuke tagged on behind the shouting, jostling mob that followed the procession, his eye on the admiral, up above in his gaudy chair.

Olderby's chest filled when he heard the proud music of the *Mississippi* and *Susquehanna* bands, and the marching of the marines was magnificent. The natives were surely much impressed! He looked back to where the one-armed man had been standing, but he was gone.

"All right, men," he said, "pull the boat up. Mason, you stay with it. Make sure the natives don't touch anything. You others may take your leisure in the shade." He pointed toward the trees, and then, trying to force some fierceness into his young voice, said, "And don't think you can sneak off for some French leave, because you can't."

The men pulled the boat a little way up the beach and headed for the shade, where crews from other boats were already relaxing and chatting, beginning their wait for the return of the procession and for news of what happened at the palace.

One of the older lieutenants was there by himself, sitting and smoking a cheroot.

"May I join you?" asked Olderby. The officer looked up with a faint smile. Lean and fit though the man was, Olderby saw that his face was deeply lined and tanned. He looked to be in his middle thirties.

"Why not? Take a seat. You're off the flagship, right? My name's Grant, from the *Mississippi* . . . gunnery officer." He held out a leathery hand and Olderby shook it, then, carefully adjusting his sword, sat down on the goat-cropped grass beside him.

"An impressive show, don't you think, sir? That should impress the locals."

Grant took out a silver case and offered it to the midshipman, who, embarrassed, shook his head and thanked him.

"Oh, yeah? I guess you're too young. Let me tell you now, a little smoke can help a man relax, but it still keeps him alert, not like alcohol." He took a long puff and sent three perfect smoke rings up toward the dark green branches. The din of cicadas droned in crescendo. Fishermen's *sabani*, slender as kayaks, knifed the incredible blues of the waters beyond the beach.

"If the Old Man gets his way, and the navy sets up a coaling station for the runs between California and Shanghai, I would not object at all to spending a little time here. Sure is pretty country. Do you hunt?"

"Not much, a few ducks and geese in the fall . . . we live close to an estuary, the Connecticut River, you know? Close to New Haven. And when I was a boy, the odd rabbit or two."

Grant smiled again. "When you were a boy, eh? Well, there are plenty of wild boar here, saw tracks myself. The fishing is good too, I'll bet."

Olderby answered enthusiastically. "Oh yes, never have I seen so many lovely fish, such colors! Those corals too, they're magnificent!"

"Yeah, it's pretty country, sure enough, and it makes me think these folks would go a long way to hold onto it, and wouldn't take too kindly to the notion that somebody might come along and grab it. Not that we came here to grab, mind you." He blew another pair of smoke rings, eyes scanning the beach. "But they don't know that now, do they? No, sir! Vigilance is the word, mister, vigilance!"

Olderby looked along the beach, seeing only a few curious brown-skinned men and boys in simple, short gowns and bare feet. It looked peaceful enough to him.

"Ever heard what happened to Captain Cook, the limey explorer?"

"You mean the man who discovered Australia, New Zealand, the Antarctic, and the Hawaiian islands? Oh yes, I've read all his journals."

158

"Then you know how he met his fate at the tender age of fifty-one, killed by hostile natives on the lovely beaches of Hawaii, and him with men and a boat right there . . . a limey navy boat, limey navy men. Now just reflect on that, those Hawaiian islands sure are pretty too, right? So we must not let prettiness throw a veil over vigilance."

Grant stubbed the cheroot into the ground, got to his feet, and brushed pieces of grass off his trousers.

"What I mean to say is, you get right back down to your boat and make sure that idle son of a whore is alert, and not lying on a gunwale toasting his socks to the noonday sun!"

Red-faced, Olderby jumped to his feet, threw a hasty salute, and stormed down the beach.

Olderby was mindful of the warnings he'd been given on the beach, and so he threw himself into the drills. Ships and men were always at battle readiness. In truth, the young man found the drills exciting, and in them he always imagined the smells, sounds, thrills and colors of naval battle.

After one drill, one of the marine officers spoke to a group of men, Olderby listening on the fringes.

"Now you men have seen those Japanese junks, and you've seen those boats with the many oars and the rowers all standing up and singing as they scull. Now which do you suppose presents the greater threat?"

When somebody suggested it was the junks, the officer scoffed.

"No, not at all. We would just set our sights right between those great ugly eyes they've got painted on them and blow them to smithereens. There'd be bits of armored hobgoblins all over the ocean. No, no, it's the boats." He paused for effect, everybody listening, knowing that this man had seen action in Mexico, and off the coast of Africa with the commodore. "You see, those boats move swift, and quiet if they want, and at night, around a careless ship, they could be up the sides like termites, and be aboard with their knives, swords, spears and such before half of the jolly Jacks had pulled their pants on. So we keep drilling, and we keep watchful. We never know what might happen when we go to the main islands of Japan. Don't be misled by the old-fashioned weapons, those fellows are fighters. If they get defeated in battle they'd rather slice their bellies open than face the shame of it. So we'll keep on our toes, day and night. Mark my words, Old Bruin knows what he's doin'."

One Saturday night the crews were beat to quarters for a night drill. The decks and the wind-bellied sails were illuminated in the bright blue glare of magnesium flares. The men rushed to their stations under the crisp orders of the officers, while lantern signals flashed between the flagship and the smaller sloop of war. Olderby, who commanded a crew of one of the sixty-four-pounder Paixhans guns, looked toward the stack of grapeshot in bags and thought again about small boats swarming around the ship. They were ready. The expedition had come in peace, but if the Japanese wanted a fight, they would surely get one. The Americans were disciplined and tough, and aboard the most modern of warships. He felt proud to be American.

On June 14, 1853, the whaling barque *Midas* was just north of the Bonins, having left that morning after calling into the islands for water, vegetables, sweet potatoes and a few goats. It was the black coal smoke from the navy ship that was first spotted by the lookout. Captain Riggs thought this strange. They had not spotted whales for a week. He felt puzzled and cheated at the luck of this other whaler, to be firing up his try pots. But, when his telescope picked up the hulls and colors of the ships and Captain Riggs knew them to be U.S. Navy, he almost forgot his dignity and whooped. Congressman Pratt, his old friend, had told him that a powerful expedition was being dispatched to force the mikado into terms of friendliness with the United States. He turned to his second-in-command, Tovey Jacks.

"Mr. Jacks, y' spy that? The only navy, am I right, to have thrashed the British at sea. Let's hope they'll give those arrogant, murdering heathen ashore a taste of powder!"

"On the Bonins, sir?"

"No, man, they'll be heading for the Japans. That's the mighty *Susquehanna,* bound on a mission to make those islands safe for the likes of us. Ten years late, but better late than never." The captain raised the telescope and looked at the second ship, whose hull was now barely visible.

"Did you say the *Susquehanna,* sir? The son of a friend of mine is aboard her. His father's a whaling captain too, out of New Haven, but he pushed the lad into the navy. Says there's no future in whaling."

Still squinting with one eye close at the brass telescope, the captain snorted. "Nonsense. What's the fellow's name? A whaling man, you say?"

"Aye, sir, name of John Olderby, originally from England, like me."

"With no intended disrespect for our erstwhile lords, enemies and vanquished foes, the man's a fool." He put the telescope down and almost smiled. "Even though the smarter ones are usually those who had the good sense to come to America." He folded the telescope with a snap and held it in both hands behind his back.

"Mr. Jacks, you and I will share a glass of sherry tonight to celebrate this sighting, and the men can have an extra ration of grog."

"Aye, aye, sir!"

As he went down to the foredeck, Jacks remembered his own encounter at sea with Japanese, and wished them no harm at all.

Chapter Fourteen

The Tsutaya was a quiet inn on the banks of the Kamo River. From his room Sadayori could watch townsfolk fishing, wide hats shielding their faces; they cast with rods for the plentiful small fish, which brought almost as many white egrets as they did humans. It was hot and humid, but a breeze fanned the room, and Sadayori could look across the river and beyond to the pine- and cedar-forested slopes of Higashiyama and to the peak of Nyoigatake. On those slopes, at the end of the Obon festival, great mystical characters were set aflame. They were the ideograms for the lotus sutra, for the holy vessel, the other-world gate, for greatness, left and right, and they guided and summoned the spirits of the dead who return, just briefly at Obon, to visit homes and loved ones. Recalling those blazing characters, and what they meant in this capital of the Son of Heaven, Sadayori softly clapped his hands twice, and bowed in the direction of the mountain.

To the left was Mount Hie. The trees silhouetted along the rims of the hills were like the fur on a badger's back. Here and there, below the hills, blue-gray in green, curved the many roofs of temples and shrines.

Just below the balcony was a tiny garden with a rock pool, beside which stood a few clumps of late-blooming iris, white, purple, pale blue and yellow, flower of lords, so common in the gardens of the nobility. Tall in form, graceful, slim, with full petals unfolding like the secrets of a silken woman, the irises reminded Sadayori of vanished joys. The soft accents of the maid interrupted his reveries.

"Yes!" he called, and the door slid open. On her knees in the corridor, the young girl bowed.

"A guest has arrived," she announced.

"Please bring him here," he said, and moved away from the window. Soon a wide-shouldered, stocky man in his thirties bowed into the room, holding his sheathed sword in his left hand.

"Ah, Itoh-san, you look as if you have traveled far. Come in, please, make yourself comfortable."

The man had not shaved for days and his beard showed as black stubble. Under his eyes were bluish half moons of fatigue and strain, but in his eyes there was no tiredness, just blank but alert agates in the deep tan of his face.

"I was not followed," he said.

Sadayori smiled. "And these walls have no ears. But come, let us sit by the window, the breeze and the sounds of the river are so cooling." And would, was the implied meaning, disguise the sound of their voices.

Sadayori noticed the slightest hesitation in the man before he took his long sword and placed it on the deer-horn rack beside the early summer scroll that hung in the alcove. The visitor accepted a cushion by the window and began to fan himself. His eyes traversed the opposite bank, noting every fisherman.

"Please excuse me." Again, the soft Kyoto accents of the maid, bringing a tray with cooled grain tea and sweet bean cakes. As she placed the tray beside him, Itoh's eyes followed her, though not with the hunger of a man, but with cold wariness.

"Your first visit to Kyoto?" asked Sadayori, waiting for his guest to take tea first.

"No," came the answer, almost rude in bluntness. Sadayori took no offense. He understood the man, had met him across clashing practice swords at a fencing school in Edo. Itoh Hirosada was a Satsuma man, one of the warlike and secretive clan who controlled Kyushu to the south.

The fencing school was open to men of all clans, otherwise their meeting would have been most unlikely. Both Sadayori and Itoh had their own clan styles, the techniques of which were generally kept secret from others. A second and more important point of contact for the two samurai was that Itoh had been another of the students of Sakuma Zosan, in Edo. Sadayori watched him.

"The city has slept for a long time," he said, "yet its dreams are those of early morning, full of changes and promise." Itoh grunted and drank his tea, not sipping it politely, but draining it like a coolie. He was typical of many

Satsuma warriors, who resented the control of the Tokugawa *bakufu*, and had submitted to the shogunate only after the devastating battle of Sekigahara, two hundred fifty-three years before. Tokugawa Ieyasu, at the head of eighty thousand men, faced a hundred thirty thousand and left thirty thousand of his opponents dead on the field. It was the pivotal battle in the history of the nation.

The Satsuma clan, with their notorious secret police, were suspicious of outsiders. They were exremely dangerous enemies, and with their virtual monopoly on the sugar market, their war chest was considerable.

"I do not enjoy Kyoto," said Itoh, with surprising frankness, even for him. "There is too much inbreeding, too much intrigue around the court, too much empty conceit. It is degenerate. You know, and I know, that this is not the time for furthering selfish desires. It is the time for steel, both in the heart and in the hand."

Sadayori nodded, and from his sleeve he produced a long letter. He unfolded it and with a slight bow said, "What you say is indeed true. Allow me to read you a personal letter I have received from a friend.

" ' . . . One of these black ships is called the *Mississippi*. It has three tall masts which carry many sails that are skillfully manipulated to use the wind best. This ship, and one other like it, can also move without wind or oars. On either side they have huge wheels, like the wheels of a water mill. These revolve through the might of great machines hidden inside the ship, from which smoke pours from chimneys in the deck, just behind the water wheels, toward the back of the ships. There are many armed men on the ships and I have made a list of those I counted. The men are dressed mostly the same, in either white or drab colors. The ones in white scramble high in the masts like monkeys, and I have seen men with guns up in the masts, so they can shoot down from a height. Their clothes are clean, and the men respond immediately to the orders of their officers. They carry long guns to which are attached long knives or short swords, so the guns become killing spears. The men who appear to be officers carry swords and pistols that can fire six times without stopping. Other men have long sharp cleavers in scabbards at their sides, with a round guard over the handles. They have long guns that do not load from the muzzle, but from the back of the gun, which has no fuse but a small hammer, while powder and ball are in metal tubes, like small pieces of cut bamboo. I have seen them fire and reload

164

with speed and accuracy. The bullets go very deep into the trunk of a tree. The ships bear large numbers of cannon, which I put on my list. The two biggest ships, the ones with water wheels, carry cannon of very large size . . ."

Sadayori paused and looked up. Itoh's eyes betrayed just a touch of surprise, and some anger. He smiled. "Your spy is good. We would use such a man if we did not kill him first."

Sadayori smiled back. "Itoh-san, these ships are not barbarian whalers, not like the scum who polluted Oshima, off Kushimoto, some five years ago. Neither are they soft-bellied merchants. They will not be easily driven away or provoked into foolhardy actions. These are the warships of a powerful nation and they have come for definite reasons."

Itoh produced a paper from his sleeve and, with difficulty in pronouncing the foreign words, began to read from the syllabic *katakana* characters.

" '. . . *Mississippi, Susquehanna, Saratoga, Supply, Caprice, Plymouth*; those are the names of those ships. They come from America, via China. As your spy tells you, two of them have huge engines which run on coal and can drive the ships against the wind or current. They are far too strong for any of our ships or guns. They have been moving in and out of Naha, but they express intentions to come to Edo."

"That is serious!"

"Yes. They intend to present a letter to the shogun."

"Do you think that is a ruse? Will they attack?"

"No. They are powerful ships and could flatten a town or destroy any number of our ships. Perhaps they could be overwhelmed by fire ships, or by numbers, or by cunning, but we would incur huge losses. Their immediate intention, however, does not seem to be war. Theirs is not a force of invasion. They claim that their intentions are peaceful, and although they have been rude and barbaric as is their nature, they have not been violent."

"Peaceful intentions?" said Sadayori with emotion in his voice. "What do you believe is the significance of them raising a flag on a hill in the Ryukyus? I have read Dutch literature about foreign ways of conquest, and such is the custom when they have defeated another nation, or when they claim the land for themselves! Even on Ogasawara they have raised their flag! Don't you see? They challenge us!"

"Perhaps. On our islands down south they have sent shore parties to look deep into the country, but these parties have been small, and they are watched every step of the way. I agree that the situation is intolerable and an insult, but I feel more anger at *bakufu* stupidity in not letting our nation develop a navy with ships equal to battle with them, to sink them before they put their big ugly feet on our soil."

Sadayori was a Tokugawa samurai, bound in allegiance to the shogun and the *bakufu,* yet his lack of protest at these words, and the pause of silence after them, signified agreement, but with embarrassment, as the words touched very difficult points for him. Also, Jinsuke, his man, had been one of the coolies who had walked with an American party. He didn't want to mention this. Jinsuke had accompanied four foreign officers, four enlisted men, four Chinese coolies. They traversed the main island on foot, making drawings and taking notes all the way. It alarmed Sadayori that Jinsuke reported the strangers being especially interested in old fortifications and castles. He was even more alarmed that other boats had been rowing freely around the harbor at Naha, making measurements of the depths of water, charting the approaches, and doing all the things that he had recommended so many times to the *bakufu* but which had been ignored. Surely, he thought, such diligent studies were a prelude to invasion.

Jinsuke's long letter went on to describe how the squadron of American ships had arrived toward the end of May. Officials of the town of Naha had gone out to greet them, under their white parasols, even as the Satsuma junks had circled the ships before heading to Kagoshima with the news.

The following day, four boatloads of presents had been sent out, including a bullock, pigs, a white goat, chickens and vegetables. The ships refused to accept the gifts. A few days later the regent had gone aboard one of the black ships to try to meet the commander, a most aloof man, who kept himself out of view. When the regent and his entourage had gone aboard, they—and the whole city of Naha—were startled by the roar of three guns, although this had been a signal of honor, without cannon balls.

All in all, Sadayori probably knew more about the ships and what had happened than Itoh. He knew too that the Satsuma had done nothing, and there would be much need to save face among them. Jinsuke's information had reached Sadayori quickly, via a route that involved the whalers of the Goto Islands, on the outer coast of Kyushu, north of the Satsuma domains, thence to a certain doctor and scholar in Nagasaki, and from there with a consignment of herbal medicine to Kyoto.

The two warriors continued to sit in silence, listening to the river. Itoh obviously would have liked to read the letter himself, but he kept his eyes away from it. Sadayori reached for his cup and sipped tea again.

"You know of course what this all can mean?"

"War," said Itoh. His fists bunched. "It must mean war!" Itoh's voice trailed off.

"War, yes, eventually, but if we want to win, then the nation must be united."

The Satsuma man snorted. "Under the *bakufu*?"

Sadayori showed no reaction to the derision. "Under those generals and men who are capable of achieving victory," he said, "under men who fully understand the nature of this threat. We, the *bushi,* cannot let our land be polluted by these hairy savages, chewed like a scrap of meat by foreign dogs!" He paused. "You know what happened in China. . ."

"The English and their opium, yes, of course we know better than any of you, but the Middle Kingdom was easy prey."

The two men lapsed into eloquent silence again. What of Japan? What of a warrior class that had not seen war for centuries? What of a so-called generalissimo who was a pampered, sick weakling? What of Edo councillors who thought of little but their own faces and necks? What of daimyos who cared only for their own small fiefs and rice incomes? Sadayori broke the silence.

"Yes," he said, "but despite those fops who surround His Divine Majesty here in Kyoto, I do not think we Japanese have entirely lost our national pride and character. However, we must unite. It is the first step."

"The first step," said Itoh harshly, "is guns, cannon, great ships, and men trained to use them!"

"And what of Bushido? What of the sword?" asked Sadayori gently.

"Of course, of course, the sword! The sword is our soul! But for centuries now we have used guns from Tanegashima, simple weapons in comparison to the foreign weapons nowadays, but those guns too have a place in war, and we must modernize and adapt, and gain weapons equal to those of the foreigners. The men who lead will be samurai, preserving the inner spirit of the sword, which, as you know full well, is self-sacrifice. Regard yourself, Matsudaira-*dono,* you carry the two swords and know their uses, and you are an expert in halberd, spear and other noble weapons. But I know too that you are an expert on Western weapons, artillery and fortifications. You are a brave but careful man, the best kind of warrior, especially in these days. You choose a place like this"—Itoh looked around with a faint smile— "because the river is at your back, and the approaches to the inn are a single, long and narrow pathway with high walls, easily defended by a man with a spear, which I'm sure you have somewhere, and hard for attackers to use their blades. Yes, easily defended with a spear . . . where is it?"

Sadayori laughed. "There is an excellent but venerable spear on the wall of the main room. This family is descended from the Fujiwara clan, long ago."

They both laughed, then looked out of the window, catching sight of the very moment an egret speared a frog in the shallows.

"Shiro sagi ya"—White egret—said Sadayori, making up the beginning of a haiku on the spot. *"Yari wa kasu na yo"*—Don't lend your spear.

And then, turning to Itoh with a serious face, he drew the character for the Land of Darkness and made a pun on the words for *frog* and *restoration*.

"Yomi gaeru"—Hades frog.

Itoh clapped with delight, then pursed his lips and screwed up his eyes.

"Naga yari ya"—Long spear—he began. *"Sasu mono wa nashi"*—There is naught to pierce.

Itoh opened his eyes with an almost boyish grin and returned the frog pun with another frog pun that also meant "return." *"Washi kaeru"*—So I'll return!

Such silly puns in poetry were the fashion of Edo, and the two warriors, friends though their allegiances were to rival factions, laughed with memories and with the relief of broken tension.

"Let us call for sake," said Sadayori, clapping his hands loudly for the maid. Then he became serious again.

"The central government has many difficult decisions to face, and to repeal ancient laws too hastily would be folly. However, there are men among the shogun's councillors who, even though they are bound to uphold the ways of our land and its purity, can see that Japan has an immediate need for foreign weapons and techniques. We will need to borrow from the barbarians, no matter how much the idea appals us. In time we will become a stronger, more united nation and can make such things ourselves. We need knowledge, and the quest for knowledge should not be against the law, as it is now. The law is outdated and wrong for the times."

A veil seemed to have been lifted from Itoh's eyes, as if their game of puns and the laughter had changed him. His deep brown pupils gleamed.

"That is a dangerous thing for anybody to say. It is even more dangerous for a Tokugawa man."

"I say it because it is true, and perhaps I know you followed the teachings of Sakuma sensei. A man like him is a true patriot, not a traitor, and a man like you, Itoh-san, who chose him to be your teacher, is no fool."

"Still, that is not the current policy of the *bakufu* and . . ."

Sadayori silenced him with a sign.

"The egrets and herons catch more fish than hooks, in my experience," Itoh went on.

"Excuse me, you called?" came the soft voice of the maid outside.

"Bring sake, cooled sake," said Sadayori, "and something simple to go with it."

"Hai," said the maid. The two men sat silently as she retreated down the corridor. Itoh continued.

"And you are a Tokugawa man. You risk being accused of treason."

"The *bakufu* is not one man, but many men, with many minds. Things will change. For the past three years I have been studying the language of the Dutch, and it has opened my eyes to many things. The advances they have made, the Europeans, in all technical and medical fields is outstanding and exciting. If they can do it, then our nation, which has purity and force, can do better. We are like gunpowder, waiting for the fire that will make us explode in a maelstrom and blow invaders back from whence they came."

"You would have dealings with the barbarians?" said Itoh quietly.

"Restricted ones, yes, for weapons and expertise and books. We should make the Dutch bring technicians to Nagasaki to teach promising young men directly. They should be under strict control, of course, as they are now, but there must be a greater flow of knowledge."

"Would that not disrupt society?" asked Itoh.

"For what reason do we *bushi* carry swords? Is it not to defend society?"

Itoh looked at him for a long time.

"Matsudaira-san, I know what a good swordsman you are, and I know that in the town dojo you keep your real skills under cover. Your reputation is remarkable, I've heard both Sakuma sensei and Yoshida Shoin of Choshu praise you. Yes indeed, many good things are said about you, Tokugawa man or not."

Sadayori laughed again at Itoh's bluntness.

"Matsudaira-*dono*, I believe you to be a man of honor, and when pressed, you would place His Divine Majesty and the purity of this land before all else. Let us make no intrigue between us, but let us both vow that when the time comes, we will die for the Son of Heaven, and for our land."

The maid appeared again, bringing a tray of dew-cooled cucumbers and a dish of miso paste to dip them in, as well as a large flagon of sake, chilled in the deep well, and promises of more tidbits now being prepared in the kitchen. She knelt beside the two men and poured sake, then, sensing that they wished to go on talking, she left. Evening colors began to tint the sky, and soon came the muffled boom of temple bells.

His forbidding countenance breaking up into a smile, Itoh unfolded his legs and switched to an informal, cross-legged position, exposing thick, hairy calves and shins whitened with a dozen scars.

"I've never been comfortable with a Tokugawa retainer before meeting you," he said.

Sadayori inclined his head at the compliment and reached out to pour him more sake.

"Tell me," said Itoh after a hearty sip, "do you practice your swordsmanship regularly?"

"Daily," said Sadayori, "like bowel movements. I find myself uncomfortable if I neglect it."

Itoh guffawed. "Bowel movements, that's good! You might start a new style, call it 'The New Matsudaira Bowel Movement Way,' and you could tell them that not only would it make their bowel movements regular and healthy, but that when faced with this style, opponents shit themselves!" He roared at his own joke and slapped his thigh. "What kind of techniques, I wonder?" He laughed again.

"Oh, the main thing in such a school would be the *kiai*, as well as a good deep stance," joked Sadayori. Itoh laughed again, and then got the double joke, a little sarcastic jibe about the Satsuma clan's own special style, Jigen Ryu, which utilized a particularly bloodcurdling fighting yell, or *kiai*. He stared at Sadayori, almost on the verge of taking offense, Kyushu men being known for lightning changes of mood. But the cloud passed quickly and he hooted with laughter.

170

"Oh yes, the *kiai*! And the deep stance! Oh yes!" He wiped his eyes, took another swig of sake and put the cup down.

"Would you care to practice with me? Not a challenge, you understand, but a practice, as we used to in Edo, with no watchers."

"I would consider it an honor," said Sadayori, with a slight bow.

"Tomorrow morning?" Sadayori nodded. "Good, good," said Itoh, then, grinning again, "but excuse me for asking, do you perform the bowel movements before or after swordsmanship?"

"Usually before," said Sadayori, "and sometimes after, but never during."

Itoh roared with merriment again, and reached over to pour sake for the man he knew, despite everything, would be his friend.

The next morning, before it got too hot, on a piece of bare ground near where the Kamo River was joined by another tributary, they practiced. A slight morning drizzle mingled with the sweat that ran freely from their faces. Sadayori's wrists were tingling from sharp but controlled strokes from Itoh's wooden practice sword, and Itoh's nose was slightly swollen from a powerful and barely blocked downstroke which brought the tip of Sadayori's weapon down past his forehead. Both of them used mainly the style they had studied in Edo, and neither betrayed his own clan's fighting techniques. They parried, stepped back, parried again. They practiced for over an hour. Wagtails bobbed along the river, and swallows dipped for insects.

"Enough," called Sadayori, and Itoh backed off, lowered the practice sword, brought it to his left shoulder, and bowed.

"Thank you indeed," he said, "that was the best practice I have had since I left Kagoshima." For Itoh, that was high praise.

They undid the white cords that tied up the sleeves of their kimonos and wiped their faces with the cloths that had been tied around their heads. As he retrieved his swords, which had been resting under the eaves of a small wayside shrine, Sadayori spoke.

"I am hungry and sweaty. Will you not come back to the inn for rice and soup, a bath perhaps?"

"I would like to, but it is best if we are not seen together too much. Some other time, yes, perhaps in Kyushu. Thank

171

you, but I'll just wash myself in the river and find some place to eat. You and I will meet again, without a doubt."

With their swords back in their sashes, they strolled along the path, which was bordered by high bamboo. A large hornet, its body as thick as a man's thumb, buzzed near them. With a swipe of the wooden sword he carried loosely in his hand, Itoh killed it. He did it unthinkingly, but Sadayori caught the movement, and thought to himself that Itoh was a sly one, for he had also studied Nitten Ichi Ryu, the style of the famed Miyamoto Musashi, who fought with a sword in each hand.

"Of course you do not have to tell me," said Itoh casually, "but at the same time I am curious. Who is this spy of yours in Okinawa?"

Sadayori laughed. "You are sometimes as subtle as an iron club. Now really, if I told you, he would no longer be a spy, would he?"

"If he is a member of our clan, it would be of serious concern to me. But if he is not, and works only for you, and not against us, it would not be in my interest to turn him in to our authorities."

"This man works solely for me. He does not gather information about the Satsuma clan, and neither is he from any part of Kyushu."

"Is that so?" said Itoh, with feigned innocence. "Then the man is an outsider or an Okinawan. Those Okinawans are passionate people, not always understanding the benefits of our protection."

"He is a man of great courage," said Sadayori, "courage that caused great loss and change to his affairs. He is a brave though perhaps simple man, and he is working to find more truth about the barbarians. I need that knowledge. I feel obliged to him, and would see no harm come to him."

Itoh stopped, turning to Sadayori with one hand on his shoulder. "In that case this Itoh Hirosada would like no harm to come to him either. Tell me who he is, and I will do what I can for him when the time comes. Should he be betrayed soon, then you know my name and where I can be found."

Sadayori looked deep into the other man's eyes, and saw that despite his studied blankness, there was a bright intelligence, as well as honesty and stubbornness, betrayed in the line of the man's jaw.

"He is a whaler who lost his left arm to a shark. Even though he lost the arm, he picked up a harpoon and killed

172

the shark. He is a man who understands ships and the sea, winds, waves and whales. His loyalty is to me. My hope is for him to go aboard a foreign ship, a whaling ship, and to bring back more details about the way they think and work, and fight."

"Hah! You have talked with Manjiro!" exclaimed Itoh.

"In secret, yes," said Sadayori.

Itoh shook his head. "I told them we should keep Manjiro in Kagoshima. Never matter. What is your man's name?"

"He does not tell me the name he uses in Okinawa, but at home he was called Jinsuke."

"A Koza man?"

Sadayori smiled. So Itoh knew far more about the fiefdom of Kii than he had shown last night.

"No, from Taiji."

"Ah yes, long ago, in the Goto Islands, we had Taiji men come to teach net whaling. Good men."

"His name is my honor," said Sadayori.

"And mine too. I will not betray him," said the Satsuma warrior, "but I would ask, please, to share any information that might harm Satsuma."

Sadayori nodded.

At the end of the path they bid sayonara, both knowing full well that the tides that pulled at Japan might in the future cause them to be either foes or allies, on a battlefield, or perhaps in some darkened alleyway or deserted dueling site. Still, Sadayori felt that Jinsuke the whaler had found a new guardian, one who had easier access to the islands of Ryukyu. Later that day Sadayori left, on horseback, for Edo.

Chapter Fifteen

An American sailor leaned down and swiped through the rope with his cutlass. He grinned at the men in the boat below, then with a hand from his mates clambered back over the bulwarks of his own ship. A growl of protest went up from the Japanese boat crew, but Sadayori and his companion, who both stood in the bow with their light lacquered helmets shielding their eyes, said nothing. A few strokes brought the boat around to the bow of the great ship. Men seized hold of the chains and several of the thirty-man crew, all naked except for their loincloths, looked to the officers for direction. Sadayori said nothing. These were not his men, and he had come because he wanted to see the ship at close quarters.

"Climb," said the other samurai. Three of the crewmen climbed up the big chains, but at the top the foreigners faced them with pistols, cutlasses and pikes. Sadayori spoke softly, without turning his head or altering his expression.

"They seem determined to keep us off," he said, thinking that these actions were pointless and childish, and writhing inside with embarrassment at the antics of his countrymen, who, typically, were turning the arrival of the black ships into a kind of festival, with nobody really able to take command and organize the right kind of attack to seize a ship, or burn it.

The samurai next to Sadayori cursed and called the three men back, and they let the boat drift off. Above them, the high sides of the boat loomed out of the water like the ramparts of a castle in a moat, and its masts above seemed so high that they poked at the clouds. With muskets in that

174

rigging, thought Sadayori, we'd get picked off with ease. The only way to take the ship would be a mass attack, at night.

Other Japanese boats sped out to the ships, their crews chanting at the sculling oars. None of them would have any success in fastening a line.

A conch sounded. Sadayori turned and saw yet another boat, with the pennant of the vice-governor, Nagashima Saborosuke, flying at its stern. As it passed, Sadayori spotted the familiar figure of Hori Tatsunosuke, a samurai whom Sadayori had met on various occasions, in Edo, Kyoto and Nagasaki.

The vice-governor's boat came alongside the ship, but the Americans still refused to lower a gangway, and the two dignitaries were reduced to shouting up at them. Finally, voices hoarse, they persuaded the foreigners to lower the gangway and the two samurai made their way up it.

Once on the deck they read from a scroll. It was in French. The only Japanese really competent in the English of marine affairs was Manjiro, and the anti-foreign faction did not trust him, as he had lived with Americans for ten years, and they thought his sympathies would lean toward them. The scroll was an order telling the Americans to go away. They ignored it, of course.

Japanese boats were now swarming around the four ships. Shoreward, the headlands and hills of Sagami were pimpled with forts. In the distance the perfect cone of Fuji was clearly visible. The ships were anchored off Uraga, on the western shores of the bay of Edo. Uraga, the customs checkpoint for all junks coming to the great city, was as usual busy with ships, scudding about their business, their crews gawking at the unfamiliar shapes of the American vessels. It was an hour or so before sunset.

The crew of Sadayori's boat sculled slowly, keeping close to the big ship, and it was not long before the vice-governor came to the side and shouted down to them.

"Keep away from the ship!" he called.

"My orders were to watch the ship, and that is what I will do," muttered the other samurai with Sadayori.

"Just move a little farther off," said Sadayori. "Should fighting start, your crew can maneuver into position easily."

Sadayori writhed in fury inside. There was no battle plan, despite the thousands of recommendations he had been making over the years. They had done nothing but argue, even though the authorities had had ample warning that the black ships were coming.

"I regret to cause trouble, but I have business ashore. I must ask you to take me there," said Sadayori. He was aboard this boat at the orders of the vice-governor, and the young samurai in charge resented it. With a curt nod he shouted an order to the boatswain, and they turned for shore. Perhaps relieved that this stern-faced, tight-lipped samurai from Kii was leaving, he posed a question.

"What do you think? Should we attack?"

"Not without a battle plan and trained sea ninja, not without special-mission ships loaded with black powder and oil. We don't have cannon of enough size and range to fight them otherwise. Do you have any special orders?"

"No. Just to watch. We have sleeping mats, quilted jackets, food and water. We will stay out here all night, although nobody seems to know what to do."

"I can give you one small bit of advice. If fighting starts, get under the guns as quickly as possible, or they'll slaughter all of you in minutes."

Sadayori jumped ashore and watched the boat back off again. He made a slight bow and turned to walk up and inspect the fortifications. Sadayori was here as a special advisor to Ii Naosuke, who now represented the top daimyo in control of the senior *bakufu* posts. Ii Naosuke was the strongman of the *bakufu* and he favored opening the country for the same reasons Sadayori espoused. However, the news of the arrival of the black ships had thrown the *bakufu* into great turmoil, with Ii Naosuke and certain other powerful daimyos being at loggerheads. Tokugawa Nariaki of Mito was the leader of a faction that wanted immediate war. *Bakufu* officials asked for advice, appealing not only to the imperial court, but to all of the daimyos, including the *tozama,* or "outside," lords. They were snowed under with seven hundred memorials. Some advocated giving in to Perry's demands. Some wanted to maintain seclusion but avoid war. Some wanted to attack immediately, believing that although initial defeats might be suffered, in the end the foreigners would be driven away. Ii Naosuke, and Sadayori, knew they would not.

It was growing dark. Signal rockets streaked into the sky from a headland, and on promontories beacon fires winked redly, all the way to Edo.

On shore the villagers and townspeople were almost hysterical. Panic could be touched off very easily, thought

Sadayori. He spent the greater part of the night walking from one fortification to the next, observing the frantic efforts to throw up embrasures of earth-filled straw bales, supported by posts and cross-balks of timber. They had cannon, but not enough, and too small. The forts were bordered with white screens of cloth on bamboo. Local officials and *bakufu* officers from Edo were everywhere, holding endless emergency conferences, or rushing about with conflicting orders. Not one single powerful leader to pull us all together, thought Sadayori bitterly. As Sadayori walked around he overheard much bravado, but he also heard one peasant tell others that the barbarians held secret rites at which they ate the flesh of babies and drank their blood.

The sudden crash of a gun shook the hills. It was one of the ships. Fires were hastily extinguished, conflicting orders shouted, and nearly everybody expected an onslaught. Steam and ash from a doused fire stung Sadayori's eyes, so he moved away into the coolness of the night air. Below, lit by many lanterns, the foreign ships swung at their anchors.

"That was only a signal gun. They fire one every night at this time," said Sadayori to a young samurai who was looking for somebody to give him orders.

These nights, to the northeast, a bright blue comet streaked in the sky, a blue sphere with a red, wedge-shaped tail. Its light illuminated the sails of the intruders, as if they were on fire. Many of the Japanese took this as an omen that the gods would come and burn out the intruders, while others held it to be a sign that there were more evil and drastic events to come.

Sadayori did not sleep at all that night, but stayed on the promontory that guarded the inner bay of Edo. The night brought a mist which still curtained the land in the morning, but no attack was ordered.

The next day, Kayama Yezaimon, governor of Uraga, went out to the ships. He was dressed in his most imposing robes, bordered with gold and silver. They allowed him onto the flagship, where he expressed his desire to meet the American admiral. He came back without seeing this mysterious person, having learned from American officers of rank that the ships had come to deliver a letter to the shogun, and that their leader would hand this letter only to a high prince of the realm, or to the shogun himself.

All that day, boats went up and down from the ships,

making soundings. They flew white flags at their bows, but the crews were well armed and stayed under the protection of the muzzles of their own cannon. Sadayori stood on an escarpment, surveying this activity. When one of the boats drew near to a shore fortification, the samurai commander had his soldiers stand in ranks along the shore, with spears, halberds and matchlock guns, but the boats made no attempt to land. As Sadayori stood at the edge of the cliff, a young *umawari* rode up and dismounted, holding the reins of his horse in his right hand, his long bow in his left.

"What are those devils doing? Why do they row up and down like that?"

"They are taking measurements of the depths of the water, and putting them on a chart, making notes of submerged rocks and such. This way they will know if it is safe for their ships to come closer to land."

The young man now glanced at the insignia on Sadayori's helmet, and bowed. "The situation is serious," he said.

"Serious indeed," said Sadayori.

"We should fight them—the sooner the better," said the young man. Sadayori said nothing, but thought that the young warrior would need more than just his bow and his courage to face these intruders. He nodded to the young man and began to make his way to where he had tethered his horse. He was determined to make his opinions about the folly of permitting the foreign charting of Uraga harbor and approaches to it known to somebody who might be able to do something about it.

The Americans waited for a reply from Edo on their request to present the letter. By their calendar it was Tuesday, July 12, 1853. For four days the decks of all four ships had been cleared for action, with cannon shotted, ammunition stacked, muskets loaded and racked.

Whenever he was not attending to his duties, Olderby spent time scanning the shore with his own small telescope, observing the activities of what appeared to be thousands of Japanese soldiers. The marine officer, the one who had lectured them on the danger of attack by small boats, joined him on deck.

"May I?"

Olderby passed him the telescope.

"Mmmm. Small guns. Badly exposed in the embrasures. Barracks and munition stores constructed of wood . . . and I

178

don't know what they think those screens would do." He passed the telescope back. "What with all those flags and finery, I would hazard that this is the biggest festival they've had in years, with or without the fireworks. However, I keep a pistol handy by my bunk and I'd advise you to do the same. If anything happens it will happen at night, and very quickly."

Three boats approached from the shores of Uraga. They were more heavily built than the swift, slender guard boats, broad in the beam and a bit more like European boats, and rowed instead of sculled. Their sails were the usual square Japanese rig. In the largest boat was a crew of thirty men, dressed in loose blue uniforms slashed with white. Across the sail of the lead boat was a black stripe, and she flew a black and white flag. The governor, Kayama Yezaimon, sat on tatami mats in the center of the deck, interpreters and other samurai all around him. As his boat drew alongside, the gangway was lowered.

He had returned to order Perry to take his ships to Nagasaki and deliver the letter from the president of the United States through the Dutch and Chinese who were permitted to trade there. The governor was told that Perry had no intention of going to Nagasaki. He left the ship to communicate with other officials on shore. Throughout the conversations between the governor, his interpreters and the American officers, Perry kept himself out of sight. The governor was very firmly informed that the commander-in-chief had no intention of going to Nagasaki, and that he intended to deliver his letter in Edo Bay, and that if this was refused then he would consider his country insulted and would take action accordingly.

That afternoon the governor returned to continue negotiations aboard the flagship. It was finally agreed that the commander-in-chief would come ashore to deliver his letter to a high prince of the realm. With negotiations on this delicate point completed, and the risk of war averted, the governor and his entourage allowed themselves to be entertained with whiskey and brandy, and then, flushed and jovial, they were taken on a tour of the ship.

Olderby was one of the several officers who snuck into the cabin to look at the swords the Japanese officials had left there. One of the lieutenants drew the governor's sword from its scabbard and, hefting it in one hand, sliced the air. He held it like a saber and made a fake lunge at a bulkhead. The others laughed.

"Damned heavy, and no guard," he said. "I'd take a navy cutlass any day, even better a good rapier."

Yet they all agreed that the sword was a beautiful thing, its steel glistening in wavy lines, with its mountings of pure gold set on sharkskin, and an edge that was finely tempered and razor keen.

"More for ceremonials than for fighting, don't you think?" said another officer.

Olderby felt the blade. "It is very sharp, and of excellent steel. I wonder if the old boy has ever used it?"

"Better put it back," somebody said. "If we nick the blade and Old Bruin finds out there'll be hell to pay."

It was a couple of days later, when the sword was carefully cleaned by one of the governor's retainers, cleaned with the finest talcum, and with great ceremony, with the man kneeling alone in a room, fine tissues in his mouth lest his breath touch the priceless blade, that the fingerprints were discovered. The retainer was so deeply shocked that he kept the discovery to himself, and spent four hours removing them. The sword had never been so polluted, except honorably, with human blood and fat, in the two hundred or so years since it was forged.

Word came that the American letter was going to be formally accepted by the lords of Izu and Iwami. Sadayori was grimly unsurprised. Toda, lord of Izu, would perform this onerous task. Preparations began, to the frenetic clamor of carpenters and laborers shouting themselves hoarse over the noise of soldiery. In the bay the government boats came and went, and seemed all too often to be scurrying about aimlessly. There were still those who urged attack, but the moderates had won. A reception hall was being built, with three roofs and a floor covered with new tatami mats and with carpets. The walls would be of natural pine, hung with violet-covered cloth. An inner chamber was built, its floor raised and covered with rich red material.

The day came, the weather fine and with a hot summer sun that quickly dispersed the morning fog. The foreign ships hauled up their anchors and moved slowly to position themselves close to the designated site of the reception of the American president's letter.

All along the route that Perry would take, the Japanese had stretched screens of painted cloth; above these, and all around, were the tall standards of the many daimyos and high officers who were present. Regiments of samurai of low

180

rank, mostly *ashigaru,* were drawn up in close lines; dressed in short, sashed, sleeveless tunics with the seals of their clans on their backs, they were armed mostly with spears.

To the left was the village of Gorihama, hustled by steep, luxuriantly forested hills that tumbled to the edges of the big bay. Inland lay hill upon hill. To the right, ranged in parallel lines along the shore, were a hundred boats manned by muscular rowers, each boat flying a red pennant at its stern.

The Japanese far outnumbered the Americans, but as Sadayori reflected on this, he looked out to where the muzzles of the guns of the four ships covered the shore and the massed ranks of the Japanese. He had no doubt that those guns were loaded and aimed, with crews standing by to open fire at a moment's notice. He watched the officials leave the shore in their barge to guide the American admiral to the reception.

Midshipman Olderby was standing to attention on the deck of the flagship. He was having trouble keeping himself from grinning, and had to bite the inside of his lip. The Japanese officials had come aboard. The vice-governor, Saborosuke, was wearing what looked like a wide riding skirt, but was in fact a species of trouser. Beneath this they could see black socks peeping out, socks that had the big toe separated from the rest like a little mouse. He was also wearing a gaily embroidered brocade dress, patterned with gold lace, and over that was a stiff collar that stuck out at the shoulders like short, starched wings, like a penguin trying to take off. The solemn-faced Japanese would have fitted perfectly as the knave in a deck of very ornate playing cards. Only by pinching his inner lip with his teeth could Olderby stop himself from giggling.

At an order from Captain Buchanan, a signal was hoisted on the *Susquehanna.* Fifteen launches and cutters pulled off from the other ships, manned with sailors and marines in full dress uniform, with flags at the bows and sterns of the boats. It took them half an hour to pull alongside the flagship. The captain then boarded his own barge, leading the procession with it, flanked on either side by the barges of the Japanese officials. The other American boats followed, two of them carrying ship's bands which blared out lively tunes across the placid waters. Facing sternward, and pulling on their oars, the American crewmen were hard put to keep up with the gleeful Japanese, who stood two to an oar, just as the Taiji whalers did, sculling with a skillful sychronization that sent their long, high-prowed craft skimming over the surface.

A wharf of strong straw rope bales filled with sand had been built in the center of the beach that curved around the bay. Guided by the Japanese boats, the captain's barge came alongside the wharf. He stepped ashore, followed by a major of marines.

The other boats disembarked in orderly fashion until a hundred marines and a hundred sailors were ashore, formed up into ranks on either side of the wharf. All mustered, with officers and musicians, the shore party numbered close to three hundred, and not since the thwarted invasion of the Khan nearly six hundred years before had so many armed strangers set foot in Japan.

Commodore Perry left the flagship in his barge, saluted by thirteen navy guns that echoed and rolled like thunder among the green hills.

Japanese soldiers were arrayed all the way from the village to the hill that bounded the bay on the northern shore; they numbered over five thousand. Behind the ranks of foot soldiers were hundreds of mounted warriors, richly caparisoned and armed with their swords, and with long bows. They looked magnificent, but Sadayori, mounted on a horse himself, looked from this army of his countrymen, armed with spears, halberds, spiked and hooked staves, swords, matchlocks and flintlocks, to the quiet, solemn menace of those ships that had crossed half the world to force this meeting, and to the tight, well-armed, well-disciplined and almost cheerfully confident group of Americans. He hated them still, but deep inside him he felt something new. He felt respect.

At the landing place the American officers formed a double line. As Commodore Perry stepped ashore and walked up between them, they fell in behind him. Two burly sailors carried the Stars and Stripes and the commodore's broad spangled pennant. His credentials and the president's letter were borne in front of the commodore by two boys. These papers were contained in boxes of rosewood, a foot long, with hinges, clasps, locks and mountings of pure gold. The documents themselves were written on vellum and bound in blue silk velvet. Each document had a seal of the Government of the United States attached to the documents by cords of silk and gold, and each seal was encased in a six-inch-diameter golden box.

On either side of the commodore marched a personal guard—two tall, magnificent black men—armed with cutlasses and pistols. Behind all this, the marines and sailors fell in, marching along in the sand, in time to the music of the bands.

The procession made its way to the newly built reception hall, by the entrance of which were two small brass cannon. A company of Japanese guards stood on the right-hand side, armed with flintlock muskets and bayonets. These men wore white headbands, but were otherwise dressed in gray. To the left was another company of guards in brown and yellow tunics. These men carried matchlocks, with the long rope fuses wrapped around their upper right arms.

The lords of Izu and Iwami waited inside. As the commodore stepped in, they rose from their seats and bowed. Armchairs had been provided and were set on the right. Everybody took his place in silence, remaining quiet as Tatsunosuke, chief interpreter, asked if the letters were ready for delivery, and said that the lord of Izu was ready to receive them. At the end of the room was a scarlet box. While Tatsunosuke spoke in Dutch, Mr. Portman, who traveled with the squadron, translated into English for the commodore. The commodore beckoned the boys with the boxes to come forward. The two black bodyguards took the rosewood-and-gold boxes from the boys, opened them, and displayed the vellum sheets and gold seals. In silence, they laid the letters and seals upon the scarlet box. Together with the letters, written in English, were translations into Chinese and Dutch.

Nobody here dared try to read the letters, but most of the high officials guessed what was in them. Promises of peace; a request to open more ports to foreign ships; protection for ships, such as whalers, which might be in trouble off the shores of Japan; trade; timber, water, coal and other supplies for ships. To the Americans simple, but to the Japanese it would mean the abrogation of laws and ways that had kept Japan safe for nearly three hundred years.

While this and other letters were presented, Tatsunosuke and Kayama Yezaimon had all the while been kneeling in the formal position. Kayama now rose to his feet and went to kneel before the lord of Iwami, and with head lowered, received a document from him. He bowed, rose, and knelt once more before the commodore, bowing before handing him the document. Mr. Portman asked what the documents were, and they were accordingly translated to him, while he in turn relayed the Dutch into English for the benefit of the commodore. It was, he was told, an imperial rescript.

> The letter of the President of the United States of North America, and copy, are hereby received, and will be delivered to the Emperor.
>
> Many times it has been communicated that business related to foreign countries cannot be transacted here in Uraga, but in Nagasaki. Now it has been observed that the Admiral, in his quality of ambassador of the President, would be insulted by it; the justice of this has been acknowledged; consequently the above mentioned letter is hereby received, in opposition to the Japanese laws.
>
> Because this place is not designed to handle anything from foreigners, so neither can conference or entertainment take place. The letter being received, you will leave here.
>
> THE NINTH OF THE SIXTH MONTH

Perry listened in silence, then through his interpreters informed the Japanese that he would leave in two or three days for the Ryukyus. He offered his services in carrying government dispatches to those places. He told them that he intended to return in April or May of the next year. Obviously startled by this, the Japanese asked if he would return with all four of his ships. With four, yes, they were told, and probably more, as they were only a part of the squadron.

The reception was over. After some brief talk about the fighting in China, the Americans left.

Hundreds of pushing samurai tried to get a glimpse of the American admiral. Sadayori, high on his horse, stayed back, but from his vantage point he saw the man. He still hated him, but at the same time he admired his cool reserve and arrogant courage, despite the ridiculous and comic dress of tight tubes and breath-restricting wrapping, all with their rows of shiny buttons. Sadayori tried to guess the admiral's age, but could not. He seemed old, yet he had a large, powerful frame, albeit on the fat side. The sword he carried, like the swords of his officers, were silly, slender, effeminate things that would surely snap if they ever tried to parry a cut from a Japanese blade. In fact, reflected Sadayori, despite their bulk and height, these officers did not look as if they would be much good at man-to-man combat, not even as good as their own men. Yet in all likelihood, they were all masters of technology and military science.

As they marched past, Sadayori looked at them carefully, noting that they walked with weight and balance high in chest and shoulders, which meant they were almost certainly weak in the hips and slow on their feet. He barely stopped his hand stealing to his sword hilt when he thought about all this.

Olderby stood beside a sixty-four-pounder gun, looking out through the gunport to the soldiers massed on the shore, and glancing from time to time at the manned American boats below, armed with howitzers and ready to speed toward the shore if fighting started. The Americans there were hemmed in, and if anything did start, it could be a massacre. But, when the commodore's barge pulled out from the shore, Olderby and his men almost sighed with relief.

"He's done it! Old Bruin has gone and done it!" One of the men slapped the gun with delight. Olderby looked at him, a reprimand changing to a grin.

Ignoring the orders delivered by the Japanese lords, instead of departing immediately, the squadron steamed farther up the bay toward the great city of Edo, the two sloops of war under sail abreast of the *Susquehanna* and the *Mississippi*.

Sadayori was traveling in the same direction, on horseback, taking the many winding routes that led from village to village. The ordered beauty and serenity of the scenes before him calmed his troubled thoughts. There were streams of pure water, gurgling down mountains and hillsides, through meadows and rice paddies, irrigating as they went, making things emerald green, going down through villages nestled in groves of trees which caught the smoke of domestic fires in their branches. Green and quiet was this land, the quietness punctuated by the sounds of running water, and of songbirds, tree frogs and cicadas. As he passed, the people bowed and offered him fresh fruit.

As the horse jogged on, Sadayori reflected quietly now on the policies that were beginning to tear at the seams of government. He respected men like Ii Naosuke, lord of Hikone, benefactor and supporter of Kii. Lord Ii was a master of sword, bow, horse, tea ceremony and other cultured arts, but he also understood artillery, guns and Western military science. He was a refined, aesthetic man, disciplined since youth to self-denial.

On the other hand, in Sadayori's opinion, his archfoe, Lord Nariaki of Mito, was a bombastic fool. His simplistic notions of denying all change and simply turning the whole country into a fortress was shortsighted and impossible.

Sadayori was convinced that Japan needed great floating castles, warships that could make forays with efficiency and speed from any number of Japan's safe harbors, attacking and destroying foreign ships that ignored Japanese laws.

The foreigners were far from home and had to be weaker for it. Also, with Japan's position in the world, with a powerful navy, she could control Asia, which was surely the nation's destiny! So why could the councillors not see this? Why couldn't they learn the lessons of China's humiliation?

The patient horse trotted, lathered with sweat. The rice paddies, noisy with frogs and busy with darting swallows and dragonflies, were not of Sadayori's fief; neither were the orchards, meadows and vegetable plots, full of bees and butterflies. To ride through here he had to carry a seal that allowed him right of way. Yet he felt all of this to be a part of him, despite the jealousies and rivalries and the various intriguing factions at the courts of the shogun in Edo and the emperor in Kyoto.

Sadayori had changed in the past few years. He now felt that the call for immediate war was the solution of ignorant and vainglorious idiots. Some of the *bushi* might achieve glory, but what of victory? What would they feel to see rape and pillage by barbarian troops trampling this peaceful countryside? No, Sadayori would like to follow the longer visions of Lord Ii, who would strengthen the country while avoiding war, who would learn from the enemy before fighting him.

From time to time, at higher vantage points, Sadayori could spot the black ships. They had proceeded calmly against the orders of a government which had controlled all of the people of this land for centuries; yet that same government, which demanded utter obedience and loyalty from all subjects, could do nothing about it. It was incredible. It was insulting. It was infuriating, humiliating. But at the same time it was intensely exciting.

Sadayori dismounted and let his horse rest and water from a small spring. His eyes followed the smoking steamers. He sat down under a tree and took out a couple of rice balls, wrapped in thin black seaweed and flavored inside with salted cod roe. He ate quickly, then drank from the spring. The lead steamer had reached a point off Shinagawa, but a short distance from the capital, and was turning back, its commander no doubt smiling to himself, satisfied with his demonstration of confident power.

The ingenuity and boldness of the Americans gave Sadayori much to think about. They could cross vast oceans, confront, demand. There was much to be learned from them. He found himself indulging in a fantasy again, of being in command of a huge floating fortress, demanding and receiving concessions from a foreign government in a distant harbor. Then he laughed at himself, got to his feet, stretched, and brushed grass and leaves from his *hakama*. As he walked over to fetch his horse, now browsing quietly, the cry of a cuckoo rang through the woods.

Chapter Sixteen

Jinsuke had found work with a salt maker, close to Naha. Again, this was made possible through introductions of his teacher, Kinjo. The salt pans were built on tidal flats, near an inlet close to the headland that commanded an excellent view of Naha harbor. Each day he took time to observe the ships and the movements around them, committing his observations to memory until he could find time to jot them down in the secrecy of his hut. Now there were eight American ships, all warships, three of them steamers. At times Jinsuke wondered how his observations could be of value to Sadayori, as by now everyone had heard the rumors of the American boldness in the main islands of Japan, and that the *bakufu* were doing little but bluster and dither. But he kept his word, sending out messages and his diary pages whenever he could.

Through the inlet a brackish stream flowed, over which were a stone bridge and a highway that led to the center of the city. There was a spot just below the bridge where at high tide junks could come in and tie up a hundred or so paces from the offices, warehouses and dwelling of the Satsuma sugar inspector, whose clan brutally administered production of sugar in these southern islands. Through an agreement with the inspector, an agreement made easier with presents of silver, dried bonito, and casks of strong liquor, the shipping of salt was also permitted, when there was cargo space, although this far less valuable commodity always had to take second place.

The same tides that enabled boats to come up the inlet flooded the salt pans. At low tide, the keelless, flat-bottomed junks were left high and dry on the red mud, giving their crews a chance to clean them of barnacles and other marine growth and to load them. Fishing boats also used the inlet, and thus life around it functioned with the tides. Fish, salt and a little sugar for local use was transported along the well-kept highway for market in Naha.

Jinsuke now lived on the other side of this inlet in a simple thatched hut, rented for a few copper coins from Jirazichi, a farmer-fisherman. Around the hut and around Jirazichi's own house and sheds was a bamboo picket fence, through which wandered a small flock of extremely agile and colorful chickens, a couple of dogs and a few cats. With each change of the wind the sharp scents of pig wafted from the pens in one corner of the compound, mingling with the smells of the flats, of drying fish and squid, of the out-of-sight workings of a sugar mill up past the bridge. Jinsuke, however, did not find it unpleasant. He was used to the smells of cooking whale.

The hut was a rude affair, although it did have a board floor, laid over with worn tatami mats. He did his cooking outside, keeping to himself, with his fine American harpoon and his beautifully balanced *sai,* his fighting iron, as well as his treasured scrimshaw tooth and Manjiro's letter hidden under the floorboards, together with a little money. He did not dare to practice with the harpoon here, but at times he brought out the *sai.* It had been forged for his own rather long forearm, with a handle bound with goat-leather thongs, and the whole weapon balanced exactly. Sometimes he carried the *sai* concealed in his short tunic.

Wages at the salt flats were poor, but Jinsuke ate well— brown rice, yams, bananas and various vegetables, supplemented with the fish he took himself with a spear in the coral off the headland and in the chasms and underwater cliffs beyond the intricate windings of the reef. There was an abundance of shellfish, clams, conches and sea snails of various kinds, and huge dishlike mussels found half buried in the sand. And, to mix with hot rice, there were always the tasty orange gonads of sea urchins. Once a week, in exchange for help with the boat, he got a few eggs from Jirazichi's wife. No less than three times he had tried pork, overcoming his prejudices by rationalizing that it was, after all, just tame "mountain whale," or wild boar, which they sometimes got in Taiji. He found he liked it, especially cooked slowly until very tender, in the Okinawan way. He had even eaten the goat meat and mugwort soup so loved by the islanders, and had gone on to try their special dish of raw goat meat sashimi.

Jirazichi had a daughter, nineteen years old. Her name was Harue and she was a childless widow, her husband having been lost in a typhoon the year before. Harue often brought Jinsuke little delicacies and leftovers, and soon he enjoyed Okinawan cooking.

Jinsuke always rose before dawn. That was the way of the Taiji whalers and their wives, for the men had to be out to sea before the sun rose. But here there was no singing, no chanting, no banter between the boats of the fleet, and Jinsuke missed them terribly, and when he went out to the headland to look at the harbor each day, and saw the sun rise redly from its sleeping place in the sea, he thought lonely thoughts.

Work at the salt flats was hot and hard. He had to use the long-handled brine rake with one hand, while others used two. His eyes ached from the glare off the grayish crystals as he raked and raked, letting the seawater evaporate in the sun.

The close proximity of the offices and other buildings of the Satsuma officials had ceased to bother him. Nobody seemed to take any notice of what he did, or of who he was. He now looked Okinawan, and as long as he kept to short sentences his speech would not betray him to outsiders, although of course he could never fool an islander. Jirazichi and the owner of the salt flats both knew that there was something different, if not dangerous, about this stranger, and they refrained from asking questions or making idle remarks about him. The Satsuma authorities used many spies.

At noon, when the workers enjoyed a short break, Jinsuke would share the shade of pine trees with the others, and take a whiff of tobacco with them, using the same smoke box. He would smile, say nothing, and be polite when it came to passing things or fetching tea. As for the other men, they knew he had studied with the master, Kinjo, and that dire consequences could befall any man who spoke unwisely about anyone connected with the teacher. It was said that Kinjo could strike a man quite lightly, at the time barely winding him, in such a way that the blow was ignored and forgotten, until six months or so later, when death came. They knew for a fact that one punch from Kinjo could smash a pig's skull, and that he was not to be fooled with. A quick glance at the calluses on the one-armed man's hand would tell them that he too practiced the secret art. They left him alone, which sometimes made Jinsuke feel depressed. As a whaler he had had many friends and comrades, and half the people in Taiji were his relatives. Back home there were always people around him, even when out on the bosom of the ocean. Now he would lie alone in his hut in the evening, staring at the underside of the thatch, and he would think of his father, his mother, his brothers, but most often of Oyoshi.

One such evening, when he was thinking of Oyoshi, he became aware that somebody was watching him. He turned on his side and saw Harue standing silently in the doorway, looking at him. Jinsuke sat up, embarrassed, trying to disguise the shape of his erection under the short, loose robe.

"I was sleeping," he stammered. She did not enter the hut. In her hands was a small package wrapped in leaves.

"I brought you some yams," she said, holding the package out to him. "I roasted them."

He took the package. It was still warm.

"I'll make some tea for you," she said, and without waiting for him to answer, she went to the ash-filled pot outside and began to fan coals to heat water. Jinsuke went outside and sat watching her face, now coppery red in the setting sun. He glanced toward the house to see if her parents were looking. Thanking her, he opened the package and began to eat. The food was delicious, and it reminded him again of home.

For a while Harue said nothing, but then, as the iron kettle began to sing, she abruptly asked if he was married.

"No," said Jinsuke.

"Aren't you lonely?"

"No."

She looked at him sideways, smiling. She had large, animated eyes with long lashes, and her eyebrows were thick, black and arched, giving her an almost stern expression, except when she smiled, and she was someone who smiled with her whole face. Her nose was small and a little flat, and she was slightly plump too, her waist beginning to thicken, although this was compensated for by the smooth line of neck and back, and by full, heavy breasts which moved as she crouched by the iron kettle and fanned the coals.

"You are a handsome man," she said. "It would be easy for you to find a woman to marry. Why don't you get yourself an Okinawan wife? They are loyal . . ." She looked at him. "And very passionate."

"What woman would want a man with one arm?" he asked gruffly.

She reached out and touched the callused knuckles of his right hand.

"Any pupil of Kinjo sensei is a man more than other men. You are not missing any other parts, are you?"

He pulled his hand away and she laughed. How could she know so much? She caught his thoughts.

"Oh, don't worry. I don't really know where you practice in this area, but I could guess. May I guess? There are about twenty of you in this area. Kinjo sensei comes only a few times a year, but there is a young master, a man of forty, whose name is . . . but I won't speak his name. There is a place up beyond the sugar fields, behind a glade of bamboo, with dense pines to the north end. The undergrowth all around is very dense, with lots of vines and snakes. It's up against the side of a hill, and there are five tombs there. In the hill is a long crack that runs from top to bottom, and if you look into the crack, which also has snakes and spiders, you'll see some very old burial jars. Several are broken, so there are bones scattered in the rocks and weeds. People are afraid to go there, and they say there are ghosts there, especially around evening time, or in the very early hours of the morning. They say that if you go there, you might not come back. It is a frightening place, isn't it?"

Jinsuke glanced around and glared at her. "Why would I know of such a place?"

"My dead husband's hands were marked like yours. He was a nephew of Kinjo sensei. Did you not know? That is why you are here. My husband was good, as a man, as a fisherman, as a fighter. He was also foolishly brave. Jinsuke-san, I think that you are good too . . . aren't you?"

He blushed. Just then her father came into the yard, carrying a heavy basket of dried bonito.

"Harue! Take these and then go help your mother. Don't bother the man. He has had a hard day of work, just like me. Now go!"

As his daughter went, Jirazichi squatted down beside the brazier and helped himself to tea.

"Ah, Jinsuke, are you well? I hear gossip that the Americans intend to conquer Edo. Silly talk. I did meet some of them down by the beach this morning, when they pulled a boat in. They gave me some tobacco, and this . . ." He pulled out a small brass button from his sleeve. "Isn't it a fine one? I got it for a few big conch shells and five parrot fish. You know, they don't seem such bad fellows once you get used to the way they look." He glanced around. "They seem better than a lot of others who have come to Okinawa from across the sea." He laughed at himself. "Of course, you're not a Satsuma man, or a spy. But do you think there will be a war on the main islands? They say the foreigners made war in China and defeated the Chinese."

"I don't know," said Jinsuke, thinking that Jirazichi talked too much.

"No, I suppose not. Nobody knows anything these days." He gestured across the inlet to the Satsuma compound. "They seem agitated. They've been asking a lot of questions around here lately. They say they are looking for Christians. I wouldn't want to be any Christian who got caught."

"It does not concern me," said Jinsuke. "I'm not a Christian."

Jirazichi sipped at his tea. "No, I know you're not, but if I were you I would not show so much interest in those ships, not every day. Somebody will notice. You are not one of us, and if they put any pressure on anybody, they will talk."

Jinsuke said nothing but inside he froze. Jirazichi slowly stood up.

"Please excuse my daughter. She does not mean to bother you. I will speak to her about it." He said it in a tone that meant that Jinsuke was to leave her alone.

Through a servant of a sugar inspector, word came that the shogun had died in Edo. His son, Iesada, would replace him as head of the *bakufu,* governing Japan in the name of the emperor in Kyoto. This news did not concern Jinsuke in the least. He was not a politically conscious man, despite his connection with Sadayori. However, there was something in the air that made him bring out his *sai* and carry it inside his robe. He practiced the moves with even greater effort and concentration. It seemed to help wash away his nervousness and isolation.

Close to the end of the year, February 1 by the Western calendar, four sailing ships left the harbor. Jinsuke spotted them leaving while he was working, and he had by now memorized the size and shape of the ships along with their names. That night, by the light of his oil lamp, he wrote the names of the ships, both in copied English letters and in *katakana.*

"Four American ships left Naha harbor on this date. They are *Macedonian, Vandalia, Lexington* and *Southampton.* I think my news will reach you too late, as it is rumored they sail for Edo . . ."

That evening he ran to the outskirts of Naha, where he had a contact, a Chinese merchant who shipped dried island

193

herbs to Nagasaki and Shanghai. The man was extremely nervous and told Jinsuke not to come again.

Six days later the three great steamers, *Mississippi, Susquehanna* and *Powhatan,* began to belch thick palls of black and gray smoke. Anchors were lifted, and with huge wheels churning water, the steamers left too. Jinsuke tried to reach his contact in Naha, but the shutters of the Chinese merchant's house were tightly closed and the only response to his knocking was the barking of neighbors' dogs. He walked home along the beach.

As he rounded the headland and went down to the tidal flats, there were four men there waiting for him. Two were mainlanders, *bushi,* one with two swords and one of lower rank, carrying one. On the kimono of the two-sworded man was a black cross in a black circle, the insignia of the Shimazu family, daimyos of Satsuma. With the *bushi* were two men who looked like Okinawans, and these men were armed with long, thick staves. They stood blocking the path that led between the mudflats and sandbars of the inlet and a grove of trees. Jinsuke stared at them, bowed, and began to walk around. The men with staves blocked his way, their weapons crossed against his chest.

"What is wrong?" asked Jinsuke, stomach tight.

"You are wanted for questioning." Questioning, Jinsuke knew, meant torture. From inside their short tunics the stave carriers produced white capture ropes, dropping their poles to bind him. Without thinking, Jinsuke reacted, sending a straight punch into one man's face, smashing his nose and snapping his head back. Soundlessly the man fell backward. The other stave bearer had deftly looped a coil around Jinsuke's shoulders, but he struggled and it slipped. Before the man could do anything else, Jinsuke kicked him in the groin. Buckling over with a deep groan, he dropped to his knees.

"Insolent oaf!" One of the swordsmen roared with anger, but his rage was small beside Jinsuke's; he turned and faced the swordsman, who had drawn his weapon and seemed to be waiting for the senior *bushi* to give an order. With a cold smile, the two-sworded one slowly unsheathed one of his own long blades. Light glinted on the steel as the sun dipped below the horizon.

Jinsuke kicked off his straw sandals and stepped back, his hand going to the inside of his robe and closing around the leather-bound handle of the *sai,* feeling the curves and hardness of the two tines at the sides that would protect the vulnerable sinews of his wrist.

In indolent confidence the young man raised his sword. He had enjoyed the right of cutting down an insolent peasant before, and the sense of power over them infused him with pleasure.

"Fish offal, you can be arrested, questioned, and then executed, or you can die now. Which is it?"

"For what will you sentence me?" asked Jinsuke, so angry now that his Taiji accent came back in full.

"For spying," said the young samurai, "and for injuring officers in the course of their duty."

Jinsuke let his shoulders slump. "Cut, if you know how, potato samurai."

Nothing could have infuriated the young man more, for it was a fact that the fief had many farmer-warriors who carried the two swords yet were so poor they also tilled the soil.

"Insolence!" he roared, slicing suddenly downward with his blade. But instead of cleaving flesh and bone, the swordsman's wrists were jarred by the contact of steel on steel. With a powerful rising block, Jinsuke had lunged forward under the blade, meeting it with the thick central tine of the *sai* along his forearm. Before the young samurai could withdraw the blade it was hooked by one of the curving guards and swept away and down. The samurai was slightly off balance and did not move quickly enough to avoid a thrusting punch, augmented by the heavy steel hilt of the *sai*. It went deep into his solar plexus and he staggered, just long enough for Jinsuke to bring his arm back, spin the *sai* in his hand, and smash it with a crash across the man's temple, knocking him unconscious.

Momentarily rooted with astonishment, the second man now swiped sideways with his sword at Jinsuke, but Jinsuke leaped straight up, feet shoulder high. As he came down he brought the *sai* down on the man's wrist, breaking it. He dropped his sword and held his wrist in agony, staring at this terrible one-armed peasant, and ran. Jinsuke could not let him escape. He picked up one of the oaken staves and hurled it like a harpoon. With a dull thud it took the running man in the back of the neck. He sprawled face down in the mud.

Jinsuke tucked the *sai* back into his sash, and was considering taking a sword when the man he had kicked in the groin called to him, voice rasping with pain. He spoke mainland Japanese, but heavily accented, like an islander.

"Don't go back to Jirazichi's place. They are waiting for you there."

"Why do you tell me this?"

"After the kick you gave me, only Kinjo sensei can help me. By tomorrow I'll be swollen like a melon. Had I known you were one of his, I'd have gotten word to you. All we knew was that you were a mainlander. If you see Kinjo, tell him you were warned. Tell him how you kicked me." He suppressed a groan and Jinsuke reached out his arm and pulled the man to his feet.

"It was a bad thing to do, I'm sorry."

"Run! If they catch you, you know you'll get your head sawn off!"

Jinsuke nodded, and ran. The only place he could think of going to was the secret training place, by the tombs. He knew that if he tried to make the long journey back to Motobu, where Kinjo lived, he would get caught. He needed to think. Apart from the odd rough wrestling and a couple of fights in Katsuura while out carousing, Jinsuke had never committed any violence against another man. It left him exhilarated, and amazed at the effectiveness of Kinjo's training.

He reached the trees at the edge of the tidal flats and looked back. Three men were on their feet, one with blood streaming down his face from a smashed nose, the other wobbling with concussion, the third using his stave to help him walk. Jinsuke ran through the trees, skirting the sugar fields, and through the glade of bamboo until he came to the training area. Somehow he was not surprised to find Harue waiting for him.

The place was eerie, with the rounded domes of tombs shining in the moonlight like white bellies, all shadowed by the walls and cornices about them, as if they might be hiding limbs. Down the side of the hill ran the awful black slash of the crevice, in which were the skulls and bones of people buried either too poorly or too hastily for a proper tomb. In the dense thickets about them darkling things seemed to be waiting. An owl hooted. Jinsuke could hear, or imagine, snakes slithering, and he heard the squeak of a grass rat.

"Come here," said Harue, beckoning him over to one of the tombs. "I knew you'd come here. Come quick, there's not much time." She pointed to the block of whitish stone that sealed the entrance of the tomb. It was the closest to the ghastly crevice. "Move this and stand aside."

Jinsuke hesitated. This tomb was the oldest of the five there, in shape slightly different from the rest. He shook his head.

"It is wrong to disturb the dead."

"This one is empty except for snakes and bugs. The bones have long since been put into new jars in another tomb. The people around here say that this was the last resting place of a young Okinawan prince who died resisting the Satsuma clan. Only a few Okinawans know about this, and until you, no mainlander. Now move the stone. Quickly, I haven't got much time!"

She spoke to him as a man might, curt and commanding. Jinsuke grabbed the edge of the big block, waist high and as thick as the length of his arm, not really believing he could shift it. It was pumice, however, and very light. He went to look inside, but she stopped him.

She put down the lantern and gathered a bundle of dried twigs and branches. With the flame from the lantern she lit the bundle and poked it, blazing and crackling, through the doorway of the tomb. In a moment, a snake, thick as a man's wrist, slithered out, followed by two more. Jinsuke shuddered; they were the deadly poisonous *habu*.

Jinsuke and Harue waited a few minutes before Harue ducked into the tomb. It was smoky inside, and she fanned her face, coughing, gesturing with the other hand for Jinsuke to come in. Reluctantly, he entered.

There was a raised platform at the back of the tomb, covered with two tatami mats, now green with mildew. In a niche in the wall was an oil lamp and beside it a large sealed jar of water.

"This is a hideout for us Okinawans," said Harue. "My husband told me. It used to be used by those resisting the Satsuma. Come out only when you hear the others practicing. They will never betray you. I will bring food every day."

"Please don't endanger yourself for me," said Jinsuke.

Harue chuckled. "Don't worry. In Okinawa we regularly leave food and drink at the tombs of our ancestors. As long as you don't show yourself I'll be all right, and so will you." She looked around. "Only brave men can stay alone here. Until I met you I never would have thought that a mainlander had that kind of courage." Her voice grew soft. "I like you," she said, and then, more curtly, "I will see that word gets to Kinjo sensei. He will know what to do."

She ducked out of the tomb and stood up, stretching. Jinsuke followed her, not really wanting her to go.

"I must hurry."

"Are they searching your place?"

"Yes. They tore up the boards in your hut." Jinsuke

197

looked startled. So they had found the foreign harpoon! "My father told them he thought you might be hiding in a sugar boat, and went off with them to look. He knows I've gone to warn you, but he doesn't know this place. When I get back I'll say I've been visiting my mother-in-law, and I'll tell my father that you are hiding and that in the morning you are going to try to get to Naha." She touched his face. "They will kill you if they catch you."

"They won't catch me. Hurry and go, and please take care, Harue-san."

It was the first time he had used her name. She smiled, picked up the lantern, and ran off.

There was a handhold in the back of the block of pumice. Jinsuke seized it and closed himself in. His shadow loomed like a hunchback on the domed roof of the tomb. Wisps of smoke blackened the stones above the oil lamp. Jinsuke lay on the mildewed tatami and stared at the low roof, listening to the sounds of his own breath. Would he have the courage to stand it? Alone?

Itoh Hirosada sat on the raised wooden step that led to the offices, the inner ones, of the magistrate of Naha. He was hot. His long sword was out of his sash and rested on the step beside him. Oh, the damned heat! A bailiff brought him tea and he nodded curtly, took the cup, and sipped noisily. The voyage from Kyushu had been a rough one and his temper was not too sweet. For the people around the island's offices of administration, Itoh's arrival was cause for concern. Itoh was a young man, but he bore himself with an air of arrogant authority, and at a glance anyone could tell that he was a master with the sword. Had his coming here something to do with the departure of the squadron of foreign ships? And why was he asking to see bills of lading for all ships? And why so many questions about the loading of sugar and salt?

An hour passed before the magistrate arrived, flanked by his armed officers. The magistrate was a thin man in his late fifties, face drawn and sallow from overwork, anxiety and a stomach ulcer. Itoh rose as soon as he heard the sound of their coming, and as the magistrate entered through the outer gate Itoh stepped out into the sunlight and bowed deeply. The magistrate did not conceal the delight in his voice.

"Why, why, it is young Hirosada! What a surprise! So you came by the boat today? Come, come, let us take some refreshments, it has been a long voyage for you and a hard day for me. I'm sorry you had to wait. Those fellows, why didn't they take you into the house?"

"Oh, don't scold them, they tried, but I wanted to greet you at the gate."

The obvious warmth in the magistrate's voice made Itoh smile. It was not many years since he had called this aging man "uncle" and had spent many afternoons with him, picnicking, angling for sweetfish in the rivers near home. The magistrate was his father's closest friend. He was also well liked by Lord Shimazu, who had sent him away to Naha because the magistrate's scrupulous honesty had earned him some dangerous enemies in Kagoshima and even in the daimyo's own court.

Itoh followed the magistrate along the polished wooden veranda, shaded by low eaves, to his rooms. They knelt on cushions and now formally exchanged greetings, and then Itoh produced a package from the inside of his kimono. The magistrate glanced at the seal, recognizing it as being that of Lord Shimazu Nariakira himself. He bowed again, took it in both hands, raising it to eye level. Then he broke the seal and with a deft flick of his hand, spread out the first dozen folds of the long paper, quickly reading the strong black characters. Itoh watched the older man's face, seeing it cloud slightly.

"The *bakufu* has made a treaty with the Americans," he said.

"Yes. They have opened the ports of Hakodate and Shimoda. The Americans refused to use Nagasaki. They ask for more open ports, including Naha, but were told the decision could not be made in Edo."

The magistrate nodded, then read on.

"This Treaty of Kanagawa has far-reaching implications, for these islands, for our clan, for the whole of Japan. The *bakufu* sought advice, did they not?"

"Yes, but most of it was no advice at all. Many of course advocated immediate war. The lord of Mito, for example."

"I sympathize; the Americans have been most oppressive in their demands, even here. However, anyone who advocated immediate war cannot be aware of the power of those ships. They would destroy all our shipping, and thus our communications and our economy. No matter how many of us left our bodies on the beaches, Naha would fall. No, now is not the time for war. That time will come, but not yet. Perhaps the *bakufu* made the only decisions they were able to, perhaps the right ones, but whatever the case, this business will weaken them."

Itoh's eyes glittered. "They may have let the foreigners in, but Japan will become strong, united in anger! Uncle, this marks a new beginning, and will surely mean an end to more than two hundred years of Tokugawa arrogance! The Tokugawa are decadent weaklings, not fit to lead us anymore!"

The magistrate held up one hand, gesturing the younger man to silence. It was enough that they both knew the rule of the shogun was doomed, but caution in speech was always wise, even in remote Okinawa. Although there might be little fear of reprisal here, friends and families in Edo for the compulsory stays were always vulnerable. Somehow all indiscreet speech seemed to make the journey, no matter how long, to the ears of the *bakufu.* The magistrate folded the paper carefully.

"The Americans have made a nuisance of themselves, mostly from their total lack of manners and good taste. It was to be expected. They were insolently bold and intolerably stubborn, but I must admit that on the whole they behaved peacefully. The danger is that they will try to spread their religion, and some of their ridiculous ideas about the honorable class system and the position in life to which a man is born. They think that all men are equal! Can you imagine what turmoil that would cause here if these islanders started to get those notions? It cannot ever be permitted. Hirosada-*kun,* may I presume that you have come to help in the investigation of these things?"

Itoh nodded. "In his letter, Lord Nariakira speaks well of you, and asks me to assist you, which of course I shall, in every way, but he gives no details of your mission. Does it have to do with the danger of the spread of Christianity?"

"Yes," said Itoh, hating to lie to this fine old man. But what Itoh had come to do was find a suitable route for importing arms, and that was against the Tokugawa laws. The daimyo of Satsuma intended to make the army of Satsuma the most powerful in Japan, and that required a great influx of foreign weapons and munitions. Itoh would, of course, make a report on Christians, and for himself he intended to investigate the matter of Sadayori's spy. Much as he liked Sadayori, he did not want word of Satsuma arms purchases getting back to him.

I would like to begin tomorrow. I need not trouble you much."

"As you wish. Of course, you must stay with me." The magistrate clapped his hands and a servant appeared. He told him to bring wheat tea, cooled by the well. Talk now lapsed into news of friends and families.

It did not take Itoh long to hear of the escape of the one-armed man, a mainlander, and a spy. It could only be this whaler of Sadayori's, and Itoh determined that he would have to somehow protect him. Already notices were posted throughout the islands, offering rewards, and warning of terrible punishments for harboring the fugitive. But the man had disappeared. Itoh, however, was one of the most efficient and most feared agents of the Satsuma clan, working on direct orders from his daimyo. He would find the one-armed whaler.

For Jinsuke the days passed far from pleasantly. The tomb was dark, musty, cramped. Jinsuke was plagued with nightmares and could sleep only in the day. In the night he moved the pumice block and walked outside, like a ghost. He did not know how long this confinement would last, and that made it worse; he constantly thought of making a run for it, of stealing a boat, anything. Only the early-morning and evening training sessions of the Okinawan fighting art gave him any release. His training partners told him that the search for him was being intensified, and warned him to lie low.

As the long days and longer nights dragged by like wounded dogs, Harue began to appear more and more in his fantasies. In almost two months of hiding he had seen her many times. One late evening, when they were standing outside, he caught her wrist and drew her to him. She felt the hardness of him against her belly and let out a little gasp.

"No, no, not here."

Jinsuke released her, but she slipped both hands inside his robe, enfolding him.

"Take me to the beach. It will be all right tonight, there hasn't been anybody around for days."

Saying nothing, hand in hand, they walked through the bamboo grove and the sugar fields and along the forest path until they reached the sea.

The feel of the warm, clean seawater against his skin was like a kiss in itself. He washed his body, with Harue beside him, seemingly quite unashamed of her nakedness, and fascinated with his. Her thighs were strong, straight, leading to a very pronounced mound that was very sparse of black hair, almost like a young girl's. Her breasts too were large, with nipples as big as the tip of a man's finger, and her belly, a little fat, was round and womanly. She pretended to be shy, and turned from him, showing a neck and back that were curved and silky smooth. She ran up the beach.

Now, with the smell of the tomb off his body, Jinsuke spread the wet robe on the sand and pulled Harue down beside him. Her body was woman, and he had felt so empty and alone. Her nipples, already hard and protruding, grew even harder in his lips, and he buried his face in the softness of her breasts, while she ran her hands over his shoulders, down his back, finally gripping his buttocks and whispering his name, over and over, pulling and pulling.

When he slipped his hand between her thighs she was so wet and open that he gasped, drew away from her in wonder, spread her thighs, knelt between them, then looked at the core of her in fascination. The lips of her vulva were a twin of the lips of her mouth, full and fleshy, and her clitoris was extraordinarily large and hard sticking out through the inner labia and the hood like a little pink nose. It was so wonderful, ready, available, that Jinsuke had flashes of clear memory of Oyoshi, with her more downy black hair, her outer labia smaller, her clitoris tinier. He put his face to Harue and kissed her, reveling in her moistness and scent, which was wetter, stronger, more sexual than Oyoshi's. Now he felt a rising urge to penetrate deeply, deeper than any other, forgetting everything for this one, thrusting moment.

Whimpering, impatient, she guided him to herself, arching her hips to meet him. Inside she was pulsing and hot and she moved with him, making him go faster, faster. It had been a long time for Harue too, and in the waves of sensation that lapped at her and in the sound of the waves breaking on the beach their lovemaking lost all sense of time. For Jinsuke the physical and emotional relief were tremendous, and although he did not love this woman as he loved another, she was here, now, urgent, everything. His seed spurted from him and she wrapped her legs around his buttocks, squeezing and screaming so that he had to smother her mouth with his lest somebody hear. Both mouths ground at him, one in muffled whimpers, one pulling, pushing, demanding.

He withdrew from her, marveling at his almost painful hardness, and with his one arm he pulled her over so that she was on her knees and elbows, rounded buttocks high, cleft wide and wet. Again he thrust into her, gasping, hardening even more, not caring now if anybody found them or not.

Four days later, Kinjo came during the night to fetch him. Jinsuke had been worried, for no food had been left for two days. As Jinsuke emerged from his somber den, Kinjo handed him a big rice ball, and he wolfed it down. Kinjo watched, saying nothing, then passed Jinsuke a stoppered gourd.

"Drink," he said gruffly, "it is not every day that a man can emerge from the grave." It was fiery, and Jinsuke took it gratefully, feeling it warm his throat and belly.

"Now follow me."

They walked through the darkness for three hours until they reached a small rocky inlet. Perhaps because of his long confinement, or perhaps because of the liquor, Jinsuke felt tired, and his head was buzzing. As they walked, Kinjo glanced back at him several times as if checking to see he was all right. The old man led the way down a steep path, his bare feet sure in the darkness. When they got to the bottom he pointed out to a *sabani* slowly bobbing at anchor.

"Jinsuke, you must know why we did this. My younger brother was a doctor, and a good one. One day they brought a man to him who was internally injured from a fall off a horse. My brother cut him open and tried to repair him, but he died. The man was a mainlander, and the Satuma sentenced my brother to death, although it was no fault of his. He escaped to Nagasaki, and there met another doctor, a friend of the samurai Matsudaira Sadayori. That samurai obtained faked passes and my brother escaped to China. I do not like mainlanders, but I owed a life. That life is yours. Swim out and hide in the bottom of the *sabani*. It is a big one and there is quite enough room to hide under the boards. The men aboard will take you somewhere. Remember, whaler, keep your secrets, and our secrets, tight in your breast. Remember too that it was we Okinawans who hid and fed you, asking nothing of you. Your mainlander brethren would kill you. Things may happen that you do not understand, but remember my training. I believe that you are a man who has gone through the gates of fear. That, and my training, will be a great treasure. Go now, in peace." He paused, and handed Jinsuke the gourd. "Take it, you will need it."

Jinsuke fell to his knees and bowed deeply, almost in tears. He said simple words in the Okinawan tongue.

"Sensei, I thank you. You are my father. I will not forget."

The old master angrily rubbed at his eyes. "Get up, and go."

Jinsuke stood and passed the gourd to Kinjo. "Let us say 'kampai' together, sensei. That is the whalers' way."

The old man took the gourd and took a large mouthful of the liquor, paused, then swallowed. *"Kampai,* whaler," he said.

Jinsuke drank and swallowed. *"Kampai,* sensei."

His legs felt leaden. He waded into the water and began to swim out to the long, dark shape on the water.

Kinjo shook his head with a sigh, stuck two fingers into his throat and vomited. He went to the sea, drank the salty water, and vomited again. He too then turned to leave, with steps now grown suddenly weary, up the steep, jungled pathway. Dawn was beginning to edge the night.

At the brow of the slope, Itoh Hirosada stepped out of the shadows. He watched Kinjo, big and powerful like an old bear, and kept one hand lightly on the sheath of his sword.

"Did he drink it?"

Kinjo glared at him with hate in his eyes. "Yes, he drank some, and will no doubt drink a little more. Now you will keep your promise and let the girl and her father go?"

"Yes, this morning. Free and unharmed, although the father has been beaten a little. As long as they keep silent they will remain unharmed."

"They will not talk," said Kinjo, and then, looking back toward the inlet, "and neither will he."

Itoh laughed. "I don't want him to talk." His voice turned cold. "Otherwise he would sing like a bird, and you would too, despite your China fists and fingers of steel."

Kinjo's thick body lowered slightly, and there was an imperceptible movement of his feet as he tested the ground. Itoh jumped back.

"Wait. The whaler will be spared. There are many things that you do not know." His left hand was on the sheath of his sword, just by the guard, and his right crossed his body to the hilt, ready to draw in an instant. He knew that nothing short of decapitation would stop the old fighter if he decided to attack.

"Wait," repeated Itoh, "there is no reason for a fight between us, nothing will be gained and it will mean a death. Should I die, which I doubt, for I have steel and youth, then the girl and her father will also die, probably after long torture. Leave it be. You have taken no money from me, and you have betrayed no Okinawan. I tell you the whaler will not die if he keeps his secrets."

They faced each other in the gloom for several long seconds before Kinjo let the tension ease out of his body, like a tiger relaxing. He felt younger and lighter now.

"I will return to my village," he said, "and pray that we never meet again. I fear neither your sword nor your youth." With courtesy that was not feigned, Itoh bowed.

Several hours later Jinsuke awoke, feeling painfully cramped. The *sabani* still rocked gently and there was an awful stink of fish. In his head was a dull, aching pain, and his limbs felt dead. Groggily he rolled over and tried to get up, but could not. As he came fully awake he realized that the cramp was not caused by the narrow confines of the hold at all—he was all trussed up with ropes. The sounds of his stirring brought attention, and the boards were lifted. Sun and light blinded him until a shadow fell. Jinsuke looked up into the swarthy features and the shaved head and topknot of what he knew to be a Kyushu samurai.

"So, you are awake? Good, I trust you slept well. We have just a short journey."

"Where to?"

"To Naha, and you to jail, where I believe there are many questions to be answered." The man knelt, and spoke softly. "Listen well, Jinsuke the whaler, we don't like spies, no matter whom they serve. But do not betray what you are really here for. I know, but others must not. If you confess to nothing I will do my utmost to see that your life is spared. If you mention another name I myself will cut your head off, after I have cut out your tongue and your balls."

He stood then, and from the sash beside his swords he pulled Jinsuke's *sai* and spun it in his hand. "Primitive, but effective . . . and most illegal." He stuck it back in the sash and grinned down.

"Bring the prisoner water," he called, and a one-sworded officer came with a flagon, holding it over Jinsuke's mouth and pouring it. "That Okinawan liquor gives a man a terrible thirst," said Itoh. "It's bad enough to poison a snake, which I swear is what these islanders use it for."

The other man laughed, but the six Okinawans at the paddles kept their mouths tightly closed. Already they were rounding the headland into Naha harbor, where a bullock cart was waiting to take Jinsuke to jail. Itoh was satisfied. The ruse with the *sabani* and the drugged liquor had let him take this man without the fight that almost certainly would have left the whaler dead, and a burgeoning friendship ruined. Now he would have to play his dice very, very carefully, and pray that the whaler was as strong as he seemed.

The week that followed would always remain as only a half-remembered dream in Jinsuke's memory. Each day began and ended in the cramped, verminous cage into which he was thrown, a space too low to stand in, too narrow to lie in. They usually came to fetch him around the middle of the morning; then they would take him into a yard for questioning. They flogged him, they hung him upside down, they forced him to kneel for hours on a corrugated board, they laid slabs of stone across his thighs. All the time there were screams and insults, slaps and punches. But Jinsuke said nothing except that he had defended himself, which brought more torture.

Then one day Itoh had a big round metal plate brought and laid on the ground in the middle of the yard. Dully, Jinsuke looked at it, wondering what new torture this was.

"Know what this is?" said Itoh.

Jinsuke shook his head. Itoh slapped him hard across the face.

"Look, and tell me what you see on it."

Jinsuke focused his blurred eyes and saw a woman with a child in her arms and a saintly aura around her head, set against a cross.

"It is Kannon-sama," said Jinsuke, giving the name of the goddess of mercy. The officers and Itoh laughed, and slapped him again.

"What is the cross?"

"Inner sign of the insignia of Shimazu and Satsuma," said Jinsuke. One of the officers kicked him in the head, knocking him over. Itoh dragged him back onto his knees.

"Do not dare associate our insignia with that. That is the cross of Christianity, as you well know."

Jinsuke did not. He had heard only vaguely of the foreign religion, and there were no hidden Christians in Taiji.

"Make him stand," said Itoh, and the officers dragged him to his feet. They pulled him over to the plate and told him to step on it. This was a ritual Jinsuke had heard about. In trampling the image of the mother of the foreign god, the Japanese showed their contempt, and their loyalty to Japan. Without hesitation Jinsuke stepped on the plate; it had grown hot in the tropical sun, and he winced.

"Hah! Se You wince to step on your barbarian god!" roared Itoh, felling him with a punch.

The questioning for the next few days, led by Itoh, was almost always about hidden Christians, a subject no amount of torture could make Jinsuke talk about, for he knew nothing. Thus was Jinsuke able to keep his secrets, and all the while the cold, unwavering eye of Itoh Hirosada was upon him.

At the end of one week they stopped torturing him and left him in the cage for almost another week, bringing food and water once a day. Then one morning they dragged him out. As his eyes adjusted to the glare of sunlight, Jinsuke was sure they were going to execute him. He straightened his shoulders, stood upright, and ignored the pain. Itoh came out of a building. He walked over and faced the prisoner, who glared straight back into the samurai's eyes. Itoh guffawed, then knocked Jinsuke to the dust with an openhanded blow.

"Such pride in a fisherman! What a funny fellow you are! Now we are going to take you to Kagoshima, where you will have even more to worry about. We are more sophisticated there."

The guards pulled Jinsuke to his feet.

After attending to the business of putting his seal to documents transferring the prisoner, Itoh bid farewell to the magistrate, promising to carry various messages of goodwill and many presents to mainland relatives and friends, and to carry personal letters directly to the magistrate's family, who were now in Edo. The magistrate came out into the courtyard to see Itoh off, glancing with mild curiosity at the battered face of the prisoner, a brave fellow by all accounts, even though a Christian rogue.

Some hours later the square-sailed junk slipped out of Naha, setting a course for Kagoshima. The great swell of the deep ocean brought a flood of memories of home, of his boat mates, of whaling, of Oyoshi, but the sound of wind in the rigging and the creaking of the timbers and mast gave Jinsuke no peace of mind. He thought too of Harue, and of his betrayal, for it must have been a betrayal, by Kinjo. He could not understand any of it.

After two days at sea Itoh came down into the hold and cut the ropes that tied Jinsuke's feet.

"Get up, whaler," he said, grinning. Damn him, always grinning, thought Jinsuke. Sullen and full of pain, Jinsuke stood up and steadied himself against the movement of the ship. He noticed that the ship's movements were fairly wild now, as if it were no longer making headway. He was pushed and prodded up and onto the deck. Sure enough, the sail was down. Two men at the big, open tiller looked at him, and they too were grinning. Two other sailors seized him.

"Watch that he doesn't kick," warned the samurai. He faced Jinsuke, speaking in a bantering tone, deliberately lacing his speech with rough Kyushu dialect. "Whaler, don't you hate this life? Would you not return to the sea, to the cool waves, find a turtle to take you down to the palace of the Dragon King? Is not death in the sea better than ending your life on an execution ground in Kagoshima? You are such an ugly fellow, and that head of yours would not look good on display."

Jinsuke, feeling both fear and resignation, said nothing.

"We would have a lot of explaining to do if we were so careless as to let our prisoner leap into the waves and commit suicide, but to the authorities, death is death, and you are such a stubborn fellow, and you would not talk." Itoh sighed, took a sailor's knife, and cut the ropes tying Jinsuke's arm.

"If you are going to murder me, use steel," he snarled.

Itoh laughed, turning to the sailors. "Such a hot temper—we must cool him off!" With that the two sailors pushed Jinsuke overboard. He spluttered to the surface, and with stiff muscles, began to swim. The waves were cool and blue around his body, and as he swam, the fear was no longer an animal lurking inside him. The sea was in his blood, and this sea was warm. Many of his ancestors had left their bones on the ocean floor, and there was no shame in that. He gazed up at the broad sky, laced with cirrus, felt his body lifted in the swell, remembered diving under whales with a rope to tie their bellies, and the first time he had cut a whale's nostril. If he turned his head he could see the junk, with the sailors hoisting up the sail again. It was leaving him, no matter, let it go. He had a few hours of life left, enough to think and remember, until exhaustion came and he would slip, down, down . . . unless . . . oh no! Sudden panic gripped him. He had not remembered until now, but the thought of sharks came to him. He yelled out for the junk to stop and started swimming after it, thrashing in the water.

Suddenly he was gripped, and he struggled in furious terror. A tremendous blow filled his head with green lights. Slowly he came round and began to struggle again, fearing the rip and tear of teeth, but instead he was pinioned in

208

huge, hairy arms, and he smelled a powerful odor of sweat and tobacco. The arms lifted him backward out of the water and dumped him into the bottom of a rowing boat. He had not seen it coming.

"Quiet, quiet, it's okay. Make trouble, I hit again. Quiet, no trouble, no hurt."

The voice was deep and gruff, and the Japanese heavily accented. Jinsuke lay still, took a few deep breaths, and looked around. The boat was full of foreigners, five of them, four pulling on oars and grinning at him, as if everything was a big joke. They rowed a little way, then stopped, while the huge, red-bearded man who had held him lifted a long bundle out of the water, then cut the cord tying it to two large empty flagons that had kept it afloat. He held the flagons for a while, as if to throw them back into the sea, but they looked useful and had some nice strong black characters on them, so he dropped both in the boat beside Jinsuke.

They began to row again, and for the first time Jinsuke spotted the masts and sails of a foreign ship, and surf breaking on the reef of a tiny flat island. It was not long before they reached the ship, and he was helped up a rope ladder. Within minutes the boat was swung inboard on its davits. Jinsuke could not believe himself. He was on the deck of a foreign ship, surrounded by foreigners, and they had saved his life. He dropped to his knees and bowed deeply.

The big man with the red beard laid a heavy hand on his shoulder. "No worry, no bow here. Stand." Jinsuke got to his feet and the man took Jinsuke's hand and shook it, smiling at him.

"We make greeting this way, not bow." He shook the hand again and let it go. Another man held out his hand and, hesitating, Jinsuke took it. This man too shook his hand. Jinsuke found himself in a circle of smiling foreigners, each taking his turn to shake Jinsuke's hand, a very strange and rather uncomfortable way of greeting, although he saw that it conveyed a sense of friendship. He had never held a man's hand since he was a small child.

"Now, get naked," said the red-bearded one. Jinsuke stared, not understanding, although the man had used his accented Japanese.

"Speak English?" asked the man, and Jinsuke nodded.

"Berry smaru," he stammered, hoping he would remember those lessons.

"Take off your clothes," said the man, slowly and patiently. "Very dirty, and wet. Take off."

Jinsuke untied the sash and stripped, feeling embarrassed. One of the sailors picked up his short kimono and threw it over the side. Another handed him white duck trousers, slightly frayed at the bottoms, but clean, and a coarse spun-cotton shirt. Jinsuke put them on, with some trouble getting his feet down the trousers and buttoning the shirt. As he fumbled, a boy with hair the color of dried straw helped him, saying words in a tongue that he did not know at all.

"English?" asked Jinsuke, then, after thinking, "American?"

"No," roared the big man. "Holland! Now you will go with us to China. You will be good. If not good . . ." He waved his huge, hairy, freckled fist in front of Jinsuke's eyes. Although Jinsuke was bigger and broader than most Japanese, this man was more than a head taller than he, and broad as a doorway. The other sailors laughed, and Jinsuke looked up into the man's eyes, wrinkles all around from sun and wind, eyes of the palest blue. Jinsuke saw no threat, even though he realized now that this was the man who had knocked him out as he struggled in the water. He waved his hand in front of his nose, rubbed his jaw.

"I be good," he said.

The man lapsed back into Japanese again.

"Fine, fine. Now you go and get a place to sleep, and some hot food. This is a good ship. Tomorrow you see captain." Then he bellowed orders to the other men, who dashed like monkeys up rope ladders strung from the masts, and pulled on ropes. There was a kind of balcony, with a roof on it, and open windows. Jinsuke could see one man standing behind a big wheel with many handles on it. The ship began to turn, wind filled the sails, and the ship started to move away from the island. The boy with straw-colored hair pulled on his arm and led him to a doorway just aft of the bows, then nudged him to go down a short wooden ladder into a cabin. Everything was cramped and crowded, with bunks all around. The boy pointed to one on which lay the long bundle they had taken from the sea. Jinsuke understood that this was where he would sleep. In the middle of the room was a table, with benches. A man in a white apron came down the ladder carrying a pot, a ladle and a bowl. He put the pot on the table and filled the bowl, beckoning to Jinsuke. The boy pushed Jinsuke to the bench and made him sit down, smiling all the time.

It was a stew, rather salty, with meat Jinsuke had not eaten before, paler than whale and darker than pork. It also

210

had potatoes, onions and beans. Ravenous now, Jinsuke ate. The boy gave him a large hunk of what Jinsuke knew to be bread, again something he had never eaten before. It was astonishingly good. Next the boy handed him a metal cup, with a round thing on the side, with which to hold it. The liquid in it was hot and dark brown, almost black. He sipped it and it almost scalded him; it was bitter at first, then very sweet. He took time to drink it, not sure whether he liked it or not. They filled his bowl again and gave him more bread, and he thought that he had never tasted anything so good, even if it was all odd. All around him the foreign seamen were smiling, watching him, their beards and hair of varying colors, their eyes blue, brown, gray, even green. He finished the mug and they poured him some more, and he saw them spoon sugar into it. Then one of them, an older-looking fellow, handed him a wooden pipe, its bowl enormous compared to the little brass pipes Jinsuke was used to. Next he passed him a leather pouch of tobacco, and the boy produced a hot coal from somewhere, holding it with tweezers.

The sailors tried to talk to Jinsuke, but he spoke no Dutch, and they knew but a few words of English, and no Japanese. Somebody hefted the long bundle off the bunk and laid it on the table, handing Jinsuke a knife. They all waited, curious to see what it was.

When he cut it open he found all those things, with the exception of the diary and notes, that he had hidden beneath the floor of his hut, plus one other small, heavy package. By the weight and shape of it he knew it contained gold *ryo* coins. While the others were exclaiming about the harpoon, and passing the *sai* around, and looking at the scrimshawed tooth, Jinsuke slipped the gold into his pocket. The boy handed the *sai* to him. They didn't know what it was. Jinsuke whirled it in his hand, showing that it was a weapon, and the old sailor who had lent him the pipe shook his head.

"No goot! No goot! You must give to captain," he said. Another man had brought in the empty sake flagons, and was tipping them one by one upside down, shaking them, making sad faces, then pointing to Jinsuke, capering around, pretending to be drunk. Jinsuke laughed with the rest of them. Yes, he thought, if I'd known I was coming I would have brought some good sake to share.

He hefted his harpoon and found another slim package wrapped around the shaft and doubly sealed in oiled paper. It was a letter. Jinsuke opened it and read it silently, much impressing the sailors.

211

"Whaler," it read, "if you come to Kagoshima we'll have to take your head. The gold is yours, from me. Passage on the foreign ship was paid for, in secret, in Nagasaki. I will tell Matsudaira Sadayorisama of what has befallen you. Yes, I knew, and you are a good, brave, stubborn fellow for not betraying him. Keep this secret too. One day, as long as it is not in Kyushu, I would like to hear the stories you will be able to tell, and will be interested in all you see and learn. Take care of your health."

The letter was not signed, but it was obvious that it was from the very same samurai who had captured and questioned him, and had him thrown into the sea.

Jinsuke carefully refolded the letter. Later he would crumple it and throw it into the sea. But he would never forget the face and voice of that samurai, nor would he forget Okinawa and its people. He knew that he could never return, not while Satsuma controlled the islands.

Everything had happened so quickly, everything was so strange, this transition from captive misery and fear to this admittedly small, smelly, yet warm, cozy and friendly place. He gazed at the faces of the animated, chattering foreigners and felt a spring of merriment bubbling up in his chest; he wanted to laugh out loud. It was like being in a room with a tribe of big, hairy, friendly monkeys, and Jinsuke liked it. Yes, he liked the foreigners, and he liked their ship.

Chapter Seventeen

Oyoshi watched him, fanning herself quietly. Saburo, she mused, finds more reality in his painting than in the world around him—but no, that was not fair, either; it was rather that Saburo transformed the world around him into his painting.

One day, a fisherman had landed a ray on the beach, a really big one. The ugly monster had lain on its back, lashing its long tail, with the deadly spines, and standing there, as if painting notes in his mind, Saburo had been fascinated by the colors of it, the white belly trimmed with orange, the orange tail tipped with black. One might think that only color and pattern were important to him, not that it was one of the biggest rays they had ever caught, or that it had been a dangerous struggle to get it in the boat, or that it would be delicious cooked in miso, or sun-dried. Yet when little Yoichi had toddled too near to the thing, it had been Saburo, not Oyoshi, who had been so fast at snatching the child out of the way of the poisonous, flailing tail.

In his seemingly distant way Saburo was always attentive, to Oyoshi, to her ailing father, to the child. He fixed things around the house, he brought little presents home, and he always did things before anyone had to ask him.

Jinsuke had been tall and muscular even for a Taiji man. Saburo had grown too, and had his brother's height, though he was more slender. Even though he had just turned twenty, he had developed a quiet maturity that drew older folk and children to him.

Saburo had kept the promises made between Oyoshi and himself when they were married. Not once had he touched her in a passionate way, nor said anything, nor made any kind of advance. Yet he was not cold. He was, as he said he would be, a loving older brother to her and a dutiful son and apprentice to her father, gradually taking over his workload.

In her own way Oyoshi had become very grateful for Saburo's presence and kindness. With him around, the house was fuller. When he ate out or worked late she found herself anxious for him to be home. Yet she didn't want him to touch her. When the child came to feed at her breast, which he still did although he was eating solid food too, the pleasant sensations of the little mouth suckling at her erect nipples evoked memories and fantasies of Jinsuke, thoughts in which Saburo figured only as a reason for guilt. When Saburo was there when the child took her breast, she pushed those thoughts of Jinsuke away, but when he was not there, she could not help herself.

Right now the child was standing and clinging with fat little fingers to Saburo's shoulder, gurgling happily as Saburo turned from the long scroll he was painting and tapped the child on the nose with the end of his brush.

"He really loves the boy," she thought, "as if he were his own." This made her feel warm and chill at the same time.

Her father often used to sketch designs out on paper before executing them on a boat, but Saburo, in the past year or two, had been spending almost all his spare time on long scrolls that folded out and told stories.

At first he had depicted the standard designs of the boats in the whaling fleet, with notes. Young Wada Kinemon, otherwise called Iori, had seen this, and praised it greatly, asking if he could have it for his office. Then when guests came, he said, he could show them the scroll and explain how each boat was different, and what its function was. He had become so enthusiastic about the scroll that he bought Saburo some fine paper from Kyoto, as well as expensive brushes and paints, and had asked him to paint more, even at the cost of his duties in the boat shed.

Oyoshi's father had pretended to be scandalized, but his delight was plain to see. After the boat scroll Saburo painted a folding scroll, four tatami mats in length, of a right whale hunt, with many scenes—the first sighting, the signals, the responses from Mukaijima, net setting, driving, harpooning, nose cutting, belly lashing, lancing. Then there were scenes of the whalers all stopping on the sea to say the Buddhist prayer "Namu Amida Butsu" for the soul of the whale, and after that the long, hard, but joyous haul as the whale was towed to the people waiting on the beach. All of it was done in astonishing detail and vivid color. When he was a boy, and out with the fleet, his boat mates were always yelling at him to quit daydreaming. But if he had been daydreaming, his mind and his eye had still been recording everything. All it needed was for him to have paper, paints and brushes, and he could bring everything back, so well that the men could even recognize their own faces.

Tatsudaiyu, his taciturn father, had almost gasped with astonishment when he saw the first part of the scroll being done, and had stayed up late that night to tell Saburo things about the hunt that he had never told anybody before. Then, every evening until the scroll was finished, Tatsudaiyu had come to check that his youngest son's memory was not at fault, filling him in on any small technical detail that might have been missed. The scroll became even more full of drama and movement.

Old Takigawa had been excited too, scolding and praising and fussing around, forgetting his bloody cough, which seemed to get worse, burning energy in trying to teach Saburo every single thing he knew.

The scroll of the right whale hunt had so pleased Kinemon and Kakuemon that they tried to pay Saburo a reward for doing it. He refused the money, though, as he had already received so many presents from them, and at this refusal they had presents of food and sake sent to the house. Kakuemon had the carpenters build Saburo a handsome working desk.

The scroll was sent to Lord Mizuno, daimyo of Shingu, and the lord himself sent a letter of thanks to Taiji, saying he would treasure it.

Saburo was further encouraged, and in the first part of that year he produced several scrolls, all of the various phases of whaling. There was one that showed the operations of flensing, cutting and boiling the blubber, breaking the bones, preparing sinews, packing meat for market, auctioning the oil. Kinemon and Kakuemon had both laughed heartily at a scene that captured the characters of the merchants—that fellow from Hiroshima with his big belly and round, fat face and his wispy beard; the sailors grimacing at the smells of whale cooking. He also did a scroll, for Kakuemon's personal amusement, of the various tricks the Taiji people pulled to hide and make off with pieces of meat.

Except for the one sent to Lord Mizuno, the scrolls were kept at the whaling office and shown to every visitor of importance. Saburo's work was praised even by well-known scholars, and several of the wealthier guests asked if this local artist could be commissioned to come and work for them.

Oyoshi put a large cup of cooled grain tea down beside him and picked up the child, who had become bored with the nose-tapping game and was now grabbing for brushes. She glanced at this newest scroll. It was quite different from all the rest. Now he was meticulously painting the obi, intricately embroidered, of a lovely girl.

"Oh, Saburo-san, it is so beautiful! Who is she?"

Saburo smiled. "She is one of the famous beauties of Taiji—Kannome, daughter of Kizaemon. Her father fought against Toyotomi Hideyoshi and was killed. After that she became a nun. Such a pity. When I finish it the scroll will also show the escape of three hundred twenty of our ancestors to the Kumano coast almost exactly three hundred years ago. One of them was a beautiful and intelligent girl called Fujiya. When the young lord of Shingu saw her he fell in love with her and begged the Wada house for permission to marry her, but she hated samurai, and ended up marrying a harpooner, Chodaiyu. So you see, it was the harpooners who got the beautiful girls in those days too."

He turned his face away from her, sadly, and pretending to ignore the last remark, Oyoshi leaned over closer to look at the painting of the willowy girl.

"Where do you get all these stories?" she asked.

"From the old folks," he answered. "Don't you see? Our village is unique in Japan! We started net whaling and it has been copied all over the country. We are descended from the Kumano sea raiders who changed history. We are linked with the fates of Genji and Heike. Our women are renowned for their beauty. There is so much that is important, but we have hardly any records. I can't write books, so I try to paint it all, to put down the life and ways of Taiji in these scrolls."

He withdrew into some secret place and sighed. "Things are changing. The whales are getting so scarce, and no new boats have been built for ages. We just repair the old ones. One day nobody will know anything about whaling with nets, or how the chase boats all had their own patterns."

"Nonsense!" snorted Takigawa from the other side of the room. Saburo smiled again.

"I hope so, Father. I really do hope it is nonsense. Anyway, what I want to say is that the few scrolls up to now have been painted by outsiders, by visiting scholars. Many are fine works, but quite often they are not accurate. My painting may not be as good as theirs, but my paintings are true." He blushed slightly, realizing that he had boasted, and bent back to his work.

"Those scrolls of yours are many times better than any I've seen done here before," said Takigawa. "Mark my words, your work is going to be treasured in this town after all of us have gone."

Saburo felt great pride in hearing this, but did not know what to say.

Oyoshi gazed over his shoulder at the beautiful lady he was painting. She wore the kimono of a rich person. She had been the daughter of a samurai, so perhaps she was wealthy. Her hair hung down to her waist. Oyoshi peered more closely at the face. She looks just like me, she thought, although Oyoshi did not wear her hair down like that, and she certainly had never worn such a rich kimono and obi. But the likeness was there, and Saburo was capturing the likeness on paper with deliberate intensity. Suddenly Oyoshi wanted to cry, for she surely knew now that Saburo loved her.

Oyoshi went to fetch her washbasin and hand towel, and hoisted the child to her hip.

"Excuse me, but if it's all right, I will go to the bath house now."

"Take care," said her father. After she left, he looked for a long time at his adopted son. "Everything is going well, isn't it?" he said.

Saburo turned slightly. "Yes," he replied, with a smile, behind which was more sadness than anyone could fathom.

The next day Saburo had to go to Moriura, the bay just around from Taiji, used very much by visiting fishing boats. There he was to meet a mountain man who was coming from the dense hill forests with a couple of tubs of tree resin, lacquer for the chase boats. He went there alone, sculling a small boat, humming a popular tune, enjoying the warmth of the early-summer sun on his shoulders and arms. As he came in close to shore he let the boat drift. There was coral in the shallows of Moriura, filled with hundreds of tiny black-and-white butterfly fish, each no bigger than a small copper coin. Along the shore were lilies, orange and white. The surface of the sea was pimpled with schools of yellowtail fry, and in the sky above were the ever-present kites, circling and trilling.

As he pulled the boat up he called out to an old man, a retired flenser, who was squatting on a rock, fishing for horse mackerel with a fine rod he had made himself, of bamboo tipped with right whale baleen.

"Catch enough for supper yet?" asked Saburo cheerily.

The old man muttered as he snatched for his line, wriggling with a small fish.

"The bay is full of these little mackerel," he grumbled, "and their flesh is too soft at this time of the year."

Saburo peered into the wooden bucket beside the man, where three horse mackerel were swimming.

"The horse mackerel are there," said the old man, "but these other greedy fellows snatch the bait each time." He threw the mackerel back in the water and rebaited his hook.

Saburo saw a movement at the edge of the trees. He reached into the boat and took out a packet of dried pilot-whale meat, dark and chewy. The mountain man did not come down to the shore but stayed where he was, just putting down the yoke and the two wooden tubs. He was a strange, almost surly fellow, a curved machete at his side, and even in the heat of summer he wore a waistcoat of raccoon dog fur. He never came into the village, but met people here, bartering resin and woven baskets for yams, meat, sugar and salt. He never ate rice, claiming that it rotted the guts. Saburo walked over and bowed slightly, handing over money and the packet of meat. From a small basket at his hip the man took out several cut sections of deer antler, handing them to Saburo without a word.

"Oh, thank you!" Saburo cried, for ground antler was one of the rare items needed to make his paints. The man stared at him, almost scowling, as if making up his mind whether or not to say something. Abruptly he jerked his head and spoke in his strange dialect.

"Pheasants be calling, all the time. Keep back from the shore. Catfish be astir. Take care, painter man. Mountain be angry, but safer."

In an instant, quick and silent as a ninja, he was gone, leaving a puzzled Saburo to carry the tubs of resin back to the boat.

He was heading back to Taiji when a strong gust of wind shook the trees on the shore and those growing thickly up the sides of the hills. Then the trees started to dance, branches waving frantically like the arms of revelers dancing to a festival drum. Boulders came crashing and bounding down the slopes, smashing pathways through thick undergrowth like raging wild boars. The trees shook with the wind . . . but there was no ruffle of wind on the waters. What the mountain man had said about the catfish now hit him. He was talking about the great catfish that lived under the earth.

"Earthquake!" He began to scull as fast as he could, to reach the town, frantic for the safety of Oyoshi, the child, old Takigawa. The hills growled. Saburo turned and saw huge slabs of rock tumble and slide into the sea off Tomyo Point. He pulled his boat up and leaped out. People were running and yelling, tiles were clattering and crashing off the roofs, people were shouting and fetching buckets to douse small fires. Saburo sprinted through the narrow streets, then stumbled and fell as the earth heaved. Like a drunkard aboard a ship at sea, he staggered his way to the house.

They were safe. Oyoshi had put out the cooking fire and taken Yoichi and her father to the temple yard. Saburo found them, hugging them in his relief.

When the shocks passed, they went back and began to tidy up the mess. A few broken tiles, some cracks in the plaster, a small cupboard tipped over, broken dishes. They were lucky that no serious fire had started in the town. With a glance around, Saburo went straightaway to fix the roof. Takigawa's face was waxen with strain and shock, so Oyoshi made hot tea and put him in his quilts, insisting that he rest. Yoichi was crying and fussing, and heavy though he was, Oyoshi hoisted him on her back, tied him with a broad sash and went to work in the kitchen.

Saburo heard her cry out with anguish and presumed that one of her mother's precious dishes had broken.

"Don't worry," he called to her, "I'll fix it for you." But it wasn't a dish. A pot of paint had fallen, the lid had come off, and Saburo's newest scroll was totally ruined. Saburo went in to find Oyoshi in tears. The beautiful lady, Kannome, had disappeared under an ugly puddle of blue paint. Saburo looked at it for a while, then put his arm around Oyoshi's shoulder.

"Never mind," he said, "when I paint her again she'll be even more beautiful. What if you help me by telling me what kind of kimono and obi she should wear?"

For some reason this made Oyoshi sob even louder.

Kakuemon and Kinemon came back from surveying the

damage at Tomyosaki. The lookout house would have to be completely rebuilt, and the shrine was damaged too. Financial worries weighed heavily on them, for they were responsible for the town. Kakuemon and Kinemon's forefathers had struggled for many years to win a rare privilege, that of freedom from direct control by the fief and Shingu castle. The whaling operations were their responsibility, and when things went badly, it would be on their shoulders that the blame fell.

However, equipment was run-down and whales were scarce. Taxes had been getting higher and higher. The fief did not control, but it certainly taxed. There was a ten-percent tax on all whale products sold; another five-percent tax on the total value of each whale caught; an inexplicable ancient tax, to be paid in silver, called "tongue money." Then, to top it all off, Taiji was forced to pay the *bakufu* a rice tax, even though Taiji had no suitable places for rice paddies. And whatever happened, taxes to the *bakufu* were to be paid, or the town officials and their families were severely punished.

This earthquake had come at a very bad time indeed.

Kakuemon felt age ache to the very marrow of his bones.

"Perhaps we should petition the castle at Shingu, ask to return to their control. They might postpone the taxes for a while if we did that, give us a little spare money to rebuild."

"No," said Kinemon firmly. "We got our independence only eight years ago. What would they think of us if we whined to give it up so soon? No, I won't give up. Let us pray for a few fat whales to put Taiji on its feet again."

His older relative looked back at the shattered town. "Yes, let us pray for whales . . ."

Chapter Eighteen

Sadayori forced his mind back, wrestling with all his memories, feelings, loyalties and beliefs. The last meeting he had had with Yoshida Shoin in Kyoto was bothersome, and what the man said, which conflicted with what he had tried to do, looped back, repeated. Yoshida was like an earnest man with a good wife he respected and treasured, falling in love with a beautiful, seductive whore he despised. Yoshida's inner conflict, like Sadayori's in some ways, was typical of the wrenching that so many patriotic Japanese were facing now.

Yoshida was under house arrest because he had tried to travel with one of the American warships. He and his teacher, Sakuma Zosan, passed a letter to a group of American officers who were strolling through the outskirts of Shimoda. Yoshida and Sakuma followed them, and then, while pretending to admire an officer's watch chain, one of them slipped a letter into the officer's pocket. It was a letter full of flattery, praising the Americans, begging them to take "two scholars of Edo" with them when they left, and to keep this secret from Japanese authorities.

That night the two Japanese rowed out in the dark. There was a heavy swell in the harbor. They reached one ship, but were told to go to the flagship. Tired and wet, they did, going aboard and letting the boat drift off. They even left their swords in the boat, so desperate were they to travel. Once on deck they pleaded with the officers, knowing that what they were doing, should they fail, carried a possible death sentence. Commodore Perry was also quite aware of the penalties proscribed by Tokugawa law, but he relayed

221

that with regret he had to deny their request unless they first obtained permission from their government.

The Americans lowered a boat, and after much pleading and a slight struggle, the two Japanese were taken to shore. Afterward they were caught by the authorities and kept in Shimoda in a cage, then removed to Edo. They were lucky, and did not receive the death sentence.

Sadayori had told them it would happen. By that time the Americans would do nothing that might jeopardize their negotiations for a treaty. In truth, he couldn't blame them for refusing the two. What if the would-be travelers had been sent by the *bakufu* to test the Americans? There were *bakufu* officials and guards all over Shimoda, so how did Yoshida and Sakuma expect to get away with it?

"But we must seize this chance!" Yoshida had said. "They are here, now, now! This is our last chance to study the powers of the foreigners!"

Sadayori knew that the two of them had also gone to Nagasaki to try to board a Russian ship, but they were too late, the ship had gone.

There were many young samurai who absolutely hated the idea of foreigners coming freely into the country, and yet held strong desires to go abroad themselves. Sadayori sometimes thought about it. The armed power and range of the American navy had stunned him and made him realize how out-of-date all his studies of war had been.

It had been difficult to arrange, but Sadayori had traveled all the way to Choshu, just across the Shimonoseki Strait from Kyushu, to visit Yoshida.

"You are fortunate to be alive," Sadayori told him. "Many spoke on your behalf, including, it seems, the American admiral."

"Barbarians! I despise them!"

"Indeed, so you often say, yet your actions seem to say otherwise."

Yoshida glared at the samurai from Kii. "They made the *bakufu* back down, and if we do not study them they will be too strong for us. That is why I wished to go abroad!"

Yoshida was allowed books. He pushed one with a marker in it toward Sadayori. Called *New Proposals*, it had been written thirty years ago by Aizawa, of Mito, a Tokugawa fiefdom on the Pacific coast, north of Edo.

"I have it," said Sadayori with a glance. "I know what it says."

Yoshida took it back, opened it, and insisted on reading

aloud: " 'Today the alien barbarians of the West, lowly organs of the legs and feet of the world, are dashing about across the sea, trampling other countries underfoot, and daring, with their squinting eyes and limping feet, to override the noble nations. What manner of arrogance is this! Everything exists in natural bodily form, and our Divine Land is situated at the top of the earth . . . America occupies the hindmost region of the earth; thus, its people are stupid and simple, and are incapable of doing things.' "

Yoshida closed the book, his eyes blazing with outrage and hatred. "Aizawa sensei is right! Absolutely right!"

"Yet you risked your life to try to travel with these stupid people and visit the hindmost regions of the earth."

"To know the enemy! Don't you see?"

To Sadayori it seemed that Yoshida's virulent hatred for the Americans would not be so violent had they taken him on board, and had he not been disgraced and punished because of their refusal. Yoshida's act of pleading with the Americans was something Sadayori could not condone. In Edo, months before, they had spent many hours discussing their mutual dislike of the barbarians, of what they had done to China with their opium and greed, of fears that they would try to take Japan, as they had taken almost every other Asian nation. These things they knew from the Dutch and Chinese who were allowed to trade in Nagasaki. For years now, although they were not allowed out of the country, scholars had accumulated and copied world maps, ocean charts and foreign books, many of them going on long and risky journeys to see somebody known to have any such a treasure, and to beg to be allowed to copy it. Young samurai like Yoshida were burning with a desire to know more, and at the same time bitterly humiliated by the Americans' display of power. Now Yoshida's hatred seemed almost insane; it was consuming him in a way that it had not before. It would prove dangerous for him and his friends.

"I went to Mito myself," said Yoshida, "to meet with Aizawa sensei. What a wonderful and wise man he is! He understood all those years ago just how vital our national polity is. It was the Sun Goddess herself who passed down the concept of loyalty to His Divine Majesty! That line, the very basis of our existence, has been unbroken for millennia. The barbarians would seek to break it, and the *bakufu* has betrayed the sacred trust . . ."

Sadayori silenced him with a gesture, and Yoshida took a deep breath, as if trying to control his passion.

223

"I know that you think the same way, Matsudaira, even though you are a Tokugawa man. You told us that the *bakufu* should have done more to prepare for the barbarians. You have spent half your life studying the problem! I say the *bakufu* must be . . ."

"Yoshida! You really are asking to be executed! Please, watch your words! This last time was a very near miss, and you are marked. As a friend from our Edo days, please, I beg you, take care."

Sadayori had traveled also to see Yoshida's former teacher, Sakuma Zosan; although he did not like the barbarians either, and was just as disappointed as Yoshida, he still favored the Treaty of Kanagawa and felt that Japan should open its ports, that it was essential for the nation to develop a strong economy, through trade, and to build up a powerful modern navy. For this they needed contact with the West. Sadayori didn't agree with opening ports, but he was a cooler and more controlled man than Yoshida, and he spent many hours discussing with Sakuma what kind of navy it should be, a topic so close to Sadayori's heart. Yoshida's rage was directed even at his former teacher now, and the two had quarreled irrevocably. Sakuma had become resigned and logical, while Yoshida had turned zealot.

All of this Sadayori had reported back in Edo, in secret, to Ii Naosuke, now the senior councillor of the Tokugawa *bakufu*. He had been called to Lord Ii's presence one night, a few days before the treaty with the Americans was signed. On first receiving the summons, Sadayori had felt a tremor of alarm. Had he been too blatant in his cries for development of a navy? He had realized that although his former plans to have whalers trained as a special attack force was a good one, he had to take the planning farther to include much more modern weapons—such as the howitzers the Americans had in their boats, the repeating rifles and pistols they carried. It was also necessary to start sweeping aside the old laws restricting shipbuilding, and begin to make a modern navy. He had written such things very plainly in his reports. Had they angered senior government men?

Sadayori had been called not for a warning, but because Lord Ii wanted him to become his secret agent, to seek out the company of anti-*bakufu* zealots and to report everything in detail, and in secret, to him. At first the idea appalled Sadayori. It required him to appear to become a *ronin,* an unattached warrior, to cut himself free from his duties to

224

the House of Tokugawa, to Kii and his fiefdom, to his clan, his lord. That was unthinkable.

Even so, Ii Naosuke convinced him. "Matsudaira-san, do you not understand that Japan is facing a civil war that will tear us apart? The foreign nations will back one side or the other with arms and insidious ideas, and then, when we are worn and battered from fighting each other, the foreigners will forcibly take control of our ports and harbors and will try to make us slaves. Oh, well I know the cry of the Sonno Joi—'Revere the emperor! Repel the barbarians!' But what that movement is really seeking is to overthrow the legitimate government of Japan, a government that has revered the emperor, protected him, and kept this nation in peace for close to three hundred years!

"Now I will confide in you. It is my belief that the next shogun will be the child lord of Kii. Work for me, and you will be working for him, protecting him and his government, his future, and the future of Japan.

"Those young fanatics, those lower-class samurai, have no right to voice their opinions on how the government should be managed. The country has been governed in peace by men of high standing and wisdom. That is the way it has been for centuries, and that is the way it must continue. Those fanatics will create disturbances and raise the heat of the emotions of the people. We must stop them. We know most of them, but we must know what they plan to do. I want you to be my eyes and ears. It will be highly dangerous and probably thankless, but you are the man to do it.

"I have long agreed with you that we must have a navy, a modern, powerful navy. You have been outspoken on that point. Serve me well, and you shall help build it. Give me your answer in one week."

Lord Ii had said many things; he had shown why he made the treaty with the Americans and how he intended to steer the course of relations with them. He convinced Sadayori that the policy of the lord of Mito, which was immediate war, would cripple the economy and delay the building of a navy by decades, perhaps forever. Lord Tokugawa Nariaki also had ambitions that his own son become the next shogun.

Sadayori saw where his duty lay, although it was one he preferred not to have. At the age of thirty-three, he would become a *ronin*, a "wave man," a wandering, masterless samurai, and he would serve, in secret, Ii Naosuke.

Almost every morning, after her chores were done, Oyoshi

would take Yoichi with her on a walk. Her family had no bossy older woman to tell her to do this or that, and Oyoshi was usually able to get her work finished early. Her father had taken to sleeping late, often not even bothering to get up for breakfast, and rather than disturb him she would take the child, encouraging him to toddle along as far as he could, then slinging him on her back when he tired. She would take a basket in hand and head for the shore or the fish market or, when the weather was pleasant, for the hillsides, where she could gather wild vegetables and mushrooms in season.

In winter Taiji was green, and rarely was it truly cold. There were flowers blooming in winter too, hibiscus, tiny yellow narcissus and many others. Oyoshi would sometimes pick the flowers and bring them home to brighten the little house, and for Saburo to sketch and paint them. Depicting the seasonal flowers of Taiji was another of his projects.

Winter. Drawing close to the New Year. Each day the watchers strained their eyes until they watered, as if they were trying to will a big, fat right whale to raise its double spout in their sight, to make all the difference to the celebrations to come. But right whales and humpbacks were scarce. Nature and the gods seemed to be oblivious to the needs of the whalers of Taiji.

Saburo was in the big shed at Mukaijima, working on repainting a boat. Weather had not been good that day, there had been wind, and the scent of a gale in the air, so the fleet, dejected and empty-handed again, came back in.

When they felt the first shocks of yet another earthquake the men rushed out of the boat shed.

"Look!" cried one man. "Look at the water in the bay!" In winter, the waters of Taiji harbor were always crystal clear. You could see rocks, schools of fish, anemones. But now the water had turned soupy with mud boiling up from the bottom, and the surface of the harbor and the bay and the waters around Mukaijima was agitated, like water in a shaken bowl. Tatsudaiyu realized the danger immediately.

"To your homes," he roared. "Get the women, children and old ones to high ground! Tsunami! Tsunami!"

There was a rush for the boats to ferry them across to the beach near the shrine. Tatsudaiyu sculled the boat that Iwadaiyu, Shusuke and Saburo, and a few others, had boarded. Tatsudaiyu called to Saburo.

"Where is Oyoshi?"

"If she's not home she'll be walking, maybe by the shore!" cried Saburo, the fear plain in his voice.

"Find them! Get them to high ground! Stop for nothing! Shusuke! Run to the house and get your mother. I'll go and get Takigawa!"

Their boat hit the shore and they leaped out, not even bothering to pull it out of the water. The men ran like frightened hares. There was no wind, yet the surface of the water was frothed with little waves. Saburo ran along the shore. Everywhere people were shouting, dashing here and there in haste to flee. Already the water was drawing back.

He found Oyoshi just beyond a small headland, with Yoichi on her back; she was staring in horrified fascination at a huge moray eel that had writhed out of its den in the rocks where the low-water mark had been. As if in a trance, she bent to pick up a small abalone left by the retreating waters.

Saburo leaped over rocks, seized her, and shook her hard. "Yoshi! Quick! Tsunami!"

Her eyes widened with horror and understanding, and flicked back to the now bare sea bottom. The sea had gone out of the bay so fast that the harbor was exposed—anchors, old fish heads, living, flopping fish. Before, there had been thirty feet of water; now there was nothing. Saburo hastily untied the sash and slung the bawling child onto his own back, pulling at Oyoshi. They ran for the nearest pathway upward. There was no time to make for the better routes with steps. The hillside shook and small stones rattled around them. Quickly, quickly, never mind the small pains and scrapes! The sea was pulling back its fist and would soon smash it toward them! Oyoshi dropped her basket, and shells tumbled out. She stopped momentarily, as if to retrieve them, but Saburo cursed angrily and dragged her on. Yoichi was screaming with terror, and slipping off his back; Saburo reached his left arm over his shoulder and seized the child by the scruff of his neck to hold him. Their chests heaved with effort, their breath rasped, knees and elbows were scraped, feet bruised. The hill seemed even steeper, the path narrower, branches grabbed at them, whipped, and thorns tore. Glimpses through the trees showed them views of the bay, its bottom bereft of water a long way out.

"Father . . ." wailed Oyoshi.

"My father went for him! Now come, Yoshi! We must get higher! The wave will come soon!"

The great wave came. It charged up the bay in an awe-

227

some wall, ripping whitely along the high cliffs from Tomyo-saki, gathering terrifying speed and height, a growling, hissing wall, sixty feet high. It raced toward the harbor, toward the huddle of houses cowering by the shore. It smashed through the warehouses and sheds of Mukaijima, spinning whale boats round and round like autumn leaves in a stream, tumbling them over and over through the wreckage. It crashed through the houses closest to the beach, sweeping them away in the white spray and boiling water and mud, wooden beams, pieces of walls, bedding, roofs, all in turmoil.

The first great wave receded, strewing wreckage everywhere. Then it roared back, as if the sea had become a vengeful army, hurling itself in suicidal charges on the fortifications of an enemy. Five times the tsunami charged and retreated, until the town of Taiji was almost totally destroyed.

From their vantage point on the hill, Oyoshi watched over Yoichi's head as she knelt and held him tight in her arms. Saburo held onto the trunk of a small tree. The ground shook from time to time beneath their feet, and they prayed that the hillside would not slip down, and that their families were safe from the fury below them. Then, almost suddenly it seemed, all was quiet but for the cries of people, the mewling of cats, skinny with wetness, the whining of a dog trapped under wreckage.

"Stay here, Yoshi," said Saburo, "I'll go look." His voice was quiet. She clung to him, weeping soundlessly.

"Saburo, no, no, I don't want you to leave us! Oh, Saburo, if you hadn't come, Yoichi and I would have been down there!" He put his arms around her and patted her back.

"You're safe, both of you. All right, let's go together. Come to Father, little boy."

He took Yoichi from her. With eyes wide and a runny nose, the boy stopped weeping and sniffled. "You're getting too heavy to carry, you know," said Saburo. Then, reaching out a hand for Oyoshi, he started for the path.

Shusuke had taken his mother and old man Toumi to safety up the steps that led past the Buddhist temple and the cemetery. Tatsudaiyu had gone to Takigawa's, woken him, and urged him to hurry. But, Takigawa had become querulous and argumentative about leaving, and in the end Tatsudaiyu had to pick him up and carry him through the narrow streets and up the steps. They were among the last to leave; the first wave funneled up through the narrowing valley and reached up like a paw, and the undertow sucked them both down the slope again. Tatsudaiyu managed to cling to the trunk of a sturdy tree, hanging on for dear life, his and his old friend's.

Bruised and battered, Tatsudaiyu fought the pull of the waters, knowing real terror of the sea for the first time, knowing that if he let go it would mean certain death for both of them. Then, as the first wave began to rush back out, Tatsudaiyu slung Takigawa, now unconscious, over his shoulder and staggered up the slope until other men saw them and helped them to safety.

The last waves had gone. With barely any change in their expressions, the men of Taiji looked at each other and at the wreckage of their homes and livelihood. Then they started down together to begin to salvage what they could, wary of another wave. Tatsudaiyu, however, was in great pain, and Takigawa was ashen and unconscious, barely breathing. They carried him to Tatsudaiyu's upland gardening hut.

Saburo, now carrying the child, together with Oyoshi picked his way through the smashed town. Nothing was left of their house. It was one of the twenty-seven houses that had been completely washed away, together with the whaling office and the warehouses. They went on up the steps, praying that they would find their families.

They reached the neat little plots of yams, scallions, burdock, beans and other vegetables that were tilled up above the town and the cliffs, and saw a little group of people outside Tatsudaiyu's hut. Shusuke ran to greet them. Onui, her face streaming with tears, was boiling water on a little fire outside. They went into the hut. Tatsudaiyu was slumped dejectedly against the wall, exhausted and in pain from three broken ribs. For the first time Saburo realized that his indomitable father was actually growing old. Takigawa, his adoptive father, lay face up on a square of matting, but they could not see his face, for somebody had covered it with a clean white cloth. Numbly, Saburo wondered how they had found a clean white cloth in all that confusion. He stood there, holding Yoichi, then dropped to his knees. Takigawa the painter was dead.

Old man Toumi knelt beside him, chanting a prayer in a monotone, a rosary of beads in his hands. In festivals and weddings the people were Shinto, faithful to the shrine at the edge of the sea, but in death they were Buddhists. Old man Toumi raised his now sightless eyes toward them.

"Your father saved him," said the old man. "They were both nearly swept away, but he carried him and hung onto him. We got him up here afterward, and dried him off and kept him warm, but he breathed his last less than half an hour ago, never coming around. He was weak. It was too much for him."

Oyoshi shrieked in her anguish, then with a low sob fell across her father's body. Saburo wept silently. He turned and laid his head on his father's knees. Tatsudaiyu put one hand on his shoulder.

"Father, thank you. You did what you could, and had it not been for your warning, Oyoshi and Yoichi would have been dead too. Perhaps all of us would have been dead. Now I will leave my wife and child and go down to the town with the other men to see what I can do."

Wincing, Tatsudaiyu got to his feet, his face gray as ash. "I will come with you."

Then, slowly and sadly, Tatsudaiyu and his two sons went down to the mess that had once been their town.

My scrolls, thought Saburo, looking across to where the whaling office had been, they're all gone, all my work . . . Then he looked around at the wreckage that had once been homes, and was ashamed of his self-centeredness.

They were not to know it for some time, but the tsunami had devastated towns and villages all along the coast of Japan. Fires that had started as a result of the earthquake had totally destroyed Osaka and severely damaged Edo.

Many said that this was all a punishment from the gods, angered as they were because barbarians had been permitted to tread the sacred soil of Japan. In Taiji they didn't care about that. There was too much work to be done.

A few days later, around new graves, small yellow daffodils nodded in the wind. Only the kites, filled with the fish that had been thrown high up on the shore, seemed at all happy with life.

Chapter Nineteen

They approached the mouth of the Yangtse River at ten in the morning. It was foggy, and the pilot's cutter took time to locate. Jinsuke noted that his shipmates were nervous: the officers had strapped on pistols, short, snubby brass cannon on swivels were mounted on the gunwales, and bags of shot were stacked beside the merchantman's small cannon. Mr. Hoek, the mate, glanced quickly about, for a second meeting Jinsuke's questioning gaze.

"Pirates," Hoek said, in English.

"Excuse?" said Jinsuke, not understanding. The big Hollander switched into Japanese.

"Pirate . . . Chinese 'wako' . . . you know? Lots around here, more upriver. They come, we fight." He drew a finger across his throat.

But there was no need for alarm. A shape appeared out of the fog, the pilot's cutter. It hailed them.

The channel to the great river was about two miles wide. On either side were extensive shoals, called by most foreigners the North Sand and the South Sand. Tides were about ten feet, and there were many groundings, for as yet no buoys or lighthouses had been placed, despite the fact that Shanghai was now one of the world's busiest ports.

By noon the fog had lifted, and Jinsuke could see the outline of an irregular group of islands. Landward, the scenery was rich, fertile, but alien and depressing. It was so unlike Japan. There were no green forested hills, no blue-water bays nestling in the arms of headlands, no clear rivers rushing and gurgling through valleys and meadows. As far as the eye could see there were flat alluvial plains planted with rice, beans, wheat, barley, potatoes. Hundreds of small boats and several large boats and junks plied the river, and the captain went carefully.

Shanghai, with its population of more than a quarter of a million, was located on the left bank of the Wampon, a tributary of the Yangtse. The Dutch merchantman anchored first off the village of Woosung, at the mouth of the tributary, where the foreign traders had built receiving stations for incoming ships. All around there were war junks, flying the flags and pennants of imperial China.

"China is a bad place, lots of fighting," said Hoek.

"Why do you come?" asked Jinsuke simply.

"For tea, tea. We take tea back to Holland," the mate answered, then tapping him on the shoulder and telling him that the captain wanted to see him. Jinsuke followed. They ducked into the narrow doorway of the captain's cabin and Jinsuke tried to stop himself from staring, for although the cabin was small, in comparison to the cramped quarters of the crew it was both sumptuous and fascinating. There was a bunk bed, covered with clean white sheets, and on one bulkhead were many shelves, filled with books. So the captain was a scholar! He sat in his shirtsleeves, a black cravat tied neatly at his neck, his hair short and graying slightly; he wore tight gray trousers tucked into calf-high black boots. He was leaning over a writing table, poring over a ledger. He looked up to face them. Jinsuke was astonished when the captain spoke in fairly good Japanese.

"Now you will go by boat with me to the city," he said. "Get your things ready. First, read this and put your seal to it." Jinsuke bowed deeply, speaking his appreciation for his rescue, for the kindness with which they had treated him. He took the paper, which was folded in the Japanese way, and unfolded it carefully. The characters had been written by an educated person, and they were difficult for Jinsuke, but he got most of them. The gist of the document was to say that he, Jinsuke the whaler, had been delivered safely to Shanghai. Jinsuke hesitated, and impatiently the captain said that if Jinsuke didn't trust him, the document could be seen to on the dock. Embarrassed now, Jinsuke stammered that he had no seal. The captain laughed. He had been used to samurai, *bakufu* officials and merchants.

"Oh, of course, I apologize. If you can write, just put your name here. If not, we will ink your thumb and make a sign."

He pushed a silver inkwell and a quill pen toward Jinsuke, who just stared at them, growing red in the face. The captain rummaged around in a drawer and brought out a Japanese brush. Jinsuke inked the characters of his name. The captain looked at the paper, nodded, and extended his hand.

"We will go and land in China now. The first time for you." He pronounced his words carefully. "Japan is a good country, with good people. In China and in foreign countries there are many good people, but many bad people too. Take care." He hesitated, as if not knowing what to say. "Things are changing in Japan, and if you ever go back to Nagasaki, go to Deshima, and leave a message for me, Captain Bloeming. I will take you to an American man, tell him you are . . ." He had lost the Japanese word for *whaler*, so Jinsuke gave it to him. The captain smiled, and quickly wrote it down. "You wish to hunt whales? It will be hard with one arm."

"I can do it," said Jinsuke gruffly, but feeling his heart lift. The captain nodded.

"Fetch your things. We go in one hour."

Jinsuke had few possessions—his harpoon, his *sai*, some gold, the scrimshawed tooth, the clothes he wore and a sailor's knife in a leather sheath, given to him by one of the crew. All of his papers, including his diary, had been lost, but he had discovered, folded up tightly and sealed with beeswax in the hollow of the tooth, another letter, written in English, one that he had brought from Edo, one that he would show only to a whaling man.

Jinsuke, the captain and Mr. Hoek left the ship and headed upriver in a hired Chinese boat. Jinsuke kept the *sai* hidden under his shirt, but the mate spotted it, tapped the bulge of the hilt under the cloth, and winked, opening his own jacket to reveal the butt of a pistol.

The waterfront of Shanghai was well constructed of cut stone, with jetties that thrust out into the water, and fine stone buildings of Western design that looked out on the incoming shipping. Since the defeat of the Chinese in the Opium War with England, the foreign residents had built considerably in the city. By 1854 in the foreign residential and business districts the streets were wide and well paved, and there were many sumptuous dwellings and beautiful gardens.

The Chinese quarters, on the other hand, had streets three paces wide, bisected with even narrower alleys. Not that this struck Jinsuke as being unusual when he finally got to see the area, for Taiji was that way too, except that Taiji was immaculately clean, while these Chinese districts were

233

teeming with humans in all states of poverty and sickness, rife with beggars and thieves, and filthy and stinking underfoot.

The three men disembarked at the jetties close to the three-story American consulate, then walked to the offices of a large American company. People stared at them. It was unusual enough to see a couple of white men in the company of a one-armed, barefoot Oriental; in addition, Jinsuke was strikingly dark and muscular, with hair pinned in the Okinawan style, and he carried a long harpoon, albeit with the head sheathed.

They strode up the wide stone steps of the building. It had double doors, very thick, with gleaming brass handles.

"Wait here," said the captain. He and the mate went inside. It wasn't long before a large, staring, gabbling crowd had gathered, everyone pointing at and discussing this odd-looking stranger. The mate came out, scattering the crowd with a few poorly aimed kicks; this profoundly shocked Jinsuke, even though he had become used to the rough ways of the men at sea.

"Come," he said, beckoning Jinsuke, who followed him into the high-ceilinged outer offices, past several shocked customers who stared and muttered as he passed, then into the inner sanctum of a portly middle-aged man with graying hair and spectacles. The captain introduced him as Mr. Rose. He smiled and spoke to Jinsuke, who picked up only a few words—"day . . . see . . . pleased"—although the greeting sounded long. The captain translated into Japanese.

"There are no whaling ships in Shanghai now. You must stay for a while. Tomorrow Mr. Rose will find you work on a ship. I told him you are a good fellow. When a whaling ship comes, Mr Rose will ask the captain for you. If a whaling ship does not come, you must go across the sea to Hawaii or California, places where there are many whaling ships."

All at once, it was too much for him. Jinsuke made a bow, not knowing how to react.

"Leave harpoon," said the mate. "When whale ship come, you take. Mr. Rose is a good man, good man for all sailors." The mate took the harpoon from Jinsuke and propped it in a corner, explaining to the merchant, who nodded and smiled again.

"We'll do our best for him," he said to the captain. "I've always envied you Dutch, always wanted to visit Japan myself. Shouldn't be too long now, the way things are going with Commodore Perry's expedition. They've been in here too, you know."

He turned and wagged a finger at Jinsuke. "You must learn English, Mr. Jinskee. English!" Jinsuke remembered that from his lessons when he first got to Okinawa.

"Yes, sir. I study," he said.

"Sayonara," said the captain, extending his hand. "Go with Hoek-san. I have business with this man."

Jinsuke bowed. He went to the door, turned, and bowed again. Outside, the mate turned and put one beefy hand on Jinsuke's shoulder.

"You good man. You stay alone in China and . . ." He made that gesture again, drawing a finger across his own neck. "Come, you need things. You got gold, we use, just little."

Dumbly trusting, Jinsuke followed. Four hours, and what seemed like a great deal of money later, Jinsuke was wearing calf-high boots of fine, supple leather; he had bought three shirts, a waistcoat of embroidered silk, a coat of fine English wool cloth that flared out from just below his groin to two tails that hung down to the back of his thighs, double-breasted, with buttons of polished deer horn, two pairs of pants of the same cloth, three pairs of cotton working pants, three rough cotton working shirts, a broad belt with a brass buckle, six pairs of socks and a duffel bag. He also had a new knife of excellent Swedish steel in a leather sheath, and the rest of his money was in a money belt inside his shirt. The greatest transformation of all, however, came about when Hoek dragged him into a barber's shop, forced him into a chair, gave orders, and watched with folded arms and a stern face while Jinsuke's hair was cut short in a Western style. The two brass pins Hoek pocketed, "as a souvenir."

When they came out of the barber's shop the mate held Jinsuke by the shoulders and examined him.

"Good, good." He stared closely at him and rubbed his chin thoughtfully. "You not like most yellow men, you got thick beard."

The mate used the correct Japanese word for beard, but Jinsuke misunderstood for a few moments, for it was also the correct word for baleen. No man in Taiji wore a beard, and baleen was something that had been a regular part of his conversation back home. The mate nodded his head and cupped his hands around Jinsuke's darkly stubbled chin, as if trying to envisage what it would be like.

"Yes. Good. A beard! But cut neat and short, yes, yes."

Then Jinsuke understood and shook his head. "No, no, I'm not hairy Ainu from up north!"

The mate pounded him on the back. "You're a sailor man! Sailors have beards! You're a man who goes to sea on a ship. Then come to shore, eat, drink, find women. Come now, sailor, we eat first. China best for eating!" He winked. "Good for women, later."

Then, with a great laugh, he pulled Jinsuke by the arm and marched off through the crowded streets, scattering people like a barge. The day ended in a glorious blur.

The following morning, armed with a note from Mr. Rose, and accompanied by the mate, Jinsuke went by boat back to Woosung, where he was introduced to an Irish-American named Fogerty. Fogerty was skipper and owner of a small steam-assisted paddle wheeler, the *Irene,* which plied the great river, taking passengers and light cargo to river ports and cities farther inland. Like the Dutch mate, Fogerty was a huge man, bearded, and with long, thick, hairy, freckled arms. He towered above Jinsuke, and had the biggest belly Jinsuke had ever seen, with the exception of the sumo wrestlers who had competed in Wakayama when he went with the whaleboats and Sadayori. He spoke Chinese fluently and wrote several hundred characters. He was reasonably honest and utterly reliable. He was a prodigious drinker too and, being of Irish stock, not averse to a fight if pushed. But this was not the reason that he was not welcomed in the polite foreign circles of Shanghai. The trouble was that he had a Chinese wife, whom he adored, and several half-Chinese children. He once insulted the wife of a prominent banker who tried to commiserate with him on how hard it would be for his children in society.

"And pray why, madam? They're bright, winsome and healthy. And madam, you said yourself to yon gentlemen that you were half English, half French, did you not? Well now, that makes you a half-caste yourself. At least, unlike some around here, you and my kids are not bastards, right?"

Her husband rushed over and remonstrated with Fogerty, but he just laughed his gay Irish laugh and walked off to raid the punchbowl again.

Jinsuke brushed off his new trousers after climbing the rope ladder up the side of the ship, a climb carefully watched by Fogerty. Now, as he straightened up on deck, he came under the steady gaze of pale blue eyes.

"You say that this fellow is a Japanee, Mr. Hoek?"

"Yes he is, Captain. We fished him from the sea ourselves."

236

"Why is he escaping?"

"They threw him in the sea themselves. We got paid good gold to bring him." Hoek shrugged. "He got enemies, he got friends. On ship he's good man, even with just one arm."

Fogerty lit a cheroot and narrowed his eyes. "If a man wants friends, good friends, then he's got to have a few enemies tucked away too, I guess. As for the arm, he came up that rope ladder nimble enough. Does he have the Chinese tongue then, Mandarin? Cantonese?"

"Not a word," said Hoek, "just his own tongue and a little English. He's willing, though."

"Well, what's your name?" asked Fogerty, in English. His accent was strange to Jinsuke and he had to repeat the question, slowly, before Jinsuke understood. Jinsuke, in turn, had to repeat his name three times. The Irishman shook his head.

"As a name, it's right enough where you come from, I suppose, but to me it makes you sound like either a drunkard or a Russian. Can't have a fellow called Gin or Somethingski on my ship. No, it won't do, won't do at all. I'll call you Jim, Jim Sky. You hear?" He pointed his big finger at Jinsuke, tapping him in the middle of the chest. "You're now Jim, Jim . . . Sky. Get it?"

Hoek laughed, and explained as best as he could to Jinsuke, pointing upward to indicate the meaning of half the name. Jinsuke felt honored; whereas before he had only one name because he was not of the *bushi* class, now he had two.

"I am Jim Sky, Japan whaler, damn good fellow," said Jinsuke, and Fogerty roared with delight, slapping him on the back.

"Fine with me. Mr. Hoek, carry my regards to Mr. Rose when you see him and tell him I'll be glad to look after Jim Sky here until word of a blubber boiler comes in. Jim can help me keep an eye on these thieving river rats. Now, from the redness in your eyes, and the pallor on your cheeks, I would think it timely for a spot of hot tea and medicine." He turned and bellowed aft.

"Wong!"

At Fogerty's bellow, a squat, pigtailed man came running. Fogerty spoke to him in Chinese, and Wong then indicated that Jinsuke should follow him to his quarters. As Jinsuke turned to go, Hoek extended his hand, while Jinsuke, now Jim Sky, took it firmly.

"Take care," said the mate, who had fished him from a

distant and long-ago sea, speaking in the last Japanese he would hear for a long time. "The Chinese will try to steal from you. Never smoke their dream stuff, be a good sailor, and obey and serve this captain. He is a good man."

Jinsuke bowed slightly. "Thank you. I am in debt to you," he said formally, feeling his chest fill with emotion at having to part with this big, friendly man, who had not only saved him, but taught him all he could in the short time available. Quickly Jinsuke followed the Chinese crewman. Fogerty took the Dutchman to his own cabin.

Later, as they sipped mugs of sweet, strong, aromatic tea, liberally laced with dark rum, Fogerty asked a question of the Dutch mate.

"Tell me, why would Mr. Rose, who lets no weeds grow in his garden, and who is a very fine American gentleman, from Fairhaven, now why would he want to take care of Jim Sky here?"

The Dutchman leaned back against the polished mahogany of the bench, which was stuck away in a corner of the cabin, below the open porthole.

"It's a long story, and I don't know half of it," he began, not wanting to mention Mr. Rose's gunrunning ventures. "But first, you know that his ships are running from here to California, and that he is one of those who believe that steamers are a thing of the future?"

Of course Fogerty knew that. He leaned over and poured more rum into the other man's mug.

"Well then," continued the Dutchman, "you also know that Perry just opened two more ports in Japan, and he's got them to sign a treaty agreeing to supply coal and provisions and not to harm American ships or men. He's not got any promise of trade yet, mind you, though we reckon that it's bound to come in Nagasaki. The Russians were fast on Perry's tail, then the French and the British."

"Ah, the bloody English," said the Irishman. "Damn their eyes!"

"Well, you see, Japan has been closed to all but us and the Chinese for nigh on three hundred years. Oh, I tell you, Captain, it's a fine country, Japan, peaceful and beautiful as a garden. Sure, the samurai are a brutal, arrogant, bloodthirsty lot at times, with horrible things they can do to a man, but I would venture to say that on the whole the Japanese are the most civilized, the most clean and intelligent race in the whole of Asia. Now they are going to open up, it's bound to come. They learn fast. Japan is going to be an important country to America. Good water, timber, coal, silk, all kinds of things."

"What you tell, I've heard before, but why this Jim Sky, and why a whaler?"

"Can't rightly tell you. He was in trouble in Okinawa, but what it was I don't know. I do know he's got powerful men behind him, and that a very important official came aboard us at night in Nagasaki, and paid us good gold to guarantee we get him here and see him safe. I can also tell you that those Orientals do not forget a favor, and if they do, it's a lasting shame to them."

Fogerty puffed on his cheroot and nodded; among his wife's family it was the same. "And the whaling business?" he asked.

"Mr. Rose has a close family friend, back in America, a ship's captain, name of William Whitfield. They were both from Fairhaven, Massachusetts. Well now, that captain picked up four Japanese who had been blown out to sea and marooned on a little island. One of them was just a boy, as bright and pleasant as a button. The captain educated him, treated him like a son, and in time the fellow himself rose up to be first mate on a Yankee whaling ship. A few years ago, this Japanese, name of Joe Mung, slipped back into Japan, through Okinawa. It was 1851, a few years before the Perry Expedition arrived. He slipped ashore in a small boat. I don't know whether it was a brave or a stupid thing to do. By all accounts he should have had his head chopped off— they do that, you know—but instead we get word that he has been given rank, made advisor to the court."

Fogerty took a hefty swig from his mug and whistled. "A smart gentleman, Mr. Rose. So it'll do no harm to make friends in Japan, will it?"

Hoek leaned across the table. "And our Jim Sky, he must be really well connected. This man, this official in Nagasaki, we happen to know he's personal doctor to the Tokugawa court, and they're the boys in charge. He said if we let any harm come to Jim, the next time we came to Nagasaki they'd find opium in our cargo and would confiscate the whole ship, and maybe have our heads too. Now this is not the way things have been until now. The Japanese don't come right out and say things like that. Things are changing, and somehow, Jim's got something to do with it, though for the life of me, I don't know what."

"Reckon he's a spy?" said Fogerty, frowning.

"On what? The Japanese in Nagasaki know everything

that's going on in Shanghai, even if they don't come here themselves. They've got regular reports coming in, from the Chinese. No, I don't know, but the Japanese are pretty hard to figure out."

"I see," said Fogerty, pouring the last of the rum into both of their mugs. "But you really think the country will open up for trade, eh?"

"Yes," said Hoek, "but there'll be some hell to pay."

Fogerty's face creased in a grin. "And the first thing those devils will pay for is guns, right?"

Hoek feigned ignorance and innocence in the talk of guns. Only he, the captain of his ship and Mr. Rose himself were supposed to know about the secret order from the Satsuma clan for several hundred breech-loading, lever-action Maynard .50 caliber rifles. But he was sure of one thing—there would be no opium in Japan. He had little liking for what had happened in China, even though the Opium War had given them some safe trading places. As Hoek finished his mug and stood to leave, Fogerty waved his hand.

"I'll look after the Japanese if he'll stand by me and my ship. Tell Mr. Rose not to worry." He paused. "You don't have to tell him this—but in my opinion the Enfield is still a more accurate and reliable rifle, and he can get them at a better price."

Hoek looked slightly alarmed, but Fogerty put his great fat finger against his lips, and winked. "Don't worry," he said, "I'm no pirate."

Although Jinsuke was impatient to find a whaling ship and begin to learn the ways of the foreign whalers, he settled down on the *Irene* and diligently began to learn the names of things, orders and methods of the ship and its captain. He was agile, immensely strong, and always cheerful and willing to work, and his own natural sense of seamanship made him an apt pupil for the big-hearted Irishman. Whenever he was yelled at, he apologized, never growing surly, never offering an excuse, even if it was not he who was at fault. Jinsuke would look for things to do. With his teeth, his knees, his feet and one arm, he could do the most intricate splicing, and Fogerty could not find a loose or uncoiled piece of line or cable anywhere on his ship. Since Jinsuke was put in charge of the decks they were spotlessly clean, despite the black smoke and smut that came from the chimney when the boilers were fired up. Fogerty recognized that here was a man who had a genuine love of ships and the great waters, quite unlike the rest of his crew, and although the captain tried hard not to show it, Jim Sky soon became his favorite.

"Ah Jim, my boy," he would say, "you'll not be working this muddy old stream for long. Time will come when you'll be facing a tempest out at sea on a blubber boiler, where the food's rotten and the smell's worse, then you'll miss the *Irene*."

Days passed into weeks, then months. Taiji, Okinawa, Edo . . . they all seemed to drift into an unreal realm of clearly remembered but discarded dreams. Jinsuke's English improved slowly, and he learned Chinese as well, helped greatly by the little Chinese engineer, Wu, with whom he communicated, in his free time, with pen and brush; although the languages of the two men were different, Japanese had borrowed Chinese ideograms, and on paper they could understand each other.

On the whole, the rest of the crew stayed away from Jinsuke. He was a stranger, for one thing, but also they saw that whenever he could, and whenever he thought nobody was looking, he practiced a punching, striking, kicking martial art, and that he was close to being a master with the killing iron of Okinawa. Some of them had seen the scars on his back, souvenirs of the jail in Naha. They sensed that he could not be bribed or threatened, and that he was not an easy man to deal with.

One morning, when Jinsuke was on his knees, holystoning the deck, he heard Fogerty cursing. He looked up, and saw nothing strange. The American warship *Plymouth* was still anchored off the foreign wharves, a familiar shape from Naha, left behind by Perry to protect American interests in Shanghai from marauding imperial troops. Two fine British warships, the *Encounter* and the *Grecian*, were also in harbor, protecting British interests. Since these ships had been around, the imperial junks had stopped their tricks, and life for honest men on the river was on the whole a lot easier. From a houseboat alongside the *Irene* baskets of live chickens and fresh vegetables were being passed up to the cook. Nothing seemed to be amiss.

Wu was out on deck, yelling down at the girl in the houseboat and at the cook leaning over the side. Captain Fogerty came down from the bridge, cursing in Chinese, yelling at the engineer.

Jinsuke got slowly to his feet, puzzled at all the shouting, for it was all in Chinese, and all very loud. Fogerty glanced at Jinsuke.

"Five of them, Jim, five! Five deserted ship, and us due to sail this morning!"

He turned back to Wu, who was pointing at five strange Chinese standing on the dock. Wu was arguing, shaking his head, and Jinsuke caught enough words to know that Wu did not want those men taken on in place of the five deserters, and that he wanted the ship to sail later. Jinsuke glanced over to the five Chinese on the dock. One of them was a tall, well-muscled man in his middle thirties. They stood, faces blank, waiting. The argument went on for some time, but in the end Fogerty waved aside Wu's objections. He went to the side of the ship and beckoned to the five men. Following the tall one, they came up the gangplank, set ready for passengers and cargo.

Later, when Jinsuke had time for a short break and went down to the engine room to share some tea with Wu, the little engineer brought out paper and brush from his little cubbyhole, and then wrote a few characters: "new," "men," "evil," "fist." Jinsuke looked at him and said the words "bad men" questioningly. Wu shushed him but nodded vigorously, and touched Jinsuke's fist, making a twisting, punching movement, similar to the Okinawan straight-armed thrusting punch. Jinsuke nodded, determining to watch the new men very carefully, and to be wary of them.

For the whole of the trip upriver he watched them, noticing that the tall one, the one who seemed to be the unspoken leader, moved with a cat-footed grace. Yet none of them bore the pronounced calluses that Jinsuke did, although they had well-developed hands, and heavy muscles in their forearms that rippled whenever they had to climb rigging or haul ropes. The other crew members seemed both afraid of and deferential toward the five new men, and several of them began to spend all their free time around them.

When they got back to Shanghai the five men went off the ship, the leader promising to be back the following day when the *Irene* was due to sail again. Fogerty watched them and the rest of the crew go ashore. Only Wu and Jinsuke slept on board while in port. As the new men walked off along the jetty, laughing and talking loudly, Fogerty beckoned to Jinsuke.

"Here now, Jim lad, look at this. What do you think it is?" He pointed to a reinforced section of oaken railing on the quarterdeck. In the top of it was a round hole lined with brass. Jinsuke shook his head, puzzled.

"Well now, it might be a good size for a little fellow, but there's no hair around it, and it's a mite high. Now take a guess."

Jinsuke looked around for some kind of peg that might fit, for hitching a line or securing an instrument, but it made no sense. He shook his head again.

"Come with me, Jim. I'll show you my baby."

Jinsuke followed the big Irishman down to his cabin. Fogerty told him to close the door. Then, from a drawer under the bunk, Fogerty lifted out a short, heavy object, wrapped in cotton material. It was not quite as long as a man's arm, six inches around at one end, and maybe four at the other. He laid it on the table and took off the wrapping revealing a stubby, large-bored brass swivel gun, with a mounting peg. He then fetched powder, wadding, a ramrod and a bag of shot, and proceeded to show Jim how to load it.

"Captain's secret," said Fogerty. "Not even Wu knows about this. It goes in that hole up on the rail. One blast and it'll clear the decks. Now this is how it works, Jim . . ."

Captain Fogerty had had the gun specially made for him. Jinsuke was fascinated. He had seen, but never handled, matchlock weapons, which were fired through a small tamped-off hole in the back of the gun by a smoldering fuse. He had seen pistols, and the swivel guns and cannon on the Dutch ship, the swivels being fired by a flint striking steel and flashing a small pan of powder. The cannon were fired by slow-burning matches. This gun, although muzzle-loaded, had a modern hammer lock that struck a small cap over a nipple in which there was a small hole. Fire went through that hole and set off the charge. Underneath the gun were a wooden pistol grip and a trigger. Fogerty eased back the hammer, fitted a cap, and again eased the hammer to cover the cap.

"See, aim by looking down the top, line up this notch and that knob at the end. Pull back the hammer with your thumb, it'll click. Pull the trigger, and bang! Now Jim, those fellows we took on are good workers, but they give me a funny feeling. Now, if I say, quite easy, 'Get the baby, Jim,' you know what to do. You come down here and bring it up, quick. Okay?"

"Okay," said Jinsuke.

Fogerty looked at him for a while, then nodded at the gun. "Can you heft it, Jim?"

It was heavy, but Jinsuke picked it up easily, cradling it to his chest.

"Good lad!" Fogerty took it from him, wrapped it, and put it back in the drawer under the bed. Next, from the same place, he took two pistols, a six-cylinder Navy Colt and a short single-barreled gun, which he slipped into his boot. The revolver went into a holster, which he hung on his belt, beneath his sizable paunch.

Next he shifted the mattress on the bunk, revealing on the side nearest the wall a heavy, well-honed cutlass. Jinsuke was overawed by the captain's show of weaponry. In Japan such possessions would be unthinkable. He passed the cutlass handle-first to Jinsuke, who hefted it, and as he did so Fogerty reached out and drew out the *sai* hidden under Jinsuke's shirt. Fogerty had seen a similar weapon in Indonesia—a man had been doing a sort of dance with one in each hand. He had been in Asia long enough to have a hearty respect for Oriental man-to-man combat. He glanced at Jinsuke, as if considering, then slipped the *sai* under the charts in the chart-table drawer.

"If you need it, you know where it is," he said, and slapped Jinsuke on the shoulder. "What you would really like to use in a fight is a harpoon, right? Pin the beggars to the mast like beetles to a board."

He laughed, and Jinsuke suddenly understood that this man kept out of trouble because he was totally unafraid of it, and made his precautions as discreetly as possible.

"You been in a fight before, Jim?" Fogerty asked softly.

Jinsuke did not want to boast, he was neither proud nor ashamed of it, but he sensed the question needed an answer. He nodded. "I fight. I get into trouble."

Fogerty nodded. Jinsuke had already told him about the shark. "Ah, I saw the marks, on your back . . ."

Jinsuke's eyes narrowed. He nodded toward the chart-table drawer. "I fight samurai, two samurai. They have sword. I have that. I win fight, but samurai catch me."

Fogerty put his hands on his hips, eyes widening with understanding. He had no reservations about Jim Sky now. He roared an oath of delight.

"You one-armed devil, I could swear you was an Irishman. Come on, Jim, you and I are going to have just a little tot of rum!"

They set sail just as the tide was starting to come in at ten the next morning. It would have seemed that Fogerty's feeling about the five men was without grounds. For the next two weeks the five new men sailed on each trip, worked hard, and obeyed orders. Gradually, with the exception of

244

Wu, the entire Chinese crew came under their influence. They would gamble in their free time, and off ship they would eat, drink, and sometimes visit the opium houses together. Jinsuke, of course, remained aloof.

The *Irene* carried passengers as well as livestock and freight, and the passengers were usually ordinary Chinese. However, on this trip she was commissioned to go farther upriver by some two hundred miles, taking a missionary, his wife, a Chinese lay preacher-interpreter, three male servants and a maid. The missionary was a ruddy-faced Englishman from Gloucestershire who had only recently arrived in China. One of the demands of the Opium War had been to permit the spread of Christianity. He had married, somewhat late in life, just before leaving England.

Jinsuke had never really had a close look at a foreign woman before, and although he did not consider her particularly beautiful, it was hard to keep his eyes off her. She had thick blond hair, falling to her shoulders in tight curls, round blue eyes and a big mouth. Her nose was straight, and all in all her face, though it seemed large, was quite attractive. She had the widest hips and most enormous breasts he had ever seen, yet she was not fat. Her waist was quite slim—Jinsuke did not realize it was tightly corseted—and her ankles were pretty. She had a loud voice, and she made her presence very obvious as the men were bringing on the dozens of trunks and suitcases, and a load of furniture. Captain Fogerty, from the bridge, kept looking down from the woman to her husband, shaking his head and muttering, "A waste, a pitiful waste . . ."

Her husband looked more like a farmer than a preacher. He was beefy and clumsy, with wispy brownish hair. He had a habit of grinning at the Chinese, and at Jinsuke, as if they were all mischievous children.

They steamed up the river in the sweltering heat, with the paddle wheels thwop, thwop, thwopping on the muddy, oily waters; there was no wind except that created by the movement of the ship. They passed junks and fishing vessels in dozens, and the scenery—cultivated fields and paddies—was monotonous and unbroken. A hot, dozy day it was, and on either bank were miles and miles of flat, flat green, spread out under leaden skies.

On the second afternoon on board, the missionary and his wife were strolling on deck, he red-faced and attentive, she hot and irritable under her layers of petticoats and her whalebone corset. Jinsuke was at the wheel, half mesmerized by the sound of the paddle wheels; he could smell the boiled-egg stink from the coal fired in the boilers. Smoke eddied down from the funnel with the barest hint of wind.

Captain Fogerty hawked, then, with a glance in the direction of the passengers, went to the side and spat over. Ahead of them, a scruffily rigged junk dawdled in midstream, its big square sail flapping grayly like a sick goose. Fogerty's eyes squinted against the brazen light. There was something wrong about that junk.

One of the new men came up the first couple of steps to the bridge, smiling blandly.

"You! Stay off the bridge! Get back to work!"

The man stopped, smile freezing. He glanced back to where his four comrades and a couple of other crewmen were now on deck, three of them facing the bridge and the others looking in the direction of the junk, which Fogerty could now see was loaded with men, its gun ports open. He cursed under his breath.

"Jim, I'll take the wheel," he said, slow and easy. "Be a good fellow and go fetch the captain's baby, will you?"

Jinsuke felt a sudden shock of alarm, but showed nothing on his face. He smiled, touched his forehead in a salute, handed over the wheel, then turned to the wooden steps that led from behind the bridge down to the captain's cabin. He was opening the cabin door when the sounds of the engine changed, and the ship suddenly heeled over. Something slammed into the side of the *Irene* and the captain's porthole darkened with a huge shape. The junk! Pirates!

Jinsuke steadied himself, dashed to the drawer under the bunk and lifted out the heavy brass swivel gun, laying it first on the bunk. There came another crash into the side of the ship, and muffled thumps. Cannon. The engine momentarily picked up as Fogerty rang down orders and tried to veer away, but the junk rammed into the *Irene* and sheered off the portside paddle wheel.

Fogerty, his hands full at the helm, had tried to turn the ship away. He saw belches of flame and smoke as cannon fired point-blank into his ship; then, out of the corner of his eye, he saw the man coming for him, glint of steel in his hand. Fogerty turned, just a little too late, feeling a sear of pain in his side, and clubbed the man with his fist in the side of the head, following with a roundhouse right that laid his attacker out on the deck. The others came in a rush up the steps, and Fogerty was able to draw and cock his revolver and fire once, twice. The man in the fore was knocked back

246

by two bullets in the chest. The others pushed over him, yelling in high-pitched voices; they did not even stop when a man only three feet from the captain was blasted through the right eye, the bullet blowing off the back of his head. Then they were all over Fogerty, stabbing at him as he went down, just as the ship lurched over with the force of the pirate junk's ramming.

The man who had been clubbed and punched, the leader of the five new crewmen, staggered to his feet. He spat at the prostrated, bleeding captain, and shouted an order in Chinese to go and kill the one-armed man.

Two of his cronies headed for the cabin, reaching it just as Jinsuke was about to come out, cradling the heavy gun. As they came, both with knives in hand, Jinsuke realized that something had happened to his captain, and he ducked back into the cabin again, slamming the door in their faces.

He dumped the gun on the bed while the two men kicked at the door. Like all the woodwork on the *Irene*, the door was stoutly made, and would not give way. Jinsuke could hear them shouting at him but could not understand. He knew that they meant to kill him, and that there would be others on deck.

Somehow, from somewhere inside him, there grew an icy calmness. He found himself grinning, and alert with adrenaline. Remembering the cutlass, he reached down the side of the bunk and felt the reassuring weight of steel.

The door began to splinter with the blows of a fire axe, and Jinsuke, forming a plan of defense, lay the captain's chair across the floor, just beyond the swing of the door when it opened. Then he made a few trial sweeps with the cutlass, hearing the heavy blade suck air. It was much like the machete, the *nata* he used as a boy to cut firewood at home, and he recalled with a grin that Tatsudaiyu had made him use the *nata* soon after he lost his left arm. Thinking of his father gave him a flood of confidence. He might die, but he would die well.

He watched as the fire axe continued smashing through the tough mahogany door. Glad of his boyhood, glad of his practice with the *sai*, he now tried moves with this new yet seemingly familiar weapon. He had never cut or stabbed a man before, only struck. Would the feel of the blade in human flesh be that different from when it entered a whale. . .

A hole appeared in the door, and Jinsuke could see the grimacing face of one of his erstwhile crewmates.

"Pig dung," said Jinsuke, in Chinese, grinning at them,

keeping the cutlass out of sight. The face disappeared while the man with the axe enlarged the hole. Then a hand, holding a pistol taken from the fallen captain, came through the hole, aiming at Jinsuke. The hammer came back and Jinsuke flung himself to one side, whipping out the cutlass from behind, slashing a split second before the revolver boomed in the close confines of the cabin, almost deafening him. Jinsuke thought he'd hit the man, or the gun, but with the bang he couldn't be sure. Both gun and hand had gone back, and the axe blows increased, until finally the door burst open.

The very tip of the cutlass had in fact cut the tendon that ran to the gunman's thumb. He came into the room, still holding the weapon but having great trouble, even with two hands to bring back the hammer, but he didn't see the chair on the floor. He stumbled into a powerful downstroke from Jinsuke's cutlass.

It's like splitting a log with a knot in it, thought Jinsuke, wrenching the blade free.

The second man came close behind, having dropped the axe in favor of his knife, a better weapon for fighting in close quarters, but a poor match for a cutlass. He had not realized that the first shot had completely missed, and was not very careful. Wrenching the blade out of the first attacker's skull, Jinsuke bent his knees and brought his cutlass point up in a straight-armed thrust, twisting his feet unconsciously, as if he were making one of Kinjo's classic moves. Now horizontal, the blade entered below the man's chin, and he felt only momentary shock as it came out of the back of his neck, severing the spinal cord and killing him instantly.

The cutlass was almost jerked from Jinsuke's hand as the second man's body sprawled over that of his comrade, and Jinsuke had to kick it over onto its back to pull the blade out, with a yank and a thrust kick to the chest. A bright flood of crimson stained the floor of the cabin. It had all happened so fast, the violence of it had been so easy for him, that Jinsuke looked around, thinking for a moment he should clean up the mess. He shook his head, squeezed his eyes shut for a second, and dismissed the notion, desperately collecting his thoughts while he wiped the blade on the dead man's tunic. He slipped the cutlass into his belt and picked the swivel gun off the bunk, cradling its weight against his chest, before stepping over his opponents and making for the companion way.

The pirates were occupied. Cargo hatches had been torn

off, passenger cabins ransacked. The English missionary and his servants, the lay preacher—interpreter and a couple of the crew had been decapitated and heaved over the side into the river. Jinsuke saw one man take a head by its long queue, swing it like a ball on a string, then toss it far out into the water. Crouching, Jinsuke darted to the bridge, and hunkered down behind the chart table. He saw his captain and took him for dead, his thoughts now on revenge and the duty he owed the man.

Wu had died fighting for his life with a pipe wrench, and two of the Chinese were now hauling the body up onto the deck, feet first, with one man holding Wu's head by his braid.

Only the women were spared, for the time being. They were both screaming.

Three men were holding the Chinese maid, a slight young girl in her middle teens, while another was raping her. Blood flowed copiously around her thighs. At first penetration she screamed, but the man with his trousers off slugged her with his fist. She lay inert while he spent himself, and was then replaced by another man.

The missionary's wife was still struggling, voice harsh from her screaming. Four men held her, a man to each limb, while her body writhed. The man who had entered her was very big and muscular, but turning fat. He supported the weight of his torso with his left arm, repeatedly slapping her with his right hand, timing the slaps with his thrusts, laughing as he did so. In every way the man was big, and from the way the others were laughing with him and cheering him on, Jinsuke took him to be the real leader. The huge, pimpled buttocks humped, and the thing moved, erect from a tangle of black, thick and purple and red.

Nobody noticed Jinsuke. Except for Fogerty, lying in his own blood, and the two men he had shot, the bridge was deserted. Jinsuke lifted up the swivel gun, fitting its brass pin into the brass-lined hole in the railing. He couldn't help but watch what was happening to the white woman. They had ripped the clothes completely off her, revealing a fine body. Her pubic hair was a mat of curling brown, different in shade, he noted, from the color of the hair on her head. She was straining against her captors, which only increased their pleasure. The man inside her grew red in the face, then, close to his climax, he punched the woman on the jaw, knocking her unconscious. Then he seized both of those large, soft, rounded white breasts and thrust furiously to the end, bellowing like a bull.

He withdrew, laughing, then ripped a rag of torn petticoat, wiping himself, joking, pointing to another man who came forward. The man the leader had selected knelt between the woman's long, outstretched legs and undid himself. Other men, eager for their turn, pushed around to watch and cheer, forming a tight knot around the two naked women. Now Jinsuke could see only one naked foot; the women's bodies were shielded. Thirteen men were bunched ten paces or so from where Jinsuke crouched behind the gun. The leader stood in the middle, goading his men, disparaging their size and performance, while the others howled with laughter; other men paused in their looting to push forward and watch. Jinsuke, although he knew there were too many of them, had to avenge his captain, and prayed that the gun would do its worst. He lined up the notch at the back and the knob at the front on the leader's head and cocked back the hammer.

It was a short weapon, and with its large bore was designed to spread its shot wide. It was loaded with a mugful of buckshot. The gun boomed and bucked in its holding, jerking against Jinsuke's fist. For an instant the smoke obscured the mayhem he had created, but soon he saw that nearly all the men around the women were hit. They sprawled on the deck, over the naked bodies of the women, some clutching their wounds, some crying in shock and pain, a few crawling. Four were dead, two dying, and several more hurt too badly to think of fighting. The leader had taken three balls, one in the back of his thick neck, one in the shoulder, one through his right kidney. He had not fallen, however, but had reeled to the side of the ship.

Jinsuke now snatched up the cutlass, and with a fierce yell leaped over the rail to the deck. The big pirate turned, face gray with pain and shock; when Jinsuke reached him, he was snatching for a short sword. Jinsuke sliced down past the side of his neck, cutting deep through the collarbone. As the cutlass bit, Jinsuke kicked the man hard in the stomach and jumped back, jerking the blade free to make a wild slash around to his right, where he had sensed movement.

He fought his way to the mast, roaring, slashing, parrying, jabbing. Time stopped. The fight went on forever, a blur of movement and strain. Then, miraculously, the pirates began scrambling over the side of the *Irene* to their own ship, and Jinsuke stood there, in limbo, his body running with sweat and blood from a sword cut under his eye and several other slight wounds on his arm, chest and legs, nothing serious, but bleeding freely. He felt utterly weary, the cutlass too heavy to lift. He looked around and saw that he had wounded at least another four. He dropped the cutlass and went up to the bridge, feeling now a terrible sense of loss, and no joy in his own survival.

He knelt beside his captain, tearing off the sweat-soaked hand towel that he always knotted around his forehead while at work on the ship. The wound in Fogerty's side was open, and still bleeding. Jinsuke pressed the towel to the wound. Fogerty's lips moved—he was alive! Jinsuke pulled the big man to the side of the bridge and leaned him against the bulkhead. Fogerty opened his eyes.

"Did you get the baby, Jim?"

"Yes, Captain, I get. Don! Big, big don! Lots pirates hit and dead. Now all gone. Captain wait, I get medicine."

As Jinsuke went to stand, Fogerty grabbed his arm.

"No, Jim, first you see to the ladies. Understand? Are the ladies dead, Jim?"

Jinsuke shook his head. "Not dead."

Something in his face told the captain what had happened. Fogerty groaned.

"See to the ladies, Jim . . ."

From somewhere came a boom, followed by an explosive crash. Jinsuke heard screams, but they did not register. Fogerty tried to stand, but Jinsuke pushed him down.

"I go see."

Although Fogerty had taken several stabs and slashes, some of them deep, his own bulk and the sheer numbers of his attackers had saved him. Jinsuke stood, not really knowing what to do, but feeling that for the women their nakedness must be the worst thing. He went down to Fogerty's cabin, ignoring the bodies, and pulled sheets off the bunk.

Out on deck again, as he approached the sprawl of bodies, the Chinese girl saw him and began to scream, covering her head with her hands. Jinsuke put the sheet around her naked shoulders, without touching her. He began to drag bodies off the white woman, still unconscious and covered with her attackers' blood. With the last body dragged to one side, Jinsuke was about to cover her with the second sheet when the side of the ship was bumped.

It was a British navy cutter. Uniformed men, all white, scrambled over the side with rifles and long bayonets. Before Jinsuke could do anything they had rushed him and he was knocked to the deck by a rifle butt to the side of his head.

"My God, sir!" exclaimed a burly marine sergeant. "The bastards got a white woman!"

The men were all staring at the naked, bloodied, spread-eagled woman. The lieutenant, pistol in hand, roared angrily.

"You men! Turn your eyes away!"

He snatched up the sheet that Jinsuke was still holding and laid it over the woman. There came another boom and a crash, then yells and a rattle of small-arms fire. A marine came and hurriedly presented arms to his officer.

"Yanks have boarded the pirate vessel, sir!"

The officer nodded. He laid the sheet over the white woman. The maid still went on screaming, hands over her head, the sheet draped around her shoulders.

"Shut up, girl!" shouted the lieutenant, shaking her, but she only tried to huddle smaller, and the screaming went on. The sergeant found a bucket and line, dipped some river water, and tipped it over her. The girl stopped, looking up for the first time to see uniformed white men, and she began to weep softly.

"Tie that one," said the lieutenant, pointing his pistol at Jinsuke. The men fetched a rope.

"Three of these others are still alive, sir," reported the sergeant. The lieutenant looked at him, smiling grimly. He was a young man, but battle-hardened from the fighting in China.

"Our American friends have strange ideas about justice, don't you think? Those scum don't really need to survive, do they, Sergeant?" The sergeant nodded to his marines who methodically bayonetted all those who showed life.

Led by an American officer, sailors armed with pistols and cutlasses came over the other side of the crippled *Irene* and saluted the British lieutenant.

"I see you've got everything under control here. We've taken the junk, but she's afire. No survivors."

The British officer saluted back and congratulated him. He yelled to two men to go and inspect the damage to the *Irene*. Another man, kneeling beside the white woman, called out.

"Sir! The lady's alive, sir!"

Both officers of this joint foray turned, giving orders, and the woman was carried below. They were more than a day's journey away from their ships, in open cutters, armed with twelve-pound howitzers, and they had been hunting this particular pirate junk for three months. While bodies were dumped overboard, the men reported the damage. The *Irene*

252

could not use her engines, but her sails were intact, and she was leaking only slightly. Two men had found the injured captain and were binding his wounds.

"This ship flies the American flag," said the British lieutenant, "so we will hand her over to you. If you need any of our men to help handle her, of course we shall oblige. However . . ." He nodded to Jinsuke, lashed to the mast. "We took this prisoner, and we intend to keep him."

The American officer nodded and yelled commands. "Bring the howitzer aboard and put our cutter in tow. See to it!"

He looked at Jinsuke coldly. "You will, I trust, invite me to the hanging," he said, and Jinsuke, struggling against his ropes, tried to protest. The British marine sergeant gave him a backhanded slap across the face.

"Shall we string the filthy animal up now, sir?"

Again Jinsuke tried to say he was not one of the pirates.

"Lively, aren't you, you chink bastard? Maybe you'd like to dance on the end of a rope?" The sergeant hit him again. There was the crack of a pistol shot, and the ball buzzed over the sergeant's head. Fogerty had pushed away the men supporting him and staggered to the railing, holding the single-shot pistol that had been hidden in his boot.

"I'll ask you to keep your hands off my bosun, you limey fool! You're lucky I didn't decide to put that ball through your pea-sized brain! Unhand my man! Take those ropes off him!"

Both Americans and British had leveled weapons at the big Irishman, who, shoving away the men who tried to help him again, lurched to the companionway that led from the bridge to the deck.

"Who are you, sir?" demanded the British lieutenant, his pistol still in his hand, but no longer pointing at Fogerty.

"Captain of this ship. Fogerty is the name. I appreciate your coming to our donnybrook, gentlemen, better late than never, but unhand that man, he's my bosun, Jim Sky, and no damned pirate."

The two officers exchanged glances again. The American saluted Fogerty.

"You're an American, sir. I'm Lieutenant Balch, of the *Plymouth*. As you're indisposed, sir, may I have permission to take over your ship and get her back to Shanghai?"

"Nobody's taking over my damned ship, Mr. Balch, but I'm glad to have you aboard . . . Now untie my bosun!"

"We seem to have made a mistake," said the British

253

officer laconically, turning to his sergeant. "Untie that fellow and apologize to him."

The sergeant cut Jinsuke's ropes, mumbling his apology, and Jinsuke, glaring angrily at them, rushed over to his captain, who leaned his bulk on Jinsuke's shoulder.

"By Jesus, Jim, you did a good job, me and you can get along without the navy, British or American, eh?" And with that he passed out. The Americans took the captain down to his cabin. Jinsuke, grayness edging his vision, was leaning over the side of the ship, vomiting. The British officer came over to him.

"I'm awfully sorry, but with you being Chinese, and on deck, we thought . . ."

Jinsuke shook his head and jabbed his own chest with his forefinger. "Not Chinese! Japanese! You know? Japanese!"

The American lieutenant, who had visited Japan with Perry's expedition, stared with amazement, then shouted to his own men.

"Damn it, help the man! Go find bandages and rum! Look at the fight he's done . . . Damn right he's Japanese! If he was in the service he'd get a medal!" He saluted Jinsuke.

"Arigato! Thank you!" he said, and with a faint grin, Jinsuke let himself be led down below.

The British led their twelve-man party into their cutter and headed downstream as American sailors began hoisting the sails of the battered *Irene*. Grounded on a bank, the pirate junk was still ablaze.

Chapter Twenty

"Anyway, Captain," said Mr. Rose, raising a brandy glass to the man who sat across from him, "I'd be mighty obliged if you could do something for him. With your contacts and knowledge of whaling, I would think that you could find him a place on a whaling ship once you get to California. As to the cost of the passage, I'll gladly pay it myself, although he is in no financial distress. The business community here got together and raised five hundred pounds as a token of appreciation for his heroism."

They had just enjoyed a marvelous dinner of roast suckling pig at Mr. Rose's house. The two men dined alone, served by the Chinese majordomo. Mr. Rose's dinner companion was a thin-faced man with blond hair and a goatee. He tapped ash from a cigar into the large ceramic ashtray in the center of the table.

"I'll do what I can, Mr. Rose. Any white man would, for a fellow who saved the life of a lady. And you say he's a Japanese whaler? You know, some years back, when we were working the Japan Grounds, we ran into a couple of their whaling boats. Friendly, they were, not like some of the stories I've heard." He raised his glass, watching the light from the oil lamps flicker and expand in the golden fluid.

"Can I get to see this Jim Sky?"

"Well, of course. That's not his real name, but that is what he is known as around here. I'll send a runner in the morning and ask him to come the day after tomorrow. He's staying at Fogerty's right now. They've sort of adopted him, and he must be quite happy there. As you know, the captain's wife is an Oriental lady."

The man ran a hand through his thinning blond hair. "Yes, and I've heard that the wild Irishman has three of the most beautiful daughters a man could ever wish to set eyes upon. I'm sure Jim Sky must be happy."

"Fogerty has a fine son as well, a bright boy, although of course it's not going to be easy for him when he goes out into the world." He sighed, drained his glass, then rang for the majordomo.

"Come, Captain. At least have another one, please. Don't worry about getting back to your ship. I'll have my carriage take you. And shall we say the day after tomorrow, in my office at ten o'clock? After you have met Jim Sky we can complete our business and perhaps have lunch together. Have you tried real Chinese food? I know a place that serves the most delicious seafood and duck, not too spicy, very pleasant."

The English captain, who was due to sail soon for California via Hawaii, quickly agreed. He had a new ship, fast and easy to maneuver, and on his maiden voyage over, everything had gone very well. He held out his glass to be filled.

"Tell me," he said, "how is the lady? The missionary's wife, or rather, widow."

"Nobody seems to know," said Mr. Rose, shaking his head sadly. "Of course, it is a very delicate business." He leaned forward and lowered his voice. "When the navy men reached the ship the lady was unconscious, rather badly beaten. Worse though, she had been, er . . . severely abused, if you follow me. Terrible thing. She has been staying with another missionary family, here in Shanghai. Hasn't shown her face at all, and only the doctor is permitted to visit. I only pray that there are no, er . . . complications and, er . . . that she may find peace of mind when she returns to England. Let us hope that the gossip won't follow her there."

"Yes," said the captain, "it would be impossible for her to remarry if it did. But I don't understand her husband, trying to go into the country with half of it controlled by Taiping and with the Chinese having no real like for missionaries either."

Mr. Rose nodded. He was not overly fond of missionaries himself. They sometimes disapproved of certain items he dealt in.

"To change the subject," said his companion, cupping the brandy glass and swirling the liquor around in it, "from what I've heard, and read in the local residents' paper, this fellow Jim Sky is quite a scrapper. Took on a whole crew of pirates

256

all by himself, did he not? I know, of course, that the Japanese are a fanatical lot, but that's hard to swallow, and him with just one arm."

"You can take it as gospel, Captain Jacks," said Mr. Rose. "Old Fogerty is quite a storyteller when it comes to spinning yarns about his own exploits, but he's a man who will never tell an untruth about another. Seems that as soon as he smelled trouble he sent Jim Sky below to fetch a damn great blunderbuss. Fogerty swears that when they came for him he shot two, only two, before they downed him. When the navy men boarded they counted nineteen dead pirates, one of them the most notorious rogue along the river, and he'd got his head half cut off by Jim Sky's cutlass."

Captain Jacks whistled. "But it must have been quite a blast he gave them first off."

"Well, Fogerty kept a loaded swivel gun under his bed. . ."

Captain Jacks threw back his head and guffawed.

"Under his bed? That crazy Irishman! Me, I never keep anything more dangerous than a chamber pot!"

The two men laughed together, both of them flushed with wine and brandy.

"Anyway, Jim went down to get the gun, and up above they bushwhacked Fogerty, knifed him quite badly, though not enough to kill that tough old buzzard, even if it has kept him in bed for a couple of months. Anyway, a couple of the rogues went down to take care of Jim Sky, who turns around and chops them both down with a cutlass, and listen to this, one of them had a pistol!" Mr. Rose raised both hands at his companion's look of disbelief.

"No, really! I spoke to the officer of the *Plymouth,* and he got the tale from the British officer who first boarded the *Irene*. He told me that there were two very dead pirates in the cabin, one with a pistol in his hand. Next thing that happens is that Jim Sky, one-handed, lugs this great brass swivel gun up top—and bang! Then, not content with that, he lays about with the cutlass. It's true—the official joint report of British and American navies, and Fogerty's testimony, are in perfect accord. Jim Sky, mind you, is too shy to say much, and his English is not that good yet, although he's coming along."

"Wasn't he wounded?"

"Slightly. Concussion, a few cuts here and there. We had him in the hospital here for a couple of days. Whatever, he's

257

been treated like a hero, invited aboard both the navy ships, toasted in the officers' mess, invited all over."

"And how's Fogerty's steamer?"

"The *Irene* is in dock, getting patched up and having a new paddle wheel fixed. The dock foreman says he can't get the bloodstains off the decks, and the ship's been swamped with reporter fellows."

"That's a rare tale," said Captain Jacks, "and if that's the way a one-armed Japanese fights, I'm not going to meddle with them. They must be sheer devils with those long swords of theirs, you know, I was talking to a fellow . . ."

The conversation went on into the early hours of the morning, and it was neither the first nor the last time that the exploits of Jim Sky were related in Shanghai.

On the morning that Jim Sky was called to the offices of Mr. Rose, he was accompanied by Lyall, Fogerty's son, a tall, handsome youth of eighteen who had become devoted to this man who had saved his father's life.

This time, when Jinsuke walked through the outer offices, the Europeans smiled their greetings to him, and some of the men called out cheerily to him. He was respected, almost accepted. He looked different, of course, with his gray trousers of expensive cloth, a white cambric shirt and a silk cravat, a dark blue jacket of fine serge, the empty sleeve neatly pinned up. The new scar under his eye did not mar his features, but gave him an air of fearlessness, one that fitted his reputation.

A secretary ushered them into Mr. Rose's office, and the merchant came out from behind his desk to shake Jinsuke's hand and to beam at Lyall.

"Lyall, my boy, how are you? And how is your good father?"

"I'm well, thank you, Mr. Rose, and Father is getting better. He's a lot thinner, and the doctor says that's done him a lot of good, and that he can get up now for a short walk every day."

"Good to hear! Now, I'd like to introduce you to Captain Jacks, of the *Swan*. Captain, this is our hero, Jim Sky. And this young man is Lyall Fogerty."

The man who had been sitting on the leather-upholstered sofa by the wall stood, his hand outstretched. Jinsuke shook it.

"Pleased to meet you, Captain," said Jinsuke, accents clipped, still slurring his *l*s, although, with daily tutoring from Lyall he was indeed making progress in both English and Chinese.

"Mr. Rose," said Lyall, "Jim has something he says he can show only to a whaling man. It's a letter, I think. I know that the *Swan* is not a whaler, but Father said that Captain Jacks used to be a whaling man himself." He turned to the captain. "It's a kind of letter of reference, sir, from somebody in Japan."

"Well, well, I don't think Jim Sky needs any letter of reference around these parts," said Mr. Rose, smiling.

"No, sir, but it seems so important to Jim, and I thought that if you like I could read the characters. I don't speak Japanese yet, but their writing is a lot like Chinese. As I said, it's very important to him, sir."

"Well, lad, my ship isn't a whaler, but I certainly was a whaling man, for twenty years." Captain Jacks turned to Jinsuke. "I'm a whaling man, Jim. Show me your letter."

Jinsuke looked at him for a few seconds, taking in the thin blond hair, the ruddy features, the eyes now slightly bloodshot from the previous night's indulgence. He noted that although the man was not large, he had a powerful set to his shoulders, and hands that seemed almost too big for him. His waist was thickening, beginning to show his years, for he was past fifty, but he had a confident, almost brusque sailor's manner about him. He looked to be a man of some means, a man of experience, and tough.

"Okay. I have letter from very big Japanese whaling man. Now Japanese government man."

To the surprise of the others, Jinsuke took not an envelope from his coat pocket, but a sperm whale tooth. He flipped his coat back, exposing a knife that he still wore, even in polite society and with his fancy clothes. Seeing it, Captain Jacks could barely suppress a grin.

"Lyall," said Jinsuke, having the usual trouble in pronouncing the name, "paper inside tooth. Please take out for me, okay?"

Lyall took the whale tooth and the knife, and with the tip of the blade he broke a beeswax seal in the pulp cavity. Carefully dropping the broken pieces of beeswax into a wastepaper basket, he handed the knife back to Jinsuke. Inside the hollow of the tooth was a piece of tightly folded paper. Lyall picked it out and smoothed its creases.

"Read it for us, Lyall. What does it say?"

"Oh, it's in English, sir!" He handed it to the captain, who read it out loud.

"'To whom it may concern: The bearer of this note is a good harpooner. He is an honest man of a good Japanese family. He comes from a whaling town that is famous in our land. He knows whales and sea currents really well. Please afford him kindness and assistance in America. Signed: Joe Mung, First Mate.'"

The captain looked up at Jinsuke and was about to ask him something when Mr. Rose took the letter and reread it for himself.

"Incredible!" he exclaimed. "Such a coincidence! This must be the hand of Providence! Captain Jacks, I have personally met the writer of this letter, at the home of my good friend, Captain Whitfield, in Fairhaven, in America! My friend rescued the boy and raised him, gave him a good Christian education. This, as far as I know, is the first any of us has heard of Joe Mung since he went back to Japan in 1851. And here we have a letter, brought to us by Jim Sky. Oh, my goodness!"

But what had caught Captain Jacks's attention was the sperm whale tooth, lying now on the desk, white ivory against polished oak, the fine black lines of its scrimshaw very clear. He caught his breath as he picked it.

"I'll be damned!" He could easily read the letters under the engraving of the ship, and on the other side was the picture of a sperm whale hunt, and his own name, Tovey Jacks.

"How did you get this?" he demanded, handing the tooth to Mr. Rose. "I did this bit of scrimshaw," he said, "back in 'forty-eight when we were working the Japan Grounds. I was first mate on the *Midas*. Did three tours with her before turning to the trade runs and working for my ticket. See . . . there's my name."

Gesturing energetically, Jinsuke told them how the two chase boats from Taiji, the phoenix and the chrysanthemum, had come upon an American boat that had killed a whale.

Jinsuke's brow creased, remembering a joke, and a word. "Supamu! Supamu!" he exclaimed. They looked blankly at him. "Supamu! Damn big supamu whale! Boat get big, big supamu!"

He talked excitedly, his English in a jumble, but he described a huge man with red hair, like Lyall's father, and a black man, and a harpoon head that was hinged, and of how the leader of the boat had tossed his tooth to them as they parted, how it had hit an oar and gone into the water, and how he had dived deep, very deep to retrieve it.

260

Captain Tovey Jacks put both hands on Jinsuke's shoulders. "Jim Sky, you're a miracle. As Mr. Rose said, it was Providence that brought us together. See the name on the tooth? Tovey Jacks. Me. It was me who did the scrimshaw, me who threw this tooth over to you."

Neither of the two men had recognized each other, but there was small wonder in that, for Tovey Jacks was no longer the scruffy, overworked whaling mate, and Jinsuke was no longer the sunbronzed, half-naked youth with the top of his head shaved and a red loincloth around his waist. Jacks told Mr. Rose and Lyall of what had happened that day, six years ago.

"Finest-looking bunch of men I've seen anywhere," he said, "and the most beautiful boats, glistening with colors and patterns, flowers and birds and stuff, and with jet-black hulls, real pretty. There were a dozen or more men in each boat, two to an oar, and they sculled those things like a dream, hardly a drop of spray, and fast—they flew over the water. Those men were good-looking fellows, built like wrestlers, with huge arms and shoulders. Clean they were too, really clean, not like the chinks . . ." He realized what he had said, coughed, and turned to Lyall. "Beg pardon, lad, no offense meant."

Lyall shook his head.

"Anyway, I recall remarking to the skipper when we got back to the ship that if we could only call into Japan and pick up a boat crew or so of men like that, then we wouldn't have to comb the docks for any scrofulous riffraff we could lay hands on, and in whaling it's boatmen you need, more than sailors. And here he is, the young fellow we met at sea, over a gam around a whale, here in your office. Mr. Rose, sir, I'll be proud to do anything I can to help this man, and if he'll agree I'll give him employment for the passage over, and I don't mean as a two-penny deckhand, either."

It was all rather too much for Jinsuke, and he did not understand what was being said. When Mr. Rose insisted that both he and Lyall should come with them to lunch at a high-class Chinese restaurant, he simply marveled.

Sometime later in the afternoon, Captain Jacks outlined his proposal to Mr. Rose. He wanted to hire Jim Sky as an overseer. Jacks was making a considerable profit from transporting Chinese laborers, at fifty dollars a head (and they brought their own food), from Shanghai to San Francisco. He hoped that Jim Sky might want to do a few trips with him, and then work as an overseer on one of the railroad projects, instead of trying to get on a whaler.

"Life on any ship is no easy ticket, even for an officer," he said, "and on a whaler it can be sheer hell. He's a good man, and I wouldn't want to see him wasted."

"I've had a few ideas for him myself," said Mr. Rose, "but he's dead set on whaling." He nodded to the corner of his office, where Jinsuke's harpoon was still leaning incongruously.

"Anyway, I'll call on Captain Fogerty myself and discuss it with him. Thank you, Captain Jacks, it is very generous of you. You know, Japan is opening up, and any small contact we merchants can make there is of value. I think Jim might be a good man for all of us to know in a few years' time."

Later, when Jinsuke was told about all of this, he was torn with indecision. He felt he could not leave his captain until he was well, although in truth he had no real work to do, for the *Irene* was still under repairs. He enjoyed living with the Fogerty family, adored Fogerty's wife, truly liked the boy, and was somewhat infatuated with all three of the girls. Fogerty too was reluctant to see him leave, but more than anything, he felt that this man Jim was not really ready for life in America. After much thought and discussion with his wife, he sent Lyall with a note to the *Swan*, begging Captain Jacks to come for supper. The captain replied that he would be delighted.

The two men sipped warmed Chinese wine, slightly sweetened with rock sugar, and Fogerty pleaded his case for Jim Sky.

"Cap'n Jacks," he began, leaning forward to take a piece of cold sliced duck breast with his chopsticks, "Jim wants to go with you, I'm sure, but he's a stubborn man, and loyal. He feels he can't leave me until I'm really on my feet again. Then I can release him. Now I can't very well turn around and tell him to buzz off, he ain't needed, can I? That would be no way to repay loyalty. What I suggest is this. You've told me you'll be back for another run in three or four months. Let me keep him for that time. I'll see that he learns more English, more Chinese, and try to teach him what I can about American ways and ships. I'm sure that you're a man of your word and that you'll see him set once he gets across the water."

Tovey Jacks thought for a moment, then stretched out his hand. "I really want him now, but what you say is just and fair, and I wouldn't want to trample on a man's loyalty. God knows that's hard to come by nowadays. He does need a bit more English, and the more Chinese he learns is all the better too. Yes, I'll wait, and yes, I'll do my best for him, although I don't know what most whaling skippers are going to say about signing on a one-armed man, even if he does fight like a two-armed Irishman." He laughed.

"One arm or two, you should see the way he hefts a harpoon or climbs the rigging," said Fogerty with feeling. "I'd sign him on any ship of mine!"

"Fair enough," said Jacks. "As I said, I'll do what I can, and in the meantime, you take care of yourself."

Fogerty smiled with relief and pleasure to know that Jim would be around for a while longer, though he knew it would simply delay the sadness they would all feel when he left.

"I'll tell him tomorrow," he said, and clapped his hands for the servants to bring on more courses, and more wine.

With more time on his hands, Jinsuke was compiling an account of his trip to Shanghai, his work on the steamer, the fight with the pirates, his visits aboard both British and American navy frigates, and his general feelings for what he had seen and felt in China. Jinsuke had changed, or rather, what had always been a part of his nature had come to flourish in this free and easy society of the Fogertys and their friends. He knew that he, Jinsuke, Jim Sky, was inferior to no man, and the respect he still felt for Sadayori was for Sadayori's scholarship and gentility, not for his class, nor for the two swords he so proudly carried. Jinsuke could never contradict a samurai, but Jim Sky could.

"The Chinese *taotae*, or daimyo, is a weak man, and cannot be trusted," Jinsuke wrote. "His ships and armies are not disciplined. Half of this great country is in control of rebels, the leader of whom thinks he is the Son of Heaven. The rebels must hire foreign soldiers to train and discipline them. Chinese generals cannot do that properly. Foreign nations believe in the right to peaceful trade, but will fight bravely if they are insulted or refused. British and American navy men and soldiers are brave and disciplined. Their ships are the finest, and our Japanese ships would be mere toys against them. Foreign gentlemen of good family and class keep their promises. I have had no unpleasantness with anybody since I showed them I was true to my captain and not afraid to die. Sensei, don't you think this is the Japanese way too? I think Japan's feeling and American and British feeling is the same, and you are mistaken to judge them so harshly when you have not lived and fought by their side. If they are insulted they will fight and never give up. We Japanese will never give up. Is this good? I think that peace is best. Fighting is easy for the men fighting but for innocent people and ladies it is horror. I think, sensei, that you are wrong to think the British or Americans wish to invade Japan. They wish to be friends with Japan because they know we are a true and trustworthy nation . . ."

Jinsuke's schooling was basic, and his brushwork was not elegant. His writing was clear and strong, though, and his sentences, lacking in flowery deference to a superior, were direct and forceful. He no longer considered himself a spy for Sadayori, but he felt that he must keep his promise and inform the samurai of what he saw and felt.

By the time he had finished and sealed the package it was very bulky. It was also heavy, for Jinsuke was returning the equivalent weight of gold coins he had received from Itoh. "With many thanks for the samurai of Satsuma who threw me into the sea," he wrote.

He addressed it in both Roman letters and Japanese characters to the doctor in Nagasaki, his contact with Sadayori, and asked Mr. Rose to put it on the next Dutch vessel bound for that ancient trading port. By now it could have gone on any vessel of the several nations to have signed new treaties with Japan, but Sadayori had specified Dutch.

With the long missive and this duty off his chest, Jinsuke felt a surge of relief, as if a dragging anchor, slowing his voyage into new worlds, was now gone. He threw himself into his studies, and enthusiastically explored the docks and city of Shanghai. For strolling in the crowded, bustling Chinese quarters, Jinsuke discarded his tight-fitting Western clothes for more comfortable Chinese dress. He had a short tunic made for himself, and loose, baggy trousers tied at the ankles. He would wear these when he worked out with the *sai,* which he had retrieved from the chart-table drawer. He also brought his harpoon to the Fogertys', and every day he would practice hurling it into a stump bound thickly with straw rope. He used the same stump to toughen his punches and strikes which he began to teach the Fogerty boy to do.

He was working out with Lyall one day in the yard when a servant was sent to bring him to the house. Jinsuke wiped the sweat from his face and neck with his hand towel and went.

Fogerty was sitting with a short, stocky, gray-haired white man. The man had a huge curving moustache set silvery gray against the seams and rugged tan of his face.

"Ah Jim, come and meet a friend, Major Tom Jenness." Jinsuke made a slight bow, a habit he found he could never break on first meeting a stranger. Then he took the major's hand, conscious of his scrutiny.

The major was a retired U.S. Cavalry officer, now a soldier of fortune, traveling through Asia, stopping where his fancy suited him, or where a man of his special talents could find work. China was just the place for him, a land where an experienced soldier need never be idle.

"Sit down, Jim," said Fogerty, "I've got a present for you." Jinsuke's eyes widened. "For me? Present? Oh, so kind!"

Fogerty took a wooden box from the low table in front of him and passed it to Jinsuke, who received it, raising it to eye level in the Japanese way, stammering his thanks, overwhelmed that again he should be receiving gifts from his captain.

"It's something I think could be useful for you in America. I hope you'll never have to use it. Open it, Jim."

He did. There, in purple felt, lay a beautiful new pistol, a weapon such as no fisherman or peasant or merchant in Japan even dared dream of owning. With this, Jinsuke thought, and with my two names, I am a samurai. He looked up from the pistol to Fogerty, his face showing his astonishment.

"A thirty-six caliber Navy Colt, six-shot. See there, Jim, it's got your name on it." Fogerty pointed to the metal just above the fine wood of the gun's stock. In the bluing was engraved: "To Jim Sky, with gratitude for life, from Brian L. Fogerty." He turned it over and, to further surprise, saw "Jinsuke" engraved in Chinese characters, and recalled Lyall once asking him to write them. The box also contained a spare cylinder, a silver powder horn, a bullet mold and tools for maintaining the gun.

"Jim, my boy, after our little adventure I got to thinking that you ought to learn to use one of these. Major Jenness is going to come here once a week, or whenever he can, and teach you and my son how to shoot." He turned to the major. "Start today, Major?"

"Right now," came the reply.

* * *

Their first lesson was in cleaning and stripping the weapon, then in loading it properly. This was an awkward task for Jinsuke, although with practice he could do it in five minutes, holding the gun between his knees.

Later, when it came to firing practice, the major found him to be an apt pupil. His strong arm and wrist and his steady eye made him a natural pistol shot, and he soon began to beat Lyall at target practice. By the end of three months Jinsuke was almost as good as his teacher. This was a skill that would drastically alter the course of his life.

"Carry the pistol with honor, Jim," said the major on their last training session together. "You won it with honor, and now you've got it, you have the lives of men in your hand." When the major said it, his blue eyes steady on him, Jinsuke had a sudden flashback of Sadayori and the deadly cold steel of his swords.

"I understand," he said. "Weapon is heaviest thing in world for man to carry."

The major clapped him on the shoulder. "I guess I don't need to teach you anything now, Jim. You've got it."

Four months later, Jim Sky, overseer, was en route to California.

Chapter Twenty-One

Early in the fifth year of the Ansei Period, 1858 by the Western Calendar, cholera was brought to the port of Nagasaki. This was the first time the disease had ever entered Japan, and it was called *mikka korori*— "three-day fall-down"—rather like the nursery rhyme from medieval England that recalled the first symptoms, and the end result, of the epidemic of bubonic plague—"Atishoo! Atishoo! We all fall down!" The disease was spread mostly by folk involved in internal trade, to Osaka, to Kyoto, then to Edo, where, by the time the last cherry blossoms were falling, some ten thousand people had died.

Sadayori once more lifted his new young friend and carried him to the *ofuro*, where he stripped him of his clothes, filthied by diarrhea, and leaned him against the wall. His own garment was smeared by the mess too, excrement that had become sickly white, the color of rice washings. Sadayori took his clothes off, then dipped warm water from the deep wooden tub over both of them. Even as he did so, the other man had another bowel movement, the eighth in the past hour.

Kuro's lips moved. His voice was so hoarse he could barely speak. "Forgive me, forgive me." Acute shame showed in his wrinkled face.

"Don't say it," said Sadayori, dipping more water and washing the watery mess away. "You'd do the same for me, wouldn't you?" He picked him up again—how light he had grown—and carried him back to the room, laying him on a clean quilt over which he had spread a thin mat and sheets. His doctor friend in Nagasaki had told Sadayori that it would help to subdue the fever by wiping the patient's body with distilled spirits made from yams, purchased by the flagon. The stuff provided the cheapest means of getting drunk, and was much used by laborers and palanquin carri-

267

ers, but now Sadayori had emptied the whole contents of a flagon into a wooden basin and was dipping a hand towel into it, wringing it out, filling the whole room with the pungent alcohol smell.

"A few whiffs of roasted garlic and this place would stink like a drunkards' lair," said Sadayori, trying to make a joke, trying to cover the dismay he felt at the sight of his young friend's wrinkled, wasted, pallid body. He finished, put fresh clothes on himself and Kuro, washed his hands, and sat beside him.

"Do you feel pain?" he asked.

"Not in the guts," croaked Kuro, "but awful pain in the back of my legs, I can't understand. I'm thirsty, so thirsty. . ."

Sadayori got up and went to the shiny blue ceramic brazier; he lifted the iron kettle quietly singing there, poured barley tea into two cups, and set the cups to cool. Sadayori had borrowed a book of medicine, in Dutch, from his friend, and he understood more than most, although he knew nothing of the true cause of cholera. He just felt that tea would be more gentle on the stomach than water, and that if Kuro could keep it down, he might derive some nutrition from it. The maid came fearfully into the room.

"Matsudaira-sama, what am I to do with the clothes in the *ofuro?*"

"Get a stick, pick them up, take them outside, and burn them."

"But we have burned so many good kimonos, perhaps if I wash them . . ."

Sadayori's face wrinkled with distaste. "No, burn them!"

His insistence was based not on medical knowledge, but on personal fastidiousness. He did not wish to wear a garment that had been so fouled, and he felt his friend would not wish to either.

He looked down at Kuro's sunken eyes, the cheekbones prominent, as in a skull, and those awful wrinkles. It was the face of an old man, yet Kuro was only twenty-six, and just five days before he had been full of strength and life.

Kuro was a nickname, acquired at the fencing school, taken from the first character of his full name, which was Kurozawa Takenosuke. The fencing master's wife happened to have a black cat, called Kuro, which she was often heard to be calling: "Kuro! Kuro! Kuro-chan! Come here, Kuro-chan!" The first character of his family name, Kurozawa, was also the ideogram for *black,* like the cat, and when he first came to the school the others would tease him, calling,

"Kuro! Kuro! Kuro-chan! Come here, Kuro-chan!" imitating the master's wife when neither she nor the master was around.

Kurozawa Takenosuke was also a *ronin,* having obtained permission to leave the service of the clan because he had radical, activist opinions and he did not want to embarrass his superiors. He also wished to continue his studies of military arts and fencing in Edo.

He had graduated from the fiercely nationalistic school of the fiefdom of Mito, and like his lord, the daimyo Nariaki, he was fervently opposed to permitting foreigners anywhere near Japan. Consequently, he despised the actions of Ii Naosuke, and was most indiscreet about his feelings, as were many young samurai.

For Sadayori to have been able to strike up a friendship with the young man was unusual. Their friendship would certainly not have been possible if Kuro had known that Sadayori was secretly serving Ii Naosuke, whom the Mito clan, from daimyo to lowest *ashigaru,* seemed to hate as heartily as they hated barbarians, Christianity, Buddhism and anything which was not, in their eyes, of pure Japanese origin.

When they had first met at the fencing school, Kuro was still in the service of the clan of Mito; he had come to Edo with a party of Mito's senior experts and officials when Lord Nariaki was charged with building the forts which were supposed to guard Edo. That was about the time the black American ships had first come.

During the year Kuro spent in Edo, he would use his free time, when he had any, to come to the fencing school. He was about twenty years old back then, an energetic but rather slow-speaking and seemingly slow-thinking young man of intense earnestness, who often slipped into his slurred northern dialect, and who was quite in awe of the fencing master and of senior students like Sadayori, who was by then a mature swordsman in his early thirties.

When Kuro first arrived at the school the others teased him, for his swordsmanship was powerful but not that well coordinated. "He's threshing rice!" they said. "No, he's chopping wood!" they jeered. Kuro would spend hours, swinging the heaviest of the thick clubs which were used to develop physical power. His efforts would make him bright red in the face, and his forearms would become so cramped that he could not even use chopsticks properly.

"Kurou suru na, Kuro," they would jibe, making a play

on words, for the word for "hard toil," with a slightly longer stress on the last syllable, was similar to his nickname. The sophisticated young bucks of Edo enjoyed making puns, and their enjoyment was heightened if an outsider could be the butt of their jokes. Don't toil so hard, they would say, and Kuro would simply increase his efforts, swing the club or the practice sword harder, giving louder battle yells that shook the rafters.

Through his efforts, he built himself the shoulders and arms of a bear. Stripped, he could be seen to be heavily muscled. The others would take him out, for he never had much money, and they would make him eat to bursting, treating him to flagon after flagon of sake. Edo folk were also known for their generosity.

"Kuro-chan, as a swordsman, you're too clumsy, so don't toil so hard. Be a good fellow, and take up sumo wrestling. With shoulders and arms like that, all we have to do is to fatten you up and enter you in the tournaments, and we can make a fortune." They would guffaw and slap him on the back, and invent professional sumo names for him, urge him to eat more and get a big belly, get him drunk, imitate his dialect, and Kuro would always smile and defer to them with modest good humor.

On the darkened, polished boards of the dojo floor they would make even crueler sport of him, for he had the habit of rushing in like a bull, swinging with powerful strokes that never seemed to be in the right place at the right time. They would dodge and parry, rap him with their white-oak training swords, often as not bringing blood to his forehead, and ugly purple welts and bruises on his forearms and ribs. But Kuro never gave up, and never got vicious.

Sadayori was above that kind of baiting, and silently he disapproved. He watched the youth carefully. The more he was taunted, the more Kuro would take out his frustration in vigorous, solitary exercise, swinging the club after the lesson was finished, the floors wiped with cloths, the others gone for their baths, their sake, their endless arguments about politics. Then one day Sadayori, quietly sipping tea, watched from aside, watched until Kuro dropped the club from his aching fingers, wrists and arms. Sadayori stepped out onto the dojo floor with a practice sword and bowed, speaking with the brusqueness of a senior, but using Kuro's full name, ordering him to fight a practice duel with him.

Kuro flashed him a look of despair.

"*Sempai,* I am so tired and so clumsy, not a good partner

270

for you. Excuse me." He bowed, sweat dripping from his row and leaving dark splotches on the wood.

"Would you refuse me? Come now, Kurozawa, you are very tired, and that is what I have been waiting for. Now is the time for you to start using a sword. You think that in battle you can turn to a foe and plead tiredness? Please honor me!"

The younger man went to racks on the wall and took a practice sword, and after the normal ritual at the beginning of a practice fight, the two started to fence.

For months afterward, whenever he could spare the time, Sadayori would wait for Kuro to finish his exercises, exhausting himself, and would then fence with him, after Kuro's bullish energy was spent. To Kuro's astonishment and delight, his swordsmanship began to improve, carefully coached by Sadayori, and once in a while—rare and precious experience—by the direct advice of the master, who had known everything. Kuro became one of the best in the fencing school, and started to thrash, with pleasant good humor, those Edo clowns who had previously mocked him. His gratitude toward Sadayori knew no bounds, and despite their frequent and heated arguments about foreign policy, they remained friends, a friendship that only the Japanese, with their *sempai-kohai* bonds, could fully understand. A senior, or *sempai*, might seem harsh, overbearing, even bullying, while the *kohai* or junior, seems to act almost like a slave; and yet the senior holds a deep sense of responsibility to his junior, and the junior's feeling for his *sempai* is almost like that of an adoring and obedient younger brother. Later these *sempai* and *kohai* bonds deepen into something as strong and demanding as real brotherhood.

As for Sadayori, he did not like to think that he used his friendship with Kuro to get to know more about other Mito *ronin*—for the friendship was genuine—but there was no doubt that his friendship widened his contacts with the anti-foreign, anti-Ii Naosuke radicals, of whom Mito had a very large share. It was in that fifth year of the Ansei Period that Lord Ii, senior councillor of the *bakufu*, had Iemochi, the twelve-year-old daimyo of Kii, elected as heir to Shogun Iesada, who had died late that summer. The Mito men felt that the son of their own daimyo should have been chosen, but they had lost, and the reins of government were securely in Ii Naosuke's hands. Sadayori understood that Lord Ii wished to use foreign powers to make the nation stronger. Kuro, like most Mito men, wanted immediate war with foreign nations. Intellectually Sadayori agreed with what Lord Ii was doing, and it was on this level that he argued, but inside, Sadayori was torn to see the treaties signed, not only with America, but with England, Russia and France too.

All that had passed between him and Kuro—their practice sessions, talks, strolls through the bustling town, the sake and food they had shared—now flowed through Sadayori's mind as he gazed at this husk of a man.

He took the now cooled tea and lifted Kuro with an arm around his shoulders, holding the cup to his young friend's lips. "Try to drink," he said. Kuro sipped noisily and began to gag. Sadayori gently thumped his back, and the tea stayed down. "Let us try some medicine," he said, lowering Kuro while he fetched a packet of fragrant powder, a concoction of poppy, ginger, cinnamon and other spices and herbs. The medicine was called *hokosan,* and in these times it was practically impossible to find in Edo. Sadayori mixed some of the powder with a little tea and raised Kuro again.

"See, it doesn't have a bitter taste like most medicine, but it is the best. Drink it and I guarantee you'll get well."

Kuro swallowed the stuff, but three minutes later he had brought it up again.

In the night, with Sadayori by his side, young Kurozawa Takenosuke of Mito died. Sadayori could not get a coffin made for him; the coffin makers of Edo were either too busy, or sick, or dead, so Sadayori and his manservant did the best they could in making one themselves. A priest came, and they carried the round, tublike casket to a burial ground, where Sadayori knelt beside the grave. For the first time since his wife died, all those years ago, he was unable to control his tears.

Taiji was isolated, and therefore not stricken by the epidemic. Neither did the town share a water source with any other community, and the basic diet of boiled yams with a little rice and soya sauce was a safe one. In bigger towns one could still buy rice balls, formed by hand, and other prepared foods, but in Taiji there was no such luxury.

Yet the great devil octopus believed to be responsible for the sickness did manage to stretch its tentacles and affect Taiji, for the price of fishery products, including whale meat, dropped like a stone. Real octopus was of course most suspect, but all kinds of fresh seafood were shunned as well. The price of vegetables and eggs rose sharply.

Although the Taiji economy was even further ruined, they

were a resilient folk. This was nothing compared to the havoc of a tsunami or a typhoon. They preserved whale meat by cooking it in a mixture of soya sauce, sugar and sake, or they cut it thinly and dried it; the meat could thus last a long time. As for eggs, the Kumano coast was long known for cock-fighting, and there were plenty of hens. Vegetables the people of Taiji grew in their own plots.

Sadly, fear of the disease kindled traditional Taiji suspicion of outsiders. One victim was an old lady from the neighboring community of Ota. For many years she had carried a heavy basket of fresh vegetables up the narrow path, over the hills and through the woods to Taiji, a forty-minute walk unladen. The soil of Ota was rich, and the vegetables always fresh and succulent, and he wives of Taiji used to welcome the old woman—before the epidemic. Now when she came Kakuemon himself came out and barred her way, shouting abuse at her and driving her back. Some people were ashamed of it, and sorry for the old woman, but most folk agreed that it had been a necessary action to safeguard the town. There was a lot of talk about it.

"This sickness doesn't come from an octopus, it's a punishment from heaven for letting barbarians into our country," Shusuke said one night at supper. Tatsudaiyu glared at him. He did not enjoy gossip in the house, nor did he believe in talk of political matters. Shusuke, although now a harpooner in his own right, fell silent at this look from his father, whose hair was now more than half gray. He held out his bowl to his mother to be refilled with cooked yams and rice, and pecked at the side dish of pilot whale meat.

After rebuilding Tatsudaiyu's house, destroyed in the tsunami, Saburo had gone to work in Shingu for a year. The Wada family had introduced him to an artisan who made sliding doors and screens, and Saburo's job was to paint decorations on them, pine trees, cherry blossoms, mountains, clouds. He enjoyed the work itself, but he missed his family, and Taiji, missed the company of Oyoshi, missed playing with the little boy. He visited Taiji every two or three months or so, and finally he returned there to build a modest little house on the Takigawa plot, going back to work for the whaling organization, doing any odd job he could, for nowadays they were building no new boats for him to paint.

Saburo had saved money in Shingu, but that was not all he brought back. He also had news of Jinsuke. He disclosed this first to his father.

"I was in the shop, and everybody else had gone out to lunch. A *ronin* came in, a very strong, dignified-looking man, not tall, but well built and fairly well dressed. I would think he was about thirty-five."

"Did you know him?" asked Tatsudaiyu.

"No, I don't think so," said Saburo, "yet there was something familiar about him, so maybe I had seen him somewhere. I asked for his name, but he only smiled and said he was just a traveler with news for us. He told me about Jinsuke and walked out. I got the feeling that it might be dangerous to follow him."

"I think you should have gone after him anyway, or gone to the officials." Tatsudaiyu was getting testy of late.

"I couldn't do that, Father. After all, Jinsuke has broken the law, if it's true, so it's best we don't tell anybody, or we'll all be held responsible. He's left the country, and that carries the death sentence."

Tatsudaiyu was silent. Saburo was right, they could not tell anybody.

"Tell me again, exactly what the *ronin* said to you."

"He came into the shop, took off his big straw hat, and asked if I was Saburo, son of the harpooner Tatsudaiyu. When I said yes, he said, 'Your older brother Jinsuke is alive and well. You can be proud of him when the time comes. He has gone to America to learn the way they hunt whales. Tell your father and mother that one day they will see their son's face again.' Then he just bowed, and walked off."

Saburo gazed at his father, who was deep in thought. "Are you going to tell Mother?"

Onui had always believed that her son was alive, and she said she knew his spirit would have come to her pillow if he had died. To tell her might be a kindness, or it might be cruel. She thought he was somewhere in Japan, but for him to be abroad was just as good as his being dead. Besides, few women could keep such a secret; sooner or later she would want to confide in just one other person, and in no time the whole of Taiji would know.

"No," said Tatsudaiyu, "I won't tell her. Jinsuke is a fool, endangering the whole of this family. Why would he do such a thing, with his mother still alive? I'm ashamed of him, and I won't have his name spoken in this house again! Saburo, I forbid you to mention this to anybody, especially your wife." He stressed the word "wife," and Saburo almost winced. He hoped his brother would never come back.

274

* * *

It was a dreadful year, that year of the cholera. Late summer in Kyoto was unbearably sultry, and tempers grew short. To make it worse, the city was buzzing with rumors. France and England had captured Canton, and the so-called Arrow War had ended in another defeat for the Middle Kingdom, with more concessions wrung from her at the Treaty of Tientsin, signed in late June 1858. Now, surely, the foreigners would turn their attention fully on Japan; the English alone were said to have a fleet of forty warships ready to sail to Edo. It was rumored that England wanted to take the great northern island of Yezo from Japan in order to forestall the Russians, whom they had recently fought in the Crimea. The Russians, it was said, wanted to get as much as they could of the northern island. The Americans reputedly wanted the Ryukyu Islands, and they would all squabble over the rest of Japan like mongrels over a bone. The country must surely be prepared for war!

Meanwhile, Ii Naosuke had been named *tairo,* or great councillor, while the thirteenth shogun, Iesada, thirty-five years old, was on his deathbed, after only five years as shogun. The trade treaty urged upon the nation by Townsend Harris, the American consul who had been making a nuisance of himself ever since he landed in Shimoda, was being pushed through by Lord Ii, without the emperor's consent. Lord Ii felt that only by signing this treaty could he keep the foreign powers from attacking Japan as they had attacked China. The new shogun from Kii, Iemochi, was only twelve years old, which meant that Lord Ii, acting as regent, controlled the country. Most of the *tozama* daimyos—the "outside lords" who were not the direct vassals of the Tokugawas —had been pushing for the selection of Hitotsubashi Yoshinobu, son of Tokugawa Nariaki, lord of Mito. This young man, also known as Keiki, was mature and intelligent, and surely would have been a better choice than a mere sickly boy.

Agitators from both factions were cajoling and bribing courtiers and nobles at the imperial court in Kyoto, and most of the Kyoto conservatives were thoroughly enjoying themselves.

Lord Ii had dispatched Lord Hotta, the man who had drafted what the *bakufu* believed to be an acceptable treaty, to argue the *bakufu's* position and the merits of foreign trade, as well as the dangers of refusing it, with the court in Kyoto. Almost en masse, the Kyoto nobles and courtiers, and certainly the emperor, were opposed to it.

For the first time in years Sadayori was sitting with Itoh Hirosada of Satsuma. They were in that same room at the Tsutaya Inn, where they had met what seemed a century earlier, overlooking the Kamo River. Itoh looked much more prosperous now, with his escutcheoned *haori* and his *hakama* of new and expensive silk and a little stoutness around the middle that had not been there before. Sadayori, on the other hand, looked poorer and thinner. He had traveled far. Itoh seemed genuinely glad to see him.

"I got word that you were here, so I came with this sudden rudeness. Forgive me."

"Not at all," said Sadayori, "I am indeed glad to see you after all this time, and, in certain matters, you have my gratitude . . ."

They both knew that he was referring to the deception of Itoh's in having Jinsuke disappear from a boat on its way to Kagoshima. Itoh waved his hand.

"Nothing, nothing," he said, and then, with a grin, "but what of that spy of yours, who sends gold and thanks to me from what must be the palace of the Dragon King, the one who committed a watery suicide—do you get reports from him?"

Sadayori lifted his eyebrows. "Reports from Hades, the Land of Roots?"

"Ho! So that's what you call America now? The young men around here might like that name! Come now, Matsudaira-*dono*, you are supposed to be a *ronin* now. You will embarrass nobody, and both of us know your whaler. Can't you be frank?"

"I have heard nothing since he boarded the ship to America, and I showed you the entire report he wrote to me before he left China. My information came, as you know full well, through Nagasaki, and it would be highly risky to get such letters now."

"I am impressed by that whaler, by the way, and from other routes I have heard how he fought and killed many pirates. The foreigners made a hero out of him." Itoh watched Sadayori's face as he said it. Sadayori's mind raced back to those young days in Wakayama, when the Taiji and Koza men had come, and when he had expounded outrageously to the councillors on how a whaling fleet could be trained as a special fighting force to repel barbarian ships. Well, he had been right about at least one whaler's abilities as a fighter! He wanted to find out how much more Itoh had learned, to know the details, but he kept quiet.

After a short silence Sadayori said, "He is no longer my informer. I am a mere *ronin*. He too is free, I suppose."

Itoh grunted. "The young *bushi* of many clans speak highly of you. You made your name not only in Edo and Wakayama. I hear you have even been to Mito, for a Tokugawa man, or an ex–Tokugawa man, that really was going into the tiger's den . . . incredible . . . Mito!"

Sadayori responded icily to this. "You know a great deal about my movements. Yes. I went to Mito. I went there to deliver the last letter of a dying friend to his family, that, his swords and a few personal effects. His family treated me with kindness, despite their grief, and I stayed one night. That is all."

"I know Kuro's cousin," said Itoh nonchalantly. "He's in Kyoto right now."

"I see," said Sadayori.

"He would like to make your acquaintance, as would many of the others. Tomorrow night we are holding a meeting at a certain house, where we drink a little, gamble a little, talk a little. It's a place where men of similar outlooks gather from all over Japan. We are all friends there, some of us simple *bushi,* some men of rank, some Kyoto nobles. Any patriot and swordsman like yourself, a man who would honor a friend as you did, despite the animosity between your fiefs, will be welcome among us."

Itoh reached into his sleeve and took out a small folded piece of paper. "Here is a map showing you how to get there. Do not, please, ask along the way. There will be several faces you recognize, and names you have heard."

"Oh? Such as who?"

"Yoshida Shoin," said Itoh, still watching Sadayori's face.

Yoshida Shoin! The most anti-foreign, anti-*bakufu* of them all! Since his arrest for trying to board the American ship, Sadayori had seen him but once, but his school in Choshu and the fanatics and radicals he was coaching there were becoming well known indeed.

"He speaks well of you. So do Hashimoto Sanai, Ohashi Junzo and the poet Umeda Umbin. They have read your publication on coastal defense, the one you did some years back."

Sadayori said nothing.

"We want you to join us," said Itoh, his eyes still riveted on Sadayori's face. "You will come?"

Sadayori made a slight bow. "Thank you, I accept the invitation, although I regret that I have neither the means nor the inclination for dice or flower cards."

Itoh smiled. "Yet you gamble with a lot of things, don't you," he said softly. He stood, reaching for his sword. With a slight bow he left the room and Sadayori let out a sigh. Itoh did not mention that the Satsuma clan had been buying large quantities of modern rifles through foreign merchants in China. Sadayori felt sure that Itoh was one of their main agents.

Sadayori and the maids stood by the entrance of the inn to see his friend depart. The Satsuma warrior clattered down the narrow alleyway on his high wooden clogs. He walked with casual dignity, as if there was nothing in the world to bother him, yet there was tension in the set of shoulders and neck. Trouble was brewing in this ancient city, and again Sadayori felt pangs of remorse for the role he was planning as informer and agent of Ii Naosuke. The hard thing about it was that he liked, even admired, many of the radicals he met, and he saw in them a reflection of his own youthful passion. Yet he saw now that their policy of total exclusion of foreigners was impossible, and could only bring disaster to the nation. Lord Ii was right. The country should be strengthened by trade, by building better ships, gaining modern technology, and only after that Japan's time would come to throw the barbarians back into the sea!

"Will you take sake with your dinner tonight, sir?" asked a maid.

"No," he said. "Thank you, no, not tonight."

Unlike the maze and jumble of Edo, the shogun's capital, the ancient capital of Japan, Kyoto, was a well-planned city; it was easy to find one's way about. Beneath an umbrella of oiled paper, Sadayori walked through the rain, his face hidden.

The house was a large one, with a big outer gateway, and it belonged to a nobleman. Sadayori gave his name at the entrance and was quickly ushered into a spacious room filled with men. Several voices called out in a friendly greeting, and one man, Yoshida Shoin, stood and came over to him, smiling. Sadayori knelt just inside the sliding-screen doorway, and Yoshida took a place beside him, facing the others in the room.

"Everybody," he began, "I wish to introduce an old acquaintance of mine, a man who has long urged the authorities to better the defenses of this nation, and urged us to grid ourselves for honorable battle instead of ignoble subservience and cowardice. This man was of high standing in the

Tokugawa fief of Kii, but he has become a *ronin* for his beliefs. He is, as some of us here from Edo well know, one of the best swordsmen I have ever had the privilege to practice with. Gentlemen . . . Matsudaira Sadayori."

Sadayori bowed deeply, speaking the first phrases of meeting.

The others bowed back, responding, "It is the first time, I beg your goodwill."

"I think introducing oneself is best," said Yoshida, "but first you must know our gracious host, Prince Iwakura."

At the head of the room, one arm leaning on a lacquered rest, sat a very handsome man with a high forehead. He smiled and bowed.

"Welcome," he said. His teeth were blackened in court fashion. Sadayori was inwardly startled. So this was not only the house of a court nobleman, many of whom were impoverished and of little real import, but the house of a very influential man indeed. Prince Iwakura was a confidant of the Emperor Komei, and had once served him as a page. There was talk too of his association with the emperor's favorite concubine, a most beautiful woman named Yoshiko, daughter of Nakayama Tadayasu.

Sadayori's mind raced, but then he had to concentrate on catching the names and faces of the other men as one by one they introduced themselves. Faces, names, voices, accents, associations. Some were pale-faced men who had never known the hardship of the roads, others were ruddy-cheeked, with the weather-beaten faces of those who had trudged the entire length of the country, men like himself. But without a doubt, all of them here were intelligent and fervent. He noted a predominance of Choshu warriors, and that made Itoh's presence something to worry about and wonder at, for the two powerful clans of Choshu and Satsuma had been at each other's throats for centuries. Umeda Umbin, the famous outspoken poet of Kyoto, was there too, a virulent critic of the *bakufu*. In one corner sat Ohashi Junzo from Utsunomiya, a samurai renowned for his scholarship in classical Chinese, discoursing now with Rai Mikisaburo, whose father and grandfather had both also been famous men of letters. Rai's father, a historian like his father before him, had long since been urging for the restoration of imperial rule. From the powerful clan of Tosa, in Shikoku, there were two *ronin*, Kasuga Mitsunobu and his brother, Tsunetaka; they were chatting and drinking with a dangerous, surly fellow from Mito, Kurozawa Yutaka, Kuro's cousin.

As he spoke his words of self-introduction, he mouthed thanks to Sadayori, but there was only ice in his eyes. Sadayori printed an image of the man on his mind; not as muscular as Kuro had been, close-set eyes, right forearm scarred, probably by a live blade. Kasuga Mitsunobu, sitting next to him, was related to a famous painter, and was known to be a brilliant swordsman and archer, as well as a master of the tea ceremony.

There were men here from Mito, Tosa, Choshu, Satsuma, all of them fiefs opposed to the *bakufu*. There were nobles too, and even one extremely wealthy merchant, a man who had gained the right to bear a single sword through public works—and, as Sadayori cynically noted, from lending money to the government. That fellow would not be here for pure patriotism. This was the most serious danger to Lord Ii, a gathering of powerful and influential men, rallying to the Sonno Joi war cry. Revere the emperor! Repel the barbarians! And this meeting was being held, with gambling as an excuse, in the house of a noble who had direct access to the Son of Heaven!

Sadayori forced himself to relax. He was a good judge of men, and he tried to get a feeling for who was the leader here. The vociferous Yoshida? No. From his quiet, confident presence it became obvious that if indeed this motley group had a leader, then it would be Prince Iwakura himself, and this network of roaming swordsmen and famous intellectuals would give him the pulse of the whole country. It was knowledge that most of the painted, effeminate, tooth-blackened courtiers certainly did not have.

Somebody spoke out, in a voice louder than the rest. "Hotta is on his way here. We know they intend to ratify this treaty of theirs, we know they have permitted an American to see the shogun, and we know what is in the treaty. Don't tell me that it isn't coming to a crisis already!"

"You are so right!" Yoshida's voice rang across the room. "Everybody hear this! I think you should all know exactly what is contained in this treaty of the *bakufu*. Please . . ." He turned to the man who had spoken first.

"For a start," said Kurozawa, "the treaty grants them three ports opened immediately, one close to Edo . . . Kanagawa. It guarantees two more ports to be opened later, one close to Kyoto. Edo and Osaka are to be opened for foreign residents within three or four years. Foreigners are to be given freedom to worship their religion, as well as extraterritorial rights."

Uproar followed.

"Hotta, Ii and the whole bunch of them should be asked to commit seppuku!"

"The first hairy barbarian that crosses my path will feel the bite of my sword!"

"Outrageous!"

Cries of anger and indignation became a babel of threats and heated talk.

"Face the truth! Hotta must be killed, it's the only solution!" Silence fell on the room, and all heads turned back to Yoshida. Even talk of killing a high official was considered high treason by the *bakufu*. All of them could be executed just for being in the same room where such words were uttered. Prince Iwakura raised his cultured voice.

"Would our new friend from Kii kindly give us his opinion?" The tone was velvet, but it hid sharkskin. They all turned to face Sadayori, who was, after all, from the clan whose boy lord had been pushed to be shogun by Ii Naosuke, and Ii Naosuke was Hotta's superior and good friend. Sadayori bowed slightly and weighed his words.

"Lord Hotta comes to Edo to explain this treaty to His Imperial Majesty, does he not? The word of the Son of Heaven is divine, and must surely be harkened to with loving hearts by all Japanese. If the Son of Heaven's word is to be carried back to Edo by Lord Hotta, then would it not be a grave disservice to His Majesty to assassinate the man who carries his words?"

"We should kill him before he troubles His Majesty with his presence!" retorted Yoshida.

"Such an action requires careful planning. Is there time?" asked Sadayori.

There was a murmur of agreement and Prince Iwakura smiled.

"Thank you. His Majesty will, gentlemen, I assure you, forbid this treaty and order the shogun to drive the foreigners out, including the American and his interpreter. I agree with Matsudaira-sama. I do not think at this stage that we should harm the man who will bear those tidings to Edo."

Yoshida began to argue, but others silenced him. When Sadayori glanced at this former friend of his, he saw the fire in his eyes, and he knew that even if Yoshida bent to advice this time, eventually he would resort to violence, because violence was what festered inside him. I wish the damned Americans had taken him when he tried to go, Sadayori thought.

In a few days, Shogun Iesada was dead, and political intrigue in Kyoto increased. Sadayori learned too that the lord of Mito had appealed directly to the emperor in a letter, an alarming and unheard-of precedent.

Sadayori's list of dangerous radicals was impressive indeed. He knew those who were active, those who were plotting violence, and the longer he kept the list to himself, the greater danger to him and the man to whom he had sworn allegiance—the *tairo,* Ii Naosuke. Sadayori believed that it placed the nation, and therefore the very person of the emperor, in danger too. After he attended that meeting, Sadayori was watched wherever he went. He could not risk trying to slip away at night. It had to be done innocently, in the day.

Sadayori's contact, also an agent of the *tairo,* was an older man, a merchant who made a habit of strolling in the gardens of certain temples and shrines. He was known to be an expert on irises, and he raised many in his own garden. Each day, late in the afternoon, he could be seen on the grounds of a temple within walking distance of Sadayori's inn.

For three days Sadayori tried to evade the men following him. On the fourth day he ducked into a small shop that sold ceramics. He knew the owner, who was a potter himself, from previous visits with his wife, long, long ago. The man greeted Sadayori with pleasure, and they shared tea and talked of old times. Sadayori decided he could trust the man, and told him he was being tailed by a *ronin* who wished to pick a quarrel with him because he was formerly a retainer of the lord of Kii. He asked if he could escape by the back way, past the kilns.

"Ah, Matsudaira-sama, of course," sighed the potter. "It all saddens me. Kyoto has been such a peaceful, beautiful place, and now they rail against the government in Edo, and I am sure they are eager to spill blood even in this city, which has known no violence for over two hundred years. It seems we are going back in time, to the days of ancient feuds. Go, and take care, this house will always be safe for you."

Nobody saw Sadayori go, and he arrived at the temple garden just in time. The merchant was sitting on a stone bench, looking at the colorful mandarin ducks and the tall irises that grew on the banks of a wide pond. Sadayori strolled by, alert for spies.

There was room for three or more on the stone bench, and it was placed to command the best view of the pond, a view artfully framed by trimmed trees, with a pavilion to the left, and green forested mountains in the background. Sadayori slipped the longer of his two swords out of the sash and sat down.

"An old pond," said his neighbor, quoting a famous haiku. "A frog jumps . . ."

"But no splash," said Sadayori, misquoting.

"Then the frog must have jumped into the reeds, so perhaps he saw a heron?" His neighbor turned to him. "Would you care for a sweetmeat, sir? They are humble fare, but a specialty of Kyoto."

The man laid a paper package on the bench between them, opening it to reveal some brightly colored sugar sweets. Sadayori took one, although normally he never ate sweets unless with green tea.

"Oh dear, how thoughtless," said the man, "I regret that I have no tissues, do excuse me."

"Please use mine," said Sadayori, taking a wad of fine tissue paper from his sleeve and laying it on the stone. The merchant took a tissue and wiped his fingers delicately.

"Thank you for the treat," said Sadayori, standing, "but excuse me now, I must leave." He slipped his sword and sheath back into his sash and made a slight bow. The merchant also stood, bowing, and Sadayori noted from the quality of the kimono he wore that he must be quite wealthy. On his head was a brown cap. He wondered about the relationship this man had with Ii Naosuke, was he another of the merchants the *bakufu* were leaning on heavily for loans they never repaid?

"Oh, sir, your tissues . . ."

"Please keep them, I have more."

The man bowed again, and as Sadayori strolled down the path that skirted the pond, he sat down on the stone bench and gazed once more at the brightly plumed ducks dabbling in the shallows and at the banks of tall, sensuous irises. After a minute or so had passed he casually picked up the wad of tissues, inside of which was hidden Sadayori's list—names of men who would use violence against Lord Ii's supporters. He slipped it into the folds of his kimono. For half an hour he stayed where he was, then got up and strolled in the opposite direction, for all the world like a rich merchant with competent clerks to carry on his business for him.

When Sadayori arrived back at the inn, Itoh was waiting for

him, together with another samurai who wore the black circle and cross escutcheon of Lord Shimazu of Satsuma on his *haori*.

"Where have you been?" asked Itoh with rude bluntness.

Sadayori knelt before the alcove and laid his long sword on the staghorn rest. He noted that both Itoh and the other man had their swords lying beside them in easy reach.

"I went to visit some of the places I had known before, when my wife was alive," he answered easily. "She was a Kyoto woman, and loved it here. However, I must warn you that for three days I have been followed by *bakufu* spies. It took me all my effort to avoid them. I don't like being watched. If it goes on and they insist, I may have to take direct action." He turned toward Itoh with a smile.

"Shall we have some more tea?" He glanced at their empty cups. He knew his story would only half convince Itoh, and that he was in a dangerous situation. Yet Sadayori's loyalty to his long-dead wife, and his steady refusal to make use of geisha or drinking-house maids, was a source of wonder to many of his friends, and it was very like him to wish for privacy in visiting places of memory of that beautiful third daughter of a Kyoto courtier, cousin of his late daimyo.

"I have some information from Edo," Sadayori said, looking at the other man, who had not yet been introduced. Itoh spoke a few words to him in their incomprehensible dialect, and the man bowed and left the room.

"How did the information get to you, and when?"

"This morning." It was true. The information had come to him from another guest who had arrived from Osaka. Sadayori quickly weighed the matter in his mind and decided it was expedient to tell Itoh.

"Hotta will carry the emperor's refusal of the treaty to the *bakufu*, but they will not accept it. The treaty will definitely be ratified, if it has not already been done so."

Itoh shrugged. It was no news to him.

"There will also be a purge, very soon, of Sonno Joi patriots, the *tairo* himself is ordering it. You had better leave for Satsuma, there you'll be safe. Try to get word to Yoshida and the others that they are in grave danger."

Itoh was silent for a while. Then he spoke. "Thank you." He paused, as if thinking over his words. "Prince Iwakura is safe, he is too close to His Majesty for the *bakufu* to try to lay hands on him. At the worst it'll be house arrest. I will try to get word to the others, but I fear their bravery outweighs

284

their intelligence. Matters are coming to a boil here in Kyoto. The emperor is on our side, he wants the barbarians out. He will write to the lord of Mito in person and ask him to force the *bakufu* to come to heel."

"I see," said Sadayori, inwardly groaning. Could His Majesty have any idea of the danger of trying to force foreign nations to forget about the treaties? They would bring their navies, all of them, America, Britain, France and Russia.

"The new shogun is definitely the lord of Kii, and you, my friend, are in great danger, even though you are our friend. There are many who do not want to take chances with you," said Itoh. He shifted and gazed out the window at the river.

"Come with me to Kagoshima."

Sadayori laughed, breaking the tension between them.

"Am I not in danger there? With a name like Matsudaira? Of the House of Tokugawa?"

Itoh grinned. "You will be my guest, and anyway, you are a *ronin*, no longer tied to Kii. Anyway, I insist. My men are waiting for you . . . and we in Kyushu can be forceful in our hospitality. Besides, Kyushu has the best food, the best wine, and the best women in all of Japan." Then, as an afterthought, he added, "And the best men."

Sadayori laughed again at this inelegant boasting, but even though he laughed, he knew that some of the radicals in Kyoto were out to kill him and that Itoh was trying to save his life.

"I will be honored to visit such a fine place, then," he said.

Itoh clapped his hands and the silent samurai appeared at the door and slid it open.

"Get the palanquin ready," he said, and then, to Sadayori, "You won't need to borrow that spear."

Sadayori began to bundle up his few possessions.

Chapter Twenty-Two

It's very hot, but good," said Sadayori, taking another piece of the orange stuff. "What is it?"

"We call it 'Matsuura-zuke.' It's whale cartilage, preserved in sake lees, red peppers and what-have-you," said Itoh, "but they keep the actual recipe a secret here in Kyushu."

"You keep most things a secret in Kyushu," laughed Sadayori, and his friend grinned and replied in dialect.

They sat by the bay, looking across to the pall of smoke and steam that hung from the peak of the volcano on Sakura Island, offshore. Behind and to the left was the castle town of Kagoshima, feudal seat of the lord of Satsuma, at present supposedly under house arrest, as were the daimyos of Owari and Tosa, and that fiery old tiger the lord of Mito, as well as his son, whom most of them had wished to become shogun.

Sadayori and Itoh often took strolls together, eating at some small place along the way, or, more frequently, with Itoh bringing a picnic lunch that usually contained some new Kyushu delicacy. Kyushu men were tough, headstrong, stubborn, and made the best of friends. Sadayori considered himself lucky.

Itoh flicked out the line and the weighted bait and stared intently at the float, as if willing it to bob. He was still an ardent fisherman.

"How long have you been here now? A year and a half? Why don't you let me introduce you to a fine girl and settle here?"

Sadayori smiled, and shook his head. Time was indeed striding by. The whale delicacy, that hot stuff they had with rice balls and tea, made Sadayori think back some fourteen years to the time when he had stood on a cliff and watched the whalers of Taiji take a right whale. Even now he could bring those colors and shapes into his mind's eye, hear the sounds of their chanting and beating, the drums, the flutes, the conches. That had been the year when Emperor Komei, the 121st in a direct line from Jimmu, had succeeded to the throne of his father. Sadayori sighed and Itoh glanced at him.

"You know, when I was young I had a solution for everything, but now the whole world seems upside down."

Itoh grunted and went back to watching his float. Sadayori envied him his apparent straightforwardness and simplicity, although he knew that beneath that lurked a very subtle native cunning.

"Do you use much whale meat in Kyushu?"

"Indeed. More than anywhere else in Japan. We have net whaling going on in several places, in the Goto Islands, at Iki, all around. When it comes to festivals or weddings, if we can't serve whale, then nothing can begin. Whale is the best food there is for giving a man strength. Come to my house for supper tonight. My wife will prepare a whale dish for you. Please come, my brother and another very interesting fellow are coming."

"Oh, but I don't want to bother . . ."

"What are you saying? No bother! Come, please."

Sadayori thanked him and they both gazed at the float, which still refused to bob. He had grown to enjoy Itoh's company and his rough humor, and to look forward to the practice sessions they had together. Yet he felt guilty about his happiness here, sad at what had happened in the rest of the country. The swords of the executioners had fallen many times in Edo and Kyoto; even here in Kagoshima, the new daimyo, half-brother of the previous lord, who had died but recently, was treating his predecessor's close confidants with suspicion and cruelty, and Itoh himself was forever walking a cautious line.

Their friend Yoshida Shoin had been plotting, as Sadayori knew he would, to kill a *bakufu* official. They caught him and cut his head off. Rai Mikisaburo also had been beheaded, in Edo, and Umeda Umbin, the poet, was reported to have died in prison after torture. Fifty-seven nobles and samurai had been arrested in Kyoto, and forty or more in Edo. Several men had been banished to islands, many imprisoned. Many officials had been summarily discharged from their duties, or were under house arrest. Now, under Ii

Naosuke's iron rule the country was quiet, at least on the surface.

The trade treaty with the Americans had been pushed through without imperial consent, and treaties with other foreign powers had followed in quick succession. In the meantime, the dangers of war with powerful nations had been averted.

Sadayori and Itoh had escaped to Kyushu just in time, for when the purge came Sadayori's name was also on the wanted list—maybe out of cunning on the *tairo*'s part, to reinforce the radicals' belief in his agent, although Sadayori was not sure anymore. Could it be that he had learned a little too much about the lines that linked directly to the imperial court?

Anyway, now Sadayori felt a strong obligation toward Itoh and to his daimyo the thirty-eight-year-old Shimazu Hisamitsu. The lord of Satsuma knew of Sadayori's presence in his city, and permitted it, perhaps because Sadayori had quite a reputation as a scholar of military science and a martial artist and perhaps because the story of his loyalty to to a young Mito friend during the cholera epidemic was also told in many circles.

Satsuma and Kagoshima were far from Edo, and pretty well a law unto themselves. Sadayori was relatively safe there. Itoh was also supposedly under house arrest, but he largely ignored it, except that he did not travel out of the domains of his lord, for that would cause embarrassment.

"No fish today," said Itoh, standing up and packing up his gear. Sadayori also stood, brushing sand off his *hakama*.

"When the fuss dies down a bit, I'm going to Tanegashima," said Itoh as they walked. "If you wish, I could try to arrange for you to be given permission to come with me."

"Could you really? I'd very much like to see the island."

Itoh glanced sideways at him. "We have some of our guns made there still, but they're not nearly as good as the American and British weapons."

It was no secret between them that Satsuma was becoming heavily armed with foreign weapons. As the ratio of samurai to other classes was about one to three, it meant that they were building up a very powerful army, rivaled only by Choshu. Sadayori had even seen a group of low-ranking *bushi* being trained to fire in volleys.

"The American guns we have are loaded at the breech and fired with a hammer and a cap, so there is no real worry about a little rain, not like our Tanegashima guns. They can

288

be reloaded and fired quickly, and have better accuracy and range. However, many of the corps leaders say that the British rifles, which are loaded by a cartridge at the muzzle, are actually more reliable, and when it comes to fighting with bayonet and butt, more rugged."

"That's the kind of fighting a Japanese will always be better at, said Sadayori."

"I agree," said Itoh, "although I'll never use a rifle myself. I still can't help feeling it's a coward's weapon." He echoed the thoughts of most samurai.

"We should be able to make our own rifles," said Sadayori. "After all, we learned to make fine matchlocks hundreds of years ago, didn't we?"

"Of course, but first we need to send some men abroad to learn the new tools and techniques of gunsmithing, or even get a tame barbarian gunsmith and put him in a cage, then feed him only if he teaches us. Also, we need to buy tools. By the way, any more word from your whaler in America?"

Sadayori shook his head. "No, not since Shanghai, but then, I haven't exactly been easy to locate, have I?"

"Think he'll learn anything useful?"

"Well, I'm sure he'll learn about foreign whaling."

Itoh snorted. "Whaling is something they can't teach us anything about."

Sadayori wasn't sure anymore, but he didn't want to think about it. In his last letter Jinsuke had been unpatriotically sympathetic to the foreigners, and Sadayori wasn't sure if he wanted to hear from him again. Nevertheless he wondered where Jinsuke was. He spoke again.

"At least the government changed its policies on shipbuilding, they're making some good big ones now."

Itoh grunted. "Not enough." They both lapsed into silence.

One of Itoh's guests was a very large man with a deep voice. The second guest was Itoh's younger brother, Tokubei, who had recently returned from Edo with news of the foreign settlement in Yokohama. For Sadayori's benefit they conversed in standard Japanese, but the big man had a very pronounced accent. This man, at thirty-two, was one of the youngest and most able commanders in the Satsuma army, and their talk over supper was mostly of military matters. The man's name was Saigo Yukinaga; his cousin Takamori was a radical now in exile on a southern island.

"You've been very quiet," said Saigo to Tokubei. "Tell us the worst. How goes it with Ii Naosuke's new foreign settlement in Kanagawa?"

"They couldn't put them in Kanagawa, it was too near the main road and the processions of the daimyo with their men, and patriotic *ronin* too, so they moved them across to Yokohama."

"Ah, I know it," said Sadayori, "a little marshy place, full of mosquitoes, with hills and a bluff up behind, overlooking the bay of Edo. Did you go there yourself?"

"Not I," said Tokubei, "otherwise I could not have kept my sword in its sheath. I got close enough to see all the ships, though. They are really moving in, lots of them, building, taking over as if they owned the land. But I've heard tales. Those barbarians are arrogant brutes, even down to the merchants. Can you believe it? Insolent even with *bushi*! Three of them have been cut down already for it, and there will be more. The *bakufu* is losing contol. Wherever young samurai gather there is talk of war, and there is robbery and violence all over the country. In the cities the people are hiring gang bosses to protect their property, because the authorities can't handle it. Many people say we must restore the emperor, obey him, drive out the barbarians . . . and to do that the *bakufu* must go."

"Can there be no compromise?" asked Sadayori, on risky ground now.

"No. Only the emperor can restore things to their proper balance," said Saigo.

"Any more news of the purge?" asked Itoh.

"Ohashi Junzo was tortured and put to death. He was in on the same plot to kill Councillor Ando. But what shocks me is that they executed Hashimoto Sanai, from Echizen."

"Hashimoto?" exclaimed Sadayori. "But he was one of those favoring opening the country for trade! I've heard him argue that point myself. He was in agreement with Lord Ii!"

"He didn't agree with him on the choice of the new shogun. He was campaigning for Keiki."

Sadayori shook his head sadly, but none of the others could guess the anguish that was tearing at him inside.

"How does our friend from Kii feel about the choice of shogun?" asked Saigo, with pointed bluntness.

"'Shogun' means 'barbarian-vanquishing leader,' does it not? How can a child of twelve, and a sickly one at that, perform that task?"

Sadayori shocked himself when the words came out, realizing that he meant them, realizing that he had been disloyal to his clan, and yet it was true. What he did not say was that he still believed Ii Naosuke to be the only man in the

290

government wise enough, intelligent enough, and ruthless enough to save the country from civil war and barbarian conquest.

"So the score of that purge is ten dead patriots," said Tokubei, and again Sadayori winced inside.

"Has the trade brought any benefit in wealth? Are the merchants making profits?" asked Sadayori. All three looked at him with amazement.

"How should I know?" said Tokubei. "I'm no merchant." He, like other men of his class, despised merchants.

"I would like to see Yokohama," murmured Itoh, "to see how far they have dared to go." His voice was quiet, but there was no mistaking the hatred in it. In that, at least, Sadayori agreed with him.

Sadayori spent the winter in Kagoshima, sometimes moving about when halfhearted attempts were made by the *bakufu* to arrest him and take him back to Edo for trial. Naturally, almost every warrior in Kagoshima knew where the renowned martial artist from Kii was, but they wouldn't dream of betraying him. Reports to Edo stated that Matsudaira Sadayori could not be found in the fiefdom of Satsuma, where outside *ronin* were not permitted anyway.

In early March, he got Satsuma clan permission to accompany Itoh to Tanegashima, that island where the first Europeans had landed, in 1542. They had brought, among other things, the knowledge of making guns.

Saburo's body was hot with exercise and cold with exhaustion at the same time, and he didn't know if he could hang on. The years he had missed actually going out with the fleet had softened him, and now this was sheer torment. Their chase boat was not one of the top three, so they had the task of towing the whale back after the kill; this one was a fat female humpback, her rotund body and long, scalloped, winglike flippers a terrible drag in the water.

"Stick to it, Saburo!" said his oar mate, as he missed the timing, and the man who gripped the same oar and stood beside him had to cover for him with extra effort of his own.

"Come on, sing the chant with us, bellow it out, it helps, you know, it really does. Just think of the song, and the rhythm will bring strength to you."

"I'm sorry, yes . . . ." said Saburo, taking deep breaths. Halfheartedly at first, just mouthing the words, he began to join in the chant. Up at the bow their harpooner led them, dancing and waving a signal stick.

They were towing against the wind and a falling tide. The whale was slung between the two carry boats, beams lashed across the broad, barnacled back, ropes under the belly, the snout rope keeping the head from going down and making even more drag. Three chase boats were out front, the one Saburo had been conscripted to in the middle. Ropes between the boats were bar tight, thrumming against wind and sea.

Winter was mild in Taiji, but at times a cold and evil wind would blow out from the land. In Taiji they called it the *yamade*, and it was feared. Luckily it had only sprung up half an hour before, and despite this adversity, they would reach the shore in an hour and hand their whale over to the men on the big wooden capstans.

Wind lashed over the waves, white and torn, and spray spattered against Saburo's legs. The water was warmish, but cooling rapidly in the wind, and his legs were red and mottled with cold.

"That's it, Saburo, you're doing fine," said his oar mate between chants. The harpooner's keen eyes had caught the barest falter in the movement of the third portside oar, and he began to yodel out an impromptu verse, a highly bawdy one, giving reasons why some young whalers were so tired in the daytime, making delightfully obscene puns that all knew were directed at Saburo. He found strength to laugh with the rest and yelled the repeating refrains louder. It really did help. Slowly, slowly, the beach grew closer, until they could make out the figures of the people awaiting them.

Shusuke saw his younger brother stagger a few steps up the beach and then sit down like an obstinate drunk. It had been an especially long haul in today, with the *yamade* coming up like that. In the past three weeks they had taken a total of nine whales, a windfall for the village, but hard work for the men.

Rain was whipping down from the hill, pocking the surface of the harbor and slicking the cloaks of woven grass that the men had slipped over their shoulders. Saburo sat there, still uncovered, with his overcoat of quilted cotton neglected in a sopping bundle on the ground beside him. Shusuke went down and slipped his coat over his brother's shoulders. With one arm he dragged him to his feet.

"Hey, come on. You'll get a cold. Let's go and have a hot bath and you'll feel better. It was hard work, wasn't it? Come on, snap out of it, let's go!"

Shusuke's tone was rough, but there was concern in his heart. Saburo's oar mate came running up, his coat on under his grass cape and his rain hat steadied with one hand against the soughing wind.

"Better get him home. He's done in. On that last stretch I thought I wouldn't last either, and I'm used to it. I swear the whale was trying to swim in the opposite direction."

"I'm sorry, I caused you trouble," said Saburo woodenly, swaying on his feet. "The only thing I can move around is a paintbrush. I'm a terrible fellow."

His oar mate affectionately kneaded the muscles of Saburo's neck and shoulder in the comradely way of whalers and nudged him into walking.

"You did fine! We all get tired, right, Shusuke-san? Most of us got fit early in the season, chasing after all those pilot whales. If you came out more often, instead of just when the whaling gets heavy, you wouldn't feel it so much. You've got a good body, wide shoulders, big hands for gripping."

Saburo barely listened. All he wanted to do was to get home and sit down. Oyoshi came to the door at the sound of their voices. When she saw Saburo, half supported between the two others, alarm flashed on her face. "Saburo! What's wrong?"

"He's just tired and cold. Get his bath things and I'll take him for a hot soak right away," said Shusuke.

"I'm all right, I just want to sit down," he said. He was embarrassed. When he closed his eyes he could still feel the boat moving under him.

"No, it's to the bath for you, it'll warm you up." Shusuke waited impatiently while Oyoshi dashed in and came back with two wooden washbowls and cloths. She thanked them both, asking them to come back afterward.

"Oh, it's nothing, nothing at all," said Saburo's oar mate, also a harpooner's younger son. "Well, I'll go and get my things. See you in the bath house."

At first Saburo could hardly bear to get into the big communal tub, so chapped was his skin and so hot the water, but as he slowly submerged, the pain of it went away; first he felt goose pimples, and then the grateful heat soaking into him. He let out a big groan, leaning his head against the wooden edge of the tub. He wondered if he could take even one more day of it.

Once thoroughly warmed, he sat on a little wooden stool while his brother scrubbed his back.

"Why don't you take the day off tomorrow? I'll speak to Kakuemon," said Shusuke.

"No, no, I can't. With father laid up with his chest again it's not right for our family to have just you working. Don't worry, I'll be fine after a good sleep."

Shusuke saw Saburo to the door of his house and was cajoled in. Oyoshi had prepared hot sake mixed with raw eggs, into which she had added a little of her precious store of ginseng. Saburo sipped it gratefully. Shusuke laughed it off, and asked for plain warmed sake. The child was noisy, romping around the little room, getting scolded, demanding his father's and uncle's attention. Shusuke wrestled him to the mats, then pushed him away while he took a cup of sake.

"This little scamp needs a brother, or a sister. He always pesters adults to play with him. He's lonely, that's why." Saburo kept his eyes down, feeling a pang of hurt and inner wrath, resenting that he should be prodded by so many people about their lack of new children.

"Oh, there's time enough for that," said Oyoshi. "One like him is all I can handle right now. He's worse than a troop of monkeys." She left them and busied herself in the kitchen, putting another couple of split kindling faggots under the rice pot. Shusuke slurped noisily.

"Hmm. It's not good for a child to be an only one," he said. Shusuke now had two children, with another on the way. Oyoshi was almost twenty-six now, and it was inevitable that the gossips were wagging their chins about her, not having a child for seven years.

Saburo and Oyoshi had kept their pact, neither of them really knowing what was going on deep inside the other, and each treating the other far better than any of their contemporaries treated a wife or a husband. It really did seem, at times, as if they had become brother and sister, yet they were closer than that, showing many signs of affection. After Shusuke had gone, Oyoshi laid out the evening meal for Saburo and the boy. Saburo spoke, with vehemence.

"I hate it," he said.

Oyoshi looked with dismay at him, and at the nicely grilled saury with grated white radish, the plate of home-

294

made pickles, the miso soup with sea lettuce and bean curd, and today, even white rice.

"Oh, I'm sorry. I'll quickly make something else for you." She went to take the fish away.

"Stupid. Not the food. I like everything you cook, better than anything else, no, it's whaling, going out in the boats. There's something about the sea that frightens me out there, it seems to tell me it's waiting to get me, to pull me down. I'm no good, I'm a useless weak worm, not a man."

Oyoshi knelt beside him and touched his arm. "No you are not, you are the finest and most honest man I know. You have great talent, and you ought to be painting. It's a waste for you to have to work like this. Why don't you start to work on your scrolls again? Or if you like, we can move to Shingu, the three of us, and you could work at that shop."

Saburo shook his head wearily. "My father would be upset, he's losing his health, you know that."

Oyoshi bit back a retort about Saburo losing his own health, but she remembered that when her own father had been ill, Saburo spent as much time as he could by his side, right up until that awful day of the tsunami. For her father, Saburo had been the best pupil, the best son and the best friend he had ever had. Her voice softened.

"Let me massage your back a little while after supper."

"Thank you, Yoshi, but I'll just sleep."

Yamamoto Genzaemon was the village headman, the *daishoya* of Taiji. His position was authorized by the magistrates of Shingu, under Lord Mizuno. When there were whales about he made it a habit to drop into the whaling office overlooking the landing beach. Kakuemon was just finishing up the day's accounts. The two men exchanged pleasantries and a clerk brought tea. It had been a long day.

Outside, the rain-moistened air was heavy with the pungency of whale blubber and bones being rendered, and the men were still cleaning up after flensing. The waters of the bay were pink with blood. To one side of the beach lay two long sides of blackish-gray baleen plates, bristle sides grayish white. Beside them, a little wagtail hopped. Genzaemon looked out at the scene.

"It's been a lot of hard work for you, but a prosperous time, for a change," he said. Kakuemon leaned back on his heels and followed the headman's gaze.

"We have been lucky. A shift in the currents offshore.

When that happens you sometimes get a little sea of cold water trapped in the warm, and the whales seem to like that. We've done well. Six humpbacks, which fetch one hundred to one hundred fifty gold *ryo* each; two gray whales, fetching about thirty *ryo* each; and then, best of all, that fine, fat right whale. That one alone is worth three hundred *ryo*.

"Three hundred, is it? Excellent! All we'd need is one of those every week and we'd be back on our feet."

The whaling master nodded sadly. "I think it's just a lucky time we're enjoying for the present. We can't hope for it to last like this. It seems there were far more whales in the old days . . ."

Genzaemon nodded. "It's become a very difficult world, I don't know what to make of it."

The two men sat and chatted for a while, then Kakuemon called for the package he knew the headman was hoping for. A few choice cuts of tail meat. As the headman left, Kakuemon thought to himself that the men really deserved some kind of bonus, they had worked so hard, and as he left for home, he wondered if the business could bear such an extravagance, what with taxes, taxes, taxes, and interest and loans, and the rising cost of everything.

In Edo, the New Year came and went. The foreigners in Yokohama had their parties and gatherings some weeks before the Japanese, who functioned on a different calendar. It was March of 1860, and a late snow was falling thickly.

Ii Naosuke had to make the short trip from his mansion to the shogun's palace. He called for guards and bearers and soon his palanquin was waiting at the front door. He got in, the bearers lifted it up, and his escort took their positions. The men wore grass capes and wide hats against the weather, and the handles of their swords were tied with bags to keep the snow from the precious blades. Otherwise the snow would melt and trickle down inside the sheaths.

As they reached the Sakurada Gate of the palace, they took no heed of a few scattered groups of loiterers, *ronin* by the looks of them. The attack came swiftly and without warning. Eighteen warriors charged them, slashing and stabbing and screaming battle cries. Hampered by the capes and the hilt bags, many of the guards fell without even drawing their swords. The attackers made a feint, running off with a head, shouting in triumph, and in the confusion, Ii Naosuke's men left the palanquin alone. Samurai rushed in, firing a pistol and stabbing through the screens. They dragged the richly brocaded, mortally wounded man out onto the snowy ground and cut off his head. Those who had survived fled into the night. Later, the attackers who still lived slit open their bellies in ritual suicide before the mansion of a member of the senior council.

They were Mito clansmen, but all had officially renounced ties with their clans, becoming *ronin,* so that blame would not fall on their lord. No, Ii Naosuke's bitter enemy, the old tiger Nariaki, would not be officially held responsible for the death of the *bakufu's* strongman.

Bakufu councillors, fearful of the gap left by Lord Ii's death, did not announce it until two months had passed, claiming that Lord Ii had merely been wounded in the attack. Not many were fooled by that, however; too many had seen the gory head, and Mito spies passed the word around.

Matsudaira Sadayori was irrevocably a *ronin* now. Nobody but Ii Naosuke had known why he had resigned from his position with the fiefdom of Kii. He could never return now.

The lord of Mito, Nariaki, did not long enjoy his enemy's destruction. He was stabbed in his own outhouse by an unknown assailant in the autumn of the same year.

Chapter Twenty-Three

The sailor walked up and looked at the gabled roof and the upper-story glass windows. The rest of the view of this Western-style house was hidden by a high fence of strongly woven split bamboo, entwined with morning glory, above which sunflowers peeked and dozens of butterflies fluttered in the sun. From a grove of pine trees opposite the house came the steady meeee . . . meeee . . . meeee of cicadas.

By the Western calendar it was July 1862. Jinsuke had been out of mainland Japan for ten years, but if the authorities caught him, if they understood in fact that he was a native, and not a foreign sailor, then they would certainly imprison and interrogate him, and probably execute him.

He checked the map again. It was crudely drawn, by a busy office worker, but for sure this was the place. He stood on a stone and looked over the fence, seeing a pillared porch, the big glass windows of the ground floor, the garden all around. It could have been a house in the suburbs of San Francisco, except for the Japanese joinery. So big! Lyall had been eighteen when Jinsuke knew him in Shanghai, which would make him just twenty-six now. Twenty-six and having a palace like this? Still dubious, he walked along the fence to the gate. He squinted through a chink in it; on one of the pillars of the porch was a small name sign, in brass: L. W. FOGERTY, ESQ.

Jinsuke stuck his arm through a hole by the latch, when suddenly the gate was charged by a big and apparently vicious dog. Jinsuke whipped his hand back out. There were few things he feared, but dogs made him uncomfortable.

The animal made a racket, and soon a servant came

running with a stick. The servant himself was impressive, a tall, fat, pigtailed Chinese in a long gown. The man looked pretty ferocious himself, with eyes glaring from narrow slits and long black moustaches. He came to the gate, quieting the dog with a gentle cuff on its nose, after which it stood by the gate, haunches bristling, a low grumbling growl sounding deep in its thick, furry neck. It was an Ainu bear dog, definitely not the kind of dog to meddle with.

"Yes? What you want?" The man spoke in English.

"I would like to see Mr. Lyall Fogerty," said Jinsuke.

The Chinese inspected him from eyes almost hidden in the folds of his eyelids. He noted the double-breasted jacket with brass buttons, the open-necked white shirt, the peaked seaman's cap.

"You off ship?"

"Yes."

The Chinese shook his head. "Mr. Fogerty don't see men off ship at house. You go to office."

"I have been to the office. He wasn't there."

The man looked at him again. "Today Saturday. Office close Saturday after five. Close tomorrow, Sunday. You go Monday."

Jinsuke's face fell. He had so much looked forward to seeing his friend, and he had brought a present for him. He held up a canvas-wrapped bundle, quite large, the canvas neatly sewn in the sailor's way.

"Please give this to Mr. Fogerty."

The Chinese did not deign to take it. "Mr. Fogerty don't buy stuff off sailors at house. You go to office."

Jinsuke's temper flared at the man's demeanor, and he spat out a string of Chinese, telling the man he was an insolent toad, and that he, an old friend of the family, had walked a mile in the summer heat to deliver a present, and that Lyall—he used the Chinese pronunciation of the name— would hear about it. Jinsuke's face was deeply tanned and rugged, and in the flush of temper the white scar under one eye showed. His features were Japanese, but he had a large nose, and most unusual, a thick black beard that was neatly trimmed. The servant, taken aback now, took a second look at the caller, and also noted that although he wore sailor's garb, the material was very good. He peered through the latch hole and looked down to see well-polished boots, of very good quality.

"Please, would Captain give name? I will inform master."

This time he spoke in Chinese, but Jinsuke answered him in English.

"Tell him that Jim Sky—got it? Jim Sky—came to call. This is a present."

This time the Chinese servant took the bundle over the top of the gate and the dog jumped up to sniff at it. Thinking that nobody was at home, and much disappointed, Jinsuke turned and started to walk back down the road he had come. At least, he thought, it's downhill.

He passed a couple of foreign ladies in bustled dresses and bonnets, accompanied by a tall, thin young man in a suit. They smiled at him as he doffed his cap and stepped aside to let them go by. The younger of the two women turned to watch him, and noted his rolling, deep-sea sailing man's swagger.

"Oh, Aunt Belle, did you see him? What an exotic, romantic-looking man! Did you see that thick black beard, and the scar? And he has only one arm . . . Do you think he lost it in a sea battle? His eyes were strange too, very black and slanted, like almonds. Do you think he's a buccaneer from Siam? Oh, Aunt Belle, I do so like Yokohama, it is full of such fascinating people!"

"Cynthia, don't prattle on, dear, and pray desist from making a fuss over strange gentlemen, what will Mr. Olderby think of us?"

Her scolding was interrupted by a shout from up the road. A figure in pin-striped trousers, white shirt and waistcoat, but no tie, had dashed out into the road and was running toward them.

"Jim! Wait! Hey, Jim Sky, wait!"

The two ladies and the gentleman stared with scandalized fascination to see this gentleman, who looked as if he had been interrupted while dressing for dinner, run down the road, waving his arms and shouting. Jinsuke turned around. Lyall Fogerty reached him and squeezed him in a bear hug.

"Jim! Where do you think you're going? Damn it, I'd have Wo Ping's head on a pole if I'd missed you. Come on back, right now. Damn it, man, it's been eight years!"

They came back up the road, the younger man talking excitedly, and Jinsuke feeling slightly embarrassed but mostly delighted at the exuberance of his welcome. As he passed the two ladies and the gentleman, he gave them a shy grin, and Lyall called out to them.

"Ah, but do excuse us, ladies, sir. Hadn't meant to alarm

you, I almost missed capturing the biggest pirate on the Yangtse."

The shocked look of the older woman and the amusement of the gentleman, who had now recognized Lyall as a business acquaintance, were nothing compared to the enraptured delight of their young visitor.

"Oh Aunt Belle," she exclaimed after they had passed, "I knew it! A real pirate!"

Charles Olderby frowned and racked his brain, but he couldn't remember where he had seen the one-armed man before.

In through the gate they went, with the big fat fellow now holding the dog at bay and bowing respectfully, and four more servants, also Chinese, out in the garden to greet them. On the porch, standing with arms outstretched, was the most beautiful woman Jinsuke had ever seen. She was slim and almost as tall as he was, dressed in a gown of watered silk, with a tiny waist and a voluptuous bosom unshaped by the corsets that were so much in vogue. Down her back and shoulders cascaded lustrous black hair, curling at the ends. Her skin was like ivory, touched with rose. Her eyes were large, but Oriental, pale brown in color, filled with life and excitement. To Jinsuke's astonishment she ran down the steps, put her arms around him, and kissed him on both cheeks.

"Oh Jim, you've grown a beard! It tickles, but I think I like it."

"Susan," said her brother, "let's get him in the house before you start flirting with him, otherwise he'll run off down the street again."

Jinsuke's memory raced. Susan? The pretty but skinny fourteen-year-old?

"You are Susan? So beautiful!"

When she laughed it sounded like water trilling in a mountain stream.

"Pray what did you expect, sir? Pigtails? I'm nearly twenty-two."

She led them into the house and ushered Jinsuke into a large, airy sitting room that looked out through drawn-back shoji screens upon a rock garden. Underfoot was tatami, over which thick carpeting had been laid. He stopped, looked down at his boots, and felt acute shame.

"Ah Jim, we're barbarians still, we wear shoes in the

house, don't fret," said Lyall, taking a seat opposite him. "I like tatami mats underneath because it's warmer in winter. Now just take a seat and tell us where you've been, and what you've been doing."

Jinsuke sat down in a thickly upholstered English armchair, and looked about the room, which was about twenty mats in size. Such a mixture! European furniture, Chinese screens, hangings and ceramics, Japanese charcoal pots, sliding doors and shoji screens, Indian tables, then a wide veranda of polished wood and deep eaves of Japanese build, and of course, those rich, colorful Persian carpets. Lyall grinned.

"This room must seem a hodgepodge to you, Jim. We like it, though."

Jinsuke wasn't sure. Although he was now used to Western rooms, with all their knickknacks, this was like being in the innermost sanctum of a temple, and it kept his eyes too busy. But the chair was comfortable enough, and the room was light and bright.

"Wait just a little while," said Susan. "It's been a hot walk for Jim. Let me fetch something cool."

While she was out of the room Jinsuke thought of where he should start. So much had happened.

"I came with a ship. I am first mate of the *Perseus,* out of Seattle."

"A whaler?"

Jinsuke grinned. "Yes, a whaler."

Susan came back with a silver tray, on which were two glasses of imported beer and a glass of lemonade for herself.

"Oh, not fair! You mustn't let him talk without me here!"

The two men laughed, and Jinsuke took the beer, a drink he'd grown to like. He drank gratefully, his face showing surprise and delight, for the beer was ice-cold.

"Like it? We have an icehouse. We bring down blocks of winter-cut ice, stored in sawdust, from Hakodate."

"In the old days, only the emperor or the shogun had ice in summer. Many men died to bring it for them." He smiled. "Now you are like a king, Lyall."

The laughter and the feel of the glass in his hand, the sights of the room, the garden, the sun playing on motes under the eaves, the sounds of cicadas and servants in the kitchen, the look on his friend's face and that of his beautiful sister—they suddenly released him from the mood of cramped ship's quarters, and from the nagging fear he had experi-

302

enced ever since setting foot on shore. He gazed for a long time at both of them. Susan settled herself on a red leather cushion, tucking her feet under her skirts.

"So very good to see you," said Jinsuke.

Lyall raised his glass. "Well, Jim, tell us about it."

Jinsuke raised his own glass, felt the chilled beer go down his throat, and sighed. It was hard to keep his eyes off Susan, who looked at him so steadily and frankly that he felt shy. He looked again toward her brother, grown much bigger now, broader in the shoulders and thicker in the neck, with a large, bushy, blackish-brown moustache, curled at the end. His chestnut-raven hair was also thick, just touching the collar of his shirt.

"Captain Tovey has been to the house a couple of times," said Lyall, "and he told us of how you worked for his friends, supervising coolies. He told us some of your adventures in California around the gold fields and in San Francisco. I hear you studied every spare minute, and I believe it—your English is excellent now."

Jinsuke shook his head. "No, I've still got an accent. I still can't say 'rice' and 'lice' properly—though I sure as hell know the difference."

Susan trilled with laughter again and he apologized for swearing. Living with men made it easy, even important, to swear, but for him the swearing was just words, like any other words, and he often used those words at the wrong time.

"Oh, don't mention it, I'm used to him." She gestured with one slim hand toward her brother.

"Well," he began, "with the Civil War and all the troubles, I guess the whalers were having trouble getting men, and Tovey, I mean, Cap'n Jacks, persuaded one skipper to take me on for really low shares. He didn't really want me, but Cap'n Jacks talked him into it. I sailed on that ship for two years, and we came off the coast of Japan, then on up to the Sea of Okhotsk. We didn't do too badly."

Jinsuke did not tell them that the captain had been delighted with the prowess of his Japanese harpooner, who though he had only one arm, compensated for it with a "lucky" boat. His new man seemed to have an uncanny knowledge about the habits and movements of the whales they hunted, and soon the captain began to start casually asking the new man's advice. He could not take advice from a nobody, so he gave Jinsuke an unofficial promotion. The captain felt guilty about the low pay, so he began to give the eager young man lessons in navigation, and his wife, who like many whaling wives sailed with the ship, also took a liking to Jinsuke. She in turn began to give him reading lessons from the Bible, which did nothing to alter his own pantheistic and vague Shinto Buddhist notions of religion, but which improved his English and his accent enormously.

Later in the voyage the bosun, the first mate and a few other men became very ill from eating tainted salt beef. From the beginning Jinsuke had persisted in eating cuts off the whales they killed, and had even converted some of the other men to the custom. With two officers incapacitated and the captain feeling ill himself, Jinsuke had kept a rough, tough and unruly crew in line with the speed and power of his single fist.

By the end of the two-year voyage the crewmen were in awe of him, and even though his was not the senior boat, they all wanted to be in his crew.

Rivalry between boats might have created hard feelings. The mate looked on Jinsuke as an Oriental upstart. But Jinsuke's natural and unassuming politeness and modesty, and his ingrained deference to a senior man, had completely won the dour New Englander over. The mate was then not to be outdone by the captain, and he took Jinsuke under his wing, teaching him all he knew—and learning quite a lot himself, though he would never have admitted it.

"Are you still with the same ship?" asked Susan.

"No, now I'm with a bigger ship, the *Perseus*. She's just five years old, a barque, with six whale boats. We sailed from Seattle up the west coast, taking gray whales and sperm whales, sometimes humpback. Then we went to the Bering Strait and hunted walrus. When the ice cleared we went into the Beaufort Sea for bowhead. In the fall, walrus again. We wintered once, but the captain said he don't like the feel of it, and we got out, came down this side, past Kamchatka and those places. We got a few right whales, a few gray whales, sperm whales, humpback. We take what we can get."

He shrugged. He couldn't boast to them that in fact their cruise, taking a different pattern from most other ships, had been much influenced by his advice. They had filled the last of their barrels in the Japan Sea, and apart from the baleen, the walrus ivory and the oil they carried, they also had a sizable harvest of fur seal and sea otter pelts, and had traded well for silver fox and polar bear skins.

"We take all kinds," he said.

"Jim, I always knew you'd do it!" Lyall exclaimed. "Dad said so too. Ah, if there were more Japanese of your kind, dedicated to a job, instead of being dedicated to killing and hating people because they're different."

Susan didn't want Lyall to get into that subject, so she clapped her hands together.

"Oh Lyall, we're being rude. We haven't opened Jim's present!"

She picked up a small brass handbell from a nearby table and rang it, bringing the big servant into the room. She spoke to him in rapid Chinese and Jinsuke saw the man's eyes widen and look at him with new interest.

"How is your Mandarin now?" asked Lyall.

"Not good," said Jinsuke in Engiish, "it's become moldy."

Susan and Lyall both laughed. He had meant to say "rusty."

"Well, Susan told him that you were the man who saved my father's life, and as they've all heard about that, I don't think you'll be treated like a sailor coming up to cadge a loan. There's some rough types, foreigners and Japanese, around Yokohama," said Lyall. "I only wish there was a way to keep them out, especially the foreigners, they make it bad for everybody, and the Japanese, if you'll forgive me saying so, Jim, are touchy and difficult at the best of times."

Jinsuke nodded grimly, then, to change the subject, said, "How is your family, are they well?"

"Mother's fine. Marlyn and Emily are both married, to good Chinese families. Father is not as strong as he used to be, and he has to take it easy. He's not drinking as much rum as he used to, which makes Mother happy, and he's still sailing on the *Irene* and boasting to anybody who'll listen about how you and he took on those pirates."

The servant entered the room, bringing Jinsuke's bundle.

Susan was looking around for something to open the stitches with when Jinsuke put his hand up behind his neck and produced a double-edged knife with a five-inch blade and a flat hilt, faced with sperm whale ivory. He flipped the knife in his hand, catching it by the blade and handing it to Lyall.

"Be careful," he said, "very sharp."

"I'm sure it is, you bloody old pirate," said Lyall, taking it and kneeling on the carpet to slit the bundle open. He handed the knife back and Jinsuke slipped it out of sight in his collar sheath.

Susan pulled out a large, lustrous sea otter pelt and held it

305

over one arm, stroking it. It was lovely. Beneath the pelt was a pair of huge walrus tusks. Lyail picked them up, looking at them with appreciation.

"Thank you, Jim," he said.

"Sorry, I didn't get it tanned completely."

"No trouble. We can get good tanning done right close by Yokohama. You know, Jim, a pelt like that is worth a fortune in China."

The servant came into the room again, asking about the meal being prepared in the kitchen. Susan stood to go and supervise, smiling at Jinsuke.

"You will stay for dinner, won't you, Jim? We've invited a few guests already, they're nice people . . ." She glanced at her brother.

"No, thank you," said Jinsuke, "I must go back to the ship, I have duties."

"Oh Jim, I'll be offended if you don't stay, and we're concerned about your status here. There has been terrible killing in Edo. They've murdered the *tairo* and every stray samurai wants to cut our heads off. Things are tense, Jim. Can we tell our guests you're American?"

Jim laughed. "With my accent, who would believe? Tell them I'm Eskimo."

Lyall spoke up. "Jim, it's serious, and you know that you've broken the law by going abroad, and you're breaking it now by wearing Western clothes. There was a man like you, a Japanese who went abroad, then came back. He got himself British citizenship, and was serving as interpreter at the British legation. He was playing with some children, helping fly kites, when a samurai came up and stabbed him in the back. He died in minutes. You've got to be careful, and you've got to think of what to tell people."

Susan paused at the door. "Perhaps the wisest thing to do, with foreigners anyway, is to tell them the truth. They know that if Jim is betrayed the samurai will come for him. Jim can pass for an American with the Japanese, but not with Americans or British. Martin is a good sort, and Natalie will keep quiet once she knows it's serious. I'll tell the servants, they know how it is too." She went out of the room.

"Stay, please, Jim. We really would be hurt if you didn't, and Susan won't forgive me if I let you run off again. We'll explain to our friends."

Jinsuke stood up. "Sitting with you and Susan I forgot how it is in Japan. I've been away a long time, and being

306

here is so different." He smiled. "I told the captain that I might be late. He'll detail somebody else. I'll stay."

"Good . . ." Lyall paused. "You're wearing a gun, Jim, not just a throwing knife. It's a hot day but you don't unbutton your coat, and although the coat is nicely cut, it doesn't hide the bulge."

The pistol was in a shoulder holster under his left armpit, beneath the empty sleeve. Of course he never wore the gun aboard ship, except when they were hunting walrus, fur seal or sea otter, but there had been times in San Francisco and out in the gold fields or with the railroad gangs when he was better off with a gun.

When the *Perseus* docked in Yokohama Jinsuke had looked through a telescope at the jumble of new buildings. Docks, factories, warehouses, with the flags of many nations flying, and ships from all over the world tied up or lying offshore awaiting their turn. It was all exciting to him, until his focus had rested on an official, a customs man, with his shaven head and topknot, his *haori* and *hakama;* the sheath of his long sword jutted out behind him, and his retainers stood all around him with swords and poles. At that moment a spasm of fear had gripped Jinsuke. He would have liked his ship to turn about and head for the open sea. It enraged him at the same time, this need for fear. This was his country, so why should he have to tremble at the sight of a man with two swords?

Grimly he went below to his cabin and checked the loading of the engraved pistol Lyall's father had given him. He determined that if they tried to arrest him, there would be five bullets for them, and one for himself.

He looked hard at Lyall and pointed to the gun in its holster. "Your father gave this to me, Lyall, and your father made sure I was taught to use it. I can use it very well now, Lyall, but I've never killed a man with it. 'Carry it with honor,' that's what I was told, and that's what I've tried to do." Jinsuke felt a touch of resentment that he had to answer, that he was in danger for returning to his own land, while this foreigner was so rich, secure, comfortable.

"We are not allowed to carry weapons in Japan, you know that. Do you know that a samurai has a legal right to cut one of us down if he thinks we've insulted him? If they catch me, dressed like this, coming off a foreign ship, they will put me in prison. A long time ago, before I go to China, those samurai take me. It was bad. Your father, and America, and the ships taught me to respect other men, but not to be afraid of them; they taught me that I am as good as the next man. I tell you, Lyall, that is the truest thing there is, more true than all the religions in the world—one man is as good as the next, if he wants to be, if he's got the guts. Well, here in this country, the samurai don't think it is true. If they try to take me, I will fight them."

Lyall nodded slowly. As a child, he had often returned home tearful, taunted because of his mixed blood. His father would take him by the shoulders and shake him.

"Boy," the red-haired giant would say, "you're no half-caste, you're half Chinese, half Irish, and with American citizenship. You're more than twice any of them. Just go out and prove it, boy. Don't come sniveling!"

Lyall put his hand out and took Jim's, shaking it.

"You've got it, Jim, you've got it! You know, one day, after we practiced, you were washing yourself off and I saw the marks on your back. I told my fither, and you know what he said? He said it would take one man to put scars on a man's face, but to scar a man's back it took many men, and in most cases the men who scar a man's back have less guts and less honor than the man who has to bear them. It distressed me then, Jim. You were a special big brother to me. It distresses me more now, Jim, that your country can't welcome you home, that your family and friends can't be at the dock in Yokohama with a big band and flags waving, 'Welcome home, Jinsuke.' "

It was only rarely that Lyall used his real name, and he hadn't heard it in years. The sound of it almost made him cry and he turned his face away.

"If they come for me, I fight." Jinsuke paused. "I hate them." He jabbed at his own chest with his forefinger. "Now I got two names. Jim"—he paused for emphasis— "Sky. Like I said, a samurai can kill Jinsuke for nothing, just for bumping him accidentally, for not kowtowing, for saying the wrong word. Well, Jim Sky kowtows just when he feels like it. If a man is a good man, I respect him and show him. Some samurai are good men, but mostly they're just two swords and a big, big pride." He patted the bulge in his coat. "Jim Sky is not afraid of swords."

"You hate the samurai perhaps, Jim, but not Japan . . ."

Jinsuke shook his head angrily. "No. Japan is the best damn place in the world!" In a rare show of emotion, he covered his face with his hand. Lyall went over to him in two strides and put his hands on Jinsuke's shoulders.

"Oh God, Jim, Jim, big brother Jim Sky, this land needs men like you, men who can make them understand. But Jim, don't hate, it just twists you. I'm like you too, Jim—half in one world, half in the other—and I started to hate too, but I had Mother and Father, and they helped, and I saw the love between them and I swore that I'd become a bridge between East and West. Jim, we're your friends, we'll do what we can. The time will come for people like us." A cloud of sadness came and went in his almond-shaped eyes. "But don't hate, Jim, they didn't teach you that in America, did they?"

Jinsuke shook his head, blinked hard and grinned. "There were a few phony bastards, but I either ignored them or taught them." He raised a big, callused fist which Lyall grabbed in both hands.

"I'll take the gun out, Lyall," he said, "and you hide it for me."

"No, Jim, wear it. I wear one myself when I go out at night. Remember? I've got one just like it. They've been killing a lot of people, cutting them down in the street, bursting into homes and murdering people who have done them no harm. The government can do nothing. We must protect ourselves. Carry the gun, Jim. There are men who would kill you for dressing like a foreigner, not to mention for being brave enough to ignore their outmoded laws. Take care, though. Anyway, I noticed the gun, and if Susan did, she won't say anything. Come on, let's go into the drawing room. Our guests should be arriving soon. I'll get you a drink. You like whiskey?"

Jinsuke laughed. "I like whiskey very much, but I might drink a lot and start singing dirty sailors' songs."

Laughing with him, Lyall took his arm. "I bet I know as many as you do . . . learned them from my father."

Lyall's concern was well-founded. Fanatical *ronin* had increased their acts of terrorism, especially since the opening of Yokohama in 1859. Russian sailors, merchants, diplomats, the amiable Henry Heuskin, interpreter to the American consul, and any Japanese who didn't agree with them—they were falling to the sword, and the killers were getting away with it.

With the *tairo,* Ii Naosuke, gone, and his successor, Ando Nobumasa, wounded, *bakufu* seniors were fearful now for the very survival of the shogunate, and to strengthen their position and mollify some of the *tozama* daimyos who had opposed the signing of treaties, they sought first a line of cooperation between the shogunate and the imperial court. Emperor Komei had been persuaded to cooperate in this, perhaps believing that by doing so he would be able to force the shogun to heed his own wishes for the barbarians to be driven out and treaties renounced. The emperor therefore agreed to give his younger sister, Kazunomiya, in marriage to young Shogun Iemochi. *Ronin* fanatics, however, were opposed to linking the court and the imperial house to a government that had, as they saw it, betrayed trust already. The fanatics wanted not only the expulsion of foreigners and renouncing of treaties, but the destruction of the *bakufu* as well. They killed to express themselves.

On the other hand, the lords of Aizu, Echizen and Satsuma supported the alliance. Itoh, Sadayori's friend and mentor, was spending much time in both Kyoto and Edo, expanding and improving the Satsuma intelligence network. His concerns were many, but one of the main ones was to safeguard the senior Satsuma officials in Edo from attack by *ronin*, many of whom he had known in earlier years.

Sadayori, after much soul-searching, had become a part of the Satsuma intelligence net, and he too was back in Edo. The fact that he had once been on the wanted list was forgotten by harried officials.

Despite all the troubles, Lyall Fogerty was prospering. Unlike most other foreigners, he did not have to use a comprador, for he could read and write Chinese characters and he was also taking daily lessons in spoken Japanese. Since his first contact with Jinsuke he had conceived an admiration for and interest in Japan and its culture, and indeed, it had taken all of his father's authority and Mr. Rose's good advice to stop him from trying to set up shop in Japan before the commercial treaty had been ratified.

Now he was importing hardware, cotton goods and Chinese medicines; he purchased raw silk, teas and handicrafts. Like many merchants, early on he had made a killing on the difference between the exchange rate for gold and silver. In Japan it had been set at a rate of one of gold to five or six of silver. Abroad it was something like one to sixteen. Both his father and Mr. Rose had long been experts in exchange, and Lyall made more profit than most.

His dealing in medicines had at first caused him nuisance, for it brought him under close scrutiny. The Japanese greatly feared an influx of opium, which had caused so much grief to China. They were determined not to let opium addiction become common in Japan. For his own part Lyall, like his parents, had a loathing for the opium trade. The more the Japanese authorities insisted on inspecting his goods, the more he cooperated with them, the more he talked about his wares, most of which they were familiar with; he would compare Chinese medicines with modern medicines and voice his opinion that the Chinese were better. Older officials were very much pleased to hear this, for Japan had been using Chinese medicines, and local versions of them, for centuries. Some of the officials began to consult with Lyall, and to get potions directly from him at a far cheaper price than could be obtained in Edo.

Being partly Chinese, Lyall instinctively knew the subtle difference between giving a gracious and thoughtful gift at the right time, and handing over an obsequious or begrudged bribe. Most other merchants never really got the hang of it. Lyall's gifts were usually small items from the Orient and the West—a music box, a set of prints, a beautifully illustrated book of anatomy, mechanical toys or dolls for children, a case of sweet sherry or port, a bottle of good brandy, some Chinese silk and, of course, any medicines the officials needed. He understood the custom of giving—and receiving—gifts at New Year's and at Midsummer.

Lyall was as Oriental in his sensitivity as he was European in stature, dress and manners. The officials, although they were Japanese and *bushi,* and he was merchant and barbarian, grew to like and confide in him, and more business moved his way. Moreover, none of Lyall's profits was lost to a middleman.

That first night of Jinsuke's arrival was enjoyable. To the Fogertys' guests, the exciting presence of the renegade Japanese was spice itself. Foreigners living in Japan had little personal contact with Japanese, and many, like the Fogertys' friends, deplored this. Not only was it dangerous, because of the fanatics, but there were severe restrictions on travel and movement.

Well warmed with wine and whiskey, Jinsuke was able to lapse into the sailor's art of yarning. He told them of his escape from Okinawa to China, he told them of San Francisco and California, of life aboard a whaling ship, of the Arctic and the coasts of Russia, but more than anything he told them of his hometown of Taiji and of his life and the whaling there.

It was ironic that those things most commonplace to Jinsuke were the most exciting and interesting to the foreigners. They had a genuine interest in Japan and asked many questions. The questions he had the most trouble answering were political ones. Jinsuke knew more about the laying of the first Atlantic cable and the beginning of the Civil War in the United States. Hearing from foreigners of the death of Ii Naosuke, whom Jinsuke had once seen briefly, and of the fanatical *ronin* who called themselves *shishi* made Jinsuke think of Sadayori, and of the letters he had sent from America, describing what he had seen there. With all this turmoil, those letters probably never reached him, he thought. Jinsuke retreated to safer ground, telling more about Taiji whaling. He barely noticed how intently Lyall listened to his descriptions.

"One whale in Taiji is worth far more than it is to Americans," said Jinsuke. "We have a saying—'A whale on the beach is wealth for seven villages.' It's true, Americans waste the best part, the meat." That led into a conversation of various viands, comparisons of Chinese and European cooking, and talk of the excellence of the wild ducks they had eaten for dinner.

"I suppose what Jinsuke says is true," said Lyall. "We would be pretty silly to shoot ducks just to make skins for greasing boots, and feathers for pillows or hats. Yes, my word," he said, spearing the last morsel on his plate, "there's more to a duck than a feather and a quack."

When time came to go, and they stepped out in the hallway, Lyall stopped Jinsuke. Their guests had departed, by carriage, accompanied by an armed guard of four men who had come to collect them.

"Jim, stay the night. It's dangerous out there after dark. We've a room for you."

Jinsuke smiled, and patted the gun beneath his coat. "Lyall, I must get back to my ship."

"Very well, then, but take care, and come tomorrow, Sunday. It'll be a day off."

"Sorry, the skipper goes ashore tomorrow and he wants me to stay aboard."

"All right, I'll come to see you, in the morning. Show me this fine ship of yours."

"She's a whaler," said Jinsuke with a shrug, "and a bit smelly . . ." He paused and grinned. "But I've got my own cabin, and she's the best whale ship in the Pacific."

Susan grabbed his arm. "Please, Jim, may I come too? I'd love to see your ship."

He looked into her eyes, and couldn't refuse.

Wo Ping, accompanied by the dog, saw him to the gate and waved him good-bye, a hundred times friendlier than before.

Jinsuke was feeling so good, so euphoric, that he did not see the figures lurking in the pine grove.

With the ship's barrels all filled with whale and walrus oil, there was no need to carry home greasy, soot-blackened try-works bricks, so the great iron pots had been scoured and stowed, and the bricks thrown overboard. Decks had been holystoned, cabins scrubbed and aired, crew's quarters and kitchens thoroughly cleaned, though of course the scent of whale, plus a certain faint stickiness, still clung everywhere.

Jinsuke had new matting brought over to put down in the captain's cabin, as well as those of the surgeon and second mate, and his own. He had also acquired some clean cotton material to cover the seats in his cabin, and although it was much better than before, and certainly superior to conditions in the foc's'le, he still felt unsure about having Susan aboard. Lyall was a man, and liked ships, but she was a woman, and might not understand that this was not so much a home to him, but more like a badger's den, a place to crawl into and hibernate until the next watch.

Jinsuke was on the dock at ten-thirty that morning, waiting with a boat and crew. As Susan stepped into the boat, briefly exposing her ankles, the men ogled her, and Jinsuke couldn't blame them, although it irritated him. She was dressed simply, with a jacket, a broad-brimmed hat with a ribbon to tie under her chin, and a riding skirt that made movement easy.

"Which one is the *Perseus*?" she asked, seating herself beside her brother, turning her face to the breeze and the sparkling off the water that lit her face under the shadows of the hat. Jinsuke pointed.

"See there? A barque, with boats hanging from the davits, dark blue and gray."

Her captain, Edward MacNeil, was the full owner of the ship, which was not so common among whalers, and as he himself went to sea in her, and made her his home and castle, he did everything he could to make her not only safe and efficient, but comfortable too. MacNeil had spent many years with the British fleet, hunting bowhead whales in the eastern Arctic. He was a Scotsman himself, but seeing the great wildernesses, even the frozen ones of the far north, gave him the urge to see more of it. After a year in Newfoundland, and another in Nova Scotia, he settled in New England and signed on with the sperm whalers. He found the American ships generally less rugged, but faster than the British ships. He also thought that having try works aboard was a far better system than the British way of cutting the blubber into small pieces and stuffing them in barrels for rendering onshore. Finally he moved to San Francisco, then up the coast to Seattle, whose climate and politics suited him better. There he had a ship built to his own specifications. This was her second cruise.

Because he used try works, unlike most Arctic whalers and the British, he had fire drills and safety precautions, which the crew objected to at first. His first mate, by now well used to discipline, taking and enforcing it, whipped the crew into shape. Fire aboard a ship in the Arctic, especially in cold weather, was a deadly danger. His first mate also introduced an innovation, a deep barrel with a copper bottom and a chimney, under which a fire of blubber "biscuits" could be lit and a hot bath provided. He taught them to soak in hot seawater, and rinse off briefly with fresh water when it was available.

Unlike the sperm whalers, the lookout did his spotting from a snug barrel built of lathes over wooden hoops, covered with canvas. This barrel had a hatch in the bottom, and a little seat for the lookout. A telescope and a speaking trumpet were kept up there, as well as a rifle, for seals.

The captain insisted that a good supply of limes or lemons be carried aboard, a British navy custom that had earned the British their famous nickname, but which by now was known by sailors to prevent scurvy.

The cook aboard the *Perseus* had let Jinsuke teach him how to prepare certain cuts of whale meat, with a marinade of limes, garlic, onions if they had them, salt and pepper. It was almost as good as steak, and it won over all but the most conservative and delighted the captain, who had long suffered from too much salt beef and pork.

She was a good ship, and Jinsuke was proud of her. As they went out across the bay, he did his best to describe the innovations and the gear they used. His captain preferred British boat equipment, such as the tail knife and the little double-handled winch for heaving lines, but the lines of the ship herself belied her extra sturdiness, and were very American. Despite the long journey, she looked new and swift.

It was aboard this ship that Jinsuke first learned to use the modern darting gun, an awkward-looking harpoon whose stock was fitted with a short brass gun that fired a pointed bomb into the whale when the harpoon struck and penetrated. Jinsuke found the darting guns end-heavy and awkward to use, and even with practice he could hurl it only half of his normal range. However, the very first time he used the thing in earnest he struck a young male humpback basking in a moderate sea in Stephens Passage, off Alaska. It was such a good strike that the bomb went between the ribs and exploded in the whale's heart, killing it instantly. They all heard the muffled "whump" of the bomb, seconds after the darting gun had been thrown, the swivel-head harpoon biting deep, the gun sounding as the trigger bar touched blubber.

That night, after the flensing, the sun still on the horizon and eiders cooing in the water, Jinsuke kept the captain talking until way past midnight, for he was excited. He dreamed of introducing these modern American methods to Taiji, to replace the need for at times fifty or more harpoons, to finish with the cumbersome nets and the long, bloody business of death-lancing. Could he dream of being a Taiji harpooner again? Using a darting gun with such deadly effect? Killing whales for his home village with his single, powerful right arm?

The next day the captain brought out a new weapon, a shoulder-fired gun that shot the same kind of bomb dart, enabling a man to finish off a whale at a range of up to twenty-five yards. Firing the gun with one hand was not that hard for Jinsuke, who had practiced in California with both a Winchester rifle and a shotgun. Perhaps because he tried harder, Jinsuke wasted fewer of the expensive bombs than any of the other mates, so the captain let him keep the expensive gun, ignoring the pleas of the others.

He was explaining this to Lyall on the way to the ship.

"In port, we lock up weapons," he said to Lyall, "but I've got the key, and I will show you. On the next trip, the skipper says, all boats get a bomb lance."

One of the oarsmen grinned a toothy smile at the passengers. "First mate here, he can shoot the pimple on a seagull's bum . . . beg pardon, miss . . . I mean, beak, at thirty yards."

Another man spoke up. "We did a lot of seal shooting, and our Jim Sky is better with that pistol of his than a lot of men are with a rifle, and he's damn good with a rifle too."

Jinsuke blushed. "Oh, can the gab, Ned."

"It's true!"

"No guff," added the first oarsman, "best shot, best mate, best whaling man I ever sailed with, and I been whaling for over twenty years."

Susan looked at Jinsuke with such obvious pride in her glance that the boat crew all exchanged envious looks.

They came alongside the ship, and eager, perhaps over-eager, hands assisted Susan up onto the deck. Jinsuke took them on a tour, leaving out only the captain's cabin and the foc's'le, where a few men were having a noisy game of cards. Then he took them to his tiny cabin, and the cook brought fresh hot coffee and newly baked biscuits with cranberry jam.

"You eat well on this ship, Jim," said Lyall, who knew what normal fare was on sailing ships.

"Best ship for everything," Jinsuke answered with pride. "The first ship I sailed on had horrible food. Rotten meat, all salt and fat, and a bad, bad smell. We get hardtack with little worms in it. But our Captain MacNeil says that good food and a safe clean ship, and clean men, make for good work and no trouble. We eat whale meat aboard, you know, not like many ships, and our cook tries hard. Sundays and Thursdays we get a hot sea pie and maybe some beer too. Once a month we get cheese. Every day we get a drink of lime or lemon juice in water, and on Saturday and bad-weather days, all the men get a tot of rum. When the weather is good, and he's not so busy, the cook makes bread and biscuits, and sometimes there's even raisins in the biscuits. Like I said, a lot of the men, and the captain too, they eat whale meat because I show them how to cut in the best places, how to cook it, how to make it tasty. The captain says it's better than beef. Sometimes we get seal liver and onions. We have no thieves, and only a couple of fights. Captain MacNeil is a damn fine gentleman!"

Lyall looked thoughtfully at his friend, seeing that here was a man who gave his loyalty so enthusiastically and unstintingly that whoever had Jinsuke under him could do nothing but treat him fairly. As Lyall's father had been, Captain MacNeil was a fortunate man indeed.

"Jim, you were talking about seals, do you mean *ottosei*?" He used the Japanese name for the fur seal.

"Oh yes," said Jinsuke delightedly, "*ottosei!* We got more than five hundred good skins, and we got oil from the blubber too! Then we got *rakko,* you know, sea otter, two hundred skins. We got lots of walrus, and eleven white bear that we shot, and we traded for more bear and fox skins with the Eskimo people."

Lyall became visibly excited. "Jim, that was a fine otter skin you gave us. Did you shoot it?"

Jinsuke nodded. "I told the captain we could try to get otter and seal on days when we don't see whales. We got lots, so the captain is happy, and he gave me some good skins for myself."

"What are you going to do next, Jim?"

"I guess we take on water, vegetables, maybe chickens, some dried squid and fish for me, a couple of new spars, and then we head back to Seattle, sell, and fit out."

He could not tell even Lyall what a torment it was for him that home was so close, yet so far, and that he dearly wanted to go and see those people he loved, yet he feared for his life, and theirs, should he try.

"Listen, Jim," said Lyall, leaning across the tiny table, shoving aside the crumb-sprinkled plate and the empty mugs, "you've got sea otter, fur seal and white bear, and I know there is a better market for them either here or in China than in America. I'm also sure I can sell the ivory, they use a lot of it here, and the fox skins. Jim, I've got lots of ideas for business. Have you got a paper and pen?"

From his tiny desk beside the bunk, above which was a shelf of navigation and nautical books, Jinsuke produced them.

"What is it, Lyall?" asked Susan, leaning over his shoulder.

"I want to invite Jinsuke and Captain MacNeil for dinner tomorrow night. I'll send Wo Ping with a carriage for them. Not only would I enjoy their company, but I want to discuss business."

Lyall wrote out the invitation in his careful copperplate style, and then from his breast pocket he brought out his name card, which he had printed in English on one side, and in Chinese characters on the other, an innovation which greatly impressed and pleased the officials he had to deal with. Jim took both, promising to give them to his captain when he returned.

"Well, thank you, Jim, and thank the cook for us. We'd better be going.

Wind was coming in against the outgoing tide, and it was a wet trip back, but Lyall's mind was too busy turning over possibilities to notice anything. Susan reached out and squeezed her brother's hand.

"Wouldn't it be marvelous if Jim could stay in Japan, perhaps work with us again?"

He looked at her and smiled.

"Susan, you read my mind."

"It's written all over your face," she said.

Chapter Twenty-Four

Captain MacNeil was not as tall as his chief mate. He had a seamed, weather-beaten face, adorned with a neatly trimmed black and gray goatee. His body was not flabby in a townsman's way, but he did have the beginnings of a paunch. His roundness, however, did not denote laziness, only a sincere appreciation of good food and wine, and a willingness to try anything.

The activity latent in him was hinted at by quick movements of his eyes and his small, well-manicured hands. His speech also was rapid, but softened by the faintest Scottish burr, giving the language a mood, an elegance, a Celtic depth.

He toyed with a sheet of paper beside his plate. The paper was covered in figures in Lyall Fogerty's precise, bold lettering.

"For your consideration, Captain MacNeil," said Lyall, "I will pay you in gold, at the exchange rate shown, and that alone will give you a fair margin of profit, without loss to me. If you prefer I can pay you also either in Mexican or American dollars, or English pounds. As I say, I would like to take all the skins, furs and ivory. I'd even venture to buy the baleen and whale oil from you, although that would be a far bigger gamble on my part, as I am not familiar with the lines of market for those things. The domestic market here is still a mystery, and almost impossible to research." He turned and smiled at Jinsuke.

"If only we could take the oil and baleen directly by sea to Jim's hometown on the Kii Peninsula, I'm sure we could sell it through the whaling management there, but that sort of thing can't happen for years, I'm afraid. But Captain, if it would be no bother, I'd like to ship a consignment of handicrafts and silk to an agent I know in Seattle."

Captain MacNeil folded the paper with neat, precise creases, lipped it into his inside pocket, and stretched his right hand across the tablecloth.

"A fair offer, Mr. Fogerty, and I'll be happy to ship anything you like, as long as it is not too large and can be well protected against the roughness of an ocean voyage and the dubious perfumes of a whale ship."

They shook hands. Jinsuke was inordinately pleased about it all and bobbed his head at them, grinning with pleasure, looking from the two men's faces to Susan, who was sitting at the head of the table, the candlelight playing tricks with the sheen of her hair.

"Excellent!" said Lyall. "I'll have a lighter ready by ten o'clock and I'll come aboard myself, bringing the gold. I've already had it assessed, at the rate indicated on my sheet, but I'll not be in the least offended if you bring along your own comprador."

The captain waved his hands. "Not necessary between gentlemen, sir." He winked. "And I'd not feel happy at having to pay one of those rogues, either."

"Well," said Lyall, "I think that this calls for a drink. Shall we move to the sitting room? It's a clutter, but more comfortable."

Lyall stood and held his sister's chair for her. Then he led his guests to the room that Jinsuke had been in before, where, on a low carved table from India, stood a tray and three glasses for brandy, and a tiny glass of Cointreau for Susan.

"Please excuse this sister of mine," Lyall said fondly, "she says that the scent of tangerine in the drink reminds her of Christmas, though why one would want to remember Christmas in summer, I cannot fathom. I promise that she won't be permitted to get indecorously drunk." He poured a fine old cognac for the men and raised his glass.

"To free trade and sailors' rights!"

"I'll gladly drink to that one," said the captain, "and to the most charming and beautiful hostess on either side of the Pacific." He clinked his glass with them and took a sip.

"Jim Sky, you've done it again. Had it not been for you, I would never have bothered with all those wee furry beasties. You've made me a fine and unexpected profit on top of what we'll make with the whales, and you've a lot to be thanked for in that too. Jim, you'll not find me unappreciative, wily Scot though I may be. It's been a good trip, Jim." He raised his glass again. "I'm going to offer you five percent of this sale."

"Let's make it seven," said Lyall, wondering if the atmosphere and the wine might not have made the captain give a promise that he might regret in the morning. "I'll give Jim three and a half, and you give him another three and a half, as commission. I'm as delighted as you are, Captain."

"Done!" said the captain with a smile. Jinsuke looked from one man to the other, not really understanding just how much money that was going to mean for him.

"I've one small complaint," said Lyall with a grin.

"Oh, and what is that?" asked the captain.

"Well, you happen to have thrown away a very valuable commodity from those fur seals."

"The meat, you mean? Even Jim doesn't take much to fur seal meat, although he's always on about whale meat; he'd have me fill my whole ship with salted whale meat in a couple of hunts, with nowhere to sell the stuff."

"I wasn't thinking exactly of meat," said Lyall, with a sideways glance at his sister. "You see, I have a very profitable little business here in Oriental medicines, and there happens to be a very valued one made from certain organs of the bull fur seal. In Japan it's known as *takeri*, and it's very expensive. Know it, Jim?"

He cocked his head, he wasn't sure, they had no seals near Taiji, only whales and dolphins.

"Well, I don't suppose you'd ever need it. They say it is most effective for chronic carbuncles, cricks, bad colds, weak kidneys, low spirits and er . . . " He cleared his throat with mock gravity. "Exhaustion after lustful behavior." Susan blushed, vividly and genuinely.

"Lyall! Please, no vulgar talk!"

"Not vulgar, dear sister, business, and very serious."

"Excuse me," she said. "I think I'd better see to things in the kitchen."

Jinsuke and the captain watched her leave with regret.

"Seriously, I'd dearly love to get my hands on a barrel of *takeri*. It's also called *kaikujin* in the ancient scripts. It is dried and salted, although if it were brought to me just salted that would be fine. Then it is roasted at high heat, but not charred. Before serving it one must seep it for a day in Chinese or Japanese wine, then bake it in a paper bag. It then has quite a pleasant smell. The final preparation is made by breaking the stuff up into pieces and infusing it with hot wine, mixed in a silver pot. If you would care to make an extra profit on the fur seals you take, and I assure you I'm very serious, then bring me back a barrel of salted genitals."

The captain guffawed. "Jim, you hear? Mr. Fogerty wants a barrel of salted seals' balls!"

"Not just the balls, Captain," said Lyall, "the whole set of three, or one and two, if you like."

Jinsuke's expression was most serious. It sounded like a very good medicine.

"Just salt them? In a barrel?"

"Right," said Lyall, "and please make sure to leave a few hairs at the base of the penis, as that's the way some people think they can tell the real thing."

The captain guffawed again. "To my way of thinking," he chuckled, taking another sip of brandy, "the equipment on a bull walrus would be more impressive to your customers. Why, the animal has a bone a foot and a half long in its penis! Much more impressive than a seal!"

"Oh yes," said Jinsuke enthusiastically, "very big, very strong!"

Lyall stared at them. "Good Lord, you know, I'll bet it would sell! It's just never been tried. A bone, a foot and a half long? That would sell just as a curio, if not for anything else. I don't believe in aphrodisiacs myself, deer horns, rhinoceros horns and the rest, that's a part of Oriental medicine that doesn't impress me. But there are a lot of dirty old men who do believe, or want to believe, and as long as I sell them what they want, I don't see any wrong in it. No, I think walrus equipment would be a big thing."

They all raised glasses to that and the captain turned to Jinsuke.

"Jim, put that on our list for our next Arctic trip . . . two, no, three barrels of walrus thingamabobs." He put one finger to his mouth. "But let's keep this a secret between us, I'd be the laughingstock of Seattle if found out."

"No fear," said Lyall, "and we don't want to flood the market, do we."

"You deal in some strange articles, Mr. Fogerty."

"Ah, but Captain, what can be stranger than valuing a whale for the baleen in its mouth to make corsets?"

"Oh, come now, sir, there's also a matter of the oil too!"

"But it is true, is it not, Captain, that there have been many whales killed just for the baleen, because the ship was already filled with oil, and the season not finished?"

The captain looked very serious. "Yes, it was true, and a disgrace at that, but those fellows did it on new grounds, where the rights and the bowheads were thick. Nowadays I doubt if anybody is filling his oil casks so easily. But anyway,

I'll drink to the whales, to the oil that lights our lamps, to the corsets the baleen makes, and most of all, to the ladies in the corsets."

"In or out of them," said Lyall, and they all raised their glasses again.

"You know, Mr. Fogerty," said the captain, "I've always told Jim here that he should think of going into business. He has the Midas touch, and guts. He looks as sweet as pie half the time, despite the scar under his eye and that black beard, but he's wily as a fox. You'd be amazed at the ways he's made himself money! Old Tovey Jacks told me this one, you know," continued the captain. "It seems that Jim here made himself a pile of dough in California from wrist wrestling the big buckos. He himself never challenged, but his friends made sure the big, tough, thickheaded ones went to challenge him. That way he got everybody on his side from the start. He'd win, every time. Then this one fool got upset, and having some drinks in him, says he'll take Jim outside and teach him a lesson. Jim says no, it's not correct to fight outside a bar, because it would give the place a bad name, which was a laugh, because this saloon had the worst reputation around, but that way he impresses the bar owner. Then Jim says he'll fight the man the following Saturday evening, after work, and bets five hundred dollars—five hundred, mind you—that he'll win. Can you imagine? The whole town went crazy, some saying the other fellow would have to tie his left hand behind his back and so on, but Jim says no, that's all right, both can fight with whatever part of the body they've got. Now I tell you, this big fellow is six-foot-three and two hundred sixty pounds, and our Jim is five-eleven and two hundred pounds. By the next Saturday the bets were flying. Mostly fellows who don't know Jim bet on the other guy. Anybody who knew Jim, well, they knew Jim. The fight didn't last three rounds. Jim broke his jaw, kicked his ribs in, and laid him out for twenty minutes." The captain slapped his knee. "How much did you make on that one, Jim?"

"Twelve hundred dollars," said Jinsuke, "but it is a stupid way to make money, and next they want me to fight all over the West Coast. I had to quit the job and head for San Francisco." Lyall laughed. "Dad would be proud of you. Are you sure you're not half Irish? But let me warn you," he added seriously, "don't let Susan hear about it, she'll rake you over the coals."

"Eh?" He didn't understand.

"Susan," said Lyall, "hates violence."

Jinsuke shrugged. How could he explain what it was like to be Japanese in those places? With the task of riding herd over a lot of Chinese, many of whom hated you more than they hated the white men? In places like that a man had to learn to act a part, to be friendly but stern, to have flair, never to provoke a fight, but never, never to run away from one. It was different from the way he had been brought up, but Jim Sky had taken to it like a seal to water. Neither did he squander his money on booze, for one day he would return to Taiji and . . .

"Jim, when are you going to come back to Japan to live?" Sprung on him while his thoughts were beginning to wander home, the question startled him.

"He can't, can he?" said the captain quietly.

"I've been considering it carefully, and I think he can," said Lyall, "but he'd have to make Yokohama his base for a while, and pretend not to be a native-born Japanese. I know a new fellow with the American consulate, a really nice guy who I think would go out on a limb to help Jim get his United States citizenship. He's very fond of Japan, and keen on doing anything that will eventually cement Japanese—American relations. Came over with Perry, actually."

The captain looked at Jim. "It's worth a thought, Jim." Then he wagged a finger at Lyall. "Sir, I think you're scheming to take my first mate away from me."

Wo Ping came into the room. "Master, there is a carriage here," he said, in Chinese.

Lyall drained his glass. "Captain MacNeil, I took the liberty of getting a carriage." He did not say how difficult that was in Yokohama. "I have no wish to end the evening, it's been such a pleasure, but you did say that you did not want to be late."

Captain MacNeil thanked him, and they went into the hallway, where Susan was waiting for them.

"Captain," said Lyall, "I have a favor to ask."

The captain inclined his head.

"We're most anxious to see more of Jim before you sail. He could help me enormously with information about this country that I can't get elsewhere. I realize it's an imposition, but . . ."

"He can have a twenty-four-hour shore leave before we sail, which will be four days from now, as long as we don't have a typhoon or something. Your office faces the harbor, so if I need him, I'll signal, and if he isn't aboard when I want him to be, I'll send a press gang."

Susan took the captain's arm. "Oh, Captain MacNeil, that is so kind of you," she said, "but what of yourself? Can you not stay here too? We've lots of room, and we'd love to have you."

He made a short bow, his hat held in front of him. "I thank you kindly, ma'am, but a captain's place is with his ship, though she be never as fair as you."

As they sat in the carriage on the way back to the docks, the captain nudged Jinsuke in the ribs.

"That young lady would make you a fine wife, Jim," he said.

It jolted him. Not the nudge, but the words and the articulation of such an idea. That evening again Jinsuke had found it hard to keep his eyes off Susan. She had worn a blue-green gown, modestly cut, but accentuating the curves of her breasts and the delicate hollow and curve of her neck, while her hair was pinned up with an antique emerald-studded comb. Jinsuke recalled her father singing a song about an emerald island, and remembered how the words had touched him, making him wonder if that island was as green as Taiji, and how the people there lived.

He sat in the gently lurching carriage, listening to the clop of horses' hooves, watching the ripple of their silky rumps and the swish of their tails, half hidden by the black serge back of the driver. The paired lanterns made weak yellow splashes of light. He tried to pull his thoughts away from Susan, beautiful, alluring, enthusiastic, exotic, gentle Susan. He had given his love and troth to Oyoshi, and only that was fitting, but Susan . . .

Ah, there had been other women, of course there had, bed companions in America and China. In America it had been white women mostly, dance hall and saloon girls, with coarse voices and manners. He'd gone for big women, with long brown or blond hair and large breasts. Even now, disgusted at himself, he saw his own muscular brown body rutting between their soft white thighs. He remembered gazing sideways in a glass, seeing a large white arse pushing and pushing up against him, and many-ringed fingers clutching at his buttocks, long red nails on smooth, pale brown skin. And breasts, he remembered so many breasts, large ones such as a man would never see in Japan, some quite huge, sagging on either side of surprisingly delicate ribs. Bodies, mostly faceless now, pushing, thrusting, grunting, moaning.

Then one morning he had done it for the fourth time with a young but shopworn whore, and she had become genuinely tender with him, thinking that his physical enthusiasm expressed a genuine liking for her. That was when he realized that all this sad, bought, yet energetic sex was somehow linked to a memory that flashed through his brain, an image that shocked, revolted, and fascinated him—the image of the white missionary's wife, writhing and screaming as the big pirate pushed his thick, wetly glistening penis slowly in and out of her. Jinsuke hated himself for it, and in the morning he paid the whore twice what she asked. He never went with a prostitute again.

He loved Oyoshi still, and felt sure that she was his. She had lain with him, and vowed to wait. And yet, he had been away for years, and she was long past the age of marriage. That thought had always tortured him, at times almost to turning his pistol on himself. He had also wrought fantasies, alone and at sea, of returning to Taiji, killing whoever might have replaced him, killing Oyoshi, killing any child she might have, killing himself. All of that was the frustration of distance. He continued to love her, but had ceased to use her in his fantasies. Now when he had those thoughts, they were mostly of women he had lain with since Oyoshi . . . that giri in Okinawa, then the tiny whore of thirteen in Shanghai, and her sister with her, who had been just a little bigger, with hands and faces like dolls, little budding breasts, bodies so silky smooth and tight and warm inside. And then there had been an incredible experience with the half-Indian wife of a drunken landlord in a small California town . . .

But the captain's words had really jolted him, for in the past day or so, Susan had been standing on the edges of his private erotic dreamworld, and he had felt so craven, wanting her to come in, but denying that wish.

"Och, don't trouble yourself, Jim," said the captain, noting Jinsuke's silence. "You're a fine man, as any man or woman who has spent enough time with you will vouch. Just like those big bull seals, Jim, men like you and I must fight for our place. Look at me, a wee tich of a crofter's son from the isle of Skye, never told you about that, did I, Jim, but I was in a boat, helping my father when I was six . . . but here I am, with my own ship. I know about fighting for place, Jim. You'll win, Jim, be sure of it."

He turned and thumped Jim Sky, first mate, on the shoulder. "Aye, man, it's hard as hell to be an exile, with home so close yet so far away. But you'll see, it'll all turn out right, but whatever you do, pick the right woman."

Jinsuke was glad his captain could not see the tears that suddenly welled in his eyes. It was not what he said, but the kindness in his tone. How was it, he thought, that in the toughest of men there was often a deep pool of understanding? How could it be that these so-called crude barbarians—how often had he heard Sadayori call them that—were so often even more sensitive than Japanese, who were so proud of their sensitivity? Jinsuke felt suddenly grateful that life had given him the chance to play the role of Jim Sky.

They finished transporting the bales of furs and walrus ivory by noon, and in the afternoon Lyall attended to customs clearance and duties, which were slight. He delighted one official with a silver-fox skin, and another with a pair of walrus tusks; the man didn't know the creature, so Lyall inked a sketch for him. Jinsuke had been in charge of bringing the goods from the ship to the warehouse, and as the last load was carried up from the lighter, he stood there, giving orders to his men in English, and gesticulating and affecting a pidgin Japanese to the local workers. He did this for the benefit of one official, who watched the whole procedure with steely, disdainful eyes.

As soon as the boat was emptied, the official beckoned Jinsuke to where he was standing, waving at him with his fan. Jinsuke looked from the official to Lyall, who was out in front of the warehouse, talking with an older and senior official with the aid of a notepad and a piece of artist's charcoal, more convenient out in the open than the inkstones and brushes he used in his office.

"Kimi!" called the samurai, using an informal, diminutive form for you." He obviously considered himself to be speaking to an inferior. With one hand hooked in his wide leather belt, and fighting a brief, panic-filled impulse to bow or to pull his eyes away, Jinsuke sauntered over, walking as casually and as much like an American seaman as possible.

"Yeah?" he said, staring right at, and slightly down at, the official, who looked coldly at Jinsuke's face and eyes, his left hand moving slowly to the sheath of his sword.

"Burei mono!" He growled the words, words that would or should strike terror into the hearts of anyone below the status of *bushi,* words that would send a commoner, a peasant or a merchant to his knees, groveling for forgiveness.

"Damn your eyes, you bald-headed bastard," answered Jinsuke with a smile, stepping back and putting his hand on his hip, not clenched, but in position for a rising punch, over the top of the sword-drawing arm and into the solar plexus. So he had been spotted as a Japanese. He would just have to bluff it out, or fight, or die. He had been accused of insolence. The samurai went on coldly staring at his face. Then he snarled, *"Omae wa Nipponjin darou!"*

Jinsuke's eyes opened wide. "Me? *Nipponjin?* No, sir. American! You know? America."

"Nippon!" shouted the samurai. Jinsuke took a great risk then. He pointed to the two swords, to the samurai's dress, to the shaven pate and topknot, thick, black and doubled back to lie down the center of his bald head.

"O-samurai-san," he said. He took off his sailor's peaked hat and pointed to his own unshaven head. He pointed to his beard, his shirt, trousers and boots, and to the sheath knife looped on his belt. He wished he had brought the gun, but that was back in his cabin, with his jacket. The throwing knife under his shirt collar was always there, and it might come in useful. In the meantime he'd stick to his bluff and, again, bless Kinjo.

"America," he said, then, in a stilted accent: *"Fune no otoko, kujira tori* . . . get it? I'm a sailor, mister, a whaler, and that's my ship." He half turned, pointing out over the water to the *Perseus* lying at anchor.

"Onoda, what is the matter? Is there trouble?"

In response, the samurai turned to bow to an older official who came over with Lyall. They had been talking and laughing as they approached and Jinsuke was astonished to hear his friend actually speaking short sentences in Japanese. So he really had been studying!

"I think this oaf is a renegade Japanese. Would it not be advisable to take him and question him?"

The older man looked at Jinsuke's face, then down to his boots, then slowly up to his face again. Jinsuke gave him a grin.

Lyall, looking from one man to the other, spoke out. "Onoda-san, you have eyes like a hawk."

Onoda transferred his arrogant stare to the foreigner and Lyall spoke in slow, polite, clear sentences.

"This man is famous on American whale ships. He is one of the best harpooners. You are right, but not right. He is American, but his grandfather was Japanese."

"What?" snapped the older man.

Sketching as he spoke, with simple, clear lines Lyall drew Japan, Kamchatka, the Aleutian chain, the western coast of North America. He pointed to British Columbia.

328

"Here," he said, "his grandfather came here." The two officials peered at the map, nodding in comprehension.

"Why?" asked Onoda.

"Kuroshio," said Lyall, writing the characters for the great current, drawing its sweep up past the coast of Japan, across and then down the coast of British Columbia. Then he wrote the characters for *stream* and *boat,* and tried to remember the word for *drifted,* which used the same character, then, giving up, wrote the character for *storm.* He flipped his pad over and wrote the characters for *capture,* then *primitive,* and afterward for *rescue.*

"His grandfather went to America," said Lyall, phrasing his words carefully and pointing at his ideograms, using them as a device to draw attention away from Jinsuke's features for a while, knowing that the Japanese, like the Chinese, are always incredulous when a foreigner can write their characters.

"His grandfather married an Indian," he said, pointing to characters for *primitive person.* "His father half Japanese. Cannot come to Japan. Old laws. Father born here, then go to America, Seattle. This man is born in America, but his father teach little Japanese, just little."

Jinsuke was dumbfounded at the ingenuity of Lyall's story, although in fact it was true that in times past Japanese ships had been blown out to sea and had drifted as far as the west coast of North America, and in British Columbia some Japanese had been enslaved by Indians, and later rescued.

"This man," Lyall pointed to Jinsuke, "can understand just a little Japanese. He can write a few characters, and *hiragana.* His grandfather taught him. He is American, good man, good sailor, good harpooner. He shot fur seals, and some white bear too. He is a good man, but half primitive, and he does not understand Japanese customs."

The older official sucked in his breath. Such an interesting story! He spoke to Onoda.

"It was astute of you to recognize his Japanese blood, despite his barbaric appearance. Very astute, I approve." With a half-hidden, prim little smirk, Onoda bowed. The older man turned to Jinsuke, whose fear had dissolved, leaving him with an urge to laugh out loud.

"Grandfather's name?"

It came to Jinsuke on the spur of the moment. "Mori Taro," he answered. Taro was just about the most common name there was, but the official raised his eyebrows. Two names? Of *bushi* stock? Surely not! He took Lyall's piece of charcoal and formed the three-tree character for *forest,* also pronounced "mori," but Jinsuke shook his head, politely took the pad, and with careful crudeness, as if he had written very little in his life, he drew the combination character with the ideograms for *metal* on the left and *tongue* on the right.

"Mori," he said. He thought it was a good joke, but kept his face straight. Jinsuke had written the character for *harpoon.*

"Indeed, indeed," said the older samurai, his mouth tightening in a smile of understanding and amusement, quite taken in by the clumsy way in which Jinsuke wrote. He turned to Onoda.

"Must have been a fisherman, skilled with a harpoon. Tell me, Fogerty-san, do those Indians over there use harpoons?"

"Oh yes," said Lyall, "they even hunt whales."

"You see, Onoda, that's how he got his nickname! Mori Taro, indeed, indeed, how fascinating it would have been to have talked with this fellow's grandfather."

He nodded at the empty pinned-up shirt sleeve.

"Bang!" said Jinsuke, enjoying the act now. *"Senso,"* war.

"Ah, indeed," said the official. He turned to his junior officer. "A civil war is being fought in America, over slaves or something. Perhaps this is a brave fellow, and anyway, I don't think we would gain anything by taking him in for interrogation. If he and his father were born in America then he would be classed as American. It would cause unnecessary fuss. Would you not agree?"

Onoda bowed again. "Thank you, sir, I have been hasty and bothered you. Please forgive me."

"No, no, not at all." He accepted the clean tissue that Lyall offered him and wiped the charcoal off his fingers. "You were most astute and watchful, and that is what an official must be. You must be recommended for it, and personally, I thank you for drawing our attention to a curious little historical detail. Mori Taro indeed, hmmm. Anyway, I think we need not bother this fellow."

Again Onoda bowed. He turned with a curt nod to Jinsuke, who took off his cap again and made a deep but deliberately awkward bow. As he went to the boat he caught an amused wink from Lyall and grinned back at him.

Later that evening at the Fogerty house, they laughed together.

"I didn't know how good your Japanese was," said Jinsuke.

"You know I've been taking lessons. But it's true, I have

heard and read stories about Japanese being washed ashore after drifting as far as British Columbia, and knowing that little prig Onoda, I figured that if we made him at least a little bit right, he'd go off with his usual smug self-righteousness. Old Miyabe is a sport, but Onoda is a constant pain in the butt. If they bother you again, Jim, stick to your story." His tone changed. "But look, what I really want to talk to you about is this—how would you like to captain your own ship?"

Lyall's plan, as he outlined it, brought Jinsuke to the edge of his chair. A ship was being built in England, a stout wooden steam schooner, similar to the two-masted ships now being built in Kimizawa, in Japan. It would be just under a hundred feet long, more spacious than the Kimizawa ships, and under steam it would be driven by a propeller, not paddles, at a top speed of seven knots.

Lyall intended to use the ship between the Japanese treaty ports—Hakodate, Yokohama, Shimoda, Nagasaki, and eventually Kobe. From time to time, in the right season, it would run to China, Formosa, and other Asian ports. When Japan opened completely, as he felt it inevitably would, the ship could be the flagship for excellent coastal trade.

". . . And it might be a good idea, when trade is slow, to try a few seal-hunting expeditions," said Lyall, "although I don't want her converted for whaling. But think of it, Jim, if we get in now, we can always build a whaling ship later. You know, I reckon that using a steamship to take whaling boats out from a shore base and then bring the boats and the whales back in would be the most efficient way to do it. We might be able to branch into that kind of business later. For the next few years, though, you'll either have to pretend to be American, or become an American citizen, at least as far as the Japanese officials are concerned. Eventually the time will come when you can tell the truth, and they'll welcome you. Then you can be either Jinsuke or Jim Sky, or both. Whatever, you'll be one of the first and best of the Japanese steamer captains. Come in with me, Jim. Think it over. You'll be sailing in a few days, so keep it in mind. But let me show you the drawings."

He went to the bookshelf, where, tucked in back, on top of a row of leather-bound volumes, was a long roll of paper. He brought it to the low table and spread it out, weighting the ends with the walrus tusks that Jinsuke had brought to them. They were schematic drawings, plans for the schooner-steamer, and as Jinsuke eagerly bent over to examine them he saw that a name had been drawn in the bow, in two scripts. One contained the characters for *big* and *sky*, beneath were the English words "Big Sky."

"It's an unusual name, Jim, but she's named for an unusual person, only we can't call a ship *Jim* now, can we?"

The color drained from his cheeks, and this time he could not stop the wetness coming to his eyes. A ship! Named for him!

He sat back on his heels and took a deep breath, making a major decision. With a sleeve of his shirt, he wiped his eyes.

"Lyall, there is a lot you don't know, and now I've got to tell you . . ."

Jinsuke told him how he, a simple harpooner, had been brought to Edo by a great gentleman of the Tokugawa fief of Kii. He told him how this man, a samurai, had given him back a dream of once again becoming a harpooner, even though he had lost his left arm. He told Lyall everything.

When he had finished, Lyall got to his feet and went to fetch a decanter of whiskey and two glasses. He poured.

"It's dangerous to try to get into Edo nowadays, Jim, so don't you try it. If we try to contact Matsudaira-san, we could very well get him into serious trouble."

"But I must tell him."

"Yes," said Lyall. "But I would think that this is what he'd want for you, for Japan, even if he is as conservative as you described. Look, Jim, write a letter to him, and I'll do whatever I can to see it reaches him, discreetly." He put one hand up. "I don't know how long that'll take, but I'll try."

Jinsuke bowed deeply, for the first time ever, to his friend. "Please."

Lyall rolled up the plans for the ship and put them back on the bookshelf.

"You know, if you agreed to become a captain for us, Susan would be pleased."

He said it quietly, but Jinsuke sensed that he was probing. Susan had gone to bed. Pretending not to respond, he just nodded.

Jinsuke could imagine the ship, sleek and new and fast. He could almost see and feel the comfort and seclusion of the fine little captain's cabin. While in Taiji, he knew only the coast from Katsuura to Wakayama, and he'd been up to Wakayama only once. He knew foreign coasts far better, and that seemed wrong to him now. As captain of the *Big Sky* he would learn the coasts and harbors of all of Japan. How marvelous that would be! What friends and discoveries he could make! A deep, aching love of his own country came back, starting in the pit of his stomach and welling up into his chest. For a few minutes he found it hard to breathe. Lyall was handing a glass of amber fluid to him, looking into his face. Tears trickled down Jinsuke's brown, weather-toughened cheeks.

"Jim . . ."

His shoulders wracked with sobs and he gasped out his thanks. *"O-kini, o-kini yo!"*

When he took the glass, drained it, and looked up, he saw tears in Lyall's eyes too.

"I don't understand, Jim, does that mean . . ."

Jinsuke's sobs turned to a laugh, and he held out his glass for another fill.

"One day, I'll sail you to Taiji, best damn whaling place in the world, and when somebody gives you a drink, you say *'o-kini yo.'* That means *arigato,* 'thank you,' in the way Taiji folk speak. Okay?"

Lyall placed his glass on the table, and put his arms around Jinsuke's shoulders and hugged him.

"O-kini yo, o-kini yo," he repeated, then, as if embarrassed at his emotion, Lyall let Jinsuke go and filled both their glasses again.

"I'll write and tell Dad tomorrow!" he said. "He'll dance a jig when he hears. Look, we can send you to England to bring the ship to Japan, or we can charter a temporary skipper if you need to be doing something else. I already have an engineer in mind. All the rest of the crew should be Japanese . . ."

They talked, almost gabbling, like excited boys, for nearly two hours.

They were discussing the kinds of cargo that would be most profitable when their enthusiastic speech was interrupted by a strangled sound, sharply cut off. It came from outside, nearby. They both looked up. The noise was followed by a shout and a scream of pain. Jinsuke jumped up and dashed for the desk, where he had left his jacket, pistol and holster. There came the sound of loud crashes, of breaking wood and glass, more yells. Through the decorated sliding-screen doors of wood and paper that sealed off one end of the room from a corridor that ran around it, two *ronin* burst through, swords drawn, white cloths tied around their heads. Another *ronin* burst through from the kitchen end of the corridor. Jinsuke stood with his feet firmly planted, mouth set in a grim line, the pistol in his hand. Sound stopped as

333

they stared at each other, then there was a loud click as Jinsuke cocked his revolver.

With a battle yell, one of the men charged at Lyall, and to Jinsuke's alarm, Lyall put himself in the way of his aim. Jinsuke roared at him, and the *ronin* gave a long, drawn-out scream and swung his sword downward. Jinsuke was sure his friend would die, but the blade thudded into a low overhead beam, barely visible in the yellow glow of the oil lamp. The blade bit deep into the wood. Lyall hurled a walrus tusk at the attacker, hitting him in the chest. A second man now rushed at Jinsuke, with the sword held out in front of him as if he intended to run him through. The revolver boomed. Fire flashed from the muzzle. Powder smoke. The lead bullet made a dark hole in the man's forehead. Jinsuke stepped aside as the man fell, face down, still holding his sword.

Lyall had picked up a little table as a shield.

"Lyall, look out! Let me shoot!"

Understanding, Lyall threw the table at the man who had jerked his sword out of the beam, and the table foiled another downward strike. The pistol fired again and the *ronin* dropped like a bundle of rags, both eyes bulging with the pressure of the bullet ripping through his brain.

Jinsuke faced the third man, cocking the pistol, seeing the chamber revolve.

"Stop!" he commanded, in Japanese. "I will kill you! Drop your sword!"

The man he faced now was young, about twenty. His eyes were full of death-wish and fear. He shifted his feet, raising the sword to the right side of his body, feeling the floor and the carpet with his feet. Jinsuke looked steadily at him. Bark on one sleeve. Mud on his bare feet. He's been sneaking around in the garden like a badger, Jinsuke thought, almost sad, feeling all of time on his side. The kimono was shabby, there was sweat on the young man's brow. He's ten years younger than I, and he's never really faced a man who will kill him before.

"Drop your sword, lad," said Jinsuke, in his own dialect.

The man tensed, like a cat, and Jinsuke shot him through the right elbow, spinning him half around. The sword left his right hand but he still held it with a fiercely gripping left. He staggered and came upright, right arm hanging useless and bleeding.

"Please, drop your sword," said Jinsuke again.

"Burei mono, shinei!" Insolent oaf, die! The young *ronin*

334

growled at Jinsuke, using the age-old insult and death threat of a samurai against a peasant.

"Insolent? Me?" said Jinsuke, taking careful aim and firing again, the bullet smashing through the young man's left wrist and spinning the sword out of his grasp. With a dreadful smile, Jinsuke lowered the gun. Spattering blood from both wounds, and with a look of understanding terror, the *ronin* turned and fled.

Lyall had seen violence before and had practiced shooting and fighting, but he had never experienced anything like this. Now he looked around at the two dead men, the broken screens and furniture, the blood spattered about, the mess of red and gray, of white fragmented bone, of shreds of hair. The deep Persian carpet was soaking up the blood, and the air was filled with the scent of burned powder.

With shock in his eyes, he stared now at Jinsuke, who had gone over to one body, still twitching, and was nudging it with his black-booted foot.

The quiet was broken by another scream. A woman! It sounded as if it came from the kitchen. Not knowing what to do, and still in shock, Lyall picked up a fallen sword and followed Jinsuke.

Another attacker had come in through the kitchen and had seized one of the Chinese maids, holding his sword against her throat, keeping her from moving with his left arm gripping around her from behind, the fabric of her gown bunched and knotted in his fist, by her right breast. Jinsuke came in, pistol cocked, as if he were making an entrance on a stage, in a well-rehearsed play. The *ronin* had heard the shots, knew what they meant. He looked from Jinsuke's blackbearded face to the pistol, and his eyes narrowed. Lyall stood behind and to the right of Jinsuke. A big copper pot of soup stock was simmering on the brazier, and on the table, the maid had been rolling little rounds of pastry. Through the coolness of a man grown well accustomed to action and danger, Jinsuke felt rage. Why had this man disturbed the peace of the scene? Was he not ashamed? Picking fights with unarmed women and servants? Why didn't he take on the warship down in the harbor, or the armed merchant vessels, or the whalers? Should a Japanese, and a man who thought of himself as a warrior, act this way?

"Tell her to be quiet," Jinsuke said in English, and Lyall spoke softly to the woman in Chinese. She still stared, the whites of her eyes showing in terror, the corners of her mouth twitching, but she calmed a little. Jinsuke then spoke insultingly in Japanese.

"You, woman fighter! If you harm her I will cut your head off, pickle it, and sell it as a curio to show what so-called samurai look like. You samurai are all cowards, useless against fighting men. Isn't that right, *o-samurai-san?*"

The *ronin* snarled and gripped the maid tighter. He too was fairly young, and Jinsuke could see from his tan that he had been on the roads. Jinsuke recognized the paroxysm of hate and fury, barely contained. Soon he would slit the *giri's* throat and charge the gun, quite willing to die. Jinsuke eased the hammer of the gun down with his thumb and lowered it.

"Wait," he said, "my companion is armed only with a sword, and he is a man. Are you afraid to face us if I put down this gun? My friend has never fought with a sword, and I have only one arm. Let the woman go, she is only a servant. If you let her go and face us, I will drop the gun. I swear. Killing your other two friends was too easy. Are we too much for you?" He raised his voice, letting the anger come out. "We are not *bushi,* but we are better men than all of you. We do not creep into homes and attack unarmed women! Coward!" Then, slowly, Jinsuke put the gun on the floor and kicked it spinning across to the *ronin's* feet.

With a curse, the man shoved the girl roughly to one side and raised his sword with the blade horizontal and facing the ceiling of the kitchen. He was confident that he could decapitate this insolent monkey in barbarian clothes, then take care of his obviously terrified friend. The kitchen had a high ceiling to draw up cooking smoke, and Jinsuke, though he had never trained with a sword, had learned the defense moves of the *sai,* and he knew that from the *ronin's* stance the sword could spin in a whirling, slicing arc left, right, from neck to knee, or straight up from the groin, or down, cleaving his skull, and with no obstructions to the whistling blade.

Lyall stood now to Jinsuke's right, knees trembling, teeth beginning to chatter, cold sweat on his forehead. He knew he had not a chance.

"Oh, my God . . ."

"Keep to my right, and don't swing wild," said Jinsuke in English, his nostrils flaring, abdomen tensing slightly.

The *ronin* yelled—"Yyyeeiii"—but his battle cry was cut short as Jinsuke, lunging to the left, yelled his own *kiai,* short, ringing sharp like the crack of a whip, his arm going up to the back of his neck and hurling his knife with blinding speed. The knife buried itself five inches, up to the hilt, in the tensed muscles of the *ronin's* solar plexus, and the arc of his blade stopped, faltered. He took one staggering step, air rattling in his throat. With a skipping jump Jinsuke went for him, right palm thrusting up at the man's chin, right leg hooking the back of his legs. He crashed to the floor and Jinsuke followed, with a descending, kneeling punch, splintering his nose. Almost casually, Jinsuke stepped on a wrist and took the sword. The man tried to raise his head, despite his injuries, and Jinsuke lanced the carotid artery with the sword and dodged the spurt of blood.

"Foolish fellow," he said, in a guttural Japanese curse.

Lyall dropped the sword he was holding and clutched at the big kitchen table, almost fainting. Thick gouts of blood were all over the stone floor. Jinsuke glanced at him, almost with pity, and bent to pick up his pistol, just as a double crashing boom reverberated in the house from upstairs. They heard the sound of pounding feet, and the crash of a body bursting through screens and rain shutters, getting out into the garden.

"Susan!" cried Jinsuke in anguish. He dashed out of the kitchen and ran to the bottom of the stairs. In a white shift, holding a double-barreled shotgun, Susan stood at the top.

"I missed. He got away," she said dully.

Jinsuke turned and leaped over the wreckage of windows, screens and shutters, and ran across the garden and out through the open gate. Although the lane was unlit, he could just see the figure of a fleeing man. Jinsuke stopped, took a breath, raised his arm, and squeezed off a shot. The range was forty, maybe fifty paces, but the man staggered. Running after him, Jinsuke caught up, realizing he had only one shot left in the chamber.

Susan had not missed completely. The *ronin* was running like a drunkard, blinded in one eye by a shotgun pellet and deafened by the blast. Jinsuke's long shot had hit just below the shoulder blade. Jinsuke shouted at the man, but he couldn't hear. He sprinted, turned, stopped five paces in front of the man, and shot him through the heart. Even then, Jinsuke had to step aside as the body took several more steps before falling.

Jinsuke walked slowly back to the house, his own heart jumping wildly in his chest.

When he went back in Susan saw him and came slowly down the stairs, one step at a time, like a child, still holding the shotgun. She had jerked both triggers at once and the recoil had knocked the trigger guard against her forefinger, tearing skin and bruising her hand badly. Lyall took the gun from her, leaned it against a beam, held her tightly, and rocked her from side to side. Jinsuke looked at them and tried to smile.

"That was the last one, and he's dead," said Jinsuke, thrusting his emptied pistol into his belt.

As if he had spoken nonsense, Lyall just stared at him over Susan's dark head. Jinsuke went through the wrecked living room, tossing the gun on a chair, and on into the kitchen. Two maids were comforting each other.

"Make hot water," he said, in Chinese. They didn't react to him so he bellowed, as if aboard ship. "Hot water, damn it! Now!"

Finding a clean dish towel, he ripped it and dipped it in cold water, then ripped another piece to make a bandage. Back in the living room he grabbed the whiskey decanter by the neck, swallowed a hefty slug, then took another one in his mouth. He took Susan's bleeding hand and blew a fine spray of alcohol over it, then wiped it with the damp cloth and bound it with the rough bandage.

"Damn Ainu dog, no goddamn bloody good," he muttered to himself, then, to the Fogertys, "Come!"

He led them into the dining room, untouched by damage, blood or violence, and made them sit down. He found a bottle of rum and three large tankards.

"Honey?"

"In the kitchen, I'll go," said Susan, her face still white with shock. The *ronin* upstairs had slashed at her as she lay on the bed, missing her in the darkness. She had escaped to her brother's bedroom, where she knew there was a gun, a shotgun, loaded and ready, and . . .

"No, Susan, stay please," said Jinsuke, pushing her back down onto the chair.

"On the second shelf," she said, trying desperately to pull her thoughts to normal, domestic things.

Back in the kitchen the two maids were still weeping and whimpering, but they had fanned coals into life and had a kettle on, glancing from time to time at the dead man and the great pool of darkly congealing blood. Jinsuke bent down, yanked out his knife, and wiped the blade on the dead man's kimono. The eyes stared up at him. He sheathed the blade behind his collar, seized the corpse's arm, and dragged him outside, almost stumbling over the body of Wo Ping. There was a well out there, and Jinsuke drew water in a bucket and splashed it on the floor. Three or four bucketfuls and the blood was mostly gone.

"Come!" he commanded. He'd found the honey, and spoons. "Come! Dining room! Bring hot water!"

The older maid wailed. "Wo Ping!" she cried, and more kindly now, Jinsuke laid his hand on her shoulder, then took two more mugs off the shelf.

"Finished now, come, come, both women, come."

They followed him into the dining room and he made them sit down while he mixed a rum-and-honey toddy for all of them. It was Captain MacNeil's remedy for men who'd been through a rough time.

The maids were fearful now of actually sitting in the dining room and drinking there at the same table as their master and mistress, but Susan smiled at them and comforted them.

Lyall smiled at his friend and took the steaming mug gratefully. Jinsuke drank his quickly and went into the other room to drag out the two bodies, laying them side by side on the lawn outside the back door. There was not much he could do about the mess, so he moved furniture to cover it. Then he went back to the mute group in the dining room and beckoned to Lyall from the doorway.

"Come," he said. Lyall put down his mug and stood.

"It is over, but we will load guns. Where is your pistol? Powder horn? Bullets? Caps?"

"Jim, forgive me, I'm useless, aren't I. They're in my study, in the drawer of my desk."

Jinsuke slapped him on the shoulder. "You're fine," he said. "Miss Susan, come into the living room and relax. You are safe now, and the maids too. Lyall and I will look around."

In Lyall's study Jinsuke loaded the six cylinders with powder and lead, wiping off the circles of lead left as he tightly rammed the bullets home, greasing the cylinder to prevent a backfire, capping very carefully, spinning the chambers and checking them one by one. Lyall fastened his own Navy Colt, a twin to Jinsuke's, to his belt.

"Have you ever shot men before with that, Jim?" he asked.

"No," said Jinsuke, adding, "no men, but plenty of seals and otters, and one walrus. Rifle's better."

At a loud clamor in the garden and surrounding the house, both men dashed for the door, pistols in hand. There were men with poles and lanterns, and an English neighbor armed with a shotgun, followed soon by a contingent of Japanese officials, five samurai and their attendants. From down the road came more noises and shouting, as other members of the foreign community rallied with arms to come on the scene.

"Quick, Jim, they haven't seen you yet, get upstairs!" Lyall's voice and manner were now calm and in control. "There'll be too many questions, Jim, quick, upstairs, get into my closet, you'll find the back slides away and there's a little hidey hole in there. I'll tell them I shot those men." He called to his sister. "Susan! Get a dressing gown on! Don't forget, I shot them! Tell those girls too!"

They left Jinsuke in the darkness for almost two hours while men combed through the bushes and the pine grove across the way. The bodies were carried away and each room searched. The officials posted a guard around the house and said they would return in the morning, offering numerous apologies. There had been five attackers. Four were dead, and one had escaped badly wounded. Lyall said he had shot all but one, with a pistol, but had killed one in the kitchen with a sword. One of the younger officials looked at him with cold respect.

Meanwhile, alone in the dark, Jinsuke was feeling the aftereffects of adrenaline wearing off. It was warm and stuffy but he shivered. He, a commoner, had done the unthinkable. He had killed *bushi*. No longer, he thought, can I be Japanese, for such actions are not in the order of things. When he fought, his spirit had been Japanese, he knew that, but his actions and coolness had been those of an American, a first mate, of Jim Sky, used to troubles and danger. It had been easier than killing a marine mammal from a boat, and certainly easier than the final lancing of a whale. Yet what he had done was truly awful, and he knew it, and he couldn't really sort out how he felt. But he knew that he had done what he must, and thinking about that man attacking Susan, alone, and in her bed, he was glad. The *bushi*, in their arrogant, xenophobic conceit, were actually vulnerable, and as for Jinsuke, they no longer terrified him. Coolness, enough space, and a pistol. And yet, he was distressed, for this country, his nation, relied on the *bushi* to defend it. Sadayori's stern face came to his thoughts, there in the darkness. I can't write to him now, Jinsuke thought, he'll never understand.

The closet was opened and the secret panel slid back. Susan stood there with a lamp. As he ducked out, pushing past the clothes, she put the lantern on the floor, flung her arms around his neck, and kissed him. She had been crying again, and her cheeks were wet.

340

"Oh, it's so nice to be able to open a cupboard and find you!" She took him by the hand and led him downstairs. Lyall came forward with a stiff drink of whiskey in his hand. A dignified-looking foreigner got up from his chair and held out his hand to Jinsuke.

"Mr. Sky, I'm Fawcett-Smith," he said. Lyall made Jinsuke sit between them.

"Jim, Colonel Fawcett-Smith is from the British legation, and a good friend. I've told him all about you, about what happened here, about you and my father, everything. He and I will talk to somebody we can trust at the American Consulate, but if there is trouble and the Americans . . ."

"Mr. Sky, you can trust us, we'll stand by you. That was a nasty bunch you handled tonight, Choshu men most probably, the same bunch that attacked the British legation." He turned to Lyall as he spoke. "According to Japanese records it'll be Mr. Fogerty who did it, acting in defense of his sister, himself, his servants and his home."

"I worry that the samurai will return," Jinsuke said. "You don't know them. Maybe brothers, uncles, even sisters, even just somebody from the same *han*—all will want revenge! Dangerous, Lyall!"

"We have been here long enough to appreciate that, Mr. Sky," the colonel responded. "We'll make sure that security is better." He shook his head with a sigh. "You two have been getting along with the Japanese so well that I never thought they'd have a go here, and Lyall is making such a headway with the language."

"It didn't help Heuskin, did it," said Lyall.

"Yes, well, those samurai are going to learn the hard way, as they did tonight, that their fanaticism will be met with fire, and civilization will win."

Jinsuke bridled inside, the bit about civilization, but he felt too tired to argue. Lyall sensed it.

"Don't worry about us, Jim, we'll be all right now. It's my fault. We were so happy, and I got too confident, but now I'll take more care. The government can't handle the samurai anymore. It'll be fine, and I'll let Captain MacNeil know." He looked steadily at Jinsuke, whose face was showing signs of strain. "That's the second time you've saved a Fogerty and we'll never forget. Our home is yours, Jim, and always will be, and don't forget our bargain, the ship . . ." He faltered. "Sorry I'm no fighter like you, otherwise . . ."

Jinsuke put his hand up. "I am not a warrior, but my life has been filled with the way of killing things. I learn to kill

341

whales as a boy, I learn to fight in Okinawa, I learn to shoot, to hunt seals, and in my life, sometimes I have fought. I am not a brave man, not a good man. I just know these things. You are truly brave, Lyall, because I see you face the samurai with a sword, and you didn't know that I was going to kill him with my knife. You are brave. I always think so. No more talk, please. Bad, bad things have happened." He looked at Susan, who was gazing at him.

"So sorry about Wo Ping."

She nodded, and sniffled. "They killed my dog too."

"So sorry, *gomen nasai . . .*" He almost whispered it, as if he, as a Japanese, were taking all the blame for everything upon his shoulders.

She got up and kissed him in front of the other two men. "God bless you, Jim."

Fawcett-Smith picked up the shotgun lying on the table. "You good people need to go to bed. Rest easily, it'll be safe now." He held out his hand to Jim again. "Mr. Sky, the whole community is indebted to you."

Lyall mixed drinks and even Susan had two glasses of strong rum toddy. Fawcett-Smith left them in the room, telling Susan to lock her bedroom door, and bade them good night.

Jinsuke lay awake on the bed in the guest room, the hot drink having barely any effect on him, despite his fatigue. He puzzled at life, at why he had twice been put in the role of hero, when inside, although courageous—for what whaler is not—he was no hero, just a brave man. He thought of the men he had killed that night, and tried to remember that time back in China, but he felt no remorse, just a numbness. They were not men, they were ghosts, fleeting, snarling horrors silenced by the boom and crash of a gun. What would come of it all? Of Jinsuke, son of Tatsudaiyu? Of Jim Sky, first mate?

Slowly his bedroom door opened. He sat up in bed, reaching for the pistol. But a voice spoke softly and she came toward him, Susan, in her nightshift, long hair loose and down over her shoulders. Moonlight reflected wetly on her face and he saw that she had been weeping again. He threw the covers off, embarrassed that he was naked, but standing and going to her.

"Susan? You're frightened? You heard a noise?"

She put her arms around him and leaned her face against his shoulder. Her breath smelled sweetly of honey and rum.

"Oh Jim, I dreamed you were gone. No, there's no noise,

342

nothing at all. It's just that I can't bear it, being alone, thinking that you might not be there anymore. Don't despise me, I don't want to do anything wrong, I'm not like that, but I want you to hold me."

Jinsuke released her and she lay down on his bed. Lowering himself beside her he pulled the covers over them. As she hugged him he could feel all of her through the thin shift and she must have been very aware of his hardness against her hips. Although he knew she would not seriously resist him, he did not want to take her now, not after what had happened, not unless everything was right. He held her, feeling an almost unbearable pleasure, yet he was surprisingly able to control himself. It was not long before she rolled over, his arm under her head, she hugging the arm. His face nuzzled the thickness of her hair, and his hand stole beneath the opening of the shift, at the neck, and cupped a full, firm, large-budded breast. Susan made a soft noise, and soon lapsed into deep, contented slumber. Jinsuke held her that way, watching dawn light creep through the window, telling himself that he would wake her and send her back to her room, in just a few more minutes, a few more minutes, a few . . . She was gone when he awoke.

Chapter Twenty-Five

It was a typical street of long, narrow wooden buildings, thin walls separating one hovel from the next, facing similar buildings across a pathway a couple of paces wide. Cracked, warping planks divided one cubicle from the next, and gave privacy from sight only. Everybody living here shared a common water source, a pipe at the end of the street, also of wood, and this particular dwelling shared a common privy with a dozen others. Not one of the paper screens was untorn, and Sadayori and Itoh were aware of peeking, frightened eyes.

In the walkway, people scattered as Sadayori and Itoh approached. There was so much violence nowadays, and a *ronin* in the presence of a hard-eyed Satsuma warrior usually boded evil for any commoner in their path.

In truth, neither Itoh nor Sadayori were swaggerers, unlike the braggart *ronin* whom, according to rumor, some Satsuma men were paying to make trouble in Edo. However, the aura of hostility about the street of *nagaya,* these long houses, simply put the two on their guard. Only children came out to stare.

Itoh stopped in front of one dwelling, no different from the rest. It had a single small room of six mats with an earthen-floored kitchen area at the back, open to the rest of the room; here there was a simple clay oven into which fitted an iron rice pot, with a smaller hole beside for a kettle. They could see that through the tears in the shoji screen. Itoh nodded, his eyes counting along the row. This was the one.

"Excuse us," he called out politely, "is this the residence of Takamatsu Hirokata of Hagi, fiefdom of Choshu?"

From inside came a scrabbling sound, but no answering call. Warily, Sadayori slid open the door and confronted a young man, face muddied, hair disheveled like a beggar's, both arms wrapped in filthy bandages, kimono torn and dirty. But in his sash was a short sword. Sadayori's eyes scanned the room, looking for the long sword, but it wasn't there.

"Who are you?" demanded the occupant.

Sadayori bowed. "Matsudaira Sadayori, *ronin*."

Itoh, close behind him, bowed too. "Itoh Hirosada, vassal of the lord of Satsuma. We were both close friends of your teacher, Yoshida Shoin-sama, now deceased."

The young man's eyes flickered over their faces, the good quality of their dress, the escutcheons on Itoh's *haori*. He had no love for either Kii or Satsuma, but he knew who Sadayori was.

"Matsudaira sensei, of Kii. When I was a boy, helping at the sensei's house in Hagi, you came."

Sadayori nodded. "May we come in?"

The young man collapsed into a cross-legged sitting position on the grimy mats, nodding weakly. In Edo, most of the fiercely xenophobic Choshu *ronin* had gone underground these past days, but Itoh's intelligence network had brought them to this place. There were certain rumors they wished to confirm.

"Why do you come here?"

"We wish to hear about the foreigner who wounded you and killed your comrades." Itoh listed the names of the four men recently killed in Yokohama. The young man stared dully at them.

"We also consider ourselves patriots," said Sadayori. "We regret the deaths of your friends. We wish you no harm. Can you tell us? It is important."

Hirokata remained sullen and silent. As Sadayori stared at him he was aware of a fat gray louse, moving slowly in the stubble of the young man's forehead. Sadayori and Itoh shed their wooden *geta* and stepped up onto the worn and dirty mats, slid the sword sheaths out of their sashes, and sat down. They looked at each other. They would wait until he gave in and talked. No help would be coming for him, and if anyone came at all it would be the officials, to take him for questioning and execution.

The once efficient police system of the *bakufu* had collapsed, and the shogun's capital was swarming with ruffians, *ronin*, agitators, gangsters, thieves, rival factions of all kinds. The Satsuma intelligence network was certainly more efficient than the government's.

They waited with stoic, unspeaking patience for two hours, when Itoh rose to his feet with one easy motion and stretched.

"My belly is empty," he said with his customary bluntness to Sadayori.

"Mine too," said his friend.

Itoh went to the door and called to an urchin playing outside.

"Hey, boy!" He tossed him a coin. "Go fetch a noodle man for us. Tell him we want three bowls of noodles and a flagon of sake, second grade. If you come back, I'll give you the same amount for yourself. If you don't I'll track you down and take your head." The children squealed and the boy smiled and bobbed, half believing the threat and delighted at this adventure in his life. He ran off, thin bare legs kicking dust, the other children following him.

Fifteen minutes later the boy came back with an obsequious old man who brought three large bowls of noodles and a large flagon of cheap sake. Itoh fulfilled his part of the bargain with the urchin and shooed the squealing children away. Hunting around in the hovel Sadayori found cups and wiped them with tissues. He poured sake for the three of them, and picked up cheap chopsticks lying on the floor by the rice pot. Itoh looked at the chopsticks with distaste, wiped them with his own tissues, then began to slurp with noisy gusto at the hot noodles in their rich, salty gravy, alternating with appreciative sips at the sweet sake. The *ronin* Hirokata just sat and stared at the bowl steaming in front of him.

"Eat," said Itoh, "it's not poisoned."

But the young man sat there, not moving. Sadayori and Itoh finished their bowls and even drained the gravy. Very often, the inexpensive noodles of downtown Edo were more delicious than anything served in more fancy teahouses and eating places. Sadayori took the sake flagon and poured for Itoh. Itoh in turn took the flagon and poured for Sadayori, then went over to the impassive *ronin*. He held the flagon, waiting for the young man to lift his cup, drain it, and have it refilled. The *ronin* did not move.

"Drink," said Itoh, "or do you disdain to drink with a Satsuma man?" His voice carried a threat. Eyes now glittering with an unnatural brightness, the *ronin* spoke; there was great bitterness and accusation in his voice.

"No, I do not disdain, and neither am I afraid of you, Satsuma man." He lifted his arm, bound thickly at the wrist by a darkly stained bandage, and showed fingers contracted like a claw. With it he touched the right arm, hanging limp and swollen.

346

"I cannot hold a cup! I cannot hold anything! I'm crippled, shot through both arms. Keep your sake and leave me alone! Is it so amusing to be able to torment a man who must die, but who cannot even take a blade to his belly? Get out!"

Itoh was genuinely distressed, and Sadayori came over to look more closely.

"Forgive us," said Itoh, "we have indeed been ill-mannered. Please, drink. Please do us a favor and drink. We did not come as enemies. In the past, from time to time our clans have been rivals, but how can patriots be at each other's throats when the barbarians are at our gateways? We are Japanese, *bushi*, and we want to share sake with you."

He lifted the young man's cup and held it to his lips. The *ronin* at first kept his lips shut tight, but Itoh coaxed him, his gruff voice soft and kind, until finally the *ronin* drank it down greedily, his throat working. Itoh refilled the cup and held it to his lips again. Sadayori, from one side, picked up the noodle bowl and chopsticks and began to feed him, like a child. He was starving.

"There now, what shame is there in taking food and drink from fellow warriors? Forgive us, but take food and drink with us and we will go. We have no reason to betray you to the *bakufu*."

He began to talk. Since his escape and the long, long walk back to Edo, the only water Hirokata had been able to take was from pools, or here, from a pot of rain water outside the back door, wriggling with mosquito larvae. He had to drink like a dog. Food had been impossible, and since that night there had been nobody to turn to. Ravenously hungry, thirsty and in pain, he finished the bowl as Sadayori fed him, drinking several cups of sake from Itoh, the alcohol now making him excited and animated, despite the fever and fatigue.

"There were five of us," he said, "and we went to kill a barbarian merchant who has been wheedling his way into the confidence of certain *bakufu* officials in Yokohama. Our plan was to kill him, take his head, and toss it onto the residence of an official called Miyabe. Then, in time, we intended to kill Miyabe too, as a warning to others who would deal with those dogs. We went at night, five days or so ago, after two of us had watched the house for several days. We easily killed a servant and a big dog they had presumed would protect them. We burst into the house. We found not one, but two men in a big room. One was the

347

barbarian we were to kill, and the other we did not know. We had seen him, but must have missed his entering the house that night. He had only one arm, and a pistol. I have never seen anyone use a pistol like that. He shot two of us dead before we could get to him. He showed no fear, didn't flinch. A strange, barbaric fellow he was, dressed like them, bearded like an Ainu, and big. He was Japanese, though, I know it! I saw my friends die, and I prepared to attack, even though I was sure he would kill me too. He shot both my arms, and the bullets knocked my sword away from me." The young *ronin* stopped, sobbing, and they waited. Finally he bit his lip until it bled, and continued. "My sword—it was given to me by Grandfather, banner bearer to the former lord of Choshu! And I left it on the floor of a foreigner's house, just as I left my comrades, and my honor and my courage, for I ran from him! I didn't know what had happened to the other two, but this was the meeting place we agreed to. They have not returned. You say they are dead?"

"Yes," said Itoh. "One was shot and killed in the road as he tried to flee. The other . . ." Itoh paused, as if not understanding himself. "The other had taken a thrust to the middle and a blade slash on his neck. It was expertly done."

Sadayori looked at him, astonished, Itoh hadn't told him this. "Not shot?"

"No. Not shot," said Itoh, "killed in close combat . . . The authorities say it was the foreigner, and in their reports there is no mention of a bearded, one-armed man, as you well know. However, one of my men saw the bodies when they were brought back to Edo, and one was definitely killed in close combat, two lethal blade wounds. You couldn't have done better yourself, old friend." He poured sake for them all, first holding the cup up to the weeping *ronin*, overcome with grief and shame.

"You are sure that the man who shot you, the one dressed like a foreigner and with a missing left arm, was a Japanese? Really sure? Tell us more."

"Yes, I'm sure. He spoke to me as if I were a servant, or a child, in Japanese. His accent I couldn't place, it wasn't Kyushu, or Edo, or Kyoto, but it sounded a bit like a Kansai or Seto Inland Sea accent. He was a big man, broad shoulders. He looked very strong. His face was dark, with a thick beard. His jaw was broad and long, and there was a scar under one eye. I have never seen a man like him. He is a devil, a devil! Grandfather, Grandfather, forgive me, please forgive me, the sword . . . I lost the sword . . ."

Sadayori patted him gently on the shoulder, a rare act from one *bushi* to another.

"We will retrieve your grandfather's sword, I swear it," he said softly.

The young *ronin* looked up, hope in his tear-filled eyes.

"You will? You promise?"

"On my sword, I swear it," said Sadayori grimly.

"Kill him, I beg you, kill him!" said the young man.

Sadayori glanced at Itoh, whose face had gone blank, a muscle twitching in his cheek.

"We understand," said Sadayori.

The young man leaned back against the wall. "Thank you. I can go with a little peace in my heart now. I know I'm dying. Both wounds have begun to rot. A few days perhaps. If only I could go with honor, instead of dragging on like this, a shame to Choshu, a samurai without his long sword, a man who ran away from an enemy."

"Seppuku?" said Itoh. They knew the young man was dying. The sweetly sick odor of gangrene was heavy in the room. Itoh looked at Sadayori. "We would help you," he said, "although we are not of the Choshu clan. Is there anybody you wish to write to? Matsudaira will write if you tell him what you wish to say. We can put your seal to it so that they will know it is you, and we can take some of your hair and nails to send to your people. I vow the letter will be delivered."

The young *ronin* let out a sob of anguish. "But I cannot hold the short sword, I cannot cut my belly. I cannot die like a samurai. Oh, you have no idea of the hell of it, wounds, rotting, pain—they are nothing compared to the shame!"

Itoh looked solemn. He laid his hand on the young man's shoulder.

"My grandfather always told me that it was a sign of arrogance and poor breeding, of mere bravado, for a *bushi* to cut his belly deeply. It is a fashion for men to do so, but not necessary to the etiquette of seppuku."

He lifted the young man's left wrist. "You can move this arm, can't you? We could bind the blade and your hand. Instead of drawing the blade across your belly with the right hand you can push it with your left. It is unusual, but if a samurai cannot use his right, what is he to do but use his left? All men of honor and breeding will understand, and we will make sure the Choshu men hear of how you died. Allow me to be your *kaishaku*. That will be a sign perhaps for cooperation between our clans, for only if Satsuma and

Choshu combine can we, with His Divine Majesty as our inspiration, drive out the barbarians. The choice is yours, Takamatsu Hirokata of Hagi. We can leave you or we can help you to do what you should do. Yes, you will die, and even if a skilled doctor could save your life, you will lose your arms, and the *bakufu*—if they find you—will execute you as they executed our friend and your teacher."

Lurching forward, Hirokata got onto his knees, letting the crippled, infected arms rest on the floor before him.

"Please do me that favor," he said, in most formal speech.

Itoh nodded. "Good. How old are you?"

"Twenty."

"First, more sake. Sake makes the blood flow freely. Sake is rice, and rice is the essence of life, rice is God. What better way to greet death than with the taste of sake on your lips? Let us face it with a light heart, for death is as light as a feather. Come, let us have sake and song, and Matsudaira will write your letters." He poured sake and lifted it to Hirokata's lips, then began to sing softly. Sadayori knelt quietly, looking at these two southerners, members of the most powerful clans in the imperial realm. For a long time had they been bitter rivals. Both clans were rebellious, arrogant, bellicose. Both had extraordinarily high ratios of *bushi* to peasants. They spoke with accents which to Sadayori used to sound uncultured, but in their hearts they were true Japanese, true warriors, and he was proud to know such men! He left them together, both singing now, and walked down the dirty, narrow lane to go and buy more sake, his heart full and heavy.

Three hours later they hired a *kago* to carry the young man to the hill at Ueno, and they found a clear spot on the grass, among tall trees. A cuckoo was singing, its cry echoing. Evening was drawing near.

Sadayori had three letters, written, sealed, and tucked away in his kimono. One was to the authorities, explaining the actions of the five Choshu men, calling for the expulsion of the barbarians and reverence for the emperor. It sounded a litle heavy and pompous, but what could one expect from a twenty-year-old about to die? The second letter was more eloquent, and was to the senior councillors of the Choshu clan, begging them to heed the principles and teachings of Yoshida Shoin. The third was more poignant, begging forgiveness for not having been an obedient son, bidding farewell to his father, mother, brothers, sisters and an old house retainer. This letter contained some of his hair and fingernail

350

clippings. Each letter bore Hirokata's personal seal, and the carved ivory seal itself was also in the wrapping of the letter.

After the two *kago* bearers jogged off down the hill, chanting, their sticks brushing bushes along the path, their bowed, muscular, veined calves springing lightly now with the lessened weight, Sadayori spread a white cloth upon the ground. It faced west, at the top of a gentle slope, where the young man's last sight would be of the red ball of the setting sun. Then, with a thick wad of tissues around the blade, Sadayori took strips of cloth and tightly bound the young man's short sword to his left hand, and slipped his kimono and the garment under it off his shoulders and down to his belly. He tucked in the sleeves so the body would fall decorously forward, and while Sadayori was performing these services, the young man talked of the beauty of his homeland, gateway to the Inland Sea and to the ancient domains of Yamato.

A mosquito landed on a bare shoulder and Sadayori was about to swat it when the young man laughed.

"No, let her be, she can drink her fill. Why not?"

Things were ready. Not having water on hand, Sadayori poured sake from a flagon down the blade of Itoh's drawn sword. He went round to the front and slightly to one side, knelt formally, and bowed to the young man.

"It may begin," he said.

The red orb, eye of the universe, mirror of the goddess Amaterasu Omikami, she who founded the line that led to the Living God . . . the sun, in all its glory, settled fatly on the rim of the world, its light catching in the smoke of evening cooking fires over the great, sprawling city, and throwing shadows and patterns on distant mountains.

"Ah! How beautiful!" cried the young man, his face radiant now. "Look at Mount Fuji!" About forty miles away, to the southwest, the sacred mountain was a perfect black cone set in orange, with a flame of cloud from its peak. Cuckoo! Cuckoo! came the call, and then the whir of a nightjar's wings, and all around the evening insects were trilling.

With awkward and difficult movements, Hirokata plunged the tip of the blade into the left side of his abdomen. He could not grip with the right hand but he brought the weight of it across the tightly bound wrist and pushed instead of drew. The blade moved across the whiteness of his belly, drawing a line of blood that formed a curtain as the wound opened. Sadayori watched impassively and the *ronin* retreated into his private world of agony and atonement, into ecstasy, while the brilliance of the setting sun filled the eye of his mind, became one with the pain, one with the stopping of time, one with the pride. He breathed harshly, held the breath, turned the blade awkwardly, and jerked it up . . . it was done, and bravely too. For a brief moment all pain left his face, his shoulders relaxed, he opened his eyes wide and gazed at the sun, a near smile on his lips. Itoh's eyes caught Sadayori's, which gave the faintest flicker.

With a tight yell from deep in his belly Itoh drew an arc with his flashing sword. Merciful blow of a trusted friend seeing in a split second the proudly stretched neck of the young man before the head was severed, life ended. He flung blood off the blade with a backward, whipping slash, executed with one hand, then wiped the steel with a wad of fine tissues. With a soft snick it slid back into its sheath.

Silently, with palms touching, heads bent, the two men said a prayer over the body.

"Let us go," said Itoh.

Down the hill they went, meeting dark-robed officials and an armed guard, magistrate's men, coming up toward them. Itoh stopped, bowed, and brought out the dead man's letter to the authorities.

"Itoh Hirosada," he announced, "vassal of the lord of Satsuma. We have witnessed the seppuku of Takamatsu Hirokata, *ronin* of the Choshu clan. You were seeking him, I believe?"

The official in the lead nodded.

"I will see to it that our men have him buried, should there be none of his clan available to do it," said Itoh. "It will be done in the early morning. I can also have Satsuma guards posted by the body until dawn." He then handed the letter over to the official, who took it politely.

"Thank you for sending word to us. We greatly appreciate the cooperation of the Satsuma clan." There was irony, if not a hint of sarcasm, in his voice. "Thank you for your trouble. I will personally see to it that his funeral is properly arranged. Should there be further inquiries, may we approach the Satsuma residence?"

"You are always welcome," said Itoh, with equal irony.

"This gentleman acted as *kaishaku*?" The official looked inquiringly at Sadayori, who wore no *haori* this day, no marks of clan distinction, and who, since becoming a *ronin*, tied all his hair back in a ponytail. Sadayori bowed.

"Excuse me. I am Matsudaira Sadayori, of Kii. No, I acted only as witness and scribe."

The official bowed again. So this was the well-known swordsman and scholar? Turned *ronin* just when Kii gained a great coup in having its young lord selected shogun! By all accounts one of the radicals, but an intelligent and moderate man. Had it not been for his brilliant reputation with sword and spear, the fanatics would long since have assassinated him, as they were killing off all the moderates. Or perhaps it wasn't just his reputation, but his extraordinary links with Satsuma? Were they covering for him? None of the thoughts going through the official's mind showed on his face, as he and Sadayori bowed to each other.

Itoh and Sadayori stood aside as the party went up the hill to the trees. It was growing dark, and from the trees behind them came the sounds of crows calling.

The next day Sadyori took a horse and rode to Yokohama to carry out his own investigations. He discovered that the ship carrying a one-armed harpooner had already sailed for America. He rode up past the house, looking over the scene and staring coldly at the guards. Those hotheads, he thought, would make poor ninja—how could they have botched such a simple job? Personally, Sadayori had a strong distaste for assassination, and he could never fully forgive the slaying of his erstwhile mentor, the lord of Hikone, *tairo* Ii Naosuke. He thought grimly of Jinsuke, of the thoughts the whaler had expressed in his letters, one from Shanghai, and one from America, of American strength, of the right of all men to bear arms, of equality, freedom, and of his general liking and respect for what he called "better-educated foreigners." So the whaler had been won over, and had killed *bushi*? Sadayori was half inclined to swear vengeance, but on the other hand, he had picked the man for his courage, and he had always believed that whalers were born sea warriors, and had argued that case in front of his daimyo. Sadayori now felt that he himself should take most of the blame, for he had nudged the whaler to go abroad, he had caused him to be trained in a fighting art. Thoughts like black clouds filled his mind as he brought the horse into a trot and headed for the highland dwelling of a *bakufu* official named Miyabe.

Mlyabe was at home, practicing his calligraphy and composing haiku. When the servants announced the unexpected guest he racked his brains for a while, trying to draw his mind back to details of his duties and connections as chief customs official. He could not place the name, so he told the servants to have him wait for just a few minutes, then bring the guest to the little tea room at the south corner of the garden. A *ronin* they said it was, who had come on a horse. Miyabe was puzzled. Matsudaira was an illustrious name, of the House of Tokugawa, so it was unlikely that this man had come to try to kill him, as others had done. Zealots were killing anybody connected with foreigners, trying to pretend they had a higher spiritual authority than a government that had kept the nation in safety and peace for nearly three hundred years. But, there was never any harm in hearing what another fellow had to say. He put his brushes aside with a sigh, adjusted his kimono, and made his way along stepping stones set in moss to the tiny little tea house where a conversation could be held with nobody in the main house hearing. He didn't bother to take his long sword.

Sadayori knelt formally at the entrance and gave his name.

The aging official was thin, slight, graying, his topknot sparse but impeccably looped and tied, his face aristocratic with none of the petty arrogance of many who served the government. He was kneeling by a simple iron brazier upon which sat a kettle whose lid was designed to rattle merrily when the water boiled. The vivid green of ceremonial tea was frothing nicely as Miyabe used the split bamboo whisk.

"Let us take tea first," he said, and indicated a cushion by the alcove, from where, through a round window, Sadayori had a perfect view of the curve of the bay and the sea. Already a slice of sweet bean cake and a tiny bamboo knife were laid to one side, ready to offset and heighten the bitter taste of the tea. During the ceremony, they spoke only the formal words required of them, and meanwhile, Miyabe's thoughts became clearer. Matsudaira Sadayori was the author of a well-known and thoughtful treatise on coastal defense; he was a former retainer of Kii, rumored to be a radical, yet with clandestine connections to some extremely important people. He had been on the wanted list, but that had blown over, and he was now known to be somehow linked with Satsuma. Miyabe stayed alive because he was never careless about people or faces, and because the chief magistrate of Edo was a close friend, keeping him both protected and informed. If he, Miyabe, was in any immediate danger from this quiet, well-mannered *ronin*, he would be very surprised.

With the ceremony over, the tea and sweets enjoyed, the minds calmed, the old official looked at Sadayori with a half smile. Sadayori bowed.

"Miyabe-sama, I have come to beg a favor," he said, "but first, I must explain things to you, as you must be wondering why I have made this rude intrusion. It concerns the recent seppuku of a young choshu *ronin* of good family, who was unfortunately involved in the attack upon the house of Fogerty, the dealer in medicines. I witnessed that seppuku and have come to you about a last promise made to him. This matter is of no concern to you, sir, except that had they killed the foreigner, his head would have been staked in front of your house."

"I see," said Miyabe, removing the iron kettle from the brazier and tidying up the tea things.

When Sadayori had finished, Miyabe sat quietly for five minutes, thinking. No, this was none of his business, and he should not involve himself in such things, and yet, neither was this Matsudaira involved, except as a samurai, and as a man of honor. Miyabe knew too that he was the only one who could approach the foreigner with enough discretion.

"Come in three days' time, an hour after dusk. However" —his eyes glittered with warning—"if there is any further attack on Fogerty and his sister, I will inform the authorities of your visit. You have strong views, and you are a *ronin* . . ."

"But no assassin, Miyabe-sama. He was only twenty, and he believed he was trying to save the country."

"He was wrong," snapped Miyabe.

"Perhaps," said Sadayori.

Miyabe got to his feet and Sadayori bowed again.

"Please . . ."

"I understand."

At first, Lyall was incredulous. Return the swords of the men who had tried to murder him and his sister? As it was, he had kept only two of the long ones, the others having been taken away when the authorities moved the bodies. They were displayed on the wall of his study, and there they would remain. Miyabe was insistent, though, as only Japanese can be, begging him time and time again to reconsider, refusing to take a negative answer.

"Fogerty-san, to you those swords are only curios, you understand? To the families of the dead men they are symbols of honor." As the difficult words got through to Lyall he began to protest in an angry tirade that was all the stronger because of his simple Japanese. Miyabe continued, quite ignoring it. When he used a hard word he would write the Chinese character for it. Swords were the honor, the soul of a samurai. The attackers were all dead, so they had paid for their crime. One young man had slit open his own belly. The swords should be returned as an act of compassion. If they were not returned the families of the dead men were most likely to seek revenge.

"If it was my sword you kept," said Miyabe, "my sons would be bound to try to kill you. Please understand. If you want a sword, I will give you one of my own, as a gift. That is different, entirely different. I beg you, do not liken yourself to a victor who keeps booty, understand?"

Finally Lyall gave in. He promised to bring them to his office the next day and asked Miyabe to bring somebody to pick them up.

"I will come myself," he said.

Back at home Lyall took the swords off the wall rack and stitched them up in the very same canvas in which Jim Sky had brought his gifts of otter fur and walrus ivory. He was very reluctant to give up the sword that had no sheath. Its blade was superb, with lovely wavy lines in the steel. The iron guard was shaped like some kind of flower, petals inset with gold. Beneath the silken cross bindings of the hilt there were jewels. It was perfectly balanced and could cut a hair . . . and had it not been for Jim, it would have killed him. It must be worth a fortune. However, if what old Miyabe said was true, it was best to hand them back.

True to his word, Miyabe himself came in a palanquin and picked them up. He tried to give Lyall a sword, but Lyall refused it, saying that he totally relented, and that he was not a samurai and would henceforth try to stay away from all weapons. The following week a very large order for ginseng came his way.

Sadayori strode up to the huge oaken, iron-studded double outer gate of the Choshu clan's official residence in Edo. Under one arm he carried a long canvas-wrapped bundle. When he pounded the door a panel in it slid open and the face of an *ashigaru* appeared and demanded to know what he wanted.

"I wish to return the swords of Choshu men, and deliver to your fief the last letter of Hirokata Takamatsu, *ronin,* of Hagi, dead by seppuku."

"Wait there," said the face in the hole, and the panel slid shut.

Sadayori waited patiently for ten minutes, until finally the great doors slid open and he was faced by a *hatamoto-*

ranked samurai and four others in formal dress. Behind them were ten *ashigaru* bearing fighting staves. Sadayori bowed and repeated what he had said.

"Enter," said the *hatamoto*.

The great doors swung shut behind him, and he stood in a wide courtyard of well-raked gravel, a mansion beyond.

"Seize him!"

The *ashigaru* came forward to pin Sadayori with their staves, but he dropped the bundle and drew his sword in a blindingly fast one-handed arc that sliced neatly through one thick white-oak staff before he brought it back, twisting it to one side so the flat of the blade cracked across another man's temple and knocked him face down onto the ground. The men backed off, and with his left foot forward, Sadayori adopted a fighting stance.

"Is this the way that Choshu treats a man who helped a young man of your clan regain his honor? A man who brings a dying man's letters to the fief and to his parents? How many of you are prepared to die now.

"Who are you?" demanded the *hatamoto*, his right hand crossed ready to draw his own sword.

"Matsudaira Sadayori of Kii."

The *hatamoto's* eyes widened in surprise and he barked orders to his men, who brought their staves to the attention position by their right shoulders. The four senior officers bowed with him.

"I beg you, forgive our rudeness. We have to deal with so many hotheads and we did not recognize you, Matsudaira-sama. You are most welcome." He glanced at the unconscious man lying on the gravel. "Thank you for not cutting his head off, and please, put away your sword." He turned to one of the samurai beside him. "Pick up the bundle and bring it." He bowed again to Sadayori. "Please, let us have some refreshments and talk." Sadayori slid his sword back into its sheath and almost grinned. Itoh had bet him that the Choshu men would boil him in oil.

Chapter Twenty-Six

They were sitting in Itoh's house, having what almost amounted to a quarrel on a subject they had chewed over at least a dozen times. In the autumn of the previous year an English tourist named Richardson had been killed at Namamugi, on the main road to Edo, close to Yokohama. They both agreed he deserved it, but Sadayori berated Itoh for the Satsuma hotheads who thought with their swords and did not stop to consider the results. The Englishman was a newcomer to Japan, and like most foreigners was totally ignorant of the nation's customs. The Satsuma men killed him and wounded two other foreigners.

It had happened that the lord of Satsuma had been asked by the emperor to escort his envoy from Kyoto to Edo, to carry the imperial words to the shogun. The daimyo's procession was beginning its long journey home, men in the lead crying, "Be below! Be below!" sending common people off to the side of the road, to make way and to show their respect for a great lord by falling to their knees and bowing low, as was the only proper and safe thing to do when any great personage, and especially the daimyo of Satsuma, passed with his hundreds of retainers. The foreigners, though, had either not understood or refused to dismount. Some witnesses said they moved to one side of the road, and some said they tried to ride against the procession. Some said that the tourists' horses were skittish at the noise and at the colorful multitude with its tall pennants swirling round, bobbing against the sky as the bearers pranced. However, most witnesses agreed that the Englishman had actually dared to look down upon a daimyo's palanquin, and to look down while seated on the back of a horse!

"Ah!" exclaimed Sadayori, exasperated, "Itoh-san, of course I understand, but such a stupid act at this time! Anyone could have predicted the consequences! The satisfaction cannot be worth the trouble that follows! Could you not have prevented it?"

"No, I could not," said Itoh gruffly. "I was behind Lord Hisamitsu's palanquin and there were too many men up front. But even had I been in the fore, I doubt if I could have prevented it. They should keep the barbarians off the Tokaido road. He asked for it."

"I know he asked for it, the ignorant fool, and I understand the feelings of the men, but why were they allowed to follow him so far, when he was wounded, and fleeing, and why were they allowed to dispatch him in front of so many witnesses? He was mortally wounded and unarmed! It makes us look like savages! They even slashed at foreign women!"

"Pah!" said Itoh derisively. "Large bones and ugly faces! How can you tell them from their ugly men? They were on horses and they refused to get down. So we men of Satsuma are not sophisticated like you! We can't understand why uninvited foreigners may do as they wish in our land. Tell me now, what do you think would happen if I and my wife and a couple of servants rode our horses down the street in the opposite direction from an official procession of the English queen? You think they would cheer and throw flowers at us? You think the English queen would get out of her carriage to talk small pleasantries with us? 'Oh, good day, sir and ladies, such a nice day for a ride.' Never! They would be worse than our men. And you know damn well, as well as all of us, just what the emperor's envoy was sent to Edo for, don't you—to *order* the shogun to expel the foreigners. Yes, and on the way back we are grossly insulted as no other person has ever, ever dared insult us before. Hateful, arrogant animals!"

Itoh slapped his meaty fist down on the tatami beside him, sending a shock wave through the floor that bounced the finely decorated china wine bottles, spilling warmed sake. He and Sadayori glared at each other for a while, then looked away. It was the first time they had had a quarrel, and it was all the more sad because each understood the other's opinion. Sadayori had said before that armed warriors, whatever the old laws said, should never draw a blade on an unarmed person, that it was effeminate and cowardly to do so. He said the foreigners should have been dragged from their horses, and had their faces ground and held into the dust until the procession had gone by, after which they should have been kicked like dogs and let go.

War had almost broken out then and there as enraged

foreigners at Yokohama, both civilians and army and navy men representing the several nations there, had gathered in force to exact revenge on Satsuma, with the Satsuma men equally eager to vent their spleen, and many other Japanese equally eager to join them and seize this chance to fight.

Yet Sadayori and Itoh and all men of intelligence could see that a war with the foreign nations at this time would end only in disaster for Japan. They had been lucky that the cool-headed British official had insisted that the matter was for his government in London to decide. The foreigners then waited for months for a ship to return with word of the London decision.

Meanwhile, following the decree of the imperial court, the *bakufu* had agreed that foreigners were to be expelled from Japan by June 25, 1863, of the Western calendar.

That very afternoon Itoh had returned to Kagoshima, bringing word of the British government's demands. The samurai who had actually used their swords on the foreigners were to die. Satsuma, through the daimyo himself, was to give a formal apology, and the fief was to pay the stupendous fine of one hundred thousand pounds, plus compensation of twenty-five thousand pounds. The alternative was war.

Itoh sighed. "Let us not quarrel. It is done. The *bakufu* got us into this position by their weakness and vacillations. The rule of Tokugawa has made us weak by isolation and ignorance. If you want to make a boy strong you don't keep him in the house. And now we are to apologize? For killing an insolent hairy ape on a horse? We would rather die first!"

"Yes," said Sadayori, "we may have to. Perhaps, after all, to bring things to a head at this point is a good thing. Of such happenings is history woven. We fight among ourselves. The lord of Hikone was assassinated by a Mito man, and his head taken. The lord of Mito was stabbed in a privy, perhaps by a Hikone man. Young patriotic hotheads kill the meaningless outsider and any Japanese who doesn't agree with them. Nothing will delight the foreigners more than for Japan to embroil herself in a civil war. That is what we keep saying, you and I."

Itoh said nothing for a long time, but he had noticed Sadayori's choice of words. When Itoh had said, "We would rather die first," Sadayori had responded, "Yes, we may have to," indicating that if it came to war, he was committed to fighting with them. Like most Kyushu men, Itoh was stubborn, emotional, intensely loyal. He clapped his hands, calling a house servant to them.

"I have been clumsy. Please clean up this mess and bring us more sake, no, make it *shochu,* and bring us something to nibble, something spicy."

He looked at his friend, with his aristocratic, handsome face and the strands of gray beginning to show at the temples, the creases of worry and strain around his eyes and mouth.

"Ah, Matsudaira, I know. You say what you always say, over and over like an old mynah bird . . . for ten years now, isn't it? To hell with the British, and the *bakufu,* if it comes, we'll take it. I want to get drunk. No more difficult talk, my head is not equal to anything but potato brandy tonight."

Sadayori looked at him, eyes twinkling. "Was your head ever up to difficult talk? You old badger!"

Of course the *bakufu* had no means to follow the imperial decree and drive out the foreigners. June of 1863 came and passed, then July. Choshu men had burned down the British legation that year, and their batteries had fired on foreign ships as they came through the Shimonoseki Strait, but the foreigners were only angered and strengthened in their resolve not to leave.

Now the summer was at its peak, a hot Kagoshima August, and Sadayori was in the midst of action, action that he had seen coming and rehearsed both in physical drills and in his mind. Now it was reality. The crash and whirr of cannon shells, musket balls and rifle bullets, underlain by the rising howl of a storm, assaulted the ears relentlessly. Exploding shells threw plumes of earth and splintered wood into the air, blowing holes in walls, roofs, buildings. Out in the harbor, seven British warships were moving in line, their tall masts leaning over in the wind, orange flashes and puffs of smoke rippling along their flanks in disciplined rhythm. The flashing and rippling were soundless, then came the scream of shells, and rising and falling with the wind, the awful thunder of those dreadful broadsides. It was all a dream he had seen before, and he felt almost relieved that it had come true.

Without armor, Sadayori found himself at a breastwork, helping a team of youths to lay a cannon. They were treating it almost as a game, shouting encouragement to each other, none of them showing any fear, only excitement.

"Wait . . . wait . . . wait until it begins to come about . . . now!" The cannon bucked and roared, rolling back. Black smoke belched back at them in the wind. The youths quickly

361

plunged wet swab poles down the muzzle, then rammed in the bags of powder, the wadding, the ball. They hauled the cannon back into position again and Sadayori lined the sights once more. Another ship began to turn and Sadayori raised his arm. The boy with the fuse rope was whirling it around, the end glowing, ready.

"Fire!" came Sadayori's command, and the boy put the fuse to the touch hole for another flash and roar. Only Sadayori was without battle armor or helmet. Along to the left, the breastworks and two cannon were destroyed, barrels tossed aside like little toys, carriages splintered, crews dead or maimed, yet the black-faced youths yelled to each other as if they were practicing fencing in a dojo, or carrying an *omikoshi*, or doing physical stunts at a festival. They were a good, well-trained team by themselves, but they took Sadayori's orders without question, realizing that this older man had experience and calm, and knew what he was doing, even if he wasn't a regular officer of their clan.

"You see?" he yelled exultantly above the racket. "We hit the mast! That's the way to do it! Cripple the ships! Don't fire too soon, too short, remember your lessons in trajectory! Steady now, up a notch, steady, steady . . . fire!"

The ships had come to exact revenge, as they said they would, for the killing of the Englishman on the horse. They were taking their toll. In the harbor, many junks, some of them from as far as Okinawa, were burning or had been sunk. Behind them, the town was in flames, women and children and older people evacuating, running and screaming to each other in the smoke and sparks, which flew like demons' tails in the wind. Undermanned fire brigades were trying to keep control, while most of the men were manning the forts, desperately wanting, most of them, to get to close combat with the enemy instead of taking this drubbing from a distance.

Sadayori turned to a teenage gunner standing beside him. While working industriously at his task, the boy kept staring with clear eyes out at the enemy ships.

"What is your name?" asked Sadayori, in a lull.

"Togo Heihachiro, sir," said the boy, barely taking his eyes off the enemy.

"What are you thinking?"

He was embarrassed, but he spoke up bravely. "I feel strange," he said, "as I stand here by this gun, looking at them, I feel at the same time that I am down there on one of those ships, by one of their guns, looking over at us. I'm not

362

afraid at all, it's so weird, like being two people in two places at once." He glanced at the older man to see if he was angry, or worse, amused. "And I was thinking that although they are the enemy, those ships are so calm and dignified and disciplined. They are magnificent! I hate them and admire them, and we should have ships like those!"

Sadayori looked at the boy with sudden affection. "One day we will have ships like that, better! And if you can think and see things that way in the heat of battle, I am sure that you will make a fine general, perhaps an admiral of great battleships."

The boy flushed at the praise, his eyes back now on the harbor. Another broadside rippled along the side of a ship, and they all braced, lining their gun to return fire.

The explosion of a shell slammed Sadayori to the ground like a giant hand swatting a bug. He struggled to his feet, nose and ears bleeding, vision doubled. Their gun was over on its side and one youth was dead. Sadayori looked around in alarm for the boy who had been beside him, but he couldn't see clearly. He shook his head, then heard a strong, high-pitched youthful voice coming through the buzz. He was calling for help to right the cannon. Sadayori dragged the torn body to one side and together they rallied, righted and reset the gun, loaded and recommenced firing. The Satsuma guns were also making hits on the tall and stately ships out in the harbor.

By now the wind was increasing in force and the ships began to tack out of the bay.

"A divine wind comes to save us!" shouted one youth triumphantly.

"Perhaps," said Sadayori sourly, "but such a wind will not save the town. Look at that blaze! Come, let us help the firefighters, before all of Kagoshima is destroyed."

For the first time since the battle began, their thoughts turned to homes and families, and they started to make their way to their houses, some running ahead, leaving others to help with wounded comrades. The dead could be attended to later.

It was not until the next day that Sadayori found his way back through the wreckage and the smoking embers and beams to an undamaged section of the suburbs, where Itoh's home was. Sadayori's face was a mask of streaked and caked blood, powder and dirt, all white around the eyes from the tears the smoke had caused, the whites themselves red and bloodshot. His kimono was pocked with holes burned by flying embers, and his hair disheveled and singed. When they recognized the apparition, Itoh's wife, rushed out and helped him inside. Sadayori's own lodgings were destroyed. All he could say was that he was so glad that Itoh's home, which was over two hundred years old, was safe. They washed him, put bear grease and mugwort salve on the burns, and put him to bed. He was exhausted and slightly concussed, and he slept as if dead.

A week later he was accorded the great honor of being called into the presence of the lord of Satsuma and thanked for "his heroic deeds and example" to the young men in their battle with the English ships. He was presented with silks, and with a full set of armor. Later that day he was invited to take a commission in the Satsuma army. As far as he knew this was the first time that the Satsuma had let an outsider into their forces. It was not a difficult decision. Of all the clans, only Satsuma and Choshu, and perhaps Tosa, were the ones powerful and independent enough to begin to try to save the country. He accepted, and the same day swore his allegiance.

Chapter Twenty-Seven

At the death of *tairo* Ii Naosuke, Wakayama castle was thrown into great alarm. It had been through Lord Ii that the young daimyo had been made shogun, causing ill feeling with the fiefdom of Mito. At the time of the assassination it seemed possible that civil war might break out between Mito and Lord Ii's fiefdom of Hikone, by Lake Biwa. Should that occur, Kii would inevitably be drawn into the war on the side of Hikone and would be expected to defend the sea approaches to Hikone via the Inland Sea. Wakayama's strong castle overlooked the broad sweep of the Kii River and the sea beyond. It was a stony, bristling fist at the throat of the sea lanes to Osaka and therefore Kyoto, and Mito, if it wished war on Hikone, would almost certainly want to come down the coast by ships. Rumors and stories were already spreading that Mito was amassing an armada.

Japan had been at peace since the Tokugawas had seized the shogunate and created the *bakufu,* and in Wakayama, removed from the violence and disruption of the foreign ships and the Sonno Joi radicals, and the trouble in Kyoto and Edo, it seemed impossible that peace could be disrupted. At least for most men. Swans still moved with graceful dignity on the still, green waters of the castle moat, and small yellow flowers bloomed in the cracks between the massive stones of the sloping rampart walls, and on the wide plains the peasants went docilely about their labors. Yet mounted riders on lathered horses brought news of more killings and complicated intrigues, of the movements of powerful foreign warships, their black, smoking funnels and menacing cannon muzzles ominous along the shores of this green and mountainous land.

Thus it was that Lord Mizuno, whose castle at Shingu defended the southern tip of the Kii Peninsula, issued orders to Taiji. Twenty whale boats and their crews had gone under command of their own *amimoto*, Wada Iori Kinemon. They were stationed at Kataura, guarding the narrowest part of the strait between the great island of Awaji and the Honshu mainland. Matsudaira's advice, long scorned by the senior councillors of the clan, was now hurriedly acted upon.

For the Taiji men it was a time of confusion and hardship. They were not trained or given weapons other than their own whaling tools, and they did not really know whom to expect to fight. For the most part they had to sleep on the beach with their whaleboats. Rations were scarce. In the beginning it had seemed like an adventure, especially for the younger men, and there was plenty of talk and bravado. But as time went on, the men, waiting, waiting, with no action except contradictory orders delivered by haughty Wakayama samurai, grew bored and resentful, and wanted to go home.

"Whaling is the most manly pursuit of all," said one young man as a group of them huddled around a driftwood fire. "War is for fools."

"And *bushi*," added another. They all laughed.

Wada Iori overheard them and spoke curtly. "What do you mean by that?"

The implication was obvious and Wada Iori perhaps had reason to feel offended, being of *bushi* stock himself, even if he rarely wore his two swords at home. But he was different, they respected and knew him, and did not fear him as they might another samurai. Never in his worst nightmares would he dream of using the privilege of his class to cut down a peasant or a fisherman for insolence.

"Oh, I have been rude," said a voice from the circle of men, "I just mean that war is warriors' business, and whaling is whalers' business, and you're a whaling man, anyway, sir."

"I can agree with that," said Wada Iori, "but take my warning and watch what you say around here. This is not Taiji."

They stayed and chafed for several weeks, but there was no war, and they were permitted to go back home to Taiji. All along the lengthy, rugged coast, and around the high swells at the cape, they sang.

That summer, toward the end of the season when they should still have been getting the few look-alike whale and various other small prey, and perhaps an occasional lone wandering bull perfume whale, the whalers and fishermen

366

themselves were thrown into panic of a different sort. A shift in the great warm current, the Kuroshio, had brought large numbers of blue sharks into the fishing grounds.

On a lazy, hot day out at sea, the fleet rose and fell with a low swell. There was no wind. The young men were cooling themselves off in the water, some trying to dive for crayfish or sporting in the water with friends from other boats. Older men, hand towels spread over shaven pates, sipped tea, dozed, and chatted, leaving one man for each boat on lookout—one eye to the sea, one eye to the signal points.

"Hey," said one young man, shielding eyes against the glare, "what's that?"

Iwadaiyu looked quickly toward the clifftop lookouts, and seeing no signals, he squinted in the direction the young man pointed. Something was lying low in the water, with protrusions like limbs sticking up from it.

"It's not a whale, but let's take a look," said Iwadaiyu. "Four oars will be enough."

When they got to it they found it was the trunk of a big tropical tree that they did not recognize, drifted from the far south. Under it were several hundred strange-looking fish. They swam with undulating movements of long dorsal and pectoral fins, large fish, with a distinctive pattern and bluish color. They schooled in the shade of the floating log, looking out with wide and astonished-looking eyes. Iwadaiyu slipped into the water to take a look. He swam under the log, then climbed back into the boat again. He was close to sixty now, but if it were not for the gray in his hair, he would have been taken for forty or less. As he was wringing out the ends of his loincloth one of the young men asked him what the fish were.

"They are called *ami mon gara,* because of that large pattern on their scales that looks like a fish net. They come up sometimes from the warm countries to the south, and always under a big log like that. It's strange that they are so close to shore this year, usually they're much farther out."

"Can you eat them?"

"Of course you can eat them, but you won't find them as good as our fish. They're very bony, but all right roasted."

"Let's spear a couple and try them," said the young man to his oar mate, and he and three others took out the fishing spears they carried for such times, and dived under the log among the startled fish. Iwadaiyu was tolerant, for there were no whales in sight. They were having their fun when Iwadaiyu spotted sharks—speeding blue ghosts beneath the

367

brilliant sea, and just a harpoon throw away, their dorsal fins breaking the water and circling the boat. His heart froze and his stomach knotted as the memory of young Jinsuke with blood spouting from the stump of his severed arm came to him. He snatched for a mallet and began pounding on an oar stem, signal for anyone in the water to surface and make for the boat. Heads appeared, and one of the men held up a fish on his spear.

"Quick! Sharks! Blood in the water!" he yelled, knowing that the blue devils would come.

They scrambled aboard, other men hauling them in.

"Look! The brute! It's as big as a pilot whale!"

The sharks circled the boat and the log, and one man leaned over the shady side of the boat, cupping hands around his eyes to try to look down through waters thick with plankton.

"I can see a whole lot of them, deeper down. You won't get me going into the water today."

The crew looked toward their harpooner and captain. Many of them remembered when his second lost an arm.

"We'll head for the fleet. Throw that fish in and perhaps they can have fun with the rest of them and leave us alone. I've never seen so many before."

The fisherman pulled the fish off the spear and tossed it into he sea. It sank slowly and in a couple of moments there was a swirl of water and it was gone, but other sharks congregated.

"Let's go!"

The men stood to their oars.

Back where the fleet lay lifting and falling in waiting formation, Iwadaiyu brought his vessel alongside the phoenix boat. Tatsudaiyu was standing up and waving.

"The water is full of sharks! It's hopeless! Look, one of them has even bitten an oar!"

The number-three oar on the starboard side was lifted out of the water to show the curve of splintered wood with one triangular white tooth embedded in it. The men looked at each other.

"Must be a big fellow to want to use an oar as a tooth-pick," joked one, and they laughed and bantered, covering up their fear.

Tatsudaiyu stood up at the prow of his boat and sounded his conch, then with his signal stick he waved to the lookout to relay the message that the fleet was coming back in. One by one the boats wheeled about and headed for home. On the way back they passed smaller fishing boats, also heading for port, and they called out to them.

"Hoy! Did you sight sharks?"

"Lots! They took every fish we hooked and rammed the boat. Enough for me. I bait hooks to catch fish, and I don't want to end up being bait myself. I'm going in too, wisest thing to do. Never seen anything like it . . ."

"Even if we took a whale today," said Iwadaiyu to his second, "by the time we towed it back there'd be nothing left but the bones, and the sharks would probably be jumping in the boats."

As the boats beached and were carried up, and equipment was being stowed, Kakuemon approached Tatsudaiyu.

"What is wrong? Why are you in so early?"

"There are many sharks out there, man-eaters, it's too dangerous."

Kakuemon scoffed. "Oh, come now, a shark is not dangerous if you stay close to the boat and if you do the nose cut and lancing quickly, and if you keep your eyes open."

Tatsudaiyu looked him in the face for a short while and then made a slight bow.

"Excuse me, sir, but were you not on the beach when they cut open the shark my son killed? Did you not see what it had in its belly? Had it not been for that accident my son would still be here, but he's gone, and what was in the belly of that monster is buried in our family grave. Excuse me, sir, but I do not need to be told about sharks. Of course, I am getting old, and perhaps my judgment is failing, perhaps I should not be chief harpooner anymore."

Iwadaiyu, overhearing, quickly intervened.

"Excuse me, Kakuemon-sama, but there are not one or two sharks out there, there are hundreds. The men won't whale, and even the fishermen are coming in."

"If you saw for yourself you would understand," said Tatsudaiyu. "The sea has something very strange about it today. There are different fish and plankton, it is warmer than usual, with a curious mixing of colors in the water."

"Perhaps something has disturbed the Dragon King," said a wizened old net mender, who despite advanced years had the hearing of a youth. "They say that when he is disturbed down there he sends his daughter and her maids out in great numbers from the palace, and they change into sharks. You fellows ignore the old rules too much, you know . . ."

"Yes, yes, all right," said Kakuemon irritably. "Today you can come in early, but I don't want any nonsense tomorrow." He stomped back to the office.

However, the next day, and the day after, and the day after that, if anything the blue sharks were even more numerous. Kakuemon himself went out to look, which was something he rarely did. He had to agree that it was too dangerous for men to go into the water, and besides, the sharks would get entangled in the whale nets, making a huge mess.

A man called Yatazaemon came to the rescue, recalling something told to him by his grandfather. He set about making a man-sized doll of straw and rope. It took him and an assistant more than a day to make it, for it had to be bound very tightly. They soaked the doll in a cask of whale oil and took it out to sea with a carry boat of volunteers.

Out on the fishing grounds they lowered the doll into the sea, secured by the thickest ropes they could get. Yatazaemon and three other men stood with lances poised, the lighter ones, used for small whales, with blades a foot and a half long, double-edged, with a shaft just over a span, and a rope that ran from a hole in the base of the blade, up along the shaft. This was placed so the lancer could thrust or hurl the weapon, then yank it back for another stroke. Saburo and Shusuke were among the volunteers, Saburo at an oar and Shusuke with a lance. They both felt a personal sense of vengeance toward sharks.

Whale oil spread a film over the water, and floating high, the straw doll danced and bobbed. It was not long before the long ghosts of shark forms appeared beneath the waves, circling.

"Wait now," said Yatazaemon, "they are cowardly vermin, and if we scare them early they might just leave it alone. If we wait and they start getting ready we can lance them with ease. If you watch, you'll see them roll over to strike. Go for the bellies and the gills, not the back."

With oars shipped, the boat drifted, four men poised with lances.

A big shark made a false pass at the doll, circled again, and started a strangely threatening movement, the front part of its body swishing from side to side, as if it was shaking its head. The shark was more than twice the length of a man and much thicker in the body. When it came, it was fast. The doll was yanked under water, and with tail thrashing, the shark tore at a rope-and-straw limb. Whale oil rainbowed the surface, scattered with pieces of straw. Yatazaemon waited until another shark closed in, its body rolling close to the surface. The first blow of the lance sliced deep into the gills, releasing ribbons of blood and exciting other sharks who now arrowed in to attack. Shusuke lanced a second one, ripping along the belly and exposing pale intestines which were then torn at by the others. Soon there was a melee, with more and more sharks coming, while each of the harpooners hurled their heavy blades time and time again. Sharks, a frenzy of them, thrashed all around the boat.

"Hey, take this," said Yatazaemon, handing his weapon to a powerful young oarsman. He then hauled out the great killing lance, its double-edged blade three feet long, and began to work with that. Now five blades flashed, and the chests of the men became runneled with sweat. Sharks buffeted the boat, and Saburo, looking over the side with fascinated horror, saw that they were even trying to bite at the boat. There were at least a hundred of the beasts now, snapping and tearing at each other, thumping the sides of the boat.

"Enough! Let's get away!" The straw doll was in shreds. The men stowed their lances and stood to their oars, having trouble in rowing at first as the sharks struck at the broad wooden oar blades. Gradually the boat moved off, and the men shouted out their chant and sped away.

"We leave them to it now," said Yatazaemon, looking back with satisfaction. "They will destroy each other."

The men all had thoughts of how it would be to have fallen in that water with the doll, and more than one man shuddered.

Whether it was due to the great slaughter, or to another shift in the water currents, within a few more days there were no more sightings of sharks, and whaling resumed. But nobody forgot, and it was a brave man indeed who dived into the water to scramble up the net-enmeshed whale and cut its nostril.

To Saburo, there was something ominous in the coming of those ugly creatures, and he had a superstitious dread that it portended something even more evil.

Chapter Twenty-Eight

Lyall Fogerty was happy with the way things were turning out, despite the hassles and risks of trading and living in Yokohama. It was January 1864. His new steam schooner was tied up at a dock, and Jim Sky, her proud captain, was happy with the trials, if not with the scratch crew.

In June and July of the previous year the whaler *Perseus* had indulged in extensive poaching, killing large numbers of fur seals crowded into the Russian rookeries. They hit several islands, including the Pribilof, Commander, and Robben Islands. Ashore they used clubs; it was brutal, bloody work at feverish speed, for fear of apprehension by Cossack guards. They hunted on the sea too, going after the seals in the water in their whaleboats, and shooting them with rifles and shotguns—and in Jim Sky's case, with a pistol too. It was so easy to get seals that year that the captain's mind was taken off whaling until they unloaded seal skins and seal oil at Yokohama. They had remembered to fill several casks with salted seal genitals, for the aphrodisiac *takeri*, a task that Jim Sky himself took care of, to the ribald amusement of the crew.

The *Perseus* delivered to Lyall Fogerty's new warehouses in early winter. Most of the skins would end up in the China trade, after being expertly tanned in Japan.

Jinsuke signed off with great sadness in his heart, for he would miss the captain, his crewmates and especially the harpooners. With a couple of seamen to help him with his trunks and duffel bag, he took a boat ashore.

Lyall and Susan were on the dock to meet him, together with a thin, sandy-haired gentleman with a waxed moustache, a handsome, aquiline face and a very upright posture. The stranger was wearing a expensively tailored double-breasted, thigh-length navy blue jacket, with neatly pressed narrow pin-striped trousers, below which were immaculate, highly polished black shoes, despite the filth of the wharves.

While the sailors struggled with Jinsuke's baggage, he clambered nimbly up the wharf ladder, pausing at the top to wipe his hand on a large red handkerchief looped into his belt. He held out the hand for Lyall to shake, but instead he was seized in a bear hug.

"Welcome home, Jim," he said.

Jinsuke's gaze rested on Susan, who looked more beautiful than ever. She too hugged him, then kissed him softly on one cheek, above the thick dark growth of his beard. He was aware meanwhile of the scrutiny of the tall, well-dressed stranger, and he felt a pang of jealousy.

"Jim," said Lyall, "this is a friend of mine, Charles Olderby. Charles is with the American consulate here, and we owe him a few favors. Right, Charles?"

Charles said no, it was nothing, and made polite sounds as he shook hands with Jinsuke.

Lyall tossed both sailors some Japanese silver *bu*, and asked them to load Jim's luggage onto a waiting carriage. The sailors did so, then came to shake hands with Jim and to wish him luck. One of them gave a wink and a glance at Susan.

"Now I see why you leave the best whaling ship on the high seas, Mr. Sky, sir. Good luck to you, it's been an honor to sail with you . . ." He paused, with another lascivious wink at his mate. "Are you hoping to try some of that there *takeri* stuff yourself, sir?"

Jinsuke laughed and pretended to cuff the fellow, but inside he felt a flush of embarrassment.

"Get away with you, John, or I'll pickle yours. Give my best to the others, and sail safely."

Lyall turned to Olderby.

"See? His English is perfect."

"Indeed it is."

"No, no," said Jinsuke, "I still have an accent, and . . ."

Lyall grinned and held one finger to his mouth.

"What do you expect, with half-Japanese, half-Indian fore-fathers? But remember that story, Jim, things are still pretty tight here. Come on, let's go up to the house, I've got a surprise for you." He held a hand up to help his sister into the shiny new two-horse carriage. It stood waiting outside

373

the fine, recentiy built warehouse and office that faced the dock. Jinsuke looked up at the big red and gold sign, reading it aloud.

"Fogerty and Sons, Merchant Venturers and Ships' Chandlers." He looked to Lyall. "Sons?"

"Maybe it's a mistake," said Lyall, guardedly, and then, "business is expanding Jim, and medicines are almost a hobby with me now. This is a marvelous country to trade in."

Jinsuke asked no more, and got into the carriage. He thought old man Fogerty had only one son. Jinsuke sat beside Susan, aware of the warmth of her beside him, trying not to remember the night she lay with him. He held his hat over his lap, angry at himself for starting to come erect at the memory. She just chattered gaily to the three of them, all the way up the hill to the house.

They had a glass of sherry before lunch, and Lyall led his two guests into the study, where on the desk was a perfect model, four feet long, of the new steam schooner. With a gasp of pleasure Jinsuke pressed his face close to the glass case it was in, like a child at a candy-store window.

"She's here, Jim, in Yokohama, and you'll see her in good time."

"A fine ship she is too, Captain Sky." Jim turned to face Olderby, raising his glass in salute.

"When can I see her?" he demanded. Lyall's grin was even wrinkling his nose.

"After lunch."

"But when did the ship arrive? Who brought her to Japan?"

Just then the study door burst open and a voice like a foghorn bellowed.

"Lyall, you little whippersnapper, break out the rum, that stuff's not fit for sea captains!"

A barrel-chested old bear of a man stood in the doorway, his red hair thinning and turning gray. His face was far more wrinkled and ruddy than Jinsuke remembered, but the lively, twinkling eyes were as they always had been.

"Captain Fogerty! Sir!" He ran to greet him and was lifted off his feet like a little boy.

"Ah Jim, but it's been a long, long time, and look at you now! Almost as fine a figure of a man as myself, and soon to be a captain! Lyall says you've got your ticket, right? I'm proud of you, lad, real proud!"

Lyall was still grinning at Jinsuke's astonishment.

"You see, Jim, the old man would not let anybody but

himself or you sail her. He brought her over. You can start running a few trials with her tomorrow, she's all coaled up and provisioned."

"Aye, and she's a beauty, Jim," said old Captain Fogerty, "and if it wasn't you who was taking her from me I'd fight for her, that I would. She's the best of both, a perfect marriage of sail and steam, and not half as smutty as my old *Irene*—the old cow."

"Sir," said Jinsuke, "you shouldn't speak of the *Irene* like that."

Fogerty slapped him on the back. "You haven't changed, have you, lad? Jim here used to smarten up my old river paddler like she was a whore invited for tea with the queen."

"Father!" Susan had come to call them for lunch. Fogerty turned and waggled a huge fat finger at her.

"Now don't you start nagging me, young lady, this is sailors' talk." He turned to his son. "And get that rum, Lyall, I'll not be sipping damned grape juice, and that's that."

"Aye, aye, skipper," said Lyall, ushering them out and heading himself for the cellar door.

Throughout the meal Lyall, Jinsuke and the old captain did a lot of talking and rather little eating as the tide marks in the decanter of dark navy rum dropped alarmingly. They talked of ships, sails, engines, sealing, whaling, typhoons, trade—trying to span the decade since Jinsuke and Fogerty had last seen each other and learn of all the things that Lyall was planning. Toward the end of the meal Captain Fogerty paused and turned to his guest.

"You must excuse us, Mr. Olderby, Jim and I haven't seen each other since soon after he massacred half the pirates in China, single-handed."

Olderby smiled. "Not at all, sir, I was fascinated. I was at sea myself, you know, before joining the diplomatic corps. I would have stayed in, but with the war, well, quite frankly, I didn't fancy the idea of having to fight fellow Americans, however noble the cause."

"Charles was in the navy," said Lyall. "He came over with Commodore Perry, back in 'fifty-three."

Both Jinsuke's and the old Irishman's eyes widened.

"Did you, now?" said Fogerty. "I thought there was a stylish cut to your jib. Now, that makes it easy for what I want to say to you, Mr. Olderby. Jim Sky here is like a son to me. Not only did he save my life and my ship in China, but here he saved the lives of my son and my daughter.

We're all Americans, and proud of it, no matter what, and I want American citizenship for Jim."

Jinsuke lay down his fork and looked from face to face, finally gazing into Olderby's eyes.

"It has nothing to do with it," Jinsuke said, "but I've seen you before, and just now I remembered when. It was at Naha, when Perry came ashore to pay a visit to the palace. You were a young officer, in charge of one boat. Your face was very red and you looked hot. You looked right at me."

Olderby's mind flew back, and he recalled seeing a deeply tanned, one-armed native, watching everything, staring at him.

"You . . . but, the beard, the hair, your clothes . . ."

"Good disguise I've got now, right?" said Jinsuke with a laugh.

"The point is, Jim, it's no longer a disguise, is it? You're one of us now."

"And what Father is trying to say, Jim," said Susan softly, "is that we don't want you ever to feel disguised again. That's why he wants you to take American citizenship, and that way you'll be safe forever from the Japanese authorities."

Olderby spoke. "Yours is a very special case, Captain Sky . . . May I call you Jim?"

Jinsuke nodded and Olderby continued.

"I've heard all about you and I've talked with the consul, and although we would really require that you'd lived all this time in America, we reason that as you have been serving aboard an American whaler, and as you have spent time in the country, and of course, because of your heroism in saving American lives and because of the delicate situation in this country, we see no reason why we can't accommodate you." Susan clapped her hands and Olderby glanced at her before continuing. "But how do you feel about becoming American?"

"I am Japanese," said Jinsuke simply, and Susan's face fell. Captain Fogerty glared at him. "Like your father, my old captain, I am proud of my country. Your father is Irish, born in Ireland, but he became American. If I can be a Japanese-American, as your father is Irish-American, it would be a great pride. But always, in my heart, I'll be Japanese too, a Japanese who loves America."

"And what if Japan and America fought, Jim, what then?" asked Fogerty.

"I've had enough of fighting, Captain," said Jinsuke, "but to protect my friends, my home, my ship or myself, I'm not

376

afraid of it, and I'd fight whoever attacked. Anyway, I reckon the sea is wide enough for me to stay out of other people's troubles. War is for fools, if you ask me."

"Would you fight for America against Japan?" asked Fogerty again.

Jinsuke looked at Lyall and Susan, then back to the old man.

"I already have, haven't I? The only thing a man could do, as I see it. They were Japanese whom I killed in this house."

Lyall spoke to Olderby. "Can we go ahead with it, Charles? Get papers for Captain Jim Sky?"

Olderby raised his glass, smiling across the table at Jinsuke.

"Let's say '*kampai*' to that, Jim. It'll take a few months, but if you want to be American, welcome."

Fogerty reached for the rum decanter again.

That afternoon, rather late, they went to visit the *Big Sky* and Jinsuke insisted on sleeping aboard, talking with Captain Fogerty and Nicholson, the wiry little engineer from Glasgow who had come over with the ship and who had decided to stay. Susan was mortified.

Lyall had not told Jinsuke, but when the schooner arrived in Yokohama, one of the very first visitors aboard was Miyabe, the customs official. At the time only the chief engineer and a boy were on duty, with old Captain Fogerty at the house, and Jinsuke not yet in the country. Lyall took the official aboard and gave him a ship in a bottle, which intrigued and delighted him. He talked to Miyabe about his ambition for a fleet of vessels running between Asian ports, a fleet based in Japan and crewed mainly by Japanese. Ostensibly the old laws still stood, but they had been much eroded. A large official party of Japanese had even sailed to America on a new steam-assisted warship, built for the *bakufu* in Holland. Her name was the *Kanrin Maru,* of about three hundred tons. If that was possible, why not a merchant fleet?

Miyabe said that it was difficult, that things changed only with great thought and care. However . . .

A month later Lyall was invited to a small teahouse just off the Tokaido road, at Kanagawa. Miyabe sent a palanquin and an armed guard of six men to escort Lyall. At the teahouse Miyabe introduced Lyall to two men. One of them had captained the *Kanrin Maru* to America and back, and the other had been elected head of the all too short-lived naval academy at Hyogo, close to Osaka on the Inland Sea. They were both young men, with spirited faces and lithe, athletic bodies. Katsu Rintaro, the ship's captain, was dressed in very expensive silks and had the air of an aristocrat. He was an extremely handsome man, with an easygoing manner rather unlike most samurai. The second man, now a *ronin*, was obviously not so well off. His *hakama* was loose and baggy, his kimono of a simple, country type of coarse silk, threadbare at the collar. They were firm friends, although once the *ronin* had intended to assassinate Katsu, a *bakufu* official who favored opening the country and learning from the Western barbarians. The *ronin*, whose name was Sakamoto Ryoma, had been typical of his type, rabidly anti-foreign, a Sonno Joi radical. However, Katsu's relaxed manner and confidence, and his brilliant arguments, had swung the *ronin's* opinion completely around. On the night Sakamoto and others determined to kill Katsu, after listening to him they put away their swords, and Sakamoto and a friend guarded Katsu's house lest other *ronin* try to attack.

The teahouse was secluded and screened from the road, with a view of the bay behind a row of pines and a sandy beach. A boat and a single boatman waited at the beach, and Lyall guessed that the two men had come to meet him in secret. They had brought an interpreter, but for reasons best known to themselves they did not introduce him. As usual, Lyall stressed points frequently with brush and ink.

"Why should you, a foreigner, take so much interest in the maritime affairs of Japan?"

Lyall looked across at Katsu's high forehead, his wide, bright eyes and his patrician nose, beaked over a wide mouth that easily broke into a smile.

"Perhaps you know that my mother is Chinese?"

They nodded, said they had heard so, made comments on how great China was, how ancient its culture, how well Lyall wrote characters.

"Of course, China was great and will be great again, of that I'm sure," said Lyall, "but now she is a mess, with colonial powers fighting over her carcass. Perhaps you do not realize that my father, who is what you call a barbarian, comes from a very, very ancient culture, perhaps as old as that of China. He was born on an island that has been colonized by England and submitted to harsh cruelties. When he was fourteen he left his home and sailed to America, a country which threw off the English yoke in a war. I see Japan as the only really free nation in Asia. Other small nations in Asia might think they are free, but they are not surrounded and protected by the sea. No, I am not Japanese, but I have come to cherish this country and have a burning wish to see it always free, to see it become truly strong. By blood I am half Asian, and I have spent most of my life in Asia. I did go to school for a few years in England, because my father, although he does not like the English, insisted that I know them well. However, I was out of place in England, and even in America, and I feel that Asia is my home." Lyall saw that he had caught their attention, and continued. "A nation like England, although small, controls and rules many countries. Why? Because of its ships, navy and merchant. Whenever a country like England wishes to colonize or explore, you must realize that it is the whalers and the merchant ships who go first, and then later the navy might follow to protect. As an Asian, I do not think that ships from other countries should control the seas in Asia. I feel ashamed that they are able to. Look at China! China has the people, the culture, the resources and the means to build a powerful modern fleet. But China is too corrupt and too conservative. Now it is Japan's chance. There can be no delay while you fight and argue among yourselves. You have a responsibility to become strong, to defend your freedom, and to lead Asia."

Katsu was smiling. He looked across to Sakamoto.

"Hey, Sakamoto, you don't think I wrote his speech for him, do you?"

Lyall continued. "I have lived in this country only a few years. I have seen that the treaties have caused political turmoil, and have myself been attacked by men, mistaken patriots, who wished to kill me and my sister. However, I believe that the people of Japan are basically good and just. If I can, I want to continue to live in Japan, to master the language and the customs, and if I do so, I would like to think that Japan benefits. But I swear on the blood mingled in my veins that I am no agent of any other country, and I desire only for Japan to exist in pride, strength and friendship.

"Therefore I ask that you assist me to get good Japanese men to crew my ships. We will train them in navigation, in sailing, in engines, in matters of international commerce. We will pay them what we would pay trained Europeans, once they have finished their apprenticeship. My ships will always be open to government inspection and we will welcome Japanese who wish to sail with us. My ships will carry only weapons that might be needed to protect them from pirates. However, it will be Japanese who operate those weapons, and they will never attack Japanese ships or towns."

379

Lyall finished and bowed in formal position, and asked for their patronage. "Gentlemen, I have a few small things I would like to give you. They are things from abroad, from the sea, or connected with the sea."

Lyall went to the door where he had left some bundles, tied the Japanese way, in squares of cloth. He put them on the mats and carefully untied them, showing fine, well-tanned sea otter pelts. The Japanese tried to hide their delight, but knew that these things were gifts worthy of a prince. To Katsu Rintaro he also gave a small working model of a ship's steam engine. Then, to Miyabe, Katsu and Sakamoto he gave double sets of mounted walrus tusks, set in black stone to make a very presentable mount or rest for a warrior's sword. Lyall drew pictures of the animals, and a map to show where they had been taken. Last of all he produced four thick, knob-ended bones, each one longer than a man's hand and forearm. This time the interpreter got a gift too. They looked puzzled.

"Are they a kind of primitive club?" asked the interpreter.

Lyall wondered if he was overstepping the mark, but he counted on the very lusty and bawdy Japanese sense of humor.

"Sirs, I hope these may be a talisman for your continued health and enjoyment of life. They are bones from the penis of the walrus. As I told you, he is an animal who lives in the coldest northern seas, and has many wives. I fear that without these bones he might shrivel, but with such a bone, one need not fear either the cold or the advance of age."

"Truly?" said Miyabe, holding his gift up erect in front of him.

"Truly," said Lyall.

They jabbered among themselves then began to laugh heartily, waving the bones around and making jokes at each other and at Lyall. He was thanked profusely, and he assured them that they were negligible things, simple gestures of his link with the sea. But he knew he had impressed them.

It was not the time to make any decisions or promises, and Miyabe skillfully led them off the topic, but used the conversation to Lyall's advantage. They talked of Chinese medicine, of Chinese classics and cuisine, and ended up with Lyall talking about how sad it was that so much whale meat had been thrown away over the past three decades, close to the shores of a nation that valued it so highly.

"There is a modern process known as tinning," he said.

380

"Food is heated and cooked in metal containers lined with tin. They are sealed so that no air is in them. In this way the food will keep for many months without spoiling. The English navy uses such containers regularly now. It is a foolish thought, but I have often wondered if the meat of whales taken by foreign ships or in distant shores could be preserved and brought to this country. Whale is one of the few meats permitted by the religion of Japan, isn't it?"

"In ancient times people ate deer and boar, some people still do," said Miyabe, "although the religion forbids eating meat of four-legged animals. In the country people eat hare, but they number them as birds, and of course, we eat chickens and ducks, also pheasants. However, whale is a very, very important meat for us. Is it really true that foreign ships throw away the meat?"

"Yes. Nobody would buy it in America or Europe, they have more than enough meat there."

They asked him several questions about foreign whaling and this modern method of preserving food, and all expressed shock at the waste that had been going on, and was still going on.

Light snacks had been provided, but Miyabe seemed agitated, and it was obvious that he was anxious to get home, and to have everybody else return in safety.

Lyall had anticipated this, and as it was a calm, clear night, with an almost-full moon, he had asked Jinsuke to bring the ship around, under power. His ears picked up at the soft pulse of an engine, and he told the Japanese that they could get back to Yokohama by ship if they liked, a short journey, much faster than by road. The two naval men thanked him but refused, but Miyabe was delighted, and went out to pay and dismiss the palanquin bearers, and to tell just two guards to wait. Katsu and Sakamoto bid them good night and went down to their own boat. Lyall, Miyabe and the two young samurai guards went down to see them off, and Lyall signaled to the ship with a lantern. Miyabe and the guards appeared nervous, and kept looking back in the direction of the main road. Seeing this, Lyall patted the little two-shot derringer in his jacket pocket, a weapon he had come to prefer over the bulky six-shooter.

Miyabe turned to one of the young men, saying something to him that Lyall did not catch. Then, to Lyall's astonishment, the young man spoke in accented, but quite correct English.

"Excuse me, sir, but may I speak of a difficult matter?"

"Yes?"

"We have information concerning a certain, er, how do you say, *ronin*. We know that this man knew one of the men who attacked your house. It is best, in the interest of peace and happiness, that your captain remains on his ship and does not come ashore, especially at night."

Lyall glanced at Miyabe, face barely hiding his worry. He bowed slightly. So the old fox had not been fooled! Miyabe had known that Jim Sky was in reality a returned Japanese, but he had chosen, at least at this point, not to act upon it!

"Thank you, I appreciate your concern. We will be cautious and discreet."

With two men rowing, a boat came ashore from the *Big Sky*. Tiny lantern twinkles lit the wharves at Yokohama, across a few miles of bay to their left, and out on the water squid fishermen with braziers blazing dotted the sea with pinpricks of light.

Lyall kept glancing at Miyabe, to see if he would betray an interest in the third man and the commander of the boat. It was Jinsuke. Jinsuke, for his part, took no more than a casual concern for his passengers, and neither did he conceal the pistol in its holster under his left armpit.

The schooner was fitted out with a small saloon, or officers' mess, spacious enough to seat eight people, and immediately adjacent to the beautiful little galley. It was normally used by Jinsuke, the chief engineer and the first mate for their meals and meetings. On the bulkheads, of knotted pine, were various prints of tall ships, and conveniently placed cabinets with sockets for bottles and glasses. At the far end of the saloon, high up on a rack were a large-bored, short-barreled shotgun and a heavy, sheathed navy cutlass. Along the portside outer bulkhead were comfortable upholstered benches, which also served as lockers, and four well-polished brass and glass portholes opened to let in cool air and light. From gimbals hung brass lamps, casting a cool spermaceti light.

Entering, they found a white tablecloth spread on a table, with bottles of light German wine, plates of cheese and biscuits, and a large red sea bream, grilled and laid on a platter. There were also Japanese pickles and rice.

"Excuse me," said Jinsuke in English, doffing his cap, "It is not much, but I thought you might like a light snack. Please help yourselves, gentlemen, we are a small ship, and have no steward. I must be on bridge."

"Certainly, Captain Sky, carry on, and thank you," said

Lyall, indicating for Miyabe and the two young samurai to sit down while he filled their glasses. The Japanese had removed their swords and laid them on the benches. Miyabe was at the far end, beneath the weapons on the bulkhead. He looked around appreciatively at the cabin. The young samurai who had spoken English spoke again.

"Your captain is kind and polite. We have also heard that he is brave, and once fought pirates . . ."

"Yes," said Lyall, "he is a hero." He switched into Japanese, stressing his words and looking straight at Miyabe as he spoke. "Several years ago he saved my father's life. He also saved the life of a white lady. He rescued my father's ship from many armed pirates, killing nineteen of them. In Shanghai he is celebrated. The navies of foreign governments know and admire him. To me, he is like an older brother, even though I am the owner of this ship. I trust him completely, in everything."

"Ah, then he is a good and brave man. We Japanese admire such men. Perhaps one day we can ask the captain to tell us the whole story . . ."

In the wrinkles around Miyabe's eyes, Lyall saw that he was actually hiding a very genuine smile. Lyall reached across the table and poured more wine for him, then for the other two. He urged them to help themselves, apologizing for the simplicity of the meal. One of the young men served fish and rice to Miyabe, then to his companion and himself. Watching them, Lyall realized that despite their modest blue and gray woven-flax kimonos, these two young men had exquisite manners, and Lyall doubted if they were of low-ranking families. He noted too the air of affectionate deference between them and Miyabe.

"Your English is excellent," said Lyall to the one who had spoken.

"Sadly, I have not had the chance to study abroad. It is book learning, and poor."

"You would like to study abroad?"

There was silence. Miyabe broke It.

"My nephew, Tetsuro, is fascinated by languages. He was formerly a pupil of the *bakufu* School of Barbarian Studies, in Edo."

Lyall smiled at the name of the school, but it was a famous one.

Encouraged by his uncle, the young man spoke again.

"I would very much like the chance to go abroad. Many of

us would. But we must obey the laws of our country. If not, there will be chaos."

He looked down at his plate. The engine throbbed pleasantly, at half speed; they would reach their destination in an hour or less. Carefully picking his words in Japanese, Lyall addressed Miyabe again. The more he tried to speak the language, the more the older man warmed to him. Lyall could not use the intricate formal speech, but if he was polite and clear in his manner it was always acceptable.

"Our ship is small, but we have one cabin for guests. Should Miyabe-san or Tetsuro-san ever wish to sail with us, you are welcome." He smiled at the other young samurai, thus including him in the invitation. "The cabin is in Western style, though, with a Western ship's bed, one up, one down, for two men. It has a locker and a basin with a tap that runs water for washing. Captain Sky serves both foreign and Japanese food aboard the ship and the meals are always good, if simple."

Tetsuro and his uncle exchanged glances and bowed slightly.

"I enjoy your ship very much," said Miyabe, "and one day would like the great privilege of sailing on her. Fogerty-san, let us drink to peace between nations." Miyabe raised his glass and the others followed suit. Lyall prayed fervently that no mishap would befall this kind, moderate, albeit cunning gentleman.

A month later the *Big Sky* had a full crew. Only Nicholson, the Scottish engineer, and the Chinese cook—and supposedly Jinsuke—were not Japanese. Miyabe, Katsu Rintaro and Sakamoto Ryoma had obtained official permission for suitable young men of *bushi* status to be selected for training on the ship. To the young samurai's delight, Tetsuro was chosen to train under Jinsuke as his first officer. The rest of the men were from coastal communities in the Tosa district of Shikoku. This happened to be the home of the clan Sakamoto had been born into, and also, perhaps not by chance, the home of the ex-Yankee whaler and the repatriated Japanese, Nakahama Manjiro, now whaling advisor to the *bakufu* government. There were twelve Japanese in all, eager young men who had studied Western languages and science, and all familiar with boats since their childhood. When they came aboard, Captain Jim Sky braced himself. No matter what their status ashore, no matter whose relative they might be, or what connections they might have, while aboard his ship they would have to learn that he was their captain, and as such, the closest thing to God. He showed them not a whit of deference above normal ship's manners. His orders were all given in English, as were his instructions in navigation.

Each of the young men was provided with a Western-style uniform and as soon as they got their gear stowed their first lesson was in how to salute the captain. He made them put away even their short swords, providing them all with sailor's jacknives. From the very beginning, the young men admired him. Only young Tetsuro knew who the captain really was.

Chapter Twenty-Nine

Jinsuke never used an umbrella. He stepped into the front offices of Lyall Fogerty's company and shook the rain off his cap. There were many people inside, some with business, some dallying to wait for the rain to stop: Westerners in suits, a couple of Japanese officials in *hakama,* swords in their sashes, and three of his own crew in their navy blue uniforms and wide sailor's collars. They bowed as they saw him, and Jinsuke waved, conscious of the sideways glances of the officials.

Out in the harbor, no fewer than seventeen foreign warships were gathered, and even in the rain, from along the quay came the cacophony of marching bands and patrolling marines, arms at slope and bayonets fixed. Yet despite the threat of an impending war to negate all treaties and drive out the foreigners, a war that the *bakufu* did not really want to pursue, the atmosphere around Yokohama was gay. War, it seemed, was almost a festival, at least when the battlegrounds were likely to be as distant as Kyushu or Choshu, way down south. Meanwhile, the foreign settlement felt itself well defended. As to rumors that the emperor himself had ordered the barbarians to be expelled, well, Japan was always a wasp's nest of rumors.

Jinsuke nodded to his crew and made his way to the front desk. A clerk, freshly recruited from Scotland, smiled and came out from behind the wooden counter.

"Well, good day to you, sir, Captain Sky. Kindly follow me."

With the faintest of bows to the people in the outer office, Jinsuke threaded his way past everybody and went upstairs, where Lyall's personal office with its large bay windows overlooked the harbor. Beside the window, on a tripod, stood a big brass telescope. Lyall was alone, poring over a chart. He looked up as Jinsuke came in and waved him over to a chair.

"You're back, Jim! It must have been a tough journey this time, and as I told your first officer already, I've ordered a new suit of sails . . ."

"Good." Jinsuke sat down and held out his hand for the drink that Lyall was making for him. He sipped it. Sherry again. Lyall took a seat across from him and raised his own glass.

"All delivered, safe and sound, I gather?"

"No trouble, but young Tetsu knows something is afoot."

"I'd be disappointed in him if he didn't," said Lyall, sipping and looking at him over the top of the glass.

Even when alone, they still spoke mostly English, although Lyall's Japanese was improving rapidly. The schooner had taken a load of copperware, raw silk and tea to Shanghai, then brought a mixed load from Shanghai to Nagasaki. They had sailed from Nagasaki with two men from Tosa, and had stopped at Susaki to unload a mysterious cargo, at night. Jinsuke had been paid in gold coin right on the beach. Modern rifles were at a premium with many of the fiefdoms now. But it was a risky business with the *bakufu* embargo on arms.

"Jim, Dad wants to go back to Shanghai, and I've another shipment for you. It's a rough trip, I know, what with the typhoons, and the word is that it's still necessary to take her around the southern coast of Kyushu. The Choshu idiots are still firing on vessels going through the Shimonoseki Strait." Lyall looked out of the window to the foreign armada. "Although, from the looks of it, Choshu is really going to get its hash settled good and proper."

He looked back at Jinsuke, who was scowling. "Come on now, Jim, firing on merchant ships going through the straits is hardly an act you would sympathize with, is it now?"

The *bakufu* had been forced by imperial command to agree to expel foreigners by June 25 of 1863, but over a year had passed and they had done nothing about it. Choshu was by now the most extreme fiefdom in anti-Western and anti-*bakufu* politics. Moderates among the clan leaders had been assassinated, or ordered to commit seppuku, or terrified into silence. Now Choshu had taken it upon itself to act out the emperor's commands, but they were having little success.

Already the French admiral Jaurés, in July of the same

year, retaliated by bombarding the Shimonoseki shore batteries with French men-of-war aided by an American warship. They even sent landing parties ashore, drove off the Choshu warriors, and spiked their guns. Now England and Holland had sent warships to teach Choshu to leave merchantmen alone, and a four-nation armada was eager to sail and teach them a lesson. Some hoped that the battle might bring the Choshu men to their senses, just as the attack on Kagoshima the year before had ended up with the British and Satsuma becoming very close; the British cooperated with Satsuma, to the dismay of the *bakufu*, making the southern clan stronger than ever. Jinsuke heard all of this not only from Lyall and his friend Olderby, but also from his young Japanese officers; although they had taken the moderate side and were learning Western ways themselves, they were undeniably patriotic and deeply troubled about the impending foreign attack, even if they did not agree with the radicals. Lyall watched Jinsuke, who just stared into his glass, saying nothing.

"Well, Jim?"

"They're fools, and we know it. Those ships, with their sixty-four pounders and exploding shells, will blow them to bits," said Jinsuke, putting his glass on the polished wood of Lyall's desk. "But I wish all those people parading about out there did not look so happy about the possibility of war." He lowered his voice. "And don't you forget, Lyall, this is the country of my birth."

"I won't forget, Jim, and I feel the same way you do. But they can't drive us out, and they shouldn't. However, with all the threats, and the government vacillating, paying court to fanatics, the emperor, his courtiers, the die-hard daimyos and whatnot, nobody in Edo can make a decision about anything. And, more important, it's bad for trade."

He stood up and looked at the ships. "It is sad, isn't it, Jim."

Ever since Jinsuke had learned that the men who had come rampaging through the peace of the Fogerty house had been *ronin* from Choshu, he had little time for men of their ilk, and he had long since despised the narrow-minded stupidity of Sonno Joi politics. And yet, inside, he was Japanese. If only men like Sadayori would listen to him! Where was the warrior now? Tetsuro, his first officer, had told Jinsuke that Matsudaira Sadayori had come to his uncle to retrieve the swords of the men killed in the attack on the Fogertys, and said that his uncle feared that Sadayori might want to kill Jinsuke. That made Jinsuke angry and sad, and frustrated.

Lyall handed him an envelope. Jinsuke opened it and began to read. He looked up at Lyall, brow furrowed.

"Kagoshima? After what the British did there? They'll blow us out of the water. Our ship is no man-of-war! You don't really want to go there, do you?"

Lyall smiled. "Haven't you heard? Things are going really well between the Satsuma clan and the British, astonishingly, so it seems. Anyway, don't worry, on this trip you'll have a young Satsuma *hatamoto* as a passenger. I got it straight from old Miyabe that the *bakufu* is lending Satsuma the money to pay what the British demanded over that Richardson affair. The British attack impressed them. They are a very martial clan, and they respect strength."

Jinsuke looked at him grimly. "Yes, I know plenty about that. And what are we carrying? Guns again?"

Lyall nodded. Jinsuke muttered a curse. "Do we have to?"

"I think so, Jim. I believe that the present government will get kicked out, and that it'll be the strong ones who'll be making decisions in the future. I like to get on the right side early."

"There are, I suppose, other goods too?" Jinsuke's voice was almost sarcastic.

"Yes. Dyes, Chinese wine, cotton goods, cutlery, odds and ends, some medicines. In Kagoshima you will pick up a load of sugar, and a few thousand pairs of scissors. And gold too, Jim, gold."

Jinsuke turned over the pages in his hand and inspected the list. Scissors from Tanegashima, sugar, even salt . . . his mind roamed back to Okinawa.

"But listen, Jim, even if they ask you, don't go ashore. We have Tosa men on our crew so I trust things there, but this is our first deal with Satsuma."

"Don't worry. Kagoshima is a place I intend to stay away from. I'll be aboard, and armed. Didn't I tell you that I once cracked a Kagoshima samurai across the head? They didn't appreciate that."

"Yes, you told me, Jim, and I do remember. The scars on your back, right? Stay cool, though, Jim."

Jinsuke nodded. The Satsuma samurai may have tortured him, but he still felt obliged to a man called Itoh for throwing him into the sea and letting him escape to Shanghai.

"You have to take Dad to Shanghai too, Jim."

"You know I like going there, and you know I like having the old skipper aboard, but Lyall, I'll caution you again, keep it tight around here—the Japanese crew are still not supposed to be taken out of Japanese waters."

"Will any of them talk?"

"No, of course not."

"Then neither will I, or Dad. He'll come aboard at night, he often visits the ship, so nobody will notice."

"But it's the second trip to Shanghai in three months."

"Jim, it's okay. Don't worry. I reckon that after Choshu gets another pounding there'll be plenty of Japanese going abroad."

He looked closely at his captain. "Dad is trying to make Susan go with him, Jim. Mother says they've got somebody for her to marry. She doesn't want to go, though, and like as not she won't sail with you to Shanghai, but she's being bullied, Jim."

Jinsuke kept his face blank while Lyall looked hard at him, then reached for a cigar from a lacquered box on the table.

"She's really fighting not to go back to China. She says she will not marry whomever they've found, even if he's the richest lord in civilization."

Jinsuke looked back at him, but waved aside the offer of a cigar.

"I think I'd better warn you that my father is maybe going to be a bit awkward with you too."

Jinsuke shrugged. "He's Irish. You know, on the railroads I met quite a few Irish. They're often difficult. It doesn't worry me, and anyway, on the *Big Sky* it's me who's the captain." Lyall grinned at him, then his expression changed.

"Jim, there is a lot I'd say if I was asked, but you never tell me anything about your personal feelings. But I do want you to know that I'm on your side."

The meaning of Lyall's comments was not lost on Jinsuke. Whenever he had come into port Susan had come to the ship, bringing small gifts, of food usually, trying to spend time alone with him. He in turn had always sent small gifts up to the house, things he knew she would like, items of handicraft, baskets of fruit from the south, fresh crayfish and fish, and once even a large hunk of whale meat, with written instructions on how to prepare it.

Lyall kept on looking at him. Jinsuke realized how much more assured Lyall was, more manly, fuller in the face, broader in the shoulders.

390

"Jim, if you don't know she's waiting for you, then I shouldn't be telling you. However"—he pointed with the smoking tip of his cigar—"don't fool around with her, or I'll shoot you myself."

Jinsuke froze inside, and returned the steady look. Lyall Fogerty's eyes were at times distinctly Oriental, his face a strange but attractive mixture, with the jaw and the lines that ran from nose to mouth haughty and Western. Had Lyall known that he had lain with Susan that night? Yet he had not taken her, but what man would believe that? Jinsuke remembered the warmly soft yet firm fullness of her breasts, the tight little buds of her nipples. He stood slowly, pulling the pistol out of his shoulder holster. He cocked it, then handed it butt first to his friend and employer.

"You want to shoot, go ahead. I tell you, though, to me your sister is a very important person. You don't understand the fact that I am a kind of prisoner. There are many things in my life that I need to settle, but can't, because of that. Susan and I have nothing to be ashamed of, nothing that you or your father can get angry about . . ."

Lyall pointed the gun at the ceiling and carefully lowered the hammer with his thumb.

"Jim, if I had to shoot you I'd use a bigger gun. Look, I'm just telling you. In everything else you are so positive, but in this you are so, so damned . . . so damned Japanese! Go and settle your life, and then make it very, very clear to my sister the way things are."

Jinsuke just nodded, turning on the blankness.

"Damn it, man, go to Taiji—that's what it is, isn't it? You've got somebody there. I'll do anything I can to help you out if you need it, but you are not going to go on sitting on my sister's heart. I agree with my father in this. It is time she was married. You may not have noticed, Jim, but there are a lot of other men who think and hope so too."

Jinsuke kept wondering if Lyall had known about that night, and he felt embarrassed, not knowing if he should explain or not.

"Lyall, with Susan . . ."

Lyall held up one hand. "I said I was on your side. But sometimes, Jinsuke, you are so damned sure of yourself I'd like to kick you. I reckon that you'll do what's right. Now get out of here, will you?"

Jinsuke holstered the gun, turning to go, deeply hurt and angry with himself, with Lyall, with the situation.

"Jinsuke," said Lyall, using his name again, and speaking softly in Japanese, "my mother is not well, and Father is worried about her, about Susan, about many things. Treat him well, won't you."

Jinsuke stopped at the door, bowed, and left.

Lyall sat down and stubbed out the cigar. There was no man on earth he admired as much as Jinsuke, but that horrible night of killing and blood always triggered in him a fear that he had difficulty controlling. Jinsuke had saved him, but at the same time Lyall had become afraid of him. Afraid, grateful, admiring. After the night of violence was over, and just before dawn, unable to sleep, Lyall had gone to Susan's room, wanting to talk with her the way they used to as children, when thunder rolled over Shanghai. Susan was not in her room. There was only one place she could be, and if she was there, she would have gone of her own accord.

As Jinsuke went to leave the outer office, the clerk dashed up to him, holding a small bag and a note. Jinsuke read it in the boat going over to his ship.

> Jim,
>
> Once in a while, engines break down. In such a case, it could be that a ship would have to head for port. I have enclosed a couple of bottles of Scotch, which I suspect you and the engineer might enjoy together over a little chat. Of course Taiji is on the way back to Yokohama after Kagoshima. Miyabe-san once told me that Taiji is a very small place, with no *bakufu* police at all. At the latest, Susan will be sailing for Shanghai a month after you get back from this next trip. Good luck.
>
> Lyall

The *Big Sky* sailed from Yokohama the day after the war fleet departed, with old Captain Brian Fogerty aboard, and with Jinsuke in a very thoughtful mood.

Just in sight of the island of Oshima, Captain Fogerty came up to the bridge. First Officer Tetsuro was pointing to the island, telling Jinsuke of its history as a place of exile for *bakufu* prisoners. He turned and saluted the old captain.

"Good morning, sir." He looked at his own captain. "Is our course to be for Ireland this time, sir? Or just to Shanghai again?" The two men looked at the young officer.

"Would you be willing to sail with us to Ireland, then?" asked Fogerty.

"Yes, sir," answered Tetsuro.

"And the others?" asked Jinsuke.

"All Japanese men would go . . . Most would like to go to England or America," he grinned. "The engineer says that Scotland is the best place in the world, though, sir, and the cook, he always wants to go back to Shanghai."

"This time, it's just to Shanghai," said Jinsuke, his voice gruff, but deeply pleased inside, "and on the way back we stop at Nagasaki, pick up a Satsuma man, a passenger. Then we will sail around Kyushu and stop off at Kagoshima."

"Ka . . ." Tetsuro bit off the question, his eyes flashing strangely for a second. He saluted. "Aye, aye, sir!"

Without saying anything more he went to plot the course. There would be two sets of charts, one for official eyes, and one for the running of the ship.

Fogerty cast his eyes to the bellying sails. "And a fine day it is, an' all, Jim," he said. "Six, seven knots?"

"Nearly eight knots, we've got a good wind." Jinsuke paused, sensing that Fogerty wanted to talk with him about something. "Lyall said that Mrs. Fogerty wasn't well, sir, I am sorry."

The old captain sighed. "Aye, well, she pines for me too, I guess, I've been away from her too long. The two of us are getting old, you know . . ."

Jinsuke looked at his old captain, and saw really for the first time how heavily age sat upon him, age, and old wounds. He was so much thinner now, almost gaunt, and his face and hands were much more wrinkled, and that once glossy red hair had grown thin and dull, flecked with wood-ash gray. On his arms, exposed now with his sleeves rolled up for the strong summer sun, the sinews and veins stood out. Among the mass of freckles and the snake-and-anchor tattoo there were many gray hairs.

"I'm sure she'll get well when you arrive home, sir, and" —Jinsuke paused shyly—"it is good to have you aboard. It is like a dream."

"Thanks, Jim, and I'm proud to be sailing with you." He gave a short laugh. "And to think that you hardly knew a word of Engiish or a scrap of navigation when you first set foot aboard the *Irene*. You know, I would have liked for you to have stayed with me, and for me to get another ship and go deep-sea voyaging, but what with the children and everything I hadn't the heart to stay away all those months. The women resent it, you know, Jim, they really do, they don't like you being away and they suspect the men feel more at home aboard ship. Then they get used to a man being away, and after a while, when the man comes back, he finds he really doesn't fit in. When you're home after a long voyage things are fine for a while, but then you get itching, wanting to sail, wanting not to hear the little nagging and the kids and the snotty neighbors, you want wind and sea again. That's why I took to the river trade, even though it was more risky in some ways." He sighed again. "And China got into my blood too, China, aye, and a fine woman . . ." Fogerty was leaning on the rail, squinting against the strong sun.

"How long have you been at sea now, Jim?"

"All my life, sir. I went out with the whaling boats when I was old enough to grip an oar."

"No, I mean oceangoing ships, not boats."

"Over ten years now, sir," said Jinsuke.

The old captain turned and smiled. "Ten years . . . I'm proud of you, Jim, you know that."

The cook called out that breakfast was ready, and Fogerty went on down below. Jinsuke did not see him for the rest of the day, as he and Tetsuro ate later.

That evening, after dinner, he and Captain Fogerty sat alone in the saloon together. On the previous voyage to Shanghai, Nagasaki and Shikoku, Jinsuke had bought a flagon of very powerful Kyushu liquor, distilled from sweet potatoes. He produced it now, setting two shot glasses on the white tablecloth, slightly dampened to stop things from slipping. The ship rolled and creaked, and glassware clinked pleasantly in its holdings. The sea was calm enough for portholes to be open, and a cool air made the saloon pleasant in the light of the gimbaled lamps.

"Captain Fogerty, we Japanese call this drink *shochu*, it's like American moonshine, made with potatoes. Most people drink it with hot water, but I reckon you'll want to try it neat."

He poured a couple of good slugs and raised his glass. The old captain raised his, gave it a sniff, grinned, and knocked it back.

"Whew! That's what I call a drop of the good stuff, not a bad poteen at all. Ah, Jim, you know the way to an old Irishman's heart. Fill it up, sir, let's not let such good stuff go rotten in the bottle!" He sank another shot, then with forearms leaning heavily on the table looked Jinsuke straight in the eyes.

394

"You've done well, Jim, and like I say, I'm proud of you. Now, lad, when are you going to get married?"

Jinsuke mumbled, words sticking in his throat. He said he couldn't think of marrying until he had seen his father, and as the laws against Japanese returning from overseas still existed, that would be difficult. Fogerty reached out and poured them both drinks.

"Jim, lad, a sailor should always take his time before getting married, should never do it before thirty. But now you're what, thirty-six, thirty-seven? A man who hasn't married at that age has got something wrong with him. You're master of a ship now, and with quite a bit of money stashed away—invested wisely, so my son tells me—so it's time you got a wife. With no wife you've got no home except the ship, and a captain like that is only good for a few years. After that he gets cranky, crazy, or becomes a booze hound. In Japan, Lyall is the boss of the company, but we are a family business, and I'm head of the family. What I say goes. So I'll come right out with it straight. What is going on between you and my daughter?" His big, bony shoulders hunched, huge hands gripping each other.

"Nothing . . . it's only that . . ."

Fogerty slammed the table with one hand. "Nothing? Don't lie to me, Jim! Susan had young men, good fellows from respectable families and with excellent futures, all around her, thick as flies. She left broken hearts in England, in Ireland, and a whole litter of them in China. She was always a good girl, mind you, a good Catholic girl, I'll vouch for that. There were plenty of young men, a couple she liked too, who wanted to marry her. Two of them came to ask me about it. Then she came to Japan, telling me and her mother it would be for no more than a year. Now she refuses to come home. She wrote to one young fellow we thought she was sweet on, one of the ones who asked me if he could marry her, and told him she wouldn't write him again, and hoped he can find happiness. Almost drove the poor fellow to blow his brains out. Now she thinks she's hiding something from me, but I know what it is, and her mother knows what it is, and her brother knows what it is, and damn you, Captain Jim Sky, you know what it is!"

He glared at Jinsuke, then angrily swallowed another shot of the fiery liquor. His eyes were starting to redden. Lips compressed tightly, Jinsuke stared back at him.

"Captain Fogerty, you have been like a father to me. I never forgot your home and family, and I always think of

Susan like a little sister. I swear that I have never done anything wrong . . ."

Fogerty waved his hand, cutting him off.

"Pah, I know that. Do you think you'd be on this ship, that I'd be sitting here and drinking with you if it wasn't so? But tell me straight, you like her a lot, don't you?"

"Yes. A lot."

"You've got another girl?"

Jinsuke flushed. "Long years ago, before I came to China, I promised to marry another girl. You don't know how it is in a small Japanese village."

"Hah! Small villages are small villages wherever you go. So you think she's waiting? You want her to be waiting?"

Jinsuke hung his head and gripped his hand around the shot tumbler until his callused knuckles whitened.

"I don't know," he half whispered.

"Then damn well go and find out," said Fogerty, "and take a good look into your own heart. In a few months I'll send for Susan and have her tied up and dragged back to Shanghai. From there I'll take her myself to America, East Coast like as not, and I'll make damn sure she never hears from you or sees you again. If you try to find her I'll have you off this ship. If you're promised to another girl, then fine, you and I can always be friends. However, after you get back from this voyage"—he paused and jabbed a finger at Jinsuke for emphasis—"this voyage, mind you, you're going to get off this ship, go up to the house and tell Susan in front of her brother the way things are, nice and clear. Now I had my say, Jim, and you can pour me another."

He downed it in a gulp, wiped the back of his hand across his mouth, grunted good night and stomped off, reeling slightly more than the movement of the boat might account for, to his cabin. Jinsuke threw his own drink away, got up, and poured himself black coffee. For a while he stood staring into the cup, then he went up on deck to gaze at the stars and the ever-restless sea. Lines of phosphorescence streamed off the bows.

What he had been told was fair and true. He should tell Susan about Oyoshi, but then, when he recalled Susan's trusting eyes and the beautiful, half-sad smiles she always gave him, something tightened in his chest. No, before telling her he would go to Taiji, and to hell with the danger. He would see for himself if Oyoshi had kept her pact with him. Draining the coffee, he went down again to talk to the

396

engineer, to see, as Lyall's note had implied, if he would help him out.

The engineer sat on his bunk, giving his captain the only chair in the cabin. As the request was haltingly outlined to him he grinned widely and stuck out his hand. Certainly, a little stop at a wee whaling village at the tip of the Kii Peninsula would be easy to arrange, and besides, there were a couple of bottles of Scotch in it, which he would accept only if he could drink them with the captain.

Jinsuke left the engineer's cabin, feeling rather like a teenager again. He was trembling, excited, nervous. He went back into the saloon and grabbed the flagon of *shochu,* intending to take it to his own cabin and drink just enough to relieve his tumbling, whirling anxieties about going back to Taiji after all this time, then lie, think, and, he hoped, drift off to sleep.

First, however, he made a quiet inspection of the ship, still incongruously gripping the flagon. One thing that frequently perturbed his crew was that although their captain wore leather boots, he could walk absolutely soundlessly, like a cat. He ended up at his own cabin door. Holding the flagon awkwardly between his knees he fumbled in his pocket for the key. Odd. It wasn't there. Reaching for the brass handle he found the door unlocked. Somebody was in his cabin, and had taken Jinsuke's big Colt out of its holster, examining it with peculiar interest. As Jinsuke swung the door open, the intruder turned to face him, holding the gun. It was Tetsuro.

Jinsuke gripped the flagon by the neck, his first instinct to fling it at him, then attack with his fist. But instead he became very cold, and full of contempt. He glared at the young officer, whose mouth and eyes were wide with alarm and shock, and sneered.

"Don't you know, mister," he said, "that to fire a revolver like that you must first cock it?"

He stepped into the cabin and put the liquor on the table. Then with his foot he slammed the door shut and leaned against it, this time slipping his hand into his pocket and closing on a little double-barreled derringer Lyall had given him, a twin of Lyall's own. Tetsuro had turned bright red. He hung his head and blurted out apologies in Japanese.

"Speak English!" Jinsuke shouted at him. It was a rule on the ship that even among themselves, on duty or not, they must converse in English. Only with a non-English-speaking passenger were they allowed to speak Japanese. As a consequence, they were all getting good at the language. Tetsuro went from red to sickly white, shaking his head, breath coming in little gasps.

"Jinsuke-sama," he said, "that is your name, is it not?"

Jinsuke now switched into his home dialect of Taiji, no longer trying to hide it.

"There was once a whaler called Jinsuke, but he died when a shark bit off his arm. Then a *bushi,* a man of your class, promised this man many things, sent him to Okinawa, as a spy. He got caught, jailed, beaten, tortured, insulted . . . by more *bushi.* All he wanted to do was to go whaling again. He got away and went to China. There he learned that some men, even when they have authority over other men, can be kind and brave. Then the man went to America. He sailed the seven seas. For a Japanese who has done this *bushi* laws demand a death penalty, correct? So there is no more Jinsuke. What I am is captain of this ship, your captain. Your *bushi* status means nothing to me. You are only a junior officer, caught sneaking into his captain's cabin. On an American or a British ship the captain would have you flogged. Now, are you trying to kill me, or shall I shoot you? Or shall I just arrest you and flog you before the rest of the crew in the morning?"

Jinsuke drew out the little pistol. It looked like a toy in his hand. He stretched his arm out straight, aiming at the young man's hand, and took one step forward, lessening the range to six feet. Tetsuro flinched involuntarily, then steadied himself, lips shut tight, as if prepared for the blast that would blot out his life. The Colt fell with a thud to the carpeted deck. With a snort of disgust Jinsuke lowered the gun.

"Go tell them," he said, again in Japanese. "That is why you came aboard, isn't it? To uncover the upstart peasant on a foreign ship? Go tell them!"

To Jinsuke's surprise, Tetsuro threw himself on his knees, touching his head on the deck at Jinsuke's feet.

"Captain, please forgive me, please forgive me, they told me I had to make sure, but they don't want to harm you, or to interfere, but they want to know. I would never let them harm you."

Jinsuke was momentarily caught between two worlds. As a ship's captain he was angry and unforgiving, but as a Japanese, to have a young man of a proud samurai family beg him like this . . . Jinsuke's mouth twitched in a half smile. He bent down and gently but firmly pulled the young man up, seeing that Tetsuro's face was wet with tears.

"Get to your feet, First Officer Miyabe," said Jinsuke sternly, reverting to Engiish, behind which shield he knew he could now control the situation.

"Captain, sir," said Tetsuro, sucking in breath and trying to calm himself. "Captain Sky, sir, I would die before betraying you. If you wish me to, I shall perform seppuku, tonight, now. I was directed to find out the truth by my uncle, but sir, he only wished to protect you."

Jinsuke sat down on the locker-bench that lined one bulkhead of his cabin. It was a trick he had learned from Tovey Jacks—if you needed to relieve tension, to delay or even stop a fight, you sat down.

"Your uncle? Just your uncle?"

"No sir, also Sakamoto Ryoma, of Tosa, and Katsu Rintaro, the captain of the *Kanrin Maru*. They said they needed to know just who you were, because a *ronin* called Matsudaira Sadayori might be seeking to kill you, because you killed some Choshu men when they attacked Mr. Fogerty's house. Matsudaira is believed to be a revolutionary, and we know he is very friendly with Choshu warriors now, and with Satsuma. My uncle told me he now serves the Satsuma clan, and you must know, being from Kii yourself originally, that this is very strange and dangeous. We know . . ."

"We, we, we! Who's we!" hissed Jinsuke, as he put both guns on the table beside the liquor flagon.

"Patriotic Japanese, like my uncle, and others, who want to see Japan strong and proud, and not torn to pieces by civil war!"

Jinsuke nodded. "Go on."

"We knew from the start that you were at Mr. Fogerty's house the day the attack came. We knew you were a fantastic shot with a pistol, a great marksman, perhaps the best in Japan, perhaps the best shot in the world, and we knew it had to be you because Mr. Lyall is a merchant, and he does not have the true Japanese steel in him . . ."

Jinsuke laughed. The young man's open admiration was almost comic. Then he growled.

"Listen, you, a man doesn't have to be Japanese to be brave. That old captain who is sailing with us is one of the bravest men I know. Mr. Lyall is just not trained to fight, I was." He pointed to the washbasin, with its small brass and wood pump.

"Wash your face. There's a towel on the rack. Then fetch two glasses from that cabinet."

Tetsuro bowed, then stiffened, shoulders back, and saluted. He washed his face and wiped it. Then he fetched the two glasses. Jinsuke unstopped the flagon and poured them each a glassful.

"*Kampai*," said Jinsuke.

"You forgive me then, sir?" asked Tetsuro timorously, just holding the glass. Jinsuke smiled. As Tetsuro swallowed the fiery white liquor he coughed and spluttered at its strength.

"You must learn to drink strong alcohol. If you can't you might have trouble in this profession," said Jinsuke. He filled his own glass again. "First, you raise the glass. Then you breathe in. You hold your breath, swallow, wait a little while, and breathe slowly out. Understand?" He poured him another drink.

"*Kampai.*"

Tetsuro did it right this time. "Thank you, Captain, you teach us so many valuable lessons."

"Now," said Jinsuke, "what made you so interested in my gun? The engraving? So you know now for sure I am Japanese, but I am also a legally qualified ship's captain, and soon to be an American citizen. So why?"

"It was Captain Fogerty, sir, before we sailed he came and drank with us aboard ship, talking with us, telling us exciting stories. He told of your great fight with the pirates, and in his wallet he had an old newspaper clipping. He boasted that it was he who gave you a pistol, and hired a soldier of great skill to teach you, but that you were now better than anybody."

Jinsuke sighed and nodded. Old man Fogerty had the gift of the gab, sure enough, and no doubt while drinking he just didn't stop to consider the implications of the characters in Japanese, and what they might mean in Japan. He reached out and picked the pistol off the table, taking it by the barrel and handing it to Tetsuro.

"What does it say on the left side, above the grip?"

" 'To Jim Sky, with gratitude for life, from Brian L. Fogerty.' "

"Isn't that enough?"

"Yes, sir." He handed the pistol back. Jinsuke looked at him.

"Over the years I've learned and read a lot. In ancient times we Japanese sailed the seas, we sailed the seas before the nation of America ever came about. I am sure that Matsudaira-san wanted Japan to have a strong navy, just like Sakamoto-san and Katsu-san. While I was in Okinawa I risked my life to send him letters. I sent him more letters from China. I described how the foreign ships and navies were. I sent him letters from America. I don't know how many of those letters reached him, and now I don't much care. What I saw, any foreigner could see and, if our country did not have such stupid laws, any Japanese could see. I betrayed nothing. I betrayed no man. I merely broke a stupid law. No, I am not afraid of Matsudaira-san wanting to kill me."

"But sir, he knows it was you who killed those Choshu men, and as I said, he has friends in Choshu. He was friends with Yoshida Shoin, a man of Choshu who was executed for plotting against the *bakufu*. Matsudaira-san returned the swords of the men you killed to the Choshu mansion. You wounded one man, didn't you? He escaped, but did the belly cutting, and Matsudaira-san was there, and Itoh-san of Satsuma acted as *kaishaku*. I have other information, sir. The passenger who will come aboard is the brother of Itoh, and it was the same Itoh who took you prisoner in Okinawa."

Jinsuke disguised his astonishment. How could they know all this and not arrest him?

"Ah," he said, "I am a simple man, knowing a few things about whales, ships, seals and the sea. What is all this about?"

"Well, sir, the clans of Choshu and Satsuma are the most powerful in the land. My uncle is friends with Sakamoto-san, but in many ways he does not agree with him, he cannot agree, although he believes that Sakamoto-san, like you, sir, and Katsu-san, are valuable men for the future of Japan."

"What does Sakamoto have to do with this?" asked Jinsuke impatiently.

"Well, sir, it is the ambition of Sakamoto-san to unite Satsuma and Choshu, and they would be very strong indeed. However, my uncle fears a revolution that would be too bloody, and he believes that the shogunate must renew itself, then enlist the powerful clans of all of Japan, and unite to serve the emperor. However, many samurai want to overthrow the shogunate and drive out all foreigners."

"I know that," said Jinsuke.

"We fear that Matsudaira-san may be one of them."

Jinsuke recalled how rabidly anti-foreign Sadayori used to be, and wondered if those long-ago opinions Jinsuke had imparted in his letters might have affected the conservative samurai.

"Well," he said with a sigh, and a glance toward the

401

pistols, "if anybody, even Matsudaira-san, comes to kill me, he'd better be quick and good, or I might kill him first."

Tetsuro's eyes glittered. "Captain Sky, sir, if anybody came to kill you, they must first kill me. Forgive me for what I have done. Permit me to serve you, this ship, because I know that way I will be serving Japan. I believe in you, sir."

Tetsuro rose, and with a smart salute, he left the cabin. Jinsuke stood slowly, pocketed the derringer, took off his jacket, and hung it on a hook. He slipped the Colt back into the holster hanging beside the jacket. His chest was a whole tangle of memories and emotions.

Chapter Thirty

Two young stokers, stripped to their loincloths, were shoveling coal. Seeing Jinsuke come, the engineer turned from a valve and wiped his brow with a red-spotted handkerchief.

"Pressure will be up in twenty minutes or so, skipper."

Jinsuke nodded toward the great black mountain they had shipped aboard with lighters at Nagasaki.

"How is the Japanese coal this time?"

"Excellent, sir, much better than the last lot. It's hard for bituminous coal, lights easy, and has a good clean ash. We should stick to this or the Formosa stuff, Captain. That last lot was too soft and smoky."

Jinsuke nodded, and left the hot, dusty boiler room to inspect the engine room, as always thrilled and even a little awed by the great, gleaming, moving parts—like dragons copulating, he thought to himself. The young Japanese second engineer was there, oil can in one hand, cotton waste in the other.

"See that those men ashore know that next time we'll get the same quality of coal. Make a note of it." He had to shout to make himself heard, but the young engineer got it, put down the oil can, and went to write in the engine room log. Jinsuke went back up on deck.

The trip to Shanghai had been largely uneventful, and the parting with old Captain Fogerty brief and sad. Now Jinsuke was eager to get away from Nagasaki, nervous about the secret load they had taken aboard in China.

A boat bumped alongside and their passenger came on deck. He was a samurai, in a kimono of fine brown watered silk and a baggy *hakama*. His short sword was tucked into his sash, but the great sword, an exceptionally long one, was gripped in one hand. Tetsuro came up behind him, holding a large cloth-bound bundle. The samurai was trying to hide his discomfort at the unfamiliar surroundings with a fierce scowl. Jinsuke touched the peak of his cap and the samurai returned the greeting with a very slight bow.

"First Officer," said Jinsuke in English, "take our passenger below to the saloon. Give him my respects and say I will join him later. Give him Japanese tea, or some lemonade, or wine or whiskey if he prefers. Please look to his comfort and then show him his cabin. I will take the ship out. You are excused watch."

"Aye, aye, sir!" With a salute, Tetsuro turned and interpreted for the samurai, asking him politely to follow him. A few minutes later Jinsuke noted with amusement that the samurai had slipped off his sandals, leaving them on deck before he went below. He called for the men to stand by to haul anchor, and noted with satisfaction how the crew jumped to his orders, and, as he glanced around the decks and hatches, that not a thing was poorly secured, not a line out of place. It made him confident that the Japanese made as fine seamen as any.

It was about a hundred miles down to Kagoshima, through some fine humpback waters, whaled by men out of the Goto Islands, who, long ago, had been taught the net whaling methods by Jinsuke's great-great-great-grandfather. Jinsuke stayed on the bridge until sunset, spotting whales and thousands of dolphins, many of which stayed and raced with the bow waves of the ship.

That evening they served rice, grilled fish, a Chinese dish of pork, green peppers, garlic and various other flavorings, as well as an extremely spicy dish of chicken livers, onions and red peppers, mixed with vegetables known only to the Chinese cook. As a side dish they had bread, small, hot, yeasty but light golden buns baked wonderfully by the cook, and they had butter, cheese and chutneys of various kinds as well.

The Satsuma samurai politely drank a glass of port, but expressed a preference for sake when he was told they had it. He ate a little of everything, but enjoyed the grilled fish and the hot dish best of all. He said very little during the meal, but was impeccably polite. To Jinsuke's relief, the chief engineer elected himself table master that evening, and with Tetsuro interpreting, told the samurai of his homeland, a mountain country too, full of fierce warriors, just like

404

Satsuma. He drew pictures in the sketchbook they always kept in the saloon to aid conversation, and boasted of great swords, of the short Scottish *hakama* of many colors, and he told of old heroes and battles against the English, and even sang a couple of songs. The samurai warmed to him as the sake took effect, and he tried some of the engineer's "water of life," his own preferred brand of real mountain liquor; this even induced the samurai to sing a song, while everybody clapped in time, a lovely sad song about a girl whose passing is mourned by the cicadas on the pine hill behind her village, of a girl who longs for a fine kimono and obi, a girl who will die by the passing of the summer festival.

Later, when the warrior expressed an interest in the engine, the Scot took him to the engine room, bellowing explanations in his thickly accented English, even though the Satsuma man knew no English whatsoever. They got along very well.

They were in Kagoshima by noon the next day, where the passenger disembarked and where they off-loaded forty long and narrow crates from the secret compartment in the hold. All went without incident, though they were very aware of the guns that menaced them from the shore. There were several new batteries, armed with modern guns supplied by the British. They were in Kagoshima for only two hours, during which Jinsuke stayed away from the bridge.

They did not have to lower their own boats to land the cargo, for a dozen boats sculled out from the town and surrounded the schooner. Tetsuro had orders to let no more than four Kagoshima men on the decks of the ship, and he executed those orders with curt but polite thoroughness.

Just as the passenger was ready to leave, and his bundle had been brought up, he bowed to Tetsuro, thanking him for the pleasant voyage, asking him to convey his regards to the captain and especially to the engineer, who had come up to see him off. They passed the bundle down to a waiting boat and he said a few last words.

"Please tell the captain that my older brother also wishes him well. He asked me to tell the captain that a man called Kinjo passed away a year ago. He died on his quilts, with his family around him. Of course, perhaps the captain has forgotten Kinjo, as he has forgotten his Japanese." He looked straight into Tetsuro's eyes, and the young officer smiled, seeing no threat there.

"Yes, sir, I will tell him. Can I take it that the captain would be welcome ashore?"

"In a few more years perhaps, yes."

The samurai went down the ladder to the waiting boat, and returned the wave of the engineer. As the long guard boat moved off, sculled by men in red loincloths, a broad pennant fluttering at its stern, he did not even look back.

As luck would have it, there was a strong wind blowing, not enough to call a storm, but enough to raise whitecaps. It took two and a half days to reach the cape of Shionomisaki, at the tip of the Kii Peninsula, and just around the bend from Taiji. The engineer came up on deck with a very solemn face.

"A wee bit of bother with the machinery, sir. I'd like to request we anchor in some nice calm bay for a while to get it fixed."

Thus it was that late in the afternoon of the third day out of Kagoshima, the schooner dropped anchor in Taiji bay, three hours before the whaling boats returned. The crew, all of them, even the engineer who was supposed to be busy, came up on deck to watch the colorful whaling fleet come in, chanting at their oars. Jinsuke was sad to note that the harpooners were not dancing in the bows; they had not taken a whale that day.

"So there are your folk, sir," said the engineer to Jinsuke.

"Aye, indeed they are," he answered, his heart full as he searched to the phoenix and the chrysanthemum boats, and the shapes of his father, of Iwadaiyu, and of his brothers, cousins, uncles, friends. As each boat came in, Jinsuke pointed them out, dropping the pretense of not speaking Japanese, switching back and forth between languages excitedly, explaining it all to Tetsuro and the engineer.

"Ah, but they're a brave sight, sir," said the Scot, "and if I may say so, I see why you're the man you are." He looked around at the craggy shores, the cliffs, the thickly forested hills, the little neat village of five thousand souls. "And it's the prettiest country I ever saw, sir, next to Scotland, that is."

Jinsuke grinned at him.

The town had changed a lot, and Jinsuke noted that all the buildings at Mukaijima were new. What disaster had befallen? Typhoon? Tsunami? Earthquake? Fire? It worried him.

As the whaleboats encircled the schooner, Jinsuke kept his cap over his eyes, but the Western dress, the beard and the circumstances of his return would probably have prevented anyone from recognizing him.

"First Officer, keep these people from boarding. See that whaleboat there? With the big man with gray hair?" He pointed to his father's boat. "Hail him and tell him we are in for the night, with engine trouble and rough seas. We will not bother the village."

Tetsuro took a hailing trumpet from the bridge, and went to call over to the phoenix boat, which glided up alongside. The whalers all looked with curiosity and excitement at the schooner with her two masts and tall funnel.

"Harpooner! Do not be alarmed. We are a merchant schooner, bound for Yokohama. We have engine trouble and would like to anchor here for this evening. Our rights to do so are covered by treaty, for we are of American registry. However, the crew is all Japanese, and we will not cause you any trouble. Please inform the authorities that I, First Officer Miyabe Tetsuro, will pay my respects and any harbor dues."

Tatsudaiyu waved. He understood. He cupped his hands to his mouth. "I understand. Who is your captain?"

Tetsuro shouted back through the trumpet again. "Captain Jim Sky, from America."

Tatsudaiyu's eyes ranged over the ship and Jinsuke gave a short wave, hardly able to control his emotions. How he wished he could just have his father come aboard to see the ship!

Tatsudaiyu spotted the figure with the peaked cap and the blue jacket, and he waved back. Tatsudaiyu then shouted orders and the boat skimmed toward the beach, where Kinemon, Kakuemon and many villagers were gathered in excitement. A few timid souls, alarmed at the sight of the ship, and remembering tales of foreign attacks, had fled to the paths behind the town. Back on the schooner, Jinsuke thanked his first officer.

"Please have a boat lowered and go to see those two samurai on the beach. Tell them we will be gone by dawn and will not bother them. No shore leave . . ." He gave a wry grin. "There's not much for the men to do here at night anyway." Taiji had no pleasure houses.

"Aye, aye, sir."

Meanwhile the chief engineer had gone below and now reemerged, wiping his hands. He smiled.

"I'll have it fixed in a couple of hours, sir. Just a spot of trouble with a valve."

Just in case, he had slipped a small metal coin into the valve, although this did not look big enough a place to have a Japanese official who knew anything about engines.

Kakuemon came back with Tetsuro in the ship's boat, bringing eggs and boiled, salted whale meat that looked much like bacon. Jinsuke acted the part and entertained Kakuemon in the saloon with coffee, biscuits and a little sherry, Tetsuro translating. Tetsuro asked Kakuemon many questions about the whaling, keeping attention away from his taciturn captain.

Evening came. The racing clouds turned orange and red, and Kakuemon stood to leave, bowing, thanking them, saying they would not have to pay any harbor dues, asking if there was anything they needed. He kept glancing at the captain, and Jinsuke grinned at him and gave a wink, a very American gesture. Kakuemon suspected nothing.

They had a quiet supper, drinking nothing, and Jinsuke seemed reluctant to move, remembering how he had been when he left Taiji, a pitied, one-armed peasant with simple, rough clothes and a meager bundle of possessions, resenting and perhaps half afraid of the weaponed samurai, loving a long-ago girl named Oyoshi, yet willing to do anything to regain the pride that came from whaling. And now? He was a well-dressed, well-booted, well-armed, well-respected captain, with more money than his father could dream of, master of a fine modern ship and a fine crew. Would going back have any meaning? Could he go back? Tetsuro sat in the saloon, toying with a half-filled cup of coffee.

"Captain, you wish to go ashore?" It was more of a statement than a question.

"Yes."

"Please let me take you. You can trust us, all of us. We will take you ashore, then return at midnight, and wait in front of that shrine facing the beach." He lowered his voice. "I have put a *yukata*, a sash and wooden *geta* in your room. If you knot a towel around your head they won't notice the hairstyle so much."

Jinsuke gave a wry grin. "And the beard?"

"After dark, I don't think there are many lights in the streets, are there, sir?"

Jinsuke shook his head. "No, it was always a quiet, sleepy place at night. The only true life here was probably out at sea, with the whales. I've missed it, though . . ." Saying such things, he realized right away, was much easier in English.

"We know, sir."

Jinsuke stood.

"It has been many long years since I saw my home. I won't forget. Thank you."

Half an hour later he was ashore, walking through the narrow streets and trying to find his way. The layout of the little town was largely unchanged, but more than half of the houses were new. A few people glanced at him, but when he called out greetings in the Taiji dialect, they just passed on by, wondering who he might be. His arm was inside the wide sleeve, and in the darkness they would not notice that the left arm was missing.

He found the turnings to his father's house, although it was different, rebuilt, and had a wide new woodshed at the side. He paused, wondering if he had found the right place, but from inside he heard his father's voice, and he put his ear to the crack in the rain shutters. Yes, it was Tatsudaiyu. With heart pounding, Jinsuke knocked on the door, slid it open and called out evening greetings. The shoji screen facing the front entrance slid open and Jinsuke was bathed in yellow-white light, whale light. At the sight of the tall, bearded figure, his mother's eyes widened with shock.

"Don't be afraid, Mother. It is I, your son, Jinsuke. I have returned."

Onui could not understand at first, could not catch the implications of what had been said, and her eyes stared at him, looking up at the stranger who spoke the Taiji dialect and looked down at her with sad, deep eyes.

"Mother, it is truly Jinsuke, your son. I have come back. Won't you let me in?"

"What is it? Who has come?" The screen was flung wider and Tatsudaiyu stood there, stripped to the waist, but with a wide cummerbund around his middle. He must have just come back from the bath, for his topknot was tied and he was still sweating. Jinsuke went down on his knees on the hard outer floor of earth, bowing deeply.

"Father, forgive me, it has been a long time."

The old harpooner was momentarily rooted to the spot, his big chest heaving.

"Jinsuke!"

"Yes." Jinsuke did not bring his head up for several seconds, but slowly, slowly he did, and found his father staring down at him.

"It is you is it?"

"Yes."

Tatsudaiyu turned from the door.

"Tell him to come in, Onui." He went to the far side of the room, by the little alcove with a simple arrangement of flowers, the hanging scroll of a lovely woman, and Tatsudaiyu's best harpoon and lance. Cross-legged, he sat on a thin cushion, glaring across the table on which were the remnants of the evening meal.

Jinsuke stood, brushed dust off his *yukata,* slipped off his sandals, and went to step up, but his mother threw her arms around his legs, weeping and sobbing, and Jinsuke, his own eyes now wet, stroked her hair. Looking across at his father he felt pride in him, sitting there, cross-legged, arms folded, back straight, face stern. Small and simple though the house was, Tatsudaiyu looked like an ancient sea king. Jinsuke gently took away his mother's arms and went into the room where once again he knelt and bowed formally to his father.

"Father, it has been too long . . ."

"You came with that ship?" he demanded.

"Yes."

"Where have you been hiding all these years? Why did you hide on the ship? Didn't you see me? It was me they shouted to."

Not knowing what to do, and quite distracted, Onui bustled in the kitchen, wondering if Jinsuke needed a meal, but no, tea first, and oh, there were dirty plates on the table, tea . . . She was silently crying, but biting her lip, trying to hide her emotion now.

"I was not hiding on that ship, Father. I waved to you, and you waved back to me. You did not recognize me, that is all."

"No, you were not there. I did not see you." There are so many lines under and around his eyes, thought Jinsuke, and his skin is the skin of an old man, and his hair, it is so gray!

"Father, you saw me. That is my ship. I am the captain. Father, my story is long, and I have spent many years in foreign lands, in China, in America, in the seas around South America, in the hot islands of the far south, and in the cold and icy seas of the north."

His father had no welcome in his eyes. They now smoldered with anger. Jinsuke slipped the loose *yukata* off his shoulders and pointed to the stub of his left arm.

"Was I not born to be a harpooner? But here in Taiji, you know that after this happened, your ways forbid that I could be what I was born to be. You of all men should see that I could not live with that." The massive muscles of Jinsuke's

410

right arm, and of his shoulder and chest, corded and flexed as he raised his arm, as if holding a harpoon. "But I, Jinsuke, first son of Tatsudaiyu, have killed more whales with this one arm than most of the harpooners in this town. With this one arm I have killed many whales by my own irons alone! I harpooned whales. I killed whales, in the seven seas of the world! That is why I went, that is why I broke the laws, so that I could be a whaler! Now I am back, and I needed to gaze upon your face. And I have not returned in disgrace or poverty, but as captain of a fine ship. So why must you look at me like that? Have you no welcome in your heart?"

Tatsudaiyu stared from great spans of time and alien ways, from the pain, the worry, the hardships he and his family had known since this man left. He took in now the lines that marked his son's handsome face, saw the scar under one eye, the thick black beard like a hairy northern Ainu, and the foreign hairstyle. He looked again at the stump of the left arm, and winced inwardly at the memory of that awful day.

Tatsudaiyu grunted. "Whales? You say you have taken whales?"

"Yes, Father! Many whales! Right whales, perfume whales, humpbacks and grays, and other sea creatures too—huge tusked sea horses from the north, hundreds and hundreds of seals, and sea otters whose fur is priceless. I was born to do so, and if our own stupid laws would not let me, then I had to break them. I am a whaler, and your son. Father, look at me!"

With a low cry in his throat, the proud old man went on his knees across the mats and hugged his son to his shoulder, sobbing, welcoming him back, and Onui came to them both and tried to enfold her two men in her now thin arms. They wept together for all the years together they had lost.

"We must call Shusuke, and his wife," she said, wiping her eyes on her sleeve.

"Oh yes," said Jinsuke, "and Saburo too!"

Onui and Tatsudaiyu exchanged glances, then Tatsudaiyu's eyes flickered.

"Yes, call them, but do not make a fuss. We must not let the neighbors know. Call Shusuke and his wife, and call Saburo . . . and Oyoshi."

Jinsuke started inside, but hid it well. His mother stood and went out, slipping her feet into sandals at the door. She was excited, but knew she must not run or show it, and she had understood Tatsudaiyu's signal. She had to give him time to tell Jinsuke about Saburo and Oyoshi.

"Your brother Saburo is married now. He married soon after you left."

An icy blackness gripped Jinsuke's heart.

"Oh? I forget, though—he is what, twenty-nine now? Any children?"

"One son," said Tatsudaiyu, "eleven years old."

That was the number of years that Jinsuke had been away. No, it wasn't possible, Saburo wasn't courting then. Tatsudaiyu looked very grave.

"Listen to me. You have been away for a long time. We did not know where you were. You caused your mother, your family and others much grief. We can forget now that it is over, but listen and think." His voice broke slightly, then with a deep breath, it regained power. "Saburo is married to Oyoshi. It is a good marriage. They have one son, their only son."

Rage and jealousy flared up from the icy blackness. "The little beast! I'll kill him! Oyoshi is my . . ."

His father's heavy hand lashed out and slammed so hard across his face that Jinsuke was knocked to one side.

"Never you dare talk of your brother like that! Beast, you say? Who was the beast? Saburo was obedient, staying here to help all of us through many, many troubles." Tatsudaiyu breathed hard, pain racking the old injuries to his lower ribs. "Oyoshi's father insisted that Saburo be adopted into the Takigawa family and marry Oyoshi. Saburo didn't want to. We made him. Otherwise Oyoshi would have leaped from a cliff, and there would have been unbearable dishonor for both families. Of all the men I have known, Saburo is the most gentle of spirit. Yet Saburo is far stronger than you, or me, stronger than all of us. Are you stupid? I told you they have one son, eleven years old. Think what that has meant to all of us."

Jinsuke went white. He hid his face in his hand. His father went on.

"Takigawa was going to kill her, although she probably would have done it herself. But it was Saburo who gave us all back our face, even though he has had no children with her. You, Jinsuke, are welcome back in my house, but don't you dare rake up old troubles or cause new ones, or, big and strong as you are, I'll kill you myself. Do you hear me?"

Jinsuke understood, and bowed. From his sleeve, he pulled

a fat leather purse. The purse held enough to keep a whaler's family in Taiji for four years.

"Father, take this. I was going to give it to you, but take it before they come, and use it as you see fit. I'll send more, much more."

Tatsudaiyu stared with distaste for a second at the purse on the mat before him and would have refused it.

"Father, had I sent money or letters before, the authorities would have punished our family, for they couldn't reach me. I'm sorry, Father, but please, take it."

Tatsudaiyu tucked the gold into his cummerbund. "We will never mention this thing ever, ever again. Understand?"

Jinsuke almost choked. Had he really expected her to wait? But for her to marry Saburo . . . He slammed an iron gate in his mind. So Oyoshi was his brother's wife. Sayonara. He hung his head.

His father looked at him. "So you didn't marry?"

Jinsuke was silent; then he spoke. "Father, I'll go, before they come. I can't face them now."

Tatsudaiyu forced a laugh. "If you have faced those sea horse things and lived with barbarians you can face anything. Come on now, be what an older brother should be. Forget Oyoshi as she was, and see her as she is. They will be overjoyed to see you, even if you did have to come sneaking back at night."

Jinsuke forced a smile, looking up. "That big two-masted ship didn't exactly sneak in, did it? I thought it caused a great furor."

"Half the idiots here thought the black ships were coming," laughed Tatsudaiyu. "Old Kurasachi's grandma was so scared she hid under a miso tub. Like as not, she's still there!"

The two of them, father and son, laughed together as they had not laughed for many years. Then, until the rest of the family gathered, Jinsuke and his father talked of whaling, and Jinsuke related how one of the foreign whalers they had chanced upon out at sea, all those years before, had been the very man who had taken him to America. He told stories of plentiful whales, and Tatsudaiyu said he wished it was still so in Taiji, for now whales were so scarce. Yet even as his father listened to accounts of his adventures, Jinsuke realized that Tatsudaiyu felt uncomfortable. This talk was outside of normal things, it was of distant seas, of whales killed by a single boat, of strange foreign lands and customs. Tatsudaiyu had never even been to Edo. Jinsuke grew quiet.

Maybe it was not right to talk so enthusiastically about such things. There was a lull. Neither spoke.

"Ah, but things are not easy nowadays," said Tatsudaiyu. "Never has the price of rice or vegetables been so high; at this house, if we can't grow them ourselves, we don't buy them. Whales too, very scarce, very scarce."

He lapsed into silence again.

Both of them were glad when Shusuke and his wife came. They babbled excitedly at how Jinsuke had changed, then soon went on about their three children, soon to be four, and about all of Jinsuke's old friends who had married, and of how many offspring they all had. All of this talk pricked at Jinsuke, although they were not aware of it.

"Well, Mother says you've been in foreign countries?"

"Yes. China, America, Alaska, and many other places, north and south. That's my ship in the harbor. She's not a whaler, but we'll go with her to hunt fur seals and sea otters again."

"Oh, let me have a ride in your ship one day. It has a steam engine, doesn't it?"

Jinsuke smiled as Shusuke continued.

"They are having a bigger steamship built for the castle at Wakayama, much bigger than yours, Kakuemon-sama told me himself. It'll have a steam engine and big cannon. Does your ship have cannon?"

"Yes, small ones, but in Japanese waters they are covered and lashed. My crew is all Japanese, except for the engineer and the cook. The engineer is from Scotland, the cook from China."

Shusuke did not have any idea where Scotland was, and he did not care, he just went on about other steamships he had heard about or seen out at sea, while Shusuke's plump little wife began chattering to Onui about a minor town dispute.

I embarrass them, thought Jinsuke. They might be happy to see me again, but I embarrass them, there is nothing really we can talk about except what happens here.

"Excuse us, good evening." It was Saburo's voice. Jinsuke moved back farther into the room. Saburo entered and bowed, very formally. How old he had grown. Jinsuke returned the bow, keeping his eyes down, mouthing formalities. They were like strangers. When Jinsuke looked up, Oyoshi was beside Saburo, and for a brief second their eyes met. She was changed too, obviously more mature, just a little fatter, but even more attractive despite the fact that the

414

girlish bloom was almost all gone. There were slight circles under her eyes, and her eyes were dark, dark brown, and cold.

"Older brother Jinsuke, you came by that foreign ship?" she asked, her voice unnaturally high and sweet, the way women's voices get when they want to hide malice.

"Yes."

"It is a beautiful ship," said Saburo. He did not say that, not knowing who was aboard it, he had already spent an hour that evening drawing sketches of it.

"Jinsuke is the captain, and they have sailed all the way from Nagasaki, and they are on the way to Yokohama, which is near Edo," said Tatsudaiyu, almost pompously. "And your brother has been whaling, to America and places far away."

His face wooden, Jinsuke looked across the room to his youngest brother.

"I have broken the law in leaving the country, but I wanted to whale. Now I live in Yokohama, mostly aboard my ship. The authorities think I'm American. Perhaps, if they knew the truth, they would execute me, so I have to stay away from Taiji, for all our sakes."

Onui put her hands to her mouth in horror at the idea, but Oyoshi gazed at him steadily, her eyes boring into him, and Jinsuke tried to fathom what was in that look. Anger? Resentment? Certainly he saw none of the soft light he had remembered and dreamed about.

"Do you speak English now, older brother?" said Oyoshi.

"If you live there, or with them on a ship, you learn. Yes, I speak, but I have an accent."

"That is wonderful, you could even be a teacher," said Saburo.

Jinsuke laughed at the thought, but inside he was tight. He wanted to ask about the boy—his son—but he subdued it, for such a question could only bring pain. A great pit seemed to loom before him, dark and lonely.

"You look like a foreigner," said Oyoshi, and there was no doubt about the spite behind her words. He bridled.

"In that case, I am. I'm American, a Japanese-American. After all, I can't be Japanese, can I, they would kill me."

"I don't like foreigners," said Oyoshi. "They have crude manners and ways, and have caused a lot of trouble to our country. Why did you have to go to barbarian lands?"

Jinsuke's old temper flared, but he bit back the words. Stupid peasant wench, what do you know? You couldn't

415

understand if it was explained to you. He glared his captain's glare at her then saw the distress in Saburo's face. He would not let her get to him, it was all over, forever.

"Yoshi!" Onui's voice cut like a knife. "You are being rude! How can you speak like that to your older brother!" Oyoshi bowed her head, apologizing. She got up and went into the kitchen.

"Older brother," said Saburo, "I . . . we missed you. I never forgot your face, and often wished you home." He smiled wistfully. "The farthest I've been is to Shingu. It would be marvelous to see all the things you have seen."

"I never forgot you either, Saburo." Looking at him Jinsuke felt ashamed—how could he think of hurting such a gentle man. Only Saburo could say something like that and mean it, despite what had happened. He has suffered, thought Jinsuke. Around Oyoshi's eyes Jinsuke had seen those lines of frustration, impatience, even spite, but the lines in Saburo's face were deeper. Images from his own life flowed and eddied in his mind. Jinsuke had certainly seen and done much, and he had suffered too, but he had always had dreams to cling to, to chase after, to hope for. I really did love her, thought Jinsuke, but never again would he think it, and if the old dreams edged into his fantasies again, he would shove them out.

Oyoshi came in with fresh tea and a side dish of sliced pickled radishes. They all sipped.

"Older brother Jinsuke," said Oyoshi in that high, oversweet voice again, "I suppose you are married, aren't you?" Jinsuke looked at her, then turned his face away.

"Oh dear, and I, his mother, forgot to ask that," said Onui, releasing tension in the air again. "Well, Jinsuke, have you a wife?"

"No. I didn't have time. I sailed the seas and never bothered."

"What?" said Shusuke, who despite the active life he led, was fond of home life and home cooking, even becoming a little paunchy. "Such a bad thing that Saburo and I have done, then, to marry before our older brother! But with me, it's too late to undo it." He patted his wife's stomach and she slapped his hand.

"I'm not married," said Jinsuke, looking straight at Saburo, ~~whose~~ eyes had not left his face, "I'm not married, but I ~~ ~~ ~~he.~~"

"~~ ~~e?" demanded Tatsudaiyu. "Does she come ~~ ~~?"

416

"She comes from the best family I know, after this one. She is a foreigner, but speaks Japanese quite well, and can write Chinese characters really well. She is half Chinese, half European, and her father is a great captain, and her brother a very rich man too. Her brother is my close friend."

Jinsuke should have predicted the reaction. They all stopped talking except for Tatsudaiyu, who waved one hand back and forth in front of his own face in a gesture of scornful dismissal.

"No good, no good, foreign women are no good."

Most of the others nodded in agreement and murmured, while Jinsuke's eyes narrowed. He saw that Saburo was still looking at him, not joining in the dissection of his life and future happiness. Jinsuke sat and listened to them begin to dismiss his Susan out of hand, and thought that none of them could even imagine how beautiful, and fine, and intelligent Susan Fogerty truly was. They talked of her as if she were a piece of three-day-old fish left over in the market. Saburo cut in.

"She must be beautiful. In the history of Taiji there are stories of how in the old days the Kumano men raided ships and took many women, some Chinese. Mixing the blood is what made Taiji have more beautiful women than most other places. And I think you are all being narrow in your hearts. Our older brother has seen many lands and many women, so if he chooses her, she must be special. Brother, congratulations."

Jinsuke's natural response was to say no, she isn't so beautiful, but then he realized that he had never even hinted to Susan that she should marry him, and he would be presuming much to be falsely modest about her at this stage. He smiled back at Saburo.

"Yes, she is beautiful, like my sister-in-law Oyoshi. One day you will meet her. And you must sail on my ship, come to Yokohama with me, bring your little boy to see a steam engine working."

Saburo went on smiling, and put his head down, pretending to reach for a pickle, but there was a moistness in his eyes. The two brothers had healed an eleven-year-old wound in a few sentences, and now all was well between them.

"I would like very much to sail on your ship," said Saburo, but both knew it was unlikely he would ever set foot on the schooner.

Tatsudaiyu waved his hand in front of his nose again. "Foreign women? Tcha! No good, no good!" There was

417

scorn in his voice, although he had never even seen a foreign woman. "Come back to Taiji, and we'll find a good woman for you. Taiji women are the best."

"Taiji women and Koza men," said Shusuke, quoting a popular saying.

But they know I can't come back, thought Jinsuke, it's just their way of trying to reject what has passed, what has become of me. I am now unlike anyone Father has ever known, and it troubles him. Tatsudaiyu went on with the annoying gesture, waving his hand in front of his nose, no good, no good. Jinsuke inclined his head slightly.

"I'll think about what you say, Father."

Tatsudaiyu grunted.

"I must go back to my ship," said Jinsuke. "I dare not get caught here, and you know how Taiji folk talk. When the laws change, then I will return properly." He paused. "They are stupid, narrow laws. This country is going to be . . ." He stopped himself from using one of Tetsuro's pet phrases, "a mighty seafaring nation." He saw his father's look and said nothing. Tatsudaiyu's lips were pursed in disapproval of any criticism of Japan.

Jinsuke turned to Shusuke. "Bring a boat out to my ship before we leave at dawn. I have a gift for you all, a modern thing that American whalers use. I'd like to show you how to use it myself, but I can't, so I'll write instructions. I must go now."

He bowed deeply to everybody, then stood. As Onui got to her feet, he hugged her. She began to cry again.

"Mother, don't weep. I'll come back."

"Please don't be sad, Mother," said Saburo. "Older brother Jinsuke is now the captain of a fine ship that can travel from any port in the world. He can come back when he likes, you'll see."

Onui sobbed. "I'll come to the beach in the morning and I'll wave. Jinsuke, you'll wave back to me, won't you?" She burst into loud sobs again.

"He's captain," said Tatsudaiyu gruffly, "so he'll be busy."

"Mother, of course I'll wave, I promise."

"Let me come with you, down to the boat," said Onui.

"No, it's too late for women to be out on the streets, I'll see him off." Tatsudaiyu looked around at them all, the old command in his voice. "You others stay here. You can go to the beach in the morning."

As they walked through the narrow streets down the hill

418

toward the bay and the Asuka shrine, Jinsuke once again asked his father to forgive him for leaving. Tatsudaiyu sighed.

"I know it wasn't your fault. That samurai from Wakayama was behind it, I know. But you did become a harpooner again, in the only way you could, and in that I'm proud of you." They walked on for a while, voices low, strolling, then Tatsudaiyu added, "but I want you to think again about marrying a foreigner."

At the beach, a ship's boat and three men were waiting. One of them approached in the darkness. It was Tetsuro, and he had donned his traditional samurai garb and two swords.

"*Sencho?*" he called softly, using the Japanese word for *captain*.

"This is my First Officer, Miyabe Tetsuro," said Jinsuke, feeling proud of the young man, and understanding why he had changed out of his Western-style ship's uniform. Because of the two swords and the man's dress, as well as the distinguished name of Miyabe, the name of an old Tottori family, together with the given name of Tetsuro, Tatsudaiyu understood not only that this was a young man of *bushi* status, but that he was of a very decent, honorable family. Tatsudaiyu bowed.

"This is my father, Tatsudaiyu, senior harpooner of Taiji," said Jinsuke. Tetsuro bowed very deeply.

"We are honored to serve under your son, our captain, sir."

It came now all of a sudden as a shock to Tatsudaiyu to realize what his son had achieved, to have a young samurai talk like that, to bow so low to an old harpooner, and say words like "serve under" when referring to his son. He could only murmur formalities in reply. Jinsuke bowed now to his father.

"Take care, Father. Excuse me, but we must go."

So they bid farewell, stiffly, for being that way was the only defense they had to contain the emotion they felt. Jinsuke helped push the boat out, then sat in the stern while the two crewmen got ready to row. Just then Saburo came running toward them. He splashed out into the water, up to his middle, and grabbed the gunwale with one hand, thrusting something at his brother with the other.

"Older brother, here, take this, something to remember us by."

Jinsuke took it, tucked it under the stump of his left arm,

and gripped Saburo's hand on the gunwale. "Saburo, thank you, take care of yourself, and the boy."

"It's something I did, it's not very good," said Saburo, and just then the boat slipped out into deeper water. Saburo sank, rose, spluttered, and swam to the shore, and stood there, bowing beside the grave old man.

"Sir?" asked Tetsuro, in English.

"To the ship," said the captain, and the two crewmen began to row. Bands of comfortable yellow lights were cast on the water from the *Big Sky*'s portholes. Leaving the crewmen to secure the boat, Tetsuro followed Jinsuke up the ladder.

"Let's go into the saloon and have cocoa, there's a chill in the air."

"Your brother, sir, will he not catch cold?"

"He's a Taiji man," said Jinsuke, gripping the thing Saburo had given him. "Come on, cocoa, with a dash of rum." One of the men who had rowed, who turned out to be the third officer, an amiable lad of twenty, with shoulders like a bull and a face round as a moon, came onto the deck just then.

"Oh, good, very good, Captain Sky, sir. I'm like cocoa."

"No," said Jinsuke, with a huge grin, "not 'I'm like cocoa' but 'I like cocoa.'" He paused. "Anyway, if I know you, Third Officer, it's not the cocoa you like, but the rum."

Their laughter rang out over the still water. It sounded so young, so easy and free, that Tatsudaiyu glanced at the shivering Saburo and nodded sadly to himself. Perhaps all things turned out the way the gods wanted them to.

Later, before turning in, Jinsuke unwrapped Saburo's gift. It was a beautiful scroll of the phoenix boat, Tatsudaiyu in the bow, closing upon a right whale, with Tatsudaiyu ready to throw, his second holding the line. Off to the right was a smaller painting of the chrysanthemum boat, unmistakably Iwadaiyu in the bow, urging his men on.

"I used to be one of them," reflected Jinsuke, proud and sad at the thought. He gazed at it for a while. Never before had he seen anything about the old ways of whaling done in such fine and vivid detail. He peered down into the righthand corner, trying to make out the highly stylized characters of the square red seal, seeing parts of Saburo's name there, then reading the three lines of black writing above the red seal.

Does the Brave Fish die
For the wealth of seven villages,
Or for the song of He who Stands?

Jinsuke noted the pun on their father's name, which meant "upright," looked a little longer, marveling at Saburo's skill, and remembering how Saburo had always loved to spend time with old man Takigawa and play with paints. It was, after all, better this way. He rolled up the scroll and put it on the top shelf above his desk.

The men were assembling at Mukaijima, and carrying the whale boats down to the water. Out beyond the headland dawn was a faint orange-yellow line. The *Big Sky*'s funnel belched black smoke, then gray. The anchor was winched aboard. Jinsuke left the wheelhouse and stood outside on the bridge wing, facing the shore. Shusuke, standing up in the stern of a little boat, sculled back toward Mukaijima and the whaling base, carrying a single long box with him. It was Jinsuke's gift to Taiji.

Jinsuke took off his blue peaked cap and waved it with large, stiff-armed movements, and Tetsuro, who had taken the wheel, reached up and jerked once, twice, three times on the lanyard. If anybody was still sleeping in Taiji—doubtful in a whaling village—they would have been awakened now by the deep boom of the steam whistle, echoing in the valleys and cliffs. A grand sound, thought Jinsuke, still waving. He could see them all there, Mother, Father, Shusuke, Saburo, Shusuke's wife, a gaggle of children—was one of them his son?—and yes, even Oyoshi. Everybody else in Taiji was waving too, although they thought they were just seeing off a ship that had chanced to visit. Nobody but the direct family of Tatsudaiyu would ever know who was aboard.

"Hard a'starb'd," called Jinsuke.

Tetsuro repeated the order aloud and swung the brass-bound wooden spokes. The ship nosed confidently out, for they had the best pilot possible in their captain.

"First Officer, go get breakfast, I'll take her out." Jinsuke took the helm, and through hand, arm, shoulder, he felt something flow—the spirit of his ship? He leaned forward and signaled on the telegraph for full speed. The pulse of the engine picked up, as if it were awakening to the swelling dawn, and wake frothed behind the ship. Jinsuke squinted as the golden edge of the sun began to slide up out of the sea, his eyes scanning right to the lookout on the clifftop, then to Fudejima, the funny little hat-shaped island below it. It used to remind him of New Year's rice cakes, a small one perched on top of a bigger one. How many times had he passed this point? Now he looked around at his immaculate wheelhouse with pride, and regretted nothing.

The figures on the beach diminished in the distance, and then were lost from view as he turned into the Enshu Nada. He could no longer see Taiji. It was gone behind the forested slopes of Mukaijima. They churned past fishing boats and a broad-sailed junk. There was a favorable wind. When the first officer came back up from breakfast, they'd hoisted all sails. Tetsuro brought Jinsuke a mug of steaming black coffee and put it where he could reach it.

"We'll be back in Yokohama in no time, sir."

Jinsuke gave him the heading, stepped back, and reached for his coffee.

"That we will," he said, smiling.

The box was addressed to Tatsudaiyu. He did not try to open it until his boat came back that evening, and the whaling carpenters and the blacksmith had trouble in figuring how to undo the brass screws. Inside, on top of the straw packing, were several pages of drawings and descriptions. The other men crowded around. Out of the box came twenty long brass tubes with sharply pointed ends. Then came a most curious device—a thick oak shaft, to which was affixed something that looked like a short gun, also of brass. There were also a short iron harpoon with a toggle head, a length of good line, a cask of black powder, a powder measure and various small tools.

"Ji . . ." Shusuke stopped himself in time. "Um . . . that captain on the ship said that with this thing a single thrust could kill a whale. He called it a 'bomb lance gun' and claimed that if a man got good with it he could kill and secure a whale with just one iron. See? When the harpoon goes in, that rod touches the whale and fires the gun. The pointy bomb goes deep into the whale and kills it."

Tatsudaiyu hefted the bomb lance, and passed it to the others. He glanced at the instructions, written in his son's hand.

"One man, with one iron? Kill a whale? That's a story bigger than the biggest whale I've seen. Here, let me have a look." Iwadaiyu hefted the thing. "Terrible balance. It's top-heavy. If you tried to hurl it, it would topple end over end."

Shusuke reached out and took it from him. "No, look, you don't hold it that way, you get up close and hurl downward, like this. But you've got to get right up on the whale." Shusuke faked a throw.

"That's not the proper way to hold a harpoon!" jeered another man.

Kakuemon pushed his way through the crowd. "What is going on? What's this?"

Tatsudaiyu held out the sheets of instructions and pointed at the heading.

"Bombu ransu ju," read Kakuemon. The first two words were in *katakana,* and the third was the character for *gun.*

"Gun?" His eyebrows raised. "He gave you a gun? Why? Here, now let me see!"

They handed it to him. Kakuemon turned it over and laid it back in the box, then examined the other things, looking with alarm at the pointed bomb cases.

"Those are bombs," said Shusuke, "they go into the gun there, and when it's thrust and fired, the bomb shoots right inside the whale and kills it, quickly."

Kakuemon made a long, deep, officious sound in his throat. "Erhummmmmm. It appears most dangerous to me." He looked sharply at Tatsudaiyu. "Why did that foreign ship give you this?"

"There were mostly Japanese aboard," said Tatsudaiyu with dignity, "and they heard that I was the chief harpooner. They gave us this present because we let them anchor last night. The captain was a whaler himself, and has sailed all over the world, hunting whales. I suppose he felt he was like one of us, and wanted to give us something that had to do with whaling. I think it must have cost a great deal of money too. It was kind and thoughtful of him."

Kakuemon pursed his lips and slipped his hands into the sleeves of his kimono. "Yes indeed, it might have been kindness, but it is most irregular. For one thing, I don't think it is legal for a fisherman to own a gun device of any kind, or bombs."

"But of course, I wouldn't accept it for myself," said Tatsudaiyu. "It was meant as a gift for the whole operation. I'm sure that is what the captain meant, but he knew only my name, because I am chief harpooner." He paused. "In foreign countries the harpooners are more important than in Japan, I suppose." The other men, not missing the sarcasm, laughed, and Kakuemon realized that he was being a bit pompous and laughed with them.

"Very good," he said, "seal it up so nothing gets lost or damaged, then bring it over to the office. Let me study these notes and talk it over with Kinemon-sama and the village headman. Indeed, it was a kind gesture on the part of the captain. Whalers are better at understanding other whalers, I suppose, and it's good he recognized how kind we were to let him anchor. In the old days we would have driven him away. Times have changed."

Once back in the box, the bomb lance was left there. Kakuemon and Kinemon studied the instructions and decided it was better to forget about it. Things in Taiji were done differently, and use of such a device would bring only criticism and trouble. Eventually the box was moved out of the office and stored somewhere in the warehouse.

Many, many years passed before it was brought out again.

Chapter Thirty-One

Sadayori boarded one of the "thirty-*koku*" river boats at Hirakata, the halfway station between Osaka and Kyoto. These long boats, which could carry as many as thirty bales of rice, in addition to passengers, were worked by two men, one fore, one aft, both wielding long, heavy poles. Passengers were left alone in a small roofed teahouse cabin amidships. The cabin had tatami mats for comfort, and sliding screen windows that could offer either privacy or a view of the river, the many waterbirds, the great fields of edible lotus, and the many other boats that plied this busy river highway that connected the Inland Sea and the ancient imperial capital of Kyoto.

He was feeling a little hung over. The night before he had gone out with friends, many of whom he had not seen for a few years. They were rowdy and boisterous, boasting of a new Japan they would build from the ashes of the *bakufu's* downfall, although some were worried about the government's dangerous new paramilitary police force, the Shinsen Gumi, whose members were often violent men, recruited from the ranks of *ronin*. The Shinsen Gumi had killed and arrested many, and their spies were everywhere. Sadayori had absorbed all this information, and he left the party before they went off roistering to the many brothels in Hirakata, choosing to sleep alone in a small inn close to the landing place.

He left on the boat the next morning, nursing his bad head, letting sunlight off the water warm his face, listening to the gurgle of the river against the hull, and the grunting chants of the boatmen as they poled the heavy craft up against the current. It was a slow, relaxing trip.

They docked at a place called Fushimi, on the outskirts of Kyoto, where Sadayori disembarked. He made his way up the broad stone steps between racks of fine-meshed fishing nets, laid out to dry and mend. Here at Fushimi a wide canal had been dug to connect three rivers, the Uji, the Kizu and the broad Yodo. Boats plied from Fushimi to Osaka and the Inland Sea on the Yodo, and all the way to Nara on the Kizu River.

It was a place of water, famous not only for travelers, but also for the water's purity. Even the canal water was so clean you could drink it. Mallards, spotbills and little teal paddled and dabbled in peace. Snowy white egrets stood by the shallows and black and white wagtails bobbed along the shore. Around here they caught many kinds of small fish, as well as the tasty long-armed freshwater prawns, and the tiny clams that were so good in miso soup.

Big, old weeping willows lined the canal path, behind which stood the high white ramparts of the great sake breweries. The sweet fragrance of fermenting rice filled the air. Sadayori normally relished the smell, but today his stomach turned. He always despised himself for overdrinking, but when he got together with the Satsuma warriors or the wild, free-roving *ronin*, it always seemed to happen.

Today he would walk to Kyoto from Fushimi, but first he had to meet a certain young samurai from Tosa who was staying at the inn facing the wharf. The Teradaya had a huge red lantern hanging outside, almost as big as a man. It was a friendly place, relatively new, and popular with travelers. Its owner was a jolly, bustling woman called Otosei, and she was helped by her adopted son, Issukei. She had taken the lad in as a waif, child of an impoverished and anonymous samurai. She saw to his education and taught him the manners and ways of the samurai class.

Issukei greeted Sadayori at the door, bowing low, delighted to meet this famous swordsman at last. He showed him into the inn, then upstairs to the room where Sakamoto Ryoma was waiting, accompanied by a Choshu man whom Sadayori had heard of but not met; he was an accomplished swordsman too, by the name of Miyoshi Shinzo.

A pretty little girl brought them tea. Sadayori sat kneeling quietly on the mats, waiting for Ryoma to speak. Ryoma was very friendly with the huge barrel of a commander, one of the most powerful leaders in the Satsuma army, a man called Saigo, cousin to a fellow Sadayori himself had met before. Ryoma was a very active fellow, and Sadayori knew that he was seeking to develop a strong naval force in Japan, which was at least one topic on which they could agree.

426

Ryoma was also trying to get Satsuma and Choshu to forget old rivalries and make a pact. However, Lord Shimazu of Satsuma still preferred to cooperate with the *bakufu*, and he held his eager young revolutionaries in check. Choshu, on the other hand, had been taken over by the radicals, who were rabidly anti-*bakufu*.

The new *bakufu* paramilitary police force was brought into existence in answer to ultra-extremist terrorists who had been killing opponents all over Japan. A group called Tenchu, or "Heavenly Revenge," was a special target of the Shinsen Gumi. Choshu extremists were very prominent in that group, which, among other things, had been responsible for the attack on the Fogerty house.

But both sides killed. In the most recent attack by the Shinsen Gumi, right in Kyoto, seven radicals from Choshu and Tosa had been cut down at a meeting, while four had been wounded, and twenty-three taken prisoner. Only two, one of them severely injured, had made their escape, aided by the geisha mistress of one of them. In that murderous attack, the samurai had even cut down a woman, the owner of the inn where the radicals were meeting.

Ryoma looked steadily at the older man, as if trying to gauge what he was thinking.

"Matsudaira-san, we need you to speak for us too. You are friends with Itoh-san, and he's one of the key men in Satsuma. He can get to see anybody he wants to, and he knows everything that is going on. Forgive me for saying it, but you were originally an outsider, and I believe your understanding of the value of an alliance between Satsuma and Choshu is clearer than anybody's. Also, you are greatly respected in Choshu." He smiled at his friend. "They have long memories, and you were, were you not, a good friend of Yoshida sensei? Will you speak for us? Work with us to unite Satsuma and Choshu?"

"I have already discussed this with Itoh-san. He knows that such a pact would be a powerful one. In fact, he is already at the Satsuma residence in Kyoto, so why don't you speak to him directly? I am a warrior, and have little access to Lord Shimazu's ear. However, you are aware that since the marriage between Shogun Iemochi and Princess Kazuno-miya, there has been a stronger movement to support the *bakufu*. It was inevitable."

Opposition to that arranged marriage had been bitter. One fanatic had killed one of the courtiers most active in bringing the imperial family and the shogunate together. He took the courtier's head and stuck it on a spoke, with a written notice as to why the man had died, and put it where any citizen could see. However, the marriage had gone through. Choshu men in particular were inflamed.

Choshu was also still reeling from the shock of having suffered a humiliating defeat at Shimonoseki by the combined foreign armada. Their batteries were utterly destroyed, their men routed. Now they were playing the same games as Satsuma, after their pounding by the British, and they were dealing with the foreigners, especially with a certain Britisher named Glover. Sadayori looked at Shinzo.

"You Choshu men must learn patience, however. Any more rash actions will ruin any hope of an alliance."

Shinzo bridled. "Rash actions? What do you mean?"

"Inciting the foreign navies to attack you, when anybody with any sense could have foreseen the outcome."

"The emperor himself issued the order to drive them out!"

"Perhaps, but you did not drive them out, you were defeated by them, and humiliated all of Japan!"

"You dare say . . ."

"I dare say what I like! You asked me to come here to speak, and speak I will!"

Ryoma skillfully smoothed over the quarrel developing, but Sadayori spoke again, his voice very soft.

"There are rumors too, that Choshu plans to march on Kyoto, and we have even heard that Choshu men are plotting to abduct His Imperial Highness. That would be a foolish move. Satsuma is still bound to uphold the Aizu clan, and they, as you realize, are charged with the defense of Kyoto, and I," said Sadayori, very tightly, "hold the emperor and his city very dear. There are many like me!"

Shinzo whitened, and exchanged glances with Ryoma. "In that outlook," he said, "I agree with you." He paused. "However, we are concerned that *bakufu* toads are getting more and more influence in the emperor's court, and they may well be clouding his imperial judgment."

Sadayori held up a hand. "Enough. I won't hear any more of that talk. We are in agreement that the powerful clans of this country must stop squabbling and unite. If fleets of different foreign nations can sail and fight together, it is ridiculous that we should be bristling to fight each other. I will do what I can." He got to his feet and bowed. "I must be on my way."

"Will you stay at the Satsuma residence?"

"No, for years now I have stayed at an inn by the Kamo River. It is quite close to the residence, though. My liver can't take too many nights with those fellows."

They laughed, and the tension was gone. Ryoma and Shinzo went to the entrance to see Sadayori off. Issukei came in from outside, his young face perturbed.

"Oh, Matsudaira sensei, won't you stay? We have been looking forward to talking with you."

"Sorry, Issukei-*kun*, not tonight."

"Look at him," said Ryoma, "he's as brown as a chestnut, fishing by the bank all day, probably for something to feed us for supper, right?"

"Oh no, Mother bought some nice prawns, and the *hasu* fish are in season, and we have the best sake in Japan."

They teased the lad, but he didn't mind, and he tried to get Sadayori to stay. Eventually, Otosei and the attractive little maid joined Issukei and the two young samurai in seeing Sadayori off at the door. He bowed, put on his big straw hat, and started walking. He saw a man down by a boat, watching him, then whispering to another man, but thought nothing of it. Perhaps the walk would clear his head.

After a bath and a light meal, Sadayori sat by the open window, looking down in the moonlight at the little garden and the river. Long, long ago, he had gazed at a similar scene with his young wife. How long had she been gone now? Twenty years? If he closed his eyes he could still see the glossy black of her long hair in the silvery moonlight. He never regretted not taking another woman, either as mistress or spouse, for her memory was just too precious to him. He sighed and spoke aloud a love poem he had written in his youth, then gave a short, soft laugh at himself.

The streets of the city were quiet and dark; just a few lanterns of drinking places glowed, and across the river, the faint yellow of lamps shone behind paper screens, in an upstairs window.

Sadayori's thoughts turned to more troubled themes. He felt himself to be like a *shogi* piece, shoved around on fate's gaming board. He had left the service of the Tokugawas at the urging of Lord Ii, believing that he could better serve them if he was free. His own young daimyo was now the shogun, and married to the younger sister of the emperor himself. Yet that same shogun was inviting foreigners, Frenchmen, to help him build up and remodel his army.

429

Now Sadayori served the Satsuma clan, even though many in the clan resented it, and would have spoken out about it, had it not been for the patronage of Itoh. Clans all over the country, but especially in Choshu, were actually recruiting peasants and townsmen into their militias, and training them to use imported rifles. Years ago, when Sadayori had advocated arming and training whalers, his clan councillors had laughed at him. So much had changed, so much was changing.

Suddenly, from the front of the inn, he heard a commotion, banging and shouting at the entrance door which had been slid shut and barred for the night. Sadayori, instantly sensing trouble, reached out and took his swords from the rack in the alcove and slipped them into his sash. He blew out the oil lamp in his room and slid open the door very quietly. The yelling and pounding went on, and Osome, the inn owner, came to the door with a lantern. The door burst open as she slid back the bar and several armed men barged in.

"What is it? Who are you?" demanded Osome, an attractive, genteel woman of *bushi* class.

"Where is the traitor Matsudaira?" demanded a burly fellow at the head of the gang. From his gloomy vantage point at the top of the stairs, Sadayori recognized him as a former *ronin* ruffian, hired now by the *bakufu* to cut down any opposition, real or imagined. So the Shinsen Gumi had come for him. Fate was giving him another nudge on the game board.

"Matsudaira sensei is not here," said Osome, with polite dignity, using the lovely lilting tones of a Kyoto woman's speech. At this the man balled up a fist and smashed it without warning into her face, knocking her to the ground, her nose broken and streaming blood. Behind, a maid screamed. Rage jolted Sadayori's guts.

"Find him!" roared the leader of the gang, stepping up into the inn, still in his dirty street sandals. There were eight men, swords drawn. They started kicking down the delicate wooden shoji screens, stabbing and slashing through the gold and black paintings on the paper of the doors, spreading out through the ground floor. Sadayori drew the short sword, saving the great sword for later. He came down the stairs so fast and quiet that the attackers, in their bellowing and crashing, did not hear or see him. Before one of them could turn, Sadayori grabbed him from behind, jerking his head back with his left arm. He stamped against the back of one leg and drove the blade between the man's ribs, into his heart. The body fell forward with a dull thud when he released it. Sadayori glided like a shadow, flattening himself against a wall. As another attacker came barging out of the room Sadayori dropped to one knee, blocking the man's right elbow, seizing it in a powerful grip, pushing it upward, the sword with it, while he thrust between the arms and into the throat. There was a horrible gurgiing noise as he withdrew the blade with a savage jerk. Then, with a one-handed push, he sent the man crashing into the opposite wall, spraying crimson.

"Here! Here!" bellowed another, spotting him and facing off with his sword, his eyes flickering now with uncertainty. Sadayori stepped onto the mats of the big downstairs room where the inn always held parties. It was almost as big as a dojo, and would give him more room. When facing many opponents, he would keep moving, keep changing tactics, do the unpredictable. The other man saw the bloodied short sword, and wondered at his confidence. He kept on yelling for the others, and soon men came in from two sides. Their leader was with them.

"You traitor, we've got you now! We know you've been plotting! Put those swords down, you can't escape."

Sadayori laughed at him. "I don't need to escape from lying bullies who pick fights with women. It is not I who is a traitor, or a braggart. Do you think you can treat one who serves the lord of Satsuma so insolently? You are nothing but scoundrels."

Sadayori slipped the short sword back into his sheath. He had no weapon in his hand as he spat out the last insult.

With a roar, the leader charged. Sadayori nimbly sidestepped, stuck out a foot, grabbed the back of his opponent's *hakama*, and heaved him sprawling face first into the mats. Scrambling to his feet, his face livid with rage, the man brought his sword to a ready position, raising the long handle up to his right shoulder. He took in a breath, ready to make a powerful arcing cut that would decapitate. He did not even see Sadayori's lightning one-handed draw, but felt the shock and numbness as the point of the long sword struck and slashed both forearms, just above the elbow, stopping the cut he was about to make. Now Sadayori had closed the fighting space in a single lunge, drawing and striking in a wide sweep from his left hip, where his sword was in his sash, out to his right. Then the blade whistled back as Sadayori took a double-handed grip, making another step to the side, venting a cry that rang like a bell as

431

he cut across and down. One arm, and a sword, fell to the mats. Shock stopped the other man where he stood, staring at the spouting stump.

"Die!" cried Sadayori, as he made a killing downward chop that cleaved the man's skull. Sadayori then jumped high in the air, avoiding another cut, whirling to face the others. He tried to get closer to the great old family spear, that of Osome's grandfather, which hung in a place of honor above the alcove, together with the old man's lacquered helmet.

"Three dead, five left. It's harder fighting men, isn't it? Why don't you run away now?"

A sword was thrust at him from the side, but he beat it down with a sharp clang of steel on steel. Another slashed at him, but he blocked it easily, then, suddenly switching to the fightng style of Satsuma, he screamed a long, ear-piercing battle yell and charged fearlessly at them—cut, cut, cut! His blade hacked at them like a machine, and the unexpected onslaught drove them back so hard that one man caught his heel against the rim of the alcove and fell backward over a flower pot. Sadayori's down cut opened him from sternum to crotch.

With another unexpected move Sadayori threw his sword, the blade slicing air and biting into one man's shins, bringing him to his knees. Now the thick white-oak pole of the spear was in his hands; he gave a jerk, releasing the sheath that protected the tip, raised the spear above his head, and began to whirl it with a low, thrumming sound. The attackers backed away in a widening circle. They had never seen such dynamic and terrifying handling of the great armor-piercing war spear before. Then the whirling stopped abruptly—its momentum changed into a sliding thrust as the polished wood flew through Sadayori's hands, the point punching deep through the sternum of the half-crippled man with bloody shins. A strong jerk, and the triangular, needle-pointed tip was questing again. With one hand, Sadayori retrieved his long sword and slid it back into the sheath at his side with a soft snick. The remaining three men fled from the room into a corridor, and Sadayori looked sadly around him at the bloody shambles he had caused in this once beautiful room. Then, gripping the spear with both hands, he stepped onto the polished wood. He'd killed five. How many more?

The spear had greater reach than the swords, and for forcing the issue in long, narrow spaces like the corridor it

432

was ideal. The swordsmen were driven back to the entrance. Osome was cowering up against one wall, hiding her bloodied face in the sleeves of her kimono. Sadayori yelled and stamped as he came, advancing step by step, with the spear tip jabbing and parrying, wounding one man in the thigh, another in the cheek.

Several of the lesser-ranked warriors, armed with staves and short spears, who had been guarding the way to the inn, started running down the narrow little high-walled lane. They smashed down the sliding doors to the inn, getting in each other's way. Sadayori's spear flickered, swords hacked at the thick, hard, ancient wood. The commotion increased. A shot boomed in the lane, then two more.

So that's the way they'll get me, thought Sadayori, giving another yell and a powerful thrust that pierced an eye. Another shot crashed loudly, and this time, one of Sadayori's opponents fell forward, the back of his head blown off. A bullet whizzed over Sadayori's head and another opponent staggered. A horrendous belly-shaking yell came—it was Itoh! Thoroughly frightened now, one of the samurai lost attention for the fraction of a second it took for Sadayori to drive a spear into his throat. Eyes bulging, gurgling, air hissing through the puncture, he turned from Sadayori just as Itoh came charging through like a wild boar.

Out in the street, Satsuma warriors, called by one of the inn's maids, were driving off the rest of the *bakufu* mercenaries. Of the eight who barged into the house, every one was killed, as well as five more outside.

Itoh wiped his blade on a wad of thick tissues and returned it to his sheath. From inside his kimono he produced a revolver.

"I've never used one of these before—it works, doesn't it?" He put the gun back out of sight, kicked off his sandals and stepped up into the inn, going from room to room, counting the enemy dead.

"They picked on the wrong man, didn't they? Quite a fight. Are you all right?"

"Yes, but the lady of the inn was hurt."

"We'll take care of it, and we'll get the bodies out. The mess will have to wait for a while, though. They might come back with more men, so we'd better get you and the woman to the residence. They won't dare attack us there."

Itoh went back to the entrance, and roared down the lane for a palanquin to carry Osome.

"Come on, you and I can walk."

433

"Wait," said Sadayori, "I must put the spear back."

"You know," said Itoh, "from that very first time I met you here, I knew you'd use that thing one of these days." He kicked at one of the bodies in the entranceway, rolling it over with his foot.

"Hmm. You must have had a lot of practice."

The *bakfu* authorities, of far higher rank than those who had called for the assault on the Tsutaya, were told that any further attack on Matsudaira Sadayori would be an affront to the honor of Satsuma. The lord of Aizu also intervened, for he hated what the Shinsen Gumi had been doing, and was secretly delighted that they had been whipped. Sadayori was allowed to leave Kyoto, accompanied by Itoh, two weeks later. Every young warrior in the Satsuma residence had begged him to relate the fight, and to them Sadayori was a hero.

Osome was recompensed handsomely in gold, enough to replace the screens and doors that had been smashed and the mats that had been bloodied, and to remove all the stains on the walls. Sword nicks in the beams were left as testimony to what had happened. Itoh gave her the revolver, which she soon put away, frightened of it as she was.

Sadayori apologized to her, and his heart was heavy. He had so many good memories of the inn, and now he would probably never go there again. The aftermath of the violence sickened him, and it took much cajoling from Itoh to pull him out of the beginnings of a depression.

Itoh accompanied him. They caught a river boat from Fushimi, leaving word and warning to Sakamoto Ryoma, another man likely to be targeted for assassination.

Going downriver with the current was much faster, and the boatmen sang as they poled and guided the long craft. The two samurai were the only passengers, so they had the little teahouse cabin to themselves.

At Hirakata, where the boat stopped and took on several more passengers, Itoh stepped ashore to call over a vendor, buying a flagon of sake and assorted tidbits. The day was cool, but fine, and they slid back the shoji screens to admire the river and the passing scenery. Other passengers were eating the vendor's treats too, and as each dish was finished, they tossed the used plate into the water.

Sadayori did not. He wiped one of the plates clean with tissues and held it in the palm of his hand.

"It seems wrong to throw them away," he said, gazing at

the blue and white design. All the dishes were of a similar shape and size, but whoever made them had a playful heart. The one Sadayori held had a little caricature of a spouting whale in the center. It made him think of the whaler Jinsuke. He too had survived an attack on his life, had he not? Sadayori felt more sympathy for him now. He picked up another empty dish. This one had a little bird in the center. The rather heavy dishes were of a style known as "banana-leaf hand," and were probably copies of the once-popular ceramics that had come from Cambodia at the beginning of the Tokugawa Period.

"They're cheap," said Itoh, munching the last piece of carrot, "I suppose it's not worth washing them."

"So if a thing is cheap, does it have to be thrown away? Used just once? Like a man's life?"

"Ah, don't get morbid again," said Itoh, passing the sake flagon. He grinned. "Hey, did you play this game when you were a boy?" He took an empty dish, and with a backhand flip sent it spinning out of the window to make it go bouncing once, twice, three times before it splashed out of view.

"I can beat you at that," said Sadayori, suddenly gay again. He tossed a dish, bouncing it over the water like a duck running for takeoff. Itoh laughed delightedly, and spun another.

Other passengers looked askance at the two middle-aged, hardened warriors playing like children on a beach.

The boat swept on toward the sea.

Chapter Thirty-Two

Saburo made his way back home. His arms, shoulders and back still ached from the heavy oar, but he had become tougher, and it was not as bad as it used to be. He still hated it, though, and wished that they were building more boats to paint, that there was work for him to do other than go out with the fleet. Old man Takigawa had gone out perhaps twice in his whole life. He loathed going out, he just wanted to paint!

He paused at the door of their house. Since Jinsuke returned, and so dramatically, Saburo feared that Oyoshi would suddenly leave him. As he stood there, the door slid open and Oyoshi looked out.

"Husband," she said, using the most familiar term, not his name and an honorific as she usually did, "why are you just standing there? I was waiting for you. Welcome home."

Saburo went in and flopped down wearily in cross-legged position in his usual place, to the left of the household shrine. A smell of newly burned incense hung about the place, and as he glanced he saw that there were fresh greenery, rice and sake at the little altar. He turned on his knees and said a prayer to the painter Takigawa.

"There are times when I feel grateful to him," said Oyoshi from behind, laying hot tea and small rice cakes—a special treat—on the little table. Saburo turned and looked at her. She seemed different. Smiling, she met his eyes then cast hers down, like a coy young girl instead of a woman of twenty-nine.

"Where is Yoichi? Out playing?"

"I said he could sleep over at Uncle Shusuke's. You know how he likes to sleep with his cousins and talk with them in the dark. He's a very lonely little boy sometimes."

Saburo's face clouded. "So he's not coming home?"

"Not for a night, perhaps two." She looked very steadily at him. "We need to talk, just you and I."

436

Saburo put down his tea and took a quiet breath, screwing his face up in an effort to say what he could not bring himself to say the night before, after they had come back in silence from seeing Jinsuke, and after he had run out and come back soaking wet.

"Yoshi, you can go, if you like. I'll not stop you, and if you want, I'll take you as far as Shingu. We can make up a story. Yokohama is not so terribly far."

Her voice became shrill as she interrupted him. "Do you want me to leave?"

"No." He wanted to shout, but it came out as a whisper.

"You don't?"

"Never, but I made a promise . . ."

She got up and fetched his washbasin and cloth, handing them to him. "Go and take your bath. You look so tired. Let's talk afterward."

Saburo just sat there, holding the things and frowning.

"This is my home. Why should I leave? If you want me to, then I will, but can we talk later? I've cooked a special supper for you tonight, and if you don't bathe and come back soon it might spoil."

So she was not going. Saburo stood, numb with relief, and paused as she called out to him.

"Husband, please hurry back." Her voice was bright again, like a girl's.

The meal she had prepared was full of his favorite things. She was never extravagant, but she had shopped well and early at the fish market, and had also bought fresh vegetables, then gone to pick wild shoots and roots on the hills. There was a dish of boiled pilot-whale intestine, sliced very thin and flavored with ginger and soya sauce. Looking at it, tears almost came to his eyes. He called for a third small dish, then placed a tiny portion before the shrine. So many times he had shared such a dish with their father.

There was saury too, pickled lightly in vinegar and made into sushi, laid and cut into bite-size pieces on hand-pressed rice, smeared with a touch of a hot green horseradish that grew in a pure, tiny stream over the hill. All kinds of small side dishes and pickles showed how much care Oyoshi had taken that day. He looked from the table to her, wondering.

"Please." She knelt by his left side, holding a warmed ceramic bottle of sake. Even more surprised, he held out the little cup while she poured it. He drank, and she waited so she could pour again. He put the cup down and picked up a tidbit with his chopsticks.

437

"Is it good?" she asked.

"Delicious," he mumbled, chewing. Again she poured sake for him and he drank it, then he took the cup and handed it to her, taking the flagon to pour. She toasted him with her eyes, and handed it back. Had she ever done that before?

"Yoshi, please, you eat too."

He couldn't take his eyes off her. Something about her made her look more beautiful, yet there was no makeup, no new dress ornament. She smiled at him, and again he was glad that she had absolutely refused to blacken her teeth, the way married women were supposed to, but instead polished them three times a day with a special frayed stick, keeping them as white and pearly as a girl's. How many times had her father and his mother scolded her for that? Now she smiled at him with a girl's radiance, and he could not help smiling back. Usually, because of her unmatronly teeth, Oyoshi smiled with tightly pursed lips, but now she took another cup of sake, smiled again, flicking her small red tongue over those white teeth and cherry lips, gazing boldly into his eyes. She was flirting with him! It made Saburo's head spin, for although he was supposed to be married to her, he had long since placed Oyoshi the female on a high shelf. She got up and went into the kitchen as he finished the meal, leaving tea for him.

"I'm going to bathe now," she called out, leaving him alone with his thoughts, of her father, of Jinsuke, of the strange but happy years he had had, posing as her husband, but acting like a brother.

She returned early, dressed in a light *yukata,* the sash tied tight and high. Still perspiring from the bath, she let the folds at the front hang loosely. Their house was not a big one, but they did have a small, waist-high dressing table, with a folding mirror, and now Oyoshi knelt before it, combing out her long, glossy, jet-black hair. It hung down to her buttocks, round and pretty as they rested on her heels. Her back and shoulders had always been straight, and the passing of eleven years had not caused her back to bend or her shoulders to slump, no matter how many heavy pots of water she carried on a pole up from the spring.

She looked at him in the mirror, curving her neck as she used the sandalwood comb.

"Saburo, have you never felt sorry that you made that promise to me?"

Oyoshi had been thinking deeply too. He had always been

such a quieting, comforting presence, always so steady, gentle, reliable. He was never demanding, and very rarely angry about anything. There was a time when Oyoshi had thought his face not to be as strikingly handsome as his brother's, but the years, inner struggles and triumphs had etched it with qualities even more attractive than the ruggedly arrogant good looks of Jinsuke. Look close, Oyoshi reflected, and anyone could see that he is a gentle, sensitive man, artistic and deeply feeling. Why had she not truly seen him before? Why had she gone on clinging to a silly girlhood dream? Saburo had always been beside her, dear, dear Saburo.

"No," he answered her. "If a man is going to regret a promise, he should not make it. I made the promise."

She turned and faced him. "You'll never know how deeply I've respected you for that."

Saburo made no reply, and she turned back to combing her raven hair. While other housewives, like Shusuke's once delectably attractive wife, grew plump and domesticated, or worse, scrawny and shrewish with their children and drudgery, Oyoshi seemed to have stopped aging physically at twenty-three. She had become more attractive, more interesting to be with and talk to, and she had become . . . he searched for a word and found an image—a lustrous, sweet, ripe plum.

"There have been many times," she said, "when I wished I hadn't made you make that promise, wished you'd cancel it. Have you never thought that?"

"What about my brother, about you and him, about what you said when we got married? Was I to forget that?"

She half turned. "He's gone. In truth, he was gone more than eleven years ago. Gone with his foreign ship, his foreign ways. There is only us, you, I, and Yoichi. Forget the beginning, will you, Saburo? I'm no longer a girl, so can you forgive me? We have a son who adores you. Then, I was young, stupid, self-centered and frightened. Had you not been kind enough to marry me I would have killed myself, surely you knew that, otherwise you wouldn't have agreed. You were so good and kind. I was my father's only daughter, and spoiled. Now I want to think about you and me. Have you never wanted . . ."

The words stuck in her throat, even though she was more outspoken than most Taiji women, who were renowned for their strong wills.

Saburo, despite his years, blushed. Once, just once, he had gone with a woman. That had been when he was working in Shingu, and the woman had been a young one, come from the pleasure quarters to the shop where he was working. She wanted some ornate screen made for her, and he went to her quarters. She flirted with him, seduced him, and when he first went to her quilts the excitement had been unbearable. I will see her body, touch it, know its secret parts, he had thought. But the harlot had not even taken off her kimono; she only spread the clothes wide, while he pawed and sucked at her breasts, stroked the dark furry sex, and then she had urged him into her and gone on humping and screeching long after he was spent, using him, her sex greedy and selfish, the caked white powder on face and neck suddenly grown ugly. Afterward he finished the work, but sent a boy to install the screens. That was the only time.

Yet for all his reticence and control, Saburo was a passionate man. The sight of a beautiful flower or the bends in the limbs of a tree, the colors of a butterfly or a freshly caught fish, all of these things could give him a tingle in the groin. Those and, of course, the glimpse of a pretty woman.

Oyoshi had always been around, but distant, taboo. He nurtured his love for her, and he loved her deeply, so that it grew in different ways.

As if catching his thoughts, she suddenly asked, "Saburo, have you ever lain with a woman?"

Should he tell her about the Shingu harlot? That one brief encounter? No, it didn't count.

"I have not, although I am a man, Yoshi, with all of a man's wants, but I know that since you married me you have slept with no other. We're like a monk and a nun, living under one roof." He laughed. "How many monks and nuns could do that?"

She put down the comb and turned to face him again. "I don't want to be a nun, and it has been several years since I began wishing that you would break that vow, but I was too proud, and I was afraid too." She looked at him with almost a challenge in her large brown eyes. How could he know the torments a woman went through at times, when her nipples swelled as they brushed against cloth, when fantasies played with her mind and body, and when only privacy and a few gasping, moaning minutes with dipping, stroking fingers could relieve it, and poor relief at that. Oyoshi often wondered if Saburo did, well, what men did, but she never found out. So many times she had lain in the darkness feeling a kind of fury inside because he, a man, would not sense her womanly wants, the battle she wanted to lose. So many times had she wanted him to roll over, say nothing, and just reach for her.

440

"Saburo, please do me a favor, it is hard for me to comb my hair at the back. Will you do it?"

Never had she asked him to do this before, and only once in a while did she ask for him to hold her obi at the back while she tied it. He went over, knelt behind her, and took the comb. Her fingers brushed his.

Her hair was long and silky, and the comb moved through it with ease. She had sprinkled a few drops of camellia oil in her hair, and the perfume mingled with Oyoshi's own fragrance. Such smooth lines of neck and shoulder, skin like silk—and he could see her face in the mirror, watching him quizzically, and he looked down over her shoulder to the valley between the hills of her breasts. He recalled those large and beautiful nipples, erect when she had fed the baby.

"Do you despise me, Saburo?"

"You know I don't," he said huskily.

"Is it too late? Have we built too high a wall between us? Yoichi needs a brother, or a sister. My monthly flows are still regular, and I think my body is young enough."

He stopped stroking with the comb, and stared at her, eyes wide. One hand was lightly resting on her shoulder. She put both hands to it and leaned her cheek over.

"Don't play games with me," he said, heart pounding.

She shook her head, let his hand go, and turned around to face him. "No games. It's late now. I'll clear away the things and set out the quilts."

Saburo went into the kitchen and poured himself some cold sake. As he raised it to his lips he saw that his hand was trembling. While Oyoshi cleared away the day things, hauled sleeping quilts and covers from the cupboard, he kept his eyes averted.

Saburo went outside and dipped water from the big earthenware pot, drinking deeply. He looked up at a sky filled with stars. An owl hooted. From a nearby street came the sounds of a few returning roisterers. The night was cool. He went back into the house, kneeling before the shrine. From behind it he pulled out a rolled-up painting. Oyoshi stared at him, never thinking that Saburo would hide anything. Without saying a word he handed it to her.

The roll was tied with silken cords, and the paper was the finest. She untied and unrolled it, gasping at what she saw. It was different from the long narrative scrolls he usually did. It was a hanging scroll fit for the alcove of a fine house, a single portrait, minutely and brilliantly painted. Tears flooded her eyes, for it was a painting of her, feeding Yoichi.

441

On her face was a mingling of pride, protection and gentleness, while the baby's face, eyes partly closed, and cheeks chubby, was all contentment. One fat little dimpled hand, tiny nails pink, squeezed the flesh by the nipple. It was by far the best portrait she had ever seen of anybody, and anybody could see that it was painted with love.

"I painted this a long time ago. Our father rescued it at the time of the tsunami. In fact, I think that's why he was a bit late in getting out of the house. He knew about it, I couldn't keep it from him. I painted it in the boat shed, when the fleet was out. Just before he died he handed it to my mother. She wanted to show you, but I said no. I always thought that if one day you left, then at least I'd have this to remember you by."

Oyoshi let out a long, pain-filled moan, and held the painting to her bosom, sinking slowly to the quilts.

"Oh, oh, oh, what have I done? Such a waste of years! Oh, my Saburo, it is so beautiful, if only I'd seen it before. How could I ever leave you?" She raised her face, eyes brimming with tears. "Saburo, dear Saburo, please forgive me!"

He took the picture from her and put it to one side, where it would not be wrinkled, then he put his arms around her shoulders. She leaned against him, sobbing. So much time wasted in pride, and yet, had their love been maturing and growing, like a strong tree, now to flower?

Oyoshi disengaged herself, went out and splashed cold water on her face, wiping it with a clean cloth. She came back into the room and pulled back the quilts. Whereas before the quilts had lain separated, now they were together. Slowly, she untied her sash and let her robe fall, standing quite naked before him, holding her arms out.

"Saburo, take me now."

He stripped off his robe and loincloth, then went to her, feeling the magic of her body against his for the first time, nipples stiffening against his chest. She pulled him down, opening her legs wide, and easily, so easily, he went deep into her, and as he did so she sighed as if all the troubles that ever beset her had come to an end.

After the first time, as they lay touching each other, she remembered the lamp and sat up to go and blow it out, but Saburo pulled her down on top of him, letting his hands explore her back, her buttocks, the backs of her thighs.

"Don't blow out the light, I want to see you."

Her hands slipped down and cupped his sac, fingers moving gently.

"I want more of your seed, deep, deep inside me," she murmured, then she moved off him and knelt on the quilts, buttocks raised, forearms leaning on the soft, padded cotton, her hair tumbling down, the tiny pinkish-brown pucker and the hairy slash fully presented to him. Her voice was muffled.

"An old lady told me that this was the best position to make a baby," she said. Saburo got to his knees behind her, spreading and entering her, looking down with joy at the sight of her vaginal lips caressing him, and above, the tight dimple of her sphincter contracting. This wasn't dirty at all, not like the lewd jokes the men were always making out on the boats. Had they never really seen or felt? It is sheer beauty! Oyoshi moaned repeatedly until he climaxed, gripping her buttocks tight to him. He was wet with sweat, and she was tight around him, moving with small, hard, bucking movements. He reached around her, leaning over her back, and stroked the wetness of their joining until she soon climaxed, pushing back so hard against him it hurt his pubic bone.

For a long time they lay in each other's arms, embracing, whispering. Then they made love again, first slowly and lazily, then fast and hard, until it was she who had to stop, saying that she was getting sore.

She fell asleep, her head on his chest, one hand gripping his penis until it too relaxed. Never in his life had Saburo slept so soundly.

In the morning, when he awoke to see sun streaming through the cracks between the rain shutters, he realized he had missed going out with the fleet. He tried to shake the sleep out of his head, hearing voices at the door. Oyoshi was apologizing to somebody from the office, saylng that her husband had a fever and could not go out. There came the mumbled sounds of a man's voice, then Oyoshi's, thanking him, and the sound of the door sliding shut. Saburo lay back. The whole night had been like a dream. Truly, why had they waited so long? So this was what it was like to be married? Was it the same for everybody? Ah, thought Saburo, such a wonderful world.

Oyoshi was out in the kitchen, kindling the fire to make rice. Then came the sounds of stirring as she made miso soup, the crisp noises of a knife cutting pickled radish, the scents of fish being grilled, fresh saury maybe, with a side dish of freshly grated radish too. Saburo lay there in euphoria. Hundreds, no, thousands of times he had heard her doing these mundane morning things, but today each sound and scent was new and fresh and tantalizing. He called out to her, and she came into the room, wiping a strand of black hair from her forehead, smiling her girlish smile again.

"Come here."

He threw back the covers and she lay on top of him, embracing. His hands slipped under her kimono and grasped her small, strong buttocks. His fingers kneaded her flesh and she moved against him. He felt her bush against his thigh.

"Breakfast will spoil," she murmured.

"No, it won't."

He spread her thighs with his knees and with one hand she reached down to guide him inside her while he filled his mouth with a hanging breast, one, then the other, and her hair fell down over him, covering his shoulders. Never had he thought it could last so long. Finally, she lay still, and he lay with his arms around her.

"I'm hungry," said Saburo, and she giggled. She got up, found tissues, then busied herself laying out breakfast and putting away the bed things. Such a delicious meal it was!

Between breakfast and lunch they made love again, and Saburo found pride in himself as a man. Soon after lunch his mother came to the door, sounding worried. She looked in to where Saburo was resting.

"Oyoshi, I heard that Saburo was ill, and no wonder too. Father told me about the soaking he gave himself the other night. I came right over. Did you send for the doctor? Do you have any medicine?"

"Mother, it is so kind of you to come." Oyoshi changed the tone of her voice. "Poor man, he was so tired last night, and getting wet, you know, and then again this morning he was so hot so I just had to keep him home and look after him."

Saburo turned his face away, trying not to laugh.

"He's got a fever?" said Onui, still worried.

"Yes, a fever, but it's gone down now. Don't worry, Mother, if it comes up again, I'll take care of him. Come in, have some tea." Onui declined, saying she didn't want to disturb Saburo's rest, and when she was gone he rolled over, smothering his laughter in the covers. He hadn't realized that Oyoshi had the humor of a courtesan.

He stayed home for two days and nights, then went out and joined the fleet again. The sea, the sky, the cheerful tumbling whistle of kites and the laughter of his mates seemed a hundred times brighter, and somehow he didn't mind going out to sea so much anymore.

444

Two months rushed by in perfect happiness. He got permission from Kakuemon to work on more whaling scrolls, and did his own work too. He even enjoyed going out on the boats. Hardly a night went by when he and Oyoshi didn't make love at least twice.

A month after the autumn festival, when even Saburo had joined in the shouting and jostling, he and Oyoshi were invited up to Tatsudaiyu's house. His father said that he had some special food, and Saburo knew that it was "mountain whale," a treat that on rare occasions he too was able to obtain from the taciturn mountain man who had warned him of the coming of the tsunami, and who brought Taiji folk raw lacquer.

The men had been out whaling that day, and came back laughing together over some incident of great amusement. Wanting to share it with the women, Tatsudaiyu and his sons waited to get into the house before talking about it.

"Who saw it first?" Saburo asked his father.

"I don't know," replied Tatsudaiyu, "all I know was that suddenly men were hopping up and down, people waving signals I'd never seen before, and yelling and pointing at a monster, a giant sea python. I just laughed at them—until I spotted it myself."

"I too," said Saburo, "then I saw the way it undulated its huge yellowish-green body in the water"—he made movements with his arm—"so long and thick, all segmented, more like a monster worm than a snake. My first thought was that the great serpent the god Susano-o defeated in the mountains must have had spawn, and that we were now facing one of its young in the sea, a giant snake that fed on whales, or worse, even whalers. I must confess, Father, I was as scared as the rest of them."

"You know," said Tatsudaiyu, "our rice boy had the same idea as you. He screamed 'yamato-no-orochi!' then tried to hide in the bottom of the boat, clinging to my legs. I couldn't have held the men out there if I tried."

Onui and Oyoshi grew alarmed, and wanted to hear more. That day the whole fleet had come racing back to port with stories of a huge sea serpent menacing them. As Saburo described the way the creature moved over the waves, its vast long body bending and twisting, the thick segments writhing, green and yellow, Onui covered her face with her hands and rocked back and forth, while Oyoshi's fingers clutched and her eyes widened.

"But never fear," said Shusuke, "one of our brave Taiji

445

men has captured it. If you like, we will take you to see it, down on the beach in front of the Asuka shrine."

"Oh, how courageous, who caught it? Was anybody killed?" asked Onui.

Father and sons grinned at each other.

"Well, you know who's always the last in? The slowest boat?" said Shusuke.

"Old Yasuemon?"

"Right," chorused both sons.

Tatsudaiyu held up his hand. "Come with us, and we'll show you the great serpent, the *yamato-no-orochi* of the ocean!"

"I'm afraid," cried Onui.

"Don't be afraid, we'll protect you, and anyway, it's quite dead."

"Don't be sure about that, Father, it had some shoots growing around the gills."

It took a lot of persuasion, but eventually the women took off their apron smocks and followed their men down to the beach, where already a large crowd had gathered. They nudged their way to the front and saw, lying upon the sand, something banded in merging green and yellow, like a snake, thick as a man's body and more than twice as long as a chase boat. It took a while to realize what it was . . . a monstrous length of bamboo that must have come from some far tropical island, riding the Black Current. No such bamboo grew in Japan.

"So nothing is as fearful as that which you do not know," said Tatsudaiyu. Then he and his sons joined in the joking and congratulating Yasuemon, and even Kakuemon the beach master was amused at the trick the sea had played on them. Then, mindful of the delicious smells that had been emanating from Onui's big pot, they went on back to the house.

Such a stew it was, with onions, big white radishes cut in circles, yams, wild mushrooms, miso and the precious mountain whale.

Onui adjusted the bamboo-and-iron pot hanger, suspended from the roof over the charcoals, so that the stew was on very low heat. When she lifted the wooden lid to stir it their stomachs rumbled in delicious anticipation.

Tatsudaiyu was telling them how, in ancient days, their ancestors often enjoyed such meat, and would join in boar drives with the wild men of the mountains. That was back in the days when the Kumano men were fierce pirates, serving only their own leaders. The animals were hunted by driving

446

them into nets, as whales were driven, then killed with spears and bows. They used dogs then too, and a big hunt was great festival, shared by the men of the sea and the men of the mountains.

"Father," said Saburo, "I've been thinking. You know that old story about the first Wada beach master seeing a cicada in a spider's web and inventing the whale nets? Don't you think that is just a romantic notion, to enhance people's ideas of our masters? Don't you think the ancient ways of using nets in the mountains was simply tried in the sea? Don't you think it was originally the mountain folk who taught the sea folk how to make nets that were strong?"

This perturbed Tatsudaiyu. He didn't like anything to shake his belief in the whys and wherefores of whaling. However, Saburo had a point. Mountain whale was wild boar. Before Buddhism, which forbade the eating of four-legged animals, was introduced, the Japanese ate deer, boar, hare, bear, raccoon dogs and badgers. Some even ate dogs, as the Koreans did to this day.

Meat of the wild boar was dark and full of flavor. It gave a man strength, like whale. "Mountain whale" was an apt name for it, and got around any religious bother. Everybody knew too that bear meat was medicine, that the dried gall bladder, used in tiny pieces, was the most powerful cure for a stomach ailment, and of course, raccoon-dog meat cured colds and stopped children from bed-wetting.

It was still a rare thing to be able to share such a treat, and perhaps, had they not been whaling people, and therefore used to meat, they might not have liked it so much.

Talk was animated and they laughed a lot, then Yoichi and his cousins came, late as usual and grubby as urchins. Yoichi was getting husky, and brown as a berry.

During a lull in the conversation, Tatsudaiyu looked at Oyoshi.

"Yoshi, you are looking healthy nowadays. Have you gotten a little fatter?"

Onui smiled, and nudged her. Shusuke's wife clapped her hands and gave a squeal of delight. Tatsudaiyu's jaw dropped, and Saburo smiled and blushed.

"Truly?" said Tatsudaiyu, his chopsticks stopped halfway between bowl and mouth.

Oyoshi nodded. "There is no doubt, it'll be early summer."

Tatsudaiyu gave a bellow. "Congratulations! Congratulations!" Shusuke joined in, and they both thumped Saburo on the back, laughing.

447

"It was the best of luck to have this meat, then," said Tatsudaiyu. "Eating this will make a fine, strong child grow of you, a son, straight and true and full of courage like a wild boar. Yoshi, give Mother your bowl, you must eat! Onui! Feed her, then fetch us sake! Sake!"

They laughed and ate, and Saburo thought he had never seen his father look happier.

When Oyoshi's swelling belly became obvious, the village gossips had many theories as to why there should have been such a gap between the first child and the second, but none guessed that Saburo's long celibacy was over.

The evening after the supper of mountain whale, after their son was asleep, Saburo drew Oyoshi gently to him. He was content and at peace. He stroked her hair and kissed her breasts, murmured his joy in her ear. She put her hand down, feeling tumescence.

"You're always so hard," she whispered.

"Ignore it, holding you just makes it that way, it'll go down."

"I want you inside me," she murmured, stroking him.

"But that's dangerous, isn't it? The baby . . ."

She gripped him with one hand and with the other arm encircled his waist.

"Come into me slowly, and let me move. It'll be all right, I'll let nothing harm this baby."

It was the first time she had made love to him that way, and Saburo thought no man could enjoy his body, or another's, as much.

And the big bamboo? That was cut and shaped and presented to Lord Mizuno of Shingu.

Chapter Thirty-Three

Kyoto, being inland, and surrounded by mountains and hills, was a bowl of heat in the summer. In his armor, Sadayori baked, adding to his general discomfort. He had slept little the night before, as Itoh's aide had roused him long before dawn with the news that a small Choshu army had marched on the imperial city and was attempting a coup d'état. Satsuma, true to an old agreement with Aizu, joined forces to repel the Choshu warriors. Sadayori had assembled his own men, coming at a run through well-laid-out streets. Overhead, a flock of crows winged in from their mountain roosts, almost as if they too were in battle formation.

As Sadayori and his men rounded a corner of a block just ten minutes from the palace, a barrage of ill-aimed bullets greeted them. He drew his sword, calling his men to a halt. He breathed a prayer that they would keep discipline.

"Firing ranks!" he bellowed. His men formed two ranks now, the front rank kneeling and aiming their rifles, the second rank standing.

"Take aim . . . fire!" bellowed Sadayori.

At his order the rear rank stepped forward, knelt, and aimed, while the men now in the rear stood, took cartridges from belt pouches, bit off the ends and rammed them home. They were armed with Enfield rifles, those used by the British army—muzzle-loading hammer-lock weapons, reliable, accurate, and with a hefty punch. The men were a mixture of *goshi*, or country samurai, and *ashigaru*, the low-ranking foot-soldier samurai entitled to carry only one sword. All of them were from Satsuma, and mostly from the countryside, so it was hard to catch what they said sometimes. But Sadayori found them to be good, brave, loyal and obedient men, and very tough.

Minié balls buzzed by like hornets and one rang on the wing of Sadayori's helmet. Two men in the front rank crumpled, rifles clattering to the cobbles, and another man in the second row spun twice around, his ramrod flying from his grasp as a ball shattered his right upper arm. Sadayori raised his sword. All the other officers of his group were dead or wounded, and although he was not Satsuma born, the men respected him, and would die for him.

"*Ute!*" The sword fell and there was a crash of gunfire and the rotten-egg stink of powder.

"Rear rank forward!" Their guns loaded, the men in back stepped forward and knelt. "Aim!" Behind them, still others were now loading. More minié balls flew and another of Sadayori's men had his head knocked back.

"Fire!" Through the smoke, Sadayori could see that the Choshu men were getting hit harder than they were, and around the cannon were several dark forms lying still. He had told his men to concentrate fire on the gun crews. As he turned to them, the Choshu cannon belched and a shell screamed a few feet over their heads, exploding in the walls of a house at the end of the street. Sadayori was thankful they weren't using grapeshot.

"Terrible shots, aren't they," he said calmly, and the men laughed. "Now load, all of you. Rear rank, fire standing; front, kneeling—got it? Aim steady, fire at the order, and then we'll give them a taste of steel.

"Aim . . . fire!" Almost thirty rifles crashed, and more Choshu gunners went down. Sadayori figured that there could be no more than thirty or forty men left alive behind the low fence they were using for cover.

"Charge!"

With his sword raised in his right hand, Sadayori led them, running swiftly despite the heavy armor, made of metal plates, of chain, silk and leather, gorgeously decorated. Close behind him, with bayonets leveled, and screaming their awful battle cry, his men charged. They swept over the low wall, through sporadic fire that took out a few of them. Sadayori leaped the fence, sword now above his head. It flashed down just as his feet touched the ground, slicing through a man's arm at the shoulder. The man looked up from filling a shell, amazement on his face, his blood mingling with the black powder now spilled over the grass. Screams and gurgles of the dying filled the air together with the clash of steel on steel, the thudding of rifle butts into bone and flesh. Many of the Satsuma men carried their own

450

swords slung over their backs, as well as their bayonetted rifles. In the heat of battle they reverted to old ways, dropping issued weapons and whirling their blades. The Choshu men did not run, as Sadayori thought they might, although inside five minutes of savage fighting not one was left standing. The skirmish was over.

One young Choshu soldier, arm dangling uselessly, knelt over the body of an officer, a mere boy, but an armored samurai. His eyes blazed and he was crying, holding in his right hand the officer's sword. There was a ring of Satsuma men around him, and upon his broad, sunburned face was a mixture of terror, grief and defiance.

"Look at him," jeered a Satsuma man, "he thinks it's a hoe. Hey, farmer, do you think we're turnips?"

They taunted him that way, perhaps even more so because most of them were not strangers to the tools of agriculture themselves. They laughed and feinted with their bayonets and swords, while the young man, crying out in high-pitched, strangled sobs, swung wildly with the sword. Sadayori finished wiping his own blade with tissues and pushed through them.

"Enough!" he commanded. "This man has fought bravely, he is wounded, and he defends his officer. Is this a laughing matter? Back off, I say!" His men, a little shamefaced, fell back. Sadayori spoke to the young enemy, who could not have been more than eighteen. "Drop the sword, lad, and give up. You were just following orders. Give up, lad, we won't harm you."

"Never! A soldier never gives up!"

Sadayori nodded and smiled at him.

"Those are the words of a true Japanese."

From the corner of his eye he saw one of the older men putting a firing cap on the nipple of his rifle. The man caught his glance and understood.

"Give up, warrior of Choshu, we respect your honor."

Pride flashed on the youth's face, and he raised the sword as if to attack. A single rifle cracked. Sadayori looked away.

"All right, load up. Stack those fallen rifles, we'll pick them up later. Put them over by the wall there."

A wounded enemy was trying to crawl away, dragging a loop of intestines and smearing the ground with his blood. Sadayori pointed with a grimace of distaste. A Satsuma soldier went over to the man, who looked only ahead, eyes clouded with shock. He put the point of his bayonet at the base of his skull and leaned on the butt of the rifle. The body went rigid, and straw-sandaled feet drummed on the ground, and it was over. Here and there Sadayori's men went about other grisly work.

Sadayori had warned them. Itoh had warned them. Saigo had warned them. Yet the Choshu clan had dared to invade the imperial city, dared to think of kidnapping the emperor and forcing the rest of Japan to rally and throw the nation into a suicidal war against the *bakufu* and the foreigners. They were fools. It had fallen to the constable of Kyoto, lord of Aizu, to repel them, and as Sadayori had warned Choshu, long ago, and as any intelligent man would have known, if they attacked Kyoto, then Satsuma was honor-bound to go to the aid of Aizu and drive them out.

Choshu had ringed the hills the night before, then attacked, confident of their modern weapons, their training and their lofty purpose of saving the Son of Heaven from wicked advisors.

Sadayori was angry, and yet so sad; his guts felt like lead. He went to a nearby knoll and looked over the city that he loved so much. His wife had been born here. Above him, the wind bent the highest branches of a tall pine. Much of the town south of the palace was now obscured by smoke. The fires were started by Choshu shells. By nightfall many people would be homeless, and many ancient and beautiful buildings would be burned, some belonging to his relatives in law, some to old friends—the potter, the kimono weaver, the maker of tiny sweets to go with tea, all linked to memories of her.

He and his men had been given a section of town to clear, and they had fought down several roads, clearing Choshu warriors and soldiers from every position, repelling their attacks, and now silencing the cannon. It had been bitter, ugly fighting.

From down the last road they had contested came the sound of a mounted warrior, his horse galloping hard, a Satsuma pennant streaming from a bamboo pole lashed to his back. Sadayori went back down to the fence and stood waiting. His men gathered their weapons and followed him. The horseman reined in. He had lost his war helmet and there was blood caked on the side of his face.

"Matsudaira-sama, that was good work, silencing those guns. They set fire to a building in the imperial compound and it is spreading out of control. The situation is most serious still. Choshu men have fought their way right to the Hamaguri Gate. There has even been fighting inside the gate, and His Imperial Majesty is most alarmed." Sadayori's men, standing close enough to hear, gasped at the sacrilege of it. The Hamaguri Gate was a forbidden gate, reserved exclusively for the Son of Heaven.

The horseman looked over to the carnage, and at the remaining men.

"Please gather your men and assist in driving them out. I'm sorry, you must be tired, but this is the most effective direction."

"I understand," said Sadayori gravely. "We will come."

The horseman pulled out a map of the city and jabbed his finger at three spots, leaning down as he did so, holding the map against the sweat-lathered neck of the horse. A soldier stepped forward and held the bridle, speaking softly to the animal, trying to calm it. A finger rested on one spot.

"If you approach them from these streets, you can hit them from behind and throw them into confusion. Unfortunately the fires are jumping from roof to roof, and it may be hard, the whole section is ablaze. Commander Saigo sends his regards, sir, sorry, I forgot." Sadayori slapped his knee with his hand.

"You rode well, thank you. Tell the commander it will be done."

He turned to his men. "Go down to that mansion. The gates are open and the owners have fled. There's a big carp pond in there, if I remember. Go dip yourselves in the water—but don't forget to take off your cartridge belts first! Soak well! Let us hurry now, we've hot work ahead of us!"

Sadayori could hardly believe it, but the men were laughing as they trooped down through the wide, roofed double gates of a courtier's house. Owners and servants had fled for the hills. The courier brought his horse around and Sadayori pointed to the cannon.

"The Choshu men are all dead there, but shall we spike the cannon?"

"No, I'll see to it that transport is detailed for them later. They might come in useful sometime." He looked around grimly, memorizing what he saw.

"It was a hard fight."

"Yes," said Sadayori, "they fought bravely and died like men."

He took off his heavy, brass-winged helmet and a gauntlet and poked his finger through the hole where the bullet had passed, grinning ruefully. "You know, these things are terribly hot, and don't stop bullets. Maybe you're better off

453

without yours—you look as if you've seen some hard fighting too."

"We all have, well . . ."

"Ride with care, comrade, I shall go and join the men. I am very sorry, but there are no Satsuma officers left here."

"We all think of you as one of us." He raised his hand in salute. "Even if you do talk funny."

Sadayori laughed, and watched him gallop off, then strode down to join the men.

They were sporting about in the big ornamental pond. It was waist deep in places, and stocked with priceless carp of many colors. The men were trying to catch the gold, red, yellow and white fish, joking that any one of them would make a meal for six, and asking if anybody had the miso to stew them with. Seeing them there, these men who had faced such danger and death, now playing like mischievous children, in a garden that normally men of their status would be unable to enter, struck Sadayori as hilarious. He guffawed, standing at the edge of the pond, hands on hips.

A curving gravel path led to a hollow water stone, a large piece of granite naturally formed into a basin, transported to the garden no doubt at great cost. It was shaded by willow and bamboo, and water was conducted into it through a bamboo pipe. Sadayori took off both gauntlets now and splashed water onto his face and neck, then drank his fill with a dipper that lay nearby. The peaceful garden was in such contrast to the violence they had just been through, so different it unnerved him, like a soft trap, pulling him, telling him to stay and forget. He looked at his hands and saw that they were trembling. Straightening up, he shouted to his men.

"Come now, stop playing. Drink as much water as you need. It may be a while before you can drink again."

They came dripping out of the pond, uniforms clinging to them, still joking, incredibly, although Sadayori could not miss the tiredness around their eyes. One last effort, he thought, and they will be spent.

The men gathered around the stone, drinking. Then they put on cartridge belts, slung rifles and swords, and followed him.

Down the street they ran, doubled over, trying to hold their breaths. Sadayori felt that he had died and plummeted into one of the Buddhist hells, a hell of fire, flames, smoke, sparks, of roar and heat and acrid smells. Here and there flames were leaping across the street from roof to roof, and all along, windows and doorways gouted smoke. He passed a dead fighter across whose body a charred and glowing beam had fallen. It ignited cartridges in his pouch—whup! whup!—they exploded like fireworks. Seeing this one man killed by fire terrified Sadayori's men more than the fighting and battle slaughter. But they continued after him, for despite his armor and his age he ran faster than they, looking like a fire demon, and they felt with an almost superstitious dread that only he could lead them out of the inferno. That thought, the thought of escaping the fire, was everything. Yelling in their fear they followed Matsudaira Sadayori.

They burst from the smoking tunnel of a street, charging straight into the enemy and taking them completely by surprise. To Sadayori's left, one of his men bayonetted a Choshu soldier through the chest, and in his excitement fired off the rifle at the same time. Other men fired from the hip, some wildly, some cool, some lifting their rifles to their shoulders to aim with precision. In the first minute or so they had cleared the gate, then became embroiled in close combat with the samurai emerging from the imperial compound.

Sadayori himself came face to face with an officer in armor. He challenged him, giving him his name. The man responded, and they stood two sword lengths apart, blades bared. His opponent wore a helmet with a fearsome mask with eye holes that slanted up, a hooked metal nose and long whiskers of bristling horsehair under the nose and above the down-curved slit of the mouth hole. The crest of the helmet was a crescent of burnished copper. Sadayori could see the man's eyes glittering through the holes, and felt suddenly very tired, hardly able to stand.

It was his sword that held him up. He felt as if he were attached to it, as if he had grown out of it, as if it controlled and moved him. Sadayori was normally a very aggressive swordsman, but this time he waited, only his feet moving, bound in straw sandals that gave him a good grip on the ground.

About them was a bedlam of shots and screams, but he and the Choshu samurai were an island. The man feinted with a lunge to the throat, very fast, then whirled the sword back; it hissed like a live thing, cutting to the side. Sadayori's sword reversed down his left arm and both blades jarred with a sharp clang. They disengaged. The Choshu warrior slowly raised his sword high and Sadayori responded with another posture, mirroring and opposite to the other's intentions. They were locked, feeling each other out, grasping at each other's sense of combat distance.

Suddenly, with astonishing agility, considering the weight of armor he wore, the Choshu warrior leaped high in the air, his sword slashing downward with great force and speed. Sadayori spun far to the left, his own sword thrusting out with his right hand, arm straight like a lance. It took his opponent deep in the armpit. The man crashed forward, actually completing his move, while Sadayori's sword jerked free, the tip reddened. He resumed his two-handed grip as his opponent turned to face him again, sword held low now, with his left arm pressed to his side in agony. Sadayori could see no blood, for it was running down the inside of the armor. Feinting left, Sadayori cut with all his force to the right, a yell rising from deep below the tightened muscles of his belly. He hardly felt a jar at all as his blade cut through the side flaps of the helmet and halfway through the man's neck. His opponent crashed to the ground, then pushed with his right hand, which still gripped his sword. He flopped over onto his back and the helmet fell off. As Sadayori gazed at his eyes, filming over now with death, he remembered that once, long ago, he had shared sake with the man, in Edo, the time he had called on the Choshu residence to return some swords. They had all sworn brotherhood then, sworn to defend this sacred nation against invasion. And now . . .

"Yahhh! Bravely done! I always said you were one of the best combat swordsmen I've ever known!"

Itoh, sword drawn, had come up beside him. His men had seized the opening provided by Sadayori's surprise attack. The Choshu men were falling back, with heavy losses. Itoh looked around.

"My brother, he was with you . . ."

Sadayori took off his helmet and bowed his head sadly.

"He fell. They shot him."

Itoh cursed savagely. "Ah, but they could never have taken him except with a bullet. Old friend, this is a damnable way to wage war. There is no chivalry in it." He put up a gauntleted hand to wipe across his eyes.

"Itoh-san, I'm sorry, you know that," said Sadayori softly, putting a hand out to rest on his shoulder. "He fought well and died bravely. Is the palace secure now?"

"Yes, but there has been damage. What with the fighting and the bullets and shells flying around, the fire brigade couldn't function, and some lead even went into the palace.

456

However, His Majesty is safe. Come, old friend, let us take a few more heads before this day is through!"

Wearily, Sadayori put his helmet back on. He called his men and followed Itoh. Those enemy that survived the fighting died by their own hand.

It was only a couple of weeks later, although it seemed like years, that the two of them were soaking aches and sprains in an outdoor hot-spring pool, in the garden of an inn. A mountain river rushed by within a pebble's throw. Neither of them had been wounded in the battle of Kyoto, but they had suffered bruises, scrapes, burns and, in Sadayori's case, a sprained shoulder. He groaned with mingled pleasure and pain as the heat and sulfur did their work on him. Between the two men floated a thick wooden tray, on which were a bottle of sake and two Bisen ware cups.

"I think I'm getting too old for running around in armor," said Sadayori. "I ache all over. And during that fight I kept on thinking—when can I take this stuff off and have a bath."

"What are you saying? You fought like ten men." Itoh was leaning against a boulder, one heavy arm draped over it, his washcloth perched on his head. Sadayori climbed out of the pool and sat on a rock in the cool evening air. On one side the pool was shielded from view by fences and bamboo, while the other looked down upon the rushing white water that filled the little valley with its music. A small place, two days' ride out of Kyoto. Sadayori had persuaded Itoh to take a few days to relax.

Overhead the first stars were peeping, and across, on the opposite side of the valley, they could see a single feeble light from the doorway of a farmhouse. Up on the hill was a glowing red spot—charcoal burners. Ah, so peaceful.

"Don't you think it ironic," Sadayori said, turning to face his friend who still endured the heat of the pool, his face as red as a boiled crayfish, "that all of us who were raised for war, all of us who did all that talk about fighting barbarians and defending the nation, should end up killing each other, and that mostly with foreign weapons?"

Itoh grunted and reached for the sake. "We had to do our duty. Those Choshu fools would have the whole country at war. I dislike the *bakufu* and always have, and it is my feeling that we should just reinstate imperial rule and have done with it. Choshu claims that is what their aim is and was. However, their methods were stupid, and we did warn them, didn't we?" He eased himself up out of the water and sat on the boulder crouching like a large red monkey. "Look at it this way . . . Japan needs both fighters and statesmen to unite the nation. Preferably fighting statesmen. The conflict we've just been through will shake things up a bit. We know the fighters. Now let's find the statesmen. My bet is that Saigo-san will win out. We've always known that he was a fighter, and now he's already negotiating, and ably too."

"I know little of politics," said Sadayori, stepping back into the hot water. "I just know that we keep on ending up in a fight with each other, when we all dream of becoming one strong nation. You say you don't like Tokugawa, and I'm painfully aware why. As for me, I served the Tokugawa clan, and the *bakufu*, for half of my life, and I still point out to you that the shogun's rule gave us nearly three hundred years of peace." He sighed. "Although in truth we were divided, a hundred little countries jealous of each other. When can we become a single nation?"

"We are. We're just having family squabbles."

Sadayori fell silent and looked down at the river, listening to its watery rushings.

"Itoh-san, what I'm trying to say is that I hate killing, especially Japanese."

His friend was no longer listening, but was singing, his deep voice echoing in the rocks around the pool, a sad, sad lullaby.

"Itoh-san . . ."

"Yes?"

"The next time we fight a battle, I'm not going to wear armor. It looks impressive, it makes a man feel martial, but it is too heavy, too hot, and absolutely no use against bullets."

Then he shut up. Perhaps he shouldn't have said that. Sadayori had gone back with Itoh to search for the body of his younger brother, and he had seen the look on Itoh's face as he gazed down at the peppering of holes in the breast-plate, waist flaps and helmet, holes punched insolently through family armor that had cost a fortune and had been revered as a precious heirloom. How proudly had the young man stood out in front of his troops, his sword still undrawn, goading them, urging not to fear the enemy with their guns. Then orders had been given on the other side to direct the first volley at the Satsuma samurai and his proud, arrogant talk. It hurled him flat on his back on the cobbles like a broken puppet. For him the fight was finished without his blade ever seeing the sun. A lifetime of pride and training, and not once did he close with the enemy.

"You're brooding about my brother, right?" said Itoh.

"Yes, I'm sorry, but how could I forget him?"

Itoh stood up and waded to the edge of the pool, then came to sit on the stone bench facing the river, the washcloth over his privates.

"Yes, a damnable way to wage war, but effective at killing men. We must just make sure not to kill too many of the wrong men. I agree, armor is outmoded. I won't wear it either, except for parades. You know what I wished I'd carried all the time we were fighting? A water bottle, yes, a water bottle, and maybe a pouch with some pads and bandages so I could help fallen comrades."

"I'm truly sad about your brother, Itoh-san."

"I know. He liked you too." He turned to face Sadayori. "Even a country samurai like me reads books," he said, "though not as much as you. However, I do recall a story describing the war they fought in America, about a hundred years ago, when they rebelled against the English king."

"Yes, they call it the 'War of Independence.'"

"Right. A war against the English, the very same English who burned our town with a single attack of their ships. Anyway, in this war the English soldiers had fine uniforms, high hats with feathers on them, bright red coats with a crossing of thick white belts. They marched out to fight the Americans in lines, beating drums and playlng flutes, very fine and correct. But those Americans just hid behind trees and walls and shot them at a distance with long, accurate rifles, weapons they were used to, because they all hunted animals to eat and take furs. Of course, from the point of view of chivalry, that was a disgraceful way to wage war, but the thing is that they won, even though outnumbered, and in winning they made a very powerful nation." Itoh raised his arms, as if holding a rifle. "Bang! One dead warrior, despite any kind of expensive finery. It works, see. Now neither you nor I would use a rifle, but if you think of it, we have always considered bows as part of the warrior's arsenal, haven't we? What's the difference between a rifle and a bow? Both kill at a distance."

"The bow employs the strength of a man's arm, not the explosive force of powder."

"And a rifle uses a man's brain, and quite frankly, as I've said before, Japanese foot soldiers can be trained to be very effective with the bayonet. Hey, let's go in and drink some more. All of it is an abomination, this business of Japanese killing each other, even if they were Choshu upstarts." Itoh fell quiet for a while. "I'm going to have a woman tonight, maybe two. How about you?"

Sadayori just smiled. How many times had Itoh asked the same question, in places all over the country.

"No, I'll just have a massage. I still ache."

"I don't understand it, you're such a man in all other ways. Come on, let's go drink. You say they have good food here?"

Later in the evening, while Sadayori's shoulder and back were being expertly tended to by a blind masseuse, Itoh was off in another room with one of the three country girls who had come to serve them drinks and entertain them with samisen and song.

In the morning, riding back to Kyoto, Sadayori teased Itoh for the circles under his eyes, and a very obvious hangover, despite another session in the hot pool before breakfast.

The air was fresh and crisp, with birds singing, groups of travelers hurrying on foot, and once in a while they overtook the palanquin and guard escort of a rich person heading back to the city now that the trouble was over. However, even though some of those people were of considerable rank, the two mounted warriors disdained to dismount.

Chapter Thirty-Four

Saburo's son, Jiro, was born in the summer of 1865, by the Western calendar, during the time that Shogun Iemochi was preparing a punitive expedition against Choshu for having attacked Kyoto, and to try to destroy them totally in the light of their vow to overthrow the Tokugawa regime. However, even though the young shogun, now nearing twenty, had originally been the child daimyo of Kii, there was no question of time of requisitioning whale boats and men. War was more modern nowadays. From Taiji only a few men were conscripted. They left the whalers alone.

The hard year rushed by with whales scarce and work arduous. Payments for meat, oil, baleen and meal shipments were slow in coming, and sometimes didn't come at all, which didn't keep the authorities from clamoring for taxes.

Oyoshi breast-fed the baby for six months, and then, despite the fact that her breasts were swollen with milk, she began to try to wean him. Several people chided her because of it, and goat milk was hard to come by. The child often screamed itself blue in the face, hating the substitute. Finally even Saburo got angry with the fuss and asked her why.

"You men don't know anything, do you?" she said, laying her hand on his forearm. "The longer I keep a baby at my breast the longer it might be before we can make another one, and I want to fill the house with your children."

He was happy.

Yoichi too doted on his baby brother, and would sling him on his back with one of Saburo's sashes, taking him on scrambles, climbs, runs and paddles that would have horrified his parents to witness.

Taiji was as full of gossip as ever, and there was plenty of comment about Oyoshi and Saburo. Some even whispered old stories. Some were perhaps jealous, for although their marriage was over a decade old, they behaved like newly wed youngsters, and a second pregnancy had not diminished Oyoshi's beauty in the least. The men also teased Saburo for being so concerned with his wife, for showing his feelings for her when other men would not, thinking such open affection to be unmanly.

Meanwhile, word had come that Jinsuke was married. Onui was happy that her son had settled with a woman, happy too that Jinsuke was rumored to be rich, with a fine house on a hill in Yokohama. Tatsudaiyu refused to talk about it. Jinsuke had married a foreigner.

It was to Yokohama, earlier that year, that Nakahama Manjiro came, the man who had spent ten years in America. As he made his way up to Captain Jim Sky's house, his feelings were mixed. On the one hand he felt strange and embarrassed because he was visiting a man's house without invitation, and because this man was posing as an American, and had a foreign wife. Oh, Manjiro had checked on it, and the fellow had gained American citizenship, but still it was strange. On the other hand he was burning with curiosity to see how the one-armed Taiji whaler had succeeded so well out in the wide oceans. The ban on Japanese wearing Western dress, with the exception of military uniforms and sea uniforms, was still in force, and Manjiro wore kimono, *hakama* and swords. He had not shaved his head again, but his hair was tied in a looped topknot.

Manjiro went to the gate and yanked on the bell cord. A servant came, and Manjiro handed him a brief, politely worded note in English, apologizing for turning up uninvited, and asked to see the captain for a few minutes.

Jinsuke went to the gate himself, and stood for a few seconds, regarding this man who had so influenced his life. He was puzzled, for he seemed to be a government official, in Japanese dress, bearing swords. Manjiro bowed, then straightened up with a grin and a wink.

"Well, Skipper," he said in English, "can I come aboard for a gam?"

Jinsuke opened the gate and held out his hand, gripping the other man's with all the welcome he could muster.

"I have studied, and at home my wife and I use English most of the time, but still I cannot speak as well as you do,

Nakahama-san. Your English sounds like an American, but I still have an accent."

"That doesn't matter," said Manjiro, "and I speak well because I went to America as a boy of fourteen and was raised by an American family. Come what may, you and I have much in common. I hope you'll forgive me for just coming like this."

Jinsuke led him to the front door, where Susan was waiting. She had heard the story of how her husband had met this man, what it meant to him at the time. She bowed formally, then with a radiant smile held out her hand. Manjiro was obviously a gentleman whichever side of the ocean he chose to be. Susan led him into the drawing room and called for tea. Manjiro sat for a while, admiring the room, less of a mixture than Lyall Fogerty's place, but still a blend of East and West.

"Captain Sky, may I be frank?"

"Of course."

"I must say that although I am with the government now, you have nothing to fear from me. Times are changing anyway. But first, tell me what you think of the American whaling ships now that you've seen them for yourself?"

"At killing whales and sailing ships they are the best," he answered, "but each time we took a whale alongside and kept only blubber, baleen and teeth, I remembered how precious the rest of a whale was to Taiji, and I felt bad. I used to think how good it would be if we cooperated. That always bothered me."

"Me too," said Manjiro, "and for years now I've been visiting our whaling stations, including Taiji, trying to tell them about American techniques, but do you think they'll listen? It's hopeless! However, soon will come the time for the young people, and they will welcome change."

He looked at Susan. "Your husband is a very important man, you know, a key man in the history of this country. Oh, not like a general or a politician, more important than that. One day the nation must recognize it."

"Perhaps, and I would like to believe so, but I'm always afraid for him. This country, and my mother's country, which is China, you know, are so volatile."

"Volatile," said Manjiro, "mmm, yes. If you take the word to mean gaseous, and easily evaporated, then I would argue with you, Mrs. Sky, but if you take it to mean 'fly like an eagle' then I would agree. The old nations of Asia will fly, like eagles."

Susan did not want to get into another of the kinds of arguments that she, Jinsuke and Lyall were always indulging in, so she smiled, stood, and asked him to stay for dinner.

"It's not much, but it would be so nice to have your company." He was charmed. When faced with situations like that in Japanese Manjiro would have declined, but Jinsuke's career and success fascinated him, as did his beautiful wife, so he answered as an American might, accepting.

Susan left the room to organize the kitchen, and the two men were left alone. A servant brought tea, and Jinsuke fetched a pipe box and fine tobacco. He still preferred the little Japanese pipes. He passed Manjiro a silver box of lucifers.

"Captain," said Manjiro, taking a puff. "I believe you have carried guns to Satsuma?"

"Why do you say that?" demanded Jinsuke, suddenly wary. The *bakufu*, although their grip was weakening in many things, still ostensibly had an embargo on shipments of arms to the other fiefs outside the Tokugawa clan. It was ignored, of course, but here in Yokohama the *bakufu* still held the power.

"I am a Tosa man. I have good relationships with Sakamoto Ryoma, and it was he who told me that you had returned, about your ship, about your, er, American papers. I assure you I have told nobody else. I come to you because the Tosa clan seeks to purchase arms . . ."

"In Nagasaki you can deal with Thomas Glover, the Englishman. There is also a Prussian company, L. Kniffler and Company."

"Yes, I know, we have been in contact with them," said Manjiro, "but for various reasons we would also like to deal abroad. I and Sakamoto, or somebody we trust, will seek to contract for heavy weapons, for many rifles and for a modern gunboat. Shanghai seems a convenient place. We hear that the American, Mr. Rose, has helped you in some dealings."

"True," said Jinsuke, "but Mr. Rose has retired and gone back to America." He stood and went over to a small desk, and wrote out the name of an English firm. He handed it to Manjiro, who read it.

"Jardine Matheson and Company, yes, of course, I know them."

"They might be the best for you. They'll sell anything," said Jinsuke, with more than a touch of cynicism in his voice. "On the other side I've added my father-in-law's address in Shanghai. If you have trouble in making contact, go to him. He knows everybody. Please understand, though, that I do not deal in arms. I have carried boxes and crates perhaps, but I do not care to know what is in them. Even that is dangerous enough." He sat down in his chair again. "I'd rather hunt seals."

Manjiro smiled. "Yes. And you go to some rather risky places for that too, don't you? But of course, I understand. Enough of business, for now at least. I hope we might enjoy your services . . ."

"Please deal with my brother-in-law. I only captain the ship. You must know him, Lyall Fogerty. But now, can I offer you something a little better than tea?"

Jinsuke wasn't telling the whole truth. Half of the ship was his, a wedding present from Susan's father.

Later, after a fine dinner and long conversation, Susan snuggled up to her husband in their big brass double bed, laying a slender hand upon his chest.

"What did Nakahama-san really want?"

"For us to carry guns, to Tosa, dealing directly with Shanghai."

"You've done that a few times already, haven't you?"

Jinsuke said nothing. Susan turned over and lay quiet for a while, then turned back to him and shook his shoulder.

"I hate you doing that, Jim, you know it."

He slipped his arm under her shoulder and hugged her to him. "I know it, but it helped build this house."

Saying nothing for a while, she stroked his nipple. "Did you read that letter that came today from Captain MacNeil?" she asked.

"I didn't have time."

She kissed him, a custom he'd gotten to enjoy.

"Jim, I love Japan, but I'm afraid. There's always fighting and killing, and you always carry a gun, and Lyall thinks there'll be a civil war. It scares me."

"Don't worry."

"I can't help it, and I want children, and I want our children to have a real home, a country. I don't want them to be like me and Lyall. Oh, Lyall is happy here and he'll never leave, because he likes learning and doing new things, but I'm different. I don't want to be foreign forever, and that's what I'd be here. But please won't you read Captain MacNeil's letter? He's moved north, to Canada."

465

"You want me to get up, put on the lamps, and read the letter right now?"

She kissed him again. "Don't you dare. I'll tell you. He says it's a wonderful place and he wants you to go there and be his partner in a shipping and sealing business. He also deals in lumber for ships. He says that where he is living now, a little place called Vancouver, is the most wonderful place in the civilized world, his words, peaceful and full of opportunity. He thinks it would be a fine place to raise children"
—she paused—"and I want children."

"Give it time, they'll come."

Now she put her head on his chest and gently bit his nipple. It came erect, like a tiny little button.

"I don't think you've been trying hard enough."

"What?" said Jinsuke in mock anger.

"Well, we haven't made love since last night, have we?" Running her hand down his chest she came to his belly, and to the dense coarse hair of him, then she folded her hand around his manhood.

"The mast is up, so if I raise the sails, will the ship start moving? I like it when it's moving."

He pushed her over and took a nipple in his mouth, teasing it with his tongue, then he kissed her again. Kissing Susan was never boring.

"Now the other one," she said, holding her other breast up to him, "it isn't fair to kiss just one, you must kiss both." He did. Perhaps it was that night that Susan became pregnant.

Two days later Jinsuke went to the office for sailing instructions. Lyall asked him to sit down, and closed the door.

"Sorry, Jim, but after this trip to Nagasaki, you're going to lose three of your men." He pushed a paper over to him. On it were written the names of his second officer, an engineer and a young third officer who had shown an extraordinary aptitude for navigation.

"We almost lost Tetsuro, but I begged them to let us keep him for at least one more year, by which time he should have gotten his certificate. The others are joining a Japanese company. You remember Sakamoto? From Tosa? He's getting ships for his clan and is forming a marine company, picking fifty men, the cream of the crop. I'm as sorry as you are, but I take it as a compliment that he wants some of ours."

Jinsuke shrugged. "We figured something like this would

happen, right? They get us to train them, and once we can really rely on them, they take them away. I got wind of it from Tetsuro, and I know that at least two of them don't really want to leave. Miyabe told you, right?"

"Right."

"He'll no doubt select three likely young men for us to take aboard on our free training voyages too," said Jinsuke with sarcasm. He hated to lose any of his crew. Lyall nodded and changed the subject.

"Jim, I want to tell you something else too—I intend to get married."

Jinsuke came to his feet, beaming and holding out his hand. "Congratulations! When? Who?"

Lyall was embarrassed, for he had kept all of this a secret from his family.

"Her name is Onami. I had the whole affair arranged, with Miyabe-san acting as *nakodo*. She came to the shop one day with her father and, well, I fell for her, Jim. She's the fifth daughter of an Edo merchant who has a branch here in Yokohama. He was an oil merchant actually. A couple of months ago he lost nearly everything in a fire, so they are rather poor now. Before that, though, all of his daughters were educated well. Things are hard for him, I suppose, and the government is always demanding those so-called loans. I'll help him out with his business." He looked into his brother-in-law's eyes. "I love being in Japan, and I want to settle here. I may be a *gaijin*, but somehow I feel more accepted here than I was in China, and certainly more than in England. She's a good girl, intelligent, bright, pretty. You'll like her, Jim, so will Susan."

Jim leaned over the desk and slapped him on the shoulder. "Lyall, you're more Japanese than I am. It'll work, I know. When's the wedding ceremony?"

"Next month. I didn't want to tell you or Susan until I got a definite answer from her father. He's agreed. And there's another thing, Jim . . ."

Jinsuke raised his eyebrows.

"I can't tell my own father, he'll not forgive me, but Onami's father insists on adopting me. I'll have a Japanese name. While Dad is alive I'll not use it in the foreign community, but I feel at heart that I'm an Asian, Jim."

Jinsuke understood. A man was what he felt himself to be. More and more he felt American, or at least, oceanic. It was as if the name of Jim Sky had gradually caused a metamorphosis in him, a change reinforced by his status as a ship's captain, and by his life, his land, home, and his cosmopolitan wife. Lyall could easily change the other way, and become Japanese. What did it matter? They were still brothers, family, two sides of the same picture. Lyall went to the cabinet and fetched a bottle of whiskey and two glasses. Jinsuke took one.

"In your case, it should be sake, but there'll be other times. Lyall, congratulations . . . but what will your Japanese name be?"

"Shimizu is the family name, it's an old samurai name. Three generations ago one of the younger sons turned to trade, it happened once in a while, you know, as with the Mitsui company."

Jinsuke raised his glass. "Here's to a new wife, a new life, and a new name—*kampai!*"

"Thank you, older brother," said Lyall, in Japanese.

To heap momentous news on momentous news was not polite, so Jinsuke did not tell Lyall of his own decision. For a day and a night he had been thinking of Captain MacNeil's offer, and remembering how he had been enraptured with the northwest coast of North America when he sailed there before. Jinsuke had decided that he would go to Canada, with his wife, stop carrying a gun unless it was to hunt, build a new home in a new country, and forget the nightmare of flashing swords that all too often troubled his nights.

No, he would wait, and tell Lyall after the next voyage.

Chapter Thirty-Five

The palanquin jounced and bumped. Sadayori would have preferred to walk, but Itoh insisted, saying that they were supposed to be officers of importance and status. Most tedious. Itoh was in another palanquin, his bulk cramped and uncomfortable. They had eight Satsuma guards, armed not only with swords, but with hidden pistols too. It was dark, a thick cloud cover hiding the moon, and the guards carried paper lanterns, but just in case of spies, the guards' faces were hidden by large straw hats, and nowhere was the cross-and-circle insignia of Lord Shimazu to be seen. Their ship was waiting in Nagasaki harbor, and they would be gone before dawn.

All in all it had been a fascinating evening. The Englishman entertained well. High-class geisha had sung and played for them. A meal in Western style had been lavishly prepared, and dark-suited, white-shirted waiters had served a dozen kinds of wines, with spirits to follow. Skilled interpreters kept the conversation moving like New Year's shuttlecocks.

Their business had been speedily resolved too, but that was small wonder. In that year alone the Satsuma war fund had spent close to four hundred thousand English pounds on foreign arms, over half of which had been paid to this balding, white-haired foreigner with his big curling moustache growing up the sides of his face. The civil war in America had created a huge surplus in weapons, so Satsuma got a lot for their money, and Itoh at least was well pleased.

Sadayori had been polite but reticent, for he despised their host and all like him, not because he was a barbarian, but because he waxed rich on the internal conflicts brewing in Japan. In the boxed-up gloom of the palanquin he tried to compose a poem in his mind on the irony of it all. Satsuma grew and refined sweet sugar to pay for weapons that would come from the civil war of the nation whose black ships had started it all. As a subject for poetry, though, it was too universal, too amorphous, and he soon gave up in disgust.

This Thomas Blake Glover, this English gentleman, had been generous, offering to supply them not only with arms, but with loans of money, as he had done, they knew, with their erstwhile Choshu foes. But then, they weren't foes any longer, were they? Sakamoto Ryoma, together with Commander Saigo of Satsuma, had effected a treaty between Satsuma and Choshu. When Sadayori thought about it, there was more to this Glover fellow than mere profit, despite his opulent mansion on the hill. The British government was behind him, and foxy as they were, they surely knew whom to back.

As for the treaty, Sadayori himself had been instrumental in that, for Saigo had sent him to Shimonoseki together with Ryoma soon after the Kyoto conflict, to see if there was any way they could resolve difficulties.

"I hate him," said Sadayori to himself. However, his hatred of Glover and of foreign interference and intrusion was not the kind of hatred that used to gnaw at his guts when he was young.

Meanwhile, forever scheming, Itoh had also tried to get Sadayori involved in affairs that he found even more distasteful. Saigo had a plan to incite the *bakufu* to rash action, while at the same time drawing their attention from his intrigues in Kyoto. He was hiring *ronin* and *yakuza* ruffians to cause trouble in Edo. Petty troubles, robberies, street fights, arson, all designed to prove that the shogun could not even control his own capital. Itoh had asked Sadayori to help in the secret organization of this, for he knew Edo better than anybody else in Kagoshima, but Sadayori had angrily refused. Itoh just smiled.

"Well, I told Saigo you'd have nothing to do with it, but he insisted I ask anyway."

"I'll tell him myself, it's disgraceful! That is not the *bushi* way!"

"Don't do that, you know what his temper is like, and anyway"—he paused—"you once said that about using foreign weapons, right?" They said no more about it, but Sadayori knew that the once peaceful, well-regulated city of Edo, one of the safest cities anywhere, was now dangerous for an honest citizen. For a while his loyalty to the Satsuma cause wavered, and he considered becoming a *ronin* again, or even a monk. When he confided this to Itoh, his friend just looked at him with a half smile.

470

"You ride a horse galloping toward destiny. Men like you must cling to the reins and grip with your knees, otherwise both horse and rider will stumble and break their necks. I don't like the Edo business either, but I do believe in Commander Saigo's aims, which are to unite this nation and make it strong and proud. I think those are your aims too. Anyway, the thought of you as a monk is a travesty, you're tone-deaf. The first time you started chanting, the good lord Buddha would flee and hide in his lotus." Then Itoh guffawed and called for drinks.

When they got back to Kagoshima, Sadayori was invited to a party given at Itoh's house for Sakamoto Ryoma, who had come to Kyushu with his new wife, the pretty little maid from the Teradaya. His right hand was still bandaged from severe sword cuts. During the latter part of the negotiations in Kyoto to affect a Satsuma–Choshu pact, Sakamoto, like Sadayori, had been attacked at night by the Shinsen Gumi. He had escaped because the girl, Oryo, had run up naked from her bath to warn him and Miyoshi Shinzon, who were just settling down to bed. After a terrific fight, during which they killed and wounded several attackers, the two men smashed their way through the wall at the back of the inn, breaking through another house, and eventually making it back to the safety of the Satsuma residence.

Commander Saigo himself was *nakodo* at the marriage between Sakamoto and Oryo, and had invited him to come to Kyushu, "for a honeymoon and rest." As all of Satsuma knew he was a marked man and now a hated enemy of the *bakufu.*

That night Saigo was too busy to come to Itoh's house, but even so, all the talk was of revolution, war and politics. At that time Shogun Iemochi was about to try to invade the fiefdom of Choshu, against all advice. *Bakufu* troops and supplies were being amassed in Hiroshima early in 1866. This time they would have no aid from Satsuma. The Choshu clan was training, recruiting, preparing. They were determined that the outcome would be different this time, and awareness of the *bakufu* attack had swept aside all the conservative opposition to the young revolutionaries in the fief.

In Kagoshima, Saigo had laid out a lavish welcome for a visit by Sir Harry Parkes, the British minister, persuading him even further to back Satsuma in any conflict against the Tokugawa regime. Satsuma men, including the young warrior Togo, were sent to train in England. Britain had even made a promise to support Satsuma against the French, should they decide to fight for the *bakufu*, who was using them to try to modernize their army.

Sadayori was depressed and decided to get drunk. Finally he threw a sake bottle and shouted.

"We're nothing but a lot of dogs in a pen," he yelled, shocking everybody into silence by his bad behavior, "fighting among each other because we're afraid to jump the fence and bite the intruders!" Sakamoto Ryoma broke the silence and came to kneel in front of the red-eyed, swaying Sadayori.

"Matsudaira-san, dogs we may have been, but now you shall see us grow to be tigers, strong enough to bite the British lion's tail off."

Itoh roared his approval, grabbed Sadayori, wrestled him to the mats, and poured *shochu* down his throat. Later he had to hoist the smaller man over his shoulders and carry him up to his room.

In July of 1866 Iemochi began his war against Choshu. It was a debacle, and Satsuma watched from the sidelines. Choshu militia, recruited from peasants and townsmen, armed with modern rifles and trained and led by samurai, mowed down their attackers.

Shogun Iemochi retired to Osaka, where in September of 1866 he died, not of wounds, but of a diet of salty and sweet extravagance, with white rice, a few vegetables, and a total lack of exposure to sunshine. He had lived through a mere twenty years, and part of his twenty-first, and had not given his princess an heir.

Keiki, the son of the ultraconservative and assassinated lord of Mito, who many thought should have been chosen in the first place, was elected to be the next shogun. One of the first things he did was to send Katsu Yoshikuni as his envoy to Hiroshima to stop the war with Choshu.

In Yokohama, with the baby upstairs in his crib, Susan was packing. The living room carpet was littered with old Japanese news sheets, crockery, knickknacks and small personal items. Charles Olderby, now resigned from the consulate and an independent artist, was sitting in an armchair, nursing a glass of sherry.

"Well, Susan my dear, if you and Jim are set on it, there is nothing I or anyone else can say, is there? You are both as irrevocable as Greenland glaciers. I must say, though, I'll miss you both. You will visit, won't you?"

472

"Of course we will, Charles. Lyall is here, and we shall miss this house."

"As far as I'm concerned, it's always yours."

Olderby had bought the Skys' house and much of the furniture in it. Unusually for an artist, Olderby had a canny sense for investment and business, and in this he was greatly aided by Lyall.

They chatted like old friends, while Susan wrapped and packed.

In imitation of a formal Japanese *tokonoma*, but set at eye level for people sitting in chairs, a wide alcove was set into one wall, lit from one side by a high, narrow window, whose light was softened by a wood and rice paper screen. The thick polished shelf of wild cherry wood held a miniature sand garden designed by Susan. Beneath the thick shelf were four cherry-wood drawers; into each was carved an ideogram for a season—spring, summer, autumn, winter. The drawers contained collections of scrolls, hung and changed regularly up until a couple of months before, when Jinsuke had brought a scroll home from his ship and hung it in the alcove himself. Susan began wrapping the scrolls for shipping, while Olderby helped himself to another glass of sherry, watching her.

"Susan dear, that one hanging, the whaling scroll, you wouldn't be persuaded to leave it, would you? Frankly, it's the best thing I've ever seen in this or any other foreign house, and it's not by one of the famous artists, is it?"

"No, it's from Taiji, so Jim says. But do you really like it? I'm not sure I do."

In truth, Susan hated it. It was not that she wanted to deny her husband's origins, it was that they seemed to deny and exclude her, and their present life. Jim had once been one of those men, she knew it, bare to the waist in red loincloths that exposed buttocks, a *happi* jacket cast off the shoulders and hanging loosely, wild hair tied with a red cloth, pate shaved, body like a wrestler, riding a gaudy boat, shoulder to shoulder with other half-naked men. Could he have loved or married her if he'd stayed one of those? No, never. She preferred him as he was now, dressed in well-fitted tailor-made jackets and shirts, his thick black hair cut rather short, curling at the ends, graying at the temples, with a beard always neatly trimmed, and with wrinkles around his eyes and mouth that deepened when he smiled, and those bulging, smooth brown muscles hidden from sight except when he lay with her.

"It's one of the best I've seen, my dear, the colors are stronger, surer, the lines bolder. It moves, it sings! Those men must be magnificent to see."

"Yes, I'm sure," said Susan gaily. "Jim was one of them, after all."

Olderby looked at her. "Yes, he was that."

"Then he lost his arm," she said, "and they didn't want him anymore. So I got him, didn't I."

She took out the little bamboo rod with a hook at the end that was used to change scrolls. She took the whaling scroll down, rolled it up, tied the cords, and handed it to Olderby.

"Here then, Charles, you keep it."

He raised his eyebrows. "You're not going to ask Jim?"

"What's his is mine, and what's mine is his, for better or for worse. Keep it, Charles, he won't mind."

She didn't know that it had been painted by Jinsuke's younger brother.

Before they set sail for Canada in that year of 1867, the Emperor Komei died in February at the age of thirty-seven, supposedly of smallpox, but reputedly of poison. It was unlikely, after all, that the Son of Heaven would be exposed to anyone in the least tainted by disfigurement, and hygiene in the imperial court was scrupulous. Mutsuhito, his son and successor to the Heavenly Throne, was only fourteen years old.

In 1867, while Lyall Fogerty was celebrating his second Christmas with his Japanese wife and their year-old daughter, his Yokohama living room gay with paper chains and mistletoe, and a big Christmas tree, a fir, decorated with tinsel and cotton wool, and bright with candles—with buckets of water ready just in case—a great fight was raging in Edo. *Bakufu* forces, enraged to action by Satsuma's subversive activities in the shogun's capital, had attacked the Lord of Satsuma's Edo mansion, his official residence, with two thousand men. Two thousand against a hundred fifty. Itoh fought, and was one of the thirty who escaped, swinging his sword right down to the dock where a Satsuma steamship was readied, roaring in anger and triumph, for the subversion had worked. Now war with the *bakufu* was inevitable. The huge residence, together with all its invaluable silks and treasures, blazed to ashes.

Vying with the standard religions of Shinto and Buddhism, new religions were springing up all over—strange beliefs whose prophets claimed outrageous things and stressed the equality of all mankind. As soon as the government put down one, another would spring up like a mushroom. Throughout the country, the people were behaving strangely.

Because of his refined accent, and because it was years since he had been seen in the city, Sadayori had been secretly sent to Edo, by land, to investigate the damage. He was mounted and armed with an imperial pass, acquired for him by Commander Saigo himself. On the Tokaido road, just outside the little town of Numazu on the Kyoto side of the Izu Peninsula, the road was blocked by a dancing, chanting mob, a thousand or more people, men, women and children, townsfolk and peasants. They seemed to have gone mad, with men dressed as women, women dressed as men, pots on their heads, many in bright or ridiculous clothes, clothes on backward, some with chalk and soot on their faces. Samisen, flute and drum beat out a monotonous tune to the wild chant that went on and on.

> "Ain't it good, ain't it good!
> If it stinks, paper it up!
> If it rents, do it again!
> Ain't it good, ain't it good, ain't it good!"

The words were nonsense, the behavior outrageous. They stormed into big houses and shops, chanting, dancing, barging out again carrying what they wanted, and the authorities were nowhere to be seen. A merchant came out shouting and striking at them, but in seconds he had vanished in a stamping, chanting melee.

Realizing that he was in as mortal danger as in a battle, Sadayori held his horse in control, and edged forward. They surged around him, clutching at his stirrups, at his *hakama*, at the reins, yelling and laughing.

> "Come on down!
> Join on in!
> Give it a go!
> Give us a show!
> Ain't it good! Ain't it good!"

They would have dragged him from his horse, but instead of going for his sword, he pulled out the pass, with the golden chrysanthemum seal, roaring at them.

"You idiots! This is an imperial pass! Would you mock and defy your emperor?"

They backed off in a circle around him, dancing and chanting around and around, still not letting him pass, when an older fellow, face and eyes painted white and black like a badger, a cloth tied over his head, came pushing his way forward, jabbing with a thick cudgel, beating a path, all the while doing a silly jig, his buttocks bared, shouting and chanting like a madman.

> "Out of the road,
> You insolent toads!
> Kiss my arse,
> The lord must pass!
> Ain't it good!
> Ain't it good!
> Ain't it just so good!"

He went ahead of the horse, jiggling bare white buttocks on which two big eyes had been painted, hitting out with the thick stick at all and sundry, hurting some, but nobody seemed to mind, for they fell back, making way for the samurai on his horse, singing, laughing, clapping, dancing.

Once past the mob, the man turned, took the cloth off his head, and bowed. "I'm sorry you were troubled, sir," he said, in the formal speech of a samurai, "it is safe now."

Sadayori was trembling with fury. "What the hell is going on? Who are you."

The man smiled under the face of a clown. "I am me, sir. The common folk cannot fight the revolution with swords, so they make revolution their own way. Banzai to His Highness!"

Then, waving his stick over his head, waggling those buttocks like a drunken fool, he went dancing back the way he came. Sadayori kicked the horse into a gallop. The well-ordered society was going crazy.

Sadayori barely made it back to Kyoto to join the combined Satsuma and Choshu armies sent to face the shogun's forces in the greatest and most decisive battle of the revolution. The *bakufu* samurai outnumbered them three to one, but Satsuma and Choshu men were better trained and better armed. When *bakufu* warriors, most of them armed with their personal bladed weapons, came at them, Satsuma and Choshu riflemen mowed them down, while their well-directed artillery pounded hell into disorganized and tightly bunched *bakufu* positions. That was at Fushimi, just outside Kyoto, on January 27, 1868. Sadayori refused to wear either armor or uniform, but instead tied his kimono sleeves back for battle, and wore on his head a light black-lacquered helmet with the cross-and-circle insignia of Lord Shimazu of Satsuma, and against all advice, he strapped a battle pennant to his back. Miraculously, he was unscathed.

Two days later, at Toba, young Issukei, the adopted son of the owner of the Teradaya Inn, fell and died, fighting for Choshu and Satsuma. And, at Osaka, on February 5, the shogun's army was again defeated. Commander Saigo, for all his cold-blooded scheming and superb battlefield tactics, showed extraordinary mercy to those who surrendered.

Effectively, the long Tokugawa rule was over; the shogun fled by ship. Imperial rule was reinstated, guided, of course, by statesmen-warriors who had brought about the revolution, and only diehards refused to accept it.

Sadayori was among the many patriots who bore young Issukei's body back to Fushimi. As he walked, still numb from the aftermath of the battle, he looked around for the familiar face of Ryoma. He turned to the man beside him.

"Where is Sakamoto Ryoma? He should be here, he was very fond of the lad."

The man turned to him in surprise. "Didn't you know? Sakamoto sensei was murdered almost two months ago, he and his friend Nakaoka."

"Where?"

"Upstairs in a soya sauce shop in Shijo Kawaramachi, Kyoto."

So they got him.

The body of Issukei, sitting upright in a wooden tublike coffin, was borne by four samurai. Incense smoke, deathly sweet, wafted back to Sadayori, but he felt no more grief.

"Madness . . ." he whispered to himself, and the man beside him thought he was praying.

Chapter Thirty-Six

Sadayori sat in the rickshaw, gripping what appeared to be a thick walking stick between his knees and staring moodily ahead over the hat of the straining, panting runner. The galloping steed of fate had run on through events that a decade ago he would not even have dreamed of. The Tokugawa regime had fallen, and there was no shogun or *bakufu* anymore. The young Emperor Meiji now ruled from the shogun's former palace, and Edo was now called Tokyo. There were no more daimyos, no more fiefs, the ancient domains had been returned to the emperor and the old daimyos were now part of a new aristocracy. Samurai were renamed *shizoku,* and no longer had their stipends of rice, and worse still, since the year before, 1876, they were no longer permitted to carry swords. To top off this calamity, in the last year the central bureaucratic government had decided to cut the samurai pensions, already but a fraction of their original incomes. For many, this new move meant a drop in income of eighty-five to ninety percent, creating unbelievable poverty and hardship. The old class system was gone.

Yes, Japan was rapidly becoming modernized, and admittedly strong, but things did not sit well with Matsudaira Sadayori. His hands tightened around the slightly curved cherry-wood stick. During the battle for Wakamatsu castle he had taken a bullet in the right leg, and now he walked with a limp and a stick, the latter concealing the blade of his sword, from which he refused to be parted, no matter what the government said.

The Meiji Restoration had come in 1867. Ten years had passed since then, and everything had changed. Now the streets were filled with rickshaws, with horse-drawn carriages, with Japanese—even women sometimes—wearing Western clothes and there were banks and new schools, outlandish buildings and customs. Even hairstyles had changed, with the topknot fast disappearing, as it was no longer mandatory. Progress had charged at them when they, the young and fervent ones who had been fighting to preserve all they loved of their country, had been thinking that progress could be held in check. The torrent of change was like a dam bursting, sweeping away so many things they had thought timeless. Yet most of them still had confidence that Japan would always be Japan, only firmer, stronger, reaching out once more across the oceans and riding the tides of history.

The rickshaw man came to a stop outside an exclusive restaurant and put down the long handles. Sadayori got out, took a purse from inside the folds of his kimono, and paid him a few coins. He looked at the young man's face, broad, young, earnest, now beaded with sweat.

"It was hard work," he said.

"It's the hills, sir, they're always hard to go up, but going up makes one strong, sir."

"Indeed. Are you from Tokyo?"

"No, sir, I came here to work so that I can go to university."

"That's excellent. Well, thank you, and don't give up!"

The young man bobbed a bow, tightened the cloth around his forehead, and picked up the long handles. Sadayori stood and watched him trot down the road, singing snatches of a snow-country folk song. For a while, even after the man had gone, Sadayori stood outside, gazing at the bold black characters of the restaurant sign, which was nailed to the gatepost of what had once been a highranking *bushi* house. An oiled-paper lantern set above it threw a faint light. His eyes shifted to the portals, to the high roof over the gates, now thrown open, and inside them to raked gravel and large round stepping stones, and a stone lantern, with moths around it; by the building was an ancient plum tree, blossoming. A woman in a kimono came out and looked at him curiously. She caught his eye and bowed.

"Are you Itoh-sama's guest, sir?"

He nodded.

"Please, sir, come this way, the gentleman is waiting."

Inside, other women knelt and bowed to him as he entered. He slipped out of his wooden *geta* and stepped up onto the polished floor. This was an old place, with huge pillars and beams, dark with age, and with tasteful ornaments and scrolls displayed here and there. He followed a woman who slid open a screen door, kneeling as she did so, announcing his arrival.

Itoh sat alone, picking at a dish of sea urchin roe with his chopsticks, a sake flagon and cups on the table, a low lacquerware tray in front of him, his left arm on a lacquerware rest. Unlike Sadayori, he affected Western dress, a dark three-piece suit with a white shirt and butterfly collar, with a neat silk tie, water blue, beneath it. His hair too was cut in the foreign fashion, slickly parted and with no trace of gray. He also sported a fine curling waxed moustache.

"Yoh! Matsudaira! Welcome! I started without you, ex cuse me. Girl, fetch more sake!"

Sadayori looked at his friend, not really approving of the way he dressed, but admiring his seemingly ageless vigor. Itoh was an official of high rank with the new Ministry of Home Affairs, and was responsible to a man named Kawaji, later to be known as the father of the Japanese police system. Now Itoh sat, not in a formal kneeling position, but with legs crossed, like a peasant.

At the entrance, they had taken Sadayori's cape, and tried to take his stick, but he had shaken his head and hung onto it. Now, entering the room, he laid the stick, and the hid den, priceless blade, in the alcove beneath a scroll and in front of a flower arrangement. Itoh watched him.

There were few in Tokyo who did not know this formida ble man, who taught at his own fencing school, and who wrote various philosophical and historical works. Sadayori took his place and the maid held out a sake cup to him; he took it, looking at his friend while she poured for him.

"Bring us blowfish sashimi first, then we'll have tem pura," said Itoh. Sensing that the men wanted to be alone, she bowed and discreetly left.

"Colonel Tani is still holding out at Kumamoto," said Itoh. "Saigo made a grave mistake in marching all the way north to take that place. You remember the castle, don' you?" Sadayori nodded. The two-hundred-year-old castle wa one of the strongest in Japan, with a moat and massive ramparts looking down steep slopes. They both sympathize with Saigo's rebellion, with the attempt to restore the samu rai to their rightful place in society, but Saigo's plan to march all those miles north in the vain belief that he coul take this stronghold with ease was ill conceived. Colone Tani, the commandant of the castle, had a garrison of fou thousand men, firing down on the rebellious samurai who attacked in suicidal charges.

"The government is sending forty thousand troops agains him, peasants mostly, mind you, and they are loading ther into steamships. If Tani holds out for another few days the

the castle will be relieved, and not only will Saigo lose that, he'll lose Kagoshima too."

Sadayori snorted. "So again, the circle turns and we fight each other. Still, I say that Saigo was right. We should have invaded Korea and expanded the empire."

"I agree."

Ever since the new conscription laws had been brought into effect, the army was now eighty percent peasant, with the *bushi* class finding less and less justification for their existence, and becoming more bitter, more impoverished. Saigo's rebellion in Kyushu was the last of a whole series of samurai revolts against the new central bureaucratic government. All other rebellions had been put down.

Neither Itoh nor Sadayori really believed that samurai from all over the country would flock to him, but it was a dream . . .

"What are you going to do?"

Itoh lowered his voice.

"When Saigo took Kagoshima, then marched north to Kumamoto, he had about fifteen thousand men. Now he has an army of about thirty thousand discontented samurai. Samurai uprisings elsewhere in the country have been crushed. Now it is spring, and I can tell you that with Tani holding out there in Kumamoto, by summer Saigo's siege will be lifted and his army surrounded. He won't get any supplies in by sea or land. Even if he manages to fight his way south to Kagoshima again, it is inevitable that the rebellion will be crushed, but I can only pray that perhaps it might teach the bureaucrats and this damned Tokyo government a lesson or two."

"You haven't answered my question," said Sadayori. "I asked what are you, Itoh, going to do?"

Itoh folded his arms and looked quizzically at this iron gray man, spare now in frame and marked by the years, yet always hard and sharp as the sword everybody knew he carried.

"Matsudaira, old friend, I dress like this because it suits what I have to do. But I am as much a samurai at heart as you are. We have fought a lot of battles together, you and I, and I'm grateful that we never had to be enemies, otherwise one of us would not be here now. Here, drink . . ."

Sadayori held out his cup, still looking at Itoh's face with the steady, unwavering gaze of a swordsman. Itoh put down the flagon.

"Saigo needs a shipment of medical supplies. I have secretly procured them. I also have a chest of gold for him. That is going to mean something, with the government over-extending itself and issuing those damn notes. Saigo was my *sempai*, I have known him since I was a boy. He became my leader, my general, and without him the emperor would not be in Tokyo. So how can I leave him? Of course I will return to Kyushu, put away these clothes and stick my swords back into my sash. It must be soon, though, the blockade is tightening."

"I see," said Sadayori. "That will mean losing everything, your house, your position . . ."

Itoh grimaced. "You think I'm another one like our precious Home Minister Okubo? Trying to live like some European princeling? Pah! Yes, of course I have a big house and servants, but they mean nothing against honor and duty and my obligations to Saigo, to the whole of our class! No, this samurai will go back and fight beside him."

"Then I will go too." Sadayori was still in a formal kneeling position, although his friend had made gestures for him to relax. He put both hands on the tatami in front of him and bowed deeply. "Please, permit me to accompany you."

Itoh knelt and returned the bow, then, coming forward on his knees, eyes filling with tears, he grasped Sadayori by the shoulders.

"Just for our old comrades down there to see your face and know that you are with them will give them the strength of lions! Saigo-san will rejoice too, and who knows, we might even win." Sadayori gave a sad half smile and reached for the flagon.

"Let us drink to that."

Itoh held his cup, then poured for Sadayori, raising a toast to Saigo Takamori, and his army of rebel samurai. Itoh clapped his hands.

"Now we will have a few geisha to entertain us, eh?"

In a carriage of the Tokyo-to-Yokohama railway, the two men sat side by side. Itoh was by the window, looking out at the swiftly passing scenery, while Sadayori stared straight ahead, sword stick between his knees. His mind was reviewing the last desperate battle he had fought in the Restoration, against *bakufu* diehards on Ueno hill. At that time the city of Edo had already been surrendered to the emperor's forces—in April of 1868—and the last shogun, Keiki, had been placed under house arrest.

Sadayori recalled that even as he had led his unit in one of

482

the last charges that swept over the remnants of Lord Oguri's forces, he felt his chest swell with admiration for the enemy's tenacity, their stubborn resistance, their loyalty. Pausing for breath in the shambles, he had thought . . . why am I here? Bullets showered him with bark from a tree a couple of feet away. Why am I here? Helping to bring down the last brave men who defend the system under which I was born and to which I am sworn? For those moments Sadayori had been unaware of the cries of his men, beseeching him to take cover from the crackling gunfire. At that battle Sadayori had reached a kind of vortex, and he felt forces swirling around him, sucking him to other levels of consciousness and understanding: "I will be sincere in what I do, at the time of doing, always—and that is enough."

The air had been alive with bullets, and with shells whining and crashing. Smoke from a blazing temple wafted over him, and he stood alone and exposed, his imperial army headdress, a lion mane of white hair, moving with the wind, sometimes catching sparks. He wore no armor, and by nature a conservative, he would discard the uniform of the army, preferring kimono and *hakama*, with sleeves tied back, and, incongruously, a water flask that hung over his shoulder on a thong. Many men had cause to remember that water flask as they lay exhausted or wounded, for he would kneel beside them, holding it to their lips. They remembered that and the detached coolness of his courage. There were many who would stand and shout defiance, glorying in valor, but never he. Sadayori merely stood, and when his men rallied and it was time to go forward again, he led them with calm and benign confidence.

Now, sitting on this foreign-built train, running over steel lines that were making ugly the garden of Japan, Sadayori wondered again what he was doing. He and Itoh were traveling for a doomed cause, and yet there was purity in the obligation, to uphold a debt of honor to Saigo, former marshal of the imperial army, forced into desperate acts by a government that betrayed the samurai who had put it in position. Yes, he now would be a rebel, but Sadayori did not think that what he would do was treachery. The real treachery was what the government was doing to the samurai, to the whole of society. Perhaps this was essentially a Satsuma fight, but they fought for the whole of the *bushi* class, for those men forced by poverty to commit seppuku, for the warriors whose daughters had been sold into prostitution, for men made to do things quite unthinkable.

He settled back in his seat. Calmness washed over him. He was fulfilling his duty, and that was enough. Once the duty and the obligation were recognized there was no question as to the path.

They took rickshaws from the station to the spacious three-story offices of Shimizu Steamships and Trading Company. Soon they were ushered into the offices of the president. He stood as they entered, and came out from behind the desk, making a polite bow, then extending a hand to Itoh.

"Colonel Itoh, it is good to see you again."

Itoh shook the man's hand and then turned to Sadayori. "I'd like to introduce Matsudaira Sadayori-san. Matsudaira-san, this is the well-known Shimizu Ryo, whom I've told you about."

They bowed to each other. Years ago they might have been enemies, for Shimizu was not born Japanese, and the actions of his brother-in-law, a mere whaler, had been very serious, for he had killed samurai.

Shimizu was much taller than either of them, with chestnut-brown hair, gray at the temples, and a large moustache. He was broad in the shoulders, and his physique hinted at strength, but now he had the florid features and slight paunch of a well-fed, well-wined merchant.

"Please, gentlemen, take a seat."

There was a round rosewood table in one corner of the office, behind which was a huge map of Asia and the Pacific, occupying most of one wall. From a window one could look out onto the harbor of Yokohama and see the ships coming and going.

A girl appeared, bringing fragrant Chinese tea and small sweet cakes, and for a while the three men made small talk, giving each other time.

To friends, Shimizu was still known as Lyall, although he had formally adopted his father-in-law's name and made him, very generously, a senior partner in the company. He was one of the rare foreigners who had obtained Japanese citizenship. That was a year after his own father's death and a few years after the Emperor Meiji had come to power. His patriotism to his adopted country was unquestioned, even if some of his ideas about Japan's future as leader of Asia, guiding the affairs of the whole of the Pacific like a benevolent older brother, seemed wild to many Japanese and absolutely scandalous to the foreign community.

He had the Midas touch, and prospered. He owned a fleet

of ten ships, all crewed by Japanese, plying trade and passenger routes throughout the East, even as far as Africa and Australia. He also had a chain of stores that sold perfumes and medicines, both Oriental and Western, and he was a major investor in several of Japan's new and burgeoning industries.

Itoh felt that this man was the only one he could go to with trust. He might well refuse, but he would not betray. Curious, but he was more Japanese in his code than many Japanese were now.

"Lyall-san," began Itoh, using the more familiar name by which he had known him for almost ten years, "you can guess what I'm going to ask you to do for us."

Lyall smiled. "It's not the first time I've been asked to run guns to Kagoshima."

Itoh held up one hand, shaking it. "No, not guns, medical supplies, that's all."

Lyall knew. He had personally opened and examined the contents of the cases in his warehouse. He held his head with his hands and stared at the carpet for a full minute. The two samurai waited.

"I can't do it, Itoh-san, it's too risky. I couldn't trust the crews to keep quiet. None of my captains would want the job, and even if they did, you know, this is a rebellion against the imperial government. No, Itoh-san, I'm sorry."

"But half of your men are from Kyushu," said Itoh.

"I know, but I've, well, felt them out. We'd lose the ship." He looked at them both, almost pleadingly. "Itoh-san, you know that General Saigo will be defeated, don't you? Even from here it's obvious to see."

Their expressions were blank, and Lyall regretted having said it. All too often he did such things, saying what to a native Japanese would have been left unspoken, but clearly understood. No matter how he mastered the language, the technique of talking without words was something he could not master.

"Forgive me. I admire General Saigo. He was one of the only truly great and honest men in the government. I just wish . . ."

"I understand. Don't worry. Well, I'm sorry we bothered you." Itoh glanced at Sadayori and they both stood. Lyall remained seated and gestured with both hands.

"Wait, please wait. There is something else."

They looked at each other, and sat down again.

"There is a ship in port now, with a captain who tells me

485

he has an old obligation to Matsudaira-san, and to you too, Itoh-san. He's willing to run the blockade."

"Can you trust him? I know of no ship's captain with any obligation to us."

"He's my brother-in-law, I can trust him with my life. If anybody can do it, he can. Not only is his a foreign ship, but he knows the coast well, and is the best captain of them all."

There was a tone of anguish shading the man's tone of voice, thought Sadayori.

"He knows Japanese waters?" Sadayori asked.

"Yes, his ship sailed for years here, under the American flag. Now she has British registry, and sails out of British Columbia." Lyall stood and traced his finger on the big wall map. "She has come here with a load of furs, then intends to head back north, to the Russian islands, to . . . er . . . take some seals."

"So this captain poaches on the Russian islands? He must be a bold man."

"He has been doing it on and off for twenty years almost," said Lyall with a grin. "Those Russians will never catch him. I took the liberty of discussing your problems with him, thinking he might know somebody. His immediate reaction was that he would do it himself, even though, frankly, I advised him strongly against it. However . . ." He turned and looked at Sadayori, who now realized who this captain must be. "If I introduce this man, Matsudaira-san must give his word that he will not try to harm him, for actions of a long time ago, taken to defend the lives of others."

Sadayori bowed slightly. "Tell the whaler that he has never really had to fear anything from me. Others misunderstood, but I know, and Itoh-san knows, that there are times when a man has to fight."

Sadayori stood, sensing that the man was here, probably just outside. "It has been a long time," he said softly.

Lyall called Jinsuke in, and Sadayori stepped forward with a smile, bowing to him as he would to an equal. Itoh stood too, grinning, widely and hugely delighted, feeling that fate and events had played some kind of long-lasting joke.

"Well, whaler, the sands of time have flowed. Broken any heads lately?"

"Not lately," said Jinsuke, "and I'm very careful when I drink *awamori*. Indeed, it has been a long time, Itoh-san, and as you see, although you threw me into the ocean, a whale spat me out again."

Itoh guffawed and turned to Sadayori. "We'd never have caught him if we hadn't drugged his liquor."

Sadayori spoke. "I am saddened to think that all these years and events have passed and we have not had time to talk. We might have understood many things about each other and the world. We are indebted to you, Jinsuke-san, or should I call you Jim Sky?"

"Either. I have a Japanese name too now. Moriichi. Jinsuke Moriichi, although in Canada hardly anybody knows that."

Sadayori cocked his head questioningly. Since the Restoration commoners had been permitted family names. But why *forest* and *one*?

"But the name is not what you think," said Jinsuke. " 'Mori', is written with 'iron' and 'tongue'—harpoon."

Sadayori slapped his thigh. "Of course! Excellent! Anyway, let me say this clearly. A long time ago I made up my mind that if I ever saw this man again, not only would I apologize for totally changing his life and no doubt causing him a lot of distress, but I would tell him that I admire what he has done in his life. Sometimes men are cursed with the need to fight. At such times, men die. It is a sad thing."

Sadayori extended his hand. "I understand that this custom came from the time of European chivalry, and showed that no sword or weapon was held. A good custom between men of sincerity, I think." Jinsuke took Sadayori's hand for the first time and shook it, while the old warrior closed his left hand over the two clasped hands, gripping tightly.

"We have much to talk about, don't we?"

"Indeed," said Jinsuke, "and let us begin tonight. We can load this afternoon and leave with the tide. Nobody suspects me. Do you gentlemen have much baggage?"

The two samurai exchanged looks. "I have need of nothing," said Sadayori, "but Itoh-san must attend to a few things in Tokyo."

"Shall we sail this time tomorrow, then?"

They agreed. Jinsuke promised to have a boat by the wharf waiting for them. Lyall went over to the window and looked down into the street.

"I anticipated this and had a carriage called." He turned and faced Itoh and Sadayori. "Forgive me if I offend, but will you not reconsider? Let us deliver the crates for you to Kagoshima, but please, don't go. Japan needs men like you."

"It is our honor and duty, we must go," said Itoh.

Lyall shook his head sadly. "Please, then, take care."

The two samurai bowed to him, thanked him, and left. Lyall lapsed into English.

"And for God's sake, you take care too, Jim, I couldn't face Susan or the kids if anything happened to you." He went to the cupboard and poured large slugs of whiskey into tumblers of Jacobean glass, holding one out to his brother-in-law. He tapped the bulge of the Colt under Jinsuke's jacket. "You bloody old pirate, you don't take chances, do you? You wouldn't have shot him right here in my office, would you?"

Jinsuke looked at Lyall with complete seriousness. "I wouldn't shoot that man for any reason. It was he who gave me this life. I carry the gun because it is risky business we're doing. It's the imperial government now, Lyall, not the *bakufu*. If they catch us I'll fight for my life."

"You can back off if you want to, Jim, nobody would blame you."

"You're Japanese enough to know that in this I cannot back off, even if I don't agree with it."

Silently the two men drank. From outside, in the harbor, there came the doleful moan of a departing steamer.

They slipped past the blockade into the Amakusa Nada and anchored off a tiny bay there. The *Big Sky* had been refitted, and was now owned by Jinsuke, who had bought Lyall's share in the ship after the death of old Captain Fogerty. Her engine ran as quietly as possible, and most of the time she sailed. Her sails were dyed blue-gray. The crew was a mixture of nationalities, and all the men were used to night operations. When Jinsuke slipped two boats ashore, loaded to the gunwales, the crewmen were neither nervous nor noisy.

Jinsuke steered the first boat in, and as it touched the sand, he loosened the pistol in its holster, jumped out, and looked around. He gave the all-clear signal and the second boat came in. The men started unloading crates, and one extremely heavy chest. Itoh, now in kimono and *hakama*, with two swords in his sash, leaped ashore and went up the beach. Soon dark figures appeared, with pack horses shod the old way, with straw horseshoes. The bosun raised the heavy double-barreled shotgun, but Jinsuke told him it was all right.

Unloading was swift and the crates were soon taken up the beach and lashed onto the horses. Itoh came back, a leather pouch in his hand, heavy with gold.

"Thank you, Captain. Have a safe journey back. This is not enough for what you have done for us, but please take it."

"No, I wish no payment for this trip." He looked at Sadayori. "Take it, please, as repayment for old obligations."

He then undid the fastenings of his shoulder holster, slipping it and the gun off. "Matsudaira-san, won't you take this? It has saved my life, and perhaps it might save yours."

Sadayori looked at him with a sad smile. How their positions had changed! Now he was a poverty-stricken rebel, going to fight a lost cause, and here, the whaler, the simple Taiji boy, was offering him the gift of a weapon!

"Thank you, Captain, but no. I'm an old-fashioned fellow, and I'll stick to my swords. Keep it. I am glad it served you well."

A young samurai ran down the beach. "Sir, we must be going."

They bowed to each other, and parted. In one direction went the soft clop of horses' hooves, and in the other the gentle dip and pull of a boat's oars.

Saigo's rebel army fought savagely for six months. Imperial warships and troops had taken his home base of Kagoshima, left unguarded during the disastrous siege up north. After many battles they were surrounded on the eastern coast of Kyushu, at Nobeoka, outnumbered, undersupplied. Saigo broke out through the government troops, killing many of them. He fought his way south to Kagoshima and retook the town. Half of his men were dead, while the government had lost a quarter of its troops. The rebellion had seen thirty thousand casualties altogether.

Knowing and accepting that this was the end, Saigo moved just outside Kagoshima, now besieged again by government troops. The very last battle was fought on the hill called Shiroyama. In the fight Saigo was wounded by a bullet and had to be carried to a place where he took the only honorable end for a samurai.

Itoh, witness to his leader's end, left the hiding of his head to Saigo's brother, wept silently for a while, then strode back to the last remaining band of a few hundred, facing an army of thirty thousand. So many had fallen, so many had fled.

To his own men he passed around a flagon of strong spirits, sharing the last drops with Sadayori, who looked tired and battered, a blood- and pus-stained bandage around his head. Itoh pointed down the slope to the positions of the army of conscripts that had been sent against them.

"For a bunch of peasants and shopkeepers, they have fought well, have they not? I think we can go now and feel confident that even with us brave fellows gone, Japan will be safe."

He stood up, immediately drawing fire. Behind him and around him the hill was pocked with craters, ruined guns, dead and wounded men, exhausted samurai. Saigo Takamori, hero of the Restoration, idol of an impoverished warrior class, was gone. The time had come for them to go too. Itoh bellowed down the hill in a voice that rattled eardrums even above the noise of the firing.

"Hey! Hold your fire! Don't waste the emperor's lead! We're coming down!"

With a grin to his men and to Sadayori, Itoh threw away the sheath of his sword. "I won't be needing that again."

Sadayori stood up and did the same. The sheath fell with a clatter on some rocks and the sun glinted off the cool, old blade. With shouts of defiance the other men did the same, throwing the sheaths away, casting life aside.

"You are going to charge?" asked Sadayori mildly.

"Of course, what else?"

Sadayori came up out of the trench, his limp quite obvious. "Look," he said, loud enough for all to hear, "you young fellows just dash down there and teach those peasants a lesson. I'm an old man, and if you don't mind, I'll just take my time and walk down behind you. Tell them to expect me, won't you? If there is anything to do by the time I get there, I'll try my best."

Then to Itoh he said, "Take care, old friend, don't trip on a stone, you're not so young yourself." The others laughed, and with swords raised, they charged down the hill at the ranks of the government army.

Sadayori did as he said, walking down, his sword in his right hand. He held it, not brandishing or threatening, not yelling, and quite unafraid. He saw his comrades fall one by one to the withering rifle fire, although a few entered among the troops and did awful slaughter until they too fell. Itoh died, shot a dozen times through the chest, twenty yards from the enemy. Those few men of his left swept past him.

The government troops were reloading their rifles and taking their wounded to the rear when they saw a single gray-haired man, head bandaged, come limping down the hill toward them.

"Hold your fire," commanded the officer. At fifty paces the officer cried out. "Halt! If you come to surrender, throw down your sword!"

Slowly, the man raised his sword into a fighting position, as if he were demonstrating moves on the floor of a dojo. Energy seemed to flow through his body, and even at this distance and from behind the safety of many rifles they feared him.

"I am Matsudaira Sadayori of Kii, retainer of the patriot Saigo Takamori. I challenge you. Long live the emperor!" Despite his limp, the man broke into a run, his now bare feet flashing over the broken ground. The soldiers threw frightened glances at their officer. During the massed charge, not one of them had flinched, but this lone warrior was terrifying. Was he really human? The young officer's sword came down and a whole line of rifles crashed.

Bullets struck even the sword, and it went flying from his hand as Sadayori was knocked backward. He lay for a while, looking up at the vastness of the sky, then with great effort he turned himself over. To his right, just out of reach, there was a single patch of miraculously untrampled grass. Above it was a swallow-tailed butterfly, yellow, white and black. It dipped and danced on delicately pointed wings. It was all beautiful, the grass, lines and skeins of green, and the butterfly's wings, moving like the long sleeves of a girl's kimono. The beauty began to darken and fade, and he tried to cry out, no, no, not yet, not until the dance is over . . .

And she whirled, in perfect time to the music, and Sadayori realized that she had been waiting for him, waiting, waiting, all this time . . .

When they walked over the battlefield the officer went to kneel by the body of the last man. Around him stood his soldiers, with their modern rifles, bayonets and uniforms.

"You all saw how this man died. Remember it. Bury him with honor, and lay his sword by his side."

A sergeant saluted. Gently, and with care not to get blood on their uniforms, they picked him up. He was surprisingly light and small.

Chapter Thirty-Seven

"It was nothing but a dream," Saburo had said, "don't let it bother you. Throw it away if you like, it isn't important." But Oyoshi could never throw away anything he had painted. Yet it did trouble her, and she carried the dread of it heavy in her heart as she mounted the one hundred eighty-eight steps that led to the little hilltop shrine on Mukaijima. Her second son, Jiro, now thirteen, her daughter Otama, who was eleven, and her youngest son Rikizo, nearly eight, followed behind her. The children stepped lightly, counting steps, carrying a few flowers, a little sake and some cooked rice. They knew nothing of Oyoshi's fears.

So, it was only a dream, but Saburo's painting was so strangely vivid that she felt she might even have shared the dream with him as they lay side by side in the night.

There was a chase boat in the dream, decorated with a dragon and with scarlet hibiscus, all set upon bands of broad black and yellow. There was no such traditional design in Taiji, nor in Koza. Fifteen men manned the boat, sculling it toward an enormous setting sun, and below the boat, deep beneath translucent water, were the curved, tiled roofs of a palace.

The leader of the boat was urging the men on, and he and all the others had shaven heads, like priests, and they wore orange robes, slipped off to hang loosely around the waist, exposing the muscular arms and torsos of whalers. The painting was a disturbing blend of images, a whaleboat heading for the setting sun, passing over the palace of the Dragon King, a whaleboat with no harpoons or lines, while the faces of the men were shining with joy, with ecstasy, with fear.

It lay tightly rolled up for a few days, then Oyoshi went and prayed to Kannon, goddess of mercy, and showed it to the kindly old priest. For a long time he gazed at it, spread on the tatami before him. To him it was quite clear, for this was surely a whaler's version of a ship of Fudara, such as solitary priests or ascetics who sought nirvana might board to drift upon the endless ocean, sailing on for eternity. But he could not tell her that. It troubled him deeply, this juxtaposing of images, although no evil emanated from its design or its colors. Was Takigawa Saburo gifted with visions? Was his true calling with the priesthood? He always was an inward-turning person, kinder and deeper and less boisterous or boastful than most.

"Allow me to keep this picture for one week," said the priest, "I wish to reflect upon it. All I can do is to advise you to pray. I believe a saintly spirit guided this man's brush."

Oyoshi prayed daily to Kannon, goddess of mercy, and to the Buddha, and to be safe she did not ignore the Shinto gods either, one of whom overlooked the sea from Mukaijima.

The path zigzagged on up, and through the thick trees they could sometimes look down into the bay, a deep bluish green now, the waters clear, for it was winter. Around the harbor there were jetty walls of rounded beach stones. Although the whaling fleet was out, several small fishing vessels lay careened, and a few others floated peaceful and still on the water, with the fishermen gathered around a fire, hunkering down and exchanging gossip and tall tales. Some children were swinging on the bars of the capstans, up from the sandy beach where the whales were landed. Out in front of the Asuka shrine the *kan-nushi,* in ordinary, everyday clothes, was sweeping. Above, the ever-circling kites.

"Mother, why are we coming up here?" asked Jiro.

"To pray at the shrine," she said.

Jiro was going to ask why, but he bit the question off. Anyway, it was nice to go for walks with Mother, even if, at thirteen, he would never admit it.

Miles away, above the hill on which the great shrine of Nachi and its famous waterfall were located, ugly gray clouds were moving, lenticular, swimming in the sky like fat, headless fish. Rain threatened, but did not come.

At the top of the hill, Oyoshi set the children to sweeping around the shrine with brooms kept there for that purpose, while she threw away the withered, dead flowers, and washed receptacles for food and drink. When all was finished she and the children clasped their hands and prayed. She prayed that she might be permitted to live many more years with her kind and gentle husband, who even now treated her like a bride.

Oyoshi had reached home when the long-awaited signal went up at Tomyosaki. There came the notes of the conch and wide waving of the signal sticks, and then the black pennant with a white central stripe licked at the wind. Right whale!

Taiji Kakuemon and Wada Kinemon both hurried to the beach, excited and hopeful, for things had been going very badly, with no whales for weeks. Kinemon lowered the telescope and shook his head, mouth tightening in a grim line. The signal had been altered. What they had seen out at sea was a female with a calf, long-forbidden prey to the whalers of Taiji.

"Anyway," he said with a sigh, shutting the telescope with a snap, "there are only a couple of hours of daylight left, and the weather is not so promising."

"Calf or no calf, we have been too long without a whale! We're on the verge of collapse, you know that! I'm going to give the signal to hunt."

Kinemon argued vehemently with his older relative. *"Semi no komochi wa, yume ni mo miru na!"* Even in a dream, look not upon a female right whale with her young. "We have been raised with that old saying! We've never taken rights with calves before, it's wrong! No good will come of it!"

"We are not dreaming now, are we, and that whale is worth three hundred *ryo,* and that calf will fetch top prices for the meat too. If we don't get those whales out there it will be a lean and hungry New Year's for all of us. I say we hunt!"

"Kakuemon, I strongly advise against it," Kinemon's voice was raised now, and several onlookers watched and listened. They all knew that it was not good luck to kill a female right whale with young. Some believed that the whale would be offended in spirit, and never again return, and some thought that the Sea God would be angered, while others said that it was that the normally docile whale would fight with fury if she had a calf with her. However, they all knew that in Taiji they did not take females with calves, and that stiff penalties were leveled against boats that killed even one calf.

Kakuemon looked at his cousin. "I accept responsibility. We need that whale."

Kinemon still argued. "If you accept responsibility, then

494

have your own way. I can't agree. We have faced hard times in Taiji before, and I don't think we are reduced to this."

He turned on his heels and walked away. Kakuemon, face lined with annoyance, gave the signal. Out on the cliff edge of Tomyosaki, the red hunt pennant was hoisted, and the chase boats, after a few brief moments of disbelief, darted forward, ready to drive the whales, mother and calf, toward the circle of nets that were already being laid.

She was a big, fat whale, and she fought. She stood straight up in the water, turning her body around, smacking her long flippers like thunderclaps on the water, getting between the boats and her calf. Several boats were filled with water and had to back off to bail out. They hurled harpoon after harpoon at her, but she arched her back into a hollow, tightening the great muscles and compressing the tough, fibrous blubber, so the iron did not bite well. At times both whales bolted to windward, the female thrashing her flukes in every direction, sweeping sideways, in vast movements. Many of the older whalers wished they had contested the hunt signal, for all of this was proving the wisdom of the old saying. But she was sixty *shaku* or more in length and round as a tub.

As the day drew to a close, and the leaden skies grew even darker, somebody managed to get in close and thrust at the tendons in the join of the tail, not quite hamstringing her completely, but certainly hampering her movements. Only then did they manage to drive her and the calf into the entangling rope meshes.

It took a long time to kill her, and meanwhile a wind sprang up, an angry, cold, wet wind. Several of the men glanced fearfully shoreward, for this was the wind they feared the most—the *yamade,* the "mountain leaver," a land-born wind, not the gentle green-scented breezes of summer, but a strong wind, born on the continent, ruffled by inland mountains, wild and furious, its belly raked into turbulence by jagged peaks.

The whale was in the net, and dying, and there was nothing to do but to finish it. They all knew it would be many long hours of work to get this one home.

From the lookouts at Tomyosaki and at Kandorisaki, the watchers could observe the fight. They too were aware and worried about the wind and kept glancing at the pennants which flapped so noisily and pointed their tails out to sea, as if saying, "There! There! Out there! Look!"

A squall came. Savage rain lashed at the thatched roof of

the lookout and drove in through the long window spaces. The wind was increasing in strength. The watchers looked at each other. Then, when they looked out to sea again, the fleet was gone.

"They're gone! I can't see them!" Toumi Kakichi cried out, and his uncle picked up the telescope. Poor light and driving rain made visibility almost nil. Kakichi was right. They signaled to Kandori, who answered that they could not see the boats either. By the time they left the lookout, it was pitch-dark, and dangerous to make their way back along the path. All night the wind raged.

Out at sea, the men were exhausted after their long battle, but now they had both whales secured between carry boats and each in tow with three chase boats ahead. They chanted as they worked the oars, but there was no joy in their song. The wind had blown them far offshore and now they had to fight wind and waves and cold to carry their whales home. Rain lashed at them like icy whips, and they were all hungry.

By the time dawn came the men's hands were raw with blisters, and their bodies ached with cold and cramp. Still they were not in sight of Taiji. One man, washing the blood off his hands in the water, cried out. "It's warm. The water's warm!"

His captain tested the water and looked with worried lines toward where the shore should be. Warm water in winter could only mean that they had been driven out into the swift, wide, warm current, a current that could flow at half the speed of an unladen chase boat with a fresh crew.

The day passed and a foul stench wafted from the bloated carcasses. With tears of frustration and shame, for never had such a thing been done by Taiji men before, they cut the precious whales free and left them to drift, and to curse them. The fleet was scattered, and by now most boats had lost sight of each other. They tried to head for home, but nobody could sing anymore.

Days later, bodies began to wash up along the coast. From the hair and the red loincloths, and from the heavy muscles, people from other villages knew that the dead men were whalers, and realized that a terrible disaster had befallen them.

It was, by the new calendar, the eleventh year of the reign of the Emperor Meiji, December 24, 1878.

Some of the Taiji whaleboats were washed as far as the

islands of Izu, and on the third day some of the men could even see the high cone of Mount Fuji, but they were unable to get to land. They had abandoned the treasured but lighter chase boats and had transferred to the broader, more stable carry boats.

To those men who could no longer stand at the oars, their comrades gave affection and encouragement. Saburo's eldest son, Yoichi, now twenty-five and with two children of his own, held his father in his arms, shielding him as best as he could with his own body from the chilling wind. Somebody stood and pointed.

"Hey! Island! Island ahead. Come, take up your oars!"

Yoichi propped his father up against the gunwale and gently slapped his face. "Father! Look, land!"

Saburo tried to speak. There was something terribly important he had to tell Yoichi, but the words would not come. Through half-closed eyes he caught a glimpse of high cliffs, ringed white with surf. Yes, it was a land, a land now encircled with a halo of exquisite and vivid colors, and the colors all vibrated with light and fragrance. They were all those colors he had quested and searched for throughout his life. Yes, yes, he knew now, his had been a life of colors, and now he was coming to the land of color he had always wanted to show to Oyoshi and the children . . . now they would be able to understand . . .

Saburo died, just before the boat was driven onto the cliffs of the island and smashed to pieces. Anguished and helpless islanders watched from the cliff tops.

Of the whole fleet, no boats and only a few men were saved, some returning months and even years later from the isolated islands to which they had been driven. One hundred eleven men died; the priceless boats of the whaling fleet and all their equipment was lost, and the net-whaling industry of Taiji ruined.

In the weeks following the disaster, as the dead washed ashore or were retrieved by other coastal communities, fishermen and sailors, and returned to Taiji in round coffins, Taiji Kakuemon was enveloped by the perfume of burning incense that lingered in every house and even in the narrow streets. He could not escape it. All around were the sounds of priests chanting sutras, bells tinging, women and children weeping. As those awful weeks passed it became clear that they had lost all but a handful of the entire whaling fleet.

Taiji Kakuemon was a broken man. He sold all of his estate, everything he had, and divided the proceeds among the bereaved. Then, to the village where his family had lived and whaled for centuries, Taiji Kakuemon bid a grieving farewell, and never returned.

On that fateful day at the beach, when the two men had argued, many had heard Wada Kinemon advise against going after the whale, so the people of Taiji laid no blame on him. The Wada family stayed and faced the hardships, going deeply into debt in efforts to raise up the net-whaling business again. However, with so many skilled men gone, and no boats, it was doomed.

Oyoshi walked home slowly. Her husband and her eldest son were among the missing. She almost envied those families whose men had been found and now sat in their round coffins with the priests chanting over them. Her own eyes were dry, because she had known. She had known the night that Shusuke's wife came weeping and wailing in despair to her house. Perhaps she had known the morning Saburo painted the picture of his dream.

Whatever, she knew that of all men, her Saburo must have gone to Paradise.

But now, what to do? Although there was no work in Taiji, at least they had their own vegetable plots, and she could help Onui, her widowed mother-in-law, with hers. Tatsudaiyu had died five years before, peacefully, in his sleep. She could sell some of the scrolls and paintings Saburo had done in the past ten years. They still remembered him in Shingu, and she had even heard a rumor that a rich American wanted to pay good money for any of Saburo's work. Yes, despite all the hardships imposed by the new tax system, there were always people with money enough for beautiful things.

Some of those paintings, though, she would never, ever sell.

Oyoshi got to the house. The children had gone tearfully to school, and it was depressingly empty. She busied herself making tea, trying to pretend that Saburo was there in the room, waiting to tell her of the things he had seen and thought during the day, waiting to share tea and time with her. Such a pity, she thought, that he had never painted a portrait of himself, and thinking of that, and of his face, Oyoshi set the hot green tea before her and wept.

At the lookout at Tomyosaki, a single watcher sadly stashed

away the flags and signal sticks, and put the precious telescope into a bag to be taken back to the office. Out of habit, he looked up and scanned the sea, then laughed at himself. What was he to do if he did see a whale? His shoulders slumped.

He walked back toward Taiji, and inside he knew that things would now change here as things had been changing all over the country. Whales were out there, he knew it, and because of them, other whalers would be born. He and others like him would carry on, for, as the old saying went, "a whale on the beach is wealth for seven villages."

By the edge of the path, a few dried stalks of last autumn's pampas grass rustled in the wind. Overhead, kites circled and whistled as usual. In the steeply sloped valleys behind the town, and all around the borders of graves, new and old, gay yellow narcissus were blooming, fresh little trumpets, proud upon stalks of brightest green. In a couple of months the first swallows would be back. Winter was short here, and mild, and the land was always green.

And somewhere offshore, even though nobody saw, didn't a whale blow? Feather of mist upon the winter-gray sea?

Chapter Thirty-Eight

Jinsuke was out by the woodshed, splitting logs for kindling, swinging the specially shortened and balanced axe. He could have gotten Joe, their Salish Indian helper, or any of his men from the ship, or even Brian to do it, but even in his early fifties, he preferred to do simple manual tasks himself.

Joe and Brian, Jinsuke's eldest son, now thirteen, had just finished scraping and salting the hide of a black bear, shot the day before by Jinsuke. One shot, from a lever-action Winchester, fired with one hand at a range of forty yards, straight through the head. He didn't often go hunting now, but the bear had come rooting around in Susan's back garden.

Nothing of the bear would be wasted. Once tanned, the hide would become a rug. The meat would be salted or smoked, some used in stews. The fat would be made into a soap that was marvelous for chapped skin. The bones would go to the dogs, and the gall, carefully dried, would be set aside as a stomach medicine.

Vancouver was only about ten miles away by sea, and a fast trip with the outgoing tides. Jinsuke had preferred the natural wildness, the great forests and the quiet of a deep, sheltered cove on Indian Arm. Here he felt his life and his family, and his ship, to be safe and unmolested. Between sealing trips he moored the *Big Sky* in sight of his house.

The shipping office was still run in Vancouver by Captain MacNeil, nearly eighty now, and Jinsuke had promised that when Brian reached the age of fifteen, he would be sent there to learn the business. Meanwhile he was taking formal schooling at a school just around the point that had been built mostly for families of the lumber business on the north shore. That education, however, placed a heavy emphasis on English history and ways, so from their mother the children learned about Asia, and once a week they had to study reading and writing Japanese and Chinese. The two boys, Brian and Sean, ten, learned also about boats, ships and the sea from their father, while Kathleen, eight, was taking piano lessons from Susan.

Their house was a big one, two-storied, built of logs and set upon a stone foundation. Beneath the outer kitchen were stone steps that led to a deep, cool cellar with stone walls and floor; it was always full of preserves, root vegetables and home-brewed beer. The front of the house had a wide veranda that gave a sweeping view of Indian Arm and the mountains beyond. The fireplace and chimney were also of stone, faced with big cuts of dark green jade that Jinsuke had brought down from the north, big enough inside to take a spit that would roast a whole pig. The kitchen had a cast-iron wood stove which also heated water for a Japanese-style bath. Jinsuke straightened up and watched Joe show Brian how to tell the age of the bear from its teeth and claws. The boy had grown well, taller and broader at thirteen than most sixteen-year-olds, his hair a dark brown, his skin tanned olive, but with freckles around the nose. For some reason Joe doted on the boy, and frequently took him home, where he loved to hunt and fish with Salish boys of his own age, preferring them to the rather stuck-up Vancouver kids.

Jinsuke scooped up another log, set it on the block, lifted the axe, and whopped it expertly in two, hard enough to split, but not so hard as to knock the pieces off the block. Whop! Whop! He nudged the quartered pieces into the pile with his boot and scooped up another log.

"Jim! Jim!"

The axe poised in midair at Susan's call.

"Jim!"

Muttering that a man could just never be left alone to do things, Jinsuke whacked the axe through the log into the block and picked up his jacket. Susan was out on the veranda with two young Orientals, one a mere boy, both skinny and with cheap, baggy jackets and trousers, cloth caps that looked like overgrown mushrooms on their heads, and neckties that made them look most uncomfortable. As Jinsuke rounded the house they bowed to him, but did not remove their caps.

"These two have come all the way from Steveston by boat to see you, Jim." Jinsuke looked down to the moorings of his schooner, and saw a small, single-masted fishing vessel.

"You came in that?" he asked.

"Yes, sir."

Jinsuke grinned. They spoke English, but the accents were Japanese. He and Susan had very little to do with the Japanese community, who were even more clannish than most whites and preferred not to mix with anybody who had a half-Irish, half-Chinese wife. Although Jim Sky was well-known and respected all over the west coast, few even knew that the big, bearded, one-armed sea captain had been born and raised in Japan. These lads obviously hadn't a clue—so what had they come for?

"Who are you?" he asked.

"I am Kakuzo Seko," said the older one, bowing again. "This is my cousin, Jiro Takigawa. Many men ask us come here. They say Captain Sky help. Eight new Japanese want go Skeena River, for salmon. White boss, he take Japanese men to Charlotte Islands for fish, and now Haida want shoot Japan men. Please, Captain, sir, you talk? You take us and talk to Indian?"

Jinsuke stared at them for a while. In the last few years there had been an increasing number of Japanese and Chinese immigrants, with many of the Japanese taking naturally to fishing, especially for the bountiful salmon.

"Yappari, kimi tachi wa Nihonjin da na . . ."

Their eyes widened to hear him speak the gruff and informal Japanese, acknowledging that he understood where they were from. They had been told that his wife was half Chinese, and that they used to live in Yokohama, but the most persistent rumor about him was that he was a pirate in the old days.

"Hai, Nipponjin desu," said Kakuzo proudly, confirming their origin.

Jinsuke walked up the broad steps and beckoned them to follow. They hesitated, but Susan, still in her apron, ushered them ahead of her into the house. She noted with pleasure that unlike her husband, who had "gone barbarian," the two Japanese lads removed their boots before stepping into the living room, its waxed floors spread with the skins of polar bear, black bear and fur seal.

Jinsuke sat down in an armchair by the fireplace, reached out, and tossed a log on the embers. He took the heavy iron poker and made an air space under the log, which glowed red then crackled into yellow flame. Nervously, the two young Japanese perched on the edge of a sofa that faced the fireplace, hats now clutched in their hands.

"Where are you from?" asked Jinsuke, switching now to an unaccented, polite form of Japanese.

"We are from Wakayama."

His ears pricked up. "From the city?"

"No, from a little place called Taiji."

Jinsuke exchanged glances with Susan, sitting across on the other side of the fireplace.

"What are your names again?" she asked, also in Japanese.

The older of the two smiled. "Oh, I am so happy that I can speak Japanese, my English is so poor. I am Kakuzo Seko, and this is my cousin Jiro Takigawa. Jiro is fifteen, and he came a few months ago. I came last year."

"With your parents?"

Kakuzo shook his head. "No, both our fathers are dead, and Jiro's big brother too. Two years ago there was a big disaster at sea. Most of our family were whalers, and they took a big right whale, which dragged them out to the Black Current, and there was a storm. It was winter, and nearly all the men were drowned."

Jinsuke's heart missed a few beats and he went ashen. In his letters Lyall had mentioned nothing of this, but then his brother-in-law had no reason to be in contact with Taiji.

"What about survivors?" he asked.

"Less than ten," said Kakuzo, "and when they got back to the village the people who had lost men despised them, just for managing to stay alive when others died. It was unfair, but they could not stay, and the government was advising poor people, especially in Wakayama, to emigrate. Nearly all the surviving men came to Canada, often as not keeping quiet about where they were going because it had been so hard for them. When they got here they found work, and they sent for us young ones."

"What were your fathers' names?" asked Jinsuke, almost in a whisper.

"My father was Shusuke Seko. His father was Saburo Takigawa. His brother's name was Yoichi."

Jinsuke didn't want to believe it. His family in Taiji never wrote, except for one letter from Saburo after Jinsuke was married. Also, he was not familiar with the name Seko, obviously a second name taken after the Meiji Restoration.

"And who was your grandfather?" he asked, his face a mask.

"He was the famous harpooner Tatsudaiyu, who died about seven years ago."

Susan stood up and put her arms around her husband's shoulders.

"I'll make us some good strong tea, with a dash of brandy in it, Jim love." Then she kissed him on the cheek and went out of the room.

"So you were sent to persuade me to take you and several other fishermen all the way up to the Skeena, like as not with a lot of little boats in tow, and my decks covered with dogs, pigs, and chickens, not to mention women and babies. Then you want me to go over and talk to the Haida, whose fishing grounds you've obviously been poaching. Right?"

Kakuzo tried to stammer explanations, that the Japanese didn't know, and couldn't explain to the Haida, and that people in Vancouver said that the Haida would trust only Captain Jim Sky. Little Jiro looked so scared he seemed likely to make a bolt for the door. It was true that Jinsuke knew the Haida well. They made excellent whalers and sea hunters, strong, powerful, fearless men, skilled with boats and far better at holding their booze than any of the other tribes. Happy-go-lucky, friendly men mostly, but God help anyone who crossed them! For years Jinsuke had been calling in to the Charlottes, doing a little trade, a little hunting for sea otter, and taking on Haida for trips up the Alaskan coast, then over to the Pribilofs, the Aleutians and the Commander Islands.

"I'll take you," he said, interrupting, "and I'll talk to the Haida. However, you must leave their fishing grounds alone. There's plenty of salmon on the Skeena and around the other islands in the Hecate Strait. Leave the Haida be. Just a few years ago they'd have either had your heads or made slaves out of you."

Susan came in with a tray of tea and sweet cakes.

"Susan," he said, in English, "they don't know who I am, and I have to tell them."

She looked into his weather-lined face, and saw the glistening of wetness in his eyes, realizing with a jolt just how much pain must lie in his heart at the years and years of separation from his family and place of birth. Oh, he was a

504

happy man, she was confident of that, he loved her and the children and their life together, but she knew too how proud he was of his origins. She put the tray down, and without embarrassment, hugged and kissed him again, then turned to face their acutely embarrassed visitors, who were not at all used to seeing a wife kiss a husband in front of others. Jinsuke stood slowly, his hand on his hip.

"For years they have called me Jim Sky," he said, "but my name is Jinsuke, the eldest son of Tatsudaiyu, the brother of Shusuke and Saburo. Onui was my mother. Kakuzo! Jiro! I am your uncle!"

Had he not said it in Taiji dialect, they might never have believe him.

Glossary

Ama. A woman diver. Also a nun, usually Buddhist.
Ami. A fishing net.
Ami mon gara. A tropical fish with a netlike pattern to its scales.
Amimoto. A net master or leader of a fishing operation such as whaling.
Ashigaru. A samurai of the lowest rank, a foot soldier.

Bakufu. The military feudal government of Japan during the Edo or Tokugawa period. The original meaning referred to government from a tent, implying that a warrior had no fixed abode. The head of the *bakufu* was the shogun, whose title originally meant "sent against the barbarians." The title was supposedly received from the emperor, but later the powerful Tokugawa clans elected their own shogun, usually through hereditary descent, and the emperor was merely required to confirm it.
Bokuto. A hardwood sword, usually used in training.
Bozu. A priest.
Bu. Silver currency.
Bushi. A samurai of the hereditary warrior class.
Bushido. A rigid code of moral and spiritual rules by which samurai were expected to live.

Daimyo. A feudal lord.
Daishoya. A village headman.
Dono. An honorific, tagged onto a man's name to indicate respect, more commonly used in Kyushu.

Edo. The old name for Tokyo. Edo was the capital of the shogun, while the emperor was in Kyoto. Thus "Edo Period" means the same thing as "Tokugawa Period."

506

Edo-mae. Food in the Edo style.
Edo Period. The period from 1603 to 1867.

Gaijin. An "outside person," or foreigner.
Geisha. A female entertainer, trained in dance, music and conversation.
Geta. Thonged wooden sandals.
Goshi. A country samurai.

Habu. A deadly Okinawan snake.
Hai. "Yes."
Haiku. An unrhymed poem, usually with three lines, of five, seven and five syllables, respectively.
Hakama. A skirtlike garment worn by samurai and upper classes.
Han. A fiefdom. Also used to indicate the loyalties of a samurai to his fief or clan.
Haori. A loose, short, formal jacket worn over a man's robe or kimono.
Happi. A jacket similar to the *haori,* but with narrower sleeves. It was worn usually by merchants or laborers, and also by firemen.
Hasu. A small fish.
Hatamoto. A bannerman or high-ranking samurai. *Hatamoto* were direct vassals of the shogun, ranking below the daimyo. Here the title also indicates high officials in the fiefdoms outside the Tokugawa clan. The word literally means "standing at the foot of the banner."
Hazashi. A harpooner of the Edo Period and before. This was a hereditary status and profession, passed down from father to first son.
Hiragana. One of two syllabic writing forms used in Japan.

Isana. The "brave fish," or whale.

Jigen Ryu. A style of martial arts.
Jujitsu. An unarmed form of combat.
Jutte. A short steel truncheon with a single tang.

Kago. A simple palanquin, usually carried by two men.
Kaikujin. See *takeri.*
Kaishaku. One who assists a person in ritual suicide by cutting off the head and ending agony.
Kami. A deity.
Kampai. "Cheers," the toast.

507

Kan. A weight measure, about 3,750 grams.

Kan-nushi. A Shinto priest in charge of a shrine.

Kata. Ritual, dancelike forms through which martial arts are mastered.

Katakana. One of two syllabic writing forms used in Japan.

Kiai. A battle yell.

Kohai. A junior student, one beneath his *sempai* in a school or company.

Koku. A measure of capacity, about 47.7 gallons.

Kujira. A whale.

Kun. A familiar honorific used by a senior or an older person to a junior or younger person, usually denoting some affection.

Kuroshio. The "Black Current." The Japan Current, a Pacific Ocean current, which warms the coast of southern Japan.

Makko, makko kujira. The "perfume," or sperm, whale.

Mikado. The emperor.

Miso. A salty bean paste used in seasoning and soups.

Mosu-bune. A "carry boat," the large boat used as a killing and securing platform, also for towing, in old-style whaling.

Nagaya. A long, usually poor and narrow town dwelling, quite common in Edo. *Naginata.* A halberd with a swordlike blade.

Naiya danna. A warehouse master.

Nakodo. A go-between.

Nata. A Japanese machete.

Ninja. One who has mastered the "art of invisibility" together with various martial arts and artifices, usually employed in espionage and covert warfare.

Nitten Ichi Ryu. A style of martial arts, especially of sword fighting.

Nunchaku. A double truncheon, connected by chains, used by martial artists, especially in Okinawa. It is believed to have been adapted for fighting from an agricultural flail.

Obon. The Lantern Festival, Festival of the Dead, the Buddhist All Souls' Day, celebrated in summer.

Ofuro. A typical Japanese bathtub.

Omikoshi. The "god-seat," a portable shrine, often lavishly gilded and carved, carried by chanting mobs through the streets during a festival.

Ono Hai Ryu. A style of martial arts, especially of sword fighting.

Onsen. A natural hot spring, often the site of a resort or inn.

Ottosei. The fur seal.

Raccoon dog. A small wild dog of Asia *(Nyctereutes proc-yonides)* that lives in a burrow, like a badger. Valued for its fur, it has a black "robber-mask" face patch, rather like a raccoon. The animal is very common in Japan, and its meat is often eaten in the countryside.

Rakko. The sea otter.

Ri. A Japanese league, about two miles. A marine league or *ri* is about one mile.

Ronin. A masterless samurai.

Ryo. A monetary unit, usually referring to an oblong gold coin of considerable value. In the Edo Period it was equivalent to one bale of rice. It is virtually impossible to estimate its current monetary equivalent—very roughly, US $400. Rice is, of course, far, far cheaper in Japan now!

Sabani. The canoelike seagoing craft of Okinawa.

Sai. A double-tanged steel truncheon, the "killing iron" of Okinawa. The weapon is found in varying forms throughout the Orient.

Sake. The rice wine of Japan. The word is often used in Japanese to indicate any alcoholic beverage.

Sama. An extremely polite honorific.

Samisen. A stringed instrument, rather like a banjo, played with an ivory fan.

Samurai. A warrior of the hereditary warrior class, entitled to carry two swords.

San. The most commonly used honorific, for both men and women.

Sashimi. Thinly sliced raw fish or whale, dipped in a sauce of soya and grated green Japanese horseradish, or ginger, or sometimes garlic.

Sempai. An honorific tagged onto a name, meaning "my senior."

Sencho. A sea captain; literally, "boat master."

Sensei. A teacher.

Shaku. A linear measure roughly equivalent to one foot.

Shinai. A sword-length training weapon made of split bamboo.

Shishi. A "noble-minded patriot" of the Restoration. Usually a nationalistic *ronin.*

Shizoku. The name given to the class formed when the samurai class and the wearing of swords were banned.

Sho. A measure of capacity, not quite one-half gallon.

Shochu. Distilled liquor, made of potatoes, yams, rice or wheat.

Shogi. A Japanese board game similar to chess.

Shogun. The ultimate leader or general of feudal Japan.

Shoji. Wood-and-paper screens.

Sonno Joi. A nationalistic, xenophobic political movement, whose name comes from its slogan, meaning "Revere the Emperor! Repel the barbarians!"

Sumo. An ancient style of Japanese wrestling.

Tairo. A senior councillor to the shogun's government and to the shogun himself.

Takeri. The aphrodisiac taken from the dried, ground genitals of a bull fur seal.

Taotae. Chinese term meaning "great leader."

Tatami. Thickly woven straw mats, of standard size, that cover the floor in traditional Japanese rooms.

Tokonoma. An alcove in a Japanese room in which precious things or flower arrangements are exhibited.

Tozama, tozama daimyo. The "outside lords," or those not of the House of Tokugawa, the hereditary clan of the shogun.

Tsunami. Wrongly called "tidal wave," a huge ocean wave caused by undersea earthquakes or seismic activity.

Umawari. A cavalry officer, a mounted samurai.

Wakame. An edible seaweed *(Undaria pinnatifida).*

Yagyu Shinkage Ryu. A style of martial arts, mostly of sword fighting.

Yakuza. Members of underworld societies or gangs.

Yamade. A wind blowing from the mountains.

Yawara. Another name for jujitsu, an unarmed martial art.

Yukata. A light summer kimono or robe.